Best Shot

Forward

Other Books by Gregory Saur

Stuck in the Past (with Jack Irish)

Otherworld: Orcish Delight

The Royal Pains & Angels in the Outhouse

Panterror! The Epic Babysitting Adventures of Rachel Pugsley

The Pond Scum Gang

Soccer Star

Diving Catch

<u>*Finding Innocence* Trilogy</u>

Finding Innocence, Book One: Strange Old World

Strange New People: Book Two of Finding Innocence

Book the Third: Strange Happenings, the Conclusion of

    Finding Innocence

Best Shot Forward

Gregory Saur

Saur
&
Saur

A Saur & Saur Publishing Project

Best Shot Forward

Copyright © 2019 Gregory Saur

First Saur & Saur Edition

Printed in the United States of America.

ISBN (pb): 978-1-949317-10-7

Cover Design by G.S. and R.S. Copyright © 2019 Saur & Saur

Photos used in cover:
© *Petrenko Andriy from Shutterstock.com*
© *Felix Mizioznikov from Shutterstock.com*
© *Polya Olya from Shutterstock.com*
© *Luis Louro from 123RF.com*
© *Jan Andersen from 123RF.com*
© *meinzahn from 123RF.com*
© *Pavel Ilyukhin from 123RF.com*
© *Pavel Ilyukhin from 123RF.com*
© *gleitfrosch from iStock.com Getty Images*
Image of silhouette: © *popay from iStock.com Getty Images*

Printed in the United States of America

To Noah, may you rest in peace.

ACKNOWLEDGMENTS

No man is an island and not every tall person is a basketball star. I have a lot to be thankful for, even if, as many friends have pointed out more than once, I'm often too tall for nothing. Thank you for all those who made me tall for something. If I couldn't do it in life, I can do it in fiction. To Ce-ce Cox of Outside Eyes Editing and Proofreading, for her amazing talent of editing, and to all early readers who made this book into something good, thank you for your time and suggestions. Thank you to Diana Cox for her time and work off the bench. To my family and my friends, thank you for always being there and never letting me sit too long on the bench. Lastly, thank you, reader, for taking a shot at reading this book. I hope it's a swish.

Chapter 1

Shiny, dark-green leaves, dappled with pale dawn sunlight, seemed to sparkle as they bounced against a gentle breeze. The air buzzed with the sounds of insects and chirping birds. The morning of another bright summer day had begun. It would be the last for some.

The slight breeze carried no warning and the mother deer had no idea of any danger. Far from the shelter of trees, a large doe grazed lazily in the midst of a clearing of tall grass. Her young fawn lay several yards away, nestled in a patch of crushed grass, completely hidden from the untrained eye. With the comfort of thick silent woods lining the edge of the clearing, the deer family had to feel safe.

As birds chirped merrily overhead, the mother calmly nibbled on the fleshy stalks, enjoying an early breakfast. Muted orange washed over the horizon, peeking just above the treetops that swayed gently around the oblivious deer. Little did she know, but death lingered not far away ... death literally stared at her offspring.

The hunter grinned as he slid a large knife from the side of his belt, carefully and slowly easing it up to his face. He lay on his belly, hidden in the deep grass. Tapping the twelve-inch blade against his grizzled chin, he imagined what it would feel like to slice the razor-sharp edge across the little fawn's neck ... The warmth of blood flowing ... The horrified reaction of the failed mother ...

The hunter grinned. The field would turn into a bloodbath and he would soak it all in.

He'd spent over two hours drawing this close. After tracking the deer to the clearing, he'd slid from the trees and crawled on his stomach like a slithering snake. Little by little, inch by inch, he'd snuck up on the unsuspecting creatures, pausing every time the mother lifted her head to search for danger. Being sure to stay upwind, he'd made slow progress, but had enjoyed every moment of it. This was the ultimate game.

Decked out in deer-hunting camouflage, the hunter had coated his boots in mud and had used more mud to paste grass and leaves all over the top of his camo ball cap. To the deer and the birds enjoying the clearing, he appeared as part of the land … part of the land that carried a very long, sharp knife.

As the breeze blew across his back, after ruffling the mother's tail, the hunter crawled a few more inches closer to the fawn. He could make out the poor little thing. It lay so still nobody would've known it was there until nearly stepping on it.

I know you're there, little guy, the hunter thought. *I know you don't see me. But I see you … I see you, buddy boy …*

He pointed the knife at the ball of brown fur, speckled with white. A thrill rushed through his body.

"Boo!" shouted the hunter, suddenly springing to his feet. The knife flashed in front of him, swiping at the air.

On his right, the doe jumped over a foot in the air. In front of him, the fawn's large eyes went wide with fright. Staring up at the hunter, frozen, it bawled in fear, sounding almost like a human child.

If it were human, the hunter would have gutted it. Instead he laughed as the mother leapt past him to defend her offspring. In seconds both were hightailing for the trees.

Twirling his knife in his hand, the hunter watched them go and couldn't stop smiling.

It would've been too easy … the game would've ended too early. The hunter enjoyed the game, more than he enjoyed the killing.

Next time, mama deer, next time, the hunter thought to himself. *Next time it won't be you. Then there'll be blood.*

As if on cue a voice rose from the trees on his left.

"I got him!" yelled a triumphant voice. "Got him good!"

The screaming sounded soon after.

Whistling, the hunter slid the knife back in its sheath and headed back for home. His ma and pa would be making breakfast just about now … he could just *kill* for some pancakes.

Chapter 2

Will Moore had the killer's touch this day. He swished every shot he took. Three pointers, fade-away jumpers, dazzling spinning layups, all found nothing but net. The crowd stood on their feet, stomping and chanting his name.

"Will! Will! Will!" they cried, none louder than Rebecca Phelps.

The prettiest cheerleader in the entire school stood from the pack and waved her black and yellow pom-poms over her head. Then she charged the court, squealing with pleasure.

Will had just caught the ball on the corner and went to launch another three when he saw her coming at him. Confused, he watched Rebecca throw away her pom-poms and shake loose her thick, dark, curly hair. With her black skirt bouncing around her knees, just below her black and yellow striped top, Will couldn't help but think she looked like the prettiest yellow jacket he'd ever seen. Then she stung him. Right on the back of his thigh.

"Ow!" he cried. He eyes flashed open and it all vanished into darkness. It had been a dream.

An inky blackness surrounded him as he found himself lying on his stomach in his boxers and a T-shirt. His sheets were tossed to the side and his pillow was wet with drool. Pain still radiated from his thigh. Something had stung him.

"Will?" asked a voice above him. "You awake? Sorry, but I've been calling your name for almost a minute. It's time to go, champ."

"Ah, Dad," groaned Will, wincing as he drew up his right knee and reached back to rub the sore spot. "What did you do, bite me?"

"Pinched you. You know, to grow an inch. Now come on, boy, we're burning daylight!"

"Hope it worked," Will mumbled. Groaning, he rolled to his side and looked down at his alarm clock. It read just before five in the morning. "Ah, man!" he groaned. "You've got to be kidding me!"

"Yeah, I am," his dad said cheerfully. "Being pinched only makes you grow mad. If you want to grow taller you need the right food and plenty of exercise. Get your lazy bones up, boy. Your mom is cooking the right food. But first I got the exercise."

"What about plenty of rest?" Will muttered. He slumped back down on his belly and yawned.

"The rest?" his dad asked, sounding confused. "Will, the rest is history. Now let's go! It's past 0500 and we've got lots to do before your bus comes! You do remember, don't you? It's your first day of school, champ!"

"Oh, yeah," Will sighed. "Great. Dad, I can't do this."

"Sure you can, champ." His dad reached down and slapped the back of his thigh.

"Ow!" Will yelped.

"Where there's a Will, there's a way. Now get way up or I *will* pull you out of bed.

His dad, Phillip Moore, a former Army captain who'd served two tours in Iraq, did not make idle threats. Early, loud, and often painful wakeups in a calm, quiet neighborhood were not a problem for him. In fact, as much as Will could gather, his dad loved them.

"Not funny, Dad."

"Wasn't trying to be funny." He delivered another sharp slap, this time on Will's blue boxers. Will jerked his head up. "All right, guy, up on your feet. I'll be waiting on the driveway. Oh, and Will?"

"Yeah, Dad?"

"Make sure you put some clothes on. I don't want you embarrassing me in front of the neighbors."

"Ha. Ha. Dad, nobody else is awake at his time. All our neighbors are still asleep."

"Is that right?" In the dull light his dad appeared more of a shadow looming above him. For a moment the shadow paused as if to think. Then Will saw the shadow shrug its broad shoulders. "Okay, then, suit yourself. At least put on some running shoes.

You still need those. But I'm pretty sure there're some young ladies about your age in this neighborhood. And it being the first day and all, I wouldn't be surprised if they're up early getting ready to meet some real nice boys ... but if they see one running in his underwear, well, don't blame me if their moms call the cops."

Will groaned. "Really? Dad ... You're so not funny."

It was the first day of seventh grade for Will Moore ... the first day at a new school in a new town ... and the first day he'd promised to work out with his dad in the mornings ... There were too many firsts to deal with. And first he still had to get out of bed.

As his dad left his room, Will gratefully sank his head back into his pillow. He shut his eyes. Rebecca Phelps would not come back. She was gone. Gone for good—left behind with all his friends in Nashville. Now he was in Washington County, Virginia, a nowhere place with no friends. Just a crazy dad.

Will did have an older sister. Angel, seven years Will's senior, had graduated high school last year back in Nashville and had just enrolled in courses at the community college. She hadn't applied to any major universities or colleges just yet, mostly because, as she said, her family needed her more. Well, Will did *not* need her at that moment. But she came into his room anyway.

Just as Will started to drift back to sleep, a figure, almost glowing in white, slipped into his room and crept to the side of his bed.

"Will," Angel whispered. "You awake?" She sighed when she heard no response. "I hope you know what you're doing," she said a little louder. It could have been spoken to her little brother or to herself.

For a moment, she looked down at her sleeping brother. Light from the hall leaked into the room and illuminated his skinny form. He looked even younger and more innocent when sleeping. "You better be making the right decision, little bro."

It had all started months before, during a Memorial Day barbecue at one of their dad's army buddies' house. They were still in Nashville then, but knew they would be going to Virginia for their mom's new job. At the time nobody felt too excited about the move, especially Will. He'd been expecting to play on the middle school football, basketball, and baseball teams with all his friends.

Now his sports career was up in the air. The main problem was Will's size. With a slight build, he remained on the smaller side for kids in his grade and just looking at him didn't give off any signals of him being a triple sport star. If the coaches didn't know him, they would probably put him down as a water boy, or just cut him. This was something their dad's army buddy calmly explained over drinks on that fateful Memorial Day. Their dad had a Coke, while his buddy sipped a beer.

Angel sat between them and got to hear it all. They were relaxing on wicker chairs on the wide back porch overlooking the large backyard where a small cement basketball court had been constructed right in the center. Sipping drinks, they watched an intense game with Will right in the middle. Though they appeared relaxed, Angel knew her dad was as tight as a guitar string ready to snap.

It didn't help that Will, the smallest on the court, played with some of the teenagers and men also attending the barbecue. Will definitely held his own using his quickness and agility, but when it came to power, he was hopelessly overmatched. Time after time Angel and her dad watched Will be shoved out of the way, backed down to the basket, and brushed aside as if just an annoying flea.

The kid matched up with Will, a few years older, stood several inches taller and had a much thicker body. He had no mercy and took to body checking the smaller boy out of the way when in possession of the ball. On defense, the guy merely stood between Will and the basket and shoved the smaller boy away whenever Will tried driving in. Will was forced to either pass or settle for jump shots. Though he did make more than a few, the point was made. Angel saw her dad's eyes narrow and mouth start to twitch. She knew what would happen next ...

The cookout ended with Angel and Will playing their dad in 21, the crazy basketball game where everyone plays against everyone else, each trying to score twenty-one points first to win. By that time Will had to have been exhausted, but he'd never let it show. Even when their dad went out of his way to bump him, foul him, and even push him outright, Will had kept on playing.

"This is to toughen you up," Angel remembered their dad saying. "You need to get your body ready for this, son. In my day, I played varsity for four years and then my team won every tournament in the army. Know why?" He paused to shove Will from the basket and slap the ball away. Will had been trying to drive past for a layup.

"Because you fouled everyone trying to stop you?" Angel asked dubiously, putting a hand on her hip. For almost the entire game she'd been ignored.

"No, my angel," their dad said, grinning. Getting the ball, he backed in toward the basket.

Will, licking his lips and wiping sweat from his eyes, grimly got up and went to guard him.

Angel cringed as their dad slammed his body into Will's, sending the boy crashing to the seat of his shorts.

"It was because I worked harder than everybody on the court and got tougher than anybody who stood in my way," her dad said, not bothering to stop, or even help his fallen son. Instead he looked at Angel, gave her a wink, and calmly went for a layup. "That's twenty-one. I win."

Angel bit back an angry reply. At the time Will had still been eleven, nearly twelve. *A boy at that age didn't need to be tougher than a man to play basketball! Lay off him!* But she never said anything.

She didn't want to make her dad angry … she remembered those days all too well. The screaming and yelling … it still caused her to shudder.

Captain Phillip Moore had served his time in the military and had served well. When he left, he took with him citations of bravery and a medal to prove it. He also took with him PTS … Post-Traumatic Stress.

For a while, he never knew about the last part. Angel had only been six when he'd left the army. The memories of the arguing and fighting would never be forgotten. Those would forever be burned deep into her heart like reverse scars—scars on the inside that nobody could see or feel, but they still hurt her.

She remembered her dad always on edge, always on the tipping point. He acted like a cell phone that never ran out of batteries. Never being able to relax, he could go off at any time … and often did.

Thinking back on it, she realized he just couldn't relax, didn't dare to feel happy. He worried about everything and expected everyone to jump to his wishes and whims. When things didn't go his way … the cell phone transformed into a monster and he raged, sometimes for hours.

But that was only part of it. If her heart bore scars, then so did her dad's entire soul. More than once she'd been awakened by his screaming from a bad dream.

Things only got better when he'd started going for treatment, about the time Will had been born. Her baby brother proved to be a calming force.

"Will," her mother once confided to Angel, "is a true blessing. If he hadn't come along, I truly don't think I could have made it with your father." On the night of Will's birth, their father had given up alcohol completely. Angel only wondered and feared if Will's coming had just been a mere Band-Aid and the calm could fall off at any moment. And when it did … what would it reveal? Could PTS ever be healed?

Angel always feared the worst.

Back at that cookout in Nashville, though, at that moment, Angel wanted to rip the Band-Aid right off. She wanted to punch her dad in the face and scream at him to leave her brother alone. Instead she watched Will slowly get back to his feet and dust off his shorts.

"Okay, old man," he said. "Let's play again."

Their dad grinned. "Sure, champ. But not just yet. First we need to go over some things …"

Angel had watched in horrified amazement as the two males of the family went back at it. Her dad gave Will the ball and started hand checking him immediately. Only this time he started issuing instructions … or, more like orders.

"Use your body, son. Protect the ball with your body. Good! Now hold your ground. Don't let me push you away!" He put a hand on Will's backside and shoved him hard. "When I do that, spin away. Use your balance and your quickness. Feel the pressure and flow around it. Make your body like water, boy. What you lack in strength you make up in speed. Use it!"

Will kept up his dribble and tried to spin, only to be knocked back to his backside as his dad's knee moved to block his path.

"Too slow, champ," his dad said, reaching down a hand.

Biting her lip, Angel was definitely going to say something, but then she saw Will's face. Her little brother thoroughly enjoyed it … He accepted the hand and started listening intently to what his dad said next … soaking it all up.

That was when Angel threw up her hands in defeat. "I'm going to find Mom," she said, mostly to herself.

As she walked across the lawn back to the house where all the rest of the company was leaving or long gone, she could only think one thing. *Boys and sports, I don't know which one is crazier …*

Now, months later, she thought the exact same thing as she stared down at her sleeping brother.

Back in May, Will had been thin, but his cheeks were full and face more rounded. Now, after a summer of working out with their dad, Will was slender, chiseled, and carried no trace of fat. He still had the look of a little boy and could probably pass for a ten-year-old, but Angel knew better. Will was one tough little kid who loved sports more than anything else.

She sighed. One day soon he would have girls all over him.

Not on my watch, Angel thought grimly. *If anyone hurts my little brother, I'll knock them back into the third grade.* And she knew that included their father.

Reaching down she delivered a hard spank on her brother's flat bottom.

"Will, wake up!"

Her brother reacted as if doused with ice water. His eyes shot open and he thrashed wildly.

"Hey!" he protested when seeing her. "What was that for?"

"For not doing the dishes last night," Angel said, smirking. "It was your turn. Now hurry up and do your punishment with Dad. He's waiting."

Will made a face at his sister and then groaned. "Thanks, Angel," he said. "You're the best."

"Don't I know it."

"I was lying."

"Lying?" boomed their dad's voice from outside the room. "Will, are you *still* lying in bed?"

The light flipped on as Mr. Moore swept back into the room like a heat seeking tornado. He stopped at the foot of Will's bed.

Both his children stared at him in shock.

"O.M.G.," Angel said, recovering first. That was the closest she ever came to cursing. "What on earth are you wearing?"

Phillip Moore, who'd just past his fortieth birthday the month before, still had the lean, hard body of a younger man. At the moment his kids got a very good look at his body—he wore skin-gripping bright green running shorts than ended mid-thigh and an old basketball jersey with shoulder straps less than an inch wide and hung down well below his armpits. A pair of white socks went up to his knees. The socks nearly matched his pale thighs, covered in dark hair.

"Dad … did you dress yourself?" Angel asked, covering her mouth to stifle a laugh.

"And you're worried about me embarrassing you?" Will asked dubiously, sitting up in bed.

Mr. Moore put his hands on his narrow hips. "Listen, champ. It's not the clothes you wear."

"Yeah," Angel said. "That's the problem. You should wear some more."

Mr. Moore turned to her and frowned. "Angel, I don't recall this being your room."

Unfazed, Angel shrugged. "Thank goodness it's not. It smells like little boy and moldy underwear."

Will wrinkled his nose at his sister and stuck out his tongue. His bedroom was the tiny corner room in the back of their two-story house. Besides his bed, there was enough space for a crowded bookcase and a dresser holding a desktop computer. A miniature closet in the far corner spilled out toys and rumpled clothes, including his nice ones for church.

In the tight space, foul odors took a while to escape. If Will ever forgot to put dirty clothes in the laundry, the stink of his room let it be known right away.

"Angel," said Mr. Moore flatly. "Go help your mother downstairs. And make sure Jimmy doesn't wake up."

Jimmy, the youngest of the Moore family, had just turned five and would be starting kindergarten that day. He slept in the room next to his parents, where they could keep an eye on him. A wild ball of energy, the longer he slept the better. If he got up now, he would insist on running with his older brother and dad.

"Sure, Dad," Angel said, smiling tightly. "But just remember, Will isn't one of the guys on the posters. He isn't a professional athlete." She nodded at the color pictures adorning the walls of Will's room.

"Yet," Will amended.

Angel rolled her eyes.

Will had two windows in his room. One faced the back and the other looked over the driveway on the side of the house. The front wall, just to the right of the door, had the bookcase crammed with books and sports trophies. Sports posters covered almost all available wall space around them. Football stars, baseball stars, and, of course, basketball stars looked down on Will's bed from nearly every direction. A giant poster of the "Splash Brothers," two sharp-shooting teammates on his current favorite basketball team, hung just above his pillow.

For a moment Mr. Moore's eyes narrowed as he gazed at this poster and then his head ducked down. He grinned sheepishly at Angel and nodded. Instantly, he relaxed.

"Yes, ma'am. I know, Angel," he said gently. "I'll keep that in mind."

For a brief moment he looked just like Will, and Angel couldn't get mad. Both had slender builds, dark brown hair, and lean, narrow faces. Often they were more like brothers than father and son. Getting mad at one meant getting mad at the other.

Angel's smile softened. "Okay, then ... I'll leave you two to the fun." She reached down and tousled Will's unruly hair. "Enjoy, kid."

"Sure," Will said, ducking his head. "But one day I'll be on a poster."

Angel slid past her dad, but stopped at the door. "Oh, you're a poster child, all right," she said over her shoulder. "You're a poster child for someone needing a reality check."

Will tried to make a comeback, but it ended in a frowning yawn. Faint daylight leaked into the room, but it still seemed way too early for him. During the summer, all of his dad's workouts were in the afternoons and evenings. School starting also meant the start of football. He would have practice in the afternoons, which left early morning as the only time to work out with his dad.

"So, champ. Where were we?" Mr. Moore asked, scratching the top of his scalp. He kept his dark brown hair buzzed short, close to his scalp to show off a well-shaped head. Lines crinkled at the corner of his eyes of his otherwise smooth, clean-shaven face.

"You were about to leave and let me sleep another thirty minutes," Will said, flopping back onto his pillow. "Then I'll get up. Promise." His eyes closed.

"No chance, son. If you can't get up, I'll have to help you. That's what dads are for."

Will eyes flew open as his ankles were jerked off the bed. "Hey!" he shouted.

"Hay is for horses, boy," Mr. Moore said. His bright blue eyes gleamed with mischief as he crouched at the foot of Will's bed, dragging his son towards him. "Today I'm the early bird and I'm getting the worm."

Weighing around seventy-nine pounds, Will had little resistance. He thrashed his arms and twisted his hips trying to break free. He even tried kicking, but his dad's grip never loosened. Suddenly his feet were over the edge and his dad had him by the arms.

In no time Will was in sitting position facing his crouched dad.

"Gotcha, worm," his dad said.

Then, all at once, his dad wrapped an arm around the back of Will's waist while grabbing his shoulder with his other arm. Pulling him forward he managed to throw Will over his shoulder and lift him easily, as if carrying a pillow … a pillow full of flapping chickens.

Will didn't go easily as he continued to thrash and kick. "Put me down!" he protested. "Let me go!"

"All in due time," his dad replied. A hand firmly held Will down, pressing against his backside. "You're getting soft, Will."

"I need to go to the bathroom!" Will cried. He could feel his face go red. "I mean it!"

"Just hold it," his dad said cheerfully. Backing out of Will's room, he turned sharply, banging Will's arm on the wall.

"Ow!"

"Sorry, I couldn't see you."

"You're about to get soaked," Will said savagely. Looking down at the back his dad's short shorts, he got an idea. Though short, Will possessed long arms for his size. Using them, he reached down and went to deliver a big whopper of a wedgie.

"Hey!" yelped his dad. "Cut that out!"

"Hay is for horses," Will replied grimly as he found the waistband of his dad's boxers.

"Bottoms up!" his dad shouted. Both his hands grabbed the back of Will's knees and lifted up, sending Will up and over his shoulder.

Crying out, Will lost his grip as he felt his whole body falling to the hardwood floor. At the last moment, he threw out an elbow and tucked his chin into his chest. As his elbow banged down, he rolled forward and ended up doing a somersault. He ended up landing on his hands and knees just in front of his door.

For a moment he paused to catch his breath.

"Not bad, champ," Mr. Moore said, coming up behind him. "I didn't think you could escape."

"What's going on up there?" yelled Mrs. Moore from the first floor. "It sounds like a football game!"

"Sorry, honey," Mr. Moore called down. "Will is just having a hard time getting to the bathroom. We might have an accident."

"Ha, ha," Will said, not looking up. "You're a riot."

"And you're a mess, son." Mr. Moore grabbed Will from under his arms and hoisted him up to his feet. He then grabbed the back of Will's boxers. "I liked your attack, but you left yourself a little exposed. Now, before you get your boxers to your ears, tell me. Who's your daddy?"

Will sucked on his teeth. He wondered what it would be like to a have a normal dad. A dad who worked during the day, read the newspaper at night, and asked his kids how their days were. "Just wait," he growled. "One day I'll get bigger."

"Sure, champ. Just don't wet yourself in the meantime." Mr. Moore released Will and snapped the back of the waistband. "I don't want a son who needs diapers in middle school."

Will's knees buckled and his eyes went wide. Turning with a squeak, he raced past his dad and sprinted for the bathroom. He made it just in time.

As he flushed, the bathroom door banged open and his dad threw in a pair of shorts and a T-shirt.

"Five minutes, champ. If you're not on the driveway by then we're doing double."

Standing over the toilet, Will threw back his head and groaned. "I can't wait for summer," he muttered.

So another typical day of Will's life had begun.

The smell of fresh pancakes greeted Will as he slumped down the stairs, dressed in loose basketball shorts and a blue tank top. The stairs led to a small foyer with a family room on the right and large living room to the left.

Angel grinned at him. She sat on the couch in the family room watching the news on the flat-screen TV above the fireplace. Just beyond her, Jimmy slumped in his chair at the family dining table. Still in his pajamas, he sat facing Will, bleary eyed, with a plate of pancakes in front of him.

Will could hear his mom in the kitchen doing dishes.

"Hey, Will," Angel said, giving him a faint smile. "Dad's waiting for you." She nodded at their little brother. "Your last wrestling match woke little guy. He made it down just in time to keep from wetting his pants. Way to go hogging the bathroom."

"I'm not little guy," Jimmy grumbled, his words slurred slightly.

"Yeah, you're tired guy," Angel said, turning back to the television. "You good, Will?"

"Yeah, whatever," Will mumbled as he sulked past.

"Hey," Angel told him, sounding serious. She turned in her seat to stare at him. "If you don't want to do this, you don't have to. You know that, right?"

Will stopped and looked back at her. Brother and sister made eye contact. Will blinked first.

He grinned sheepishly. "Yeah … I know. It's good."

"You sure?" Angel lifted her eyebrows. "You know, Dad really enjoys this. It is good for him."

"It's good for me too." Will licked his lips. "Just wait. By October you're never going to beat me in basketball again."

Angel snorted. "Yeah, right. I'll destroy you, little bro." She didn't sound like she meant it.

Angel took after their mom in height. She loomed several inches over Will, but had the same slim athletic build. In high school she had starred in volleyball and soccer. She'd played basketball for a church league and had dominated there too, but had never really enjoyed the competition part.

To her, sports meant meeting friends and hanging out. The athletic part came naturally to her and never really inspired her to do better. She played more for fun than for winning. She took after their mom in that way, too.

"Will, is that you?" Mrs. Moore called from the kitchen. "If you want to eat first, I have loads of pancakes ready!"

Will yawned. "That's okay, Mom. I'm not too hungry." Then his eyes blinked open. It had to be close to five minutes since his dad dropped off the clothes. "Uh, I got to go."

"Can I come?" Jimmy asked sleepily. He yawned. "I'm almost done …" Then he promptly put his head down on his plate of pancakes and began to snore.

Will and Angel looked at him and then at each other before cracking up.

"You go and run your little heart out," Angel said. "I'll take care of sleepy … though, now he should be called sticky. That's some hair gel he's going to have."

Chapter 3

The cool morning air already hung thick with humidity as Will hopped off the front stoop of the house. His dad stood stretching on the driveway and nodded at him.

"Going to be another hot one, champ. We should've left by now to beat the heat."

Will only yawned. Southeastern Virginia summers were steamy and sometimes lasted, according to Mr. Franks, their next-door neighbor, until October or even sometimes November. Stupid global warming. The average that week was in the mid-90s.

"You ready to run?" his dad asked, a wicked gleam entering his eyes.

Will breathed out deeply. "Shouldn't I stretch first?"

"Nah, you've stretched your mouth long enough. Let's go!"

His dad took off in a quick trot and Will quickly made to catch up.

Ordinarily, Will hated running. Running just to run made no sense to him. Unless he had to get someplace in a hurry, why bother? The only time he truly loved running was playing a game, where it served a real purpose. In basketball, football, baseball, and even the few times he played soccer, running felt great and he could do it forever. But running on an empty road in the ugly crack of morning? Only his dad kept him going. Running with his dad just felt right.

They quickly left their driveway behind and started up their street past rows of dark, silent houses. They'd moved into this neighborhood just a few weeks before, in early August. So far, besides their neighbor Mr. Franks, they had yet to meet anybody. Filled with mostly newer houses with a few older structures scattered in, the neighborhood remained a sleepy area with more trees than houses. Farther down, the street led to a narrow creek that eventually fed into a larger river.

Will knew there were kids around, he'd seen bikes in front of houses, but none were yet spotted. Either they had been on vacation all month, or they'd been glued to video games. In a way, it felt good to be starting school. Video games were cool, but not if you lacked friends to play them with. Will missed talking with kids his age.

There were no sidewalks and, as usual, Will ran close to the road's edge with his dad on his left, protecting him from any oncoming traffic. Will breathed a sigh of relief as his dad slackened the pace. Soon all he could hear was the slap of sneakers on pavement and the steady breathing of him and his dad. And that was what made it worthwhile. Jogging side by side with his dad was something worth getting up early for.

Several houses down, they came to a house with lights shining through the front windows. The aroma of frying bacon drifted into the street.

Mr. Moore nudged Will's shoulder.

"See, Will," he said, "we're not the only ones up at his hour."

Will grimaced. "Dad, those are just weirdos who never sleep."

That earned him a sharp whack to the back of his shorts. Mr. Moore never broke stride as he swooped low and delivered the strike, sending Will leaping into the air.

"Don't call anybody weirdos, son," his dad said severely. "The odds of two weirdo families living on the same street are highly unlikely."

Will recovered his stride and made a face. "Ha, ha."

Minutes went by and sweat started dripping down Will's cheeks. His dad continued leading, going up the hill at the top of the street before turning right into a side neighborhood. Mr. Moore never changed pace and kept his arms pumping like a machine. This side neighborhood looped around in a circle and after a few more minutes of running they were back at the top of the hill.

"Let's do the loop again," Mr. Moore said, not waiting for permission.

"R-right," Will said, gasping for air. Tightening his lips, he started after his dad to run the loop for a second time. By now cars were beginning to back out of driveways as the work week slowly started to take form. Yesterday had been Labor Day and the holiday was quickly becoming a distant memory. Back in Nashville school would've started weeks earlier, but in Virginia, mostly due to the tourist season, it began after Labor Day.

"You tired, champ?" Mr. Moore asked as they reached the start of the loop again. His eyes, a deep cobalt blue, sparked with delight as he slowed his pace. "Let's take break." Other than a thin sheen of sweat on his forehead, he looked as fresh as when they'd started.

Will's hair, on the other hand, lay plastered to his scalp, drenched with sweat. Perspiration dripped down his face and neck, soaking the front of his shirt. He gratefully nodded and stumbled to a stop, instantly bending over to rest his hands on his knees.

Mr. Moore ruffled the back of Will's hair and grunted. "Son, you need a haircut."

"Ha," Will breathed out, too tired to say anything else. He'd had a haircut that Friday—clipped sharp and short in the back and on the sides while longer on top. The front of his hair hung just above his eyebrows. His dad preferred buzzed all over.

"Now," his dad said conversationally, "drop and do some pushups."

Will now looked up incredulously. "Are you serious? I thought this was a break!"

"It is! Break another sweat. Let's go! At least do twelve, one for every year of your life."

Groaning, Will got down into a pushup position and started going down and up. When he'd asked his dad for help in sports, he'd never realized what it would entail. Still, he had to admit, the results couldn't be argued with. Will easily finished twenty quick pushups. Of course, his dad just stood over him watching.

"Great job, sport. You barely did ten, but they'll have to do."

"Hilarious," Will gasped.

A red sports car drove by, slowing almost to a stop when it passed them.

Guess the guy doesn't see a kid doing pushups on the side of a street every morning, Will thought through gritted teeth. He went to stand back up when his dad's sneaker rested on the small of his back.

"Not yet, champ. Do four more, one for every foot you've grown."

Will sucked in his breath. His dad wouldn't let him lift any heavy weights. "Not until you reach your teens," he kept telling him. Until then Will could only do pushups, and that he did … over and over and over. Back in May he started doing ten pushups a night and had increased the number since. Now he was up to forty-five a night. With all the extra pushups his dad made him do during the day, he had to be doing close to a hundred a day before his head touched his pillow to sleep. His arms, though boyishly skinny, had well-defined muscle.

"Just so you know," Will puffed, not being able to hide a grin, "I measured myself yesterday." He did three more pushups and then strained hard to finish two more.

Finished, he rested his legs and stomach on the warm pavement and looked up with a satisfied grin. "I'm close to five feet … almost up to four ten."

Mr. Moore jerked back his head as if startled. "Really?" he asked. "Are you sure about that?"

Will slowly got to his feet and brushed off his knees. Then he stood his tallest and looked up at his dad. His dad stood five feet eight inches and still towered over his son. But Will would catch up … catch up sooner rather than later. He grinned wider when he saw his dad's worried look.

"Positive. I checked twice." He didn't mention he had to round up, and that it was actually four feet seven inches, but it was *close* to four feet ten inches.

"Oh, great," groaned his dad. "I was afraid this day would happen."

Will just had to ask. "Afraid what would happen?"

"You've been wearing your mother's high-heeled shoes, haven't you?"

Will's shoulders slumped. "Ha, ha, Dad. You're a real riot. Know what would be really cool?"

His dad raised his eyebrows. "Yeah?"

"If I had a funny dad."

"Yeah, well, at least I have a funny-smelling son." Mr. Moore reached down to slap the back of Will's shorts and started off on a jog. "Now let's get going again, munchkin!"

"Ow!" complained Will. "Why is everyone hitting me there today?"

His dad looked over his shoulder. "Sorry, son, but you got the wrong name."

Will struggled to keep up, but managed to pull alongside his dad. "Huh?" he asked.

"We didn't name you Rod. The Good Book says spare the Rod. Nothing about the Will. Besides, in the army, everyone is always saying fire at Will. So …" He raised a hand as if to deliver another blow.

Will rolled his eyes. "Dad, can we run faster? I just want this to end. Your jokes are killing me worse than the running."

"Sure thing. When we get back, I want you to shoot at least thirty baskets."

Will nearly stumbled to the ground. He looked up with his eyes wide. "B-but Dad, we're in football season!"

"Exactly. That's why you need to practice basketball here. You won't be doing it at school until winter."

Will could only roll his eyes, now stinging from sweat.

They headed back down their street, picking up the pace the closer they got to the house. When about a hundred yards from their driveway, Mr. Moore looked down at Will.

"You ready, champ?"

"Bring it, old man," Will said, his eyes narrowing in determination.

"Okay, then … go!"

All their runs ended this way. The last part turned into a dead sprint, a race to the driveway. As usual, Mr. Moore let Will get several lengths ahead of him only to come back at the last second and win by a smidge.

"And the old man wins again!" crowed Mr. Moore slowing to a trot, raising his arms in victory.

"Not today!" cried Will. Still sprinting, he charged and leapt onto his dad's back, wrapping his arms around his neck.

"Oh, no!" Mr. Moore moaned. "I have the sweat monster trying to drown me!"

He lurched and swayed. Reaching back, he took the back of Will's thighs and hefted him up to a piggyback. "When you get inside, buddy, you go straight to the shower. If your mom sees you, or smells you like this, she'll spend the rest of the day airing out the house and will have to miss her work."

"Sure, Dad, but you don't smell much better."

"No thanks to you. Oh, and don't forget those thirty shots before school."

Will only groaned.

Hearing the door open, Mrs. Moore came out of the kitchen to greet her sweaty husband carrying her son on his back. She wrinkled her nose when seeing them. Then her hand went to her mouth.

"Phil!" she cried. "What happened to Will? He's not hurt, is he?"

Mr. Moore looked at her with a surprised face. "Oh, you mean our son? I'm afraid he got an awful wedgie near the end and I had to carry him the rest of way. Don't worry. With the proper care he should be fine. Do you have any tweezers?"

"Dad!" Will protested. "That's not funny!"

"Just listen to the little guy," Mr. Moore said in mock sympathy. "Hear how high his voice is? Stephanie, are you sure he isn't our daughter?"

"Dad!"

"Oh, you boys," Mrs. Moore said, sighing in relief. She headed back to the kitchen, shaking her head. "I have three little boys to deal with."

"Dad, just put me down!" pleaded Will.

"Sure, but you're the one who jumped up there in the first place. Now go shower up before breakfast and don't forget to use soap this time. Toilet water isn't working for you."

"Hilarious," Will mumbled under his breath as he slid from his dad's back. He quickly retreated up the stairs before his dad could say something else.

Whistling, Mr. Moore headed into the kitchen where he caught his wife in a quick embrace and planted a quick kiss on her cheek. "Hello, darling. You ready for more of that?"

"Phillip!" Mrs. Moore cried, her eyes going wide. "I'm dressed for work!"

"Yes, ma'am," Mr. Moore said, stepping back and delivering a crisp salute. "I'm dressed for work too."

Eyeing his tight-fitting clothes, drenched in moisture, mostly from Will, Mrs. Moore rolled her eyes.

Stephanie Moore stood the same height as her husband, but there the similarities ended. Three years younger, she had silky smooth hair, the color of honey, down to her shoulders. With a small mouth and narrow, slightly upturned nose, she'd shared many of her features with Will.

Her large, deep-set eyes, chestnut brown with flecks of green, glittered with amusement as she stifled a laugh. "I'm afraid what you call work is what I call fooling around."

"Fooling around?" Mr. Moore said, his eyebrows twitching. "Do you mean it?"

Angel, who stood at the sink getting a glass of water, groaned loudly. "Come on," she said. "You two need a room, or something."

Mrs. Moore blushed and smoothed down her gray suit jacket and matching business skirt. She taught at the same community college Angel would be attending and would be working almost all day.

Mr. Moore hadn't worked regularly since leaving the army. He'd tried different jobs, but nothing stuck. Now he helped part-time at a gym owned by a fellow veteran. Once a month he would meet there with his PTS Support Group. Nobody there, and certainly nobody in his family, ever called it PTSD—the D stood for disorder. What Mr. Moore dealt with was not a disorder. It was the natural reaction of a human being witnessing terrible atrocities that he had no control over.

Just knowing that helped him tremendously, almost as much as knowing his family still supported him and stood by him in his worst, darkest of times.

Mr. Moore cleared his throat. "Speaking of a room, you should go to yours, Angel."

"Sorry, Dad," Angel replied sweetly. "But I'm going with Mom and will be starting class today. We'll be leaving in a few minutes."

"Honey," her mom said, "just go up and make sure Jimmy is ready for school. And get Will out of the shower quick. His bus will be here in less than an hour."

Angel sighed. "Okaay … Sure, Mom. I know when I'm not welcome."

"You're always welcome," Mrs. Moore assured her.

"Just not now," Mr. Moore added, smiling cheekily.

Angel stuck out her tongue at him as she left.

Left alone, he turned to his wife. Reaching past her, he snatched up a pancake. "Well, I really think he enjoyed it."

"Phillip, that's for Will!" admonished Mrs. Moore. "There're more in the pan keeping warm for you."

"Ah, the boy can have those. Seriously, though. It went real well."

Mrs. Moore smiled and flicked hair from her eyes. "I'm glad, Phil. I just hope it continues to do so. You know, once homework starts coming and football kicks in, he's going to be a busy boy."

Mr. Moore leaned in and kissed her. "Ah, Will can handle it. I'm telling you, he really likes this workout stuff."

Shaking her head, Mrs. Moore went to the pan to replace Will's pancake. "I can't imagine why. What twelve-year-old wants to give up sleep to run miles with his crazy father?"

Mr. Moore winked. "I'm just that great of a guy. You know that."

"That's why I married you. You're so modest. But really, are you sure he can handle this on top of school?"

"You take care of his school work. I'll take care of his sports. Trust me, he loves this."

Mrs. Moore smiled. "Of course I do. I just wonder why."

Will stepped from the shower and grabbed his towel. Wiping his face, he wrapped it around his waist and surveyed himself in the mirror. At first he eyed his slender frame with mild distaste. Then he sucked in his breath and flexed his arms. Though long and skinny, his arms were lined with veins and boyish muscle. Across his flat belly was a clear six-pack faintly turning into an eight-pack. For a moment he flexed and admired the look when a sudden pounding at the door caused him to nearly jump out of the towel.

"Will!" bellowed his sister's voice. "Stop admiring yourself in the mirror and hurry up!"

Embarrassed, Will made no reply as he hastily dried and got dressed in his new school clothes. He'd almost forgotten it was the first day of his new school.

Just thinking about it as he tugged on his T-shirt made his stomach suddenly do a double somersault. Right. First day of a new school. He glanced in the mirror and sucked in his breath before letting it out.

"Are you ready for this?"

"Yes!" shouted his sister from just outside the door. "Hurry up!"

"Hey! Stop listening outside the door, you creep!"

Angel only laughed and dashed away as Will hastily turned on the sink to cup a handful of water he meant to throw in her eavesdropping face.

Several minutes later Angel skipped out of the house carrying her car keys and pocketbook. Her mom decided at the last minute that she wanted to take Jimmy to his first kindergarten class and so would go to the community college later. Since her first class didn't begin until late that morning it would work out fine. But Angel had a math class starting at 8:30 a.m. Hearing this, her dad tossed her his keys and told her to take his car.

"Just don't drive it up a tree," he'd said on her way out.

Though Angel didn't always understand him, she couldn't help loving her dad. Even when he did act like an overgrown kid, he still had the best intentions toward his family.

She started for her dad's old Corolla parked on the side of the street when she heard the familiar sound of a bouncing ball.

Feeling free and happy, she nearly skipped around the garage to find her little brother shooting baskets at the hoop their dad had installed on the first day of the move.

"Every home needs a basketball hoop," he'd said when erecting the hoop in the midst of the movers. "It's not a home without one." Angel's bed wouldn't be set up for another three days …

"Hey, Will," she said in way of greeting. "Let me guess, you're doing part of Dad's workout plan."

"Not anymore," Will said as he lined up another shot. "Now I'm just waiting for the bus." Biting his bottom lip, he bent his knees and went up in perfect form for a jump shot that found nothing but the back of the iron.

"Isn't that what they call a brick?" Angel asked, pausing to cross her arms.

"Ah, your hot air messed up my shot." Will trotted to retrieve the rebound and dribbled out for another shot.

Angel eyed his backpack lying haphazardly in the flower bed in front of the garage, right in the midst of their mom's petunias.

Will missed another shot and made a frustrated face.

Angel watched him in slight amazement. Will never missed two easy shots in a row. It then dawned on her. Of course. First day at a new school. Will, her perfect, sports-crazed brother, was nervous.

"Do you want me to take you to school?" she asked kindly. "Dad's letting me drive his car so I can drop you off on the way to class."

Will pulled to a stop near her, almost twenty feet from the basket. Eyeing the rim, he heaved up another shot that rattled in.

"Nah," he said. "I'll take the bus. I don't want whiplash."

"Hey, I'm getting better with the brakes! Besides, I know the real reason," Angel teased. "You're just afraid all your new friends will drool over your gorgeous sister."

Will turned and looked at her as if confused. "Huh? Since when did I have a gorgeous sister?"

"Hey, you!" Angel dropped the keys and her pocketbook before reaching over and grabbing the back of the collar of his new button-down shirt. She pulled him close and wrapped both arms around his shoulders, giving him a tight hug. Leaning her chin over his right shoulder, she said, "You be careful in your new school, Will. I mean it."

Will tried to pull from her arms, but she didn't budge.

"What?" he teased. "You mean don't get a girlfriend the first day?"

"Will, you'd better not! You be careful with middle school girls. They can be ugly!"

"Really? Angel, I promise. I won't date any ugly girls."

"Not what I meant, and you know it!"

Will sighed and relaxed in her grip. "Okay. Fine. I promise, Angel. I promise I'll never date more than two girls at once. Is that better?"

"Ooh!" Angel released her brother and gave him a quick kick in the seat of his new khaki shorts. "You're as bad as Dad!"

Laughing, Will raced for the ball that had rolled to the trees lining the driveway. Picking it up on the run, he bounced it once before doing a perfectly executed layup. His nerves seemed to be settling.

Watching him, Angel bit her bottom lip. She worried about her younger brother. He looked too young and innocent to face the terrors of middle school. She knew what kids could be like, especially to new ones. Growing up, she had to switch schools three different times, all before high school.

Will turned to see her watching. Crossing his eyes, he wiggled his nose and Angel's worries instantly melted away.

With high cheekbones, their mom's slightly upturned nose, small mouth, and his deep pair of dark eyes, so brown that they appeared black, Will had nothing but good looks. He had little to worry about.

Best of all, Angel knew he had a good heart and wouldn't fall into the social pitfalls of school life. All he really cared about were playing sports and winning. She just hoped no girl would come along and derail him.

If that happened … Angel clenched a fist. *That,* she promised herself, *will never happen.*

"So," she said casually, "I'm guessing Dad already gave you the 'first day' lecture, right?" Angel deepened her voice and gave her best Dad impersonation. "Remember, on the first day always lie low. Scout the area and establish a perimeter. Identify the good kids from the bad kids. Find the ones you want to be friends with before making first contact. Engage only at the right moment." Her voice broke into laughter. "Engage when you're past thirty."

Will looked at her with real respect, pausing where he grabbed the ball. "Yeah, but I never get the last part. Why is that so funny?"

"Dad humor," Angel said. "Seriously, if you want any advice, kid, I've been to new schools plenty of times."

Will smirked at her. "Why is that? They kick you out a lot?"

"No way, kid. They couldn't handle my natural beauty and amazing intellect. Really, Will. Middle school won't be bad. Just remember to be yourself and not worry. Things will fall into place." Then her face turned into a frown and she looked at him critically. "But first, are you wearing a T-shirt under that? I mean, really."

Will looked down at his blue and white checkered button-down shirt. "Yeah, why?"

"Unbutton it before the bus comes. Trust me. You don't want to start your middle school life as a geek."

Looking self-conscious, Will stared down at his shirt and let the ball fall from his hand. "Really?"

"Yes, kid. Really. Nobody goes to school looking like that after the third grade." Angel sighed as Will frowned. "Kid, you need help."

Bending down, she pulled out her cell phone from her pocketbook and checked the time.

"Tell you what," she said, returning the phone and moving her keys and pocketbook to near Will's backpack. "It's only 7:20, so your bus won't come for another fifteen minutes. Keep your shirt buttoned. Let's play 21. If I win, I drive you to school and you unbutton the shirt. If you win, and that's a big if, you take the bus and be a geek for the day."

Will's favorite game remained 21. He didn't even blink. "You're so creamed!"

Chapter 4

"It's 7:20!" bellowed a rough voice from somewhere above. "Get your sorry behind out of bed before I kick it out! I mean it!"

Jared Cook blinked his eyes open and instantly regretted it. "Oh, man," he mumbled to himself. "It's the first day of school already ..."

"Jared, get out of bed!" bellowed the voice, now just outside his room. "Mom's been calling for twenty minutes!"

"I'm awake," Jared said loudly, sitting up in bed. The shades were pulled low and it was still dark in his room. He glanced blearily at the nightstand by his bed and saw it blink to 7:22.

His door banged open and his roommate, older brother by two years, George glared in at him. "You're still not out of bed."

Jared yawned and nodded. "I'm going, I'm going ..." Then he blinked and looked up at George. "I thought ... Doesn't high school start already?"

"I missed the bus!" George shouted, slamming the door, acting as if it had been Jared's fault. Then just as quickly, he opened it. "Oh, and by the way. The new shirt you wanted to wear today? Jack is wearing it. So don't go whining to Mom."

"What about my shorts?" Jared asked, already knowing the answer. George wore them.

Jared had gone with his mom to buy new clothes for school the week before, but his brothers had both refused, saying they couldn't be seen clothes shopping with their mom. Apparently they didn't like their mom's choices for him. The khaki shorts she'd picked out for George were short and tight, especially on tall, lanky frames. Though older than Jared, George was only a half inch taller and a little bit thicker in the waist.

"What shorts?" snarled George. "They're mine. Find some clothes yourself and get your ugly behind downstairs. You have to make sure Kelly is up and ready before Mom gets back."

"Huh?" Jared asked. "Gets back from where?"

"From taking me and Jack to school, idiot!" George yelled. Then he slammed the door again.

Their father worked in computers for a firm in Virginia Beach, over an hour's drive away. He'd left before dawn, leaving their mother to do any school driving.

Jared groaned as he wilted back down to lay his head on his pillow.

"I don't know what is worse," he said aloud. "Starting a new school year, or being a middle child in this family."

He'd woken up a whole hour early, all set to get ready for school. His new clothes had been laid out on the dresser and his bathroom supplies had been organized right next to the sink. Then, just as he'd slid from his bed, George had growled from behind him. "Wait your turn." George had shoved past Jared and had stalked to the bathroom, slamming the door.

A half hour later it'd been Jack's turn. Jack was a high school senior while George was just starting his freshman year. A few years earlier they'd been best pals to Jared, letting him play all their games and even hang out with their friends. But recently that had all ended. Now they wanted nothing to do with Jared—they only spoke to him in grunts or, mostly in George's case, to yell at him for something.

Jared sighed and forced himself out of bed. "I hope you're up, Kelly," he said to himself.

About the same time as his brothers ceased talking to him, Jared had started talking to himself. It probably wasn't healthy, but it kept him sane. Truth be told, Jared had few to zero friends, which, he reasoned, was why his brothers didn't want to be around him. Having a loser brother did little for high school popularity.

Groaning as he stretched upwards, Jared shook out his arms and stumbled to his door. It had been a hot night and he only wore boxer briefs. Switching on the light, he glanced at the dresser set against wall between his and George's bed. Sure enough, his brand-new clothes that he'd set out for himself were missing. Even his socks were taken.

Shaking his head, Jared scratched his skinny ribs. He stood just over five feet seven inches, a giant among seventh graders. Finding clothes that fit him properly was never easy.

The problem was he carried little meat on his tall frame and had even less confidence to carry it. When in public, especially when in school, he constantly ducked his head and did his best to look smaller and, if possible, invisible. He preferred long, loose clothes, clothes that he could hide in and that nobody would really notice.

It was quite sad, really. Jared had moved to Washington County in the summer before his fourth-grade year. In the three years since, he had yet to make a real friend. Part of the issue, Jared knew, was that he was just naturally shy. For some reason, he just didn't quite feel comfortable around people, especially those his own age.

As long as he could remember, his life felt as if stuck in the background. He never quite fit in with his peers, never knew what to say and when to say it. It had never made him outcast, but it kept him away from friends. In truth, his peers didn't know what to do with him, or make of him.

Jared loved sports, more than anything else. He played soccer every fall and spring for the county and had surprisingly quick feet. He also had a good set of hands and proved dangerous in PE class during dodgeball and football.

However, his personality never let him fit in with the jocks. Besides sports, he also loved to read and would always have a book with him. During indoor free time, instead of chatting with peers or playing a game, he would sit back at his desk or, preferably, in a corner and read the entire time. More than once he'd gotten so lost in a book that his class and the teacher had forgotten all about him. He'd look up from a page to find himself sitting alone with the rest of the class back in their desks twenty minutes into a math lesson.

The kids around him always treated this behavior with some amazement and more amusement. Finally, they just ignored him and Jared became part of the background. By the fifth grade he became a loner and accepted it. Lately, it had become harder.

At home, when younger, he got to play with his brothers, but when they lost interest in his company and didn't share his passion for sports, he often ended up playing by himself. And he still did it even now.

Football, soccer, and baseball, Jared found a way to play them all without a single teammate. For football, he threw the ball up in the air and pretended he was the receiver. Catching it on the run, he would dart through the trees in the backyard, pretending to juke out defenders. For soccer, he dribbled the ball through and around the same trees, once again make-believing that they were defenders. He always ended up back on the small patch of grass where he'd shoot on "goal," which in reality was the air-condition unit. When playing baseball, he used a tennis ball that he threw against the back of a small wading pool he'd propped up against a tree. This he did to simulate pitching. When he wanted to play outfield, he threw the same ball against the brick chimney, so it came back down like a fly ball. For hitting, he had a long skinny Wiffle ball bat that he'd filled with dirt in the hole in the bottom to add weight. He was forced to toss the ball up himself, which, he was embarrassed to admit, usually caused him to strike out. Pitching, he decided, was his best position in baseball.

His ingenuity and imagination were lost on others. Whenever his brothers caught him playing, they either laughed at him, or ordered him to stop before the neighbors saw. His sister Kelly, a year younger than him, only shook her head and wondered aloud how she could be related to such a weird brother.

Kelly … thinking of Kelly made Jared groan all over again. Kelly would be starting middle school in the sixth grade. They would be riding the same bus and be stuck in the same school.

Jared hated, absolutely hated school. Kelly, on the other hand, loved it. She had good reason. Kelly, taking after their mother, had soft, curly blond hair, a small button nose dotted with light brown freckles, and a wide mouth that never seemed to close. Her bright blue eyes seemed to light up every room she entered. While Jared always wanted to be invisible, Kelly wanted every eye in the room to look only at her. And mostly she got her wish. She had more friends than Jared could count and even managed to convince their parents to allow her a Facebook account. At the moment she was working on getting her own phone, but so far she hadn't managed it. Jared imagined by Christmas their parents would cave. Kelly could be relentless when she wanted something.

"If only I could be the same way," Jared mumbled. "If only I knew what I really wanted." He started fishing in the cabinet for suitable clothes, but had no luck. His brother Jack stood three inches taller than him and much, much wider. Unfortunately, Jack had discovered that tight shirts revealed his pecs. That meant any decent shirt of Jared's tended to end up in Jack's closet.

"Great," Jared mumbled to himself. "Just great."

"Jared?" Kelly's voice called from the hall. "Are you up?" She sounded bright and chipper.

"Uh, what?"

Jack could hear Kelly's exasperated sigh. "Are you *up* yet?"

"Uh, yeah. I'm up."

"Can't you ever answer a question the first time?"

Jared felt his ears burn and he made no comment.

He'd never known it until the fourth grade, but he had a funny accent when he talked. In his head, his words came out fine, but for some reason nobody ever understood them. It wasn't until one day when his brothers were recording themselves telling jokes like standup comedians that Jared heard what he sounded like. He sounded like a baby talking without front teeth and all his 'r's came out as 'w's.

It proved to be an eye-opening experience. Since then, he'd started asking a "what?" question in response to any question directed at him. This allowed him time to come up with a clear, articulate answer. It also drove people crazy and made them less likely to ask him more questions, which suited Jared just fine.

In school, kids tended to think of him as either super smart, because of the books he read, or just plain stupid, because they heard him talk. Mostly, as a tall, quiet kid he was left alone. Hopefully this would continue in the seventh grade, but … was that what he really wanted?

He had to admit, deep down inside, what he really wanted, what he really needed, was a friend … Somebody he could hang out with. Somebody to share his good times and bad times. Somebody who would listen to him and not make fun of the way he talked. Somebody who would share his love of sports and would join his games instead of being embarrassed by them. That was what he truly wanted.

He sighed. What he wanted was something only an imaginary friend could give him. He wasn't that far gone … yet.

Kelly's annoyed voice brought him back to the present. "Well, Mom's gone. She has Carey with her, so you'd better get down and eat your breakfast. The bus will be here in ten minutes."

Carey, their two-year-old sister, never left her mother's side. When she did, she would bawl her eyes out until the situation was fixed. Having their mother take Carey was a huge relief.

"Uh, okay. Thanks." Jared quickly pulled out a wrinkled T-shirt with a bald eagle on front and a pair of ripped jean shorts. Quickly getting dressed, he rushed out of his room to head to the bathroom only to see the door slam behind Kelly's back.

"Kelly!" he cried with a groan. "But you're already dressed!"

"I just need to fix my hair! Use the downstairs bathroom!"

"But I need my hairbrush and … other stuff."

"You don't need your acne cream, Jared. You don't have any zits yet. And *please* don't use any cologne. This place *reeks* of it. I think George used a whole bottle! Yeech!!! Boys stink even when they try to smell nice!"

Jared sucked in his breath and then sighed. He'd begged his dad to buy him a bottle of cologne the past week. "I just wanted to wash my face," he growled. "Why can't I get any respect here?"

Grumbling to himself, he went down the stairs and into the bathroom by the kitchen. After using it, he washed his hands and stared into the mirror.

"What are you looking at?" he murmured. He'd been reading westerns lately and liked to imagine himself as one of the heroes who never let life bother them, even when faced by a gang of outlaws holding their darling hostage in a cave full of poisonous snakes. He eyed himself dangerously in the mirror.

"You're nothing but a no good, two-bit, washed-up seventh grader about to get his block knocked off, that's who you are." He tried glaring, but only ended up rolling his eyes.

His mother always called him handsome, with his deep blue eyes reminding her of the ocean. Jared couldn't see it. All he saw was a tall, thin kid with a shock of thick, curly, black hair bunched up on his forehead. The sides and back were cut short, but would never stay neat. Stray curls kept springing out in random places. Grimacing, Jared rubbed his large nose and then flicked his thick lips.

On his last dentist visit he'd been told that he needed braces. His mother disagreed and said his teeth were fine. Jack had gotten braces a few years earlier and his parents had yet to finish paying for those.

"I think I hear the bus coming!" Kelly's voice called, breaking Jared's attention from the mirror.

"Great," he muttered. "There goes breakfast."

When his mother, Mrs. Cook, returned from dropping off his brothers, Jared had just stepped out of the house with his backpack in hand. She'd just parked the Ford minivan and had taken Carey from the car seat. Kelly already stood at the end of the driveway looking dainty and pretty in lime green capris and a white blouse with a floral design on front.

At seeing Jared, Mrs. Cook's face twisted in a frown. Then her eyes went wide. "Jared, what are you wearing?" she asked in horror.

"What?" Jared asked, his belly quickly filling with dread.

"Th-that shirt! Where did you get it? The trash? You can't wear that!"

"Yucky," Carey murmured, standing behind Mrs. Cook, sucking on her blanket. "Ugly."

Jared's face burned. George had been teaching Carey the "ugly" word. "They're just clothes," he mumbled.

Jared's mom dropped her pocketbook right on the front steps. "They're not just clothes. They're just ugly. I'm sorry, Jared. Carey's right. That's the truth."

They lived in a spacious, two-story brick house, with a large front porch, overlooking a bare patch of dirt that ended in a line of trees that enclosed much of the yard. Once upon a time there'd been grass on the bare patch, but after years of kids running, biking, and falling, the grass had given up the fight and was no more.

At the moment, Jared felt like the grass. Fighting his mother on fashion was hopeless. He would only be trampled. He peered mournfully through a thicket of trees at where Kelly stood, safe from their mother's wrath.

"No son of mine is wearing that on their first day of school. What happened to the new shirt and shorts I bought you?"

Jared turned to his mother and couldn't keep the whine from his voice. "George and Jack took them! They take everything that's mine!"

"But I bought them their own!"

"I know, Mom, but Jack wanted his shirt extra tight, so he took mine. And George thought the shorts you got were too tight, so he took mine too! This is all I had left! Mom, the bus is coming. I'm going to miss it!"

"Then I'll take you to school. Now turn around and march yourself straight back upstairs and find decent clothes. Jared, right now you look like a hobo who wrestled his shirt for a meal and lost."

Jared made to argue, but remembered the grass. Breathing out loudly, he dropped his backpack, threw up his hands, and turned back to the house.

Mrs. Cook stood no taller than five feet, three inches, but towered over her household. She carried a slim, petite figure, but possessed an iron resolve that would bend to no amount of arguing from her children. Usually she was sweet, mild mannered, and full of understanding. Usually didn't count when it came to fashion and her children making a good impression. "A family's reputation is important," she always said. "Do nothing that would embarrass yourself, or embarrass your family. In this world, the only people who really care about you in the end are your family, don't forget that."

After five minutes, when Jared could find no suitable replacement, Mrs. Cook went up to help. By this time the bus had come and gone. Of course Kelly never asked the driver to wait for Jared. Jared ended up being driven to school ... wearing a blue dress shirt meant for church and a pair of his dad's dark blue shorts, several sizes too wide and several inches too short. Only a belt saved him from total embarrassment.

Chapter 5

Angel eased the Corolla to a gentle stop on the side of the school where student drop-off was directed. She turned to Will, sitting in the passenger seat beside her.

"Okay, kid," she said cheerfully. "This is it! What do you think?"

"It's like all the other schools," Will said sullenly. "It looks like a prison."

Angel chuckled. "Maybe, but look. At least it has a gym. Now, would you like some music to accompany your exit?" She turned on the radio to a heavy metal station. "Listen," she teased, "that's what your homeroom sounds like right now."

Will rolled his eyes. "I still should've taken the bus," he said with regret.

Angel shut off the radio. "I know. Too bad you were so busy celebrating your victory you never saw it coming. This was you." She crossed her eyes and stretched down her mouth while shaking her head, mimicking Will's victory dance.

Will just stared at her and shook his head before losing control and breaking into laughter. It had been funny.

The game of 21 had turned intense and neither sibling noticed the bus zoom by, going to the end of the street to turn around at the creek. Will had won the game on a nifty reverse layup and immediately started leaping for joy. His joy quickly faded when he heard the rumble of the bus returning from the creek. He saw it zip by without slowing, heading up the street without him. From victory to defeat in a matter of seconds …

"Okay, sis," Will now said, grabbing his backpack and opening the door. "I'll see you tonight."

"I'll smell you first, kid. After that 21 game, you need another shower."

Will only smiled as he stepped from the car. "It's the smell of victory. I bet I'll beat you home!"

"Not if I can help it. My last class ends at two, so there! Oh, and Will? I see you unbuttoned your shirt. Looks better. One final piece of advice. Stay out of the funny smelling bathrooms. Especially the smoky ones."

Will smirked. "Uh, Angel, you haven't been in many boy's bathrooms, have you? They're all funny smelling."

"Not as funny smelling as you, Will. See you, kid!"

Will made a funny face, crossing his eyes, and waved.

Beeping once, Angel pulled away and headed for her first class in college.

Will paused to watch his sister drive off and felt a pang of loneliness creep into his gut. His dad looked out for his sports. His mom looked out for his grades. But often it was his sister Angel who looked out for everything else. Then he sighed. All in all, it wasn't a bad life. He just hoped it wouldn't change with the start of his new school year.

Slinging his backpack on his shoulders, he headed down the sidewalk to the front of the school. Most of the kids being dropped off for school headed straight for an open door on the side, but Will didn't know where to go and figured his best bet at finding directions would be at the front. Besides, as his dad had suggested, he needed to scout his new school.

Washington Middle School, like most old schools, stood as a large brick edifice with a flat roof and long passages turning at sharp angles. Will knew the halls made a rough shape of a rectangle gathered around a courtyard. He knew about the open area in the middle because his dad had taken him two weeks before, to practice football routes, and a janitor had let them inside to get water.

Thinking of football caused Will to bite his bottom lip. The football field was surrounded by a cracked concrete track being overrun by weeds, and lay way in the back of the school. To be truthful, Will wasn't too impressed.

But like his sister said, at least it had a gym. His old elementary school in Nashville had no gym facility and the kids were forced to use the cafeteria on rainy days. If you were unlucky enough to have PE during lunch block and it rained, well, you were forced to play board games on the stage at the back of the cafeteria. It was not a fun time for kids who loved to run around.

The gym at Washington Middle resembled a giant brick block. It towered over the rest of the school, rising up near the left side of the main building, almost right inside the front entrance. Will wanted to head there first and take a peek at the basketball court. His dad always said you could tell a lot about the quality of a school's team just by looking at where they played. They both had already agreed the football team had to stink. He hoped the basketball court would be in better shape.

"Yo, man, wait up!" hollered a hoarse voice to Will's left. He turned to see a taller boy with a large, black T-shirt and super wide cargo shorts rushing toward him. Long, auburn hair flowed past his shoulders, bouncing behind him. Judging by his deepening voice and faint shadow of a mustache sprouting on his upper lip, Will guessed him to be an eighth grader.

"Move it, kid," the youth grunted at Will, shoving by him. "Sorry," he yelled back, sounding anything but. "Sixth graders have to give way to the upperclassmen!" Whooping, he ran to a trio of bigger kids just heading from the buses.

Will just widened his eyes briefly and kept moving. He soon joined the flow of students pouring out from the line of buses parked in front of the school. Most were dressed in brand-new clothes and wore nervous or too bright faces. Nobody gave him a second glance. Many were catching up with old friends, but many others had their heads pointed down at their feet. It was as if they were being herded along in a trance. The first day of school held excitement and fear.

One boy did catch Will's eye. He stood out in black Adidas track pants and a bright white collared shirt, but that wasn't what caught Will's attention. Instead of joining the crowd of kids heading into the school, this boy stood off on the grass facing the busy road in front of the school. He wore a dreamy expression and seemed to be humming. A bright blue backpack rested by his feet.

Will slowed his walk and stared more out of curiosity than trying to be rude. The boy had strikingly good looks and almost angelic features. With a delicate build, he still had a few inches on Will and reminded him of a young willow tree.

Golden blond hair, cut short and sharp around his long narrow head, gleamed in sun. His small, straight nose and tan skin gave him a little boy look. What drew Will's attention were his startling emerald green eyes, drooping down slightly on his narrow, smooth face. They gave him a sad, forlorn look. However, his small mouth stretched into a mischievous smile.

Will couldn't tell if the boy looked lost, or was just playing a game nobody else knew about. He looked to be on an island by himself with a sea of students flowing by, happy and sad all at the same time.

Will blinked. None of the other kids seemed to notice him. It was as if the kid was invisible.

Then he saw the eighth grader with long hair turn from the school's entrance and go toward the boy. His trio of buddies followed. They all walked with a swagger, taking up the entire sidewalk, forcing other kids to go around them.

"Hey, there he is!" said the long-haired eighth grader, laughing. "That's the retard who started stripping during music class last year!"

"Yeah he is," barked one of his companions, a shorter kid with short, bleached blond hair and pinched face. He spoke loud enough for everyone around to hear. "I was there. Man, in sixth grade he pulled his shirt right off during art. He tried to go farther when the teacher had to stop him. He ended up bawling like a baby and had to be dragged to the office. It was classic, man!"

"Classic retard," added another of the trio. The other guys cracked up.

"Yo, John!" called the long-haired eighth grader. "Aren't you hot in those clothes?"

The dreamy boy, John, tilted his head toward the hecklers, but never turned. His expression remained the same as he kept his eyes focused on something off in the distance, probably something that nobody else saw but him.

"John, I'm talking to you! Can't you look at me, or are you too stupid to even turn around."

Will, licking his lips, started toward the boy. His mom taught classes for upcoming teachers at the community college. One of her first rules was to always treat students with respect, especially if they appeared or acted differently. He didn't know what he meant to do, but he wasn't going to let the kid John face the bullies alone.

He dodged and slipped between kids, reaching the edge of the sidewalk.

A few gave him odd glances and some gave looks of pity towards John, but others actually stopped to watch with more than hint of glee in their eyes. Just as Will stepped from the sidewalk, a girl darted past him and ran up to the dreamy boy.

"John, there you are," she said, breathless. "I couldn't find you. You were supposed to meet me at the office!"

"Oh, look," the long-haired eighth grader said, "it's the retard's girlfriend. Maybe she can get him to take off his shirt."

The girl's pale face flushed red and she turned to the long-haired eighth grader with a look of fury. John still hadn't changed his expression and barely acted as if he noticed the girl.

Will certainly did. Even he stepped back when seeing her face.

"Excuse me, what did you say?" the girl asked, a dangerous tone deepening her voice. She wore a black T-shirt and long black jeans. Both matched her dark, wavy hair that hung loose at her shoulders. Will could almost see a black cloud form over her head.

Despite her dress and manner, she actually had a pretty face, with long eyelashes and thick lips … smeared with black. Now her eyes were narrowed into slits and her mouth a grim line of fury. She looked ready to unleash a set of claws.

"You heard me, goth girl," the long-haired eighth grader said, not sounding quite so confident. He licked the corner of his mouth and folded his arms across his chest. "You're always hanging around that retard, Angie. How come?"

"For your information, Brad," Angie spat, "I only hang around intelligent life. That's why you never see me near you. And if I ever hear you use that 'r' word again, I will personally cram my fist into your nasty fat mouth and rip out your vocal cords. If you can't be civil, don't be anything!"

By now a crowd had formed and more than one kid gasped. A giant "Oooooo" arose and all eyes turned to Brad.

Brad wrinkled his nose and looked flustered for a moment. Then he cracked a sick smile and shrugged. "Sheesh, we were just trying have a little fun. You know, trying to get John engaged on the first day. That's all."

His companions had backed off and were nervously looking for a way to gracefully escape.

Angie only curled her lip and whirled to the kids watching.

"That's it," she said loudly. "The show is over. Go inside and actually learn something, like how to treat others with common decency." Her eyes settled on Will and for a moment she glared in something close to hatred.

Swallowing, Will quickly backed off and hurried toward the school. As he did so, a teacher stepped out of the building and clapped his hands loudly.

"Come on, everyone inside!" he called loudly. "Let's go! Leave John alone." He stared over at Brad and his companions. "And just for everyone's information, in case any of you people forgot over the summer, John still happens to be the son of our principal. So before you decide to talk to him, think real carefully about what you're going to say! Now come on, inside! Move it!"

About Will's father's age, the teacher wore athletic shorts, a Washington Middle football shirt, and a whistle around his neck. Will at once thought football coach and decided to stick around to ask about practice. As he did so, he quickly became engulfed in a crowd of kids, all hastily trying to cram their way inside the school. Stepping out of the mob just outside the door, he heard Angie coax John to the school and toward the teacher.

Gulping, Will decided to meet the teacher later and slipped back into the crowd. He paused just inside the door.

"Thanks, Mr. Hackett," Angie said sourly, "but I had it handled."

"Any time, Ms. Robinson," the Mr. Hackett said pleasantly. "I heard Mr. Drydon had kept you employed to watch over John this summer. Guess it extends to the school year?"

"Yeah, but that's not why I'm doing it," Angie said fiercely. "John is a whole lot nicer than any other kid in this stupid school."

"Give it time, Angie," Mr. Hackett said, taking no offense. "You might be surprised and meet some very nice kids here."

"Yeah, right," Angie huffed. "Come on, John."

Will waited for the girl to enter the school with John and then slipped back out and edged up to Mr. Hackett. "Um, excuse me, but I'm new here. Is the gym open right now?"

"Huh?" Mr. Hackett asked, looking down at him. "What's that? The gym? Sorry, son, but you have to check in at homeroom first. Besides, most sixth graders don't have gym today. That'll most likely be tomorrow, bud."

Will tightened his lips. "I'm in seventh grade."

The teacher looked at him dubiously. "Well, in that case you'll either have it first period after homeroom today, or second period tomorrow. We have block scheduling here, so odd classes are today and even classes are tomorrow. See you then, bud. To find your homeroom, just go inside these doors and look on the papers posted on the wall. You can't miss them. They're right where all the other kids are crowding around ..." Mr. Hackett glanced at Will again. "Are you sure you're not in sixth grade?"

Will raised his eyebrows and decided not to ask about football. "Um, thanks," he muttered.

Jared made it to school just in time to miss the tardy bell and be counted as late. Waving goodbye to his mom, he slipped inside the building as the bell rang loud in his ears.

"Well, if it isn't a Cook," a sardonic voice greeted him. "Late like your brothers, I see. Not a good start, bud."

Gulping, Jared looked up to see Mr. Hackett, one of the PE teachers, staring at him. He felt his face burn as he pulled at the waistband of his shorts, stumbling to a halt in front of the office.

Mr. Hackett was a middle-aged teacher with intense gray eyes and a hard demeanor. Jared heard a lot about him from his brothers. One of the football coaches, Mr. Hackett liked discipline and demanded things be done his way ... and as long as he liked you, things were great. But if he decided to not like you ... he could make your life miserable. Jack used to complain all the time about Hackett's favorites and how they got away with everything. Jack had played football his seventh-grade year, but skipped playing in the eighth grade. He'd blamed Mr. Hackett for his year off.

"Are you just going to stand there, Cook?" Mr. Hackett asked.

Jared nervously swallowed and shook his head. "Uh, what?"

"I asked if you're going to stand here. Don't tell me you're another George."

"Uh, no ... Uh, where do I go if I'm late?"

"Don't worry about that today. There're so many lost sixth graders wandering these halls we'll be finding some in March, still trying to find their homerooms." The teacher snorted and ran a hand through his dark hair tinged with gray. "Some of them even think they're seventh graders. Just go and find your teacher. Get to class. I have no doubt I'll be seeing you in a few minutes for gym." It almost sounded like a threat.

Jared nodded and hastily made his way to the class lists posted on the wall near the doors. He found his name and room number and quickly started down the hall. Mr. Hackett's voice stopped him after only a few feet.

"Hey, Cook? Don't be late again. I don't like kids who're tardy."

Now that *definitely* sounded like a threat. It was going to be a long year. Jared could feel sweat starting to build under his arms. He'd forgotten to put on deodorant that morning.

A minute later, Jared found his room, down the side hall on the right side of the school near the auditorium. He knew from last year that all the sixth-grade core classes were in the back. Briefly he wondered how Kelly fared … probably had already made a bunch more friends.

Then, taking a deep breath, he edged into the open doorway to his homeroom. He hated being late. As soon as he walked in, he knew he would not be making friends anytime soon.

"Yo, teach," said a loud, sardonic voice. "There's a walking beanpole here."

Gary Jenkins sat in the front desk closest to the door and leered at him. A shock of sandy blond hair hung over his freckled face, but couldn't hide his cruel sneer.

Jared had known Gary since elementary school and had even been sort of friends with him then. In middle school everything changed. The year before, Gary had suddenly acted as if he'd never seen Jared before. He started hanging out with more popular kids and had quickly figured out a great way to be cool—putting down unpopular kids with sharp insults that made others laugh. For the most part, Jared had managed to avoid Gary in the sixth grade. No such luck in the seventh grade.

Feeling like an idiot, Jared stood just inside the door and tried desperately to find an open seat without having to look anybody in the eye. He felt the whole class staring at him.

"Look at him," Gary said, speaking loudly to the boy sitting next to him. "I think he thought he was going to church today. Nice clothes, man. Only I wonder if your shorts pass dress code. Any shorter and we'll be seeing your undies, man."

Jared's face and ears burned and he knew he was turning a shade of red.

"That's enough," the teacher said severely, looking up from across the room. "We're all new students here today, so let's be kind." She rose from behind her computer near her desk and looked at Jared. "You must be Jared Cook, is that right?"

Jared nodded miserably. There were four columns of desks in front of him, all filled with kids. He didn't see one open seat anywhere.

"You're my last one, Jared," she said cheerfully. "My name is Mrs. Donavon, nice to meet you. Go sit in the back, in front of Mike, sweetie. Mike, will you raise your hand?"

A dark-skinned kid in the back of the column of desks closest to Jared looked up briefly. Breathing out in disdain, he flipped up a hand, as if to shoo away an annoying fly.

"Thanks, Mike," the teacher said cheerfully. To Jared, she said, "You haven't missed anything yet. All we've done is take roll."

"Hey, sweetie," Gary whispered as Jared went past. "I shouldn't mention it, but you have a big booger in your nose."

Jared felt his face burn as he tried to ignore him as he went to the open desk in front of Mike. Big Mike, the silent legend, never looked at him. Big Mike was built like a tank and looked much too old to be in middle school.

Only a few inches shorter than Jared, his broad shoulders were thick with muscle and his large hands could palm a regulation-sized basketball. Jared had seen it. His neck seemed as thick as Jared's waist and he had a square head with a broad, flat nose and a strong jutting chin. Under his boxlike haircut, his expression of disdainful indifference almost never changed. Jared had been in his sixth-grade English, math, and PE classes and had literally only heard him speak ten words. Mostly Big Mike kept to himself. Jared had only seen him interact with others when playing basketball, which he dominated in. When teachers called on him, Big Mike tended to ignore them. The other kids, except for his select group of basketball buddies, left him alone. They only talked about him when he was not around, and when they did, it was mostly in awe.

As Jared took the seat in front of the legend, he squirmed a little, but then relaxed. With Big Mike close by, he doubted Gary would bother him much.

Sure enough, for the rest of the class Jared was able to slip into the background and become an observer. He listened idly as Mrs. Donavon started going over the standard rules and procedures.

A rather stout woman in a floral printed dress, Mrs. Donavon looked to be in her late twenties or early thirties. She had a kind face, but didn't seem to put up with much. Whenever Gary tried to make faces, she gave him a hard look and he quickly stopped.

She explained that seventh grade had been split into two teams, the Pathfinders and the Trailblazers. They, Mrs. Donavon announced proudly, were the Pathfinders. "In middle school," she said, "it's important you find your path and take it. Find out who you really are."

Gary snorted loudly. "What happens if you don't find it?"

"Then you end up repeating the seventh grade," Mrs. Donavon told him, causing laughter. Not batting an eyelash, she continued her explanations. The only times the teams would mix would be during the elective classes and lunch. "All your core classes, math, English, science, and history, will be with the kids grouped in your team," she said. "Don't worry. You'll soon enough find out who else is on the Pathfinders. The Trailblazers are all the way on the other side of school, so you won't see them much. I'll be your English teacher and homeroom teacher. That means you'll come here each morning, but you may not be together for English."

"That's a relief," Gary muttered under his breath.

Mrs. Donavon ignored him. "The bell will be ringing soon, so let me pass out your schedules and you can see what electives you have. Remember, your odd electives are today and even ones will be tomorrow. That means half of you will go to gym next and the other half will have gym tomorrow morning. If you need help finding your next class, there will be teachers placed in the hall to guide you, so don't ask me …"

As Mrs. Donavon started passing out the schedules, Jared glanced around the room at familiar faces and a few new ones. Nobody looked his way. When he got his schedule, he saw he had PE next.

Maybe there, he thought, *I could find a friend there.* It was the first day. Anything could happen.

Chapter 6

Usually, on any typical day, PE would be the best class of the day. But on the first day of school, it became nothing but plain, horrible, mind-numbing torture. With the block scheduling, having only three classes a day, each class lasted nearly two hours. For the first day of PE there would be no dressing out and no exercising. Instead, as the students arrived they were immediately directed to sit in the pulled-out bleachers. After a quick introduction by the PE teachers, where they introduced themselves and called roll, the kids were left with nothing to do but talk. For two straight hours.

Jared bowed his head and massaged his thighs in frustration. In his rush to change clothes that morning, he'd forgotten to bring his book from home. Now he sat by himself in the upper middle section near the side door, a safe distance from the main crowd of kids. Mostly there were seventh graders, but a single class of sixth graders and another class of eighth graders were mixed in. He was relieved to not see Kelly among the sixth graders. But two hours of this? He wasn't sure he could make it.

Loud, raucous laughter a few rows above him caused him to take a quick glance back.

Gary Jenkins sat with a small, scrawny kid that Jared remembered as Ray Sawyer. Ray was another class clown with little class and a lot of clown. With sloped shoulders and a long, skinny neck, he had puffy cheeks that made him look like the cross of a pencil and a chipmunk. For some reason the girls loved him, which made him great friend material for a guy like Gary.

"Hey, church boy," Gary said nastily, catching Jared's eye. "You want to come up here and get some? I got you some fresh weed!" His voice had broken over the summer and came out rough and hoarse.

"Yeah," added Ray, his voice smooth and sardonic. "I picked some from my yard this morning."

Jared quickly turned back around and stared across the gym at the stark white wall. The two boys laughed over him. Sighing, Jared tuned them out. He idly surveyed the gym that hadn't changed much from the year before.

The George Washington Middle Patriots had been around for nearly fifty years, but had yet to win anything significant in sports. The only banners hung were covered in dust and were for field hockey back in 1990 and baseball in 1981. These were hung high up on the wall over the boys' locker room door, facing the bleachers in the far-right corner.

The girls' locker room door was across from the boys', right next to the bleachers. Above it, painted on the wall, loomed a giant mural of a man with a ponytail waving a tri-corner hat. Above his hat read the words *LET'S GO PATRIOTS* in the school colors of red and black. So far, not many of the school's sports teams responded to the call.

Last year their football team had showed promise and had made the playoffs, but most of the team now played for the high school. Jared remembered some noise about the basketball team, too. They apparently were doing really well when the coach had abruptly resigned near the end of the season, supposedly over some disagreement with the principal.

Since Jared never attended the sporting events, and didn't even care about basketball, he never did get the full story. He just wished the school had a soccer team, or that he had the guts to go out for football.

Gary and Ray's conversation drifted back down and he listened with morbid disinterest. They were speaking loudly and obviously wanted other kids to hear them.

"I'm telling you," Gary was saying, "These sixth-grade babies are so lame. I sold some stuff to a kid just last week, told him it was a bag of weed. All I did was pour some basil in a bag and he bought it all! He even asked for more!"

Ray snorted. "Hey, speaking of lame, go look at John. You think you could sell some to him down there? Do you think he even knows what weed is?"

"Yeah, probably. Look at him! He's always smiling and stuff. I bet he uses the real stuff every day and night."

"Sure would explain a lot!"

Jared wrinkled his nose and looked down below him to where the principal's son sat happily on the floor at the edge of the school basketball court. As usual, he seemed oblivious of his surroundings as he stared up toward the rafters, smiling as if listening to hidden music.

John had been in his math class for sixth grade, always sitting in the back and always, somehow, scoring As and Bs on all his work. A lot of kids thought he just got the grades because of his father, but Jared wasn't so sure. Beneath the distracted, whimsy exterior, John possessed an intelligent mind. He knew this because of Angie.

Angie Robinson had been Jared's seat neighbor back in the fourth grade. Back then she'd often complimented him on his choice of books. She'd even asked him for reading suggestions. But then, of course, middle school came and, like some weird disease, it changed her entire personality. In elementary school Jared remembered her as sweet, outgoing, and always wearing princess shirts and lots of pink. Looking at her now, sitting on the front row of the bleachers next to John, she wore all black clothing and looked angry enough to spit in anybody's eye who dared to approach her.

Only with John did her sweet side come out. She'd taken to him the very first day of sixth grade and somehow managed to be in all his classes. Quickly, she established herself as his guide and protector.

One time last year they had a group math project. Jared, naturally, had no friends to partner with, so was forced to group with Angie and John. For a very short time Jared had thought he'd reconnected with Angie. Working together on the project in class, they'd started talking about good books and had even set up a study time at Angie's house. Then Jared had to ruin everything by asking what John would do for the project, since he couldn't do the work. Could he maybe draw some pictures?

Just thinking of the look that Angie had given him still made Jared's face go red. "John is perfectly capable of the work," she'd seethed acidly. "And he's sitting right beside you, so why don't you ask him yourself?"

Shocked and tongue-tied, Jared had fumbled for a response, but had only ended up ducking his head, mumbling nonsense. His stomach had clenched so tight that he couldn't swallow and his mouth muscles had stopped working. Deeply embarrassed, he'd silently listened as Angie tore into him. Even now he remembered her words clearly.

"I thought you were different, Jared," she'd said, actually sounding more sad than angry. "I thought you didn't judge people without knowing them, but I guess I was the idiot. I judged you as someone better. Boy, was I wrong. Just so you know, John got a 104 on his last test. What did you get?"

Jared remembered getting a "C," but had never said so. The project had ended with Angie and John doing all the work without Jared's help. They'd gotten a 98 for the grade.

Since then Jared had left Angie and John alone. Middle school made no sense to him. He just knew it changed people … changed people a lot. Looking around, it was amazing to see all the kids he knew from elementary school that he now, just a few years later, could barely recognize.

Sarah Power sat next to Angie. He remembered Sarah as a little, plump, shy girl who used to pick out books with him in the library. Now she sported a shaved head dyed green and sported a nose ring. Her black T-shirt matched Angie's, but hers had writing in blood red on the back. It said, "If you're a vampire, BITE ME." She and Angie sat next to each other, but neither one spoke a word. Sarah, like the majority of kids, had her phone out.

Jared bit his bottom lip. Every kid in the school probably had a cell phone except for him. At his house his parents didn't even have cable or home internet. If he wanted a phone he would have to do what Jack did, get a job and pay for it himself. Jack and his friend Rick worked at a coffee place together and almost all of Jack's paycheck went to his phone bill.

Jared glanced over at the clock above the main doors that led to the front of the school. "Great," he muttered. "It hasn't even been a half hour yet."

Resting his elbows on his thighs, he supported his chin on his fists and looked around. He noticed all the kids who'd been friends last year were reconnecting and catching up. Down in the center were Stephanie Baker and Giselle Garcia, two of the prettiest girls in the grade, talking and laughing with a gaggle of other girls, all wearing nice outfits that showed off tanned legs.

Jared gulped and forced himself to tear his eyes away. He knew none of those girls, all of them cheerleaders, would ever give him the time of day. A few rows below him on his right he saw Ben Mallard, Ryan Mahome, and Nick Kelly deep in a conversation about sports.

Jared sighed. Just a few years ago he could've been in that conversation. Nick, a large, rotund boy about Jared's height, had once played soccer on Jared's team. His head, always shaven, was shaped like a melon with dark fuzz on top. Many thought of him as just a fat kid. Jared knew better. In soccer, Nick had once collided with him in practice when they'd both gone after the ball. Nick had felt like a freight train and had sent Jared flying. Back then, they were friendly, especially when they'd discovered they were both Redskins fans. But once soccer had ended, they'd stopped talking and now Nick acted as if he'd never seen Jared before.

Ben and Ryan were two boys that Jared knew from PE last year. Ryan had rich brown skin and black curly hair cut short to his well-shaped skull. With a broad nose and chiseled cheeks, he looked the complete opposite of Ben. Fair-haired and with skin as pale as milk, Ben sported a bowl-shaped haircut and had otherwise unremarkable features. Watery blue eyes set far apart, rounded cheeks and a weak chin, he reminded Jared of a plain mop.

It wasn't fair. Without Ryan around, Ben would be useless. His parents were devout Christians and Ben was never allowed to curse, or even have friends who cursed. This had caused all sorts of teasing in the locker room during the sixth grade, until one day Ryan had stepped up to defend him. "If he won't curse, then I won't curse," he'd announced loudly. As the fastest kid in the grade and football star for the recreation football team, Ryan's words carried weight. The teasing had immediately stopped and Ben and Ryan were best buds ever since.

Jared often wondered what would've happened if he'd tried something like that—standing up for somebody being picked on. "Probably nothing …" he muttered. He was like wallpaper, everybody saw him, but nobody ever seemed to notice him. He figured the only time people realized he existed was when he didn't show up. Then they would wonder what was different. In any case, nobody ever stood up for him, or went out of their way to be his friend. Life, he decided, definitely didn't care about him.

Looking around the gym, he saw only a handful of kids like him, sitting alone with nobody to talk to and not having a phone to hide their loneliness behind.

"This is actually my chance," he mumbled quietly. "On the first day of school nobody really knows everybody … It could be a time for a fresh start."

He looked around trying spot any kids new to Washington Middle. If he could find another kid sitting alone, he could introduce himself and perhaps make a friend just like that.

He spotted Big Mike sitting silently at the top of the bleachers above him with a bunch of the eighth-grade boys, all wearing baggy clothes and gold chains. All looked down with either contempt or total indifference.

That, he knew, wouldn't work.

Then he spotted a kid he hadn't seen before. His pulse quickened.

Sitting just a row above him and five yards to his right, a slim, wiry boy sat looking comfortably bored. Wearing khaki shorts that revealed thin, muscular legs, he had on an unbuttoned shirt revealing a dark blue Nike T-shirt. He also sported bright red Nike sneakers with black socks. Beneath a sharp haircut, his thin boyish face appeared friendly and intelligent, but definitely bored. Jared watched out of the corner of his eye as the new kid glanced curiously around the gym with dark eyes that seemed to miss little.

Jared swallowed and then licked his lips. This could be his chance … He could tell the boy knew nobody here and would welcome company. If only he could just get up and introduce himself … but how? Biting his lip, he stared down at Nick and his friends, wondering how he should approach the new kid without being too obvious.

"You think the Patriots will win it all this year?" he heard Nick say loudly.

Ryan snorted. "You mean the Washington Middle Patriots? You bet, as long as they let me play quarterback."

Ben laughed, causing his hair to bounce on top of his head. "Good luck with that! I hear the coach only lets eighth graders play."

"Nah, come on, man," Nick said. "I mean the New England Patriots. Can anyone stop them?"

"Well, I know the Redskins sure won't stop them," Ryan said crossly. "They couldn't stop a shopping cart stuck in mud."

"What?" Nick asked. "What are you talking about, shopping cart stuck in mud? Where did you get that from?"

"Your mom," Ben shot in. "That's where. I saw her at K-Mart yesterday."

"Seriously, guys," Nick pleaded. "Can't I have a decent conversation about football?"

"Only if you talk about the Cowboys," Ryan told him. "That's the team this year."

"Oh, yeah," Ben agreed. "You get them going, and look out!"

Nick frowned. "Whatever, the Cowboys su—I mean, stink. Just ask anybody."

Jared swallowed hard and felt his heart start to pound. This was his chance. He could jump in the conversation and support Nick. That way he would look as if he had friends, and then he could just walk up to the new kid and ask what team he liked. It was that simple. He felt his palms go sweaty and he hastily rubbed them on the sides of his dad's shorts.

"Come on, Jared," he mumbled. "You can do it."

Then, just as he was about to get up, he felt a tap on his shoulder.

"Hey," said an unfamiliar voice. "Is this seat taken?"

"Uh, what?" Jared instantly asked, feeling his body tense. For a second he thought maybe the new kid had come to him. But then he turned and saw a *different* new kid standing behind him. Much shorter and pudgy, this boy had dark hair in a buzz cut and a rather blank face that gave away little. His eyes, the color of mud, blinked at Jared, waiting.

"I said," the kid said, "is this seat taken? Can I sit here?"

"Oh, uh, yeah. I mean, no … this seat is not take—you can sit down." Feeling his face start to burn, Jared hunched his shoulders and settled back in his seat.

"Cool," the new boy, taking the space on Jared's right. "I'm Chaz."

"Oh. Uh, I'm Jared." Jared cleared his throat. "Are you, uh, new?"

"New as a baby's birth," Chaz said smoothly. "What about you? I saw you talking to yourself."

"Uh, what?" Now Jared really felt the blood rushing into his face.

"It's okay," Chaz said, grinning slyly. "No problem. I notice things. Tell me. What's this school like?"

"Oh," Jared said, wishing with all his might that Chaz would leave. "It's okay."

"Cool," Chaz said.

Jared flicked a look past Chaz and felt his blood go cold.

Nick, Ben, and Ryan were all sitting around the new kid with red sneakers and … asking him about his favorite football team. Jared had blown his chance. His shoulders drooping, he turned to Chaz. Maybe he could still salvage a friend, he thought.

"So," Chaz was saying, "are you a Pathfinder or Trailblazer?"

"What? Oh, I mean, I'm a Pathfinder."

"Cool. Me too."

Jared suddenly found new hope surging. Maybe the other new kid could be a Pathfinder too. They could be in the same core classes. Clenching his fists, he said a brief prayer to make it happen.

"You okay?" Chaz asked. "You look like you need the bathroom, dude."

Jared shook his head. "What? Oh, uh, no. I'm just, uh, tired."

"Cool." Chaz wore long jean shorts that went over his knees and a black buttoned shirt, untucked. He didn't seem like the type who would immediately pick somebody like Jared to sit with and this made Jared a little uncomfortable.

Jared looked down at his blue dress shorts that ended above his knees. Trying to make it look natural, he tugged on his shirt, trying to get it untucked. Chaz didn't seem to notice as he glanced around the gym.

"Cute girls here," he said, smacking his lips.

Jared grunted a reply and caught himself staring down at Stephanie again. Her brownish blond hair, tied neatly in a short ponytail, matched her rich, tanned legs. Slim and petite, she didn't seem aware of her own beauty.

Coughing, Jared quickly looked away. His parents always taught him to be respectful of girls, and having a younger sister made him very aware of what that meant. If any boy looked at Kelly too long, he always wanted to punch him.

"Let's move closer," Chaz said. "You know, just in case one of them gets lonely."

"What?" Jared asked, raising his eyebrows.

Chaz pointed to Stephanie and her friends. "Come on, dude."

Jared bit his bottom lip and looked back once more where the new kid with red shoes now talked with Nick and the guys.

"Yeah, sure," he said glumly.

They hadn't been assigned lockers yet, so he grabbed his backpack and followed Chaz to a space a few rows behind the group of cheerleaders. When they plopped down, Chaz nudged Jared. "Do you know any of them?"

Jared shrugged. "So, uh," he said, trying to change the subject. "Where're you from?"

Chaz stared at the girls as he answered. "Not too far. I went to Hamilton last year."

Jared made a face. Hamilton Middle was on the other side of the county and served as Washington Middle's archrival. "Oh."

Before Jared could continue the stimulating conversation, a commotion broke out on the floor to their left.

"Hey, who's that guy?" Chaz asked, his face cracking into a grin. "And what's that kid *doing*?"

"That guy" turned out to be the principal of Washington Middle, Mr. Drydon. A middle-aged man in his early forties, Mr. Drydon still carried a youthful appearance with him. His slicked back auburn hair showed off a high forehead and a long, square face. With just a hint of gray, a neatly groomed beard and mustache covered the lower portion of an otherwise smooth face. Currently, he wore a gleaming white dress shirt with rolled-up sleeves and dark gray slacks, causing him to look more like a father coming home from work than a principal running a busy middle school.

"The kid," of course, turned out to be his son, John. As soon as he saw his father walk through the side door, John had jumped to his feet, chirping in delight.

"Daddy!" he cried.

Ignoring him, Mr. Drydon started walking to center court where the four gym teachers had congregated to discuss and update their class rosters.

John rushed to intercept him, clapping his hands and grinning from ear to ear.

Most of the kids in the gym were used to John, but nearly every eye turned to watch.

"No, John," Mr. Drydon said firmly. "Not now. Go sit. Sit."

"Come back, John!" Angie cried, rushing after the boy. "Come sit back down! Your dad's busy."

John wouldn't listen and threw himself at his father's chest, wrapping him in a giant hug. "Daddy!" John cried happily.

Chaz laughed in Jared's ear. "What in the …"

"That's not funny," admonished Giselle from a few rows below. Dark curls hung down her slim, Hispanic face as she turned to glare up at Chaz and Jared. "That's Mr. Drydon's son and, like, he has special needs. You shouldn't laugh."

Chaz instantly swallowed his laughter. "Oh, sorry," his said, looking at Giselle, instantly sobering. "I didn't know. Really. I'm new here."

The girl only wrinkled her nose in distaste.

Jared ducked his head, biting his lower lip. He couldn't help but feel ashamed as if he too had laughed … that was because a year ago he probably would have.

On the court, Angie had caught up to John and now led him back to the bleachers.

Mr. Drydon pulled on his beard and spoke to Mr. Hackett, who'd come over to help. Whatever he said didn't make Mr. Hackett very happy. The PE teacher glanced at his colleagues and then gestured at the students, speaking tightly, but too low to be heard. Finally, he turned to Mr. Drydon and threw up his hands.

"Next time," he could be heard saying. "I promise."

Nodding sharply, Mr. Drydon turned on his heel and marched from the gym without a single look toward the students, or his son.

"Man, what was that all about?" Chaz wondered aloud.

Giselle sighed loudly, flipping back her hair to expose her dainty neck. "If you must know," she said, obviously bored, "I'll tell you."

She put away her cell phone and turned in her seat to face Chaz. Stephanie and the other girls also shifted to face the boys and suddenly Jared found eight attractive girls all looking at him. He immediately ducked down to stare at his backpack, not daring himself to speak.

"Last year the school's test scores were low and Mr. Drydon is feeling the pressure," one of the girls said. "If he doesn't raise the scores he'll be fired."

Giselle sniffed. "That's only part of it. A few years ago his wife left him. She ran away with a history teacher because she couldn't handle John any longer."

"Actually," cut in a boy behind Jared. "I know the true story. My mom used to work for Mr. Drydon when he was principal at Berkshire. That's the school way out west past Richmond—"

"We know where Berkshire is," Giselle said disdainfully. "We play them in football and basketball every year." She didn't sound happy to have her story interrupted and corrected.

The boy drew himself up, sitting tall, and nodded. "Very well." He spoke in a deep, clear voice and obviously was another new student.

Jared took a look back at him and winced. He thought his clothes were bad. This kid wore a pressed blue dress shirt, a red tie, and black silky pants. The pants ended just above his ankles, showing off white socks and large boat shoes.

Tall and gawky, the boy had uncombed blond hair hanging over his ears and thick round glasses. The only thing missing was a pocket protector.

"As I was saying," the boy continued, clearing his throat, "my mom worked for Mr. Drydon there. His wife did leave because of John, but she married an art teacher and moved to California."

"How do you know that?" Giselle asked, clearly not liking the boy. "Who are you, anyway?"

"I'm Marshall. Marshall Guthridge." Marshall actually bowed, slightly rising from his seat and raising a hand in front of his face like he was in front of royalty. "And I just moved from Berkshire myself."

"OMG," Giselle muttered. "Can you move back?"

The girls giggled, but Marshall shook his head, oblivious to the ridicule. "I haven't finished my story. You asked how I know about Mr. Drydon. I know this because my mom got a wedding invitation to his ex-wife's new wedding. That is why Mr. Drydon came to this school, you know. He wanted to get away from Berkshire with John. It was quite the scandal."

"Are you sure he didn't want to get away from *you*?" Giselle asked.

"Speaking of scandals," murmured one the girls. "Your fashion, ouch."

Chaz laughed at that one.

Then Stephanie stood up with a frown. "That's terrible!" she said, her hand on her hip. "Poor Mr. Drydon. I can't believe his wife would do such a horrible thing."

Immediately, the girls murmured in agreement.

Giselle pursed her lips and glanced at Marshall. "Yeah, sorry about that," she said. Then she looked over at where Angie still struggled to get John to sit down. "Now I know why Angie left us and helps him so much."

Stephanie scratched her hip thoughtfully. "Maybe we can help too."

A conversation instantly started on the best way to help. Uninvited, Chaz slipped away from Jared and joined the girls.

Left alone, Jared leaned back and stared up at the rafters. As usual, he'd been forgotten and ignored. He glanced back up the bleachers, but couldn't spot the new kid with the red shoes. "I really hope he's a Pathfinder," he muttered.

"Excuse me?" Marshall asked him. "What did you say?"

"What? Uh, nothing."

"Well, I'm a Pathfinder," Marshall told him seriously. "Perhaps we'll meet again."

Jared ducked his head and pretended to tie his shoe.

After gym ended, Jared's misery only continued. He never saw the kid with the red shoes for the rest of the school day. Both Chaz and Marshall were already in two of his classes. And he got his first homework assignment of the seventh grade: write a two-page essay on how to help Washington Middle School be a better place for all students.

"That's easy," Jared muttered as he climbed onto the school bus to finally take him home. "Tear it down."

He plopped down on a seat near the back and glanced out the window just in time to see the boy with the red shoes exit the school with Nick, Ben, and Ryan. Instead of heading for the buses, they made their way to Mr. Hackett. The PE teacher stood by the cafeteria directing student traffic.

"Oh, just great," Jared groaned. Resting his knees against the seat cushion in front of him, he slouched down as low as he could. As he did, Kelly hopped up onto the bus stairs, talking up a storm with three girls behind her. "I really hate school," Jared muttered.

His mood never lifted once at home. If anything, it sank lower. As soon as he got off the bus, Kelly started talking about how awesome her new school was and how she couldn't wait to go back.

"It's so cool we don't have to walk in straight lines anymore!" she gushed. "I'm telling you, Jared, it's like, like, freedom!"

Jared merely grunted and hurried across the lawn and up the porch. Inside his house he found his brothers slouched over the table eating huge ham sandwiches and cookies. His mom hefted an overflowing basket of laundry up the stairs with Carey crawling after her, trying to grab her skirt.

"Hi, Jared," greeted his mom. "How was the first day?"

"Hi, Mom," Jared said. Then he quickly kicked off his shoes and hurried up the stairs to help. "Let me get the basket for you."

His brothers never looked up from their food.

"Oh, I got it ... well, thank you." Gratefully, Mrs. Cook passed the clothes basket to him and quickly reached down to pick up Carey. "I've been busy all day trying to get everything ready. I have cooked pasta on the stove. Your father called and won't be home until late. I'll be leaving at 4:30 to take Kelly to dance, so supper is on your own."

"What?" hollered Jack, now looking up with his mouth full of food. "I thought I could borrow ... the van tonight!"

"Swallow your food first, Jack," Mrs. Cook admonished him. "You can have the van only if you want to give your sister a ride to dance, but then you'll have to wait for her and bring her back."

"Nah, I'm good," Jack growled. "I'll call Rick and ask him for a ride."

Mrs. Cook sighed and gave Jared a smile and then a quick kiss on the cheek. "I hope your first day went well, dear."

"My first day was, like, awesome!" Kelly loudly announced, barging through the front door like a returning hero. "Mom, ohmygosh, you have to let me go to a party on Saturday. Marisa Saunders invited me and, like, it's going to be amazing!"

Jared rolled his eyes and started up the stairs with the heavy load of laundry in his arms and his backpack on his shoulders. It felt as if he carried a lot more weight. After dumping the clothes on his mom's bed, he gave a big sigh and dropped his backpack. He ended up folding the clothes himself.

"What else could I do with my life?" he asked aloud. "I mean, really. Why else am I here?" Having no answer, he finished folding the clothes, grabbed his backpack, and retreated to his room. There, he found his book and started to read.

Four hours later, he woke up with a start. He lay on his bed still in his school clothes. The sun had started to pack it in for the day and murky light covered the windows. Groaning, he pushed his book onto the floor.

George grunted above him. "Finally, you're awake," he said. "Too bad you missed supper. I think Jack ate the last of the pasta. You'll have to make a sandwich, or something. You'd better hurry, though. Mom is coming and she'll want to say prayers and go to sleep. I have to get up early."

Jared sighed. "Great," he said. "My first day was just great."

George snorted. "Who asked you?"

Chapter 7

Will arrived home in a pensive mood. He'd been dropped off by the activity bus at the very top of the street and had to walk a half mile to his driveway. His first day had been … interesting. He'd met some pretty cool kids and seemed to have okay teachers, but football didn't quite work out so great.

When he'd met Nick, Ben, and Ryan during PE, he'd mentioned going out for the team. Ryan and Nick shared a look and then gave him the bad news. Football had started the week before and he would have to walk on late. Thankfully he had a doctor's physical already filled out in his backpack, so he'd at least been allowed to practice … without pads.

Mr. Hackett, the PE teacher who still believed him to be a sixth grader, just happened to be one of the football coaches.

"We already have five running backs," Mr. Hackett had said dubiously when Nick, Ben, and Ryan had introduced Will right after school. "Come on out and practice, though. We can, uh, definitely maybe use you next year … You sure you're not a soccer player?"

Thinking about it, Will tightened his lips and stared at the basketball hoop at the top of his driveway. He already couldn't wait until basketball season.

Walking up to the front door, he'd just pulled it open when a wild scream blasted in his face.

"Got you!" yelled Jimmy, leaping up into his arms.

Stumbling back, Will barely managed to catch his little brother, dropping his backpack in the process and stepping on it.

"Hey, little dude, what was that for?" Will asked, bouncing his brother in his arms. "You trying to start a fight?"

"Yeah. A poop fight!" Jimmy then smacked Will in the face. "Got you again!"

"Ow!" Will said. "You hang around Dad too much."

"Who's that, Jimmy boy?" called Mr. Moore from the kitchen. "If it's one of the Bible people, tell them we've already watched the movie and are still waiting for the sequel!"

"Ha, ha, Dad," Will said, plopping Jimmy down. Crouching, he reached back to snatch up his backpack. Going into the house, he shoved a hand in his brother's face, pushing him away. "Go find Angel," he grumbled.

Jimmy responded by baring his teeth. "I'm a pooping dinosaur and I want you!" Growling, he attacked Will's leg, his head coming awfully close to the private area.

Shaking loose, Will stiff-armed his brother and ran to the kitchen.

"Go get extinct, pooposaurus!"

Jimmy gave chase and was about to attack again when Mr. Moore leapt from around the counter and swooped him up in his arms. "Got you, you poopy pants!"

Jimmy screamed with delight and mock horror.

Will leaned against the counter and rolled his eyes. Now he knew why he didn't see his dad's car parked out front. Angel had probably escaped to the library for peace and quiet.

The opposite of peace and quiet, Jimmy was a human ball of energy that only stopped when he slept or watched television. He had the same large brown eyes as Will, but a slightly rounder face, taking more after their dad in that area. He even had the same buzz cut as Mr. Moore.

"Throw me up, Daddy," he demanded.

"Throw you up? Are you sure?"

Jimmy nodded emphatically.

"Did you hear that, champ?" Mr. Moore asked, turning to Will. "Your brother wants me to throw him up."

Will just lifted his eyebrows. "Is Mom back yet? What's for supper?"

Mr. Moore winked. "Hold on, champ. Let me get it right now." Then making horrible vomiting noises, he pretended to eject Jimmy from his mouth.

"No, Dad, not that!" protested the little boy. Too late, he ended up lying belly down on the dining table.

"How about regurgitated brother for supper?" Mr. Moore asked. "Sound good?"

Jimmy giggled. "You can't eat me! I'll poop in your mouth!"

"Ha, ha," Will said wearily, pulling out a chair from the table and taking a seat across from his dad.

Mr. Moore frowned at him. "Hey, champ, that doesn't sound like you had an all-star day. What's up?"

Will licked his upper lip. Despite all his juvenile behavior, his dad always seemed to know his mind. Will could never hide his feelings from him.

"Ah, not much …" he said.

Mr. Moore turned back to Jimmy and gave him a quick smack on the back of his shorts. "You go and watch some TV and learn something, guy. I'll be there in a minute to throw you up again."

"All right," Jimmy said with a huff. Crawling off the table, he raced to the couch, diving face first onto the cushions. "Can I watch wrestling?"

"Not with your mom coming home soon. Go watch something violent, like Sesame Street."

Jimmy rolled his eyes, something he'd learned from his older siblings when dealing his dad's sense of humor. The year before his dad had nearly convinced him that the Sesame Street characters were really alien invaders trying to take over the world—all the letter lessons were really secret codes.

"Oh, all right," he said.

"There's a big man."

Soon the sound of Big Bird and Oscar the Grouch filled the background.

"Okay, grouch," Mr. Moore said, moving to sit across from Will. "Tell me about football. What position did the coach put you at?"

Shrugging, Will told his dad the bad news. "The worst thing is," he said, finishing, "my friends say the coaches like to play eighth graders … and there're three running backs in the eighth grade."

Mr. Moore grunted. "At least you have friends." Then he frowned. "But they haven't even seen you play yet."

Will shrugged again. "Yeah," he said glumly. "Tell me about it."

"I guess that means you'll just have to outwork everybody. Prove to the coaches you're the guy." Mr. Moore banged his hands on the table. "Hey, I'm not due at the gym until eight. Tell you what. You dump your backpack in your room and let me finish up the dishes. Then let's you and me go out back."

Will groaned. "Dad, not another workout! I just finished running in football, and then I had to walk the whole street to our house!"

Mr. Moore tilted his head and made a goofy face. "Ah, poor baby," he said, reaching over and mussing up Will's hair. Then he laughed. "Don't worry, I promise. We'll just play pass and run some routes. That's it."

Will looked up, his eyes sparking in hope. He loved catching the football from his dad. "You promise?"

"Definitely. You'll only do ten pushups for every dropped pass and twenty for every route you run wrong."

Will groaned, but he quickly got to his feet. "Fine," he said. "Deal."

He wore a red tank top shirt and loose athletic shorts, having changed from football practice. His nice school clothes were stuffed in his backpack. "I'll get the ball and wait for you."

"Hey, champ!" called his dad. "You forgot your backpack!"

"I have forms you need to sign, that's my only homework!" Will called back.

"Oh. Well, let your mom do it. Hey, Jimmy boy, I know you just took a bath, but you want to go outside and play some football, right?"

Hours later, after a shower and a supper of his dad's chili and cornbread, Will lay on his bed in his boxers and T-shirt. Completely worn out, but happy, he patted his flat belly and stared up at the picture of the Splash Brothers on the wall just over his head. Curry and Thompson, two of the greatest shooters in basketball history, he thought. *One day, I'll join them.*

His daydream came to a resounding halt when Angel banged on his door and opened it without waiting for an answer.

"I saw your light, can I come in?"

Will jerked with a start and gave her a sheepish look. "Isn't it too late to ask?" he said. "You're, like, already in."

Angel grinned. "I just wanted to see how my little brother is doing. How's middle school?"

Will made a face and wiped his nose. "It's not bad. Football could be better," he admitted. "The school is all right."

Angel smiled. "Yeah, I heard Dad say you're playing 'left out.'"

"Ha, ha. Dad is hilarious. How are your classes?"

Angel came over and sat on Will's bed next to him. He rolled to his side and rested on an elbow. She often visited him like this, always checking in and offering advice when wanted, comfort when needed.

"Not too bad," she said. "College is a lot like high school, just without the drama. I mean, you're paying to learn, so I might as well get my money's worth." Then she sighed. "Honestly, though. It's going to be a lot of work. Some nights I might be busy studying, but if you ever need anything, just call me, okay?"

"I can't," Will said with a straight face. "Dad won't let me have a cell phone yet."

Angel snorted and reached her arms down, tickling Will's stomach. "You're worse than Dad!"

Squirming, Will flipped to his stomach in defense. "So are you!" he said.

"Oh yeah?" Angel abandoned her tickling and gave him a hard whack on the back of his boxers. "You deserve that one! Now go to sleep."

"Ouch," Will said ruefully. He rubbed the sore area. "That's just how my day started."

Angel stopped at his door and turned to him. "Get used to it, kid. Middle school is like that. It pounds you in the behind, and keeps on kicking. Get ready for that, kid." Then she flipped out the light, plunging him into darkness.

A long time later, as thick darkness covered the windows, the hunter got a phone call.

"'lo," he drawled into his cell. "Who is this?"

"*I've got a job for you,*" a voice told him flatly. "*I need some help with a problem ... something needs to be ... eliminated.*"

"Go on, but go real slow. First tell me who you are and how you got this number. If I don't like what I hear, I'm hanging you up."

What the hunter heard next, he liked. He liked it a lot. A wide smile spread across his rugged features. When the speaker had finished, the hunter sucked on his teeth. Then he said, "Okay, you got yourself a deal. You just find a way to get me in, and I'll take the planning from there. Just be real careful who you let in on this. If I find somebody else crowding my space, I'm gone faster than spit on a griddle. Got me?"

"*I understand,*" spoke the now familiar voice. "*Just one question. How do you plan to make it happen? It has to be an accident with no connection to me.*"

"Be patient. I'll text what I need."

The phone call ended with both parties satisfied.

Putting down his cell phone, the hunter leaned back in his easy chair and sighed with contentment. It was official. He had found new prey. This, he knew, was going to be fun …

Chapter 8

Jared had to wait two more days until the next gym class. In the day between he'd only once spotted the new kid with red shoes. He'd found they'd shared the same lunch block, but definitely not the same table. Just thinking about lunch made Jared grow tense.

To Jared, lunch at Washington Middle School had little to do with food. Instead, it had everything to do with social status, more importantly, the social ladder—finding where you belonged among your peers. And Jared knew his place.

Entering the cafeteria during lunchtime felt like entering a loud, boisterous zoo, only instead of cages there were tables. The food lines were to the right and vending machines were on the far wall. Rows of long, narrow, rectangular tables, interspersed with smaller round tables, crowded the large boxlike room between them. Divided in the middle by three massive pillars, the cafeteria had two sections, the "cool" area and the "uncool" area. The first section, closest to the entrance, was unofficially reserved for the popular kids, the ones with the cool clothes, lots of friends, and little time for nobodies like Jared.

The farther away you sat from these tables the less popular you were. Along the far side wall, way back in the second section, were a series of the small round tables. This was where Jared had found his place, sitting alone, forced to listen to a series of noisy conversations, none directed his way.

On the second day of school he sat with his back to the wall, facing the popular tables. He knew he'd have to get used to the view.

Sweeping his gaze across the tables before him, he imagined he was observing animals in a zoo. There were the large, powerful football players, crowding the first tables and acting like lions, the kings of the cafeteria. The graceful, gorgeous cheerleaders preened at another table like vain swans, where no ugly ducklings were ever allowed. Gary, Ray, and their bunch laughed like hyenas at another table. Other kids, the want-to-be athletes, rich kids, studious bores, kids dressed in black, and so on, all sat at tables in groups of their own kind. They reminded Jared of either packs of wolves or herds of sheep. They meant to dominate, or to follow meekly.

Jared sighed. Thinking of the cafeteria as a zoo was a little funny, until he realized that doing so would make him a cockroach—something unwanted and only fit for garbage. He wondered how he'd missed out belonging to a group.

He spotted Sarah in a black leather jacket sitting at a crowded table of kids covered from head to toe entirely in black. Outside had to be well over ninety degrees, but the boy next to her wore tight black jeans and a long-sleeved death metal shirt, not to mention black lipstick.

"Guess you got to do what you got to do to fit in," he muttered to himself. "Even if it means going to the extreme to be different, just like everybody else." But he would never do such a thing. Nope. He would just sit alone and blend in with the bare walls covered in chipped paint.

True, it had only been two days, but Jared knew things wouldn't change. Last year it had been the same. The round tables in section two were for the outcasts and rejects. It was another of the unwritten rules that nobody broke. And once you found a lunch spot, you almost never changed it.

At least Jared wasn't *totally* alone. Marshall also sat by himself. He hunkered down at the table just to Jared's left. Hunched over his newly issued science textbook, eating a white bread sandwich, the boy seemed totally unconcerned with his total lack of social status.

Jared felt relief mixed with shame when glancing at the tall, awkward boy. Marshall had provided a great service for Jared. He'd ended up in every one of his core classes, and Gary, being a classic bully, quickly turned his focus on the new kid, forgetting all about Jared.

Poor Marshall didn't help himself. In less than two days he'd already established himself as a know-it-all with poor fashion sense. These were two big mistakes in middle school. Jared wasn't sure if he should feel sorry for him, or be thankful to have him around. With Marshall, kids like Gary would never have time to pick on Jared.

Angie and John sat a few tables down to his right. In the far corner, they sat with their backs to the rest of the cafeteria and ate facing the wall.

A few other kids were scattered at other round tables, but these at least had a friend or two, or at the very least had cell phones to hide behind. Jared had nothing.

He had, again, forgotten to bring his book. That's when he spotted the new kid with red shoes. The boy entered the cafeteria with the Trailblazers, talking and laughing with Nick, Ben, and Ryan, like they'd been buddies for years. All carrying their lunches, they'd gone straight to the second long table where the football players sat. There Jared had lost sight of him. Jared's only consolation, the new kid had yet to see him sitting alone like a total loser.

"That's what I am," Jared said, just before taking a bite of the school's macaroni and cheese. "A first-class loser."

"You're a what?" Chaz asked, appearing at Jared's elbow. "Did you just say you were a user?"

Jared nearly choked. Coughing, he quickly took a gulp of milk.

For some reason, Chaz kept following him. He'd sat either next to him or behind him in all their core classes so far, and kept up a continuous line of questions about the kids in the school.

Jared didn't really know what to make of him, but he had a feeling Chaz wasn't looking to be best friends. If anything, he had the feeling Chaz just didn't want to be alone. Once he found better friends he'd leave Jared in a snap. Jared couldn't shake the thought that Chaz was always secretly laughing at him.

"Uh, hey," he managed to say as Chaz put down his tray and took a seat, uninvited.

Chaz ignored him as he started munching on a fry and surveying the cafeteria.

"Food is pretty good here," he said, nodding toward the long table in the first section where the cheerleaders had gathered.

"Yeah," Jared said, stabbing more macaroni. "It's much better than in elementary school. And here we get more choices. You can have a cheeseburger every—"

"I'm not talking about *that* food," Chaz said, licking his lips. "I'm talking about *that* food." He nodded his head at where Giselle and Stephanie headed to the vending machines.

Jared frowned and dropped his gaze to his tray. He didn't say anything else for the rest of lunch. If he still wanted a chance to make a real friend, he'd have to wait for gym class. He would have to rise above cockroach and become something better. But what?

He scrapped the zoo analogy when tossing his garbage. He just wanted to be a friend. It would not be easy, he knew.

When gym class finally arrived, Jared, of course, faced more disappointment. All the bleachers were closed when he walked in and the kids were directed to sit on the floor in their classes. Jared and Chaz ended up with Mr. Hackett as their teacher. In the other half of the gym, the new kid with red shoes sat in his class with Coach Swopes, the old track coach, as the teacher. Just like that, Jared knew he would be friendless for another year.

"Okay, listen up," bellowed Mr. Hackett after taking roll. "Usually, you all would be on the bleachers today and we wouldn't start until next week. However, our esteemed principal doesn't like to see his kids being lazy. Therefore, as soon as I call roll, you all will have a choice. You can go sit on the top of the bleachers and socialize, or you can play some basketball. What you cannot do is talk while I'm speaking. Ray and Gary, I'm talking to you."

Gary, sitting two kids in front of Jared, quickly turned away from Ray and coughed. "Sorry, but I was just wondering aloud. Are you allowed to wear ties when playing basketball?" He jutted his chin over at Marshall.

Marshall, sitting in the front with his back bent over, looked back and wrinkled his brow. "Are you referring to me?"

"Yeah, I'm referring to you, you big ape."

"Quiet!" barked Mr. Hackett. Then he wrinkled his brow. "In basketball, there are no ties, so no. Ties are not allowed." He looked at Marshall and clicked his tongue. "By the way, that's a nice watch you have, son. You might want to lose that with your tie if you want to participate in PE."

Marshal grunted and held up his left hand, showing off a glittering silver watch. "My dad gave this to me. I really don't think

I need to take it off to view people bouncing a ball and throwing it into a little circle."

Big Mike, sitting behind Jared, clicked his tongue and snorted loudly. The rest of the class either stared in shock or laughed in their hands.

Mr. Hackett frowned as if he had a bad taste in his mouth. "Suit yourself, bud. But just know this. When we start dressing out next week, I don't want to see any ties or watches from daddies or mommies."

"I hardly think I'll wear a tie and watch when dressing out," Marshall said.

Mr. Hackett grunted. "Lovely. Okay, guys. Get up and do some stretching and stuff. The balls will be out in a minute." He turned on his heel and headed into the locker room.

"Hear that?" Ray said crudely. "I think he means John is stripping again. This time he'll go all the way!"

Gary laughed scathingly.

Then Chaz spoke up in front of Jared. "If Marshall tried it, nothing would be out! He doesn't have any!"

Jared didn't get the jokes and frowned as other kids laughed.

"Oohhh!" Gary cried out, covering his mouth with his hand. "Good one, man!"

Ray pounded the floor with laughter.

"You guys are gross," one of the girls said, giggling.

Jared just shook his head and quickly headed for the bleachers.

When pushed against the wall, closed up, the bleachers left only the top row open for sitting, about six feet off the ground. Using both hands, Jared pulled himself up and slumped back against the wall. Basketball always seemed the first activity PE teachers went to during downtime. Like always, he chose to watch.

When hearing they would be playing basketball, Will's eyes lit up. Sitting in the middle of the first row of kids, he spun to his right to find Nick two rows over. Grinning, he mimicked a shot and pointed at the main basket over their teacher, Coach Swopes.

Nick frowned and pointed at a side basket.

"Before you get up," Coach Swopes's gravelly voice said. "I'll be coaching the boys' basketball team this year." He cleared his throat and for a moment looked bitter.

With thin, white hair, stooped shoulders, and more wrinkles on his face than a crumbled piece of paper, Coach Swopes appeared well past his coaching days. But his voice rang strong and his watery gray eyes were bright. "If any of you boys want to make the team, now's a good time to start trying to impress me."

Will licked his lips, even more excited.

"What about the girls?" Angie's voice asked. "Do you care how we do?"

Coach Swopes blinked and focused on Angie. "Next time, raise your hand, Ms. Robinson. To answer your question, you already do impress me. You keep looking out for John, young lady. I may have a place for him on the team as manager. The rest of you girls, if you care to sweat, can impress Ms. Turner. She's with the eighth-grade class next to you and will be coaching the girls' team. Now let's go play ball!"

Nick quickly got up and went over to Will.

"Come on," he said. "Grab the side basket before some other kids take it."

"What's wrong with playing here?" Will asked, nodding at the main hoop with the clear rectangular backboard. All the side rims had white rounded backboards and no foul lines.

"That's where the eighth graders and basketball stars play," Ben told him, joining them. "They'd never let us join, and if they did, they'd cream us."

"Well, some of us," Ryan added, playfully shoving Ben on the shoulder. All four boys were Trailblazers and had Coach Swopes as their PE teacher. Ryan and Nick also were on the football team, with Ben serving as one of the managers. The three boys had quickly welcomed Will into their group.

"All right," Will said, disappointed. "Let's get a ball and play."

Over his shoulder he watched Brad, the long-haired eighth grader, dribble a ball to the main hoop and do a layup, slapping the backboard as he went up.

"Oh, yeah, that felt good!" he crowed, flexing his arms as he landed.

Tightening his lips, Will shrugged and turned to the side hoop. His time would come.

Chapter 9

Jared actually enjoyed watching basketball in gym. At home, with no cable or internet, he followed every sport aired on regular TV. All his family had was a digital antenna that got eight channels worth watching. Thankfully, the major networks showed sports on the weekends. He loved to watch games on television and then go outside to copy what he'd just watched. It got to the point where he could watch any game of any sport at any level and, just as long as it proved competitive, find pleasure in rooting for a team.

For PE basketball, he always watched the "main game" played by all the school's basketball stars. Just like last year, it was at the hoop near the front gym entrance. If you weren't on the team, or weren't at least best friends with a team member, you were simply not allowed there. Nobody ever said this out loud, but even on the third day of school it was a well-understood fact. Another unwritten rule. Big Mike and his group gathered there, mixing with some eighth graders.

All the players were tall and athletic and handled the ball as if it was an extension of them. A few had trouble moving, because they wore baggy shorts that kept slipping down. Trying to dribble and shoot while pulling up your shorts took impressive skill. After some jostling and messing around, they shot for teams and started an intense half-court game.

A few other games broke out around the gym, but nothing too serious. Some kids just shot around or dribbled balls off their feet. Gary and Ray were shooting with some girls at the basket to the right of Jared. Sixth graders got a game going in front of him, but none really knew what they were doing. A couple of times Jared had to dodge an errant shot from one of them. The majority of the kids, especially the girls wearing nice clothes, sat on the bleachers with Jared, or gathered in groups in the corners of the gym to socialize.

Settling in his seat, Jared turned to focus on the "main game" when he swallowed hard. At the hoop just beyond the "main game" he saw Nick shoot up a brick. A small kid in red shoes soared up for the rebound.

"Great, just great," Jared muttered. "Why can't I be in that class?" Placing his elbow on his knee, he rested his chin and watched glumly.

The new kid was good. Real good. Taking the ball out, he turned and fired a shot over Ben and hit nothing but net. It was two on two, Nick and Ben against Ryan and Will. Quickly it turned into a rout with Ryan and Will easily winning.

Jared wished he could be out there with them … maybe Nick and Ben would let him play on their team, making it three on two. Then it would be more even. Instead he moped and felt sorry for himself.

"You want to play?" asked a voice next to him.

"Uh, what?" Blinking, Jared wasn't too surprised to find Chaz sitting next to him.

"You wanna play basketball?" Chaz asked again. He nodded his head at the sixth graders. "I bet we could take them."

"Oh … uh, that's okay. I don't play basketball."

Chaz looked at him and frowned. "You're tall enough. What's wrong? You scared?"

Jared shrugged, his face burning. "I just play soccer."

Chaz snorted a laugh. "Whatever, man. Soccer is a sissy game." Getting up, he pulled up his shorts and hopped off the bleachers.

"Yo, dude!" cried Gary. "Little help!" He'd shot a clunker off the side of the rim and the ball rolled toward Chaz.

Chaz picked up the ball and looked at Gary. "Is this yours?" he asked.

"You know it isn't Marshall's," Ray said loudly. "He doesn't have any!"

"But I do," Chaz said, grinning.

Gary laughed and waved Chaz over. "Come over and shoot with us," he said. "You don't want to hang out with the losers over there."

Without looking back, Chaz dribbled the ball to a new group of friends.

Jared bit his bottom lip and turned his attention back to the games on the far court. The kid in the red shoes now played with Ben against Ryan and Nick.

Ryan had a good six inches on Will, but that didn't stop the smaller boy. Will had been playing against taller, bigger opponents almost all his life.

His cheeks were flushed, and sweaty strands of hair hung over his brow. Gripping the ball with both hands he pivoted away from Ryan and looked for Ben to cut. The blond-headed boy had never played organized basketball and it showed. Standing still, he waved his arms ineffectually. Nick's massive size blocked Ben away from the basket.

"Okay, man," Ryan said, grinning through sweat. "What you gonna to do now? Just you and me, man." Crouching low, he waved an arm in Will's face. "And I got you guarded like the secret service, man. You're locked up tighter than Fort Knox!"

Tightening his lips, Will kept his eyes on Ben as if he meant to pass, but then took a quick dribble to the right. Ryan stepped with him, so Will quickly crossed to his left. Again, Ryan's quick feet moved to block him from the basket. "I'm too tall for you, little man," he crowed.

Smiling, Will crossed back to the right and dribbled hard to the middle. As he did so, he leaned into Ryan, creating space. Then, when just in front of the hoop, he stepped back and launched a high-arcing shot. Ryan stumbled past, caught off guard as the ball splashed through the net before bouncing on the hard floor.

"Yes!" shouted Ben. "We win!"

"Oooh, Ryan, he got you," Nick said, shaking his head. "Fort Knox just got robbed!"

"Da—I mean, man!" Ryan said, slapping the side of his shorts in frustration. He'd already explained to Will how they weren't allowed to curse around Ben, but sometimes he had trouble remembering. "How'd you do that, man?" he asked. "You're like a mini Jordan."

Will smiled and wiggled his hips in celebration. "Small guys rule," he said. He wiped sweat from his brow and looked ruefully down at his blue golf shirt and gray shorts. "We also sweat too much." His shirt, soaked with moisture, clung to his body. Yanking out his collar to wipe his mouth, he grinned. "So, ready for another?"

"No way," groaned Nick. "We have football practice, remember. I need a break."

Ryan frowned at him. "Aren't you trying out for the basketball team this year?"

"Yeah," Nick told him, "but that's in the winter. It's only September." He slumped to the floor and lay back, stretching out his arms. "Whooo-wee. Besides, I reek."

"Yeah, you do," Ryan said. "In more ways than one. You best be practicing now, man, or this little dude is going to take your spot."

"If he does, I'll just sit on him and crush him," Nick said. His large chest rose and fell as he sucked in air. "Dude, I don't think I can get up again."

"I'll play," Ben said. "I'm definitely going out for basketball, so I need a lot of work."

Will lifted his eyebrows. "Want to play 21?"

Ryan sighed. "Yeah, let's do it. But this time, I'm going to be stuck to you like fly paper!"

Later, at lunchtime, Will slid into a seat between Nick and Ryan, plopping his bulging bagged lunch in front of him.

"There he is," Ryan said in greeting. "Dude, you tore up the court today. I never had somebody steal the ball from me like that. You got the hands of lightning."

"Ah, you just think you're good, Ryan," Nick said, pulling out a sandwich from his bag. "Dude, I'm so hungry after PE I could eat three of these."

"You can always eat three of anything," Ryan said, tearing open a bag of chips. "That's the problem. Maybe if you didn't eat so much you could move faster and play longer."

"Not a chance," Nick said, taking a huge bite of roast beef and bread. Chewing with his mouth open, he threw back his head in satisfaction. "Thath is good."

"And gross, man," Ryan said. "Close your mouth, dude. I hate see-food." He looked at Will. "What you got in that bag, five sandwiches?"

Will gave him a sideways smile. "Maybe. My dad packs my lunch, so I never know what I got."

"Open up and let's see," Nick said, taking another large bite.

Ben, having bought his lunch, joined them, taking the seat across from Ryan. "If you don't want it," he said, sliding into the conversation with ease, "Nick will eat it."

"Heck yeah, I will," Nick agreed, already halfway done with his sandwich.

Will licked his lips. That morning his dad had looked way too happy when he'd handed him the lunch bag on the way to the bus. One time last year, Will had opened up his bag to find a half roll of toilet paper, a bottle of water, and five dollars to buy food.

Opening the bag now, he pulled out a package of pink marshmallow cupcakes with a Disney Frozen greeting card taped to the top.

"What the he ... I mean, what is that?" Ryan said, his eyes going wide.

"Princesses think big thoughts, but when life becomes a burden ...," Nick read.

Sucking in his breath, Will flipped the card open.

"Let it go!" finished Ben, cracking up.

The card was signed, *Love and kisses, your Biggest Fan.*

"Dude, are you sure you don't have your sister's lunch?" Ryan said. "I mean, that's some cold sh—stuff."

"Ha, ha," Will said sheepishly. "My dad's a failed comedian and takes it out on me. Here." Ripping the card off, he tossed the cakes to Nick. Then he pulled out two squished sandwiches, an apple, a giant homemade cookie, and a box drink. He was relieved to see the sandwiches had only ham and cheese, not leftover chili. He jammed the card back in the bag.

"Yo, how does it all fit in that tiny bag," Ryan said. "Can you eat all that?"

"Just watch me," Will said grimly. After basketball, the boys were more than a little smelly and wore rumpled clothes. They also had ravenous appetites.

Minutes later, Nick licked the last of the cupcakes off his fingers and stared at Will, who was finishing his last bite of his second sandwich. "Where does it all go, man?" he wondered. "You're like a matchbox kid."

"Who's a matchbox kid?" boomed a voice, joining them. "I haven't played with matchbox cars since I was in kindergarten." A tall, well-built boy with thick blond hair, neatly combed, set down a tray of two cheeseburgers and two servings of fries. "How are the seventh-grade babies doing?" Sitting next to Ryan, he looked past him and saw Will. "Oh, er, what's a sixth grader doing here?"

Nick nodded at him and burped. "Hey, Glen. We're *all* seventh graders here," he said.

Ryan nodded coolly. "You're the only one *not* in the seventh grade," he added, implying that Glen didn't belong.

They were at the end of the first table, just next to the table where the majority of the football team sat. Yesterday they'd sat with the team, but had found it too crowded and noisy.

If Glen noticed the hint, he ignored it. "Hey, that's right! I recognize you from practice! You just joined the team, right?"

Will nodded, not recognizing Glen at all, which wasn't surprising. Most of the practice Will had to sit out while all the other guys did drills in pads and helmets.

"Well, let me introduce myself. I'm Glen Baker. I'm the quarterback. My sister is in your grade, did you know that?"

"Yes," sighed Ryan. "We know that."

"I was talking to the new kid," Glen said, grabbing a cheeseburger. "You guys ready for our first game next week? You should be. You'll just be sitting on the bench."

"Yo, Glen, whatchya do'in?" hollered a voice from the next table. Brad, the long-haired eighth grader, threw up a hand in disgust. "Come over and sit with us, not those pansies!"

"Uh-oh, that's my call," Glen said, giving the seventh graders a wink. "Make sure you boys sit here nice and comfortable, start practicing your bench warming." He stood and paused to stare at Will. "Are you sure you're not just the water boy? I doubt you're big enough to warm a twig."

Will stared at him. "Ha. Another failed comedian."

Glen just laughed and carried his tray away to the next table. "Yo, Brad, lookout, star quarterback coming through!"

Ryan glared after him. "That Glen," he said, "is such a punk."

Nick frowned. "Ah, he's not bad," he said. "You just have to get to know him. He likes to joke around, but he doesn't mean anything."

"You're just saying that because you like his sister Stephanie," Ben told him.

"Yeah, of course I do," Nick said, shrugging his wide shoulders. "She's hot."

"Who's his sister?" Will asked.

"You'll see her," Ryan promised. "She's one of the head cheerleaders. She and Glen have some rich parents and they get whatever they want. If Glen wants to be quarterback, Glen gets to be quarterback." He spoke with unfeigned bitterness.

"What about Brad?" Will asked. "Does he play football?"

"Brad Williamson?" Nick asked, wiping an apple on his shirt. "Nah, man. Brad is going to be your competition in basketball. He plays point guard for some hotshot travel team. He doesn't want to get injured so stays away from football." He crunched into the apple and chewed ferociously.

Will nodded thoughtfully and glanced over at where Brad and Glen laughed over some joke.

Ryan followed his gaze and wrinkled his nose. "Just look at Glen. He really thinks he's the star quarterback. What a joke."

"Dude, don't be so sore at Glen," Nick told him, swallowing. "He's in eighth grade. Of course he gets to start over you."

Ryan abruptly stood. "Whatever, man. I got to go to the bathroom."

"What was that all about?" Nick said after Ryan left. "Why's he so pi—uh, so mad?"

Ben leaned forward, looking uncomfortable. "Look, guys, I'll tell you, but you have to promise to keep it a secret." He licked his lips. "You have to understand, Ryan's family … He doesn't have a dad and I think his mom struggles with her work and stuff. Ryan wants to get a football scholarship in high school. It's probably his only way to get to college. No way can he afford it otherwise."

Nick blinked and put down his mostly eaten apple. "Oh, man. That's heavy. I didn't know that."

"Just don't tell him I told you guys," Ben said quickly. "He doesn't want anybody to know about him, you know, being poor and all."

Will nodded. "Sure, dude. I got it."

"Yeah, man. Me too," Nick added. "I play offensive line and I'll block for whoever is back there, but if Ryan gets the QB job, I'm blocking double hard."

"Good," Will said, tossing him his cookie. "Then you get a cookie. I'm full."

Chapter 10

Jared spent the lunch block barely touching his food. Sitting alone at his table, he spent the time thinking about basketball …

Someway, somehow, he had to start playing. By the time the bell rang, an idea formed in his head. For the first time in five years he couldn't play soccer in the fall. Kelly had tried out for the winter's performance of the Nutcracker and had landed a key solo. Now she had rehearsals on top of her regular dance schedule. His mom had apologized profusely and promised to make it up, but Jared had shrugged it off. He was pretty much used to everything going wrong in his life. But now he had a spark of hope. He may have just found a way to replace soccer for the time being.

Jared went to work as soon as he got off the bus. Giving his backpack to Kelly, he raced for the garage.

"What are you doing?" his sister asked, perplexed. "Like, do you need the bathroom that bad, or something?"

"Just tell Mom I'll be in later," Jared called back. "I need to do something."

"Suit yourself," Kelly called after him. "But George and Jack will probably eat all your supper again!"

Jared ignored her. Finding his father's saw and an old paint bucket, he carried them to the backyard and started searching the trees bordering the patch of dirt with tufts of grass. He found what he wanted in the midst of a young holly tree growing just beyond their driveway. About eight to nine feet from the ground, a thick branch extended over the yard with long arms of leaves spreading out in two directions.

Jared set up the bucket below the branch to use as a stepstool. Hopping on, he lifted up the saw and started cutting small twigs and leaves from the branch. He ignored the sharp, thorny leaves scraping his face and arms as he worked. He kept cutting until he created a bare v-shaped space at the end of the branch. Satisfied, he hopped down and quickly returned the bucket and saw to the garage. Next he found one of his soccer balls and went back to his branch.

He grinned. "There's my hoop and here's my ball."

Bouncing the ball on the dirt twice, he stared at the "hoop" and tried a jump shot. It hit the back of the branch and dropped into the v-shaped space.

"Yes!" Jared said, happily retrieving the ball. Grabbing it, he leapt up and did a two-handed slam on the branch. "Yes, yes!"

Jared snatched up the ball and dribbled it like a basketball, going all over the backyard before returning to the branch to do a layup. He'd seen basketball on TV, mostly after football season ended, so he knew the basics. Still, seeing layups and jump shots was a whole lot different from actually doing layups and jump shots, especially when using a branch and a dirt-packed backyard as the court.

Jared spent the next hour practicing and playing an imaginary game. When his Mom left with Kelly for dance, he had sweat dripping down his face and arms, but a big smile running up his face. Not only had he found a place to practice, but he thought he'd just found a new sport to love.

Will entered his front door after another frustrating football practice just in time to hear an upstairs door slam.

He'd heard shouting from the driveway, but had hoped it had come from the TV. No such luck. Both his mom's and dad's cars were parked out front, so everybody was home. That meant one thing ... another argument.

"How could you leave all the breakfast dishes in the sink?" screamed his mom's voice from the kitchen. "You don't even have supper ready! What were you doing all day?"

"What?" roared his father's voice. "How am I supposed to know you were coming home early? You should've called!"

"What, so you could've ordered a pizza? That's what you always do! Our kids need real food and they need a dad who can be counted on!"

"What's that supposed mean, huh? You don't think I'm a good father? Is that it?"

"That's not what I said!" His mom's voice dropped and sounded close to tears. "Oh, Phillip, don't you get? I'm tired, okay? That college has me working to the bone."

"Then maybe you should quit."

"And then what? Quitting won't help our family. We need a paycheck!"

"Then what do you want?"

"I want you to be more supportive! Help me out!"

Sighing, Will dropped his backpack and started for the stairs when he heard a whimper from the couch.

"Jimmy?" he said. "Is that you?"

Jimmy's head peeked over the cushion with tearstained cheeks. "Mom and Dad are mad," he said.

"Yeah," Will agreed. "Let's go upstairs to my room."

Jimmy climbed up on the couch and allowed Will to lift him up to his arms. For once he didn't fight back as he snuggled his cheek in Will's shoulder.

"Man," Will groaned. "You're getting big, Jimmy." Still, he held him close and patted his back. He turned for the stairs when his mom's voice hit him.

"Do you know why I'm home so early? Jimmy's school called and wanted to know why my son had only brought fruit snacks and juice for lunch."

"Why did they call you? I'm the homemaker," his dad said bitterly. "Besides, I made him a sandwich."

Will closed his eyes and groaned. He remembered his two sandwiches for lunch. His dad had been so focused on his prank that he'd messed up the packing. He turned for the kitchen wondering if he should say something when his dad stalked out and saw him.

"Will, go upstairs. Now. Your mother and I are having a discussion."

"No," said his mom. "Be truthful. We're having a fight."

"Fine," Mr. Moore snapped, turning to the kitchen. "We're having a fight! The kids can come in to sit and watch. Maybe they can keep score!" His chest heaved and his face was tight with emotion. "They can see their terrible dad falling apart. Their dad who can't even support his family. Is that what you want?"

"Oh, darling," Mrs. Moore said, coming out of the kitchen. "That's not it at all. You're a great father, it's just ..."

"Just what?!" roared Mr. Moore. "What?!" He breathed heavily and then threw up his hands. "I can't take this!"

Jimmy scrunched tight against Will's chest and squeezed his neck hard.

Squeezing his lips tight, Will quietly made his way up the stairs and headed to his room. Angel's door was firmly shut. Heavy rock blasted from the other side. Below him, his parents continued fighting.

In his room, Will gently set Jimmy down on his bed and went to close his door. Before he could, the front door from downstairs slammed shut and he knew his dad had stormed out. A minute later he heard his dad's car roar to life.

Will licked his lips, giving his head a shake. His parents hadn't fought for a long time, not like this, not that he could remember. Going over to his bed, he looked down at his little brother.

"Okay, little guy. You can rest here. It'll be all right."

Jimmy nodded and curled into a ball, closing his eyes. In moments his breathing evened out as he fell asleep.

Will wished he could just lie down and sleep his troubles away. Instead he quietly left his room and went back down the stairs. He found his mom sitting on the couch, crying.

"Mom," he said tentatively. "Are you okay?"

Looking up, she wiped her cheek and smiled. "Oh, Will, honey, I'm so sorry you had to see that. Come here. You're not too big to sit with your mother, I hope. I need a cuddle right now." She sighed and wiped her eyes. "I shouldn't have lost my temper like that. I just had such an awful day at work. And your poor dad ... he didn't need that."

Will moved around the couch and sat with his mom. Leaning against her shoulder, he tucked in his knees. "Is Dad ever going to get better?"

"What, you mean from PTS? I don't know, Will." She stroked his shoulder and looked down at him. "It's not like some sickness that just goes away, I think." She shook her head. "But you don't worry about him. You just do your best to enjoy school and growing up. I'll always be there for your dad. We'll mange. He said he's going to the gym tonight. He had to leave now anyway."

Will nodded. "Jimmy is sleeping on my bed."

Mrs. Moore squeezed Will's shoulder close to her and gave him a kiss on the top of his head.

She immediately made a face and wrinkled her nose. "Will!" she cried. "You smell like a pile of dirty laundry! And your hair is greasier than your dad's chili!"

"Sorry, Mom," he said guiltily. "I just had football practice and played some basketball earlier."

Mrs. Moore pursed her lips but then chuckled. "Well, I guess it's too late now. But you'd better wash up before supper." She coughed. "I, er, told your father I'll order a pizza."

"Sure, Mom," Will said sleepily. He closed his eyes and relaxed …

Angel came down the stairs minutes later to find her mom picking at Will's messy hair. He lay with his head draped over her lap, breathing gently.

"Ew, Mom," she said. "What are you doing?"

"Your brother," Mrs. Moore said dryly, "needs a shower. And now, so do I."

"Is Dad gone?" Angel asked. "He hadn't been drinking, right?"

Mrs. Moore closed her eyes and breathed out heavily. "I know you've been through rough times, Angel, but your dad is a good man. He stopped drinking years ago. He'll be back just the same as always."

"That's what I'm afraid of," Angel muttered.

"Angel, not now, please. Come, help me move Will and let me order us supper."

"Sure, Mom." Angel moved to the front of the couch and leaned over Will's sleeping form. "Hey, kid," she said loudly, smacking the side of his shorts. "Go up and take a shower. You reek."

"Angel!" cried Mrs. Moore. "That's not what I had in mind!"

Will woke up with a start and then grinned. "It's okay, Mom," he said groggily. "She has to practice hitting on boys somehow."

That earned him another smack, only much harder.

Late that night, close to midnight, Mr. Moore knocked softy on Will's door and crept in. Leaving the light off, he called softly. "You awake, big guy?"

Will had been lying on his pillow staring up in the darkness. Now he sat up and stretched out his back, feeling tension leave him. His father sounded like himself. He hadn't been drinking.

"Yeah, Dad. What time is it?"

"Time for a workout, of course. Let's go."

"Ha, ha."

Mr. Moore sighed. "I know, guy. I … I kind of blew it today, didn't I?"

"I did have two sandwiches," Will told him. "They were pretty good, though."

"What about the card? Did you like it?"

"I let it go. In the trash."

Mr. Moore chuckled. Then he coughed. "Um, Will. About tomorrow … you don't want to do a workout, do you?"

Will licked his lips in the darkness, thinking. "No, not really."

"I … I understand."

"I think we should save it for Saturday," Will said. "You know, make it doubly as long."

Immediately Mr. Moore's voice perked up. "Is that right? You mean that?"

"Sure, Dad. Next week I get my football pads and I'm last on the depth chart. I need the practice, but I'm too tired for tomorrow morning."

"In that case, champ, what are you doing still awake at this hour? Get some sleep."

"Ha, ha, Dad. Hilarious."

The lights flipped off and Will fell back in his bed, exhausted, but relieved. Angel had warned him about their dad's drinking days and had confessed she feared they would return. So far, their dad had made it. He'd managed to wait at least another day.

Chapter 11

Football never did go as planned for Will. All the coaches thought him too small to play, and joining the team late made it difficult for him to prove them wrong. By the time he got his helmet and pads, the depth charts were filled and he ended up standing on the sidelines for the first three games. Even being one of the fastest players on the team didn't help. He often finished in a dead heat with Ryan during team sprints, but the coaches chalked it up to him getting more rest on the sidelines, so he wasn't as tired.

September ended and finally, after their fourth loss in a row, Mr. Hackett, the defensive coach, let him start at cornerback. Their next game was against Hamilton, their archrival who had a pass-happy quarterback.

"Use your speed and keep the receivers in front of you," Mr. Hackett had told Will during the last practice before the game. "And if any big guy comes at you with the ball … just duck low and go for the ankles. Slow him down and wait for help. Got it?"

Will had just stared at him. Then during the game he made four open-field tackles, two pass deflections, and a diving interception. The red and black clad Washington Middle Patriots still lost by the score of 24 to 12.

All the coaches at least took notice and went out of their way to smack his shoulder pads and tell him great job. Still, Mr. Hackett only moved him up to third in the depth chart for cornerback. Nobody asked him to play running back.

"It's the tradition," Ryan told him the following day at lunch. "Only the eighth graders get playing time, especially the ones with rich daddies who donate money to the team." He glared in the direction of Glen.

"But don't they want to win?" Will asked, incredulous. "I mean, we haven't won a single game yet."

"We're used to that," Nick said, licking ketchup off his fingers. It was corn dog day and the burly boy had two on his tray, in addition to his packed lunch. "Last year we had our first winning season in ten seasons. My brother played here years ago and he never won a single game, man."

"Great," groaned Will. He put down his sandwich and felt his shoulders slump. "I can't wait for basketball to start."

Ryan smiled without humor. "Just be careful. The last coach quit because he didn't like how things were done here. So expect more of the same in basketball. If you're not in eighth grade, you're probably on the bench." His eyes hardened. "To tell you the truth, I'm ready to quit football right now."

Will kind of felt the same way, but of course never did. His dad continued waking him up before school for runs and pushups. "Stay the course, champ," he kept preaching. "Your time will come. And when it does, you're going to be ready."

Mr. Moore made it a rule to never interfere in his children's sports. He attended all of Will's games, but always stood silently on the sidelines just watching. Still, Will knew his dad was just itching to ask his coach for more playing time. A lot of other dads did, causing all sorts of embarrassment to their sons.

Coach Marsden, the head coach, was a burly bald man with a huge, bushy, black mustache. When he chewed gum during games, his upper lip looked as if it held a caterpillar crawling on a treadmill. He always wore slick athletic pants and a Washington Middle football hoodie, no matter the weather. Whenever the parents started barking at him about his play calling or for not playing their sons enough, he would simply pull up his hood and stare intently at his whiteboard, chewing vigorously, never responding or giving in.

October crawled past and the leaves started changing to vibrant colors before littering the ground with bright yellows and reds. What didn't change was Washington Middle football. Entering Halloween week, they stood at 0-8. In the latest game Will played defense and special teams. He had yet to touch the ball on offense.

When Halloween arrived on a Friday, they were 0-9 and had a single game left. The day before they'd lost 35 to 0 to Berkshire. They would not be making the playoffs.

"I knew I should've quit," Ryan said, kicking the outside door of the locker room as he stepped out. "This is embarrassing! Everyone laughs when they see me wearing my football jersey."

Nick grunted in agreement as he followed after him. "Yeah, I wore a sweater over mine yesterday."

It was after school and they'd just finished changing into their pads and now headed for the practice field. This meant exiting the back of the gym and walking through the rear parking lot before crossing the baseball field to reach the football field.

Will brought up the rear, carrying his helmet loosely beside him. He made no comment as he listened miserably to their cleats crunch and clump on the asphalt. That pretty much summed up his thoughts. Crunch, crunch, there went his football season.

The players were all required to wear their game jerseys on game day, to try to drum up school spirit. Instead, all they managed to drum up was ridicule. When washing his hands in the bathroom the other day, a kid had come up to Will and had slapped his back. "I didn't know they let sixth graders play football," he'd said. "No wonder we can't win a game. Hey, what's the difference between your football team and a vacuum?" Will had ignored him. "I'll tell you. You both suck, but a vacuum cleans up and you guys *get* cleaned up. Good luck today, loser!"

The memory still caused his cheeks to burn. As they reached the grass to the baseball outfield, Will noticed a familiar figure standing on the sideline. Dressed in a heavy camouflage jacket and jeans, he threw a plush football to a little kid in a bright blue winter hat, black hoodie, and Adidas warm-up pants. Will recognized the clothes immediately.

"Dad?" he said. Breaking into a run, he left Nick and Ryan to race the rest of the way to the field.

Mr. Moore saw him coming and turned to meet him. "Hiya, champ," he said, grinning. "Surprised to see me?"

"What are you guys doing here?" Will asked. Still on the run, he dropped his helmet and leapt into his dad's arms, pads and all.

His dad caught him and staggered back. "Whoa, watch it, guy. You have cleats on, don't forget."

"Seriously, Dad, why are you here?" Will demanded. His dad had never been to one of his practices before. Will always had to take the activity bus home.

Mr. Moore lifted him high and then set him down. "What are you talking about? I just took Jimmy out to toss the ball around." Jimmy waved from where he crouched over the plush ball, like he'd laid an egg … or pooped it out. "We came here for the space. The question is, what are you doing here? The last I heard, you didn't play football. You just sat on the bench."

"Ha, ha."

Mr. Moore mussed up the front of his hair. "Man, you need a haircut."

"I just got one last Saturday," Will said, ducking away.

"Really? In that case I need my money back."

"One day, Dad, you're going to tell a funny joke."

"Yeah, and one day you're actually going to play running back in a game. I just came to see how practices are run. That's all. I promise. I'll keep away from your coaches. I won't be a crazy dad."

Bending down to retrieve his helmet, Will looked back at him and grinned ruefully. "Too late for that."

Mr. Moore aimed a playful kick at his backside. "Don't tempt me, bud."

On the field the whistle blew and the coaches started calling everyone to line up for stretching.

"Go get them, champ," Mr. Moore said, giving a swift slap to his shoulder pad. "Oh, by the way, if you have plans tonight, cancel them. I bribed Jimmy that if he came with me you'll take him trick-or-treating."

Will had started to run onto the field, but now stopped. "But Dad, you said I could go with my friends!"

"And you can," Mr. Moore said, smiling. "And so can Jimmy. Aren't I a nice dad?"

Will jammed on his helmet. "You, nice? Now that was almost funny."

Jared rubbed his eyes as he stared at the computer screen in front of him. For his elective he'd chosen typing class. For his midterm exam he'd been assigned to type a two-page letter without a single error in less than three minutes. That had been the week before and he'd ended up with five errors in two minutes, thirty-four seconds, good enough for an F for his final grade. That meant now, on a Friday, Halloween night, he sat stuck at school redoing the exam.

Ms. Jackson, a short, no-nonsense lady with dark ebony skin and a voice of flint, had suggested he do so if he wanted to pass her class. You did what she said, or risked watching sparks fly. Then you'd only end up burned. At the moment she sat at her desk reading something on her computer as Jared readied himself to start typing.

"Are you ready, Jared?" she asked, not looking up.

Two other kids were in the room with him, but they were still practicing their form and would be taking the test a little later. Jared was in a hurry because he'd called his mom for a ride home. Kelly had dance that night and if he didn't finish by 3:30 he would be stuck at school, forced to use the dreaded activity bus.

"Uh, ready," he mumbled.

"What was that? Speak up," his teacher demanded. A tough but fair lady, Ms. Jackson expected the best from everyone at all times. You toed her line, no exceptions.

"I'm ready, uh, ma'am," Jared said louder.

"Okay, I'm going to start the timer. Tell me when you finish. Ready, go!"

It took two more tries before Jared managed to get the letter typed without errors. By that time, it was well past 3:30 and he would have to wait over an hour before the bus would take him home. Only one activity bus ran, so the ride home could take anywhere between five minutes to an hour—it had to go all over the place.

Jared was tempted to walk home, but that meant crossing a busy street and walking over two miles. Instead, he asked Ms. Jackson if she needed help with anything.

"You're a dear, Jared," the teacher replied kindly. "What you can do is take my recycling to the dumpster. Just make sure you put it in with the cardboard and not the trash."

Jared grunted. Most teachers had no qualms about dumping old paper in the trash, but Ms. Jackson had an old milk crate she used for recycling. When Jared got to it, he found it overflowing with paper. Bending, he had to strain to lift it.

"You got it, Jared?" Ms. Jackson asked. "It's not too heavy, I hope."

Jared bit his bottom lip and shook his head. He would never admit it even it was too heavy. Apparently, a lot of kids failed Ms. Jackson's typing exams. He felt honored to be on her good side. "I got it," he wheezed.

"Thanks, Jared. I'll get the door. You know, this is a great way to earn extra credit."

"Yes, ma'am," Jared said through gritted teeth. The crate wasn't really *that* heavy, but the plastic sides dug into his hands and that was a problem. He made it out the door and quickly headed up the hallway to the rear doors near the dumpsters.

The main section of Washington Middle was constructed in sort of a horseshoe shape with the gym in the middle area near the left, with a later hall added on to the back to close the horseshoe. The computer room was on the right hall of the horseshoe and Jared had a long walk to the back doors.

Midway down the hall, another addition of an intersecting hall ran off on Jared's right. This led to the Pathfinder classrooms and ended at the auditorium and band room. As he reached the intersecting hall, Jared started to feel the burn in his fingers and arms. Sucking in his breath, he hurried up the hall, now passing the eighth-grade classrooms.

When three rooms from the rear door, his hands begged for mercy and he abruptly dropped the crate. It landed with a sharp, resounding crash. Immediately a frightened squeal erupted from the classroom on his right.

Surprised, Jared gave a start and froze.

"Wh-who's there?" a timid girl's voice asked. "Is, is that you, Mr. Drydon?"

Jared frowned and coughed loudly, clearing his throat. "Uh, uh, it's me," he muttered. "Uh, hello?"

Angie stuck her head out the doorway, her scared face framed with dark curls. Seeing Jared, her whole face relaxed and she practically launched herself at him, stopping herself just a foot away from him. "Oh, thank goodness it's you," she said, sounding out of breath. "I was so scared."

Jared could only bite his bottom lip and stare, very confused. "Wh-what are you doing here?" he stammered. "I mean, why are you scared?"

Angie swallowed hard and looked back down the hallway. "I'm always here after school," she said, wiping a strand of hair from her face. "Mr. Drydon pays me to watch John. I'm supposed to take him trick-or-treating later."

"Uh, so where's he now?"

"Mr. Drydon took him out to McDonald's for his supper. He asked if I wanted to come, but I don't feel right going out to eat with the principal, even if John is there. Besides, I wanted to get my homework done for the weekend." She spoke fast and nervous, but suddenly stopped. Then her eyes grew hard. "Any way, what are *you* doing here?"

Taken aback by her sudden animosity, Jared stepped back. "What?"

"Why are you here? Have you been following me? Was that you?"

John bit his lower lip as he fumbled for an answer. "I, uh, I was with, uh, typing, I don't know what you're talking about. I was with Ms. Jackson redoing my midterm," he finally managed to say. "I dropped the paper by accident."

Angie stared at him and suddenly ducked her head. Jared was sure he'd seen tears in her eyes.

"What's wrong?" he asked, surprised to feel a rush of confidence flow through him. Having two younger sisters made him naturally protective, especially when around crying girls. "Did something happen?"

"Oh, I don't know … I was in Mr. Drydon's office using his computer. Everyone left early for Halloween, so I was alone … but I didn't *feel* alone. Somebody, or something, was watching me. I could feel it." Angie shuddered and took a deep breath. She wore a black frilly blouse over blue jeans and now crossed her arms over her chest. "It was the creepiest feeling I ever had. I even called out, but nobody answered." Now her eyes closed. "Then something fell outside the door. And I heard … a voice. That's when I freaked. I ran out of there so fast and went into the hall."

"It could've been a janitor," Jared said doubtfully. "Or another teacher."

"Maybe," Angie said without conviction. "But I don't think so." She shivered. "In the hallway I still felt like I was being watched. That's when I came over here." She looked at Jared. "You didn't see anybody, did you?"

Jared shook his head. "No, but I just left the computer lab. I'm bringing her paper to recycle." He saw Angie was still spooked. He remembered that she enjoyed reading vampire novels and other spooky stories. He figured Halloween probably had unnerved her.

Clearing his throat, he said, "Ms. Jackson's still here if you want to wait for Mr. Drydon there."

Angie widened her eyes and looked at Jared. "You do believe me, right?"

"Uh, yeah … of course. School is scary enough during school hours."

Angie smiled and relaxed. "Perhaps it was just my imagination, but just in case I'll go sit with Ms. Jackson." She ducked her head shyly. "Thanks, Jared."

Just like that, Jared's confidence left him. Tongue-tied, he bobbed his head and grunted. Then he hastily stooped down and grabbed up the milk crate. "I, uh, I better go. But I'll wait here to see you get to Ms. Jackson's okay," he finished hastily, feeling his cheeks burn red.

Angie smiled at him and headed away. Jared waited for her to reach the computer lab. She waved just before disappearing into the doorway.

Breathing out a sigh of relief, Jared lifted his burden and staggered the rest of the way to the rear entrance, using his back to open one of the doors. Exiting, he stumbled onto a sidewalk and had to catch his footing. The sidewalk led to the rear parking lot at the back of the school. It flanked a small service road on his left leading to the dumpsters at the rear of the gym.

The shrill sound of whistles from the football field let him know practice had yet to end. The high outer wall of the band room on his right blocked his view of the field.

He didn't really care. The team stank. He just wanted to dump his load of paper and get back to Ms. Jackson's room.

Thinking of Angie sitting there frightened caused his forehead to break out in sweat. Would she talk to him again? Or ignore him like she'd been doing since the sixth grade. And did he *want* her to talk to him? What should he say?

"This is so confusing," he murmured. Still, a slight thrill ran down his back.

As he approached the dumpsters, straining with the heavy crate before him, trying to puzzle out what to say to Angie, he heard a noise.

Immediately, he went still. It sounded like something scraping or clawing at metal and it came from the dumpster in front of him.

Nervously biting his lower lip, he took a hesitant step forward. Again he heard the noise, only this time louder. It definitely sounded like claws scraping metal. What if Angie *had* heard something?

His imagination took over and Jared felt his knees start to tremble. His hands started to shake and he dropped the milk crate, spilling paper in all directions.

Chapter 12

"Hey!" cried a high-pitched voice. "Who's there? Is that you, Will?"

A small boy darted out from behind the dumpster carrying a stick.

Jared gasped with relief, feeling very foolish.

Seeing Jared, the boy stopped and stared at him with wide brown eyes. Dirt stains smudged the knees of his black athletic pants and he had a dark smear across the chest of his hoodie. Reaching up, he tugged on a blue winter hat. "Who are you?" he asked, quickly recovering from his surprise.

"What? Uh, I'm just, uh, Jared. I'm, uh, dumping the paper."

The boy's eyes narrowed. He looked to be five or six. "Dumping? Do you mean pooping? Hey, tonight's Halloween. I'm going to be a ninja."

"Oh, uh, that's great. Are your, uh, dad and mom around?"

"Yeah." The boy smiled mischievously. "They're pooping somewhere."

Jared rolled his eyes. "Okay," he said. He wondered if he should offer the kid some paper for wiping, but thought better of it.

Gathering up the spilled paper, he stuffed it all back in the crate. Picking it back up, he walked past the poop-obsessed boy and started shoving the paper into the dumpster marked for recycling. First he had to pull open the side door. It screeched as it slid open, causing the boy to cover his ears.

"That sounded like a dinosaur," he cried. "Do it again!"

"Hold on," Jared muttered, grabbing up paper. Little kids were more annoying than bothersome.

"Jimmy!" called a man's voice from around the side of school. "Where are you, little man? Will, go find your brother. I think he might be dumpster diving again."

The boy wrinkled his nose. "Uh-oh. That's my dad. Bye!" He raced to the edge of the band room, dropping his stick behind him.

Jared went still. He didn't want to be caught at the dumpster.

"There you are, Jimmy," a boy's voice said. He sounded slightly younger than Jared with a pleasant, high voice. Something sounded familiar about it, but Jared couldn't place it. "Don't run off like that! All sorts of weirdos hang around dumpsters."

Jared felt his face flush and he slipped behind the dumpster.

"I was just looking for something to use as a ninja sword," he heard Jimmy explain. "There's a whole bunch of stuff back there."

"Yeah," the older boy said, "and you're wearing some of it. What's that on your shirt?"

"Poop!"

"Yep, sure looks like it. Let's go see Dad. If you want to come trick-or-treating you'd better hurry. We need to be showered and changed in thirty minutes."

"Race you!"

Jared waited for the voices to move off before he came out from behind the dumpster. Feeling like a total loser, he hefted the empty crate in his hand and trotted to the end of the band room to satisfy his curiosity. He knew the older kid's voice from somewhere.

Peering around the corner, he saw the back of a slight boy in football pants running behind Jimmy, herding the little kid to a man holding a helmet and pads.

Jared's eyes went wide. It was the new kid he'd never made friends with … With school work piling up and separate classes, he'd nearly forgotten about him. Friendship this late in the year seemed impossible. Yet, he had a chance and had just blown it.

"Just great," Jared muttered. "At least I know he has an annoying little brother. And that I'll never get another chance to meet him again."

Angry and embarrassed by his shyness, Jared swung the crate irritably as he went back to the school doors. Why did he have to hide every time people came around him? Why couldn't he just act like a normal kid and not be so afraid of talking?

And then he found the doors locked. Groaning, Jared leaned his forehead against the door and kicked it with his toe. "I'm such an idiot."

He'd forgotten. All outer doors were locked for security. During a school day he would just have to push a button and somebody in the main office would open it for him. But Angie had said everyone had left. And he'd never asked Ms. Jackson for her key.

Muttering in frustration, he stepped back, resisting the idea of throwing the milk crate against the doors. Instead he stalked down the sidewalk, going to the left to take the long way to the front of the school, the opposite direction that little Jimmy and his brother had gone.

As he left, the back doors clicked open, but Jared never heard. He also never knew he was being watched with every step he took. Cameras were everywhere.

When he arrived at the front of the school, he slumped down on a bench by the main entrance to wait for the bus. The crate clattered beside him.

He'd planned to go trick-or-treating by himself that night, but now knew it was hopeless. He wouldn't get home until after six and still needed to eat and shower. Besides, he had nothing to wear for a costume. And what loser went trick-or-treating by himself?

So focused on his problems, he never noticed he wasn't alone until he felt something tickle his right ear. Thinking a spider had dropped on him, he leapt from the bench, tripping over the milk crate as he did so. He ended up sprawling on his hands, banging his knees on the concrete.

Harsh laughter burst out from behind him.

"It is you," crowed a harsh voice. "It's church boy!"

Turning to a sitting position on the pavement, he looked up with a stricken face.

Gary stood behind the bench pointing down at him, his mouth twisted in a cruel smile.

"Nice one, Chaz," Ray said, leaning on Gary's right shoulder, still bent over in laughter.

Chaz stood beside the bench, smirking down at Jared. A leaf dangled in his hand.

"You okay, man?" he asked cheerfully. "You looked awfully worried there, so I thought I'd lighten the mood. At least lighten the bench. Uh, nice landing."

Jared only swallowed and didn't move. He hadn't had much contact with Chaz since he'd started hanging out with Gary and Ray. Just as Jared predicted, as soon as Chaz found more popular friends, he'd dropped Jared like a moldy hot potato. Even now he acted as if he didn't know Jared's name.

"Hey, church boy," Gary said, moving up and leaning over the bench to leer down. "You don't happen to want any weed, do you?" He reached lazily in his pocket and fished out a small plastic bag. A quarter of the bag was filled with dry, shredded green leaves, almost looking like paper. "This here is the good stuff."

"Yeah, and since it's Halloween and all," Ray added, "we have a special deal. It could be a trick, or a treat. Want to try? Five bucks for a hit. We take cash."

Jared felt his arms and legs shake. He didn't trust himself to speak, so just looked down at the concrete below him. From inside his jeans, he could feel blood trickling down his knees.

"Look at him," Ray said. "He's scared stiff."

"I think he's doing a mannequin challenge," Ray offered. "Either that, or he's so tight he's going to snap. Come on, Jared, this stuff will loosen you up. I got it fresh today, straight from the bottle. It's spicy."

"Let's just leave him," Chaz finally said. "He's about to spray in his pants and we got things to do tonight. Halloween, baby."

"Loser," Gary said, stuffing the bag into his pocket.

Laughing, the trio turned from Jared and disappeared back into the bushes, heading down the side of the building toward the rear parking lot.

Jared still didn't move until they were well out of earshot. Then he slowly picked himself up and limped to the front of the school. As he leaned against the door, he felt tears start to trickle from his eyes.

He hastily wiped them away as a car pulled up in front., a shiny, red Honda Civic.

He watched nervously as Mr. Drydon climbed out from the driver's seat, wiping a sweaty brow. Even though a cool day, the principal's hair seemed dark with sweat.

"Okay, John, let's go," Mr. Drydon said, not seeing Jared. His voice sounded impatient and a little strained. "Now, son. Angie is waiting for you inside. You like Angie, remember?"

The rear door opened and John stepped out. He wore a pirate's costume, but had the eye patch around his head facing backwards.

Mr. Drydon grabbed John's shoulder and guided him to the sidewalk toward the school. "There you go," he said. "Now, don't forget. Angie is taking you trick-or-treating tonight. I'm going to go home. You'll meet me at her house later tonight, okay? But first, if you need the bathroom while trick-or-treating, you go to the school. You understand? I don't want you in any stranger's house. Angie has a key and knows to take you here. Understand? I'll be at her place at eight on the dot. Stay with Angie until then. But remember to use the bathroom at the school. Got it, John?"

John appeared not to hear as he smiled lazily at the school. Then his eyes met Jared and he smiled wider, lifting up his hand in a wave.

Jared, feeling caught in a place and time where he did not belong, gave a quick, timid wave back.

Mr. Drydon saw him and looked startled. Quickly he recovered and frowned. "Excuse me, but are you a student here?"

Jared had never spoken with the principal before and found his mouth too dry to speak now. Dumbly, he nodded, too nervous to speak.

Mr. Drydon stared for a long second, scrunching his mouth in disapproval. "Well, if you're waiting for the activity bus," he finally said, "it won't be here for another half hour. You should wait inside."

Biting his bottom lip, Jared nodded again. Coughing, he finally found his voice. "I, uh, got locked out."

"It happens," Mr. Drydon said, grunting.

Perspiration gleamed from his forehead and he appeared a little unwell. Jared guessed he must be sick and that was why he wanted Angie to take care of John that night.

John walked over to stand right by Jared's shoulder. Smiling brightly, he said, "Hi, Jared."

"Oh, uh, yeah," Jared said, surprised that John remembered him. "Uh, hey, John."

"Hey," John said, too loudly. "Are you going trick-or-treating?"

Mr. Drydon raised his eyebrows. "You two know each other?"

"Yeah, uh, I was in his class last year," Jared said, feeling his face grow warm. He hid his embarrassment by retrieving the empty crate.

"Huh," said Mr. Drydon, losing interest. "Well, come on in." He took out his badge that acted as a key, but before he could use it, the door clicked, the lock popping free on its own.

Mr. Drydon's face froze for a second. Then he snorted. "Must be the custodian in the office," he mumbled, hastily pulling open the unlocked door. "John, you stay with me." To Jared, he said, "Go where you need to be and nowhere else. Got it?"

Jared nodded and followed the principal and his son into the school. He didn't know what to say, so said nothing.

John stayed close to his father and didn't seem to notice Jared any longer.

Keeping his head down, Jared left them at the office to return the milk crate to the computer lab. He walked gingerly, his knees still stinging.

Halfway down the front hall to the lab, the loudspeaker crackled and Mr. Drydon's voice boomed from overhead. *"Angie Robinson, to the main office."* Like outside, he sounded impatient. *"We're back. Angie Robinson, come to the office immediately."*

As the speaker died, so did Jared's willpower. After what had just happened, he didn't want to have to face another person, especially Angie.

Quickly he ducked into the nearest boy's bathroom in the front hall and waited until he heard Angie's footsteps rush past. Then he went to a stall and grabbed a handful of toilet paper. He left the milk crate by the sink as he soaked the tissue. Then he returned to the stall, slumping down on the toilet seat.

"This is my worst day yet," he muttered.

It only got worse when he found his jeans were torn at both knees. They were his best pair.

He carefully pulled down his jeans and washed the bloody scrapes on both knees. Thankfully, they were superficial and he didn't need any bandages. Finished, he pulled up his jeans and got up to throw the bloody clump of paper in the toilet. Flushing, he stared down at the swirling red clump and couldn't help but imagine that it resembled his life. It was all going down. As the water filled back up, he sat back on the toilet, hanging his head.

Now, hidden away, he let his tears roll. Halloween night and he had no friends, just bullies. Remembering Gary, Ray, and Chaz, he shuddered. He couldn't remember feeling so alone before.

He wasn't sure how long he sat there, but after a time his eyes finally went dry. Before he could stand up, he heard soft footsteps enter the bathroom. A shoe scraped the floor.

Jared's breath stopped and he felt his heart start to pound. Somebody stood outside his stall. He didn't dare move. Out of habit, he'd chosen the farthest stall from the door, where he could have the most privacy. At first he feared it was one of the bullies, but a heavy breathing told him otherwise. It sounded like an adult. It felt like something worse. Jared got a bad feeling.

Mr. Drydon wore hard soled shoes that made a clicking noise against the floor. This person barely made a sound when he walked. Perhaps it was only his imagination, but Jared could almost feel the temperature drop as if something sinister lurked outside the stall. The heavy breathing continued. Whoever it was wore strong cologne. A sharp, chemical smell filled the bathroom and Jared felt his eyes start to water. He immediately started to feel dizzy.

Then the person, definitely a man, snorted through his nose and spat in the sink. After running the water for a few seconds, he left just as quietly as he came in. The sharp smell slowly dissipated, drifting after him.

His head spinning, Jared waited at least two full minutes before getting up. He staggered from the stall and over to the sink. He shook his head at the mirror.

"This has been one rotten day," he said blearily, staring at his bloodshot reflection.

The fumes were stronger by the sink. Picking up the milk crate where he'd left it, he hurried from the bathroom, breathing deeply in the much fresher air in the hallway. He nearly fled to Ms. Jackson's room, only to find her already gone.

His backpack sat outside the door with a note on top. Picking it up, he read aloud, "Jared, where did you go? I waited, but have to rush home for Halloween. I know you're taking the bus, so you'll be back. Enjoy your weekend, Ms. Jackson."

Sighing, he crumpled up the paper and dropped it in the crate to be recycled.

Leaving the crate in the hall, he snatched up his backpack and headed out front. He left through the front doors closest to the lab, avoiding the main entrance. He'd rather not face anybody right now.

Thankfully, he exited just in time to see the activity bus pull into the spot where Mr. Drydon's car had parked. It, Jared reflected, had been a long, strange day. And he still had Halloween night to get through. He doubted he would be up for trick-or-treating. He'd already had enough scares for the evening.

Chapter 13

Will rushed out of the bathroom in just his boxer shorts, still dripping wet.

"Dad," he cried. "Where's my costume? We're going to be late!"

"I have it here in your room," his dad called. "I picked it out special."

"Great," Will muttered. "I bet you did." If his dad had a princess costume, or something …

"Jimmy is downstairs waiting," Mrs. Moore called, almost too cheerful. "He's all set!"

"Hurry up!" Jimmy hollered. "I want candy! Candy, candy, candy!"

Muttering to himself about the injustices of having little brothers, Will hurried to his room.

Nick lived in a fancy, upscale neighborhood, just behind the football field at their middle school. He promised some serious candy there. Ryan and Ben were also going, but Ben wasn't allowed to dress up. His parents didn't celebrate Halloween, but at least allowed him to tagalong with his friends. The plan was to meet up at the school and walk across the field for the trick-or-treating.

Mr. Moore raised his eyebrows when Will dashed into his room. "Oh, I see you got your own costume. With your white chest you look just like a ghost."

"Ha, ha," Will said, covering his pale skin with his arms. The summer tan had faded and only his arms and lower legs remained brown from football. "Where is it?"

Mr. Moore tossed him a single-piece black outfit with a white skeleton printed on the outside. It looked like something more in Jimmy's size.

"Seriously," Will said, holding it up doubtfully. "A naked skeleton?"

"Hey, guy," his dad said with a shrug, "everyone says you're skin and bones. Now you can just be bones. Honestly, it was the only costume left in your size. The rest were way too big."

"Only little kids wear costumes like this, Dad!"

"Um, bud," Mr. Moore said, clearing his throat. "I hate to break it to you, but you're still—"

"Bye, Dad," Will said. "You can get the car ready."

"Wait, you forgot the best part." Mr. Moore reached in his pocket and pulled out a flat, round container and a cylinder the size of a pen. He grinned. "White makeup and black liner for your face. Your sister could help you put it on."

Will caught the containers against his stomach and made a face. "A naked skeleton with makeup," he muttered. "Wow. Thanks, Dad."

"You're welcome, champ." His dad winked at him. "It's safer than using a mask."

His dad left whistling a happy tune. Frowning, Will put down the containers and hastily pulled on the nearly skintight costume. It had a zipper in the back with a long nylon string that ran up all the way into a hood. Contorting his body, he managed to reach back and yank it up. It took effort, but he managed to get everything set. Then it was time for the worst part …

Angel was getting ready for a party later that night, but was only too happy to take a break to put makeup on her little brother. She ushered him into her room and sat him on her bed.

"Let me see," she said, picking up the makeup. "You sure you don't want a different color? Something to bring out those big brown eyes?"

"Just hurry," Will pleaded. "I'm going to be late!"

"Okay, kid. Just hold still." She scraped up a handful of white goo and smeared it all over his face. "I always dreamed of this day, Will," she told him, rubbing his cheeks and forehead with the white. "I wanted a little sister that I could dress up and put makeup on …"

"Just finish already," Will growled through clenched lips.

"Hmmph. Just for that ..." After rubbing in the white, Angel used the liner. After giving Will a black mouth with stitches, she added two huge black eyes and black nostrils on his nose. When finished, she yanked up the hood on the back of his costume and stepped back to admire her handiwork. "Not bad, little bro. I almost wish I was going with you."

"If you want," he said hopefully, looking up with big eyes, "you can take Jimmy to your party."

She flicked him on the head and pulled him off her bed. "That's okay. Just bring me back some candy." She pushed him to the door. "I love the sour gummies, so save me those."

"Hurry up!" shouted Jimmy's voice from below them. "I need candy!"

Will sighed. "Sure."

Angel smacked his shoulder. "Seriously, though. Have fun, little bro. Don't let Jimmy rattle your bones."

Daylight savings time was still a week away, so as Will stepped out of the front passenger seat of his dad's Corolla, the sun was just about to set. His dad had pulled up to the curb at the back of the school near the baseball and football fields. Jimmy impatiently waited in the backseat for Will to open his door.

"You guys be careful," Mr. Moore said from behind the wheel. "I'll be at the gym until 1900 and meet you right back here at 1930. Got it?"

"Yes, Dad," Will said, pulling up his hood. His white face gleamed with excitement. His parents had never allowed him to go trick-or-treating so far from home before. Not even Jimmy's presence was going to ruin it. Yanking open the passenger door, he stepped aside. "Okay, little guy. Let's go."

"I'm not a little guy," Jimmy said ferociously as he climbed out to the sidewalk. "I'm a ninja! I'll cut you up into poop!"

He had on his white karate costume with a black belt over a skintight athletic shirt with a hood and mask attached. The shirt was meant for cold weather sports, something Mr. Moore had found at his gym. With his hood and mask, Jimmy did resemble a mini-ninja. He also carried a long plastic sword with an extra-large pillow case.

"Hi-ya!" he exclaimed, attacking Will's backside with his sword.

"Hey, dude!" Will said. "Stop that, or you'll have to stay with Dad."

"Nope," Mr. Moore said cheerfully. "He's all yours." His voice grew serious. "Will, do you want my cell phone?"

"That's okay," Will replied, rubbing the stinging area on the back of his costume. "If Jimmy doesn't behave, I'll just take all his candy."

"No!" cried his brother, instantly lowering his sword.

"I mean just in case you have a real emergency," Mr. Moore said, gripping the wheel tightly.

"Oh." Will shook his head. "The other guys will have theirs. It'll be okay, Dad. Really."

Mr. Moore breathed out and nodded. "I know, champ. I just … Well, I don't want anything to go wrong. If anything does, call me first. Before calling your mother. Got it?"

Will nodded. "Sure, Dad. I will." He knew his dad couldn't help worrying.

His father relaxed and grinned. "You'll be careful. I know that. Go have fun with your friends."

"Where are they?" Jimmy complained. "We need candy!"

The other guys were already waiting on the small metal bleachers at the football field. Seeing Will and Jimmy, they called out and waved.

With a final wave, Mr. Moore beeped the horn and drove off. Will and Jimmy hurried across the baseball outfield to the football bleachers.

"Nice face, Will," Nick said in way of greeting. "You look like a sick cow."

"Ha, ha," Will said. "What are you? I can't see a costume."

Nick wore ripped jeans and an old T-shirt with his face painted pale green and spotted with fake red sores and blood. "I'm a zombie, man," he said. "So you guys are safe with me. No brains to eat here."

"Funny," Ryan said. He had a monster's mask pulled up on his head and otherwise wore a dark hoodie and jeans. Now he pulled down the mask, showing off a nasty red face with sharp teeth, warts, and deep scars on the cheeks. "And I'm your mom, Nick."

"Hey, man!" Nick cried. "Take that back!" He swiped at Ryan, who quickly dodged back.

"Do that again," Ryan said in falsetto voice, "and I'll send you to your room!"

"You jerk!" Nick snarled, running at Ryan.

Jimmy grew shy and hid behind Will as Nick chased Ryan across the field.

Will reached back and patted his head absently. "Uh … We'll be going soon, Jimmy. I think."

"This isn't the way to treat your mom!" Ryan yelled back as he ran past them, going in circles.

"I'm so going to crush you!" Nick roared back, just a few feet behind.

Ben hopped from the bleachers where he'd been sitting. He wore his normal clothes, blue jeans and a sweater.

"I'm glad you finally came," he said to Will with little enthusiasm. "We've been waiting." He looked slightly envious at seeing Will's costume. Unlike the other boys, he didn't carry a pillow case or bag for candy. "My parents won't even let me get the candy," he explained ruefully when he saw Will notice his empty hands. His face twisted into something dark for a moment. "They won't let me have much of anything."

"You can have some of mine," Will told him. "Definitely take all my sour gummies."

Ben grunted, but looked pleased.

Nick finally gave up the chase and came back, breathing hard.

"I give up," he wheezed. He glanced at Will and snorted. "Hey, man," he said. "Seriously, where's your costume, dude? And how come you didn't put any clothes on?"

"Ha, ha," Will said. "Let's just get candy."

Jimmy giggled and shuffled forward. "My brother is a naked skeleton. He poops candy."

"And you're going to be a black and blue ninja if you don't be quiet," Will told him, pulling him back into a headlock.

"Okay, I give!" Jimmy squealed.

The other guys had met Jimmy at football practice earlier and were okay with having the little kid with them. "We'll get more candy with a little kid with us," Ryan had reasoned. "That'll be cool."

"Yo!" Ryan now called from the middle of the field. "It's well past 6:00! We going, or not!"

The group of boys laughed and jostled each other as they crossed the field and found a short trail through the trees separating the school property from an upscale neighborhood.

"Wow," Ryan said as they came out on the other side. "You didn't tell me you were a millionaire, Nick. Now I really wish I was your mom."

"Ah, it's not so great," Nick assured him. "A lot of people here are d—uh, not very nice."

If that were true, at least for one night the people of Nick's neighborhood came together and proved to be very nice.

Already crowds of trick-or-treaters were going house to house. Laughter and excitement filled the air as parents escorted smaller children and packs of older kids roamed the streets. All the houses were huge and were well lit, making Halloween seem more like a cheerful carnival than a spooky night.

Nick hadn't been lying about his neighborhood having good candy. After only two short blocks, their bags were loaded. Houses were giving out full-sized candy bars, or handfuls of smaller candies. Gummies, suckers, chocolates, caramels, marshmallow candies, and more were piling in.

If they did find a house decorated with scary or spooky images and props, they skipped it, out of respect for Ben.

"Really, guys?" Ben asked when they bypassed the first house shrouded with fake fog and tombstones in the front yard. "I'm with a zombie, a monster, and a walking skeleton. Aren't you guys being, like, hypocrites?"

"Don't forget the ninja," Jimmy said.

"Just shut up and eat some candy. Both of you," Ryan growled, shoving a chocolate bar in Ben's chest.

The sun finally called it a night, sinking low and giving way to a brisk chilly darkness. As it did, Will finally realized why his dad had chosen the skeleton costume. The bones turned an eerie green in the dark, making him a ghostly skeleton, clearly visible in all directions. His dad, though he hid it with his strange sense of humor, was all about safety.

"Ah, cool," Jimmy said when seeing his glowing brother. "I want to be glow in the dark, too!"

"If you're like your brother, just take your shirt off," Nick said, chewing on a Hershey bar. "His chest shines like a beacon in the darkness."

"Ha, ha," Will muttered. "A comedian zombie, just what we need."

Near the end of their night, Nick led them up a long driveway to a particularly large brick house, blazing with lights.

"I saved this one for last," he said, not looking at his friends. "It's Stephanie Baker's house. I'm, um, hoping she's back from trick-or-treating by now."

Ryan gave him a look and groaned. "Oh, I get it! You want her to open the door and see you! That's why you put makeup on! Sorry, Nick, but while I think your face is a big improvement, I still don't think she's going to go for it."

"Shut up," Nick growled. Leading the way up the porch, he rang the doorbell and wiped his sweaty palm on his pants. "You all just shut up," he muttered. Then his eyes went wide as the door swung open.

Instead of Stephanie Baker, her older brother Glen answered. Chewing on a candy bar, he leaned out the door and grinned widely, recognizing Nick.

"Hey, fat Nick!" he cried. "Aren't you too big for trick-or-treating?"

"Oh, hey, Glen," Nick said, obviously disappointed. "Where's, uh, Stephanie?"

"Not with you, that's for sure!" Glen said, laughing. "What are you doing here, man?" Then his eyes swept over the other boys. "Oh, I get it. You're the babysitter for these clowns. Isn't it past their curfew?" His eyebrows rose when he saw Ben. "And what's your costume? A loser?" He laughed. "Just joking, man."

Ben shuffled backwards, dropping his gaze toward his sneakers.

Immediately Ryan shoved up his mask and stepped in front of his friend. "You recovered from practice yet, Glen?" he asked, forcing his mouth into a tight smile.

Glen had thrown two interceptions and been sacked two times during scrimmage that day. He glared at Ryan, but then snorted. "If my line wasn't so fat and decided to block, I would've done better."

"Who's that?" called a voice from inside the house. Brad sauntered in from another room, joining Glen at the door. Looking out, he frowned. "Just give them some candy and let's go, man."

Glen grinned. "Sorry, boys. But we're having a party here and little kids aren't invited. Here you go." From a large bowl in his arm, he took a handful of mini chocolate bars and dumped them on the porch. "Make sure that skeleton gets extra," he said. "He needs to grow a bigger rear end to cover more bench."

The door then slammed in their faces.

"Uh … that was rude," Ryan said.

Nick sighed. "Yeah, man," he said dejectedly. "Sorry about that, guys. Glen is usually a cool dude …"

Jimmy tugged at Will's sleeve. "Should we take the candy?" he asked.

"No," Ben hissed fiercely.

In the end, Ryan took the candy, but he didn't keep it. The others watched curiously as he first removed all the wrappers from the chocolate bars, sticking the papers in his pocket. Then taking the pile of chocolate in both hands, he squeezed it all together, twisting it as tight and hard as he could. Finished, he threw the melty lump of goo on the porch, right in front of the door, wiping his hands on the welcome mat.

"Ew!" Jimmy said, giggling. "That's poop!"

"Yep," agreed Ryan. "That's Glen."

Nick nervously scratched his shaved head. "Yeah, man. And he's my neighbor. Let's get out of here. I think it's time to head back to school anyway."

By the time they reached the football field, stars lit up the sky and their good mood had returned. Loaded with candy, definitely on a sugar high, they ran across the grass, laughing and whooping.

Jimmy had started to complain about being tired and now rode on Nick's back. His plastic sword was stuck in the back of his belt and Will carried his candy. "Faster!" he urged Nick. "Faster!"

"I'm trying," huffed Nick. "Just watch that you don't press the ejection seat."

Then, as they crossed midfield, they heard a girl's faint cry from the back of the school.

Immediately they all stopped, frozen. Will felt an icy tingle run up his spine as a cold wind blew from behind.

Chapter 14

"Um, what was that?" Nick asked.

"Is there anybody there?" cried the voice. "Help! I need help!"

Whoever it was sounded desperate and scared.

"One way to find out," Ryan said grimly. Dropping his candy bag, he cupped his hands and called out. "Where are you? Who are you?"

"Just come over here, please! I'm at the school!"

"That sounded like Angie Robinson," Nick said. "Let's go!" He bent low and let Jimmy slide down. "Here," he told the smaller boy, "hold my candy." Then he broke into a run, following in the wake of Ryan and Ben.

Will stayed behind with Jimmy, but pulled his brother's arm, urging him to go faster. He left the candy bags behind, telling Jimmy they'd come back for them.

Angie Robinson, a fellow Trailblazer, shared some of their classes with the principal's son, John. She never really bothered with them, but if she needed help it had to be for one reason. John.

John Drydon had become sort of a mascot for the Trailblazers. The girls always went out of the way to be nice to him and the boys made sure all of the other kids in the school left him alone.

Angie didn't like this, saying John should be treated the same as anyone else. "You should talk to him because you want to know him, not because you feel sorry for him," she liked to say. This didn't make her very popular, but if not for her, the boys ran for John.

They found Angie standing, distraught, at the back entrance to the school, near the dumpsters. A streetlight from the parking lot lit her in a wash of dim light and exposed her as a mess. Her hair looked to be a tangle of curls and she wrung her hands in front of her, a nervous wreck. Her eyes wild, she kept staring at the school doors as if she expected them to spring open and unleash a monster.

"What is it?" Ryan demanded as Will and Jimmy were the last to arrive. "What's wrong?"

"It's John," Angie said, confirming their fears. "We were trick-or-treating over in the neighborhood and he had to go to the bathroom. Mr. Drydon had told me to take him here, so I did." Tears welled up in her eyes and her words came out rushed. "But now I can't find him. He's vanished! It's like the school swallowed him up!"

"Maybe he just got lost," Nick said. "Or could he be playing a game? You know, like hide-and-seek?"

"No," Angie said, shaking her head vehemently. "Mr. Drydon is supposed to be meeting us at my house in like fifteen minutes. John knows that and I barely left him for like two minutes. Besides … something in that school … it creeped me out." Her voice started the shake. "Th-the lights w-went out too."

She shuddered and looked again at the doors, as if they contained something terrible. The boys grew still as they followed her gaze. Through the narrow paned windows of the doors, all they could see was an inky darkness—like two bottomless eyes staring back at them.

Will felt the short hairs rise on the back of his neck. As if a giant invisible hand just passed over, covering the night with a shroud of fear, an ominous dread settled over them. All at once the fun and excitement left and the terror of Halloween returned in full force.

Jimmy pressed against Will's side, whimpering softly.

"Can you get in?" Ryan asked, breaking the silence. He spoke extra loud, as if trying to break the somber mood.

Angie swallowed and nodded. She held up a pass key. "Mr. Drydon gave me a card that unlocks the doors." She stood up straighter. "But I'm not allowed to let anybody else in."

Ryan snorted. "Yo, do you want us to help, or not?"

"If you want," Nick offered. "I can call the police."

"For what?" Ryan asked, almost caustically. "John could just be wandering the halls, man, or stuck in a stall or something."

Angie nodded in misery. "I don't know what happened," she said. "Earlier today I just felt like I was being watched and even followed in school … And I got the same feeling when John vanished." She tried to smile, but failed. "It could be just my imagination. But I'm really glad to see you … If I let you in, will you help me look for John?"

"Yeah, sure," Nick said. "Right, guys?"

"Somebody might have to stay behind with Jimmy," Will said, "but I'll go."

Ryan and Ben nodded grudgingly and, clearly relieved, Angie turned to unlock the doors. As soon as she opened one, her nerves started to fail.

The deep darkness seemed to roll out of the school, swirling before them. It felt like looking into a bottomless pit.

"Uh, what exactly happened to the lights?" Nick asked.

Not even the emergency lights were working. Only a single red exit light provided an eerie red glow that seemed more evil than helpful.

"Yeah, and what about the janitor, where's he at?" Ryan wanted to know. "I know there's supposed to be one working every night."

"How do you know?" Nick scoffed. "Maybe they get Friday's off."

"My mom used to be one," Ryan snarled, angry. "She never got Fridays off, that's how I know!"

"Hey, stop fighting!" Angie said sharply, her confidence returning with the boys' presence. She held the door open with her back as she crossed her arms in front of her. "Mr. Harold *is* supposed to be working, but I don't know where he went." She paused to blow out her breath. "The lights were working before, but they suddenly cut off. That's when I sort of freaked and ran out. When I heard you guys, I just started calling."

"Where did you leave John?" Nick asked her.

"I didn't *leave* him," Angie said acidly, turning on Nick. She moved her hands to her hips and practically snarled. "I went to the girls' room and he went to the boys' room. When I got out I couldn't find him." All her acid turned to fear. "I-I felt something watching me. I even thought I heard somebody laugh. I called John and then for Mr. Harold, but nobody answered. Then the lights went out and I … sort of freaked."

"Yo, man," Ryan said nervously. He stared down the dark hallway and stepped back. "You know, this is how a lot of horror movies start. Maybe it's not such a good idea to go in there."

Ben cleared his throat and spoke up. "I don't watch horror movies," he said, his voice cracking. "So maybe I should stay outside, just in case John comes out."

"It'll be okay if we stick together," Will said, trying to smile. "Come on, guys. It's just a school. We, like, spend half our lives there during the week."

"Will's too little to watch scary movies," Nick said. "He doesn't know what he's talking about."

"Yeah, and besides, schools are scary enough in the daytime," Ryan said dryly. "Nick, you go first. You're the slowest."

The larger boy grunted. "What does me being the slowest have to do with anything?" he demanded.

"If anything bad happens," Ryan explained, "you'll be the first victim. Then the rest of us can escape."

"Quiet!" Will said loudly, his voice going shrill. "Just listen."

The kids went still and strained to hear. The school stood as silent as a grave.

"Nothing," whispered Ryan. "And I don't know why I'm whispering."

"Wait!" Will pleaded. "I thought I heard something in there."

"Okay, now I'm really getting freaked out," Nick said. "Let's just call the police."

Jimmy hugged Will's waist even tighter, burying his face in his older brother's side.

Ryan cupped his hands and leaned inside the doorway. "Yo, John!" he shouted. "Are you in there?" His voice bounced off the walls and echoed back, but no response followed.

"He could just be scared," Angie said. "When he gets scared, he curls up in a ball and shuts his eyes. He'll never answer if you yell at him, especially if you're not somebody he really knows."

"Sounds real convenient for him," Ryan said with a grunt.

"It's not easy for him," Angie said defensively. "He calls it going into his hidey hole. When he doesn't know what to do, or what's going on, his mind sort of retreats there."

"How do you know all this?" Nick asked. "I mean, are you like his shrink?"

"It's because I asked him," Angie said, her voice going hard. "I talk to him. He calls it his 'hidey hole' because he loves Bugs Bunny, okay? Inside it he imagines all the things he likes so he's not so scared. Does that answer your question?"

"Uh, yeah," Nick said, ashamed. "I need to go crawl in my hidey hole now."

"Okay, I'll go in," Will said, looking down at his green glowing costume. It wasn't as bright as before, but still could be seen in the dark. "You guys can follow if you want, but somebody has to wait outside with Jimmy."

"Suits me," Ryan said. "I'll stay out. You go be the hero."

"I'll wait too," Ben added quickly.

Nick breathed out and groaned. "Fine, I'll go with you, Will. Let's do this. We find John and then get out. Pronto."

"I'm coming too," Angie said. "John has to see me, or he probably won't come out."

Will licked his lips and pried Jimmy loose, passing him off to Ryan. "I'll be right back," Will told his brother. "Dad will be here in a minute, okay?"

Jimmy had pulled down his hood and mask. Peering up at his brother, his bottom lip trembling, he nodded and then reached back and pulled out his plastic sword. He solemnly handed it to Will. "You might need this, Will."

"Uh, thanks," Will said, taking it. "I'll give it back to you, free of blood. I promise." Rolling his eyes, he shoved it at Ben on his way into the school. "Just in case the monsters come," he muttered.

Ben nodded seriously and gripped the sword tightly.

Stepping inside the dark, silent school felt like stepping inside the mouth of a giant beast. The first steps forward were small and timid. At any moment the darkness threatened to crash down and swallow them.

With Will squished between them, Nick and Angie carried their cell phones before them like weapons. Equipped with small lights, the phones allowed a few feet of visibility, but otherwise destroyed their night vision. And it was what they couldn't see that unnerved them the most. Moving deeper into the hall, they could imagine all sorts of strange creatures and monsters leering at them.

Will, his costume still emitting a faint, eerie, green light, felt as if he was suffocating in the middle. Nick pressed tightly against his right shoulder, aiming his light on one side with Angie gripping his left arm, shining her light on the other.

They'd walked this hall over a hundred times, but never had it felt so long before, or so terrifying.

"Yo, Will!" Ryan called from the doors, sounding very far away. "Your glow-in-the-dark costume is fading, man! You look like a green blob, but we can barely see you!"

"Just keep Jimmy with you!" Will yelled back. "We'll be good."

"Got it, dude!" Ryan's voice echoed and then died. "See you soon!"

"I hope," Angie finished softly as the echoed died to nothing. "This so feels like stepping into a scary movie."

"Not helping," Nick muttered.

They stepped farther into the bleak darkness.

"Man, I hate Halloween," Nick said. "I'd rather take a math test than do this."

"We should find a light switch," Will said, squinting in the dim light. He could feel sweat start to run down his face. "Maybe somebody just turned the lights off."

"Maybe," Angie said doubtfully. "All the lights went off at once." Her fear seemed to be returning with every step. "Something isn't right about this."

It was a chilly night, but with adrenaline pumping, moving through the dark cavern-like hall felt smothering.

Despite all the tension, Will couldn't help notice that Angie stood a good two inches over him. Being the smallest made the others lean on him more. Both Angie and Nick pressed even closer against him, squishing him.

"Room, please," he muttered.

"I already checked the boys' room. He went on this hall," Angie said, her voice catching. "But we can check again. That's where I last saw John and I ... I didn't go too far in there."

"You two go do that," Nick said. "I'll go find a light switch. I know there's one by the janitor's office down here. I'll also check if Mr. Harold is here."

"Are you sure?" Angie asked. "You want us to split up?"

"Yeah," Nick said. He tried to chuckle, but ended up coughing uncomfortably. "I have a light and we'll only be like ten yards apart. Let's find John and scram out of this place."

Will cleared his throat. "You know in horror movies, splitting up is always the dumbest plan."

Nick bumped Will's shoulder. "Thanks, man. You always know the right thing to say. Besides, you're too little for scary movies."

"Ha," Will replied, his eyes wide. "Then why do I feel like we're in one?"

They reached the side hall leading to the auditorium and paused to look into the darkness. It seemed as if it stared right back, waiting for them.

"Man, I'm not going down there without the lights back on," Nick said. "You two check the bathroom while I check the lights, okay?"

"John!" called Angie. "Where are you?"

As her echo bounced to nothingness with no reply, they followed the plan.

The boys' room was a little farther on their left near the computer lab. Leaving Nick, Will and Angie peeled off to enter the dark cavernous doorway. Angie went first, holding the lit cell phone in front of her.

"Gross, I hate that smell," Angie said, breaking the tension as she shined her light on the pale tiled walls. She yanked up her front collar, covering her nose.

"What smell?" Will asked, sniffing.

"Boy urine mixed with gross cologne."

As soon as she said it, Will smelled it. A sharp, pungent chemical smell hit him in the nose like a punch. Instantly he reeled back and felt his eyes start to water.

"Yep," he coughed, wincing. "That's bad. You don't think something died in here, do you?"

"What's worse," Angie said grimly, "is that the light switch won't work here." She tried the switch multiple times to no avail. "Are you in here, John?" she called. "John? Oh, I can't believe I'm in the boys' bathroom at night."

"And with a good-looking boy," Will said, grinning. "I won't tell if you don't."

"Don't be gross," Angie said, checking the stalls. "He's not here."

"Okay …" Will wiped his nose as the smell started to give him a headache. "But, um, now that we're here, I kind of have to go …"

"Seriously?"

"Hey," he said defensively. "It's been a long night, and I'm more than a little nervous."

"Fine," Angie said with a huff. "Do you need the light?"

Will moved to stand by a urinal and squirmed. "Ah, no, I'm okay. I don't mind the dark, really. You can go outside."

Angie sighed loudly. "Hurry up, then. I'll be out in the hall with Nick."

As soon as she left, Will did his best comply. He didn't want to stay in the pitch-black darkness any longer than necessary. Unfortunately, his stupid costume had other ideas. Being in one piece, the costume had no zipper in the front below his waist.

"How does Spiderman do it?" he mumbled to himself as he danced impatiently. Reaching back, he yanked the nylon string from the top of his head and down his back before pulling off his hood. Then he had to peel the entire front part of his costume down. It took several anxious moments, but Will managed to strip to his waist in time.

Finally, sighing in relief, Will finished and fumbled in the dark to flush. Then he attempted to zip back up.

"Great," he groaned as he bent his back and tried to reach back with both hands for the zipper. Just as he got the zipper half way up, he heard a noise behind him, like a shuffle of feet.

"Is that you, Nick?" His voice went higher than normal, sounding very much like a scared little kid. "It'd better not be Angie."

Turning, he stifled a grunt as a faint mist sprayed in his face. All at once the harsh chemical smell assaulted his senses, stronger than ever.

"Wha—" Reeling back, he bumped into the urinal and felt his knees start to buckle. An overwhelming desire to sleep descended and he never felt the hand gently cover his mouth with a damp handkerchief. His eyes were already closed as his body went limp and fell into waiting arms. Without a sound, he was dragged into the darkness.

Chapter 15

When Angie and Will headed into the bathroom, Nick started humming to himself as he shined his light along the wall, searching for the light switch. He hated silence, especially when alone in a dark, creepy school.

Hearing Will's and Angie's faint muffled voices from the bathroom, he grimaced. Maybe he shouldn't have left them. It'd sounded brave at the time, but now … Nick shook his head. He was sure Angie was just exaggerating and John would be fine.

Near the end of the hall he came to the janitor's office and saw the door cracked with faint light leaking through. A radio played softly on the other side. Nick sighed with relief. John was probably sitting inside with the janitor.

"Mr. Harold?" he asked, knocking. Hearing no answer, he pushed the door open. "Mr. Harold? Are you there?"

Nick stepped in and immediately felt a wave of dizziness crash over him.

"Huh?" he muttered, stumbling into the office. Immediately he barked his shins on something hard that he dizzily identified as a chair. He barely registered the pain as he dropped his cell phone.

Strong fumes swirled around his head, pulling him down. Groggily, Nick surveyed the room, trying desperately to clear his head.

The light emitted from a small lamp on a desk on the far side of the office. Before Nick could wonder how the light worked, his knees buckled.

Catching himself, he managed to collapse back into the chair just before his head dropped to his chest and his eyes slid shut. In seconds he slid into unconsciousness.

Across from Nick, Mr. Harold, an older man with thin white hair, sat slumped over the desk. He snored quietly as a fan blew silently from a shelf just above the desk. A small bowl of liquid was set up in front of the fan. It smelled strongly of chemicals.

Angie exited the bathroom surprised not to see Nick's light.

"Nick?" she called tentatively. Figuring he must've turned the corner, she started down the hall after him.

"Where are you?" she called louder. "Did you find the switch? I don't think the lights are working. Nick?"

She frowned when hearing no answer. Then suddenly a beeping sounded from the computer lab on the left. Startled, she nearly dropped her phone. Then she gasped, recognizing the sound of a timer going off. John liked using timers and loved computers.

"John!" she cried.

Quickly she hurried to the lab. She was surprised, but also relieved, to find it unlocked. Ms. Jackson always locked it at the end of the day, but this definitely would be a place John would hide if scared. He always felt more comfortable with technology than people.

"Where are you, John?" she called, banging open the door, nearly falling into the lab.

The beeping came from the back corner, but she couldn't see anybody in the darkness. Rows of tables were set up in the center of the room holding the desktop computers. All the chairs had been stacked for the weekend, blocking her path. John could be lying under one of the tables.

"It's me, Angie." Kicking an empty crate out of the way, she moved carefully around the chairs, heading toward the beeping. She held up her light as high as she could, desperately hoping to see the blond boy smiling up at her.

Then the door slammed hard behind her, causing her to stifle a scream and lunge forward. Striking the front of a table, she fell sideways, landing awkwardly with a hard crash. Her hip flared with pain as her phone flew from her fingers, skittering across the floor.

The beeping continued without stopping. Whimpering in fright, Angie didn't move for several moments.

With an arm draped across the boy's chest, the hunter dragged the slight, unconscious body back to the sink. His free hand slipped the handkerchief and small spray bottle into his pocket. As he did so, he swore softly under his breath. This was not part of the game. Somebody cheated. He stopped at the sink and avoided looking into the mirror. This wasn't going well.

Keeping his hands supporting the boy, he crouched down and rested the boy on his knee as he gathered his breath and thought what to do. Who were these kids? So far he'd counted three, including the girl. More importantly, what to do with them?

With a grunt he grabbed the back of boy's thighs and lifted him up before plopping him into a sitting position on the edge of the sink. The boy's body sagged against the hunter.

"What do I do with you," the hunter muttered.

Growling slightly, the hunter moved his hands to hold the kid's shoulders and pushed him back. The boy's head lolled back, exposing a slender throat. The hunter eyed the throat and bit his bottom lip.

"Whoever you are," breathed the hunter. "You're part of the game now. And for you it's game over. You're dead meat, buddy boy."

At the same time, a trickle of sweat rolled down the side of his face. Everything had been under his control until now. He hadn't planned for so many stupid kids to be running around. He hated surprises. And this surprise could prove very dangerous. Usually danger provided a thrill, but on this night he only felt fear. His carefully crafted game seemed to be rapidly falling to pieces, slipping from his control.

When first seeing the three kids enter the school, he'd nearly panicked. He'd thought he'd sent the girl running for help, but hadn't counted on her coming back so soon, and with the stupid boys. Keeping back in the shadows he'd watched and waited. Only at seeing their stark fear did his confidence return. He still held the power and so had then waited for an opportunity.

He'd lucked out when they'd separated and the big one walked right into the trap he'd rigged for the janitor. But that left the other two. After seeing the big kid turn into the janitor's office, the hunter had slipped into the lab where he'd found a bowl full of timers just inside the door. Earlier he'd unlocked it to shove in an abandoned crate left outside the door—he hadn't wanted to trip on it in case he needed a quick getaway. Inside the lab, thinking quickly, he'd set a timer for a minute and tossed it into the corner. Then he'd slipped out and had waited in the shadows.

He'd watched the girl come out first and start toward him. Ducking back in the shadows, he'd started counting seconds in his head. When the timer went off, she'd reacted liked he'd hoped. Once she'd gone inside the room, he'd waited a few seconds before slamming the door.

After watching her for days, the hunter knew the girl's tendencies. She'd now be totally freaked out and wouldn't dare move. That had left the boy. And now he had him. But now what?

Dressed from head to toe in black, he wore night vision goggles and a black painted mask over his nose and mouth. For all intents and purposes, he was a shadow—part of the darkness. Shadows didn't panic.

Through the greenish tint of night vision, he viewed the limp boy in front of him and made a decision. The boy had dark smudges around his eyes and mouth and wore a skeleton costume. He grinned. Apparently the kid had dressed for the part. He'd soon be as dead as a skeleton.

Crouching and leaning a shoulder into the boy's chest, he scooped his hands under the kid and lifted him up.

"Okay, buddy boy," he whispered as he dumped the boy over his shoulder. "Let's end the game for you."

The girl would eventually emerge from her fright. He only had a few minutes to finish this.

Hugging the wall, he swiftly exited the bathroom, moving right. As his right hand pressed the limp body against his shoulder, his left hand flexed under his glove. The tingling sensation spread from the tips of his long, nimble fingers all the way to his thumping heart.

Feeling the beating against his ribs, the hunter smiled. Sometimes the feeling leading up to the kill proved more powerful than the kill itself. He could still do this.

Then he heard a scrape from behind him. The girl in the lab.

Crouching low, he paused for a moment, listening. His right hand gripped the back of the boy's costume tightly. The unconscious boy would only be under for a few more minutes. He needed to think this through. The moment of exhilaration passed and panic returned. What if he was caught? Even if a kid caught just a glimpse of him all could be lost. He needed more time to plan it right. The game had to end on his terms without causing suspicions.

Snarling, he used his free hand to yank down his mask and push up his goggles. He needed fresh air. It may have saved him. As his eyes adjusted to the darkness, he saw the side of the kid hanging over his shoulder faintly glowing. The bones on the costume gave off an eerie light that spooked him to no end.

Grunting in fear, he quickly rose to his full height. If anybody looked his way he'd be spotted easily. That settled it. It wasn't going to be his night.

Hastily, he carried the glowing body to the side hall, using his elbow to scrape the wall to let him know where he was. Finding the corner, he slipped around it and paused. He was surprised to find himself breathing so hard. The game had really gone south.

It had started so well—putting down the janitor, cutting off all the electricity on that side of the school except for the janitor's office, snatching the prey from the bathroom, and scaring the girl out. All he'd had left to do was make a tragic accident. But then the girl returned with her friends, ruining everything.

Catching his breath, he listened for any pursuit. Only darkness and silence followed him. Apparently, the girl remained too scared to move.

Letting out a sigh of relief, the hunter lowered his googles and felt his good humor return as the world lit up a bright green. He boldly walked the rest of the way down the hall toward the auditorium. The limp arms of the boy swung gently against his back. The skeleton would live for now.

The hunter knew he would have to start his plans over. And that wouldn't be a bad thing. He would actually quite enjoy it, especially now that new pieces might be in play. He slapped the back of the boy's thigh.

"You win this round, buddy boy," he hissed, "but perhaps there'll be another time."

At the end of the hall, he dumped the comatose body from his shoulder and laid the boy against the wall of lockers. He looked down at the pale, painted face before him.

"Nice looking kid like you, I hope we meet again." He ruffled the boy's hair and then stood up. "I'm sure we will. And when we do, you just might end up a real skeleton. How about that?" Grinning, he faded back into the darkness.

Angie finally found the nerve to get on her hands and knees and crawl to her phone. Her hip screamed with pain from where she'd smacked the table, but she ignored it. With a trembling hand, she picked up the phone and tried to make a call, but had no cell signal. The thick concrete walls blocked out cell service, and unfortunately all the computers in the lab were wired to the internet. There was no wireless service in the room, so she couldn't use that as backup.

She brushed back her hair and took a deep breath. Then she slowly forced herself to aim her light toward the beeping. She was relieved to see nothing. No boogeyman waited in the corner, just a small plastic timer. Crawling to it, she turned it off and saw it had been set for one minute. Her blood froze. That meant somebody had set it just before she'd gone into the room.

"Nick," she hissed, loudly. "If this is some sort of joke, I'm going to strangle you. Nick? Will?"

No answer came.

With a pounding heart, she got to her feet and started to the door. She stopped when she heard a noise out in the hall. A door closed and somebody whistled.

Immediately, Angie sank back down and hid under a table. Shortly after, the lights suddenly snapped back on.

Will woke up with a splitting headache, not knowing where he was or how he got there. Blinking groggily, he groaned as bright light burned his eyes. He had a foul metallic taste in his mouth and a fuzzy memory of being in the bathroom.

Now he lay with his cheek pressed against a hard, cold floor and his left arm squashed under his body.

Groaning, he rolled to his stomach and tried to make sure all his limbs still worked. Then he gingerly pushed himself up to his knees and looked around.

Shaking his head in confusion, he saw that he knelt in the hallway between the band room and auditorium of his school. All the lights were on and for a second he thought it had to be Monday morning. Then he saw his skeleton costume and remembered going into the school with Angie and Nick.

He had no idea how he got there or how long he'd been there. Wincing, he leaned an arm against the locker on his left and forced himself to his feet. His body sagged against the row of lockers. He felt exhausted. Then his eyes went wide. From where he stood, he spotted another boy curled up on the floor in front of the band room.

"John?" Will said.

John Drydon opened his eyes and blinked blearily up at Will.

Will had a problem. He somehow had blacked out in the bathroom and woke up to find John in a totally different area of the school. And now John looked to be deep in his hidey hole.

After seeing Will, John had sat up but then started to shake. His hands flapped and his mouth started muttering gibberish.

Will was reminded of a panicked puppy his mom had nearly hit back in Nashville one night. The animal lay trembling in the middle of the road until his mom tried to cradle it. Then all at once it snapped sharp teeth, nearly taking off his mom's hand, before racing into the night.

"John, it's okay," Will said gently. "It's me, Will. From your class." He crouched next to the boy and licked his lips. "Um, I don't know what happened, but it's okay now. Angie is here." He spoke to John the same way he spoke to Jimmy after one of his dad's tirades. "You ready to get up to find Angie? It'll be okay."

At the mention of Angie's name, John's eyes went wider and his shaking arms slowed. "Angie," he said. "Where's Angie?"

"Come on up. I'll help you find her. We have to get up first."

John still muttered gibberish, but he allowed Will to help pull him to his feet. John closed his eyes and shook his head a little bit. Then he blinked and looked at Will, as if seeing him for the first time.

"Will, you're a skeleton."

Will breathed a sigh of relief. "Yep, I feel like one."

"I'm a pirate. But I lost my candy."

"Um, Angie has it. We, um, both got lost. Are you okay?"

John swallowed and his eyes still held a panicked look, but he nodded. "I just want Angie and my candy."

Nick stumbled from the janitor's office holding his head. "Man," he groaned. "What just happened?" He blinked rapidly at seeing the bright lights.

"Hey!" shouted Ryan, coming down the hall toward him with Ben and Jimmy in tow. "What's going on, man? I mean, what the heck?"

"That's what I want to know," Nick said, wincing. "I, I think I fell asleep or something. Ah, man, I feel horrible."

"We saw the lights go on," Ben said accusingly, "but we couldn't see you. Where're Will and Angie?"

Nick just looked around, helplessly. "Good question, man."

Jimmy looked around with large eyes. He clutched his sword again.

The three boys joined Nick and waited for some sort of explanation.

Nick started to explain how he reached the janitor's office, but kept getting stuck. "I-I don't know what happened … I just woke up in a chair. Man, I don't know where Will and Angie went." He groaned. "They went to check the bathroom and I …"

Angie tore open the computer lab's door, causing the boys to give a start. "I'm right here," she said icily. "What was that, some sort of prank?" She was livid. "It wasn't funny!"

Nick just stared at her. "Wh-what?"

"You know what!" Angie nearly screamed. "You set the timer in there and shut the door on me to scare me!"

Nick's mouth dropped open. "I did not!"

Angie wiped a tear from her eye. "And we didn't even find John, yet!"

"Guys, I found him," Will's voice, slightly muffled, called from a side hall behind Ryan and Ben.

The group turned to see Will stumble out behind them. He blinked sheepishly. "I think I found him … or maybe he found me. I dunno."

John Drydon trailed right behind him, looking lost. Seeing Angie, his eyes lit up and his mouth broke into a huge smile. "Angie!" he cried.

"John!" Angie cried. She rushed over and gave the boy a hug. "Where did you go?"

Before he could answer, a bang came from the janitor's office.

"Hey!" shouted a harsh voice, thick with sleep. "Who's out there? Who's there?!"

"Mr. Harold!" Nick shouted. "Let's get out of here!"

"Wh-what?" Angie protested. "Wait!"

It was too late. Ryan and Nick bolted for the back door. After a brief hesitation, Ben and Jimmy followed, joined by Will. John, thinking it a game, also gave chase, leaving Angie no choice but to also run.

Coughing and clearing his throat, Mr. Harold stumbled from his office as the back door of the school slammed shut.

"I need to drink more coffee," he mumbled, wiping his bleary, red-rimmed eyes.

Seeing no kids around, he retreated back to his desk. For all he knew, he could've dreamed the voices out in the hall. Taking a seat, he snapped off his lamp and rubbed his eyes. It was time for him to go home. He'd been working in the school for thirty odd years. Maybe it was time for him to retire. "Ghosts in this place," he muttered.

Out in the parking lot, the children were relieved to find two cars waiting for them. Mr. Drydon and Mr. Moore stood on the sidewalk, talking, when the highly agitated kids tore out of the school. At first there was a lot of confusion and talking at once, but Mr. Moore raised his voice and shouted for quiet. Then Mr. Drydon calmly asked Angie for an explanation.

Beneath his calm, the principal looked shocked and even a little scared at seeing the children. He stood with John at his side, but stared at Angie hard.

Swallowing, Angie didn't really know what to say. She explained about losing John and the lights going out and getting the boys to help her, but then stopped. Truthfully, she had no idea what happened inside that building. Nick seemed genuinely confused, and how did Will get from the bathroom to John?

"I, uh, think things got confused in the darkness and everything," she finished lamely. "I don't know what happened, but we found John and then Mr. Harold yelled at us. We," she continued, glaring at Ryan and Nick, "sort of panicked and ran."

Nick and Will were similarly confused. Both admitted to waking up and not really remembering going to sleep. Will insisted he had no idea how he ended up near John.

"I think somebody came up behind me," he said, "but that's the last thing I remember. It could've been John …" He winced. "Or it could've been nobody."

"It was a miracle," Ben solemnly. "While you guys were in there, I was praying constantly." Nobody said anything, but they all turned to look as Ben continued. "I think this may have been a warning about Halloween." He ducked his head. "Guys, I don't think I want any more candy. I want to go home."

Mr. Drydon cleared his throat. "Okay, kids, I think we all need to go home. I'm just thankful everything turned out okay." Sounding relieved, he spoke in his pleasant, slightly nasal voice. He now had John in front of him with his arms wrapped securely around his shoulders. "I know sometimes Mr. Harold turns off the lights to save electricity. I'll talk to him about that. We'll also check for any gas leaks." Both Will and Nick mentioned smelling something strange before losing consciousness, but neither could agree on what it smelled like. "But what I'm thinking is that you boys had a long, hard day and then a lot of sugar. You had football practice, right? You boys were just exhausted, full of candy, and then overly stimulated about Halloween. What you need is some good rest."

Mr. Moore kept silent during the explanations, but nodded his head in agreement. "This is one night where imagination tends to run wild, I guess. I think we should call it quits. Does everyone have a ride home?"

"Uh, yes sir," Ben said. He shivered. "My mom is meeting me here. I already texted her. I'm telling her I'm never going out on Halloween again."

"I'm going with Ben," Ryan said, putting an arm around his friend's shoulder. "He's my prayer buddy."

Angie frowned, clearly not satisfied with the explanation. "I live just over there," she said, pointing across the football field. "Mr. Drydon, I thought you were picking up John at my place."

"So did I," the principal said, giving a rueful smile. "I was on my way when I got a text from a parent saying some kids were messing around the school. I pulled in to check it out when I found Mr. Moore. Next thing I know, you kids come running out like you saw a ghost." He chuckled, but it sounded forced. "Only on Halloween does stuff like this happen."

Mr. Moore crossed his arms gruffly. "Young lady, do you live far?"

"Not too far," Angie said. "Just through the trees and down a block."

"I live over there too," Nick said. "I can walk with her."

Angie glared at him. "I can walk by myself."

Mr. Moore nodded. "I feel like I need a walk myself. What about it, champ?" he asked Will. "You and Jimmy up for one more round of trick-or-treating?"

Jimmy's eyes went wide. "Our candy! We left our candy on the grass!"

Mr. Drydon grunted. "I'd go too, but I'd better get John home. It's already past his bedtime, and apparently he's already sleepy. I'm real sorry this happened, but I'm also thankful I have good students to count on in times of trouble." He forced a chuckle. "Thanks for all your help, guys. Come on, son."

The boys and Angie said their goodbyes and John, back to good spirits, waved as his father led him to the car.

Ben's mom pulled up in a minivan just as the principal left, and Ben and Ryan quickly climbed in the back. Nobody spoke to Ben's mom. The feeling of disapproval wafted from the front seat like an invisible dark cloud.

"What about your candy, Ryan?" Nick asked, just before the door slid shut.

After looking quickly at Ben, Ryan told Nick to take it all. He didn't want it anymore. Nick was happy to oblige.

"After what happened tonight, I need some sugar," he said as the van shot forward. "Sugar is medicine to the soul."

After they'd gone, Mr. Moore led a subdued group back across the football field. He carried Jimmy on his hip with the boy's head against his shoulder. Exhausted, the small boy quickly fell asleep, but only after they'd retrieved the bags of candy.

As they entered the path through the trees, a ghostly fog descended, blanketing the ground before them. Will shivered slightly. In the rush to go trick-or-treating, he hadn't put anything on under his costume. Still, it was the atmosphere more than the temperature that caused his body to quake. He hugged the two bags of candy close to his chest.

"Great," Nick muttered. "Could this night get any spookier?"

"Let's hope not," Angie said. She eyed Nick with suspicion.

Nick grunted, looking away. "Yeah, whatever."

It was the first time they'd spoken to each other since Angie had accused Nick of scaring her.

Angie sniffed and made no other comment.

Neither one seemed to trust the other.

"My house is over there," Angie said, nodding to the left as they entered the neighborhood.

It was just after eight o'clock and trick-or-treating had officially ended, but a few stragglers, mostly older kids, remained. From a distance, through the fog, they looked like ghosts and sounded like ghouls. Their laughter carried a spirit of meanness rather than one of mirth.

"I'm that way," Nick said, pointing to a street to the right. "I can get home from here."

Mr. Moore nodded. "We'll just watch from here until you both get to your houses."

Angie left without saying goodbye. Now that she saw her house she started resenting the fact she needed to be walked home like a little kid.

"See you Monday, Will," Nick said, glaring at the back of Angie.

"Yeah, see you," Will said in return. He stood with his father, watching his friend hustle into the fog. As they were swallowed up in mist, Mr. Moore put an arm around Will's shoulder.

"Let's go, boys," he said. Turning, he led his two boys back to the path through the trees.

Behind them, an egg spattered against a window followed by howls of laughter.

Halloween night continued for some, ended for others. Will couldn't wait to get home.

Chapter 16

Once on the road, Mr. Moore cranked up the heat and looked at Will.

"Okay, champ," he said, "tell me what really happened."

Licking his lips, Will explained everything again, the best he could. He still had no answers as to how he got from the bathroom to the side hall.

He looked up at his dad, his brown eyes questioning. "Do you really think it could've been a miracle, like Ben said?"

"I do believe in miracles, son. After what I've seen in the army I have to." He clicked his tongue, keeping his eyes on the road, but his mind somewhere else. "But this one … I don't know. Things seem a little fishy. Do you feel okay? You don't feel faint or dizzy, do you?"

Will shook his head. "I have a little headache, that's all."

"Well, just in case, you're staying home from school tomorrow. You and Jimmy both.

Jimmy sat in the back, still fast asleep.

"Ha, ha," Will said. "Tomorrow is Saturday."

"You're right," his dad said. "You guys better stay home for two days."

Jared spent his Halloween reading in bed. Kelly had gone to a friend's house after her dance class and would be sleeping over after a night of trick-or-treating. Both George and Jack were at separate parties. Neither one had invited Jared. Like most nights these days, he was left alone with nothing but his books and a deep longing for a friend. In the years past he'd gone trick-or-treating with George, but knew George would've laughed snidely if Jared even suggested the idea this year.

After a while, he put down his book and picked up a soccer ball. Lying back in his bed, he started tossing the ball up with his right hand with the flick of his wrist. In his mind it became a basketball and he was shooting bucket after bucket, hitting nothing but net every time.

The hunter's phone rang just as he got out of his car. Staring at the number, he grunted. "Patience, my friend," he muttered. Accepting the call, he put the phone to his ear and listened. Then he spoke one word in response.

"Berkshire."

Hanging up, the hunter smiled grimly. The planning would begin that very night. They would have to get some help, but it could be done with no more problems.

With Halloween in the past, November quickly took over and with it came the end of football season. By the time Thursday rolled around, the day of the final game, Halloween night had become a distant memory. School continued on as before and only Ben still talked about the night, claiming it had been a miracle. Angie and John kept their distance from the boys and they were okay with that. They had enough to worry about, like having to end their football season on the bench. Of the three, only Nick had any significant playing time on the offensive line.

But somehow, things changed. Will had no idea how his dad managed it, but in the final game, with the team down by four touchdowns early in the third quarter, Coach Marsden sent Will in at running back. On his first carry, a simple dive play to the right, Will bounced to the outside, outraced three defenders to the corner, turned up field and scampered eighty-five yards untouched to the end zone.

The entire team went crazy and mobbed him as he returned to the sidelines. Coach Marsden turned and stared thoughtfully back at the small group of parents who'd made the trip to the Patriots side. A road game an hour's drive north of Washington

Middle, not many had made it. Standing in the front, Mr. Moore grinned and waved.

Quickly the coach turned back to the field and pulled up his hood.

Will finished the game with five carries for 154 yards and three touchdowns. The Patriots lost 42 to 28, but Will had gained respect from his teammates and his coaches. His speed and strength had turned heads.

On the way to the bus, Will saw Coach Marsden run down his dad. Curious, he hung back and fumbled with his helmet strap so he could listen.

A sharp smack landed on his shoulder pads and a swinging helmet knocked him in the backside, the ultimate football compliment.

"Sweet running, man," Glen said, stopping beside him. He shook his head. "I tell you what, man, for a benchwarmer, you got some wheels. I mean it. Next year with Ryan at quarterback, you guys are going to rule."

Surprised, Will looked up at him. "You mean it?" he asked.

"Heck, yeah." Glen ducked his head. His helmet in hand, he used the other to scratch his sweaty hair. "Shoot, man. I know I give you guys a hard time, but my playing days are over here. I never really wanted to be quarterback, but once I got the job, I wasn't going to give it up." He grinned. "I'm just waiting for basketball to start. That's my game."

Will raised his eyebrows. "Yeah? Mine too."

Glen lifted his right hand. "See you at tryouts?"

Slapping it with his own, Will nodded. "See you at tryouts."

Then as Glen started off, Will stepped in and kicked the back of the larger boy's padded pants. "Just getting you used to that," he said grinning.

Glen snorted. "You wish! I would kick yours, but you don't have one. You just ran it off!"

By then, Coach Marsden was shaking hands with Mr. Moore and Will had missed the entire conversation. Yanking off his helmet, he waited for his dad to catch up to him.

"What did you and Coach talk about?" he asked casually.

Mr. Moore smiled mysteriously, grabbing the helmet from Will. "Oh, he just wanted me to get your autograph for him. I told him I couldn't do it. You haven't learned to spell your name yet."

"Ha. Dad, really, what did he ask?" Will started unbuckling his shoulder pads, waiting for a real answer.

Scratching the back of his head, Mr. Moore sighed. "At your last practice I asked him why he didn't play seventh graders. He told me some bull story about school tradition and how seniority mattered here. Well, I said, talent would matter more to a good coach, and then stomped off." Mr. Moore grinned. "I think he put you in today hoping to see you get your block knocked off. He wanted me to watch you getting smeared all over the ground to teach me a lesson. Good thing, champ, you didn't let your dad down."

Will looked up, his eyes widening. "Really? Your plan was to get me potentially smeared?"

"Hey, I wasn't interfering. I was just relieving some of my curiosity. If your coach took it the wrong way, that's his fault. In any case, today your coach asked if I wanted to join his staff next season. Don't worry, I said no thanks. I told him I'm more of a basketball man. Speaking of which, make sure you take thirty jump shots when you get home, all from at least fifteen feet."

Will pulled off his pads and grinned. "Only if you play me in 21 afterwards."

Mr. Moore mussed up his hair, making it spiky from sweat. "Sure. But if I win, you get a haircut."

Needless to say, the football team did *not* make the playoffs. Will didn't care. Basketball tryouts were only a week away.

The next day was Friday and a PE day. Mr. Hackett didn't just serve as the PE teacher and defensive football coach, but also served as a bus driver for the sports teams. Still recovering from the ride from the football game, he convinced the other PE teachers to allow a free day. After dressing out, where everyone changed from their nice school clothes into wrinkly, smelly, gray cotton shorts with Washington Middle T-shirts, the kids quickly went through stretches before Coach Swopes pulled out the rack of basketballs.

"Play, or sit," he barked to the classes, "but everyone participates!"

By this time of year everyone had formed their groups of friends and the same kids played at the same baskets. Most of them just gathered in groups and socialized, so there was always at least one open hoop. Jared, of course, hadn't found a group to play with. However, he'd given up just watching. Grabbing a free ball, he found an unused basket at the far end of the court on the side.

Behind him, on the main court, an active game broke out with seventh graders against eighth graders. With basketball tryouts fast approaching, a lot of trash talking was flying back and forth. Big Mike, Brad, and the other basketball stars, already assured spots on the team, played their own game on the opposite side of the main court. They viewed any other player with disdain and didn't have to use talk trash to let it be known.

Ignoring them all, Jared started shooting. With no formal training he just copied what he saw other players do on TV. So far he thought he had a decent shot, but found it hard to hit nothing but net. He always seemed to hit the rim, either shooting too hard or too soft. Every so often he got a lucky bounce and the ball went in.

What he did discover, though, was that he had a pretty good layup. The week before, Mr. Hackett had the class do a short basketball unit. One of the tests was doing as many layups as possible in a single minute. At first Jared had been nervous, thinking he'd fail. But he'd been amazed to find how easy it was to lay the ball up on the backboard, sending it into the hoop. He'd finished with nineteen baskets, one of the higher scores in the class. It was since that day that he started going out on the court during free time, to shoot baskets instead of sitting out.

After getting a rebound, Jared dribbled out and lined up another shot from a few feet from the basket. Just as he was about to shoot, he noticed John standing under basket watching him. The boy grinned and just stood there.

"Uh," Jared said, "want a shot?"

John's face lit up and he eagerly hopped out onto the court.

Taking that as a yes, Jared bounced the ball to him. John awkwardly caught it with both hands against his chest. Then, his tongue sticking out in concentration, he turned to the rim and threw up a high shot with both hands. The ball sailed over the rim, missing everything entirely.

"That's a miss," John said, grinning.

"Just try again," Jared told him, running to chase down the ball. It felt good not to be shooting alone. Briefly he wondered where Angie was, but didn't look too hard for her. He hadn't been near her since Halloween. Retrieving the ball, he passed it back to John. "Just aim at the rim," he said. "You can do it."

John scrunched up his eyes and sent up another shot. This on bounced off the backboard and Jared quickly snatched it from midair.

"You're getting closer," he assured John.

It took five more attempts, but John managed to bounce one in. As it fell through the net, he immediately jumped up and down, pumping his fists.

"Nice shot!" Jared told him.

John turned to him and grinned ear to ear. "You did math with me," he said.

Surprised he remembered, Jared nodded. "Uh, yeah. Want another shot?"

"Your turn," John said, still grinning.

Jared's shot struck the front of the rim, went flying up, and then fell down through the hoop.

"Hey, big guy," cried a voice. "Nice shot! You want to play over here? We need another guy."

Jared felt his heart jump and his mouth grow dry. Turning, he saw the boy with the red shoes looking at him expectantly.

Swallowing, Jared, managed to find his voice. "You mean me?"

"He don't mean John," Ryan said, standing near Jared, bent over with his hands on his knees. "Man, you playing, or not?"

"Uh, yeah," Jared said. He looked back to pass the ball to John, but he had already taken a seat on the floor behind the side basket. Leaving the ball behind, Jared clumsily jogged to the main court. His heart beat a mile a minute and he felt his palms grow sweaty. Nobody had asked him to play before.

"You're taking my place," Nick said, walking by him. "I'm flat-out tired."

"Don't you mean 'fat out' tired," Ryan said snidely. "Yo, man, you need to stop eating the burgers and play more ball before tryouts."

"Shut up, man," Nick said. To Jared, he said, "You got Will," he said, pointing at the kid in the red shoes, "Ben, and Ryan on your team. You're against the eighth graders."

"Fresh meat," one of the eighth graders said, grinning wickedly. "I got the human toothpick."

Jared ignored him as he fought to steady his heartbeat. He'd never played a pickup game of basketball before and he was doing it with the kid he used to dream of becoming friends with. It was a chance he did not want to blow.

"We get the ball first," Will said at the top of the key.

"Oh, no way!" protested the eighth grader guarding him. "It's our ball!"

Will just stared at him with is his large dark eyes and then lifted his eyebrows. "Fine. Let's shoot for it."

"No way," the eighth grader, a medium-sized boy with short, curly, blond hair, shook his head empathetically. "You never miss. Let the new guy take the shot."

Will shrugged. "Sure. Hey, big guy, here." He tossed the ball to Jared, who caught it by reflex.

In his mind, Jared still couldn't believe this was happening. He had barely even known the boy's name until now.

"Uh, where do I shoot?" he asked.

The eighth grader by him, a tall, burly boy with dark, hairy arms and long, shaggy hair, groaned. "From the foul line, idiot. Hurry up!"

The other two eighth graders looked like twins. Both were solidly built kids of medium height with buzz cuts and heavy acne. One of them had a mustache starting on his upper lip.

"Just aim right above the rim," Nick called from where he sat under the basket. "You got it, man."

Jared moved to the line and bounced the ball once, trying to steady his thundering heart. Then, eyeing the basket, he followed Nick's advice. Aiming at the front of the rim, he sent up a shot that caught nothing but net ... the bottom of the net. He'd been so nervous he'd forgotten to bend his knees and had shot way short.

"Airball!" crowed the shaggy, burly boy. "Our ball."

Ryan threw up his hands and gave Jared a dirty look. "Should've picked John," he muttered.

Seeing the ball bounce to the wall, Jared dropped his head and bent over in shame.

"No problem," Will said. He stepped forward and smacked Jared's back. "You just need to warm up. Let's get these guys!"

Nodding, Jared stood, grateful for the support. He turned to Will and waited for direction.

"You guard Bigfoot," Will said. "I got Curly."

"I'll take Mustache," Ryan said. "Ben, you can have his brother."

"We're not brothers," the boy with the mustache said. "We just look alike"

Jared bit his bottom lip and jogged over to the shaggy boy. Taking a deep breath, he tried to steady his nerves. Putting his airball out of memory, he focused on defense. Jared knew he wasn't great on offense, but he knew he could play defense. His favorite college teams to watch on TV were Duke and UVA, two teams who prided themselves with swarming, aggressive defense. Also, in soccer, he usually played in the back and often marked the other team's best forward. He had quick feet, long legs, and long arms.

"Okay," the curly-headed boy said. "Make-it-take-it. Take it back past the three-point line if it hits rim. Ball in."

The game started with a pass in to Bigfoot. Perhaps thinking Jared a complete pushover, the shaggy eighth grader pivoted to the basket and went up for a shot.

Jared stood an inch taller and had much longer arms. Rising up, he easily blocked the ball in the boy's face and then grabbed it as it bounced loose.

"Oooh!" Nick shouted from his seat. "Toothpick got game!"

"Nice!" Will shouted, running down the three-point line. "Here, big guy! Pass!"

Jared threw the ball out to him and Will launched a high-arcing shot that splashed into the net.

Bigfoot hung his head and groaned. "Man, nobody blocked my shot before," he complained.

That didn't stop his friends from ragging on him. Jared couldn't help but feel good.

After that, the seventh graders dominated. Jared kept down low, blanketing Bigfoot on defense and snatching every rebound from missed shots. Twice he stole errant passes, reading the play and jumping in the lane to intercept the ball. Each time he quickly got the ball out to Will.

On offense he mostly acted as a decoy, setting up near the basket, but twice Will found him with perfect bounce passes. Once

Jared went up too fast and hit the ball off the backboard too hard, missing the rim completely, but the other time he converted the layup perfectly. Otherwise he only scored on two put-backs—easy buckets on offensive rebounds. If he didn't have a shot, he always looked to pass out to Will. The smaller boy seemed to be everywhere, always calling for the ball and always open.

While he cleaned up the inside, Will and Ryan controlled the perimeter. Ryan easily broke down his defender with the dribble and either passed if defensive help came, or went in for a layup if left alone. Ben played in the middle and set picks if needed. He had developed a decent midrange jumper and if left open would get a pass from either Will or Ryan.

They played two games, with the seventh graders winning both in blowouts.

"Man," Bigfoot said, gasping for a breath after the second game. "You guys run around too much. I'm dripping buckets here."

His friends agreed and refused a third game. "We can't get too sweaty like you dudes," said the curly-headed boy. "Girls actually like us." The eighth graders tried to keep their heads up as they trudged off the court.

"I guess we showed them," Ben said, shaking out his mop of blond hair. He couldn't help grinning. "Are we ready for tryouts, or what?"

Will twisted his mouth in a frown. "Ah, they're just a bunch of hangout ball players."

"A bunch of what?" Ryan asked, jerking his head back and scrunching his face. "What's a hangout ball player, man?"

Will shrugged. "You know, one of those guys who just likes to hang out instead of playing. All they do is talk, dribble a little and then shoot. They don't play defense and barely ever pass. You know, like those guys who play on the outdoor court after school. We saw them all the time at football practice."

Jared hid a smile. He knew exactly what Will meant.

"What are you smiling at, toothpick?" Ryan said to him. "You don't play football. You don't know what he's talking about."

Jared hastily bit his lip and looked away. He didn't have to be on the football team to know. Most of the kids in PE played what Will called "hangout ball" and Jared had been watching it for a very long time.

In "hangout ball," the real skill came in trash talking. The playing was more of an afterthought. "Hangout ball" players were so scared of being beat off the dribble and made to look silly that they just didn't play defense at all. Instead they'd just stand around talking trash while somebody dribbled around until getting bored and throwing up a shot. Every once in a while it went in, but nobody really cared. If anybody broke a sweat, it was more by accident. To them, basketball acted as more of a social activity than a sport.

Jared had seen this version of basketball many times when sitting on top the bleachers. Still, he kept his mouth shut. He didn't think Ryan liked him very much.

Ryan had already turned from him. To Will he said, "If you're looking for a real game, man, you should go try the Shady Farms Apartments." He nodded at the game on the other side of the court. Big Mike just stepped back and knocked down a contested three. "That's where Big Mike plays. There's always a game there."

Will turned to watch. Cocking his head, he licked his lips thoughtfully. "Is it far from here?"

"Nah, it's just up the road after Nick's neighborhood." Ryan's voice grew bitter. "Once you get past all those fancy houses you'll get to some pretty sorry apartments. I used to live there and, man, am I glad I don't anymore."

"Hey, guys," Ben said. "What about now? Are we playing, or what?"

"I'm good," Ryan said. "Man, I need some water."

"Where's Nick?" Will asked.

Ben snickered. "Ah, he left to sit near the girls. He keeps trying to get Stephanie Baker to look at him."

"Great. Hey, big guy," Will said, as if suddenly remembering Jared. "You still want to play?"

"Uh, yeah," Jared answered. "Sure."

"That makes only three of us," Ben said.

Will grinned. "Want to play 21?"

Ryan turned back from where he'd headed off the court. "You guys playing 21? Count me in. I'll be right back! I need the bathroom and water first!" He ran into the boys' locker room.

Jared had never played 21 before, but wasn't going to say anything. He quickly figured out it was every man for himself. If you scored a bucket you got two points and got to shoot free throws for a point each until you missed. Then the rebound became a live ball for anyone to grab. At first he played hesitantly, but quickly realized that if he just kept his eye on the ball, like in soccer, he just needed to react. Soon his play picked up and he became a strong defensive force.

"His long arms!" complained Ryan after returning to the game and facing Jared. "I can't see anything!"

He'd split Will and Ben on the dribble and had reached the basket where he ran into Jared on the blocks. Every pivot move he made, Jared followed, both hands raised high. Finally, he threw up a wild shot that hit the backboard and nothing else.

"Man, it's like he's got Go-Go Gadget arms," Ryan grumbled.

Will laughed as he chased down the ball. "What about me?" he said. "I can't even see over big guy's waist!"

Nobody had won when Mr. Hackett blew the whistle to put the balls up.

"So," Ben said, panting heavily. "Now are we ready for tryouts?"

"You bet," Ryan said, slapping his back. "You'll make it, man. If not, I'll kick you on the team myself."

Sweaty, face flushed, Jared started heading to the locker room feeling elated. In 21 he'd managed nine points and even had swished a free throw.

Will's voice stopped him. "Hey, big guy! Nice game. You going out for basketball next week?"

Jared stopped. "What?" He'd never considered school sports and much less ever considered playing basketball.

"Basketball tryouts, string bean," Ryan said. "They start next Wednesday. With your height you might make it. But if you do tryout, you'll need to get your sports physical on Monday."

"Uh, okay," Jared said, feeling his heart to pound again. "I'll try."

Ryan grunted. "Sure you will. Come on, guys, I need to get out of these stinky clothes."

Chapter 17

Jared walked to his locker in a daze. He couldn't believe it. It was like, out of the blue, he'd just won the lottery without knowing he even had a ticket. Not only did he play basketball, but he'd played well, and had, just maybe, made real friends.

His walk in the clouds didn't last long. After changing into his regular clothes and snapping his locker shut, he went to line up by the main doors on the left side of the gym. As he walked across the basketball court, he scanned the kids where the Trailblazers lined up on the opposite side of the gym, searching for Will. He spotted him in conversation with Nick and Ryan. None of them looked his way.

Then he heard Mr. Hackett calling him. "Mr. Cook, a moment please."

Swallowing, Jared turned and trotted over to where the teacher stood just outside the locker room. Mr. Hackett didn't look at him as he busily scanned a clipboard.

"It seems like our friend Marshall is having some trouble. Go in the locker room and check on him."

Nodding, Jared headed back with a sigh. The boys' locker room reeked of cologne and body spray mixed with straight musty sweat. It smelled like a dead animal rolled in chemicals and left in a corner to rot. Even after two months of school, Jared had yet to get used to the stench.

Pale light and a faded olive-green floor only added to the dirty, depressing atmosphere. He went through a short hall past the teachers' offices and into a wide room filled with long, skinny lockers. There were two rows of lockers, one on top of other. They ran along the walls in all directions. An island of more lockers dominated the center of the room, with long benches running between the island lockers and side wall lockers on either side. In the middle of the back wall another small hallway opened that led to toilets on the right and to another room of lockers past the bathroom. This back room also had the shower stalls that, to Jared's knowledge, had not been used in years.

At first Jared thought he was alone. All the kids had changed and were gone, but then he heard a whimper and a loud sniff.

"Great," Jared muttered. "Why does it have to be me?"

Marshall had been making things hard for himself since the first day of school. By now everyone in the school, teachers and students, knew about him. Nobody liked him. He kept an appallingly arrogant attitude and seemed to go out of his way to say the wrong things. Way back in September, when given his gym clothes, he loudly told Mr. Hackett he couldn't change in the locker room because there were too many dirty people around. When Mr. Hackett ignored him, he took to waiting until everyone else left before he changed in and out of his clothes.

He easily remained Gary's favorite target and was mercilessly teased. Always sitting alone at lunch, Gary or Ray would come up and leave him fake love letters from girls they'd made up. At first Marshall had actually believed them and once had loudly asked his homeroom class who knew Ineesem Weedman.

He at least stopped wearing ties every day, but his pants were always too short and his shirts remained more appropriate for business meetings than school. In short, hanging around Marshall, unless you were teasing him, meant you were a total loser.

Jared, after his great time playing basketball, did not want to be here. Quickly he followed the sound around the island of lockers and found Marshall.

The tall, awkward boy sat on the filthy, stained, chipped, floor with his back against the bench, sobbing. His face lay buried between his knees that were wrapped in his long arms. Still in his gym clothes, he did not look up at Jared. Behind him, a single bottom locker was open with papers and jeans strewn out in front of it. Marshall's backpack lay open and upside down beside it.

Jared coughed and squeaked his sneakers against the sticky floor, but Marshall ignored him.

"Uh, what's wrong?" Jared finally asked. "Are you okay?"

Marshall picked up his head and looked over his shoulder at Jared. His eyes were red behind his glasses. "They stole my watch," he said, his voice shaking. "They stole it …"

"Oh," Jared said, taken aback, not knowing what else to do. He knew locker thefts happened.

Already three times he'd heard kids complaining of missing money and jewelry. Usually somebody had forgotten to snap the lock shut, or so Mr. Hackett said.

"You don't understand," Marshall said, his voice loud and deep as always, but now shaking with emotion. "My dad and mom … They gave me that watch for my birthday."

"Uh, should I go tell Mr. Hackett?"

"No!" Marshall nearly yelled. "Why would you do that?" he said, his voice turning bitter. "He won't care! He'll just say it's my fault for bringing it to school and not locking my locker. I know how to lock a locker! Somebody broke in. They even took my shirt! They're dirty monsters!"

"What are you going to do?" Jared asked, feeling at a loss. "If you want, I, uh, can find a shirt for you from the bin."

The bin was a huge laundry basket kept parked outside the teacher's office. Inside were all the old clothes leftover in the locker rooms over the years. If any kid forgot their gym clothes, they were allowed to grab some from the bin. Most chose to get a fail for the day instead. Mr. Hackett claimed that the clothes in the bin had been washed, but it certainly didn't smell like it.

"Don't bother," Marshall said, taking off his glasses and wiping his eyes. "I'll just wear my gym shirt." His bottom lip jutted out. "I'll not let them terrorize me and I won't bow down to their evil!"

"Uh, okay …" Then Jared grimaced. "Uh, I think your pants are ripped too." He spotted a good size hole from where he stood.

"What?" Marshal spun around and grabbed his jeans. Holding them up, he shook them out and revealed a long slit cut right where the two legs met in the back. "The monsters!" Marshall said, his eyes blazing. "They have no shame!" He whirled on Jared and glared. "I'll just wear my gym shorts too."

Jared nodded and edged away. "Okay then," he said, relieved to be retreating. "I'll, uh, let Mr. Hackett know that you'll be out soon …"

Marshall ignored him. Kneeling, the awkward boy muttered fiercely under his breath as he started stuffing the ripped pants and papers into his backpack.

At lunch, Jared took his time finding his usual spot. Leaving the line with his tray carrying pizza and chocolate milk, he walked along the outer edge of the cafeteria, pausing near the front long tables as if searching for his friends.

If he expected Will to invite him over for a seat, he was disappointed. He saw him sitting with his back to him talking to Ryan across the table. Nick sat on his left, leaving a seat open. But as he stared at the open seat, wondering what would happen if he sat in it, Ben brushed by without a glance in his direction. He sat next to Will and that was that.

Embarrassed and feeling like an idiot, Jared made the long walk to his round table and plopped into his chair.

At the table on his right, Marshall sat in his gym clothes ferociously stabbing at his salad. During class a lot of kids had given him a hard time, ribbing him about finally finding decent clothes to wear. "And nice cologne you got on," Gary had said mockingly. "What's it called, 'Musk for Losers'?" Marshall had just gritted his teeth and ducked his head.

At first Jared had thought it a little funny, but then he remembered Marshall sitting on the dirty floor crying. Jared's father constantly worked late and often had to travel for weeks at a time to conferences and out of state meetings. He knew the importance of gifts from parents and how much they meant. On his last birthday his father had given him a book about Native American art he'd gotten from a trip to New Mexico. He'd never cared about art before, but he still kept the book as a treasured possession, often flipping through it at night when his father was away. He'd felt sorry for Marshall and made sure to look away from the teasing.

As he stared down at his pizza, a shadow fell over him. For a brief second he thought Nick or Will had come over and his heart jumped, but when he looked up he saw Angie standing beside him.

"Hey," she said. "I just want to thank you for letting John shoot baskets at PE today."

Jared immediately swallowed hard and felt his face grow warm. "What? Oh, uh, yeah," he managed to choke out. He found it hard to look Angie in the face. "He, uh, he did good."

"Yeah, he really likes basketball. Look, Jared," Angie said, brushing a strand of black hair from her face, "I think you're a nice kid." Jared gave a start and stared up at her, his eyes wide. Angie ducked her gaze and then glanced back toward the long tables. "Listen, I also saw you playing basketball with some boys. I'm just giving you a warning. You should stay away from those kids. They're bad news."

Jared felt as if he'd just been hit with a hammer, right between the eyes. "Wh-what?" he asked. "Do you mean … Ryan and them?"

"That's exactly who I mean. Ryan, Will, and Nick." She sighed. "Even Ben. They're nothing but jocks."

Jared shook his head, not believing he was hearing this. Angie came up to his table and said she might like him and then warned him against making friends?

"How do you know?" he asked, the question jumping from his mouth. He was surprised to hear anger in it.

"I'm a Trailblazer," Angie said. "I have class with them. They're like all the other jocks in this school, stuck-up showoffs who think they're better than everybody else. But you know what? All they can do better is maybe bounce a stupid ball. They're not nice, Jared."

Jared just shook his head. "Why are you telling me this?" he asked tightly.

"I-I told you. John likes you and, well, you're not like the others." She nodded over at Marshall. "You don't make fun of people just because they're different."

"Neither do they," Jared said. He took a deep breath. "They let me play with them today."

Angie snorted and abruptly sat down next to him. "Sure they did, but where are they now? If they were so nice, Jared, then why did they leave you alone at lunch?"

Jared frowned and looked away. He had no comment.

"Besides that," Angie continued, "I think there's something wrong with them … Do you remember Halloween?"

Jared coughed and nodded. "Y-yeah," he stammered, remembering how he hid in the bathroom from her.

"Well, that night I had an incident with them … You know there are thieves in this school, and I think they might be part of it."

Jared felt his face go tight and heart jump. He whirled on her, forgetting his nervousness. "What?" he cried. "What proof do you have?"

"Well, none," Angie said, drawing back, surprised at his reaction. "Not yet. I-I just have a feeling. They, they tried to scare me that night … they just don't seem right, okay?"

"Yeah, well," he growled. "It sounds like you're the one being judgmental."

Angie's face reddened. "What? How dare you say that!"

"First you judged them as jocks. Now you're trying to call them thieves."

"You don't even know them, Jared," she said bitterly. "You're defending kids who probably don't even remember your name and definitely won't remember you tomorrow. Maybe I'm wrong, all right. And maybe I'm wrong about you! Goodbye."

Shooting to her feet, she stalked back to her table with John.

Shaken, Jared pushed his tray away and stared at the table in front of him.

"I'm still going out for basketball," he muttered to himself.

That afternoon, right after school, he went to his tree and practiced his crossover dribble using his soccer ball. Tryouts were coming and he had to be ready.

That Sunday night at supper, Jared cleared his throat. "Uh, Dad? Can I have money for tomorrow? Like fifteen dollars?"

Sunday was the only night of the week where the whole family still gathered together to eat. With Kelly's dance schedule, Mr. Cook's work, and the boys' school, the rest of the week was eating when you could with whoever was around. Mrs. Cook always made a big pot or dish of food on the weekend that lasted for the rest of the week. On this night, she'd made spaghetti and meatballs.

At the head of the table, Mr. Cook, tall and lean like his sons with a shock of dark, curly hair, leaned back in his chair and pushed up his glasses. He rubbed his square, clean-shaven jaw.

"Um, maybe," Mr. Cook said. "Is this for school?"

When younger, Jared used to think his dad looked like Clark Kent, but as he grew older the Superman image had begun to fade.

"It's certainly not for a hot date," George quipped, sitting on his father's right.

Next to him, Jared felt blood rush to his face. He looked over at his mother just to the left of his father.

"Please?" he begged.

"What's it for?" Mrs. Cook asked, bouncing Carey on her knee. "You'll have to let us know. Money doesn't grow on trees."

"I, uh, am trying out for basketball and sports physicals are tomorrow after school." Jared kept his gaze on his mother, not daring to look at his brothers' reactions.

He didn't have to look.

George barked out a laugh.

Jack, at the end of the table, grunted loudly. "You?" he said. "You're going out for basketball?"

"Awesome!" Kelly said, sitting across from Jared. She smiled wide. "I hear there're some really cute boys going out for the team. I can go watch them, I mean you, play!"

George scoffed. "No way are you going out for the team. You can't play basketball. Dad, just save the money, or give it to me."

Jared ducked his head. "I can play," he said.

"Yeah?" George said. "Maybe if they had a branch for a basket you could play."

Jared had just started to take sip of milk and now coughed hard, spraying milk across his plate of pasta.

"Careful!" Mrs. Cook said. "George, leave your brother alone."

"No, Mom, I can't," George said. "He's an embarrassment to the family. Just ask Jack."

Jack glared at his younger brother. "Hey, don't get me involved." He stood up and wiped his mouth. "Oh, can I be excused?"

"Already?" Mrs. Cook asked, sounding disappointed. "Don't you like the meatballs?"

"Oh, uh, yeah," Jack said rubbing his stomach, "but Rick is picking me up. We have a project due in history tomorrow."

"Can't you work here?" Mr. Cook asked him.

Jack shook his head. "Sorry, but we have no internet here." He'd been pleading for his parents to subscribe to internet for years and always made sure they knew it when he needed it for school.

Mrs. Cook sighed, pulling her hair out of Carey's mouth. "No, dear," she told her. "Eat spaghetti, not hair." To Jack, she said, "Okay, go ahead then. You can have more to eat when you get back."

"And make sure to be back before ten," Mr. Cook told him.

"Sure," Jack said, taking his plate to the sink. As he went by Jared, he bopped him on the head. "You go out for basketball. Just don't shoot any stick balls."

George cracked up and Jared's face burned bright and hot. Their parents just stared in confusion.

After Jack headed out the front door, Mr. Cook wiped his mouth with a napkin and turned to Jared.

"Now, what's all this about stick balls and basketball?" He asked.

"Nothing," Jared mumbled.

George snorted. "Nothing? I don't think so." He glared at Jared, heat entering his voice. "Don't think we don't see you, Jared. Almost every day after school he goes out back to bounce a stupid soccer ball in the dirt and then throw it at a tree while talking to himself. I don't think he needs to go out for basketball, Dad. I think he needs to go see a shrink. I'm serious."

"What?" Mr. Cook asked, scrunching his eyes. "Is that true, Jared?"

"It's not that bad," Kelly said, speaking up. "I think it's kind of cute."

Jared had enough. Slamming down his fork, he got to his feet. "Forget I asked. I don't need the money."

"Jared, wait," his father said.

"I can't. I have to study for a test." Jared raced from the kitchen and went straight to the stairs.

"Let him go, dear," Mrs. Cook said. "George, that was cruel. He's your brother."

"Don't remind me," George said, stifling a snort.

"George!" Mrs. Cook cried.

Jared paused on the stairs to listen, his heart hammering in his chest. He'd never felt so embarrassed before. All his dreams were crashing down. At that moment he wished his life would just end.

"What?" George exploded. "What's cruel is having a socially challenged brother who has imaginary friends and plays imaginary games. He needs to grow up, Mom!"

Gritting his teeth, Jared had heard enough. He raced up to his room and threw himself on his bed. Then the tears came. For a long time, he just cried into his pillow. Eventually he must've fallen asleep because the next thing he knew his brother was standing over him.

Chapter 18

"I, ah, I'm sorry," George mumbled. "I just had a bad weekend, and stuff … but you still shouldn't play stupid imaginary games. Anyway, 'night."

Jack looked at the nightstand and saw it was close to ten thirty. He'd been sleeping for over three hours. Not saying anything, he rolled out of bed and stalked to the bathroom.

After using the toilet, he washed his hands and splashed water on his face. Staring in the mirror, he saw a tall, curly-headed loser with bloodshot eyes.

"You're not a basketball player," he said. "You're trash. A loser." Sighing, he flipped off the light and left his dreams of basketball glory behind.

Stumbling downstairs, he went to the living room and flipped on the TV to watch football. Jack, he guessed, hadn't returned yet. He sat in a big rocker and tried to relax. Without cable, Sundays were the best days for sports because the broadcast stations had most of the NFL games, including the night game. He'd missed the end of the afternoon late games so was just catching up on the scores when his mother came in.

"Jared!" she exclaimed when seeing him. "I thought you were in bed!"

"I was," Jared mumbled. "I just woke up."

Mrs. Cook came over and knelt beside her son. "I'm sorry about George … he didn't mean what he said."

Jared shrugged and kept his attention on the game. "Where's Dad?" he asked.

"Oh, he had to go to the store for some things … I needed. Um, well, he'll be back soon. Jared, dear, don't you think you should go shower and get more sleep? If you have the physical tomorrow—"

"I don't have any physical tomorrow, Mom." Jared grabbed the controller and snapped off the TV. "I don't have anything, okay?" He flung the controller across the room, smacking the back of the couch.

"Well, you should. You certainly have good aim."

Jared stood and bit back tears. "Good night, Mom," he said. "I need a shower." He quickly ran from the room before his mother could see him cry.

The next morning, George shook Jared awake. "Get up, man," he growled. "And watch your step. You might step on your stupid dream." Then he stalked to the bathroom, slamming it shut.

Confused and bleary eyed, Jared sat up and swung out his feet. He hit something soft and looked down. Lying next to his bed, under his feet, was a brand-new sports bag. A new pair of basketball shorts and a folded blue T-shirt rested on top. Jared blinked rapidly. Under the shirt he saw his physical form sticking out. Snatching it, he saw it was signed by his mother and had a twenty-dollar bill attached by a paperclip.

Jared's mouth dropped open. Now he knew where his father had been the night before. He'd been shopping for him. Flopping back in his bed, Jared rested the physical form on his chest and stared up dazedly. He couldn't quite say it about his brothers, but he had the greatest parents in the world. Maybe his dad really was Superman.

Jared's rekindled hopes and dreams were nearly dashed as quickly as they'd been reborn. Before school he'd stuffed the twenty in his pocket to keep it safe. He thought of nothing but getting the physical. All morning in homeroom he kept pulling out the money to stare at it, just to make sure it wasn't all some dream. Twenty dollars was a lot to him, the most money he'd ever had before at one time.

Monday, being an even day, meant he had no PE. During his second block, he sat in Ms. Jackson's typing class staring at the computer screen. The constant clatter of fingers striking keys filled the room, but Jared's own fingers lay idle on the table. He was supposed to be working on training his fingers to stay on the "home" keys, but all he could see was him in a Washington Middle basketball uniform taking a pass from Will ...

"Hey, dude," whispered a voice over to him. "You got your physical today?"

Surprised, Jared turned and saw Ryan standing behind him.

"What?" he said reflexively.

He'd almost forgotten the dark-skinned boy also had typing that period. Ms. Jackson didn't tolerate talking during class and all the computers had cardboard walls dividing them. The only time he really saw other kids was when lining up to leave, and nobody ever spoke to him then.

"Are you trying out for basketball? The sports physical is today after school. You have to pay for it."

Jared immediately slapped his jeans' pocket. "Uh, yeah," he said. "I got money."

Ryan grunted. "Cool." Despite the fact Ms. Jackson had cranked up the heat, he wore a loose-fitting gray jacket, worn at the collar. Both hands were in his pockets. "Good luck," he mumbled.

"Uh, thanks," Jared replied, surprised.

"Who's that talking? Is that you, Jared Cook?" Ms. Jackson's sharp voice demanded from her desk.

"What?" cried Gary in mock astonishment. He sat at the computer closest to Ms. Jackson, so the teacher could keep an eye on him. "Jared the beanpole talking? Is that possible?"

"Sure it is," Chaz said from one the back computers. "He was just talking to himself. He does that, you know."

Jared's face burned.

"Quiet, you two!" snapped Ms. Jackson. "You know I don't tolerate any talking. Get up and move to the back corner, Mr. Cook. Right now. Ryan, you'd better find your seat before you join him. The rest of you better be typing or you won't have much to be thankful for when you see your grades."

Jared knew better than to argue. Getting up ruefully, he left his blank screen and headed to the last row of computers. As he did so, he saw Gary staring at him, grinning.

Ignoring the bully, he went to the far corner computer where he saw Ryan sitting across from it. Ryan looked up briefly to give an apologetic shrug.

Jared gave a nod and slid in front of his new screen. Inside his chest, his heart did a little dance of joy. Ryan had acted friendly toward him. He rubbed his pocket holding the twenty and bit his bottom lip. Things were definitely looking up. Then he got down to typing …

As he got into his keyboard drills, his eyes started to droop. He could smell a faint fragrance and wondered if Ms. Jackson had some sort of air freshener set up here in the corner. Whatever it was, it started to give him a headache. The smell and constant clacking started to lull him to sleep. The letters on the screen in front of him started to blur and his head began nodding.

Shaking it, he sat up straight and tried to focus. He'd been so upset last night that he hadn't slept well.

"Come on," he murmured softly. "Stay awake …"

Jared had nodded off in school before, but had never fallen fully asleep. He just needed to rest his eyes for a second … Leaning his keyboard against the computer screen, he pushed his chair back and laid his head on his arms on the table. His eyes slid shut and he went out …

Jared woke with a start.

He'd been dreaming of playing basketball against a giant, two-headed monster. With the body of a lizard, the monster had Gary's and Chaz's heads. Standing eight feet tall, the monster had been waving bags of basil at him while the heads had mocked him, calling him a weed-eating beanpole. Then it'd started shouting his name.

"Jared! Jared, wake up!"

He sat up with a jerk and found himself staring at a computer screen. Ms. Jackson stood beside him, staring down at him worriedly.

"Jared," she said angrily, "class ended twenty minutes ago. It's lunchtime!"

"Oh, uh …" Jared shook his head, trying to clear away a headache. "I'm, uh, sorry," he mumbled.

The teacher's voice softened into concern. "Jared, I've never seen you like this. Talking in class, and now sleeping in class. You're one of my better students. Is everything okay?"

Jared rubbed his eyes and nodded. "Uh, yeah …" He had a nasty taste in his mouth. Swallowing, he made a face. "I, I guess I didn't get enough sleep last night."

"I'll say so. I tried to wake you for almost a minute." Then she frowned. "And I expect you to stay after school, young man. You didn't do any work today."

"Wh-what?" blinking, Jared looked at the computer screen and his mouth dropped open. All the work he'd done had been erased. Only one word remained. In large font, it read THANKS.

All at once, Jared slapped his jeans and checked his pocket. His twenty-dollar bill was missing.

"No," he said, panicking. Standing up, he checked his other pocket and then his back pockets.

Ms. Jackson frowned at him. "Now what's wrong? You need the bathroom?"

Jared just shook his head. Desperation gripped his insides. He frantically searched the table and floor around the computer. "I … I, uh, lost something," he mumbled. He fought back tears as he slowly stood with the realization that he'd been robbed. "It's … gone."

"Well, next time don't sleep in my class. Now you'd better go off to the cafeteria. I'll write you a pass to your teacher explaining you were helping me, but not again, Jared. Give it to her after lunch. Now go get some food. You look pale."

Jared nodded dumbly and followed her to her desk. Taking the pass, he stumbled from the computer lab with a sick, sick feeling. He'd been robbed. And now he had no money for his physical.

"Gary," he mumbled, squeezing his eyes shut. Gary must've seen him pull out the money during homeroom and then had waited for his chance. Either that or it was Chaz. He could see Chaz being a thief more than he could see Gary. They'd probably worked together. Finding him sleeping, they'd pulled his money.

Jared never made it to the cafeteria. Going to the office, he asked to use the phone to call his mother.

Seeing his stricken face, the assistant merely waved him to a phone on the counter and went back to typing on her computer.

"Mom," he said miserably when she'd answered. "I … I lost the money. I don't know what happened to it …" He managed not to cry, but it wasn't easy.

His mother listened as he told her about falling asleep and then quickly reassured him. "Don't you worry, Jared. Things like this happen. You go to your physical. I'll come by and drop off a check. You don't have to worry about a thing. Okay, honey?"

As he hung up, Jared still felt the pain and hurt, but also the love of his mother. Biting his bottom lip, he clenched his fists and remembered Marshall. Now he knew how the tall, gawky kid felt. And like him, he wouldn't bow down to their evil.

"I will make the tryouts," he said grimly.

Chapter 19

Wednesday afternoon, after school, found over thirty boys sitting in small clumps in the bleachers. Big Mike and his group of friends looked down on the rest from the top, almost with contempt.

As soon as Jared walked into the gym, he knew he'd made a big mistake. There was no way he belonged here. There was no way he could make it over so many other boys. He stood just inside the doors on the far side from the bleachers. Staring at all the boys sitting and with more coming, he had every urge to quietly back out and find Ms. Jackson for typing

Glen Baker and Brad Williamson sat on the bottom row of the bleachers, cracking jokes about some of the boys' chances.

"I see some butterballs coming in here," Brad said, loudly, tossing back his hair. "I sure hope they don't think there's free food when we're done."

Nick had just entered from the doors opposite of Jared. Walking in front of Brad and Glen, he paused to lift his leg and pass gas.

"Here's something free," he said. "Ah, that felt good."

"Gross, dude," Glen said, wrinkling his nose. "What did you eat, raw fish?"

"That's just your talent you smell," Nick told him, walking on.

"Get out of the way, fatso," Brad said. "You're blocking the wall."

"That's just your ego," Nick called back, going up into the bleachers.

Jared had just started to turn, when Glen called to him.

"Hey, kid! Are you here for tryouts? Because if you are, we're over here."

Caught, Jared bit his bottom lip and hastily started for the bleachers.

"He looks scared," Brad said, laughing. "Yo, man! What are you wearing? You expect to run in that?"

Jared wore jeans and a sweater over a T-shirt. He carried his backpack and sports bag carrying his shorts and the new basketball shoes his mother had picked out for him the day before. Blinking, he realized all the other boys had already dressed out in shorts and T-shirts.

Making a quick pivot, he hurried to the locker room. His face felt hot and he wished he'd never decided to go out for the team.

Glen's and Brad's laughter followed him.

Then, just as he reached the locker room, Will came dashing out, calling over his shoulder.

"Beat you, Ryan!" Seeing Jared, he gave a quick grin. "Hey, big guy! You made it!" Trotting by, he jumped up and slapped the top of Jared's head. "See you out there, dude!"

Jared had stopped short when seeing him. "Uh, yeah," he said to Will's back. He took a deep breath, feeling better.

Ryan walked out next, nearly bumping into him. "Yo, dude. I see you got your physical. You better hurry. Coach won't like if you're late." Then he followed after Will without a glance back.

Jared quickly went into the locker room. Mr. Hackett was unlocking the supply and medical room to the right of his office. Seeing Jared, he straightened and raised his eyebrows. "Mr. Cook, don't tell me you're going out for the team. That's a bold step. It's about time you used your height for something."

Not sure if he'd been complimented or insulted, Jared continued to his gym locker and quickly spun the combination on his lock. The thefts had been continuing, and just the other day the gym teachers had a big lecture about trust, never sharing your combination, and stop bringing expensive items to gym. After changing, Jared made sure he locked everything up. As he turned to go, he saw Chaz sauntering into the room.

Seeing Jared, the plump boy's mud-colored eyes lifted in surprise. "What are you doing here?" he asked. Then he smirked. "Don't tell me, are you going out for the team?"

"Uh, yeah," Jared muttered. He kept his eyes down. He hadn't had any proof of who'd taken his money, but still suspected Chaz.

Chaz laughed. "You don't play basketball. Remember? That's what you told me." Then he shrugged. "Well, cool. I guess I'll see you out there."

Jared nodded and quickly exited. He refused to let Chaz throw him off. Back in the gym, he kept his head low as he jogged to the first open spot he saw, the front row closest to the locker room. Sitting down, he propped his elbows on his thighs and held his forehead, staring at the ground.

For a moment he concentrated on taking deep breaths.

"I can do this," he muttered. "I can do this."

"Do what?" Chaz asked, sitting next to him, appearing out of nowhere. "You really think you're going to make the team?"

Swallowing, Jared picked up his head. "What? Isn't that why you're here?" *Or,* he thought to himself, *is it just to put me down? Did you take my twenty dollars?*

"Well, yeah," Chaz said. "That's why I'm here." Then he grinned. "Oh, I get it. You're one of the managers. You and that retard over there."

Jared looked up and saw John helping Mr. Hackett pull out a rack of basketballs from the locker room. Angie stood on the opposite side of the gym watching. She didn't look very happy, but John seemed to be having the time of his life.

"Hey, Mr. Hackett?" called Brad. "Can we shoot while we wait?"

"I'm not the coach," Mr. Hackett said gruffly. "Sit down and wait for him." He directed John over to Angie and headed back to his office.

Chaz snorted. "The retard's girlfriend isn't bad looking. Too bad she's so weird."

Jared dropped his gaze to the floor and ignored him. He started to wonder if Chaz really did take the money. If he did, he had no shame.

A minute later, Coach Swopes shuffled into the gym from the main doors where Jared had first entered. Stooped over, he carried a clipboard in front of him and never looked up. As he walked, he absently scratched his thinning white hair, appearing disinterested in the thirty-odd boys suddenly growing quiet and staring at him with rapt attention.

Finally, he came to a stop right at center court and lifted his head.

"Wow," he said. "That's a lot of boys being quiet in one spot. And they're all looking at me like I'm a swimsuit model."

He waited for the chuckles to die down and then lowered his clipboard. "I should have everyone's form. If I do, then I have you on my list. If I don't, I need them now."

All the boys had to turn in forms with parental permission to tryout. A few kids got up with folded forms, sheepishly bringing them to the coach. Jared had given his the other day at gym, so he knew he was already on the list. It felt good to have done something right.

"Okay, boys," Coach Swopes said once he'd gotten all the forms. "I'm going to give it to you straight. I only got fifteen spots open, and from that, only about ten can expect playing time. And just so you know, I already penciled in six slots. That leaves only nine of you boys left who can make the team. If you don't like the odds, get out now before you need a shower. If you do like them … line up. Everyone who thinks they can play for my basketball team, get on the end line facing me. And get ready to run your rear ends off. Basketball is a running sport, not a walking sport. Let's move it! If you're walking, just walk straight to the locker room and get your stuff and clear out!"

Jared quickly jogged to the end line, joining the murmuring crowd of boys.

"I miss Coach Hicks," one of the boys mumbled on Jared's right.

"Yeah," another boy said. "Too bad the retard got him fired."

"Less chatter, boys," Coach Swopes's voice called, "and more hustle!"

During PE class, Coach Swopes always spoke in a soft voice and always seemed laid back, if not a little muddled. Often he called kids by the wrong names, and he never made his class do all the stretches like the other teachers did. Now, though, the mild-mannered old man transformed. His voice came out like thunder and his eyes blazed with intensity.

Moving to the sideline, he stared down the row of boys. "I got my eye on those who can run. I mean run! If you can't keep up, don't come back. We're going to do what are called suicides, but I don't think we're allowed to call them that anymore. If you don't know what one is, follow Mr. Williamson's lead." The coach glared at Brad. "Because he'd better be the one leading." He raised a whistle to his lips.

Brad frowned and bent low in a runner's stance. At the blast of the whistle, the pack of boys took off, sprinting to the first foul line. Then all at once they stopped and sprinted back to the end line.

Jared had no idea what to do, so he followed the mass of bodies. Eventually he figured out a "suicide" run was running to each line on the court, one at a time, returning to the end line before turning again to race to the next line. That meant sprinting to the foul line and back, then to the midcourt line and back, followed by sprinting to the opposite foul line and back, and finally, sprinting to the opposite end line and back.

Jared quickly realized where the term "suicide" came from. All around him boys were gasping for air and bent over in pain.

"Again," Coach Swopes said. "This time faster!"

When Jared first started the running, his nerves were all over the place, jumping like popcorn. But as the whistle blasted for the second time, he felt calmness wash over him. Racing to the length of the first line, he leaned forward and slid to a stop, quickly pivoting back to the end line. It became like a game he could perfect. Lean forward, run hard, slide to a stop, pivot, and repeat.

By the middle of the second cycle of runs, he realized he was among the leaders. A surge of confidence shot up his spine and down into his legs. He could do this. Sure, he wasn't the fastest, but he was far from the slowest. More than that, he wasn't getting that tired. He also noticed, at the head of the pack, wearing bright red shorts with his red shoes and a white shirt, Will led the way.

Coach Swopes had them do one more "suicide" run and then allowed a break.

"You got five minutes," he barked. "Then I want two lines at center court facing each other. I want eighth graders in one line and seventh graders in the next." He turned to John and Angie. "If you don't know John, he's our team manager, along with Ms. Robinson. Angie," he called. "Give a wave!"

Angie lifted her hand halfheartedly and didn't smile. She was helping John wheel out a cart carrying a large water cooler and paper cups.

"If you want off this team, show our managers disrespect. Otherwise, I expect you boys to be gentlemen. John's father, I'm sure you all know, is our principal. He'll be checking in. If you didn't bring your own water, go line up at the cooler. But now you only have four minutes, so move it!"

The coach shuffled toward the locker room as the boys quickly either went to the cooler, or to the bleachers for their water bottles.

Jared bit his lip and stayed back. He hadn't brought his own water, but the line looked too long and he didn't really want to be near Angie. Standing near the end of the bleachers, he surveyed the gym and saw Will and his friends gather under the basket.

Crouching down, he tried hard not to feel left out. Nobody gave him a glance. In a room full of boys, he felt very alone.

"Oh, man," wheezed Nick. "I think I'm done. I can't take another step." He collapsed against the padding on the wall behind the basket.

"I feel you," groaned Ben, going to his knees next to him. "I think I'm going to puke chicken nuggets any second." His thick blond hair had turned dark with sweat and now matted against his head.

Ryan leaned back on the pads above Nick and chuckled. "You dudes are in for a long day. Coach Swopes used to coach track, remember. We'll be running our rear ends off before this is all done." He wiped sweat from his brow and turned to Will. "You went out fast, dude. You need to pace yourself, man."

The slighter boy gave an impish grin, bouncing on his feet as if ready to run again. He'd finished first each time.

"What?" he said innocently "I thought that was just warm-ups."

Nick groaned. "I hate little kids. Hey, Will, help me up."

Will's boyish enthusiasm proved infectious. As he extended a hand to Nick, the larger boy grabbed it and pulled Will down, sending him across his lap.

"I'm going to warm up your skinny rump if you don't bring me my water bottle, you little creep."

Laughing, Will rolled free and shot to his feet. "Which one is your water, fatso?" he called, trotting to the bleachers.

"The big blue one with my name on it!" Nick called. "Now hurry and run, I'm dying of thirst!"

"I wish I had his energy," Ben said. He stood up and grinned. "Can you imagine if we all make the team?"

Nick shook his head. "No way, man. I might die first."

As Will reached the bleachers, Brad stepped in front of him, throwing out his chest, bumping him back. Will's head came up to the older boy's nose and Brad made sure the height difference was apparent.

"Hey," he said. "I didn't know sixth graders were allowed to try out. You're here to be another manager, right? Go over there with the retard and fill water cups. You don't have to try out for that. Just prove you won't drool in our water."

Glen stepped up beside Brad and pulled him back. "Hey, man. You're just sore the little guy finished before you. Don't be, dude. That kid is as fast as lightning. He's pretty good."

Brad snorted and sneered at Will. "Yeah? Good at what? Coloring inside the lines?"

Will just lifted his eyebrows and kept quiet. Then, shrugging, he leapt up the bleachers for the water bottles. His dad always taught him to ignore trash talk. The best way to unnerve an opponent is to act as if he didn't exist and then show him up during game time. Will meant to let his playing speak for itself, loud and clear.

Brad stared after him. "I'm going to cross you up, kid!" he called.

Glen shook his head. "I'd watch him, Brad. He played football and knows how to hit, and he runs like crazy. He's got wheels, dude."

"Whatever. Your football team was a joke. This is basketball. I'm going to wipe the floor with him."

Glen just shrugged. "We'll see, man."

"Yo, the water boy is back," Ryan said as Will returned with Nick's water bottle. "I saw you and Brad getting into it." He punched Will's shoulder. "Good luck with that one."

Will grinned tightly. "He's the one who's going to need luck."

"Yeah," Ryan said with a grunt. "Too bad he got the inches on you."

"Hey, water boy," Nick called. "I need some water." Still seated against the wall, he tilted his head back and opened his mouth.

"Ha," Will said. He pulled open the nozzle and stood to the side of Nick, gripping the bottle with both hands. "Here you go, big guy." Squeezing hard, he sent a squirt right in Nick's eyes. "Oops, I missed."

"Hey, you little jerk!" Nick swatted at him, but Will jumped back. "I'm so going to get you for that!" Showing renewed energy, he pushed himself to his feet and gave chase.

Laughing, Will danced away. "Here, Ben! You can have water, too!" He tossed Ben the bottle and ran for the center court.

"Hey, give me that!" Nick demanded, pivoting to Ben. Ben only grinned and took a long sip of water. "Want it? Come and get it!" As Nick went after him, he tossed the bottle to Ryan.

"Yo, Nick, I hope you're not thirsty," Ryan said. "There's not much left when I'm done with it."

The game of keep away ended when Coach Swopes blew his whistle sharply. Coming out of the locker room he demanded why there weren't two lines waiting for him.

"I gave you boys an extra two minutes! That's two more suicides we're doing in the end!"

Quickly all levity ended and the drills began.

"I never got my water," Nick muttered as he trotted toward center court.

Will smacked him in the side. "Sorry, dude. Water just makes you weak."

Nick only grunted. It would be a long tryout session.

Chapter 20

The first drill consisted of one versus one. Coach Swopes would toss a ball toward the top of the key and the first two players in line had to fight for it. Whoever got it first played offense and tried to score, while the other had to stop him.

Jared was relieved to be last in line. That gave him a chance to watch the others go and gather his nerves. Chaz stood in front of him, but didn't say anything. He'd struggled in the running and didn't look too pleased to see Jared barely sweating.

"We'll start with eighth grade on eighth grade on one court and then seventh grade on seventh grade on the other," Coach Swopes told them after explaining the drill. Then his eyes twinkled. "In the end we'll do eighth grade on seventh grade, for anybody who's willing. I want Glen Baker and Mike Thompson to go first, to show all the newbies what I'm talking about."

"Yo, coach," Glen said. "Big Mike is in seventh grade."

"Good," Coach Swopes said, grinning. "Then you should put him in his place."

"Yeah, right," Glen muttered. "He's in the seventh grade going on NBA."

Big Mike stepped to the front of the line looking bored. He didn't glance at Glen. The eighth grader, about the same size, but not nearly as built, edged next to him, crouching low.

"Go," said Coach Swopes, tossing the ball out.

Jared was sure Glen would get the ball first, but as soon as Coach Swopes's hand moved, Mike shot forward faster than Jared could blink. Using his wide body, he cut Glen off from the ball, grabbing it with two hands. Glen tried to go around his back to knock it free, but the big seventh grader spun away. Taking one dribble, he easily laid the ball into the hoop. Then, without a word, he trotted to the back of the seventh-grade line.

"Hey, man," Chaz said, "nice move."

"Shut up," Big Mike growled, not looking at him.

Jared swallowed and suddenly wished he wasn't last in line any more. He could feel Big Mike's disdain, rising off him like steam.

The drill quickly started. Coach Swopes tossed in a ball to the eighth-grade side and then immediately after tossed one to the seventh-grade side. He watched some boys intently, but other boys he seemed to totally ignore. Nineteen seventh graders had come out for the team, so Jared had time take it all in.

Will got matched with Ryan. Both arrived at the ball about the same time, but Ryan's longer reach managed to knock the ball to the side and he quickly tracked it down. Will went into a defensive crouch and put his hands out, blocking Ryan's path to the basket.

"You have ten seconds to score," Coach Swopes called.

Ryan dribbled right, going to the middle and then tried to crossover and move left. Will hopped back and shuffled his feet, keeping in front.

"Okay, little dude," Ryan said. "I see you." Shifting his back to Will, he crouched low and backed into him, trying to use his power and size to bull his way to the basket.

"Five seconds," Coach Swopes called.

Will put up a fight, refusing to back down, and Ryan ended up pulling back to throw up a shot that hit rim before bouncing down.

"Man!" he said. "Next time I got you!"

The two slapped hands as they trotted back to line. After two more pairs, Jared went up against Chaz.

"Uh, oh," Coach Swopes said when seeing them. "It's David versus Goliath."

Jared barely heard him. He looked at Chaz on his left and saw the shorter boy was also nervous, but was trying hard not to show it.

Crouching, Chaz looked at him and winked.

"Remember," he whispered. "You can't play basketball." Then he leaned into Jared's body, trying to get in the way.

Coach Swopes tossed out the ball. "Go!" cried the coach.

Just as Jared started, he felt Chaz's hand grab the bottom of his shorts and tug down.

Jared stumbled and nearly fell, reflexively using his right hand to hold up his shorts and left hand to catch the floor. By the time he recovered, Chaz had the ball and headed for the basket.

Jared immediately sprinted after him, his eyes locked on the ball as his long legs ate up the distance. His adrenaline spiked as he saw Chaz pick up his dribble and take two steps, readying for an easy layup. At the last second, Jared jumped in front of Chaz, twisting his body in the air while keeping his eyes on the ball. His arm came up and slammed into the ball, sending it crashing down with force.

With a loud thump, the ball knocked into Chaz's face before bouncing skittering to the side.

Caught completely by surprise, Chaz stumbled to the floor as the entire line of seventh graders roared.

"Bam!" shouted one of the eighth graders. "He packed him for lunch!"

"Facial!" cried another as several boys hooted and called out.

"Woohoo!" cried Coach Swopes. "Nice recovery! That's what I want to see!"

Jared felt like he was walking on air as he jogged back to the line.

"You fouled me," Chaz said sullenly, cutting in front of him. He blinked rapidly and rubbed a red spot on his forehead. "You jerk."

Jared just ignored him.

After another round, where everyone faced a different partner, Coach Swopes called for a halt and asked if any seventh grader dared face the eighth graders.

Jared had gone against Nick the second time and had actually gotten to the ball first, but didn't know what to do on offense and ended throwing up a clunker that hit the back of the rim. He didn't want to try his luck against eighth graders.

Ryan immediately stepped forward. Will, Nick, and four other boys followed him. Big Mike just snorted and kept his place. Jared figured Big Mike already had a slot with his name on it and had nothing left to prove.

Jared sighed and bit his bottom lip. He had a lot to prove. If he wanted any chance of making the team, he'd have to face eighth graders sometime. With little enthusiasm, he joined the group.

"Big guy is with us," Will said, seeing him. "Nice block, dude."

Nick slapped his back. "Hey, man. It's nice having another tall guy."

Jared immediately felt better and gave a tight grin.

"Here's the deal," Coach Swopes told them. "There're eight of you. Every basket you score is one lap around the court the eighth graders have to run before the next water break." He held up his hand as the boys started cheering. "At the same time, the seventh graders have to run a lap for every bucket the eighth graders score." He turned to the twelve eighth-grade boys. "Pick your best and brightest and let's see what happens."

"I got the sixth grader!" Brad shouted. "Let me take him!" He pointed a Will and grinned.

Glen and six of the bigger eighth graders joined him. Among them, Jared saw Bigfoot and Curly from PE class. He hoped he went against one of them. He at least knew he could defend them without too much trouble.

Brad demanded that Will and he go first.

"I've been waiting for this for some time," he said, wagging his tongue out of his mouth.

Will gave him a small mischievous smile. "Me too."

As the ball was thrown in, both boys went full speed after it.

Will went off a little quicker and cut slightly in front of Brad to cut him off. Just as he reached the ball, Brad put a hand on his back giving him a slight nudge. Will ended up sprawling on his stomach, but managed to bat the ball in front of him. Quickly, he lunged to his feet, slapping the ball downward with his hands, causing it to bounce up. Picking up the dribble, he moved out toward the midcourt line.

Cursing under his breath, Brad immediately switched to defense. Squatting low, he put both hands in front of him, setting up at the top of the key. "Come on, kid," he growled. "Let's see what you got."

Will dribbled toward him, bending low and switching hands with every bounce. Then, when a few feet away, he suddenly got taller and bounced the ball between his legs. Feinting left, he crossed to the right. Then with a flurry of hands, he did a double crossover, feinted again to the left before dashing to the right, catching Brad flatfooted. The eighth grader tried to recover, but stepped the wrong way and ended up on his backside as Will laid the ball up and in with a finger roll.

It took a long time for Coach Swopes to calm the boys down before the next pair went.

At the end of the drill, the eighth graders jogged three laps and the seventh graders went around four times. Ryan and Nick were the only other seventh graders to score. Jared was just proud to have kept Bigfoot from scoring, taking one lap away. Still, everyone was talking about Will taking down Brad. The eighth grader still fumed as he ran.

"I just stepped the wrong way!" he said loudly to Glen. "The little punk just caught me by surprise. That's all!" He glared back where Will jogged with a large group of seventh graders. "I'll get him back."

During the next water break, Will made it a point to get a cup from John. Then deliberately drooling in it, he held it up for Brad. The eighth grader just glared. Grinning, Wil drank the water and tossed the cup away.

Jared was surprised to see a number of boys missing after the second water break ended. They had slunk back to the locker room. Chaz was among the missing, which didn't bother him at all. He was actually having fun.

After a shooting drill and some scrimmaging, practice ended with more sprinting drills. Twenty-six exhausted, sweaty boys stood panting on the end line when Coach Swopes finally called them to the bleachers.

"Check tomorrow morning in the gym for cuts," he said when the boys had all collapsed to a needed seat. "If you see your name on the list, show up here, same time tomorrow. Final cuts will be posted on Friday. Now go get changed and get out of here. If you're taking the bus you have an hour, but don't be late!"

Jared entered the locker room feeling great. He'd managed to hit two shots in the shooting drill and held his own in the scrimmage, getting four rebounds and even scoring on a put-back. Will and Nick had been on his team and both had given him encouragement and advice.

As he reached his locker, Jared saw Glen standing in the way and dropped to the bench, breathing hard.

"Hey, dude," Glen said, opening the locker above Jared's. "You didn't do too bad out there. Can you dunk yet?"

Jared shook his head. "Ah, no."

"Well, one day, man. If you make the team, I'll show you some moves. We need a good center."

"What I need right now," Nick gasped, staggering in behind Jared, "is a shower."

An eighth grader named Darius heard him and laughed. He was one of Big Mike's crowd, but, unlike Big Mike, had a friendly smile. "Yeah, man, it reeks!"

"Want some spray?" Glen asked, pulling off his soaked shirt. He grabbed a can from his locker and started to spray it all over his chest and stomach.

Jared immediately turned away, coughing.

Nick shook his head and went to his locker in the back. "No, thanks. I don't need to smell worse than I already do."

Will sat on the floor leaning back against his locker when Nick came in. He lifted his hand, giving a limp wave.

Nick looked down at him and sighed. "Finally, man. You look like total sh—uh, you look tired, man."

Ben groaned from where he'd yet to start getting changed. "I'm too tired to care if you cuss now. And I thought we had practice until five. My mom isn't coming until then."

"That's okay," Will said. "I'm taking the bus. I'm definitely stuck here."

Ryan sat on a bench shirtless, looking disgusted. "I don't want to put a clean shirt on now. It'll just get soaked."

They were the only boys from tryouts who had lockers in the back room. With the heat on for the winter, and the room being filled with soaked, sweaty clothes, the smell of unwashed bodies was overpowering.

"I tell you," Nick groaned. "We all need showers."

Will perked up and he pulled his knees to his chest. "Wait. We have showers here, right?"

"Yeah," scoffed Ryan. He nodded across the room where five shower stalls were lined up against the wall.

"We should use them," Will said, his boyish enthusiasm returning. "We're all stuck here, right?"

"No way," Ben said, seeing Will was serious.

"Why not?" Will asked enthusiastically. "We all have, like, an hour to kill, right?"

"Yo, man," Ryan said. "They were probably last used by the original Patriots who beat the British. There's a shower George Washington used."

Nick, though, caught Will's eagerness. "So what? That means they should be clean, right?"

"No, dude," Ryan said, rolling his eyes. "It means they probably don't work."

"One way to find out," Will said, jumping to his feet. Kicking off his sneakers, he hurried to the closest stall, pulling back the curtain to reveal two knobs and an intact showerhead.

"Do they work?" Nick asked.

"One way to find out." Will turned one of the knobs and icy water immediately shot out, catching him in the face. Yelping, he jumped back. "Oh, yeah. They work!" he cried.

Nick laughed. "That's payback for my water bottle."

"One problem, dudes," Ryan said. "I didn't bring any shampoo or soap. Did any of you?"

Will turned off the water and quickly started pulling back shower curtains. The third stall had a large bottle of almost new shampoo.

"Bingo!" cried Nick. "We have shampoo!"

"Who'd leave shampoo here?" Ryan asked with a frown. "How old is that thing?"

Will opened the cap and sniffed. "Smells like herbal essence garden to me," he said. "And it promises to better fortify your hair and leave it fresh for forty-eight hours."

"Sounds great," Nick said with a grunt. "Count me in."

Will licked his lips and grinned. "Let's do this!" he exclaimed, holding up the shampoo like a trophy. "Shower party time!"

"You guys are crazy," Ryan said, but his mouth broke into a grin. "I guess I could use one. You in, Ben?"

"Uh, I don't know," Ben said worriedly. "Are you sure we're allowed to? I mean, I could definitely wash away some bad memories of me getting schooled, but I don't want to get in any trouble." He'd been the unlucky seventh grader who'd had to face Big Mike on the second one versus one drill.

Nick was already yanking off his shirt. He revealed a massive tanned chest already starting to sprout hair. "Yeah, man," he said, smacking his firm, round belly.

"Dude, get in the shower before you go any farther!" Ryan yelled at him.

"Sorry, guys, but I have to show off my manly body." Nick tossed his shirt toward his locker before strutting around the room. "If you don't like, close your eyes."

"Seriously, guys," Ben said. "Do you think we're allowed?"

"Why wouldn't we be?" Nick said, stretching as he stepped into the first shower stall. "That's what these things are here for." He pulled the curtain closed and started humming. His shorts flew over the curtain soon after.

Will sat on the edge of the slightly raised shower floor, pulling off his sweaty socks. Looking up, he said, "I'll go check if there's any teacher around." Tossing away his socks, he ripped off his shirt and put it on the hook behind him.

Ryan immediately covered his eyes as if blinded. "Yo, man! You're ripped, but come on! Get a tan already!"

Self-conscious, Will snorted. "Ha, ha. I still have my football tan," he explained. "You'll have to wait until spring for my real tan."

"At least your mom can save money on T-shirts," Ryan said. "Nice abs, though."

Will's flat, trim stomach and chest were pale, almost white. They matched his arms from his shoulders down to his forearms. There, below the elbows to his fingers, he had a light tan, but the tan line was so stark it looked as if he wore a skintight, gleaming white T-shirt. Having boyish muscle didn't help his cause.

"You're hilarious," he grumbled, scratching his ribs.

"Too bad you're not naturally tan like me!" Nick called from behind the curtain. "You guys want to see?"

"No!" his three friends shouted at once.

"Besides," Ryan said, standing up and stretching his own abs, showing off his own tight stomach and muscular arms. "Will might got the skinny, but I got the muscle! Yeah, look at that." His arms were just starting to mold into hard muscle. He admired the twin bulges as he flexed his arms.

Will rolled his eyes. "I think you need a cold shower, dude."
He raced from the room before Ryan could hit him with his shirt.

Chapter 21

After Glen had dressed and left, Jared remained seated on the bench for a few more minutes, letting it all soak in. He still couldn't believe how much fun it had been. He'd even enjoyed the running. Being with other kids, all going at it as hard as they could, it made him feel as if he belonged … almost like he was already on the team.

Finally, as one of the last kids left, he got up and yanked off his sweat-drenched shirt, peeling it from his skin.

Breathing out, he heard a commotion behind him. Turning, he was surprised to see Will, dressed only in his red shorts, racing from the back room, his bare feet slapping against the floor.

Seeing Jared, the small, skinny boy slid to a stop and grinned. Jared could see his ribs sticking out from his bony chest. "Hey, big guy! Is the coach or any teachers around?"

Swallowing, Jared blinked and then shook his head. "Uh, no. Uh, why do you ask?"

Will's large brown eyes gleamed with mischief. "No reason. We're, uh, having a shower party. Hey, you should join in! There's room for one more. Come on!" Turning, he scampered back the way he came.

Jared was left staring stupidly. To kill time before the bus arrived, he'd been planning on going to Ms. Jackson's class and see if he could do some typing. The way he smelled, though, she'd probably not be too happy to see him.

"Wait," he muttered. "What just happened?"

His heartbeat jumped a little as he realized Will had just treated him as one of his friends. He couldn't let the opportunity slide.

"But," he wondered to himself, "what did he mean 'shower party'?"

Excited and nervous at the same time, he tentatively followed after the smaller kid. In the hall by the toilets he could hear water running and Nick's loud voice trying to sing opera. Eyes widening, he kept going until entering the back locker room. Then he stood still in shock.

Will had just started to shuck out of his shorts when he saw Jared. Yelping, he jumped into a shower stall and slid the curtain closed. "Last one is yours!" he cried.

Four curtains were closed with running water blasting behind them. A fifth stall curtain was open in the back corner.

"What's that?" Ryan's voice called from one of the middle stalls, echoing over the running water. "Is that you, Will? Is someone else there?"

"Just big guy," Will called. "He needed a shower!"

"What?" Ryan cried. "Why'd you bring him here?"

"He's like the rest of us!" Nick's deep voice answered. "He stinks!"

Jared was just about to back away and leave when Nick's head popped out from behind the curtain of the first stall. "We got some shampoo, man. Hop in and we'll pass it down. The water is great!"

"Ha," Will yelped, his voice going higher as his water shot to life. "Yeah, right! It's freezing!"

"It gets warmer," Ben said. "Oh, Will. Here's the shampoo."

Jared watched as a green bottle appeared above the third stall and fell with a thump in Will's shower stall, clattering to the ground.

"Ow!" Will cried. "That was my head!"

"No kidding, man," Nick said. "You put shampoo on your head, dummy."

"Ha, ha," Will said. "Hurry up, big guy. You get it next!"

Not really believing he was doing it, Jared found himself kicking off his shoes and going to the last stall and closing the curtain. Muttering how stupid he was, he got undressed, sticking his dirty clothes on the hook outside the stall. He gasped when he turned the knob and cold liquid blasted him in the chest.

"Cold, right?" Will called to him. "It's nice after a while. And there's great water pressure."

"And peer pressure," added Ben. "Everyone has to use two rounds of shampoo. It says so on the bottle."

"Yo, hurry up with the shampoo, man!" Ryan called. "I need another round."

"Big guy is next," Will said. "Bomb's away!"

Jared looked up to see the shampoo bottle fly over his stall's wall. He managed to catch it one handed and quickly poured a gob on his free hand. "Uh," he said. "Who wants it?"

"Send it to Ryan, three stalls over," Will called. "Shoot it like a three-pointer!"

"You'd better not!" Ryan yelled. "If I get bonked by that thing, I'm suing!"

Not sure of what do, Jared stood for a moment with cold water beating on his head, a gob of green goo in his left hand, and a bottle of herbal shampoo in his right. It was a situation he had never imagined as ever possible two hours before when he'd first showed up for the tryouts.

"Hey, big guy," hissed Will's voice next to his curtain. "Give the shampoo to me. I'll get it to Ryan." A small wet hand reached into the curtain and Jared quickly gave it the shampoo.

"Two-pointer," Will sang out, almost immediately after.

A loud bang sounded as the shampoo bottle landed near Ryan.

"Yo, dude!" Ryan protested. "Are you crazy!" A second later he laughed. "Yo, it's like we barely touched this bottle. There's still a ton left! Let's use this bad boy up!"

The banter continued over the running water as the boys slapped gobs of shampoo on their hair and bodies. Jared washed his hair and then got the bottle back to wash the rest of his body.

After several minutes the bottle was still over half full.

"It's like magic," Ryan said in wonder. "It never goes away."

"Hey, you know what?" Nick called. "We should do this tomorrow. Let's keep the shampoo in our locker and do this again."

"Yeah!" Will agreed. "We can be the shower brothers!"

"That sounds so lame!" Ryan complained.

"I'm okay with it," Ben said. "I mean, if we all make the cuts tomorrow."

"Of course we will!" Nick assured him. "We got shower power on our side!"

"What about the new guy?" Ryan suddenly asked. "Is he invited?"

Jared froze, knowing exactly who Ryan meant.

"Are you kidding?" Nick said after a moment. "Did you see him pack that shot?"

"Yeah, besides, we need a fifth player," Will added. "Not only are we the shower brothers, we're the shower team! Hey, big guy. What's your name, anyway?"

Jared wiped water from his eyes and took a deep breath. "It's, uh, Jared." He had to almost shout to be heard over the water and his voice echoed in the room.

"Hi, Jared," Nick sang out. "Are you a showerholic? Welcome to our club."

"Wonderful," Ryan said with a groan. "You dudes are such idiots. Who wants more shampoo?"

"Uh, guys?" Ben said, sounding slightly sick. "What do we do about towels?"

Almost immediately all the showerheads were shut off. For several seconds, Jared could only hear the sound of dripping water.

"Uh ..." Ryan began, finally breaking the silence, "I know they keep towels in the training room by Coach's office."

"Yeah, but that's kind of far away," Ben said.

"Not it," Nick quickly said. "I ain't going out there, no way, man."

"Send the new guy," Ryan suggested cruelly. "If he wants to be with us, then this is his initiation. Make him get some towels."

Jared felt his chest tighten. But before he could talk, Nick came to his rescue.

"No way, man. He doesn't know where they would be! Besides, this is his first day with us crazy idiots. We should go by size. Who's the smallest one here?"

"Ha, ha," Will said. Then he gave a heavy sigh. "I'll go. But you guys better not look!"

"Ah, we won't see anything," Nick said.

"Yeah," Ryan said with a snort. "Your skin is so white you can blend in with the wall. Even if anybody is left out there they'll never see you."

"Well," grumbled Will, "if you hear any screaming, you'll know you're wrong."

"Just don't be cheeky, Will," Nick told him.

"Ha, ha," Will muttered. "You guys are awesome."

Moments later, Will slipped from the shower, grabbing his dirty shorts and holding them in front of his waist, covering his front the best he could. Licking his lips, he darted to the doorway and peered through.

"I think we're good," he hissed behind him. "I don't see anybody."

"J-just hur-ry," Ben called to him. "I'm st-starting to freeze."

"Just take another shower, dude," Ryan said, turning the water back on. "Hurry back, Will. We'll be waiting!"

"You guys are the worst friends in the world," Will said as water puddled around his bare feet.

Nick only laughed and turned on his shower. "Hey, Will," he called. "Take my flip-flops, man. My locker is open. They should be on the bottom. You don't want to get any disgusting fungus on your feet."

"Now you tell me," Will grumbled, looking down at his toes. He hurried to Nick's locker and found the flip-flops, but they were several sizes too big. "I can just wash my feet when I get back," he called.

"Fine," Nick hollered. "But you're going to get ringworm!"

"Only if I wear your flip-flops!" Will yelled back. Licking his lips, he crept into the hall, leaving his showering friends behind him. As he left, he heard Nick laugh.

"Will is such a little kid, man. I can't believe him sometimes."

"Yo, but he's doing us a service," Ryan said. "He's little, but he's got guts!"

Will grinned. He didn't mind being little. It made people underestimate him, especially in sports. Still, as he stood clutching his sweaty shorts and having nothing else against his skin, he suddenly felt very foolish. All at once he was very conscious of how small and exposed he must look.

"Hello?" he called softly toward the bathroom area. "Anybody there?" Hearing nothing, he tiptoed into the main locker room. He sighed with relief when seeing the room empty.

It felt amazingly free, incredibly terrifying, and absolutely stupid—all at the same time—to be sneaking around without clothes. Also, he couldn't help but feel a sort of thrill race through him. He'd always liked dares.

As he reached the island of lockers in the center of the room, he heard a door open. It came from the office area. Just like that, he only felt the terror. Holding his shorts closely in front of his waist, he went as still as a statue.

"Mr. Hackett?" he heard a familiar voice say. "I know you're there. We need to talk."

"Mr. Drydon," he heard Mr. Hackett's muffled voice say from his office. "What brings you here? Who's that with you?"

"This is a friend," Mr. Drydon's slightly nasal voice said. He spoke in a monotone, neutral tone, but Will could tell the principal was not very happy. "He and I would like some words with you."

Curiosity won over fear as Will tiptoed to the edge of the island of lockers and slid down to his haunches. With his back to the edge of the lockers, he twisted his neck and peered around the corner.

Mr. Drydon, in a blue suit, stood in front of Mr. Hackett's office with a man next to him. The man stood just beyond Mr. Drydon in a shadow and Will couldn't make him out, but something was strangely familiar about him ... like he'd seen him before, or something.

"May we come in," Mr. Drydon said, not really asking. "Trust me. You'd rather have *me* talking to you than somebody else."

Not sounding very happy, Mr. Hackett's voice beckoned the principal in.

Before entering the office, the principal glanced toward Will and the boy quickly ducked his head back. The last thing he needed was to be caught spying, without clothes, by his principal. That would be something he would never be able to live down.

He waited until he heard the door close with a sharp click and then peeked around again. Seeing the coast clear, he got up and quickly dashed to the large bin of old clothes by the offices. He jerked to a stop there, only to have his wet feet slip out from under him. All of a sudden, with a sharp breath, he landed on his backside and slid several painful inches. He'd managed to keep hold of his shorts, which he covered himself with, but for an instant he froze. His eyes went wide with terror.

"What's that?" Mr. Drydon's muffled voice called.

Will heard furniture moving and somebody fumbling for the doorknob. Instantly his body shot into action. Propelled by fear and adrenaline, he shot to his feet. He had nowhere to go.

Without thinking, he raced for the island of lockers. Behind him, he heard the door swinging open, banging sharply against the wall.

Will launched himself up at the lockers, leaping as high as he could. His shorts fell in his wake as he reached up, managing to catch the top of the lockers with both hands, his body banging against the side.

"Hey?" barked Mr. Drydon's voice. "Anybody out there?"

Will's feet kicked wildly as he scrambled to the top. Instantly, he crawled forward before flattening his body against the flat roof of the island lockers. It took only a few seconds and he'd made it, just as Mr. Drydon called out for a second time.

"Anybody there? Go and check it out. I thought I heard something."

"You did," grunted Mr. Hackett's voice. "I heard it too."

Will didn't move a muscle. His arms were bent forward at the elbows, he pressed his hands down next to his face and waited.

The lockers hadn't been washed in probably forever and he had to ignore the filthy grime sticking to his wet skin. Inches from his face he saw several pieces of chewed bubble gum growing fuzz.

Ignoring the filth, he tried his best to lie still as his heart hammered against his ribs. This would not be his best moment if found now. His body seemed to melt to the sticky metal surface.

"Who's there?" he heard Mr. Hackett's voice call.

"What is it?" Drydon called, sounding as if still back in the office. "You see anything out there?"

"Shh!" hissed a voice nearly right below Will.

The boy's muscles tightened and he pressed his cheek tightly against the grimy metal. For a long moment he dared not even breathe.

Will didn't hear, but rather felt a presence just under him. It slowly traveled the length of the room before stopping and coming back. He spotted the top of a man's head, full of greasy blond hair, passing just below him.

If the man took a single step back and looked up, Will would be totally exposed—totally bare and in the open. For the first time, he felt very happy to be short and skinny. Water from his body soaked into the grime under his skin and thankfully didn't drip down.

"It's all right," called a thin, reedy voice. "You got some boys taking showers back there, sounds like. We must've heard them."

"Idiots!" Mr. Drydon snarled.

Will couldn't agree more. He pressed his lips tightly together and wondered briefly if he'd break into laughter. His dad would love to hear this story, but if he did, it wouldn't be from Will.

"Basketball tryouts just ended," Mr. Hackett's voice said, sounding like a whine. "They're still kids around. Maybe we can do this later."

"Sure," snapped Mr. Drydon. "But we're not. Get back in here and close the door. Let's get this over with pronto before the showering fools come out."

The presence grunted, still very close to Will.

The boy dared not breathe. In his head he prayed as hard as ever not to be seen. It felt like forever, but the presence moved on. He waited until he heard the door click shut. Finally, he let out a breath and felt his body go limp. He'd barely made it.

Groaning, he carefully rolled to his back, moving his hands to cover his dignity. For a moment he lay there, staring up at the ceiling. He'd never noticed all the spit balls stuck up there, now dry as spackle.

"Next time," he wheezed. "Somebody else gets the towels."

After his breathing returned to normal, he slowly sat up and made sure he remained alone. He winced at seeing the blackened grime and gray dust covering his legs, torso, and arms. He really needed a shower.

Cautiously he moved to his hands and knees and crawled backwards to the edge of the lockers. Taking care to be quiet, he carefully lowered himself down while gripping the filthy locker top. He dropped the last short distance and managed to end up landing on his backside again. This time he was ready and rolled quietly to the side, making little noise.

Besides, the raised voices from the office masked any sound he made. He spotted his shorts where they'd fallen and snatched them up. Once again his heart hammered against his chest as he crept past the bin, into the front hall past Mr. Hackett's office.

As he reached the office door of Mr. Hackett, he crouched down and crawled under the window. It was covered with a poster with the Washington Middle football schedule, but Will wasn't taking any chances.

He gripped his dirty shorts in his right hand and knew if anybody walked into the locker room right now he was in for it. As he passed by the office he heard Mr. Hackett's elevated voice, sounding indignant, but also a little scared.

"What are you talking about? I did no such thing!"

"We know it was you, Frank." Mr. Drydon's voice sounded calm and reasonable. It also sounded adamant. "You got it from the supply room."

"Do I need to make a phone call? You're both just as guilty. I know I didn't put it there."

"Relax, Frank. We aren't here to get you in trouble. We have a deal for you. Hear us out."

Will paused for a moment, listening, but then he heard a noise just behind the door. Quickly he pulled himself past the door, jumped to his feet and dashed to the supply room. He was relieved to find it partially open with the light on.

Inside was a table used for medical taping before games, a beat-up washer and dryer, and all sorts of PE supplies. In the back, just above the dryer, he saw a small shelf holding stacks of white towels.

Sighing with relief, he darted to the dryer and hopped up on top. From his knees he started grabbing towels and small washcloths.

As he took a handful of towels down, he saw they had hidden a glass bottle filled with clear liquid. It sat next to a small fan and chipped ceramic bowl. Curious, he put the towels beside him and picked up the bottle. Will peered at it closely. It smelled slightly of a chemical … a very familiar smell that he couldn't quite place, but knew he didn't like. Instantly he felt dizzy.

Behind him, he heard a muffled shout and he nearly fell off the dryer. Replacing the bottle, he whirled around and hopped down. Dancing with nervousness, he gathered up the towels and cloths. No longer caring about stealth, but just wanting to be back with his friends, he dashed from the room and past the office.

Not until he reached the shower room did he realize he'd forgotten his red shorts, back in the supply room.

Chapter 22

Jared stood under the shower washing his hair for the fifth time when he heard Will's excited voice announcing his return.

"Man, what took you so long?" Nick hollered over the running water. "My fingers and toes are pickled to pieces."

"Yo, did you run into some cheerleaders or something?" Ryan joked, switching off his shower.

"You don't want to know," Will said breathlessly. "Dudes, just so you know. I'm never doing that again."

"You don't have to," Ryan assured him. "Tomorrow it's new guy's turn."

Jared kept quiet, but he felt his heart skip a beat.

"No way," Ben said. "Tomorrow we bring our own towels."

"Fine," Ryan agreed. "Whatever. Now where's my towel, Will?"

"Hold on," Will said, his voice high with excitement. "I'm cleaning up first. Man, I need another shower."

"No way, man!" Nick cried. "Just give us our towels. It's freezing in here!"

"Hey, you try running out there with no clothes and tell me it's freezing," Will said indignantly. "Besides, you've no idea what I went through! I barely made it."

Nick chuckled. "You were bare, all right. Hey, but we came up with a new name for you, Will. Now you're called Running Bare."

"Ha, ha," Will said. "Fine, you can look now, but this is all I got. Hey, big guy, you get first dibs."

Jared sighed with relief. Once Will had left, the other boys had forgotten about him. As they joked and talked amongst themselves, Jared felt completely out of place. He felt like an awkward lump that needed to disappear down the drain but was too big to fit. He'd feared Will wouldn't remember a towel for him and he would be left stranded.

Sticking his head out of the curtain, he saw Will standing in the middle of the room wrapped in a towel holding a large white towel in one hand and a handful of washcloths in the other. Seeing Jared, Will grinned mischievously and tossed him the large towel.

Jared blinked as he caught it. The small kids' boney chest was smeared with dark grime and he had grayish gunk smeared on his right cheek.

"Yo, where's mine?" Ryan demanded, sticking his head out of the shower.

Will quickly made his face innocent and shrugged. "Sorry, dude. This was all they had." He tossed Ryan a washcloth.

"What, are you serious?" Ryan cried, snatching the cloth from midair. "You have to be joking!"

"No way, man!" Nick cried, ducking his head out to see a tiny cloth sail his way. "I'll need like fifty of those and still be soaked!"

Ben peeked out and groaned. "I knew we never should've done this."

Will's impish grin widened. "Well, I might have some more towels out here, but I left them by your lockers. You'll have to come out and get them."

Nick responded by soaking his washcloth and flinging it at the smaller boy. "You're a class-A jerk, man!"

Ryan also fired a wet washcloth, causing Will to duck and cover his head, laughing. He went back and retrieved the towels before tossing them over the shower curtains to his grumbling friends.

"But you guys have no idea how hard it was getting these," he told them, dropping his towel and hopping back in his shower stall.

"Thanks, man," Nick yelled as he started drying off. "This feels good! So what happened? Why are you so filthy? You got gunk all over you, man."

"I nearly ran into the principal and Mr. Hackett," Will said, his voice turning serious. He flipped on the water and yelped. "Toss me the shampoo. I *really* need it this time."

Nick burst out laughing, but Ryan yelled for quiet. "What happened?" he demanded. "Did they see you?"

As he washed, Will quickly related the story of his near discovery and hiding on the lockers.

None of his friends believed him at first, but Jared could hear real fear beneath Will's story, especially about how Mr. Drydon and the stranger went to see the gym teacher.

"Guys," Will said, his voice going higher than normal. "I think Mr. Hackett got busted or something." He finished sheepishly about losing his shorts.

Ryan groaned. "Oh, man. You're so lucky they didn't spot you."

"Yeah," Ben added, awed. "Hiding on the lockers … wow."

"Ah, they wouldn't have seen much," Nick said jovially. "Hey, Will! Now you're Running Bare, the Naked Ninja!"

"Ha," Will shot back. "And you're Nick, the big mouth with a small—"

"Okay!" Ben instantly shouted. "Let's not go there."

"What?" Will said innocently. "I was going to say brain."

"Shut up, dudes," Ryan said, his voice almost snarling. "Everyone just get dressed. We need to be out of here." He'd gotten out of the shower first and was already halfway decent.

"Okay, man," Nick said. "Just calm down, dude."

"Calm down yourself!" Ryan barked. "You done, Will?"

Will shut off his water. "Yeah, uh, I just need a clean towel."

"I got you," Ryan said. He seemed to have lost his humor as he retrieved a towel and tossed it over the curtain to Will.

Jared sighed with relief that it hadn't been him out there. He quickly dried himself off in the shower and wrapped the damp towel around his waist. As he stepped out, he realized he had another problem. His school clothes were back in the gym locker room and he hadn't packed any clean underwear.

Ben, it seemed, had also forgotten an extra pair of underwear.

"Ah, man," he complained, breaking the silence. "What am I supposed to wear now?" He stood in front of his locker holding up his soaking boxers, looking disgusted. His free hand kept a wet towel tight around his waist.

"Sorry, dude," Nick told him, exiting the shower with his own towel held tightly around his waist. "But in football you learn, always pack an extra pair, because you never know where and when you need another to wear."

"Such poetry," Will said dryly.

"I was only the manager," Ben wailed. "I never needed to change!"

"Yo," Nick said, "just put on your pants and don't worry about it. Your mom should be here soon. Speaking of that, the bus is coming, guys. Will, you'd better get a move on."

Jared cleared his throat. "I, uh, left my clothes in the other room … I, uh, see you on the bus."

"Not me," Nick said, giving him a wave. "I'm walking home. Good practice today, man."

"See you, big guy!" Will said, exiting the shower with the clean towel around his waist. "Don't forget, showers after tryouts tomorrow!"

"Yeah, if he makes the cut," Ryan grunted.

Jared's ears burned as he left the room. After all the water from the shower, he needed the bathroom and stopped at the toilets. As he finished and stood washing his hands, he heard Ryan's muffled voice from the back room.

"Yo, what do you think about Jared? I really don't trust him."

Immediately Jared went still and strained his ears to listen. At first he could only hear his own heartbeat thump and the sounds of a locker slamming.

"He's okay," he then heard Nick say. "I knew him from elementary school. He's a bit of a dull stick, a little slow I think."

"Big guy?" Will asked. "He's tall and he plays hard. Now toss me my shirt. It's freezing."

"Hmmph," Ryan muttered. "If he wasn't tall he'd be nothing."

"Ah, man," Ben moaned. "I'm so not comfortable." Jared heard him break wind loudly.

Laughter immediately broke out.

Feeling numb, Jared quickly went to his locker to change. He wasn't sure if he'd made any friends that day or not. It didn't sound like it. Uninvited, tears sprang to his eyes.

"Who am I kidding," he muttered. "I have no friends. I'll never have friends." Feeling hurt, he hoped he didn't make the cuts for basketball. Will hadn't exactly put him down like Ryan did, but he certainly hadn't defended him either. Neither had Nick. They all thought he was just a tall loser. A stupid stick. Now he knew why Will had given him the big towel, because he'd felt sorry for him, meaning he wasn't part of his group.

"My life," he mumbled, "stinks."

Angrily, he pulled his jeans up under the towel, mindful that the principal still might be around. As he sat down to put on his socks, he heard a door opening at the offices.

"Mr. Drydon," he heard an unpleasant, slightly high-pitched man's voice say. "I think we have a problem."

Jared's anger quickly evaporated and came down as panic. Quickly he stood and quietly closed his locker door. Grabbing his socks and shirt, he then scooted around the island of lockers and stood still. Something about that voice gave him the chills.

"What is it?" Mr. Drydon's voice asked.

"Puddles," the voice nearly purred. "Looks like footprints right outside the door. They go to the supply room and out, I'd say."

"So?" asked the principal.

"They weren't here before," the voice continued, sounding more pleased than worried. "I noticed some water near the lockers earlier, but not out here. Looks like we had a visitor."

The way he talked made Jared think of a snake, flicking out its tongue when on the hunt. If snakes could talk, he thought, they'd sound like that voice.

"Check the supply room," Mr. Drydon snapped. "Just to be sure."

"Don't worry about that," Mr. Hackett's voice said, sounding slightly shaken. "Remember, we had basketball tryouts today. It was probably just the jokers who found the showers. That's all. They probably came for towels."

"I got some very smelly shorts in here," the unpleasant voice called from farther off. "Definitely a kid."

"Interesting," Mr. Drydon said. "It'd be a shame if some little joker heard something. Take the shorts, Mr. Hackett. Find out who they belong to and let me know by tomorrow. Don't e-mail me, but come directly to me in my office. Got it?"

The PE teacher sighed heavily. "Yeah, yeah, I got it."

"Don't let us down, Frank," Mr. Drydon said, his voice carrying a hidden warning. "You're with us now. Have a good night."

"Yeah," the PE teacher muttered. "I'm with you."

Jared started breathing again only after he heard the office door close and a long pause of silence. He didn't know what he'd just heard, but it didn't sound very good.

Quickly he finished dressing and grabbed his sports bag and backpack. He wanted to tell the other guys what he'd just heard, but at the same time didn't know if he could face them. His dilemma was solved when he heard Ryan coming towards him.

"Yo, Jared!" Ryan called. "You still here? Where's your towel, man? I'm bringing them all back before we get busted."

Jared chewed his bottom lip and retrieved the damp towel from the bench where'd he tossed it after he finished dressing. Turning, he saw the dark-haired boy staring at him with unfriendly eyes. Then Ryan quickly dropped his gaze to the pile of wet towels he carried under his arm like a football.

"The other guys went out the back door to make the bus. You'd better hurry. It, like, leaves in five minutes."

Jared took a deep breath and made sure to have a blank face.

"I, uh, heard, uh, Mr. Drydon talking," he muttered.

"What's that?" Ryan asked, cupping his ear. "You need to stop mumbling. Don't worry, I know Mr. Hackett. Give me your towel and I'll take care of everything." He grinned without humor, staring at Jared. "I'll even grab Will's shorts."

As Jared left the locker room soon after, he heard Ryan knock on Mr. Hackett's door. He didn't hear the door open as he rushed, very alone, to the front of the school. The hallways were as empty as Jared's feelings. Ryan didn't want to hear anything Jared had to say. Pushing open the front door, he saw the bus still waiting, but with its engine rumbling.

Jared kept his head low as he climbed up on the activity bus, already crowded with boys, mostly from basketball tryouts. The girls' team had their tryouts at the elementary school, so it was a very male-dominated bus ... and very loud and smelly.

"Everybody sit and be quiet, or we ain't leaving!" hollered the bus driver, a skinny old man with an Adam's apple the size of a golf ball.

Jared scowled as he slid in the first open seat he came to, right behind the bus driver. He knew it would be a long, painful ride.

Thirty minutes later he sat staring out the window watching Big Mike walk across the road to a brick apartment complex. The large boy kept his head down and wore large headphones. Jared could almost hear the heavy beat from inside the bus. The boys walking with him looked just as tough.

Jared blew out his breath. There was no way he could ever compete with Big Mike. He was just thinking how he would never make the cuts when he felt a tap on his head.

"Hey, big guy," Will said, peering over his seat. "I didn't see you get on. I thought you got a ride home."

Surprised, Jared shifted sideways in his seat and sat up. "Uh, yeah. I mean, no, my mom takes my sister to ballet. Uh, weren't you sitting in the back?"

"Yeah, but we're almost the last ones left." Will ran a hand through his damp hair, brushing spiky strands from his forehead. "So, how long have you played basketball for?"

"What?" Jared gave a start. He couldn't believe Will was actually talking to him.

"Have you been playing long?"

"Actually," Jared admitted, "I just, uh, started." He waited for Will to laugh.

Instead Will lifted his eyebrows. "Dude, really?" He whistled. "You're pretty good." Then his voice turned eager. "Hey, do you ever want to practice together? I mean, like on the weekends?"

Jared wasn't sure he heard right. But he didn't ask a question, just in case it was a dream. "Uh, yeah ... I mean, that would be cool."

"I've been trying to find a good game and I hear they play back at those apartments every Saturday morning. Think you could make it?"

The bus had rolled on, but Jared saw Will nod back at where Big Mike had exited. He remembered seeing fenced basketball courts in front of the apartments. The boyish face looked so hopeful that Jared nearly thought it must be a joke. At any moment Will would burst out laughing and say he was just kidding. Why would Will ask him?

Instead of saying yes, he cleared his throat. "Uh, what about the, uh, other guys?"

Will pressed his lips together. "Ah, I don't think they want to go there ... Maybe it isn't a good idea."

"No, no, I can do it."

"Really?" Will nearly jumped over the seat. He eagerly stared at Jared. "Your parents wouldn't mind?"

"Oh. I'm sure it'll be cool." Jared actually had no idea what he was saying now. Playing basketball at Shady Apartments with Big Mike and his bunch …? He took a deep breath. "But I don't think I could get a ride …"

"No problem, dude." Will licked his lips. "What if you come over to my place on Friday? You can sleepover and my dad can take us Saturday."

"Uh … sure." Jared felt like his head might explode. How did that happen?

He'd just been invited to a sleepover, just like that.

Chapter 23

Jared stumbled off the bus in a daze. Will had gotten off two stops earlier, but not before giving Jared his phone number and telling him to call that night, so their parents could arrange things for Friday. Just two days away.

Jared shook his head in disbelief. Daylight saving's time would bump the clocks back an hour that weekend, so the sun still barely peeked over the horizon as he stumbled off toward his house. The bus had dropped him off at the top of his street, so he had a long walk. But he didn't mind. He needed time to process his crazy day.

It had been a cool, brisk day so he wore only a sweater with his jeans. Now with nightfall fast approaching, the temperature took a dive and he shivered. As he did so, he reached his hand into his pocket and grabbed the paper with Will's information, squeezing tight just to make sure it really existed. That gave him all the warmth he needed as he continued the walk.

"This is so crazy," he mumbled as he reached his driveway. He couldn't help breaking into a grin. He'd gone out for basketball and possibly made a friend. Instead of entering the house right away, he stood outside and took it all in.

His mother had yet to return with Kelly, and Jack had left for work. His dad, of course, would be working late. As soon as his mother returned, he would ask her about going to Will's on Friday. He knew she'd let him. She always asked about having friends over. Friends … Jared liked the sound of that.

He'd been invited to birthday parties back in elementary school, but that was usually when his whole class had been invited. Nobody had ever asked him for a sleepover. He just couldn't believe how fast everything moved in middle school. He'd gone from feeling like a total loser to being on top of the world in the snap of a finger. One second he was feeling sorry for himself on the bus, and the next second he had a sleepover invite from the one kid in the school he longed to make friends with.

"What," he wondered, "will happen next?" Then, just as he made his way to his porch, he froze.

He'd been so elated and surprised about being friends with Will and playing basketball at Big Mike's apartments, he'd forgotten all about telling Will about Mr. Drydon and the stranger in the locker room.

He decided not to worry about it too much. After all, Ryan would take care of things …

Jared furrowed his brow when thinking of Ryan. That was one kid who probably would not be his friend any time soon. Jared didn't know why, but Ryan had something against him.

Shrugging, he jumped up the steps to his house and entered, whistling cheerfully. He couldn't carry a tune, but didn't care.

George greeted him from the kitchen table eating leftover spaghetti and meatballs.

"Stop whistling, man," he grunted. "Uh, how did the, er, tryouts go?"

Swallowing, Jared coughed. "What?"

"I said, how did tryouts go? Your basketball?"

"Oh," he said neutrally. "They went okay. I'm going to take a shower. Uh, can you tell me when Mom comes in?"

"I'm not your slave. You'll figure it out when she comes."

"Yeah …"

Jared hurried up the stairs and made sure to take a long, hot shower. He washed every part really well, especially his feet.

As predicted, Mrs. Cook was more than happy to let Jared spend the night at Will's place. And she wasn't the only one in his family excited.

"You know Will Moore?" Kelly practically squealed after Jared came down in his pajamas to break the news about the sleepover.

She'd just arrived back from dance and still had her hair in a glossy tight bun. Sitting at the table eating the last meatball that Jared had forgotten about, she dropped her fork and stared at her brother with wide, sapphire eyes.

Jared stared owlishly at her and slowly nodded. "Yeah … uh, he's trying out for basketball with me. Why?"

"Oh my gosh, Jared. Like, he's the cutest boy in the school! Every girl in my class has a crush on him."

Jared closed his eyes and opened them. "Really, Kelly?"

"Jared," his sister said. "I'm serious. You, like, have to introduce me to him."

"We're trying out for a basketball team, not running a dating service," Jared muttered. He reached down and patted Carey's head. She was unsuccessfully trying to pull his toe from a hole in his sock.

Mrs. Cook lifted her eyebrows and frowned. "In that case, Jared," she said dryly, "I'm glad you're going to his house and he's not coming here. You'd better give me his parents' number before your sister gets a hold of it. Oh, give me Carey while you're at it. It's time for her bath."

"Well, you boys should start a dating service," Kelly told him, picking her fork back up. "Some of the girls think you're cute too."

Blushing, Jared lifted his little sister and handed her to his mother and then quickly gave Will's paper to her. "Make sure Carey doesn't eat it. I, uh, will be upstairs," he stammered.

"I'm serious, Jared!" his sister called after him. "I told them they needed glasses!"

Jared just shook his head. "I'll never understand girls," he muttered.

George never looked up when he entered their room, and Jared climbed into bed without another word. He missed saying prayers that night as the exhaustion of the crazy day finally caught up to him. Even so, he felt sure his prayers had already been answered.

The next day Jared made sure to get up early and be ready for school long before the bus arrived. Kelly joined him at the end of their driveway, yawning as she flipped back curls.

"Really, Jared," she said. "Like, what's the hurry?"

Jared kicked at the pavement. "I just need to get there early to see if I made basketball cuts," he murmured.

In jeans and a navy-blue long-sleeved shirt under his gray jacket, he carried his sports bag slung over his right shoulder so it rested against his backpack. The bag actually weighed more than his backpack at the moment. Early that morning he'd stuffed in extra boxers, two towels, flip-flops, and socks, as well as his basketball shorts, T-shirt, and shoes. Just in case he made it to the team and the shower, he would be ready.

Kelly grinned brightly, smoothing down the sides of her pink hoodie. "Can I go with you? I want to know if you made it, too."

"What?"

"Jared, like, it would be the coolest if you made the team. Then I can say, 'what's up, girls? My big bro Jared plays basketball with Will Moore. Look at me!'"

Jared grinned as he saw his sister was joking. "Yeah, sure," he said. "Why not?"

To be honest, he didn't want to be alone … just in case he didn't see his name.

As soon as they got off the bus at school, Jared and Kelly pushed through the throng of kids, heading straight to the gym. A large group of boys milled around the entrance. Most wore disappointed faces, but Jared saw Glen and Darius laughing with Bigfoot. Bigfoot couldn't keep a relieved smile off his face.

"Jared," Kelly said, following close behind him as he made his way through the crowd, "how many boys make the team?"

"Only fifteen," he mumbled behind him, feeling his stomach fold up in knots.

She wrinkled her nose. "There're, like, a hundred boys here, and they all reek of cologne."

Jared ignored her. There were a lot of boys, much more than he remembered seeing at yesterday's tryout. Doubt filled his belly. Could he really have made it through?

His answer came when Will and Nick greeted him at the rear of the swarming pack of boys, all desperately trying to look at the posted list of names.

"Hey, Jared Cook," Will said casually. He wore a white long-sleeved wrestling T-shirt and black athletic warm-up pants with his red shoes.

Next to him in loose jeans and a Redskins jacket, Nick laughed when seeing Jared's face. "Go look for yourself, man. All the shower brothers made it!" He slapped Jared's shoulder as he and Will moved by. "Awesome job, man!"

"See you this afternoon," Will called behind him.

Kelly bumped her knee into Jared's backside. "Um, big bro? You, like, totally forgot to introduce me."

Jared had to wait, but eventually he found a path to the list and, sure enough, the second name from the bottom read *Jared Cook*. His elation was short lived when he heard Brad Williamson snort loudly.

"Lot of seventh-grade losers on the list," he said loudly.

"Yeah," snickered one of his friends. "And one of them is that small fry who broke your ankles yesterday, dude."

"Shut up!" Brad snapped. "I slipped! Besides, none of those losers would've made it if you and your posse actually had decent grades. Why don't you go read a book, or something?"

His friend laughed. "Poor Big Mike," he said. "He's going to be out there alone with a bunch of pansies. You better pass him the ball, man."

Turning, Jared saw one of the boys from Big Mike's group standing with Brad. Taller than Jared, the boy had a long neck with a head of thick black curls sticking several inches up, his skin a light shade of brown. Seeing Jared, he smiled, revealing two sparkling gold teeth. "And you, boy, had better learn to shoot!"

Jared's morning was a blur after that. It was Thursday and he had PE, but the classes were separated so he never saw the other "shower brothers." He did see Chaz, though. The shorter boy came up to him sullenly as they changed back into their school clothes.

"You know you fouled me," he said. "Yesterday."

Jared shrugged. "Maybe," he said, not wanting to fight. "I, uh, didn't see your name on the list."

Chaz snorted. "Coach Swopes is an old geezer. He can't see past his farts. Besides, it's not a basketball team he's making. It's a track team. You'll get cut today, anyway." He grinned nastily back at Jared as he walked away. "If you need something to help you relax afterwards, let me know."

In the cafeteria at lunch, Jared found his usual seat, sitting against the back wall of his round table, with his tray carrying a ham sub, a bag of chips, and an apple. Usually he hated school food, but famished and knowing he had basketball tryouts later, he started eating with zeal. When halfway done with his sub, he got surprise visitors.

As Will and his friends entered the lunchroom, they immediately noticed a change.

"What the heck, man," Nick said. "What are those losers doing?"

Their usual spots were taken by a loud, obnoxious group of eighth graders, most of them from the football team.

In the middle of them, Glen waved when seeing the boys in the cafeteria's entrance.

"Hey, dudes!" he shouted. "We saved you seats. Come join us!"

The eighth graders had sat with one empty seat between them, taking up the entire table. They all looked at the boys and waved. Some of them wagged their tongues and made faces.

"Wonderful," Ryan said with sigh. "We get to eat lunch with the eighth-grade dog pound."

"No way, man." Nick shook his head. "I know those guys. They'll try to eat our food. Let's find another place."

Ryan gave him a look. "Like where, dude? If you haven't noticed, the eighth graders have taken up all the tables here."

"Well," Nick said, "we can try sitting with the cheerleaders. Right?"

"Only in your dreams," Ryan told him.

One of the lunch monitors, a wrinkled lady who looked as if she drank lemon juice for breakfast, motioned for them to move along.

"You kids! Find a seat!" she yelled, coming at them from behind the group of eighth graders at their normal table. "You can't stand there!"

Hooting, Glen smacked the table next to him. "One of you kids can sit right here!"

Ryan frowned. "I bet Brad came up with this one."

Ben grunted. "You guys figure out where to sit. I'm going to go buy lunch."

"I'll go with you," Ryan said. "I need more chips. Good luck, Will." As he left to follow Ben, he muttered under his breath, "This is because of what you did at tryouts yesterday."

Will pursed his lips as he scanned the cafeteria. Brad sat at the first long table, but pointedly kept his back to them.

"What a jerk," Nick said. Then he coughed. "Okay, man, it's just us and that old witch is giving us the evil eye. If we don't move, she's going to turn us into frogs, or something."

Will's eyes suddenly brightened. "Hey, look, there's big guy!"

Nick looked at where Will pointed and groaned. "Will," he said. "I don't want to break it to you, but over there is where all the losers sit."

"Ha," Will said, nodding over at Brad. "If you can't beat them, then you're a loser. Let's go."

Chapter 24

Jared looked up from his book in surprise when he heard Will's and Nick's voices. The two boys were heading straight for him. Putting down his sub and closing his western novel, he hastily took a sip of chocolate milk and swallowed hard, barely keeping himself from choking.

"Hey, big guy, mind if we join you?" Will asked, putting down his lunch bag and sitting across from Jared.

"Hey, Jared," Nick said, not sounding nearly as enthusiastic. "What's up?" He slumped to the seat on Will's left.

Jared only stared and finally managed to clear his throat. "Uh, hey," he said, not knowing what else to say.

"Hope you don't mind if we sit here," Will told him.

"Yeah," Nick muttered. "We needed a break from our fan club." He started unpacking his lunch, keeping his shoulders hunched.

"Hey, your mom called last night," Will said to Jared.

Nick snorted. "Is that a punchline?" he said, unscrewing a bottle of fruit juice. "What did she call you?"

"Ha," Will said, elbowing Nick in the shoulder just as the larger boy went to take a drink.

"Hey!" Nick spluttered as red juice ran down his chin. "Not funny, man!" He wiped his face with the back of his sleeve. "Seriously, what did Jared's mom call about?"

Will glanced sideways at his friend. "Jared and I are going to play ball at Shady Farms this Saturday. Want to come?"

Nick choked and slammed his juice bottle down. "Ar-are you serious?" he croaked. "No way, man. You really going to play with Big Mike and his guys?" He looked at Jared and then at Will.

Jared felt his face flush and he took a sip of chocolate milk before nodding. "I could use the practice," he mumbled.

Nick shook his head. "Yeah, well, count me out. I got to do yardwork this Saturday."

"Oh?" Will asked, raising his eyebrows innocently. "It's not because you're chicken?"

Nick elbowed Will in the chest and immediately winced. "Ow, man! You got armor under there?"

Will rubbed his chest and grimaced. "I need armor to sit next to you."

"Whatever, man. I think my elbow hurts worse. I forgot how boney you are. Tell me something, Will. How does a little shrimp like you with no meat on your bones get to be so ripped? Seriously, man, what do you do?"

Will shrugged as he dumped out his lunch bag, spilling a sandwich, juice box, bag of chips, and a giant cookie. "Thank my dad for that," he said ruefully. "He used to be in the army and likes to do exercises in the mornings." He looked across the table at Jared. "If you want, on Saturday you can join in."

"Wait, Jared is going to be at your house?" Nick jerked up his head as if mortally offended. "Man, thanks for the invite. We've been friends for how many months and I've never seen your place."

Will gave him an exasperated look. "I just did invite you, but you said you had yardwork. Remember? But, hey, if you want to come, we're sleeping over at my place Friday night."

"Now you're talking," Nick said. "I'll go for the sleepover, but count me out of any Shady basketball. Seriously, you two dudes better be careful there."

"Who'd better be careful?" demanded Ryan's angry voice. "And what idiot decided to sit over here?" He stalked their way carrying his lunch tray.

"That would be Will," Nick said, munching on chips. "He and Jared are organizing a playdate."

"Oh," said Ryan, stopping short at seeing Jared. He looked even less happy. "Are we seriously trying to sit here?"

Jared just ducked his gaze and started picking at his mostly eaten sub.

Will took a bite of his sandwich and shrugged. "Better than standing."

"Yeah," added Nick. "You can always choose another table." He gestured over at where Marshall sat, tilting back on his chair while staring up at the ceiling with his arms stretched out. "He could certainly use the company."

"I'd rather sit with John," Ryan muttered, flicking his gaze toward the table where Angie and the principal's son sat.

Nick shuddered. "But that would mean sitting by Angie."

Shaking his head, Ryan slammed his bagged lunch and chips down in the space on the other side of Will. "Yo, that girl needs to get on her broom and fly to Sarah Power and her gang."

Sarah Power, still with a clean-shaven scalp, sat with her clan in the corner opposite of Angie and John. Body piercings, black clothes, and no smiling seemed to be the dress code there. Jared stared over at her and looked quickly away. With Ryan burning with hostility at the table, Jared kept his mouth shut.

Ben joined the table, sitting next to Ryan. Jared found himself facing the four boys. He didn't know if he should bury his head in his book or try to follow the conversation. He chose to pretend to keep drinking from his empty milk carton and eat crumbs of his sub. Making friends, he decided, was hard work.

His ears did perk up when Nick asked Ryan how it went with Mr. Hackett the other day. "Basically, man, is it on this afternoon? Do we get to shower?"

Ryan nodded. "Dude, you always need to shower. Of course it's on."

"Hey, did you figure out why Mr. Drydon was there?" Will asked, pulling out his cookie.

Ryan squirmed briefly and nodded. "Yeah, Mr. Hackett doesn't want anybody to know, so don't say anything, but he was speeding when driving the bus. Remember our last game at Berkshire? Some parent was following and said he was going too fast." He shrugged and stared down at his barely touched turkey sandwich. "No big deal, really. He just can't do it again or he can get fired."

Jared narrowed his eyebrows and clenched his fist tight. What he'd heard the other day didn't seem to match with Ryan's story. The stranger didn't sound like a concerned parent ... more like a concerned predator.

Ryan looked up and grinned at Will. "He even washed your shorts for you. I'll pick them up at tryouts."

"Hey, man," Nick said, eyeing Ryan's food, "if you're not going to eat your lunch maybe you can eat them."

"Ha," Will said. "Eat my shorts. You're hilarious. Have a cookie." He tossed his cookie at Nick and yawned.

"Thanks, man!" Nick's eyes lit up. "Your dad makes awesome cookies. I'm definitely there on Friday."

Will nodded. "Sure, dude." He yawned again. "I think I'm going to take a nap. Wake me up when lunch is over." Pushing back his trash, he put his head down on his arms and closed his eyes.

"He is seriously not being serious about taking a nap," Nick said, biting into the cookie.

"Not if you keep talking," Will mumbled, his eyes still closed. "That's why I like big guy, he doesn't talk …"

Ryan snorted. "He doesn't do anything. Sometimes, Will, you remind me of John. Nothing seems to bother you."

"Ha," Will muttered. "You're bothering me right now."

"Speaking of John," said Nick, his mouth full, "somebody should seriously rescue him from Angie. I mean, look at them. The poor kid has to face the wall. He can't even look at other kids with her around."

Ryan snorted. "That's just to protect him from seeing your ugly face."

"Why don't we invite him over here?" Ben asked, sitting up. "I mean, it's too late today, but what about tomorrow? He can eat with us for a change."

"Come on, guys," groaned Ryan. "Let's just focus on making the team this afternoon." He eyed Jared. "And not trying to make every school reject into a friend."

For a moment there was an awkward pause. Jared didn't dare say a word, but he felt his legs start to tremble.

Then Nick belched. "Whatever, man. I think that's a good idea. Why? Because Ben said it and he's a good Christian. Right, Ben?"

"Just as long as I'm right," Ben said, shrugging.

"Fine," Ryan growled. He glanced down at where Will actually appeared to be sleeping. "But what's this about Shady basketball?" When he heard about the sleepover plan from Nick and playing basketball with Big Mike, his eyes bulged. He made to protest, but suddenly relaxed. "Dude, that's … that's crazy. Count me out, but good luck."

Will sat up and blinked. "You too?" he said. "What about you, Ben?"

Ben also decided to skip out. "I'll pray for you," he told Will, only half joking.

Lunch ended soon after, Will promising to see Jared at basketball. Nick and Ben nodded while Ryan rolled his eyes. Jared didn't know what to think of his new lunch buddies … but he hoped to see a lot more of them at basketball practice.

"Yesterday," Coach Swopes barked to the twenty boys sitting on the bleachers, "was about if you could do it. Today is to see if you can make it. I'm looking for skill, teamwork, skill, and more skill. Show me you have what it takes to at least learn and I can use you. But if you do the skill, skill, and skill without the teamwork … then do me a favor. Leave now."

It was after school, the final day of tryouts. The tension lay think in the air like a heavy blanket on a hot day. Some of the boys were already sweating as they stared, grim faced, at the stooped-over coach. Even those players assured spots looked grim. Brad adjusted a hair band he'd added for his long hair and glared over at where Will sat behind Jared. To Will's left, Nick, Ben, and Ryan all sat with heads bowed as if in prayer.

Jared saw Brad's glare and blew out his breath. He couldn't think of the bigger eighth graders, or anybody else, for that matter. If he wanted a chance to stick around, he needed to worry about just himself. After getting changed in the locker room, he'd headed off to sit alone, but Will had tugged on his shirt and told him to sit with them.

It felt good to be a part of the group, even if Ryan hadn't been too happy to see him. Nick had even offered advice. "Keep your eye on the ball and focus on either stopping it from going into the basket," the big fellow had told him while waiting for Coach Swopes, "or putting it in the basket. If you're on offense and can't put it in yourself, pass it to somebody who can. That's all there is to it."

Will just shook his head. "Better advice," he'd told Jared, "is to kick everyone's, um, behinds."

Then Coach Swopes appeared with his clipboard, calling all attention to him without saying a word.

"So," the coach said, "I see nobody is leaving. Okay, then. Everybody who's staying, line up on the line! Let's see who I can make throw up today!"

All twenty boys got up and rushed to the line. Each one knew that for five of them, this was their last chance to impress their coach.

Five rounds of "suicide runs" later, Jared hadn't thrown up, but he'd wanted to. Afterwards, he'd no reservations about getting water from John and Angie. In his haste to pack for the shower, he'd again forgotten a water bottle.

Trotting to the water line, he came up in time to see Brad, Glen, and Bigfoot push their way to the front.

"Here you go," John said cheerfully, holding out cups of water.

"Thanks, spaz boy," Brad said softly, "but I don't want your water. It might make me like you." Leaning forward, he deliberately spat in one of the cups. "Go manage the girls' team."

Glen gave a sickly smile. "Hey, Brad, that's a little rough, man."

John stared at Brad, his smile slipping and confusion clouding his face. "If you didn't want water, why did you spit in it? You shouldn't spit in cups of water."

"And you shouldn't be here," Brad hissed. "Come on, guys. Let's find our water bottles."

"Just a second," Angie said, furious. She'd been busy filling up more cups and putting them on the cart by the cooler. "You heard what Coach Swopes said yesterday. You leave John alone."

"What, goth girl?" Brad sneered at her. "Are you going to go tattle on us that your poor boyfriend has no other friends? Remember Coach Hicks from last year? You know why he quit? Because this loser," he nearly spat when pointing at John, "wanted to be a manger, his daddy tried to force Coach to make him part of the team."

"What's wrong with John being a manger?" Angie said, crossing her arms and glaring. "He just wants to help."

Poor John looked from Angie to Brad and still held his cups of water out. "Does anybody want water?" he asked.

Brad ignored him. "If he wanted to help, he'd leave us alone! This is a basketball team, not a babysitting service. We lost our coach because of him, and now we're stuck with old man Swopes, who can't even stand up straight, much less coach basketball. Do you know he cut eight of my friends because of their grades already?"

Angie snorted a sharp laugh. "If they're your friends, it's no wonder. Obviously they're stupid."

"No, actually," Brad said, his voice rising, "they live in the apartments. They're not rich like you, you self-righteous—"

"Hey!" called Coach Swopes from across the gym. "What's going over there?"

"Nothing!" Angie yelled, glaring at Brad. "Absolutely nothing."

Brad jerked his head towards her, flexing his muscles. "Nothing is right," he muttered. "Come on. All real basketball players don't need water."

"Uh, I do," Glen said.

"Then you can have some from my water bottle," Brad told him, walking towards the bleachers. "Come on."

The line of sweaty boys shuffled uncomfortably for a second and then started following Brad, leaving John still holding the water and Angie looking ready to throw the water cooler at Brad.

"Uh, I'll take a cup," Jared said, ducking his head. "The, uh, one without the spit."

"Oh, hi, Jared!" John said, his smile returning. "I'll save the spit water for later."

Angie turned her wrath on Jared, gritting her teeth. "You see what I mean about jocks," she fumed. "You really want to be one of them?"

"I just want to play basketball," Jared muttered, accepting the offered water from John. "Brad's just mad because he lost to Will in the running again." He quickly drank the water and returned the empty cup. He could feel Angie's seething eyes burn into his back as trotted away.

Chapter 25

The first drill after the water break was about shooting and boxing out. While the eighth graders practiced on one end of the court, supervised by Brad and other returning players, Coach Swopes had the seventh graders gather around him at the far basket.

"I want to be clear, boys," Coach Swopes told them. "If I have any doubts about which players I pick, I'm going with experience. That means those big eighth graders over there have a leg up. If you want to be on this team, you have to show me something."

Besides Jared, Will, Nick, Ben, Ryan, and Big Mike, there were six other boys in the seventh-grade group. Jared couldn't help but notice, while Nick had the biggest bulk and Big Mike the strongest, he was the tallest. A solidly built Asian-American boy with short spikey hair named Tom stood about an inch shorter than Jared as the next tallest. Will, not surprisingly, was the shortest and slimmest.

"I want three teams of four," the coach explained. "There's going to be one shooter from outside the paint and offensive three rebounders against four defensive rebounders. Here's how it works. The shooter gets five shots. Every basket made counts as one point. Every rebound of a miss counts as two points. This drill is about rebounding and establishing position. After five shots, the teams switch and the offense becomes defense and vice versa. The third team stands on the end line and watches. See what works and what doesn't work. After both teams shoot, the team with the most points stays on the floor and the loser sits out. We'll keep going until everyone has a chance to shoot. Sounds simple, right? Good! Line up and let's make teams!"

Jared ended up with Ben, Ryan, and a boy named Kyle. An average-sized kid with a light complexion and compact build, Kyle was a Trailblazer, so Jared didn't know him too well. And quickly became glad of that fact.

"You stay down here and don't let any ball get by you," Kyle told him, physically shoving him to the block to the right of the rim. He twisted a sweatband on his right wrist and flicked back the front of his buzzed dark hair as if it made a difference. "I got the other side. That's my side. Remember, if the ball comes your way, grab it!"

"Yeah, okay," Jared muttered, too softly for Kyle to hear. The boy was already moving on to tell Ryan and Ben where to stand.

They were assigned as defensive rebounders against a team composed of Nick, Will, Tom, and a quiet boy with glasses named Ed. Ed was a Pathfinder and took English with Jared. A good athlete, he used to play with Jared in elementary school at recess. Since Middle School started, he only hung out with the football players, but he still treated Jared okay.

Big Mike and the other three kids looked on from under the basket. Big Mike appeared bored and unhappy to be there.

"Okay, boys, let's get it rolling," Coach Swopes called, tossing a ball to Nick, the first shooter. "Remember, box out!"

"Definitely," Ryan said. "Nick's shooting."

"Hey, man," Nick said, spinning the ball in front of him, "I heard that. I'm going to swish this thing so pure you're going to hear music." He stood just to the right of the foul line, and after sizing up the basket, he took a high-arcing shot that clanged off the front of the rim.

Jared watched it come towards him and lifted up his hands for the easy catch.

Just before it reached him, a body flew into him, knocking him aside. Stumbling back, he saw Tom going up with the ball, scoring an easy put-back.

"What are you doing, man?" Kyle demanded. "What was that?"

Ryan threw up his hands from where he'd boxed out Nick. "Yo, dude, this isn't a show. You're not supposed to be just watching. Get the ball!"

Coach Swopes blew the whistle and walked in from where he'd been watching behind Nick. "Hold up, let's hold up."

"Nice music," Will told Nick, covering a grin. "It sounded like a brick hitting a metal bar."

"Man, I missed that one on purpose," Nick said, getting the ball back from Tom. "I just wanted the two points."

"Everyone, listen up!" Coach Swopes said. "I don't think I made myself clear."

Jared grabbed the front of his collar and wiped sweat off his upper lip, but really he just wanted to hide his face in shame. He should've had that rebound, but Tom seemingly had come from nowhere. His side still hurt from where Tom's hip had plowed into him.

"This is about boxing out." He turned to Jared. "What's your name, Jared, right?"

Jared nodded miserably, trying to keep his stomach from clenching any tighter.

"Come here, son. Stand where you were before the shot."

Jared did so and immediately felt Coach Swopes's hand on his shoulder, spinning him to face the basket.

"When the shot goes up," the coach said, "this is where you face. Now, spread your legs and get lower. Use your rear end, son." He slapped Jared on the hip. "Don't be shy. Use your backside and block anyone behind you. Don't give an inch, got it?"

Jared nodded, feeling his face go red again.

Coach Swopes turned to the other players. "That goes for everyone. You have your rear end for more than one reason. Use it here!"

Nick reached over and patted Will's shoulder. "Sorry, Will," he said. "That means you can't do this drill. You don't have any rear end. Your whole back is flatter than a pancake."

Will shrugged away from Nick. "Ha," he said, slapping the back of Nick's shorts. "You have two rear ends. One on top and one on bottom."

Ryan cracked up. "Yeah, you do! We can't tell if you're talking or passing gas."

"Funny," Nick said. "Not!"

"Yo, just watch it," Ryan said. "Will's rear is tiny, but powerful. Remember when he brought that chili to lunch?"

"That wasn't me, guys," Will said, blushing.

Ignoring them, Coach Swopes slapped Jared on the back. "I know you're new at this, son," he said in a low voice, "but I've got my eye on you. You got real potential."

Immediately having his spirits lifted, Jared clamped his teeth on his lower lip in concentration and got ready for the next shot. This time he looked at where Tom stood and made sure to position his body in front, blocking any path to the basket.

The next shot from Nick bounced high off the back of the rim, heading toward the center of the paint. Jared had immediately turned to face the basket as soon as Nick went up. Now he backed his way into the paint. As the ball descended, he leapt high in the air, snatching it from the air with both hands.

"That's it!" Coach Swopes said. "Nice rebound!"

Kyle grunted when Jared passed the ball to Nick. "I had that one," he muttered. "Stay on your side."

Nick put up three more shots, making only one. Ben managed to slip by Kyle for a rebound, but Jared nabbed the last, snatching it over Tom and Will, who'd come crashing in.

Frustrated from losing a rebound to Ben, Kyle quickly volunteered to shoot first for their team.

"If you shoot as much as you talk, you're probably pretty good," Ryan mumbled to him, tossing him the ball.

Ryan, Jared could tell, wasn't happy to be stuck on a team with him and Kyle. He watched Ryan frown as he went to the lower block under the basket next to Nick.

Ben took a position near the foul line and briefly made eye contact with Ryan. The two friends traded looks. Ryan looked away first. Seemingly confused about Ryan's attitude, Ben kicked at the floor.

Ignoring it all, Jared moved to the other block where Tom immediately pushed him back with his body, sticking out his backside. Will and Ed set up at the top of the foul line to block out Kyle and Ben.

Will saw Jared looking at him and grinned. "I'm coming, big guy," he said. "I'm jumping over you."

"Sure," Nick scoffed. "If you brought a ladder."

Kyle then proceeded to drill the first four shots. The fifth shot caught the back of the iron and bounced straight back.

"I got it!" Will cried, rushing in as the ball went over the heads of Nick and Tom.

Without thinking, Jared, his eyes on the ball, moved into the center and nabbed the rebound over the smaller boy's head, one handed.

Will jumped his highest, but just bounced off Jared's chest and stumbled to the floor.

"Yo!" Tom protested. "That's over the back!"

Nick chuckled as he reached down and pulled Will up from under his arms. "More like over the head. Come on, dude." He smacked the back of his shorts. "Next time use your rear end."

"Ha," Will muttered. Then he blinked. "Wait, did we just lose?"

Ryan sighed. "Oh, yeah. It was a loss."

In the next game Jared had to rebound against Big Mike. The shorter, but wider and stronger, basketball star pushed Jared all over the paint when Jared's team went on offense. Ryan acted as the shooter and made the first two baskets, but missed on his last three.

Frustrated, he yelled and glared at Jared like it was his fault. Jared at least had the satisfaction of keeping Big Mike from an offensive rebound. He grabbed one miss and Ryan the other four. The poor shooter on Big Mike's team looked nervous and afraid. After every shot, he stared at Big Mike as if waiting for a rebuke. Once again, Jared's team held on to the floor.

Jared's joy quickly faded into dread when Ryan tossed him the ball as Will and Nick led their team back on the floor.

"Here," Ryan said, his eyes unfriendly, "it's your turn to shoot."

"It's okay, Jared," Nick called. "I'll grab your misses."

Jared's first shot missed everything. He'd set up at the left corner of the foul line and the ball landed over the rim, not even touching the backboard.

"Are you kidding!" Kyle cried.

"Airball!" yelled one of the kids on the end line.

Tom hid a laugh behind his hand and threw back his head. "Tall man can't shoot!"

Big Mike grabbed the ball and stared at it in utter contempt. Without looking at Jared, he fired it back.

Feeling lower than dust, Jared caught it with both hands. Swallowing hard, he bounced it front of him.

"Take your time," Ben told him. "You got it, man."

It felt nice having one person on his team support him, but it didn't help. His next shot struck the side of rim and fell to Tom.

"Two points for us!" he crowed.

Jared blew out his breath and took the ball again.

He still hadn't quite figured out what to exactly aim at when shooting. Most of his swishes, when they came, were by accident.

"Hey, man," Nick told him. "Relax. You'll get this one."

"Yeah, right," Ryan said. "I'll bet you my chips tomorrow he misses."

"I'm in on that," Nick said. "Remember, I like barbecue!"

Will stepped towards him, licking his lips. "Don't worry about them," he said quietly. "Just pretend the basket is a cookie jar. Every time you shoot imagine you're putting your hand inside. Pretend you're almost grabbing the front of the rim."

Jared nodded and looked back at the rim. Going up, he followed Will's advice and watched the ball splash into the net for a swish.

"Hey, man!" Nick cried, catching the ball on the way down. "Why didn't you give me that advice when I was shooting?"

"Then," Ryan said dryly, "you would've eaten all the cookies in the jar."

Will only shrugged. "Ah, I'll give you a cookie tomorrow."

Jared made one other shot, but felt elated when moving in to rebound. He'd finally figured out a strategy for shooting that he could practice … and he felt he actually had friends supporting him.

"Good job," Ben told him, slapping his back as he passed. Ryan only looked away and shook his head.

Will went to shoot next with his team up four points to two points. His first shot went too strong and bounced to Ryan to tie the score. He calmly swished the next two, but left his fourth shot short and Jared grabbed it as it fell off the front of the rim, right in front of Nick.

"Man!" Nick said, slapping Jared's back "You're too tall." He looked back at Will. "Okay, man. This is it. Score is tied and you have last shot. This is for the win, man. Don't blow it!"

Will nodded and wiped his mouth with his front collar. Jared could tell he wanted the win.

"No pressure," Kyle called. "We're going for three in a row! Don't mess up on the rebound, man," he said to Jared.

Ryan only shook his head. "This drill is taking forever."

Will dribbled twice and then threw up a jumper that hit nothing but net.

"Yes!" cried Nick. "We did it! We finally won a game!" Putting up his arms in victory, he stood in the paint and yelled.

Will, grinning, took a running start and leapt onto his back, joining the celebration.

"Yeah!" he crowed. "We're the champions!"

Ryan shook his head and came up behind them. He smacked Will's backside hard.

"Congratulations, dudes. Now you get to face Big Mike."

Will slid free of Nick and rubbed his stinging rear. "Hey," he grumbled. "I thought only the losers are supposed to be sore."

Big Mike proceeded to hit all five of his shots and grab every rebound from Tom's misses.

Chapter 26

After a quick passing drill and a dribbling drill, the tryouts ended with three on three fast break scrimmages. A team of three had to race down the court with the ball, where they had ten seconds to score against three defenders. If they managed to score, they kept the ball and raced back to the other side of the court where three different defenders waited. If the defenders got the ball on a turnover or a rebound, then they became the offense and raced to the other court to try and score. That meant there were three lines of players on either side of the court.

The eighth graders did their best to make sure they teamed up together. Needless to say, it became a fast, lively game with more than a little intensity.

After several rounds, Jared dripped with sweat, but felt elated. He'd held his own in the passing and dribbling drills and so far had been effective in the fast break. He'd scored once off a nice pass from Ben and had gotten three rebounds. Looking at the lines ahead of him made him feel even better. In the next round he would be grouped with Will and Ben.

Out on the court, down on the other end, the team of Brad, Glen, and Bigfoot, who Jared learned was really named Teddy, was making short work of a seventh-grade team led by Tom. After passing the ball around the perimeter, Brad blew by Tom, faked a pass to Glen, and then nailed a short runner in the lane.

"That's one!" Brad's voiced boomed. "Who's next?"

The next three players were already out on the court. Big Mike stood at the top of the key with Nick and Kyle. They fared only a little better. Brad didn't even try to go at Big Mike. Dribbling to the side, drawing Big Mike out, he lobbed a pass to Glen. Guarded closely by Nick, Glen backed in towards the basket, acting as if he was going to shoot. Then, at the last moment, he bounced a short pass to a cutting Teddy, formerly known as Bigfoot. Kyle had been caught watching the play and slammed his hands together in disgust as Teddy laid the ball in for an easy bucket.

"The seventh grade has nobody!" hollered Glen. "Let's get another one!"

Big Mike just shook his head and stalked to the back of the line.

The eighth grader in front of Jared turned around and grinned. About the same height as Jared, but much burlier, he wiggled his eyebrows. "Hear that, string bean? I think he wants you guys next." He turned to the middle line and looked where Will stood. "You too, small fry. Go on out there."

Will pressed his lips together, but gave a slight nod. Jared and Ben followed him on court. As soon as he stepped over the end line, Jared's heart started hammering. This was the real test, he knew. Down on the other end, Brad nailed a three-point shot. Then he had the ball and was coming for them.

"I get the ball," Will said, rubbing his hands together. "Ben, you watch my back and look for cutters. Big guy, you get down low. Make sure there're no layups."

Hearing Will's cool directions calmed Jared and he quickly assumed a defensive posture with his hands at the ready and feet spread wide. "Just like soccer," he muttered, "only easier. Remember that." In soccer he could never use his hands and there were more players to account for. But the idea was the same. He just had to keep the ball out of the net.

Seeing Will in front of him, Brad smiled and slowed up. Switching hands, he dribbled to the left, keeping his body between the ball and Will. Then he abruptly swiveled his hips, slashing to the right on a quick crossover.

Will pivoted his feet with the sudden turn and jumped back, keeping in front of the ball. Brad leaned in and bumped Will's upper chest, sending the slighter boy tumbling to the seat of his shorts.

Chortling, Brad kept going to the basket, leaping for a layup. He never saw Jared until too late.

Jared had been watching Glen, but when the older boy drifted out to near the left corner of the three-point line, he'd cheated back toward the basket, moving up to block any passing lane from Brad to Glen. Seeing Will go down, he immediately filled in the space. As Brad took off for the layup, Jared jumped up with his right hand outstretched.

Brad saw Jared in midair and panicked. Twisting to his side, he tried to throw up a wild shot, but lost control. He ended up colliding with the floor on *his* backside while the ball fell right in front of Jared.

"Hey, big guy!" Will cried, scrambling to his feet. "Pass!"

Glen and Teddy both hesitated and the ball was lost.

"Foul!" Brad yelled, slapping the floor. "Come on, man!"

"No foul!" Coach Swopes yelled. "Not unless it was on you for pushing off! Great help on defense!"

Will, meanwhile, took the outlet pass from Jared and sprinted down to face the next three defenders on the other end of the court. He faked out the first with a brief hesitation move, drew out the other two to guard him near the foul line. Then, jumping, he tossed a no-look pass towards the basket, right in the path of a racing Ben. Ben had sprinted down the right side of the court behind Will and was never picked up. He scored an easy bucket.

On their return trip back up the court, none other than Brad waited for them. He'd switched spots with the tall, burly boy and went out to meet Will who dribbled over center court. Jared and Ben both went down low, but were quickly guarded by Brad's teammates. A boy with a thick waist and mop of black curls put a hand on the back of Jared's shirt and shoved him away from the basket. "Not today, string bean," he said gruffly. His breath smelled of garlic.

"I got you now, small fry," Brad said, hunching low as he faced Will. "No tower is going to help you now!"

The small boy ignored him. His dark eyes surveyed the court as he slowed his dribble. Crouching low, he kept switching hands.

"Seven seconds!" Coach Swopes hollered from where he stood in front of the bleachers with his clipboard and a stopwatch.

Jared took a quick glance at the coach and saw John and Angie sitting right behind him. Angie had a look of disgust on her face, but John sat on the edge of the first row watching the action with a happy grin.

"This is for you, John," he muttered. In truth, once the game started all his nervousness and awkwardness vanished. It became all about his team, and right now his team was being bullied by a class-A jerk. Jared had never been taught how to do a pick in basketball, but he'd seen it plenty of times on television. He knew you just stood still next to a defender and covered your private area.

Biting his bottom lip, he moved up and assumed the position to Brad's left, spreading his feet under his shoulders.

Will never looked at him, but after feinting right, he moved behind Jared.

Brad followed the move. Seeing Jared, his eyes lit up and he tried to plow into him with his shoulder, running him over.

Jared had a secret he never liked to share. He'd been born with a protracted chest that stuck out right between his pectoral muscles. As he matured, it'd turned into a rock-hard bone that served almost as a plate of armor. When playing tackle football with his brothers, they'd learned to avoid hitting him in the chest. When they did, they were the ones who paid the price.

Brad paid the price now. He struck Jared full in the chest, but somehow found himself lying on his back staring up with a dazed expression. He'd bounced back a foot and, with his hair flying, had crashed to the floor while Jared hadn't budged an inch.

Jared stood over him and quickly realized what he'd done. He'd just pulverized one of the star players during tryouts.

Nearly every boy in the gym cried out and yelled, mostly in delight.

"Boom!" Nick yelled. "Big guy took down Brad!"

Coach Swopes blew the whistle as Brad tried to get up, but lay back down and groaned.

"Oooo," the eighth grader moaned. "I can't move …"

Suddenly afraid, Jared backed up and wiped his hands on his shorts. He didn't mean to hurt anyone. He'd just wanted to send a message.

Will had kept up his dribble, but now let the ball fall and roll towards the basket. He looked at Jared and grinned. "Man, I'm glad you're on my team."

Jared nodded, his face growing red, when suddenly boys were crowding around him, slapping his back. Even Kyle came up and gave him a whack on the back of his shorts.

"Seventh graders, baby!" he crowed. "Seventh graders rule!"

"Where did that come from?" wondered Nick, shoving Jared. "Man, you put him in his place!"

"What did you do to him?" Ben asked, his voice almost in awe.

"I, uh, nothing," Jared mumbled, embarrassed by all the attention. "He, uh, hit me."

Ted laughed. "Man!" he cried. "He hit a brick wall, man!"

Even some of the eighth graders joined in the crowd, but more than a few, Glen included, glared at Jared.

"He elbowed Brad," Glen said loudly. "I saw it."

"His hands were in front of him," Nick told him, laughing. "Jared is just a brick wall!"

Only Ryan and Big Mike appeared unmoved. Big Mike sat against the wall with his hands on his knees staring up at the ceiling. Ryan had his arms crossed as he stood under the basket. He was staring toward the locker room with an unreadable face.

Coach Swopes blew his whistle again and ordered everyone off the court and to the bleachers.

Instantly the boys complied, growing quiet. They'd forgotten about the tryouts.

"You okay, Brad?" Coach Swopes asked, leaning over the fallen boy.

"Oh, uh, yeah," Brad said, wincing. He sat up and suddenly glared. "That's twice he fouled me! I'm going to break that toothpick in half!"

"That's enough!" Coach Swopes barked, his voice growing hard. Looking up, he spoke to everyone. "No more trash talk, gentlemen. It ends now!" He looked down at Brad and glared. Then he sighed. "You're supposed to be a leader of this team," he said. "Go join the rest and listen well." Once Brad had made his way to the bleachers, trying hard to show he had no ill effects from his fall, Coach Swopes tore into the boys.

"I hear seventh graders and eighth graders in here. What I don't hear is a Washington Middle School basketball team!" Jared saw spit fly from the coach's mouth. Old and stooped, Coach Swopes still had fire inside of him. His voice rang off the walls of the gym and the boys heard him loud and clear. "Trash talk is for the trash can. And if I hear any more of it, your can is going to be trashed on the bench. Go it? I mean this! I have a lot to think about before I make the final cuts, but you can make my job a whole lot easier by talking trash. Now everybody on the line. If we can't run this drill properly then we'll just run!"

Brad came up to Jared after the final sprint and the boys were starting for their lockers. Everyone dripped with sweat and looked ready to fall over. Coach Swopes had run them hard.

"Hey, dude," Brad muttered. "No hard feelings, man. Nice pick."

Jared looked up in surprise. "Yeah, uh, sorry," he said.

"For what?" Brad asked him. "You did the right thing. Next time I'll get you back. Don't worry. See you on the court."

It wasn't until Jared had reached his locker that he realized what Brad had meant. Brad fully expected Jared to be on the team.

"Yes, finally!" Nick said with a groan as he staggered into the doorway of the back locker room. "It's shower time."

Will prodded the back of his shorts, coming impatiently behind him. "Get your big backside out of my way."

"Hold on," Nick said. He let loose a loud fart. "There, that felt better." He moved out of the way. "You may pass."

"Oh, man!" Ben cried from beside Will. "What did you eat?"

"Not enough," Nick answered. "I'm starving. We ran so much …"

"Yeah," Will said, wryly, "but somehow you still have gas left."

Nick groaned. "Stop it. I'm too tired to laugh. Who has the shampoo?" He parked himself on the bench and started untying his shoes.

"That would be Ryan," Ben said, standing behind Nick opening his locker. "And I brought a towel today. Did you guys remember?"

"Oh, man," Nick said as he kicked off his shoes. "I knew I forgot something."

"Gross! Pass more gas," Ben pleaded, covering his nose. "Your feet smell worse than a dead skunk."

Will laughed as he sat back against his locker. Thoroughly exhausted, he spread his feet in front of him. "Well, dude, I'm definitely not fetching any towels today."

"It's the new guy's turn, right?" Ben asked.

"Yeah, but where is he?" Nick wondered. "And where's Ryan with our shampoo?"

"I'm right here!" Ryan called, coming into the room. He tossed a pair of red shorts in Will's lap. "Put those away before you forget them. In your backpack."

"Yes, Mom," Will said, not moving from the floor.

"Hardy-har-har," Ryan said. "I'm serious, dude. Mr. Hackett doesn't want to see them again. He says they're the ugliest shorts he's seen since the 1970s."

"Hey, man, while you were with Hackett, did you pick up any towels?" Nick asked him. "I forgot mine."

"That's Jared's job," Ryan said, turning away and going to his locker. "But we'd better hurry in the shower. Old man Swopes kept us twenty minutes late!"

"Yeah," laughed Nick. "All because Jared pasted Brad on the floor." He started struggling to pull off his shirt. "Where's he at?"

"I just saw him. Yo, Jared!" Ryan called loudly. "You coming? The showers are ready!"

Will groaned. "Yeah, but are we ready?" Sighing, he scooted away from the locker and started peeling off his shirt.

"Ready for what?" Ryan asked him. "A tan?"

"Ha, ha." Will said, finally pulling his shirt free. "Didn't you use that one already?"

"Watch it, man," Nick said. "If Jared comes in and sees you messing with little dude, he might clean your clock. He's got Will's back, man."

Will frowned, but then rolled his eyes. "At least somebody has it."

Ryan just shook his head, muttering under his breath. "We'll see how long that lasts."

Nick then slapped Will's bare back hard. "See, man? I got your back too!"

Chapter 27

Jared joined the shower bunch wearing his flip-flops and carrying his bag of fresh clothes and towels. The other boys were already in with the water running full blast.

"Man, feels so good!" cried Nick. "This water is like the water of life! I can move again!"

"Just toss me the shampoo!" Ryan told him. "Remember, we need to use it all today!"

"You there, Jared?" Nick called. "I hate to mention it, but I forgot a towel, man."

"Yeah, me too," added Ryan. "You'll have to fetch some when we're done."

"Or get them now," Will said. "Don't worry, dude. I brought one."

"No, man!" Ryan said. "That ruins the fun. Besides, Jared, you brought a towel, right, man?"

Going to the open shower stall, Jared was surprised to hear Ryan talking to him so much and actually being somewhat friendly. He thought perhaps Ryan was getting used to him being around.

"Uh, yeah, no problem," he said. "I can get the towels after showering. I can change first, no sweat." He put his clean clothes outside the shower and started shucking off his shirt.

"Don't mention sweat again," Ben said. "I've had enough sweat today."

"Man, can you imagine showering in somebody's sweat?" Nick asked. "What if we're doing that right now?"

"Yo, really, dude?" Ryan said. "You're disgusting."

Thirty minutes of showering later, it took six shampoos each for the boys to finally empty the bottle. Nick announced the great achievement with a wild yell and tossing the empty shampoo bottle over his curtain into Ryan's stall. "We did it!" he cried. "Our showering is complete! Alleluia!"

"Hurry up, Jared!" Ryan called. "Get our towels, man! This is your initiation time!"

"Just make sure to change first!" Nick hollered at him. "We don't need any more Running Bares."

"Ha," Will said. "You guys are so hilarious. Hey, big guy, you know where to go?"

Grabbing his towel, Jared wiped his face and started toweling off his hair. "Uh, yeah … the room just past Mr. Hackett's office, right?"

"Want me to go too?" Ben asked. "I can—"

Ryan's yell cut him off. "Yo, hold up, dudes! There's still more shampoo on the bottom! We need to clean this thing out! Everyone but Jared, one more round! We'll have it done before you get back!"

After pulling on his boxer shorts, Jared stepped out of the shower and quickly added a shirt and pants. Stepping into his flip-flops, he left his friends singing and laughing as they completed one last shampoo with gusto.

It felt good. Real good. After a good tryout, a fresh shower, and knowing he'd actually made some friends, Jared didn't mind fetching towels. It made him feel like part of the gang, especially since one of the towels would be for Ryan. Ryan, it seemed, was finally being nice. Amazing.

Not being able to hide a grin, he headed into the main locker room in high spirits. As soon as he entered, his nose started to twitch. The strong sharp odor of body spray mixed with unwashed bodies smacked him in the face. It served as a stark contrast to the herbal shampoo scent.

Jared blinked and felt his eyes start to water.

"What cologne do those guys wear," he muttered, coughing a little. In the appalling odor he got a whiff of a familiar chemical …

Jared suddenly felt his legs go weak. It was the same cologne he'd smelled back in the bathroom on Halloween, only this time much stronger. Just as he had this thought, he felt his senses being overpowered. A terrible drowsiness hit him like a ton of bricks and his eyes started to slide shut. He was so sleepy …

Jared never saw the figure step out from behind the lockers in front of him. He sort of felt himself being lifted up and then dumped upside down. The last thing he remembered was his fingertips brushing the floor …

Jared opened his eyes without knowing what had happened or where he was. Blinking drowsily, he had a hazy memory of going to fetch towels, but then … He lifted up his head and found himself lying stomach side down on a padded table in brightly lit room full of gym supplies. His right arm dangled over the side and a towel cushioned his cheek. His eyes slowly came to focus on a rack of basketballs and he remembered the tryouts.

He pulled himself up with a start. What had happened? Groaning, he twisted to his side and put a hand to his head as pain shot through his skull. It felt like somebody had dribbled his head like a basketball before slam dunking it.

Faint traces of the sharp cologne still hung in the air and just sniffing it made Jared nauseous. "Tryouts must have really wore me out," he muttered.

"Hey, big guy!" he heard Will's voice yell from outside the door. "Where are you?"

"Uh … here," Jared croaked, his throat dry and scratchy.

The slighter boy dashed into the doorway a few seconds later. "Dude, what happened to you? You never came back!"

Jared just stared blearily at him and shook his head. "Must've fallen asleep," he mumbled.

Will widened his eyes. He wore a thin sweatshirt with a hood, a winter cap, and Adidas warm-up pants. His face looked flushed as if he'd just finish running. "Man, the bus is leaving! I had to beg the driver to wait while I ran back to find you!"

"Wh-what?" Jared asked stupidly. He looked up at a clock hanging over the door and was shocked to see it was well past five. He'd been sleeping for over twenty minutes. He stiffly got to his feet and stretched. "Where are … the others?"

"They already left, dude. Ben's mom picked up him and Ryan and Nick had to get home to walk his dog. Man, Ryan and Nick weren't too happy about you disappearing." He grinned. "Luckily I still had washcloths from yesterday." Will suddenly frowned. "What's that smell?"

"I don't know," Jared muttered as he stumbled away from the table. "But it's giving me a headache."

"Yeah …" Will's face clouded. "I had something like this happen to me before … Come on," he said abruptly. "Get your stuff and let's get out of here. This place is starting to give me the creeps."

Jared couldn't argue. He quickly went to his locker and gathered his backpack. Will had already packed his old clothes in his sports bag and had it ready. "That's why I knew you were still here," Will explained. "I thought Mr. Hackett busted you or something."

Jared only grunted. He took a deep gulp of fresh air as they left from the back entrance of the locker room. The dizziness started to pass as a chilly November wind greeted him. Behind the trees, across the football field, the sun started to sink for the evening, leaving behind a colorful sky of reds and purples. Jared immediately felt better as the cool air cleared away the fumes and fuzziness in his brain.

Will nudged him forward. "Come on, the bus will be leaving. Ben went to go look for you," he explained, "but heard Mr. Hackett talking in his office. Ben said he sounded real mad, so he ran back, but then you never showed up. By the time everyone got changed it was time for the bus and Ryan said you ditched us."

Jared blew out his breath in relief when they hurried around the school to find the bus still waiting. By the time he climbed on, muttering an apology to the glaring driver, his head had fully cleared and he started thinking.

Why had Ryan wanted him to get those towels so badly and then say he'd ditched them? And how did Jared end up in the supply room? Thinking of the horrible smell, Jared was convinced it wasn't just cologne. Something had knocked him out. Jared grimaced. Definitely something fishy was going on …

Will sat behind him again, but neither boy seemed to be in the mood to talk. Jared spent the ride staring out the window, coming up with all sorts of scenarios and arriving at only one firm conclusion. Ryan, he knew, was not his friend.

"Hey, big guy, are you still up for tomorrow?" Will asked as the bus slowed to stop at the top of his street. "You're still coming over, right?"

Jared quickly sat up. "Oh, uh, yeah. Of course. Oh, and, uh, thanks for going back to find me."

Will grinned and smacked his shoulder as he gathered his bag to get off. "Hey, dude. You got my back at tryouts. I was just returning the favor. See you tomorrow, big guy!"

By the time Jared prepared for bed that night, he was convinced it was just his active imagination running away with him. He'd just been overly tired and the horrible locker room smell had just been too much. He'd made it to the supply room and had fallen asleep on the table without remembering doing it. There was no way Ryan had rigged some sort of trap for him. Even if he did, which seemed pretty impossible, what would have been the purpose?

Sighing, he stood at the bathroom mirror, running a hand through his thick curls. Barefoot in his pajama pants, he'd just finished another shower and had brushed his teeth.

George banged on the door behind him. "You done yet, man?" he hollered. "Let me in to at least get my toothbrush! You're worse than Kelly in there!"

"The door's open," Jared said tightly. "Come in and get it."

"About time," George said, pushing open the door. Seeing Jared, he wrinkled his nose. "Great. You're admiring yourself in the mirror."

Jared ignored him and quickly replaced his brush in a cup by the sink. As he did so, he heard George grunt.

"What in the world, man," George said. He slapped the middle of Jared's back. "You got some weird friends in basketball."

"What are you talking about?" Jared said, doing his best not to flinch.

"Watch your back."

"What?"

"Who did this to you?"

"Did what?"

"Turn around and look at your back in the mirror, dummy. Somebody wrote on it in sharpie, it looks like."

Jared twisted his body and looked back in the mirror. In twisted black ink, somebody had scrawled across the small of his back, just above his waistline.

WATCH YOUR BACK.

"Hey, little bro. Are you awake?" Angel's voice called softly as she slowly pushed open Will's door.

"I am now," Will muttered from under the covers in his bed.

"Sorry, kid." Angel stepped next to his bed and knelt down. With Will's sports and school work and her college work, she'd seen little of him since September. It was hard to believe that Thanksgiving was just around the corner. "I just wanted to check on how you're doing."

"Just trying to get some sleep."

"Ha, now who's being funny?" Angel poked his side. "Besides, it's almost time to get up. This is your big day."

Will grunted. Lying on his stomach facing her, he opened his eyes. "Are you here tonight?"

"What? Am I invited to your sleepover too? No thanks, little bro. I'm too old to have a party with twelve-year-olds. And no, I'm not going to date one of your friends."

"Ha, ha," Will said, shifting to his side. "Seriously, though."

Angel slapped his leg. "I'll be around, little bro. You know Dad is getting all geared up about it."

Will rolled his eyes. "That's what I'm afraid of."

At first, when Will had asked his parents about having Jared and perhaps Nick over for Friday night, they were hesitant. His mom had said she had a dinner meeting that night and would be home late. It wouldn't be fair to his dad. Mr. Moore had just licked his lips and mentioned the house being too dirty for company. Only Angel had saved the day. Reminding their parents that Will had yet to have friends over since the move and promising to help clean the house, she'd convinced them to allow the sleepover.

Then, last night, when Will mentioned that his friends would like to participate in Mr. Moore's workout on Saturday, his dad perked right up. Now he acted more excited than Will about the sleepover.

"It'll be good for him," Angel said. "He can be like you guys' drill sergeant."

"Right." Will rolled over and sat up, leaning back against his headboard. "Was Dad always like this?"

"Do you mean like a stay at home parent worrying about a dirty house?" Angel grinned. She and Will had spent most of the night before vacuuming, cleaning bathrooms, and straightening the place up in preparation for the sleepover, all under the close supervision of their dad.

"Well, yeah. Maybe. But I mean, he can get really mad really fast for no reason."

Angel sighed and reached over, tousling his hair. "Don't worry, Will. He won't get mad tonight."

There had been a few flare-ups over the months with their dad, but nothing too catastrophic. Will had asked to limit the running and exercising to three times a week and Mr. Moore hadn't argued. At the same time, their dad could be like a ticking time bomb. You never knew when he might go off.

"It's the PTS," she said. "It's probably scary for him. But you know he loves us." She suddenly grinned. "You should be more worried about Jimmy. He's going to jump all over your friend."

Will groaned. "Please, Angel. You have to lock him up somewhere."

"Tell you what, little bro. You give me ten bucks and I'll babysit Jimmy for you."

"Not fair! I don't have any money!"

Angel slapped his knee and stood back up. "Then I guess you better be really, really nice to me and obey my every command for the foreseeable future. Now get some more sleep. I woke you up an hour early. You're going to have a long day."

"Wow. Thanks, sis. Isn't it a little too late for that?"

"You're never too little to get up too early, little bro," Angel told him. "Don't forget that."

Will threw his pillow at her, "Go away, Angel."

Laughing, Angel left her brother to slump back on his mattress and think. He hoped it was a good idea to have the sleepover. The plan was to run with his dad early Saturday morning, eat breakfast, and then get dropped off at the middle school to play basketball. He never told his dad the real plan—to leave the middle school on foot to reach the apartments and play ball with Big Mike.

Chapter 28

At lunch later that day, Jared took his usual seat and had just started eating his fries when he saw Nick and Will coming his way. Not far behind were Ryan and Ben, stopping at the lunch line. Jared suddenly lost his appetite and slid his tray away. His stomach clenched and he could almost feel the writing, still faint even after constant scrubbing, burn against his back. Which of them, of his "so-called" friends, would have done such a thing?

It couldn't have been Will. No way. Jared refused to believe it. But the others? Nick and Ryan had been the ones insistent that he went for towels. Ben had gone to check on him and claimed to have heard Mr. Hackett. And Will had been the one to find him. Jared blew out his breath. In truth, every one of them, Will included, could have been the culprit. The question was, how did he fall asleep so quickly and not wake up when somebody wrote on him? And how had he even gotten into the supply room? He had vague, hazy memories of being carried, but that could have easily been part of a dream.

He said little as Will and Nick set down their lunch bags, taking the same seats as the day before.

"Hey, man," Nick said. "Will said you fell asleep yesterday. Must've been exhausted from rocking the tryouts."

Jared grunted, feeling his stomach give another spasm. That was something else he had to worry about. The final cuts had yet to be posted and should be up this afternoon after school.

"You okay, man?" Nick asked, concern in his voice.

"What?" Jared asked.

Nick gave him a look. "I asked if you were okay."

"Ah, he's just upset you won't be coming to the sleepover tonight," Will said, pulling out his lunch. He rolled his eyes at Jared. "Nick says he has to stay home to babysit his dog instead of staying up all night playing video games."

"Who says I won't stay up playing games all night anyway?" Nick said. "Alfie is just a puppy. My parents are going out late, and if we leave him alone he'll tear up our house. Besides, I'll look for you online, man. We playing NBA 2K?"

"Only if you want to get wrecked," Will told him. He looked at Jared. "You ready for tonight?"

"Oh, uh, yeah." Jared had all his stuff in his hall locker, but to be honest didn't feel ready at all. He snuck a glance at Nick, searching for any sign of guilt. Appearing unconcerned, the large boy propped his elbows on the table, holding a thick ham sandwich in front of him.

Ryan and Ben arrived a few minutes later. Both gave Jared a cool look as they sat.

"Yo, man," Ryan said. "Thanks for the towel yesterday. I heard you used it as a baby blanket." He looked at Will and smiled. "You're going to have one awesome sleepover tonight, man. Jared won't say a word all night, but at least he'll sleep."

Jared's face flushed. "Actually," he said without thinking, "somebody wrote on me yesterday."

The boys in front of him stared for a second. Then Nick lifted his eyebrows.

"Uh, come again?"

"Yesterday," Jared said, feeling all his anxiety boiling to the surface, "when I fell asleep somebody wrote on my back."

"What did it say?" Ryan asked. "Stop snoring?"

Jared shook his head and told them about the message.

"Next time, just grab the towels and come back," Ryan told him with a snort. "Then things like that wouldn't happen and I won't have to dry off with miniature washcloths."

Nick licked crumbs off his lip and opened up his bottle of juice. "Probably Brad or one of his friends," he said. "They saw you snoozing away and decided to send a message. I'd just ignore it, man. Don't let them get to you."

Jared blinked. He hadn't thought of that. A lot of the eighth graders rode the activity bus, so they would've been around at the time. Ryan, though acting a little hostile, didn't exhibit any definite guilty signs and Ben seemed more disgusted than shamed. Will just chewed his food thoughtfully.

"Hey," Ben said, changing the subject, "What about John. Aren't we rescuing him today?"

"Yeah, man!" Nick said, quickly getting to his feet. "I almost forgot. Coming, Will?"

"Oh, yeah. Sure." Will put down his sandwich and soon Jared was left alone again.

He sank back in his chair, shaking his head. A headache pulsed through his skull, very much like the one he had when waking up the day before. He had no idea what to think …

Will walked casually over to the table where Angie and John sat, licking his lips. Nick, Ben, and Ryan stood watching several feet away. Being the smallest, and since John seemed to like him, he'd been sent as an emissary to offer the lunch invitation. In reality none of the others were brave enough to face Angie.

Moving to John's back, he put on a smile and tapped the boy's shoulder. "Hey, John," he said. "We, er, were wondering. Do you want to come sit at our table for lunch?"

Angie had a Tupperware full of salad before her. Hearing him, she dropped her fork and turned with a start.

"What are you doing here?" she demanded.

Will ignored her, keeping his eyes on John. "It's just me, Nick, Ryan, and Ben. Oh, and there's Jared. You know, from basketball."

John's eyes lit up and he picked up his bag of teddy grahams. "Sure," he said brightly. "I'll go eat lunch with you."

"No you won't," Angie said sharply. "Leave us alone," she told Will.

"Hey!" Nick cried, coming to join Will. "This is a free country. John can sit wherever he likes. You're not the boss of him." He patted John's shoulder. "Do you want to sit at our table, man?"

"Sure!" John answered. "Come on, Angie!"

Angie gritted her teeth. Picking up her fork, she gripped it tightly and for a moment both Nick and Will backed away, afraid she meant attack them.

"I'm staying here, John," she said firmly. "You can sit with me, or go with those … boys."

"Oh. I'll go sit with Jared and Will," John said. "They play basketball!"

Angie stabbed her salad fiercely and made no other comment as John left with Nick and Will. She glanced over once and glared right at Jared.

As a Pathfinder, Jared's lunch ended five minutes earlier than the Trailblazers' lunch. He'd spent his time eating quietly as John happily sat next to him eating teddy grahams and grapes while the other boys engaged him in conversations about favorite basketball players. John, it turned out, was a big Golden State Warriors fan.

As Jared got up to throw away his trash, Will stood to join him. "You're still coming home with me, right?" he asked as they walked to the center of the cafeteria to the trashcans.

"Oh, uh, yeah. Of course. I already got my bus pass."

"Good." He licked his lips nervously. "I have to tell you something on the bus. I'll meet you at the gym so we can see the basketball cuts before going to the bus. See you, big dude." Will tossed in his garbage and went back to the table.

Jared scratched his curls and wondered what Will had to say. Before he could think too much about it, he felt a tug on his arm.

Turning, he looked down, right into the livid face of Angie Robinson.

"Thanks a lot, you big jerk," she spat, curling her upper lip.

Shocked, Jared stepped back. "For what? What did I do?" He felt his heart thump wildly, seeing her dark hair pulled back from her furious face. She wore a black, heavy metal T-shirt and dark blue jeans, ripped at the knees. Jared couldn't help but notice how good she looked. Instantly his face flushed and he dropped his gaze to her sneakers, which he noticed had pink shoelaces.

"You know what you did!" Angie growled. "You stole John from me, that's what! You and your stupid friends snatched him away."

"Huh? They, we just asked him to sit with us. We treated him nice!"

"Sure, because all you jocks are super nice. Isn't it funny, Jared, that they never cared about you until you proved you could pick up a basketball? If they really liked you, why didn't they sit with you before?"

Jared stared at her, feeling himself getting angry. Why did Angie come after him? He hadn't come up with the idea. The cafeteria had three columns in the center and they were against the middle one, thankfully hidden from view from most angles of the cafeteria. All around them, chattering voices kept their quarrel from being the center of attention. "They didn't know me before," he said tightly. "I met them through basketball."

"Yeah, just like you met John. Only, wait. You met him a long time ago. Why didn't you ask him to sit with you before? If you were so lonely, why didn't you ask *me* to sit with you?"

Jared frowned, feeling blood rush back to his head. "I never thought you ever wanted to sit with me," he muttered.

"Because you never asked! And now I lost John. Did you ever think, Jared? Do you see me with lots of friends? John is all I had. If John is gone, who am I supposed to sit with?

Jared kept his head down. "Why don't you go sit with Sarah's group," he mumbled.

He could hear Angie gasp. Looking up, he saw her staring at him, shocked and hurt. Then it all turned into anger. "Is that what you think? That I'm a freak and that Sarah's a freak and all the freaks should be together? Really? Don't you know anything? Did you know that Sarah's parents broke up last summer? That maybe her hair and her piercings are actually her wanting some help and understanding? Instead of judging people you should start caring about them."

Jared stepped back as if slapped. "Well, I didn't see you care about me when I sat alone for two years!"

Angie's mouth dropped open and for a second she looked confused. Then all once she looked ready to cry. "Oh, I can't do this."

Jared quickly swallowed and pursed his lips. He'd never gotten angry in school before, especially with a girl. Angie just drove him up the wall. "I, uh, I'm sorry," he mumbled.

Taking a deep breath, Angie tossed back her hair and looked at Jared. "Come with me," she said, grabbing his arm and pulling him toward the cafeteria's exit. "I have to tell you something and don't want to make a scene."

"Too late for that," Jared mumbled. He was very aware of several pairs of eyes directed his way.

"Look at that," he heard Brad's mocking voice. "The string bean basketball star got in trouble with the retard's girlfriend!"

Out in the hall, Angie continued leading Jared to the front entrance area where she pushed him against the wall. "This isn't funny, Jared," she said.

Jared, his face flushed, ducked down his head. "No kidding," he mumbled. "What's the big deal?"

"I'm scared, that's what." Angie took a deep breath.

Jared frowned. "Scared of what people are saying about you?"

Angie gave him an icy look. "No, I don't care what they say. They're jerks. Do you know why I stay with John? Because he's not like them. He's good and innocent. He represents everything good in this crummy world of evil, Jared. And I'll always protect him for that."

Jared looked up at hearing the vehemence in her words. Then Angie stared up at him and her bottom lip started to tremble slightly. Swallowing, she licked her lips and glanced around.

"I'm telling you this, because I really think evil is out to get him." Jared could only stare as Angie rushed to continue. "I haven't told anyone this, but I think somebody is watching us. John and I. Somebody who wants to hurt him. I babysit for Mr. Drydon a lot. Remember Halloween? Well, since then I saw a pickup truck following us two times when taking John for a walk." She crossed her arms in front of her chest, ducking her own gaze. "And, I don't know, but I feel this presence sometimes. Even in school. I don't like staying late here anymore." She shuddered.

"Have you told Mr. Drydon?"

"I tried, but all I have are feelings. Strange things have happened, but I haven't any proof of anything. The pickup could just be an old neighbor driving too slowly. So far it has never come close enough for me to see the license plate. Besides, Mr. Drydon is always busy … and, I don't know. Sometimes when I get to Mr. Drydon's house, John is sleeping a lot … He never used to take naps during the day. And when he wakes up, he's super groggy. I think he's getting some medicine just to make him sleep."

Jared felt his entire body tighten. "Um," he croaked. "That's, uh, interesting."

"I need to keep an eye on him, Jared. And I need to find out what's going on. Is it my imagination, or is something bad going to happen? And if you're going to get involved, then you'd better do the same. You need to keep an eye out for John."

"Uh, okay. Sure."

"Good. In that case, I'll start sitting with you guys tomorrow. Thanks for the invite." All at once she turned and walked away.

Jared was left gasping for air and wondering what in the world was going on. He *really* wished he had somebody to talk to and share his worries. He'd wanted to the previous night, but had failed.

George had just snorted, and said something about Jared needing new friends, before stalking out of the bathroom with his toothbrush. His father had come home late and had been too tired to listen, while his mother, as usual, had been too busy with Carey. He guessed he could've gone to Kelly, but after her dance lessons she'd locked herself in her room to talk on the phone with her friends. Not having a cell phone, she'd brought the extension phone up to her room, so even if Jared had somebody to call and talk to, he couldn't have done it.

And now Angie dumped all of this on his lap. More like, she hit him upside the head with all this.

"I have too many questions and no answers," he muttered. "And nobody to even ask the questions to *find* the answers." He had serious misgivings about the sleepover, but at the same time couldn't wait for it.

Chapter 29

Jared's mixed emotions of the day spilled over to joy and relief when he met Will in front of the gym and heard the news. They'd made the team. Not only that, but all the shower brothers had made it. Coach Swopes had gone with chemistry and youth in his selections. Big Mike, Tom, and Kyle joined them as the seventh-grade members of the middle school basketball game. That meant of the fifteen spots on the team, over half were filled by seventh graders.

Jared's excitement at making the team caused him to put aside his worries about being targeted by an unknown bully. It felt as if he floated on air as he followed Will out to his bus. He couldn't believe it. He'd made the team, had Will as a friend, and was going to a sleepover, the first in his life, all on the same day. At any moment he expected to wake up and find it all a dream.

On the bus, Will picked seats near the front and sat on the inside, giving Jared room to stretch his legs in the aisle. It was Friday afternoon on a chilly November day, a little over a week before Thanksgiving break. It was a time to be rowdy and excited, but Will ignored the other kids who clamored on the bus after them. They all headed to the back, where they could be loud and obnoxious without drawing the wrath of the driver. Will and Jared were left alone in relative peace. After putting his backpack under his feet, Will turned to Jared with a serious look.

Jared immediately sobered, remembering that Will had wanted to talk.

"Hey, er, look, dude," Will said. "Do you really not remember what happened yesterday when you fell asleep?"

Jared took a deep swallow and coughed. "Uh, no," he said shaking his head. "I honestly have no clue." He peered toward Will, biting his lip nervously. Then he dropped his gaze. "Just tell me. Do you know who wrote on my back?"

"No way, man. That's creepy." Then he sighed. "I had something similar happen to me." As the bus pulled away from the school, Will started telling Jared about his experiences on Halloween and how Mr. Drydon acted a little fishy. "My dad called the school about any gas leaks and got nothing. He even got one of his army friends, who works for the police, to check Mr. Drydon's past."

Jared felt his breath quicken. "Uh, is there, uh, anything? Our principal isn't some sort of crazy criminal, is he?"

"Ha." Will shook his head. "I don't think so. My dad said the only thing about Mr. Drydon happened way back in his high school days. He went hunting with some friends and they ended up shooting a neighbor's dog, or something. Probably an accident."

Jared raised his eyebrows. "Man," he said at last. Then he told Will what Angie told him about John, how she felt somebody watching them.

Will shivered slightly. "Dude, I think we'd better keep watching each other's backs."

Jared felt a flush of pleasure rise up. "Yeah, and we'll keep an eye on John."

Will nodded and licked his lips. "The next stop is my house. Um, Jared? When we get there, don't tell my dad anything about what we talked about. Don't even mention going to the apartments tomorrow. Okay?"

Puzzled, but ready to do just about anything for Will, Jared nodded. "Sure, no problem."

Will's sleepover started with a flash.

As Jared hopped off the bus, he saw Will lived in a cozy two-story house with pale yellow siding sitting on a half-acre of land dotted with trees. A clump of towering trees grew directly in front of the house and were just starting to lose their colorful leaves.

"We can drop off our stuff and come back out," Will told him as they walked from the bus.

Jared coughed. He'd been caught staring up at the trees decked out in all their glory of deep reds and bright yellows. He and Kelly used to have fun chasing the falling leaves on days like this. It was something he hadn't done in years and had no idea why he thought of it now.

Hefting his sports bag, now carrying his overnight clothes and supplies, he bit his bottom lip. He did *not* want to say the wrong thing now.

"Yeah, uh, sure," he finally managed to say. Excitement filled him, but also fear. This weekend he would either cement a friendship with Will, or potentially destroy it for good. He did not want Will to think of him as some sort of loser.

As soon as Will opened the front door to lead Jared into the foyer, a bright light blinded his eyes.

"Hi, champ!" boomed a deep voice, aiming a cell phone at his face, just inside the door. "Nice picture. Now I have proof you need a haircut."

"Dad!" Will cried, blinking. "Really?" He ran a hand through the short brown hair on top his head, disheveled in the front. "What was that for?"

Startled by the blinding flash, Jared nearly jumped and he ended up stumbling into the house. Closing the door with his sports bag, he stood awkwardly behind Will.

"Huh?" Mr. Moore shrugged, sliding his cell phone into his pocket. "I was just trying to take a picture of the door and you barged right in." He looked over Will at Jared. "Well, don't just stand there. Introduce your friend. They still teach manners in school, right?"

Will sighed and turned to Jared. "Jared, this is my dad. He's a failed comedian, so don't laugh at any of his jokes. It only encourages him."

Mr. Moore smiled pleasantly and nudged Will to the side to shake Jared's hand, squeezing his hard. With a similar build to Will's, he had muscular arms and close-cropped hair. "Great to meet you, Jared. I hope my son warned you about our house. We have a cockroach infestation, all the food is gone, and I forgot to pay the power bill so expect the lights to go out sometime around 5:00."

"Ha, ha," Will said. "We're just dropping off our stuff and then going outside."

Mr. Moore ruffled Will's hair. "Well, bring him up to your room. Don't mind the cockroaches, Jared. Before you came along, they were Will's only friends."

Jared nodded clumsily. "Uh, yes, sir."

Will rolled his eyes. "Dad, one day you'll be funny."

"Yeah, and one day you'll be five feet, champ." He clapped Will on the back and then gave him a quick smack on the back of his pants. "Shoes off before going in the house, remember. When you both are ready, I'll have cookies and milk. There's baked ziti for dinner, so make sure you're both hungry." He winked. "And eat a lot, because you'll need the energy tomorrow."

Whistling merrily, he left the boys, heading back to the kitchen. Jared could smell fresh cookies baking, mingling with the scent of tomato sauce and cooked meat. His stomach rumbled.

"Come on," Will said, kicking off his sneakers. "We're sleeping on the floor in my room. My dad's letting us borrow his sleeping bags." He led the way up a flight of stairs directly in front of the foyer. "You can take the bed if you want. My room is kind of small," Will confessed.

Jared just shook his head. "No, this is, uh, great."

Will pointed out the bathroom, his little brother's room, which he advised never to enter unless he wanted his feet impaled by tiny Legos and metal cars, his parents' room, and his older sister's room. "She's in college right now. You'll meet her tonight," he told Jared, leading the way to his room in the back corner of the floor.

After dumping their bags, the boys went straight back down and soon were on the driveway shooting baskets.

"Why do you keep looking at the trees?" Will asked Jared, catching the taller boy gazing upwards again. A few leaves flew down, carried by a slight breeze.

Both boys wore light hoodies and pants. Jared had loose jeans while Will wore another pair of tight-fitting Adidas warm-ups.

Embarrassed, Jared shrugged. Then, feeling self-conscious, he explained how on windy fall days he and his sister used to have contests on who could catch the most leaves before they hit the ground.

"You have a sister?" Will asked.

"Yeah, she is, uh, in the sixth grade." Jared swallowed. "She, uh, well, she dances." He decided not to mention her school crush.

"That's cool. Here, it's your shot."

After a few warm-up shots, they played a game of horse, easily won by Will, and then 21. Using his height and long reach, Jared proved much more competitive. He had trouble with his dribble and had to rely on posting up, or throwing up wild shots. Will played him tough, but had no answer for Jared's height. Jared's best move was to miss a shot, grab the rebound, and score on a quick put-back. On defense, he limited Will to outside shooting. Will finally won the game on a nifty crossover that moved Jared out of the way and then putting in a reverse layup, just in front of Jared's outstretched hand.

Laughing, Will stumbled and dove in the grass behind the hoop. Jared leaned down with his hands on his knees panting. "Lucky," he gasped.

Will rolled on his back and sighed happily. He wiped sweat from his brow. "I wish you lived closer. Then we could do this all the time."

Jared grunted. He wished the same thing.

A sudden gust of wind sent the trees around them swaying and a swarm of leaves started to fall. One drifted down, landing on Will's stomach.

"Got it," Will cried, snatching the leaf. "I got one point."

"Huh?" Jared asked.

Will sat up suddenly. "Hey, let's play your leaf game." He reached back and stuffed the leaf in his hood. "Every leaf you catch goes in your hood. Whoever has the most gets to pick out what stupid thing we do next."

Jared couldn't help but grin. "Okay. If you say so …"

The two boys spent the next several minutes running around Will's yard, chasing falling leaves. Catching a twirling, spinning leaf was not as easy as it looked.

Several times they were left in frustration or laughter as they spun in circles, sometimes falling in their attempts. With a strong breeze and plenty of trees, there was an abundance of opportunities.

The game finally ended when Will, exasperated at missing another leaf, reached down and picked up a handful of leaves. Running down the unsuspecting Jared from behind, he stuffed the leaves down his back. "Slam dunk!" he yelled.

"Hey!" Jared cried, arching his back and going to his knees. "What was that for?"

"You win," said Will, laughing. "Let's do something else."

Jared tore off his hoodie and spent the next several minutes emptying leaves and dirt from his shirt. "What about showing me some moves with dribbling," he suggested.

Will's eyes gleamed. "You're on, dude."

Will rarely had an audience for his drills and he made sure he showed everything he knew to Jared. He dribbled two balls at once, going through his legs and behind his back, and then put on a nifty display of crossovers, feints, and fakes.

Jared watched and tried, but was happy just to put a single ball through his legs and complete one crossover without losing control.

Jimmy's bus pulled up in front of the house as the two boys were in front of the hoop, dribbling through a series of cones set up by Will.

Seeing Jared, Jimmy ran up and stopped. Squinting at him, his eyes suddenly widened. "I've seen you before! You were the trash man!"

Picking up his dribble, Jared coughed embarrassedly and looked at the small boy. "Uh, yeah," he mumbled. "Hey."

Will only lifted his eyebrows. "Um, this is my brother Jimmy. He's just about to say goodbye and go inside."

"No I'm not," Jimmy said. "I want to play too."

"Go inside right now and setup the Xbox," Will told him. "Do it right now and you can play with us in a minute."

Jimmy stared at his older brother suspiciously. "Promise?" he asked.

"Either that," Will told him, holding the basketball like a baseball, "or we'll play dodgeball. Us two against you."

Jimmy frowned. "I'll poop on you if you hit me!" he said. Then he ran to the front door. "I get to play first!" he hollered back.

Will grimaced. "Sorry," he said. "Jimmy isn't too bad ... when he's sleeping."

Jared only shrugged. "You should meet my brothers." Playing 21 and then the leaf game had released all his tension. Seeing Will go after fluttering leaves and actually enjoying it had brought down most of Jared's walls. He suddenly felt relaxed and free. That was why he really loved sports so much. You got to know a lot about a person when playing them head-to-head in games. "Should we keep going?"

"Nah, we'd better go in. Jimmy will never forgive me if we don't. He might poop on me."

Jared had never played video games before. He also had never spent an evening with a family like Will's. As soon as they'd entered the house, Jimmy had run from the TV room and threw himself at his brother's chest, nearly knocking him down.

"Hey, little guy," Will cried, smacking his brother's bottom after he caught him. "Don't you have a room to lock yourself in?"

Jimmy only squeezed his brother around the neck and held on tight. "But I want to be with you."

Will rolled his eyes at Jared. "Then let's play Xbox. Just remember. No pooping."

Jimmy responded by making a disgusting noise with his mouth against his brother's shoulder.

Chapter 30

Shortly after, using his dad's cell phone, Will called up Nick to get him to join them online, but the big fellow said he couldn't because of dog duties. *"Sorry, man,"* he told Will. *"I hope you're not bored out of your mind with Jared."*

Will just held up his cell phone towards the TV where Jimmy was trying to climb up Jared's legs to reach his head. Laughing like a hyena on helium, he had a hand on Jared's right sleeve and a foot on his knee.

"Okay, I give up!" Jared called. "I give up!"

"Then let me climb on you!" Jimmy told him.

Will sighed. "Next time I have a sleepover, Jimmy is sleeping at your place. He and your dog would get along great."

"Man, I'd never torture Alfie like that. Good luck, dude."

After hanging up, Will tried playing an NBA basketball game on the Xbox, but quickly realized Jared was hopeless. Once he realized that Jared had never used a game console before, he chose Mario Kart, a multiplayer racing game for a Wii console. "You just press a few buttons and move your hands to move. It's easy," Will told him.

It was never easy when Jimmy, also playing, picked inopportune times to jump on him, or attack his brother, which usually happened whenever he started losing.

Mr. Moore came to the rescue, coming from the kitchen to announce dinnertime. Angel arrived just as the ziti was brought to the table. The evening passed with a delicious dinner followed by watching *Space Jam* while eating cookies and milk. Afterwards Mr. Moore carried Jimmy up for a bath, leaving the boys with Angel.

"So," Angel asked. "Did you guys make the team?"

Jared had forgotten all about the basketball team. It had been a fun, exhilarating day. Now as he relaxed on Will's couch, it started to sink in. He'd made the middle school basketball team … and had made a friend.

Will just looked at his sister. "What do you think?"

"A lot of things, little bro," Angel responded. "But I confess, not much about basketball."

Just then she was interrupted by Mr. Moore calling from upstairs. "Angel, I could use your help up here! Is your mom back yet?" His voice sounded a little strained.

"No, not yet, Dad!" Angel yelled up. She got up and offered an apologetic grin to Jared. "I'd better go up. You boys don't do anything stupid like burn the place down." She flicked Will's hair as she moved from the couch.

"Ha," Will said. "Don't forget your promise to keep Jimmy away."

"Sure," Angel said cheerfully. "And don't forget you have to be my slave next week. See you later, Jared."

Will took the TV controller and turned on a basketball game, showing Jared the power of cable. Jared couldn't remember the last time he got to see a sporting event on a Friday night.

When he said so out loud, Will stared at him in horror. "You're not joking, are you?" he asked when Jared explained his home situation. "No cable, no internet, *and* no video games? How do you survive?"

Jared grinned wryly. "I play stupid games like catching leaves. But mostly I read."

"Dude," Will said, staring at Jared in almost reverence, "and I thought I had it rough."

Just then Mr. Moore's raised voice carried from overhead. "I can't do it all, Angel! Your mom should be back now!"

"What am I supposed to do about that?" Angel's voice snapped back.

"I can't take this!" barked Mr. Moore.

"Dad!" cried Angel. "Don't forget Jared's here."

Their voices dropped after that, but Will stared down at the rug under the sofa. He didn't say anything, but did turn up the volume of the game.

A few minutes later, Mr. Moore came down with his shirt soaking wet in the front. "Hey, champ," he said. "The bathroom is open if you or Jared need showers." He had a smile, but his voice came out tight. A wild gleam had entered his eyes.

Will licked his upper lip and nodded. "Sure, Dad." He looked at Jared. "Let's go up to my room."

Jared said nothing as he followed Will. He could tell Will felt embarrassed, but didn't know what to say. All of a sudden he reverted back to the quiet, awkward kid who didn't know how to make friends.

As they went up, they heard Angel reading Jimmy a story from a room down the hall. Will went straight to his room, shutting the door firmly as soon as Jared followed him in.

"So, that's my family," he muttered, flipping on his light and falling back on his bed. "Now you know why I like sports so much. It keeps me busy."

Jared stared at all the posters in the room and settled on the Splash Brothers above Will's head. He knew what his mother would say. To make a friend, you had to be a friend. This was the first time, he realized, that he'd ever seen Will actually needing a friend. He'd always thought Will had to have the perfect life, with no problems. The realization was mind numbing.

"I understand," he heard himself say. "I think your family is really nice."

"Ha." Will told him. "You haven't heard anything yet." He sat up and pulled his feet up onto his bed. Hugging his legs, he rested his chin on his knees, suddenly looking very young and very lonely. "My mom and dad don't always get along. You might hear some shouting when she gets back." He sighed. "My dad was in the army and ... and it hasn't been easy for him since he got out."

Jared nodded. "I have an uncle who was in the navy. He goes crazy when he's in one spot for too long." He reddened and quickly coughed. "But I don't think your dad is crazy, or anything."

Will rolled to his side and flipped to his stomach. Neither boy spoke for a while. Then he turned his head to Jared and gave a sheepish smile. "Sorry, man. You probably regret coming here."

"No, not at all," Jared said, honestly. "It's been good. Really. I, uh, think every family has problems."

"Ha." Will rolled to his side and sat at the edge of the bed. A tiny room, there was just enough space on the floor for two sleeping bags, so close they were almost touching. "Sure you don't want the bed?" he asked.

"The floor is fine," Jared told him. "Really."

"In that case you can have first shower." He managed a wider grin. "We don't have any herbal shampoo, but there're towels already in there. I promise."

Later, dressed in sweatpants and a T-shirt, his hair still damp, Jared brushed his teeth at the sink with Will. The slighter boy wore basketball pajama pants and a sleeveless T-shirt. He'd just finished his shower and his hair still dripped water. Jared couldn't tell, but Will's eyes may have been leaking a bit too. Down below, the muffled voices of angry parents were clearly heard. Mrs. Moore had returned.

Neither boy spoke.

Will shut off the light as soon as Jared slipped into his sleeping bag. Crawling over his bed, he searched for his own sleeping bag and ended up stepping on Jared's face.

"Er, sorry," he mumbled.

"It's all right," Jared said. "Really."

Will only sighed as he lay down. The arguing, though too faint to make out, continued below them.

"My dad might wake us up early," he muttered. "Then if you want he can drive you home. I guess you don't want to go to the apartments tomorrow."

Jared stirred in his sleeping bag. He'd never heard Will sound so down before. Jared had always thought *he* was the one who needed a friend to ease his pain. It never occurred to him that Will also had pain. He knew he couldn't let Will down.

"Hey," he said. "I get sad a lot. Sometimes I even get mad. But you know what? I always feel better after playing sports. We have to go to the apartments tomorrow." He took a breath. He'd never opened up like this before, but lying down, surrounded in darkness, knowing he had somebody listening to him made it easy … it felt good to unburden himself. "When I said I understood, I meant it."

Jared started talking about his home. "I don't see my dad very much. He's always busy working. And my mom is always busy with my sisters. I, uh, actually have two, but one is still a baby. They're both really busy, but I do know ... well, I know they love me. But then I have my two brothers."

Jared's voice rose as he spoke about George and Jack. "I don't understand them at all. I mean, sometimes they act like the biggest jerks in the world, but I'm always the jerk if I say anything about it. I mean, they eat all the food and never save me any, they leave all their dishes in the sink so I have to clean up after them, and, well, I'm sick of it! They only like me if I do what they want, but I don't really think they care about me. All they talk about is cars and girls and how great they are." He paused for a moment. "What really makes me mad, though, is that I don't think they care about all the work my mom and dad do for us. I mean, I know they care, but they just don't show it."

Jared went quiet. He wondered if Will had gone to sleep, or was biting down laughter. In any case, he'd said his piece and had felt good about doing so. He'd been holding that in for a long time. "Well, in any case, I definitely think we need to play basketball tomorrow."

"Jared?" Will's voice said softly. "Thanks, man. I always wanted an older brother ... but not yours."

Jared smiled. "Yeah."

The two boys talked long into the night, mostly about their favorite sports and which teams they liked in each sport. Finally, they both drifted off to sleep.

Hours ticked by. At the crack of dawn, Mr. Moore cracked open his oldest son's room and peeked in. He saw the bed with wrinkled covers, but empty. In the dull light drifting through the windows he made out two forms lying in sleeping bags, both snoring softly.

"Hey, champ," he whispered. "Will, you awake? It's just about sunrise. You boys up for some running?" He ran a hand through his cropped hair. "Will?"

One of the forms, closest to the door, rolled over in his sleep and Mr. Moore saw a head of dark curls.

The other form, his son, didn't move. "Well," Mr. Moore said. "I'll be downstairs making coffee if you change your mind." He gently shut the door and quietly crept away.

Will sat up in his sleeping bag and stared at the door, his face a blank mask. Jared continued to snore, but Will felt wide awake.

His dad had ruined the sleepover. He didn't deserve a second chance.

Will tried to fall back asleep, but found it hopeless. He sat up and rubbed his eyes. A soft tapping on the door caused him to quickly lie back down and feign sleep. He heard Angel's soft voice call his name.

"You awake, little bro?"

Grumbling, Will got up, disentangled from his sleeping bag, and crawled up onto his bed to get around Jared and reach the door.

"What do you want?" he muttered, cracking the door open.

Angel knelt on the other side and was nearly eye level.

"Well, for one, for you to smile and say good morning," Angel told him. She sighed when Will only looked at her. "Look, kid. I'm sorry about last night. Dad gets worried easily, and when he gets worried he doesn't handle it well. It's not your fault. Now he's really sorry about it."

"So?"

"So it would mean a lot to him if you went down and ran with him. You know, like two dudes sweating it out."

Will licked his lips. "Yeah, right."

"I'm serious, Will. He wants to say he's sorry, but doesn't know how. Exercising with you is his way of apologizing. But it takes two people to forgive. You have to let him." She looked past him at Jared. "You have a good friend, Will." She looked down, guiltily. "I, um, sort of went by your room last night to check on you guys … I heard a lot of what he said."

Will stared at his sister. "What?" he cried. "You—"

Angel quickly clamped her hand over his mouth. "Shh!" she hissed. "I didn't mean to, it just happened. But really, Will, you should make sure he's still your friend after today. End the day on a good note."

Jared sat up, groaning. "Uh, I guess we're even," he croaked sheepishly. "I've, uh, been awake." He blinked at the siblings guiltily. "Sorry."

Angel ran her hand up from Will's mouth into his unruly hair, giving it a tug. "Never trust boys," she said.

"Ha," Will said. "Never trust big sisters. Even when they're right."

"I knew you'd do the right thing, little bro." Angel clapped him on the shoulder and stood back up. "Now," she yawned, "I'm going to my room to get some beauty sleep."

"You need it," Will said, grinning.

Angel stuck out her tongue over her shoulder as she left.

Chapter 31

When Mr. Moore saw Will come into the kitchen moments later, he nearly spilled his coffee.

"What's wrong, Will?" he asked, his voice hopeful and frightened all at once. "Is your friend okay?"

"He's in the bathroom," Will said, rubbing his hair sheepishly. "I, uh, we were wondering if you're still running this morning."

"Uh, yeah, of course." Mr. Moore put down his coffee mug and straightened up. He'd been leaning against the counter looking as downcast as the cloudy morning outside the window. Now his eyes sparked with enthusiasm. "Only there's one problem, champ."

Will gave him a look. "What's that, Dad?"

"You can't go running in pajamas and your sticklike arms. It's kind of cold out there so find a sweater at least."

"Ha, ha. For Christmas I'm getting you a joke book."

"Fine, son. It'll look good under the tree next to your booster seat."

Will cracked a smile and turned to go.

Mr. Moore cleared his throat, stopping him. "Will, before you go upstairs, come here."

Will went to his dad and got wrapped in a big hug that lifted him off the kitchen floor.

"I will always love you, Will. I'm sorry about last night … I, well, your old man still has growing up to do."

"Not as much as me," Will said when his bare feet touched the floor again.

"You'll get there, champ," Mr. Moore assured him, giving a quick smack to his thigh. "Just don't be in a hurry. Being a grown-up isn't all that exciting."

Jared breathed in the cool brisk air and shivered. He and Will both wore long-sleeved T-shirts and shorts. Will's shorts went past his knees and he had long socks pulled up, covering his legs entirely in black. Jared's shorts ended right above the knees and his socks ended at his ankles. His legs paid the price.

"H-how cold is it?" he wondered.

"Don't worry," Will assured him. He blew in his hands. "My dad likes to run faster when it's cold. It'll warm us right up."

"Can't wait," Jared muttered.

The sun had yet to break through the clouds, but Mr. Moore had promised them no rain that day. That was because, Jared thought, it would snow.

They now stood under the basketball hoop waiting for Will's dad while trying to loosen up. After a few stretches both boys felt too cold to move much more.

Finally, Mr. Moore called from the front door and met them carrying two white winter hats. "For you, kids," he said, tossing them. "You'll be seen by cars better and they'll keep your ears from falling off." He waited for the boys to put on the hats and then smacked his hands together and ran toward the road. "Okay, let's go, chumps! It's six in the morning! We're late!"

"Great," Jared muttered, breaking into a trot. The hat made his scalp itch, but he did appreciate the warmth.

"Don't worry," Will told him. "If we're late my dad runs faster, so if you don't like this, no problem. We'll be done quicker."

"Not helping," Jared told him. "Now I'm worried. How often do you do this?"

"Mondays, Wednesdays, and Saturdays. Sometimes we do pushups and stuff."

"Less chattering back there, chumps! Pick up the pace; you're falling behind!"

"If I catch you, Dad, I'm kicking you in the behind!" Will called.

"Just enjoy the view, champ!" Mr. Moore hollered back. "If you're not careful, you might just see a moon today."

Will groaned and made no comment back.

Jared couldn't imagine doing this with his own dad, or even his brothers. It actually felt good. Shoulder to shoulder with Will, he followed Mr. Moore up the street on the chilly November morning. In the lawns on either side, a thin mist covered the dewy grass, littered with brightly colored leaves. A few song birds, not yet gone for the winter, lit up the air with their chattering.

They were just reaching a slow-rising hill, when an old faded red pickup appeared over the top driving their way.

"To the side, boys," Mr. Moore called, slowing his pace. "Off the road."

Will and Jared both left the road and jogged onto the grass in front of a one-story brick house. The pickup did not slow and it did not move over.

Mr. Moore frowned. "What the …" All at once, he turned toward Will and Jared, his face set hard. "Down!" he roared. "Duck and cover!"

Jared had barely noticed the pickup, but now his eyes went wide. The front grill seemed to be heading straight at them. Panicking, he veered away and then saw Mr. Moore diving at him.

Mr. Moore tackled Jared and Will together, throwing them onto the grass and landing on top of them.

The pickup spat dirt and gravel as it roared past, never slowing. Jared could almost feel the paint scraping his shoes.

Silence then descended.

After a moment, Mr. Moore got to his knees and sighed heavily. "You boys okay?" he asked.

Will waited for Jared to get up first and then rolled slowly to his side.

"I'm … I'm okay," Jared said, still shaken.

"What was wrong with that driver?" Will groaned.

"I would hope he'd have seen us," Mr. Moore said grimly. He looked at the boys a little sheepish. "Sorry about that, boys. For a second I thought I saw the driver with a rifle." He shook his head. "My army days kicked in."

Jared felt himself grow cold. "W-wait," he said. "D-did you see the license plate?"

"It was covered in mud," Mr. Moore said darkly, sounding worried again. "It could be one of our rowdy neighbors, the Pherrins. I was warned about them."

"Who are they?" Will asked. "I never heard of them."

Mr. Moore grunted. "Three brothers who moved here from way out in the woods. Apparently they have crazy parents who believe all civilization is evil and never taught their boys right from wrong. They live on the end of the street and like to go hunting in pickups … where it's not legal. I've been told their idea of hunting is running into deer with their trucks."

He wiped his mouth and narrowed his eyes. "Whoever it is, they have to come back eventually. There's a dead end at the end of the street. Let's get on home, boys. I'll keep an eye out for that pickup. If we see it coming back, we head for the trees. Got it?"

Jared and Will exchanged glances. Both of them thought of the pickup Angie had told Jared about. They both wondered if it had been a red Dodge.

When they arrived back at Will's house without further incident, they were greeted with the smell of cooking pancakes. Mrs. Moore met them at the door, wearing an apron and wide smile. Jared had yet to meet her and was shocked at how young she looked. He could definitely see the similarities between her and Will.

"Sorry I missed you last night," she said, shaking his hand. "Angel told me we had a nice visitor and that I needed to make sure you felt welcomed to come back again." She never blinked or batted an eyelash about the night before. It was as if the arguing had never taken place. "Now you two boys go wash your hands and sit down. I understand you'll be playing basketball later, so don't worry about showering. This won't be the first time I had sweaty boys sitting at the breakfast table."

After a giant breakfast of pancakes and eggs, Jared and Will spent the morning entertaining Jimmy with the Wii until a college football preview started. Then, just before the first kickoff, Mr. Moore offered to drop them off at the middle school. "I tried to find that pickup," he told them as they climbed in the back of his Corolla, "but it either snuck past or it's parked out behind somebody's house. You guys better be careful at the middle school. I'll give you my cell, Will. Call your mom or sister when you need to be picked up."

Shady Farms Apartments were constructed in a big open space just behind a main highway and on a stretch of road with more gas stations and corner shops than trees. It was a twenty-minute walk from the middle school after cutting through Nick's neighborhood.

Jared and Will spent the walk talking about all the strange things that had happened. The crazy pickup that had almost run them down just added to the puzzle. Was it an inattentive driver, or something more sinister? And if it was, how did the pickup know where they would be at that time? Neither boy could come up with a good explanation. It was like they had pieces from three different puzzles and were trying to put them all together. Nothing seemed to fit or appeared remotely related. Items were being stolen from gym lockers. A strange sleeping gas seemed to be getting loose in the school. Mr. Drydon hung out with mysterious characters and threatened PE teachers. Angie felt like somebody was stalking her and John.

It was all too much and Will groaned in frustration when Jared listed all the mysteries. "That's not to mention Brad and his bunch bullying John because of last year's coach," Jared said. He didn't dare mention his suspicions about Ryan. Those he would keep secret until he found proof.

"I wish we could ask somebody," Will said. "You know, find somebody who could tell us something."

Jared grunted and shrugged. Suddenly he brightened. "I know somebody," he said, excitedly.

"Yeah?" Will said. "Who?"

"Wait until Monday and you'll see," Jared said. He bit his lower lip. "Actually, I'll have to figure something out first."

A group of kids around their age already occupied a court when Jared and Will reached the apartments. From the sidewalk in front of the fence they saw Big Mike and several kids from their school shooting at a basket, mixed with several older teens from high school. All of them wore tough-looking faces and didn't seem ready to welcome company. Most wore baggy shorts and sweaters. Big Mike stood out in wide gray sweatpants and a matching hoodie with its sleeves cut off. His thick muscular arms grabbed a rebound as Will led the way around the fence to the entrance.

Watching Big Mike go up and snatch the ball, Jared gulped and started having second thoughts. Big Mike's face looked ferocious, his nose curled up in a snarl and his eyes narrowed with determination. Even just shooting around was a competitive match with these guys.

"Are you sure about this?" he muttered to Will, and to himself.

Will licked his lips and shrugged. "No, but let's do it."

They both had the same clothes on for the run, with Will sliding his warm-up pants over his shorts. Will pulled off his white hat as he passed through the fence onto the green-topped court. Jared did the same and copied Will, tossing the hat to the side.

"Yo, yo, hold up, man!" called a voice from the court. "Look what we have here?" Jared recognized the tall, long-necked kid with the gold teeth. Scratching the side of his thick curls, the boy looked over at Big Mike. "Do my eyes deceive me, or do we got some of your teammates here, man? What, they lost or something?"

Big Mike fired up a long three that hit the side of the rim. Turning, he saw Will and Jared and gave them a look of absolute disgust.

"What are you pasties doing here," he demanded loudly.

Will kept his face neutral as he stood at the edge of the court. "I thought we could play some ball," he said.

"Not here," Big Mike said. "Go play at the school!"

Will didn't budge.

"Ah, let them play," the tall boy said, grinning, showing off his gold teeth. "They make ten players, and besides, man. If they're going to play with you, they're going to need the practice. Let's see what the fresh meat got."

"They ain't playing with me," Big Mike growled, turning his back on Will and going to get another rebound.

The other guys stared at Jared and Will with unfriendly looks, but the tall boy just waved a hand at them, still grinning. Going up to Will, he put out his hand for a high five. "Hey, dudes. I'm Mario. Welcome to Shady basketball. You two ready to play?"

True to his word, Big Mike made sure to be on the opposite team from Jared and Will. Instead of shooting for teams, he and Mario picked the sides. Jared and Will were Mario's last picks. Big Mike never even looked at them.

"We play to twenty, doing ones and twos," Mario said cheerfully as they moved into positions on the court. "Inside the line is one point, outside the line is two points. Call your own fouls, but no crying. It's full court, so pick a man and stick with him. I got Bigmouth Mike."

"Shut up, Mario," Big Mike muttered, walking the ball to midcourt. His team would get the ball first.

On the first possession, he took the ball right at Will. His teammate guarded by Will set a pick on Mario, leaving Big Mike facing down the smaller, slimmer boy.

Jared stood under the basket next to a large kid a couple of years older with a scar on his left cheek. He bumped Jared with his large belly and grin wickedly. Jared tried his best to ignore him.

"You got him, small dude," Mario said to Will, sounding a little amused. "Just keep him in front of you, man."

Big Mike just grunted as he dribbled, facing Will. After briefly hesitating, he lowered his shoulder, taking Will to the hole. Will went with him, but when he tried to go up for a block, he took a shoulder to the chest. Big Mike flashed by and scored an easy layup as Will crashed down to the seat of his pants, skidding on the paved court. Jared had started to block the basket, but Big Mike had been too fast. Jared stood helplessly as Big Mike scored in front of him. Going over to Will, he stuck out a hand to help him up.

"You okay?" Jared asked him.

Nodding, Will took the hand, but didn't say anything. Standing, he winced and rubbed his landing spot.

A lot of the other boys laughed, even some on their own team.

"Roadkill!" cried one of the kid's on Big Mike's team.

Big Mike scowled. "Shut up, Lou. You guard roadkill and see what happens."

Mario retrieved the ball and now tossed it to Will. "It's in your court, dude," he said, winking.

Lou, a cocky, scrawny kid wearing wide blue shorts and a faded red tank top, swaggered forward. "Any time of any day of any week, man. Come on, skinny boy. Let's see what you got!" Waiting at center court, he stood a good three inches taller than Will.

Jared thought about a pick, but saw Will flick his eyes toward the opposing basket, waving him away. Jared trotted down to the other end of the court, very mindful that this could end very badly.

Will brought the ball up at a jog, dribbling high. Then, just as he reached center court, he suddenly went low and faked right before crossing left.

Lou, caught by surprise, hesitated and then moved his feet left, only to see Will cross back to the right in a blur. He tried to match the smaller boy's move, but ended up tripping over his own feet and falling.

Will blew by him, driving into the paint. The large, round boy quickly went to meet him, throwing his weight forward and extending his right arm up. Seeing him coming, Will went toward the basket, but then laid a bounce pass right under the large boy's arm, straight to Jared. Jared almost didn't catch it. He'd been caught watching the play. Thankfully his reflexes kicked in and he was able to snatch the ball and put it up in the basket before anybody else could react.

"Ohhh, man!" Mario shouted. "Game on, dude!"

Lou got up sheepishly. "All right," he said. "Little dude got some moves … I see that that now."

It became a back and forth, hard-fought game. Big Mike kept his head down and body moving. When his team had the ball, he ran the offense. Mario had the height advantage, but Big Mike proved quicker and stronger. After Big Mike scored a layup and a short runner, Mario started playing off him more, protecting the basket, forcing Big Mike to take a contested outside shot or pass.

Jared's man, the large boy, proved to have deceptively quick moves. When Big Mike passed him the ball the first time, he acted slow and cumbersome. But when Jared moved to guard him from the basket, the large kid suddenly spun around him in a blink and scored an easy layup.

"Just watch the baseline," Will told him, smacking Jared's back as the taller boy shook his head. Will grinned. "We got this, big guy."

Biting his bottom lip, Jared nodded and ran up to be on offense. Once he scored his first basket, he'd stopped worrying about being at Shady Apartments playing with tough-looking guys. He quickly discovered he was just playing basketball with kids who loved the game. And it was fun.

Chapter 32

Will played point guard for his team and proved just as effective as Big Mike. Quicker and faster than Lou, he constantly beat him off the dribble. The only problem, Lou's teammates knew this and were quick to provide help, swarming the smaller boy. He often had to pass out to Mario, but still kept his eyes out for Jared. Jared learned to read Will's moves and tried to set himself up in a good passing lane.

The problem came once he got the ball. Unless Will made a super pass that caught everyone napping and Jared had an easy layup, he proved hopeless with the ball. The large kid, named Kashawn, bumped Jared away from the basket, cut off his shot with his long arms, and proved to be a mountain when it came to pushing back. Lowering his backside, Jared tried to fight for position, but couldn't budge Kashawn an inch.

After twenty minutes, Big Mike's team led by three points and needed only four more for the win.

Will brought up the ball and surveyed the court. His eyes found Jared's and then moved on.

Jared swallowed and moved out toward the foul line. The two had formed a connection. Whenever Will made eye contact like that it meant he was looking to pass his way.

Sure enough, Will dribbled right, drawing out Lou, and then suddenly whipped a pass to Jared. He immediately sprinted to the top of the three-point line. "Big guy, pass!"

Jared caught the ball and immediately bounced it to the spot Will ran to. Left wide open, Will took the long shot and drained it.

"Woowee!" Mario shouted. "The pasties have got game!"

The teams continued battling on, and in minutes it was tied 19 to 19.

"You have to win by two!" Mario called. "Let's do this, dudes! Lockdown defense!"

Big Mike dribbled at him, his face a mask of disdain. At the same time, Jared could see his eyes bright with excitement. Big Mike, he knew, was enjoying the game just as much as everyone else. He just wasn't showing it. As he reached the three line, he suddenly pulled up, going for a shot. Mario jumped to contest it, but at the last second Big Mike switched the shot to a pass, sending it down to Kashawn.

Jared reacted instinctively, sticking out his hand, knocking the ball away. He immediately chased after it, catching it at a run and found himself leading the break to the other basket.

"Stop him!" Lou cried. "Big dude can't make a layup!"

Jared actually agreed with him. He was going way too fast and his dribble was a little wild. He had to keep his eye on the ball and didn't even see the rim.

"Over here, Jared!" he heard Will call to his right.

Past the foul line, Jared jumped and turned toward the voice, throwing the ball out. Big Mike had caught up to him and also jumped for the block. He crashed into Jared's back.

Jared found himself flying forward about to face-plant into the court.

Strong arms suddenly caught him by the waist, breaking his fall. He ended up stumbling to his knees as he landed with Big Mike falling on top of him before rolling off.

Meanwhile, Will calmly took the ball and nailed a long shot for the two points.

"Game over!" Mario yelled. "We win with the dagger from small dude!"

As Mario and his other teammates mobbed Will, Jared let out a deep sigh of relief. He'd nearly been splattered on the court. "Th-thanks," he said to Big Mike as he got up.

Big Mike sat with his knees up, arms resting on top, and just shook his head. "Shut up," he muttered.

After the game, most of the kids left and adults started coming on the court to start a game. A few of them stared at Will and Jared with less than friendly faces.

"You dudes better leave soon," Mario told Jared and Will.

They were shooting around with the remaining members of the game, including Lou and Kashawn. Big Mike sat under the basket against the fence, still glowering.

Mario nodded at the newcomers approaching. "Next bunch isn't so friendly as us."

"Sure," Will said. "Can we come back?"

Mario grinned and shrugged. "Ask your teammate Bigmouth Mike."

Big Mike glared up at Mario. "Shut up."

"If you do come back," Kashawn said, looking at Jared, "you'd best learn some defense. And some moves, man. You got the height, but you lack game."

Jared nodded and ducked his head. He'd scored three easy layups from great passes and had pulled down some rebounds, but that was it. "I'll try," he said.

"Try nothing," Kashawn told him. "You better do."

"Shut up, Kashawn," Big Mike suddenly said. "He can take you."

Kashawn laughed. He had the ball and fired up a shot, hitting nothing but net. "Since when?"

Big Mike growled and stood up on his feet, moving like a cat. "Come here," he said, barely looking at Jared.

"Uh-oh," Mario said. "Here it comes."

"Ignore them," Big Mike growled. He positioned Jared on the post and proceeded to teach him different post up moves, including the spin move Kashawn had used. He then showed him how to block the baseline and steer the ball back to the inside where help could come. "Find out what your guy does best," Big Mike told him, "and then take it away. Make him uncomfortable. Make him hate playing you. Then you got him."

The other boys watched the lessons in silence, some of them nodding.

"Big Mike," Kashawn said to Will, "is the best coach out there, man. He taught me everything I know. Too bad he talks too much."

"Yeah," Lou added. He nudged Will's shoulder. "But I think I still got things to learn, man. You're a bad small dude with the rock."

"Shut up," Big Mike growled at them. He shoved the ball into Jared's stomach and pushed him under the basket. "Now show a hook shot." He put a hand on Jared's backside, playing defense, guiding him away from the basket. "If you can't do nothing else, just turn and throw up the shot over your head, man. Nobody will be able to block it."

Jared practiced a few hook shots, finally making one.

"Hey, yo!" shouted a man wearing an old shirt wrapped around his head from the other side of the court. "We playing, or not!"

"That's your cue to leave," Mario said, his face turning serious. "Games can get rough out here. A lot of guys come from the outside and they try to be tough."

Big Mike grunted. "You two pasties get out of here."

Will and Jared gave no argument, especially when they saw both their hats had vanished. The guy with the shirt wrapped around his head had a bulky hoodie with a bulging pocket in front.

After exchanging fist bumps and high fives with all the kids but Big Mike, who merely grunted toward them, Jared and Will quickly left the courts for the sidewalk.

Will had wisely left his dad's cell phone at Nick's house on the way there, so they had to call for a ride from there.

Just as they left Shady Farms, they heard footsteps pounding the sidewalk behind them.

"Yo, pasties!" called a voice. "Wait up!"

Jared and Will relaxed when turning to see Mario racing up to them. "Let me walk with you dudes for a bit. You know, just to make sure you make it out okay." He grinned as he slowed to a walk. "Now that you know our secret."

Will raised his eyebrows. "Secret?" he asked as Mario caught up to them.

Mario waved his hand behind him. "Yeah, the dump we live in. Now you know why Big Mike and us boys play ball like we do, man." His humor grew dim as he ducked his head and started walking with the two light-skinned boys.

"Let me tell you something, man." Mario threw an arm around each of their shoulders and ducked his head. He spoke without making eye contact, but sounded deadly serious. "For you guys it's just a game, man. For us, it's life. Big Mike? The only chance he got out of this mess is through playing ball. Man, I tell you. He's going to be the best that ever played, and the rest of us

… we're going to rise with him. We play to make him play harder. It's all we got. Man, it's ball or nothing in these parts."

Mario suddenly clapped the boys on their backs and dropped his hands to his side. They were away from the apartments and nearing the turnoff back to Nick's neighborhood. "I just wanted to let you pasties know, just in case you ever come back. Don't expect easy games here, man." He grinned and winked.

"There, now you boys are in the safe zone. See ya!" Smacking their backs one final time, Mario turned back to his apartments and the life of ball. "Come again and we'll kick your pasty tails!"

"Uh, thanks," Jared said to him.

"Yeah, and we'll be back," Will called to him.

Mario looked back a final time and flashed a grin, his gold teeth glinting in the sun. "I count on it, pasties!"

Will and Jared finished their walk to Nick's house in high spirits, all their troubles pushed aside for the moment. Basketball suddenly meant something more. For Will, he'd found a place where he could play the way he wanted, where passion and skill ruled the court. And for Jared, he'd not only found friendship, but had also discovered a genuine love for basketball. For the first time he felt accepted on the court. Yes, Mario was right. Basketball was more than just a game.

Nick had told them he would call the police if they weren't back by dark, so was surprised when they returned to his house with flushed and excited faces. He met them on the front porch of his three-story house with a medium-sized but compact dog tugging on its leash.

"You guys seriously played with Big Mike and his group?" he kept asking while pulling back his overly excited dog. "Really? He let you shrimps play?"

Alfie, though only a puppy, weighed around forty pounds and kept trying to jump on Jared to lick his face. A brown and white mutt, he somehow decided Jared should be his best friend.

Will took a seat on the top step and leaned on the railing, while Jared stood next to him, eyeing the excited dog uneasily.

"I told you," Will told Nick, shrugging as if no big deal. "They don't play hangout basketball there. It was cool."

Nick frowned and tugged on the leash. "Yeah, man, you won't catch me over there. Hey, you mutt! Alfie, stay back! Leave Jared alone!"

Will shook his head, watching Jared jump back from Alfie's tongue.

"Watch your step," Nick warned. "He pooped somewhere at the bottom of the steps and I haven't cleaned it up yet."

Will lifted his eyebrows. "Maybe my little brother is part dog. That would explain a lot."

Jared kept on the steps and looked a little sick.

The three spent the rest of the afternoon playing chase with Alfie, running around Nick's backyard. Jared finally returned to his house with the sun setting and his body totally exhausted but also totally happy.

For the first time in a long time he knew what it felt like to have friends who cared about him. Will and Nick were like two new brothers. He felt a pang of sadness when Will's father finally came to pick them up. Suddenly, he couldn't wait for school to start.

During homeroom that Monday all the boy basketball team members were called down to the gym. Coach Swopes met them at center court with a bulky cardboard box in front of him.

"Come on, gentlemen," he said, waving his hands as the team started trickling in. Jared entered from the main entrance and walked over to where Will and Nick were coming in from the side. Ben and Ryan followed close behind. Will and Nick both gave a brief wave to him, but Ryan looked away and Ben stared at the floor.

"This is a tradition I have with the track team," the old coach said. Reaching down into the box, he pulled out a black basketball jersey with a red collar and the letters WMS outlined in red on the front. Below the letters was an outlined number 1.

"Uniforms, man!" Nick said, shaking off any tiredness he'd brought with him. "Awesome!"

Coach Swopes grinned. "I want you boys to wear your jerseys today, let the school know about you and get them excited. Our first game is in three weeks. Practice starts today, but until then, celebrate a little. Here, Brad." He threw the jersey to the long-haired eighth grader. Brad caught it, but immediately dumped it on Glen's shoulder. "No way, man. I'm number 23."

"I usually give number 1 to my captain," Coach Swopes said, but then shrugged. "But suit yourself. I have the jerseys on top and the shorts on bottom." Reaching in, he took out a pair of black shorts with red trim. "Find a pair your size. Later on I'll pass out our second set of white jerseys and red shorts. But these will be our home and road uniforms as much as possible."

"What number do you want?" Nick said excitedly to no one in particular.

"Man, I don't care," Ben said, leaving Ryan. "I'm just glad I get one."

"Find me 21," Will said. "That's mine!"

Nick groaned. "Of course," he said. "Your favorite game."

Jared just looked at the uniforms and smiled.

It took a while, but soon the fifteen members of the team had gathered around Coach Swopes with each holding a jersey and pair of shorts. The eighth graders had first pick. Besides Brad, Glen, Darius, and Teddy, there were three other eighth graders, each who had more size than talent. Curly, whose real name was Bob, had made it, along with a plump, pale-skinned boy named Scott, and Howard, a tall, lanky kid with brown skin and a shy smile. Scott openly admitted to joining the team to lose weight. He didn't expect to play and had nabbed number 0.

When the seventh graders got the leftovers, Jared had grabbed number 4 and like Ben was just happy to have a jersey. Will managed to find 21, but looked a little embarrassed. The closest size shorts to fit him ran past his knees and looked two sizes too wide.

"Told you, man," Nick said when eyeing Will holding up the wide shorts to his narrow waist. "You have no rear end." Then he shrugged. "But I have the opposite problem. I'm going to need to lose a few pounds for mine to fit."

Coach Swopes overheard him. "You'll lose it starting today, Nick," he said. "Don't you worry about that. We have a lot to do." He raised his voice and spoke to the whole team. "Now put on your jerseys and get to class. If you don't have a shirt underneath that matches, just grab your gym shirt … if it's clean. Just remember. Wear them with pride and don't forget you're representing your school, your teammates, and yourself. If you can't handle that, I'll take it away. That means, boys, good grades and good behavior. Got it?"

The team responded with a loud "yes, sir!" and started either for the hall or to the locker room. Jared slipped his jersey over his gray hoodie and immediately felt a glow of pride. He'd done it. He was now officially part of the Washington Middle boys' basketball team.

Ryan shoved past him, knocking into his shoulder, and left the gym through the side entrance without a glance back. He had his jersey and shorts over his shoulder.

Frowning, Jared turned away to head back to class. Big Mike stalked towards the door ahead of him, his jersey and shorts balled up in his big hands.

"Hey, Mike!" Will called, hustling after him. "Good game on Saturday, dude."

Big Mike didn't turn or slow down. "Shut up, man."

Will widened his eyes and parted his mouth. "Uh, okay," he said, stumbling to a stop.

Big Mike turned to him. "Be more like Jared and don't talk," he snapped. "Just because we're teammates don't make us friends."

Will nodded slowly. "Okay, sure … I won't talk to you. But are you playing again this Saturday?"

Big Mike's eyes twitched. "You're too much, man," he muttered. Then he turned back for the door. "See you Saturday," he mumbled.

Will crossed his arms in satisfaction. He looked over at Jared and grinned. "I think we'll do good this year."

The last member of the team to get a jersey was John Drydon. The manager came in last with Angie at his side. He happily took the number 1 jersey that had been discarded on the floor next to the box. Angie glared at the departing players and made no effort to find a jersey of her own. Nobody offered her one either.

Chapter 33

Later that morning, Jared entered English class on a mission. All during PE class he'd watched Marshall while keeping an eye on Gary and Chaz. It had been football day and the classes were split so he didn't get a chance to talk to Will or Nick. He'd spotted Ryan glaring at him during stretching, but had chosen to ignore that. Marshall, for once, had been left alone. But Jared knew his time would come. He rehearsed what he would do all of last night. Finally, he got his chance when Mrs. Donavon had the class look up vocab words while she ran across the hall to pick up copies from a printer. As soon as she left the room, Gary, sitting in the front row, looked across the room at Chaz and grinned.

Sliding out of his seat, he sauntered over to the middle of the room where Marshall sat with his big frame hunched over a dictionary and notebook.

"Hey, Marsh," Gary said. "Could I borrow a pencil?"

Marshall didn't look up. "No, Gary," he said loudly. "The last time I gave you a pencil you broke it and threw it in the trash."

A few of the kids snickered as they stopped their work to watch the show.

Giselle sat two seats in front of Marshall, and whipped back her hair, turning to watch. She shook her head and rolled her eyes. Marshall had infamously asked her to the fall dance right in front of everyone a month before, even going on a knee in front of her desk. Swallowing hard, she had quietly gotten up with her arms bent in front of her clutching her stomach before rushing out the door and bursting into laughter. Marshall had been left red faced and flustered. Since then Giselle took personal pride in seeing him humiliated.

"Come on, man," Chaz said. "Don't be such a … you know … one of those things you don't have."

Jared shot to his feet. He sat in the back behind Marshall. Taking a deep breath, he stepped forward and cleared his throat. "Cut it out."

Gary looked at him in surprise. Then he leered. "What is it, beanpole? You want a pencil too?"

"Leave him alone," Jared said, ducking his gaze. He stared down at his basketball jersey and suddenly felt stronger. He no longer felt alone. He had a team behind him.

"What's that?" Gary asked, surprised.

Clearing his throat, Jared took a deep breath. He remembered Big Mike's words. To play defense, you wanted to take away what your opponent did best. For Gary it was preying on the weak, finding an audience and putting down those who couldn't or didn't know how to defend themselves. Gary's strength was finding an audience and a target. Jared would no longer be a target.

"Leave Marshall alone," he said, his voice growing stronger. He looked straight at Gary. "He never bothered you."

The class grew silent and Gary's freckled face pinched inward. "Excuse me, beanpole? But Marshall pretty much bothers everyone in this school. Stay out of this."

"No," Jared told him.

"What a loser," Chaz said, remaining in his seat. "Just because he made the sorry basketball team …"

Gary glared at Jared and then smirked. "You think you're hot stuff with that stupid basketball jersey, don't you? But I know what you really are. You're just a snot-nosed, beanpole loser."

Jared reflexively wiped his nose but didn't back down.

"I don't care what you call me," Jared said, meaning it. "Just leave Marshall alone. He has too much class to fight back against slime like you."

"What if we don't?" Chaz asked, getting to his feet. "What are you going to do about?"

"He won't have to do nothing," growled a tough voice. Big Mike suddenly loomed next to Jared, seemingly coming out of nowhere. Jared looked at him in surprise. He wore his jersey under a heavy, black, zippered hoodie. Yanking down the zipper, Big Mike glowered at Gary and then Chaz. "You punks go smoke your basil elsewhere. You heard Jared. Leave Marshall alone."

Gary meant to say something, but scrunched up his nose and huffed. Turning, he stalked back to his seat. Chaz also sat, busily scratching his head while staring at his desk.

The entire class watched in quiet amazement. Giselle turned back to her desk, shaking her head.

Meanwhile, Marshall stared at Jared and then at Big Mike with his mouth wide open. "You didn't have to do that," he finally started to say, but Big Mike quickly shut him down with a glare.

"Shut up, Marshall," he snarled. "Go read a book." Then he stalked back to his desk.

"Okay," Marshall said. "Thanks."

Jared took a deep sigh of relief and returned to his seat feeling utterly drained. But he'd done it. He'd stood up for somebody, and more importantly had somebody he could question.

Mrs. Donavon returned to find a subdued class actually doing their work. She still didn't know what had happened when the lunch bell rang.

Before going to sit at his table, Jared dropped his lunch tray off and went to crouch near Marshall's seat.

"Uh, hey, Marshall," he said.

Marshall looked at him and frowned. "Jared," he said, nodding his head. "I want to thank you for back there. Next time, I will handle it, but if you ever need something from me ..."

Jared bit his bottom lip and nodded. "Yeah, of course. Uh, Marshall, I wanted to ask you something."

"If I can repay you, sure. What is it?" Marshall pushed up his glasses and leaned forward with his arms on the table, nearly bumping foreheads with Jared.

Jared had squatted down, but now quickly took a seat next to Marshall, scooting back a little.

"I was just, uh, wondering. What else do you know about Mr. Drydon? You know, you said your mom used to work with him."

"Hmm," Marshall said. He sat back and actually crossed his legs, resting his right ankle on his left knee. "There's not much to tell, really. Just some gossip."

"Uh, that's what I want to know. Please, Marshall, tell me anything you know."

"Well, before he resigned to come here, my mom said he might be in trouble. Teachers were accusing him of adjusting test scores and … I shouldn't say this, Jared, but some thought he was being too friendly with one of the assistant principals. She used to babysit John and spent a lot of time at his house. But that's all gossip. Why do you want to know all of this?"

"Oh, uh, I just started hearing things about him. Does he like John? I mean, I never see him really around him that much."

Marshall stared at Jared. "I don't know what or who he likes, Jared. John is his son, so of course he probably likes him. Now I'm going to eat my lunch. If you want to know more, why don't you ask Mr. Drydon?"

"Uh, maybe later. Thanks, Marshall."

Jared turned back to his table and was surprised to see Angie sitting in his seat with John next to her. She'd pushed his tray to the space next to her and now looked at him with a challenge in her eyes.

"Remember?" she said when Jared gave her a frown as he sat in the seat at her side. "If John sits here, then I sit here. Now what was that all about? What did you talk to Marshall about?"

"Tell you later," Jared mumbled. The other guys were coming, including Ryan.

"Hi, Jared!" John said brightly. "Hi, Will! Look at my basketball jersey!"

Lunch began awkwardly as Nick stared at Angie and immediately backed away.

"Don't worry," Angie said to him. "I won't eat your food."

"I'm more worried about you biting me," Nick mumbled. "Come on, man," he said to Will. "We have to find a better seat."

Will shrugged. "We're all on the same team now, right?"

"Everyone except for her," Nick said. But he sighed. "Fine, but I'm sitting as far away from her as I can."

Ryan and Ben joined them, but Ryan barely said a word the whole time. He kept his eyes on his food and kept twisting his shoulders like he had spiders crawling all over his back. Ben kept looking at him and then at Jared. He looked thoughtful and confused at the same time.

Jared didn't know what to think, but decided to stick close to Will and Nick. They were all part of the same team, but it sure didn't feel like it.

Three weeks of practice went by in a blur. Jared's schedule became a grueling, but ultimately fulfilling, routine. He woke up, ate breakfast, suffered through school (besides lunch and PE), went to basketball practice, took a long bus ride home, showered, ate supper, did his homework, and went to sleep, only to repeat it the next day, five days a week.

He barely saw his family except on Sundays at church and suppertime. His mom always had Carey with her and kept busy bringing Kelly to and from dance. With the Nutcracker looming, Kelly's schedule got even crazier and sometimes she came home later than their dad. Jack worked and hung out with his friend Rick, and George spent most of his time playing computer games. They had a computer without internet connection setup in the hall outside their room, and George spent hours playing strategy and world domination games. Days at a time passed with Jared saying barely five words to his mom and even less to his brothers. Kelly was really the one member of the family who took an interest in Jared's life, talking to him while waiting for the bus in the mornings, but mostly she just asked about meeting Will.

Jared didn't mind it at all. Basketball became his escape from all of life's problems. The players became his new family and he could hardly wait for practice to begin. Of course, Brad still acted like a jerk and went out of his way to ignore John and to make the seventh graders, especially Will, look bad, but the rest of the team accepted him. Glen called him an up and coming superstar. Even Ryan started leaving him alone. In truth, Ryan started leaving everybody alone. With the shampoo bottle empty, the showering tradition never continued, and Ryan drifted from his friends. During lunch he no longer sat at their table, joining Kyle and Tom's group on the other end of the cafeteria. Ben tried to talk to him, but Ryan told him to cool it, he just had to think things over. He still played with their group during scrimmages, but his spark had diminished. He no longer joked with Nick and Will and mostly went through the motions on the court. Often he passed up open looks, and seemed to want the ball out of his hands as quickly as possible. He seemed distracted and distant.

Jared didn't have time to worry too much about Ryan. He was too busy trying to learn all the drills and plays thrown at the team by Coach Swopes. He did talk to Angie and let her know about the rumors surrounding Mr. Drydon, but she admitted nothing suspicious had happened lately and that maybe she'd been imagining things.

Mr. Drydon visited practices often and went out of his way to sit near John and offer encouragement to the players. Will also seemed to put the mysteries on hold. He, Nick, and Jared continued to click on and off the court. With Will as point guard and Nick and Jared down low, the three ran a form of the triangle offense and were at times unstoppable. Jared, with practice guided by Big Mike, developed a decent hook shot and continued to work on spins to the basket.

Thanksgiving came and went—Jared spent the time eating turkey, watching football, and dreaming about basketball—and less than two weeks after, on Monday, December 8, the Washington Middle Patriots had their first game of the season.

"Okay, boys," Coach Swopes said to the team, looking down at his clipboard, a few minutes before tipoff. "We have nine games ahead of us. Nine. As you know, there are only ten teams in our district and only the top four move on to the playoffs. Every game counts." He stood in the middle of a small locker room in the gym of Herfton Middle, a small school in the lower side of Washington County. The boys sat on old wooden benches listening to him intently.

Jared could feel his nerves start to jangle. He could hear the muffled roar of the crowd as the girls' team was finishing their game. The boys always played after the girls. From the sound of it, the Patriot girls were not faring well.

"Last year, Herfton had a young team," Coach Swopes said. "I didn't get a chance to see them play in person, but I watched some tape. They've a tall point guard who knows how to handle the ball and can shoot. We're going to have to contain him. We'll also have to watch their big men. They have a guy who can probably touch rim just by standing on his tippy toes."

"Don't worry," Nick muttered from Jared's right. "We won't be starting and may not even play. He'll start the eighth graders and Big Mike."

"No sweat," Brad said loudly. "That tall guy has no coordination. I remember him from last year."

Coach Swopes looked at Brad and then shrugged. "Let's hope so. Here's the starting lineups …"

The team ran out moments later. The Herfton gym looked very similar to Washington Middle's, with the same high white walls and pull-out bleachers. At the moment the bleachers were packed with kids and plenty of adults. Their cheerleaders were in the middle of a routine in the center of the court, and the boys' team, the Herfton Warriors, in forest green uniforms with white lettering and trim, were doing layup drills on the far end.

Jared jogged onto the floor feeling a mixture of relief and disappointment. Nick had been right. All the starters were eighth graders except for Big Mike.

"Layups, boys," Coach Swopes called. Angie and John started tossing balls from the team's travel bag onto the court from the Patriots bench.

Seeing Jared, Angie stopped her work and walked over to him, giving him a smile.

"How's it going, jock?" she asked.

Jared gave a slight grin in return. "I probably won't play much, but I still feel like my stomach is ready to jump out of my mouth."

"You'll do fine, Jared." She grimaced. "You better do better than our girls. They lost by thirty."

Jared raised his eyebrows. "What?" he asked. "You said 'our' girls and you want us to win." He grinned. "Are you becoming a jock?"

Angie made a face and looked over to where Brad was directing where the layup lines should stand. "No way. I just watched you play a lot in practice. You really like this game. Honestly, you'll do fine." Her mouth twitched. "On the other hand, your friends may be in a little trouble." She nodded her chin to where Nick stared openly at the Patriots cheerleaders.

The cheerleaders, in black and red skirts and tops to match the boys' uniforms, sat to the right of the Patriots' bench watching the Warrior cheerleaders' routine. Stephanie Baker and Giselle Garcia were in the front middle. Nick stared right at Stephanie, as if willing the girl to meet his gaze.

Jared groaned when he saw Will move to stand next to Nick. Nick had been talking about Stephanie just about every practice and Will kept badgering him to talk *to* her instead of talking about her.

"There she is, Nick," Will now said, elbowing his larger friend. "Just go up to her now."

Nick blinked and peered down at him with a look of horror. "Are you joking, man? Now?"

"Why not?" Will asked. "She's stuck right there with the other cheerleaders. She wouldn't be able to escape you even if she wanted to."

Nick shook his head and muttered. "No way, man."

"Chicken," Will said. Then a ball rolled from the Warriors' side, heading toward the Patriots' bench. Will's eyes lit up and he looked up at Nick impishly. "Let me help."

Will trotted to the ball just as it reached the front of the cheerleaders and kicked it back to a Warrior's player, giving a brief wave. Then he turned to Stephanie and grinned.

"Hi, Stephanie," he said. "I, uh, have a message from Nick. He wants to ask you something—here he comes n—"

Nick charged after him, his eyes wide in shock. He wrapped his left arm around Will's shoulder while smacking his right hand over his mouth, cutting him off. "Sorry, girls," he blurted. "Will's late for layups. You can get his autograph later." He then bodily lifted the smaller boy and carried him away.

Most of the girls just stared and started giggling. Stephanie blushed and stared down at her pom-poms.

"I hate you, man," Nick hissed as he carried his friend to the layup lines. "Absolutely hate you." Setting Will down, he slapped the back of his shorts. "If we both get on the court, I'm going to be the first player in history to get a flagrant foul on his own teammate."

Will hopped away from him. "Ha! You'll thank me later. Now Stephanie at least knows what you look like!"

On the sideline watching, Angie blew out her breath and shook her head. "Jocks," she muttered.

Jared bit his bottom lip. "I don't think that's the best way to prepare for a game," he finally said.

"Hey, Cook!" Brad yelled, causing Jared to jump. "Are you a manager, or what? Get your rear in gear and get in line!"

Chapter 34

The games were played in four quarters, eight minutes each with a fifteen-minute break at halftime. The eighth-grade starters with Big Mike were Brad, Glen, Bigfoot Teddy, and Darius. They faced the Warriors' lineup led by the tall center, who had to be three inches taller than Jared. All the Warrior players looked tall and lean, ready for the game ahead. They did not look like a developing team.

In the first five minutes of the game, the Patriots quickly learned this to be true. The Herfton Warriors were now definitely a developed team. The tall center, a light-skinned kid almost as skinny as Will and taller than Jared, easily won the opening tip, knocking it out to their point guard, a dark-skinned boy with blond dreadlocks. The center scored seconds later off a great feed from their point guard. Soon after, he rejected a shot from Glen, skied for a rebound over Big Mike, and scored two more buckets, one a hook shot and the other a layup after a lob pass from the guard, who proved to be quick, smooth, and flashy. Very quickly it was 12 to 2 in favor of the Warriors.

Jared looked over at Will, who sat two seats down from him, Nick in the middle.

Will just grabbed a towel from the back of his chair and nervously clutched it in his lap like a security blanket.

Coach Swopes called a time out and called the team over. "Looks like that tall guy found some coordination since last year," he said mildly.

Brad glared, but didn't say anything. He adjusted his hairband and rudely turned his back on John as the boy offered him a water bottle.

"Don't worry," Coach Swopes said. "It's their first home game and they have the crowd. Just settle down and they'll fizzle out. Same players out there, but take your time on offense. Pass it around and look for a good shot. Then, get in gear and get back on defense. Let's go!"

The crowd roared as the players returned to the floor. Jared had never expected to see so many people at a middle school game. In his soccer leagues, only the parents showed up for maybe half the team. The entire stands were packed, mostly in Herfton green. He did see Will's dad in a small section of Patriots supporters. When he mentioned the crowd size out loud, Nick grunted.

"Get used it, man. A lot of grown-ups come to these games. My dad calls them basketball junkies. They go to the middle school games to see who the next high school stars will be."

Ryan spoke up from the end of the bench, surprising Jared. "Yeah, but there're lot of travel coaches watching too. They're always scouting these games looking for players." Then, as if remembering he was supposed to acting distant from them, Ryan grunted and turned away.

Will just kept his lips tight, watching the action.

Coach Swopes proved right as the Warriors missed their next three shots and started struggling in the half-court offense. Just as the first quarter ended, Big Mike hit a three in the corner, making it a 14 to 7 lead. The Patriots were trying to claw back.

Midway through the second quarter, Coach Swopes called for subs. First he beckoned two eighth graders, Matt Holby and Charles Fisk. Then he looked down the bench and made eye contact with Jared. "Jared and Will, you're in too. Let's see what speed does. Will, you're in for Brad. Jared, go in for Glen."

Jared lurched to his feet in shock. He barely felt Nick slap his shorts as he stumbled toward the scorer's table. He was so nervous he didn't even hear who Matt and Charles were replacing. At the next whistle, he found himself walking onto the court with Will, Matt, and Charles. Matt, a hefty blond kid with acne who had a surprising burst of speed, replaced Teddy and Charles, a slender boy a few inches shorter than Jared, took over for Darius.

Glen, sweat dripping down his face, gave Jared a fist bump and told him to box out the tall center.

Brad glowered when he went off the court, not even looking at his replacement.

The Warriors had the ball and hadn't made any substitutions. Their coach, a young guy with a suit and tie, clapped his hands loudly. "Let's take it to them!" he yelled. "This is our time!"

"Look at the shrimps they're sending at us," Jared heard one of the Warrior players say from the bench. "Look, they're sending a sixth grader against us!"

Smelling blood, the crowd clapped loudly. The score was 20 to 15, Warriors. They wanted to see their team run it up and put the game away before halftime.

Will picked up the flashy point guard as soon as he crossed backcourt. Jared settled down low, making sure to keep his body in front of the tall center, but slanted so he could guard the basket if necessary.

The tall kid snorted when Jared pushed back on him. "Yo, Jimmy!" he called. "Lob it in!"

The point guard ignored him as he tried to break Will down with the dribble. He underestimated Will's speed. Dribbling in front of him, he relaxed slightly and Will struck like a cobra, swiping upwards at the ball. Making contact, he knocked the ball loose, sending it bouncing into the backcourt. Before the point guard could turn, Will already had the ball on the run and took it in for the basket. The point guard whistled and didn't even give chase.

"You got me that time," he said as he jogged by Will to retrieve the ball and pass it in. "Nice steal, kid."

"Stop fooling around!" the Warrior's coach yelled. "Send it in to Derrick!"

Jared assumed the tall kid had to be Derrick. Sure enough, on the next trip up the point guard dribbled to the right, on Jared's side, and lobbed the ball in.

Jared was expecting it. He'd set up behind the tall center, and when the ball came in, he quickly moved around and threw up his hand, deflecting the pass.

Playing down low on the left, Matt snatched the ball and came down clutching it with both hands.

The few Patriot fans yelled their approval and, his face flushed with pride, Jared jogged to the offensive side. He set up on the right block in front of the tall center while Will brought up the ball. Matt was on his left while Big Mike and Charles set up on the corners, giving Will the middle space. It looked like it would be an isolation play with Will taking on Jimmy, the Warriors' point guard.

Jimmy bent low and grinned, looking for payback for Will's steal. Ignoring him, Will whipped a pass to Big Mike in the right corner. The big man barely had the ball before he sent it inside, right to Jared.

Caught by surprise, Jared fumbled the ball, recovered and turned to put up a quick shot. His fumble saved him. The tall center jumped as soon as Jared got the ball and bumped into Jared on the way down. Jared's shot never made it to the rim, but a whistle shrieked.

There were two refs for the game. One always stayed high near the midcourt line while the other ref watched baseline. The ref on the baseline pointed at the center. "Foul on green!" he barked. "Two shots!"

The crowd groaned and Jared wanted to join them. He'd never attempted a free throw outside of practice. And inside of practice he was mediocre at best. A little over three minutes remained in the first half of a tight game.

Will walked over and wiped his mouth with the front of his jersey. "You got this, big guy. Just remember you're grabbing a cookie from the jar."

"Come on, Jared!" Nick yelled from the bench. "Put it up and in!"

Jared sucked in a deep breath, biting his bottom lip as the ref bounced him the ball. Ever since joining the team he'd stopped talking to himself. But right now he could've really used some advice from himself. Looking at the basket, he tried to block out all the yelling from the crowd.

Big Mike and Matt were set up on the blocks between taller Warriors' players. Letting out his breath, Jared bent his knees and went up for the first shot. It hit nothing but air until striking the floor. His first foul shot ever ... was an airball.

Almost the entire gym seemed to laugh and Derrick, the tall center, leaned back his head, chortling.

Jared felt his face go red. From the bench he saw Brad toss up a towel in frustration.

"That's okay," Will told him, going over to him. "You got the bad one out of your system. This one will be good."

Big Mike glared at Jared. "Just put it close to the rim," he growled.

Jared nodded. His next shot bounced off the side, going to the right.

Immediately, Big Mike stepped into the paint, stepping in front of Derrick. Then he threw in his hip, checking the tall, slender boy out of the way. Jumping up, he caught the ball and put it back up into the basket before his feet touched the ground.

"Foul!" yelled Derrick, stumbling back. "Come on, man!"

The ref shook his head. "He was quicker than you, son. Next time less laughter and more focus."

Jared finished the half with no points but did have three rebounds and managed to keep Derrick from doing too much damage. Will added a three pointer and two assists. The score at halftime was 27 to 26, the Warriors leading only by a point.

In the second half Jared remained on the bench as Nick went in with Will in the fourth quarter. He didn't really mind. His ears still burned from his airballing the free throw. When the final buzzer sounded, the Patriots escaped with a 54 to 50 win.

The handshake line was supposed to be just that. The two teams line up, shake hands, say good game, and call it a night. It didn't quite go as planned in the Herfton gym that night.

After slapping hands with the Warriors' players and coach, Jared trudged to the locker room to gather his bag. While in the line shaking hands, the tall center Derrick had smirked at him. "Nice air, man," he'd said, deliberately missing Jared's offered hand. Brad, who'd been standing behind Jared, had laughed.

So preoccupied about his stupid airball, Jared went straight to the locker room without stopping to talk with any of his teammates. He collapsed on the bench and stared down at his sports bag waiting for the rest of his team to show up. As he did so, he missed all the fireworks … which started as water works.

As the players lined up, John and Angie had started cleaning up the bench area. While Angie carried the bag of balls toward the back entrance near the bus, John was unscrewing a water bottle to dump it in a nearby water fountain. Just leaving the handshake line, Brad came up behind the manager and bumped him in the back.

"Oh, excuse me," the Patriots team captain said as John stumbled forward, losing control of the bottle. It crashed to the gym floor in an explosion of water. Quickly, a huge puddle formed in front of the stricken boy.

Brad snorted and kept walking. "Looks like our manager just wet the floor," he said. He'd had a decent night with ten points, three rebounds, and three assists, but still smarted after watching Will, in less than half the minutes, score nine points and record four assists.

Nobody had seen the bump, aside from one fan way up high on the bleachers. He watched the incident with great interest. The hunter had once again begun stalking his prey.

The Herfton coach had just finished shaking hands with Coach Swopes when he saw John standing there, frozen, with a look of horror on his angelic face. The coach had already had a rough night with losing his home opener and was just turning to argue with the officials about some of the calls. Instead, he unleashed his anger on the Patriots manager.

"Hey!" he yelled. "What do you think you're doing! You can't mess up my floor like that!"

John's sad green eyes filled with tears and his knees started to tremble.

Angie turned and saw the coach going after John with his tie flying up in his face.

"Leave him alone!" she shouted, dropping the bulky bag and running toward the scene.

The other Patriots players looked on with mild interest and shock. Then Will rushed from where he and Nick had been trying to catch Stephanie Baker's eyes.

"John, it's okay!" he said, going to the manager's side. He looked up at the livid coach. "It was an accident."

"The only accident I see is standing in front of me," the coach snarled. Instantly he caught himself and, clearing his throat awkwardly, pointed down at the spilled water. "It's right there! That's what I'm talking about."

"Watch your mouth," Angie cried, going to the other side of John. "He's doing the best he can!"

The coach glowered at her. Just under five feet with a stocky build, he jutted out his sharp chin aggressively, his mane of brown hair flipping up on his head. "That's what I'm afraid of. Why is he here in the first place? What sort of team is this?"

"A team that beat you," Will said coolly, immediately earning the coach's wrath.

"That's enough out of you, kid. You get that, that boy off my court."

Will just widened his eyes and stared uneasily at the Warriors' coach and at Angie. He put a hand on John's arm, but didn't budge.

Angie made a fist and looked ready to step in and slug the coach.

"What's the problem?" Coach Swopes said, shuffling from center court.

"Your managers are the problem," the coach snarled. "They just ruined our floor, we just had it fixed up for the game!"

Mr. Moore suddenly appeared at Will's side. He'd seen the commotion from the stands and ran onto the court without hesitation.

"Let's settle down now," he said calmly. "It's just water. The way I see it, you just had a tight game and came up short. It's over now. Go back to your team." He nodded toward the home bench where the Warriors' players were watching with interest. Some looked ready to rush over and support their coach, but most looked a little ashamed and even disgusted. Their coach faced down a poor trembling kid standing in a puddle of water, a slightly built boy who looked all of ten, even if he played much bigger, and a single girl. Rushing to his aid just seemed … wrong.

Taking deep breaths, the coach still didn't back down. "Who are you?" he demanded.

"He's my assistant," Coach Swopes said, shuffling his feet. "I understand you're upset about the game and the water, but it's over. Let's not turn this into an incident you'll regret, mister. You lost fair and square. Let's just end the night like that."

Suddenly realizing what he must look like, the coach breathed out and seemed to deflate. Coughing, he said, "Fine, but now I have to stay late to do the floor again." Turning, he flipped back his hair and stalked back to his bench.

Angie immediately started comforting John.

"It's over, John," she soothed, patting his back. "It's all over now. You don't have to be upset."

His lips trembling, the boy just shook his head, and then grabbed Will's arm, not letting go.

"Um, it's okay, John," Will told him, slightly embarrassed. "It's all over now. You can let go now."

John only held on tighter and shook his head again.

"Will," Mr. Moore said softly. "Why don't you walk John to the bus, okay? I'll get your stuff and bring it in the car. I'll see you at school." He patted Will's shoulder and ruffled his hair. "Nice game. I won't even make you get a haircut."

Coach Swopes sighed and ran a hand through his thinning hair. "You know, if you do want to be an assistant, I can really use one."

Chapter 35

Jared sat slumped in the front seat just behind Coach Swopes on the bus ride back to Washington Middle. He heard from Nick what had happened with John. The fair-haired boy sat next to Will a few seats back, happily staring out the window like the incident had never happened. Jared knew he should've been there, if only he hadn't felt sorry for himself about his stupid free throw.

"I let you down," he muttered. "It won't happen again." He didn't know if he meant Will, Angie, or John. He just felt bad.

In front of him, Coach Swopes's cell rang and the coach answered it after a grunt. "Hello? Mr. Drydon? Oh, hi. Yes, it was a good game. You what?" The coach sighed, sounding tired. "Well, okay, if that's what you want. Yes. I'll be there." He put down the phone and sighed again. "One more year to retirement," he said, surprising Jared. For the first time the coach sounded as old as he looked.

Jared climbed down the bus and started scanning the waiting cars and parents and didn't see his mom or her car. He groaned. Kelly, most likely, would be at dance right now.

Moving to the sidewalk away from the parents, he bit his bottom lip and waited for Will so he could ask to borrow his dad's cell phone. Maybe his dad would be home …

Will climbed down with John and awkwardly said goodbye. "Uh, you better find Angie, John. Okay?"

John nodded and waved. A second bus carrying the girls' team and cheerleaders, along with Angie, had pulled up. Angie jumped off first, as soon as the doors swung open, rushing to meet John.

"John, are you okay?" she asked, bending down and giving him a hug.

"Hi, Angie," John told her, smiling. "I rode with Will on his bus."

He'd gone to Herfton with Angie on the bus carrying the girls' team and cheerleaders. He'd been the only boy allowed on the girls' bus.

Angie grinned tiredly at him. "Yes, I know. But now you're coming home with me. Your dad is picking you up from my house. You ready?"

"Yes!"

Jared watched the two managers go off to Angie's mom's minivan feeling a pang of hurt. "I should've been there," he muttered. He went to find Will when he saw the boy waiting by the bus door, crouching by the front tire. As soon as Nick stepped out, Will leapt on his back, sticking up his knees in a piggyback style.

"Let's go, Nick!" he cried. "Stephanie Baker awaits!"

Nick staggered under the added weight. "Hey, man! Get off! You're ripping the strap to my bag!"

Laughing, Will hopped down. "Dude, I'm serious. We just won, now's the time to talk to Stephanie."

Nick shook his head and mumbled something.

Sighing, Jared turned away. He longed to be friends like that, but knew it wasn't the case. He spotted Coach Swopes going into the gym and got a good idea. He could borrow the coach's phone and maybe practice his free throw shooting while waiting for a ride. Coach Swopes had told the team that the gym would always be open during off-practice times as long as he was in the building.

He quickly hurried after his coach.

Inside the school, Jared frowned. Something didn't feel right and he got an uneasy feeling. While the hall seemed clear, it felt as if somebody was watching him.

"Coach Swopes?" he called. Hearing no answer, he headed into the gym and heard muffled voices. He knew he should probably just back out now and find Will, but he remembered Coach Swopes's strange phone call. Saying a quick prayer that he wasn't doing something incredibly stupid, Jared put down his bag near the wall and crept across the court to the locker room, toward the voices.

When just outside the locker room, he paused, straining his ears to hear.

"I want him doing something other than spilling water all over the place," Mr. Drydon's face was saying. "I heard all about what happened tonight. That's an embarrassment to our school and an embarrassment to me."

"It wasn't anything but an accident," Coach Swopes said back, sounding angry and frustrated. "The other coach overreacted. End of story. Now I think you're overreacting."

"I'm a father and the principal here. I'm trying to do the best for my son and the school. It isn't easy, believe me."

Jared heard Coach Swopes sigh. "So you want John to be on the bench as one of the players now. He loves being the manager. If you cared about your son, you'd know that."

"What's that supposed to mean?" Mr. Drydon asked icily.

"Nothing, I'm sorry … I'm just tired."

"Then do what I say. I want John to ride the team bus permanently from now on. Maybe if you ever have a blowout you can even put him in a game."

"Yes, sure. Why not?" Coach Swopes didn't sound like a winning basketball coach. He sounded utterly defeated.

"Good. Now, tell me. Who is this Will character? Why is he always around my son? I hear he eats lunch with him now with some of your other players."

"Hold on, now," Coach Swopes said. "Will is a good boy."

"I'm sure he is, but I'm trying to be a good father."

"In that case you should be happy he has good friends like Will."

"For your information, having a son like John is not easy. Usually his 'good friends' are the ones who plan all sorts of bad things for him to do. Remember last year in art? Some of his 'good friends' got him to think he had acid on his clothes. They thought it was funny for him pose in the—"

"Okay, okay," sighed Coach Swopes, giving up. "But I don't know what you want me to do. You want him to be part of the team, but you don't want players to be around him. What exactly do you want, Mr. Drydon?"

"I told you. I want what's best for John and my school."

Mr. Hackett's voice coughed and cut in. "How about this," he said.

Jared's eyes went wide. Apparently there were three teachers back in there. He wondered if the mystery man also was present.

Mr. Hackett's voice continued, "John rides the bus with the basketball team and I'll be the driver. That way there'll be an extra set of eyes around and I'll keep them on John. Would that work?"

"Sure," Coach Swopes's voice said, sounding defeated. "If it makes this night end, sure. Why not?"

"Sounds sensible to me," Mr. Drydon's voice said.

Feeling slightly ashamed for listening, but puzzled, Jared quickly hurried from the locker room and ran back to his bag. He didn't notice anything wrong until much later that night.

After his mom finally came, apologizing for being late due to Kelly's rehearsal, he went home, showered, and ate supper. Then, as he unpacked his bag to get it ready for practice the next day, he saw something written in black ink on top. Just above the zipper, it simply read, *OOPS*.

The Patriots had two days before their next game that Thursday. The day after their close victory, their practice could only be considered lukewarm at best. Coach Swopes appeared worn-out and not into his coaching duties. After a few laps of running, he had the boys do the same drills as the last practice and then break up into teams for scrimmaging. At the conclusion of practice, instead of a pep talk, he announced no practice the next day and for everyone to show up on time for their game Thursday.

"Coach Swopes has lost it," Brad said when the players were dismissed and the coach headed for his office. "His old age has caught up to him."

"Lay off him, man," Glen said. "He's not Coach Hicks, but he's all right."

"Yeah, well," Brad grunted, "we'll see."

On the activity bus Jared told Will about overhearing Coach Swopes and Mr. Drydon. He just left out the part about Mr. Drydon asking about Will.

Hearing it, Will frowned. "Why would Coach Swopes be mad about John being on the team?" he wondered when Jared had finished.

"I just want to know," Jared said, "why Mr. Drydon wants his son to be on the team so badly. Remember, last year he made the old coach quit."

Will shook his head and shrugged, dismissing it all. "Who knows, dude. But right now we'd better worry more about Knox."

Jared grunted. On Thursday, after a day with no practice, the Knox Middle Cannons were due up next on their schedule.

Will came home the next day to find his dad sitting at the table with a cup of coffee and wearing a shocked expression. "Hey, champ," he said, barely looking up when Will walked in. "Guess what happened today?"

"You told a funny joke?"

Mr. Moore smiled. "Kind of. Your basketball coach called me up. He wants me to help coach the team starting tomorrow … Says he isn't feeling well."

Will dropped his backpack and stared at his father. "Really?" he asked. Then he grinned. "Dad, that's awesome!"

Blinking as if surprised, Mr. Moore looked up from the table. "You really think so?"

Will rolled his eyes. "Of course, Dad! Now you can put me in the starting lineup."

Mr. Moore nearly started choking and then cracked a grin. "Okay, champ. Now who's being the funny one? More like I'll ride your little behind on the bench all game unless you clean up your room."

"Ha," Will said. "Not if you want to win your coaching debut, you won't. You're going to need me."

Mr. Moore's grin faded slightly. "Yeah, well … I'll need you all right, champ. I haven't done anything like this since the army."

Instantly, Will sobered and he went to his dad, leaning against his knee. "It'll go fine, Dad. The guys will like you."

"Sure, champ." Mr. Moore patted Will's back. "That's one good thing about you. You're still small enough to sit on me without crushing me. Too bad you smell. Now get up there and shower. Then go clean your room. If it's not spic and span, you're grounded after school tomorrow."

"Ha, ha, Dad. You're hilarious."

The Knox Middle Cannons came into Washington Middle having won their first game by blowing out Lincoln Middle by a score of 62 to 34. From Lakeland County, just north of Washington County, all the players were tall, rangy, and looked ready to play in college. The large crowd that'd gathered for Washington Middle's first home game didn't seem to faze them in the least. Knox's coach and most of the players had dark skin and were from a poor farming community. To them, basketball served as the best part of life and they knew the value of hard work.

The Patriots were not prepared for them. Having little practice and a sudden, unexpected coaching sub didn't help matters. The blue- and yellow-clad Cannons liked to play a fast up-tempo game where they thrived on pressuring the ball, forcing bad passes and quick shots. Very quickly they jumped to an 11 to 2 lead.

Brad slammed the ball with his hand in frustration when Mr. Moore called a timeout after an easy Knox layup off a Patriots' turnover. The substitute coach had gone with the same starting lineup from the first game, and so far they'd produced more turnovers than shot attempts. Brad had three turnovers himself.

"It'll be fine," Mr. Moore said, clapping his hands as the Patriot players gathered around him.

"No, it's not," Glen said. "They're destroying us on the break."

"And just listen to the crowd," Teddy muttered. "I wish we were on a road game."

The teams' benches were set up across from the bleachers, but they could still hear the muttering and murmuring of concerned parents. Worse, just behind their cheerleaders, Gary, Chaz, and Ray sat in the front row. They were cheering every mistake the Patriots made and kept calling for beanpole to play. There were rules against heckling, but they weren't supposed to apply to fans of the home team jeering their own players.

"Don't worry about any of that, boys. Focus on the game," Mr. Moore said. He knelt with a whiteboard and marker in the middle of the huddled players

"Who's this guy?" Brad muttered. "We have some random parent step out the stands and act like he's John Wooden." He said it under his breath, but was clearly heard by the team.

Mr. Moore looked up at him and smiled. "You know," he said, "we could just forfeit the game right now and go home. Is that what you want?"

Brad opened his mouth and then closed it. Ducking his head, he coughed. "Uh, no, sir."

"Good," Mr. Moore said. "I know I'm not part of the team, but that's okay. Because I'm not on the floor. It's the players that have to come together in times like this. Now, here's what I want you to do. Brad, you get the ball and move it up court."

"Yeah, I know," grunted the eighth grader. "Then they trap me with two players and I have nowhere to go."

Mr. Moore tightened his lips and put down the whiteboard and marker. "We just need to slow the game down and make good passes."

"I'm trying," Brad said. "I need some help!"

"Mike will come to help," Mr. Moore said calmly. "Get him the ball when the trap comes." Will's dad turned to Big Mike. "You either slow it down, or look for a quick pass to an open player down low. I want Glen and Teddy to stay on either side of the basket. You two try to lose your man. Let them get sucked up high to pressure the ball. Darius, you roam around the perimeter and look for cuts to the basket. If you get the ball in space, put up a shot. Glen and Teddy will fight for any rebounds. I know it's not perfect, but right now we need to slow the game down and look for easy baskets. But whatever happens, once we score or lose the ball, get back on defense. Pronto. They like to shoot quick, so keep your hands up and be ready to box out. Got it? Let's go."

Brad sighed as the huddle ended. "Where's Coach Hicks when you need him?" he muttered.

Mr. Moore ran a hand through his cropped hair, now damp with sweat. He turned around and grinned at Will, who'd just sat after the timeout. "How am I doing, champ?"

"Better than us," Will told him truthfully.

His dad winked. "Don't worry. Things will improve. They're going to tire. Eventually."

Jared sat on Will's right and glanced down to where Mr. Hackett sat on the end of the bench. He served as the school's official coach, since Mr. Moore was never hired to coach and didn't officially work for the school. So far the PE teacher just watched silently with mild interest. John still worked as a student manager with Angie, but had his basketball jersey on with jeans. He sat on the floor next to Mr. Hackett's feet watching the court intensely. Angie stood over him with her arms crossed. They'd both offered water in the huddle, but nobody had accepted it.

On the court, the whistle blew and Jared turned his attention back to the game.

"Let's go, Cannons!" yelled Ray obnoxiously as Brad took the ball in from Big Mike. "Blast the Patriots!"

"Wreck them!" Chaz added.

Brad shot them a dirty look and then headed up the court. As two Cannon players blasted toward him, he threw a quick pass across the court to Big Mike. He never saw the third player lurking at midcourt. A small, wiry guard, this player leapt in the passing lane, snatched the ball, and raced for another uncontested layup.

"What are you doing, Coach?" yelled an angry father from the stands. "You're feeding them the ball! They're killing us! Someone help out, because the coach isn't doing a blasted thing!"

Brad heaved a sigh and looked toward the voice and then at Mr. Moore.

"That's okay," Mr. Moore said, sweat dripping down his brow. "Keep your head up. You and Mike take the ball up together."

The play continued and the Patriots managed to get back in the game a little bit. Big Mike started setting picks for Brad and then rolling to the basket. When the pressure started swarming Brad, he tossed the ball Big Mike's way. Once Big Mike had the ball, the pressure seemed to bounce off. Using his wide body and thick hands, he held off a double team and either dribbled through or found a wide-open teammate. Glen scored two easy buckets off his feeds down low. Darius started making darting cuts through the middle of the lane, exposing holes in the Cannons' defense. He scored on three straight possessions. On defense, the Patriots rushed back and limited the Cannons to only a single basket for the rest of the quarter. As the whistle blew for the second quarter it was 15 to 12 in favor of the Cannons, but the Patriots had the momentum.

"Keep it going, guys!" called the same loud father from the stands. "You're doing great! Don't let up!"

The crowd responded with loud cheering. Gary and his group went silent.

Chapter 36

In the second quarter things started falling apart. Mr. Moore went with the same players and the Cannons responded with an eight-point run. He sent in Charles and Matt for Glen and Teddy.

Glen wiped sweat from his face and accepted a water bottle from John without thinking. "Man," he breathed, sitting with his chest heaving. "I'm exhausted."

Teddy sat beside him and shook his head. "We have no chance," he muttered.

It looked that way. By midway through the second quarter, the Cannons had increased the lead to 31 to 17.

Gary, Chaz, and Ray were back on their feet, giving the visiting team a standing ovation after another Patriots' timeout ended with another turnover.

"The Patriots need to wave the flag!" Ray called loudly.

"The white flag!" Gary yelled.

"I'm so going to pound those twerps," Nick growled as he slouched in his seat.

"Okay," Mr. Moore said. "Let's give the boys a breather. Will, come here." Will practically leapt from the bench to stand beside his dad. Jared could tell he couldn't wait to get in the game. The entire time his hands had been twitching and his feet tapping as if he were imagining dribbling the ball on the court. Crouching, Mr. Moore put a hand on his son's back. "You know what to do, right? Keep the ball until over midcourt, don't pick up your dribble, and pass the ball around. Keep it moving."

Will licked his lips and nodded. "Who else is going in?"

Mr. Moore blew out his breath and looked back at the bench. "You know, I think it's time to give the seventh graders a chance." He smacked the back of Will's shorts. "Go get them, champ."

Brad, his hair dark with sweat, tore off his hairband and tossed it at the floor, nearly hitting John, as he stalked to the bench. "Great!" he spat. "We're giving up! We're putting the scrubs in before halftime."

Big Mike only grunted and collapsed onto a seat.

Out on the floor, Jared, Nick, Ryan, and Ben had joined Will. It was the first time the "shower brothers" played together all at once.

"Hey, man," Nick said to Ryan as they left the bench. "You with us today?"

Ryan gave a look that first appeared angry, but then he sighed. "Yeah, man. We're going to lose any way. Let's go down swinging at least."

Ben tossed the ball in to Will and it was game on.

Plenty of fans grumbled and murmured when seeing the substitutions. The loud father had cried out as if in physical pain. "You're killing us, Coach!" he yelled. "What're you doing! Little kids and fat kids won't help us!"

"Get the sixth grader out of there!" hollered a mother.

The only home fans who enjoyed the moves were Gary, Chaz, and Ray. They immediately started to mock cheer and laugh. "Here comes the beanpole!" Chaz cried. "Don't snap in half out there!"

"I want to see you dunk, beanpole," Gary shouted.

The Cannons also sensed blood in the water. Seeing Will, one of the smallest and slightest players with the ball, they immediately sent two players at him. Jared started to go to give support and maybe set a pick, but Mr. Moore waved him back. "You guys, spread out! Go to four corners!"

Nick pointed for Jared to go to the right corner down low while he set up in the left corner. Ryan and Ben stayed on the perimeter, but both near the sidelines, leaving the middle void of Patriots players.

"What's this?" hollered the father from the stands. "Are you kidding me? Are we running out the clock?"

Some of the fans started to boo, but Mr. Moore just crossed his arms, tapping his clipboard against his side.

After getting the ball, Will had walked slowly toward midcourt while Ben ran to his position. Now with the two Cannon players looming, he suddenly lowered his head, put on a flurry of moves and split the defenders, tearing up the court at full speed. He went right down the middle. He wasn't challenged until the Cannons' center, caught trying to guard both Jared and Nick, jumped in late as Will went for a layup. Bodies crashed, but Will managed to get the ball up and off the backboard before it swished into the basket. He then banged onto floor, landing on his side and rolling to Jared's feet.

"Did I make it?" he asked as Jared rushed to help him up.

The roar of the crowd let him know the answer.

"Foul on yellow!" shouted the ref standing near Will. "Basket counts, one shot!"

Ryan rushed in and bumped Jared out of the way. "You got it, little dude!" he cried, reaching down and hoisting up Will by his wrists. "Nice one! You good, man?"

Will grinned and rubbed his right forearm. "Good enough. Thanks, man."

Jared bit his bottom lip and went to setup for the free throw. Ryan rubbed Will's head and pushed him toward the line. He didn't look in Jared's direction.

Will swished his free throw.

"Back, back!" Mr. Moore cried. "Keep the ball in front of you!"

Jared raced back to the lower right of the basket and found himself guarding a kid three inches shorter than him. If he'd shaved off his box haircut, he would be lowered another two inches. However, what the kid lacked in height, he made up for in lower body strength. The Cannons wore yellow jerseys with blue shorts. The back end of the blue shorts that crashed into Jared's thighs felt like a bowling ball. Wincing, Jared stumbled back.

The guard with the ball faked a pass to the left, causing Will to commit in that direction, and then fired in a hard pass to Jared's man. Jared watched helplessly as he turned for an easy bucket, but Nick rushed in to help, throwing off the shot in the last second. Jared quickly jumped for the rebound, snatching it from the air above everyone.

Immediately two players in yellow converged on him, trying to knock the ball free. Holding the ball high over his head, he avoided the swiping hands and looked for an outlet. Seeing Ryan streaking down court he thought of a long pass, but then Will ran open to his right. Jared quickly passed it to the short guard.

"Yo, come on, man!" Ryan said, throwing up his hands. He threw a dirty look toward Jared. "I was open!"

Ducking his head, Jared trotted back to the offensive side. Maybe he should've gone for the long ball to Ryan, he knew, but he'd been afraid to make a mistake and had played it safe.

"Pressure!" shouted the Knox coach. "He's just a little kid! Get the ball!"

Will held the ball for a second, as if waiting for the pressure. Then, as it came, he dribbled once toward the middle, before darting back to the right, streaking past the two Cannon players and going up the side of the court. When a third Knox player tried to cut him off, Will flipped the ball over midcourt to Ryan. Ryan then turned and fired a hard bounce pass to Nick, right under the basket. The big man put the ball up and into the hoop. The Knox Cannons were beat at their own game.

The second quarter continued with the Knox players continually trying to pressure Will into turnovers. They quickly found they were wasting their time. Will had spent his whole basketball life going up against bigger, longer defenders. Keeping low to the ground, he navigated the pressure like a bloodhound following a trail, time after time dribbling through the defenders into open areas. When double teamed, he always found the open man and soon Ryan was feasting off his passes. Either he got an open shot, or found a wide-open Ben at top, or Nick down low. He never once passed to Jared. Jared's only bucket came when Will faked a pass to Ryan before cutting in the lane and bouncing a perfect feed to Jared's hands as the center went to challenge him. Jared rushed his shot and put it up short, but grabbed the rebound and got it in on the second try. It wasn't pretty, but it made his heart soar. He'd scored the first official points in his life.

Without their pressure working, the Knox Cannons began to falter on offense. Jared and Nick controlled the inside while Will and Ben badgered the ball on the perimeter. Ryan patrolled the middle, cheating up high and constantly getting in passing lanes.

The Cannons started settling for outside shots and soon Jared had six quick rebounds.

Near the end of the quarter Big Mike went in for Ben and Glen replaced a tired Nick. Brad, fuming, remained on the bench. When the buzzer sounded for the half, the score had been cut to 35 to 32.

The crowd, except for Gary and his bunch, gave the Patriots a loud ovation as the team trotted into the locker room. The fans for Knox, a small contingent on the far side of the bleachers, also cheered their team, but they sounded worried. Their team relied on speed and quickness over size and strength, and at the moment, the young point guard for Washington Middle was beating them at their own game.

"Okay, we're back in it," the loud father yelled from the stands.

As he left the floor, Jared risked a peek at him and saw a balding man with gray hair and a large belly. He stood next to the bleachers near the entrance in a blue and white tracksuit.

Cupping his hands, he yelled, "You'd better put the starters back in so we can win this!"

"Who's that guy?" Kyle asked. "What a jerk." He'd gone in for Ryan and had scored on a short jumper from the side.

Brad heard him, and scowled. "Watch your mouth, you little punk. That's my dad."

Kyle instantly turned red and ducked his head. "Sorry, man," he said.

"It's okay," Mr. Moore said. "Everyone gets excited during games."

Brad just ignored them both.

Brad got the start for the third quarter, but came out with a chip on his shoulder. His chip seemed to be directed at Mr. Moore rather than his opponents.

The Patriots got the ball to start the half and Mr. Moore called out instructions to work the ball around and go inside. He wanted to wear out the Knox players. Brad instead dribbled one-on-one against his defender, beating his man off the dribble. Going into the paint, he put up a shot that missed, but a whistle blew for a foul on yellow. Brad made both free throws and slapped Glen's hand on the way back down the court. "This is my game now!" he shouted.

After that, whenever he had the ball, Brad looked to score. He ran right into the pressure thrown at him, drawing fouls or taking two defenders on at once. He scored six straight points for the Patriots and then missed a contested three he took off the dribble.

"Come on, man!" Big Mike growled at him as the Cannons grabbed the long rebound and rushed the other way. They ended up with a fast break layup as Brad trailed the play and let his man run down the lane unguarded.

Mr. Moore sent in Will to replace Brad. Throwing up his hands and yelling toward the ceiling, Brad walked off the court without looking at Will.

Brad's father covered his face as if he couldn't believe it. "He just scored six of your points! What are you doing! You're not a coach! You're a parent showing favoritism!"

Mr. Moore's ears turned red but he gave no other reaction.

"Get out of my face," Brad snarled at John when the boy tried to offer him water.

Jared glanced at Mr. Hackett who sat watching it happen, but the PE teacher just looked down at his watch and seemed unconcerned.

John blinked for a moment and then put the water bottle down and clapped his hands. "Will's playing!" he said.

Angie nodded and smiled at him, but then she stuck her tongue out at the back of Brad's head.

Brad sat heavily on his seat and covered his head with a towel. "How wonderful," he muttered loudly. "Daddy's boy gets to play some more."

Mr. Moore turned and looked at him. "I'll put you back in when you're calm enough to listen and think straight."

The game became a back and forth affair, both teams looking to grab control, but neither quite doing it. Each time one team went on a run, the other team would answer. With Will on the court running point, the Cannons settled back and played a tight zone. They were forced to loosen when Big Mike started hitting threes, but still held firm. The final quarter started with the score even at fifty-one points apiece. Then, with less than five minutes remaining, the Cannons went on a six-point run.

"Okay, Brad," Mr. Moore said. "You're in. Go in for Darius and help Will bring up the ball. You two work together and find some good shots."

Brad took off his towel and frowned. "Sure, *Coach*."

On the court, Glen went to toss the ball in to Will from under their basket when Brad rushed in and grabbed the ball from the seventh grader.

Will's eyes widened in surprise, but he lifted his hands over his head, letting Brad take it.

"Just stay out of my way," Brad grunted.

Glen threw back his head. "Come on, Brad," he said. "We need to do this together! Let's not blow this thing."

"Then let's go," Brad said. Not looking back, he started dribbling up the court.

Glen and Will hurried after him.

"Take it, Brad!" yelled his father. Most of the crowd now stood on their feet. It was the home opener and plenty of students, parents, and fans in the community had attended. The smaller Knox crowd was easily drowned out. Gary, Chaz, and Ray had left during halftime.

"He's going to blow it," Kyle muttered from next to Jared.

Jared grunted and wished he could be out there instead of Brad. He'd played a few minutes in the third quarter, but had missed his only shot attempt. He did get a block and two more rebounds.

Brad dribbled at the top of the key, staring at the basket. Will set up on his right while Glen moved down low, parking himself on the right block. Nick, who'd played big minutes in the second half, moved up to set a pick. Before he got there, Big Mike rolled from the left corner toward Brad, but suddenly cut to the basket, slashing through two defenders.

Brad saw him in the corner of his eye and threw a pinpoint bounce pass. Big Mike caught it and laid it in, cutting the lead to four.

"That's it!" Mr. Moore called, clapping his hands. "Nice pass, Brad!"

Knox tried to run down the clock on the next possession, but Will tipped a lazy pass and Brad rushed forward to scoop it up. Will immediately sprinted to the basket, but Brad instead dribbled to the right, slowing down.

"It's okay!" Mr. Moore yelled. "Set up for a good shot!"

Brad passed out to Big Mike, who immediately whipped the ball around to Will in the corner. Immediately a taller defender rushed him. Will faked a shot, causing the defender to leap in the air, and dribbled down the baseline. Glen's defender rushed over to cut him off and Will bounced a pass to Glen underneath the basket. Feeling pressure coming in, Glen threw the ball back out to Brad.

"Why didn't you shoot!" Brad yelled at Will. "Come on, man!" Dribbling once, he stepped into a high-arcing three. It clanged off the back iron to the groans of the crowd. But then Nick's outstretched hand tipped it up. Will crashed in and managed to nab the rebound. As he landed with his back to the right of the hoop, he immediately felt hands on his back, shoving him out.

"Yo, man!" he heard Big Mike call behind him.

Without looking, Will fired a behind the back pass toward the voice.

Big Mike grabbed the ball on the baseline and almost in one motion rose up for a shot, sinking the short jumper. The lead was only two.

"Defense!" yelled Brad's father. "Stop them here!"

The entire gym seemed to be rocking now as everyone in the bleachers and on the players' benches were on their feet. The cheerleaders of both teams had given up any routines and were just waving pom-poms, adding their voices to the screams. The Patriots had a good chance of winning, if they could stop the Cannons here.

Chapter 37

Will wiped his upper lip as he crouched, picking up his man at midcourt. The guard in the yellow jersey had a quick first step, but had struggled with his jumper all night. Will knew he would probably drive in if he didn't pass. Knowing this, he backed up.

The Knox guard crouched low, dribbling from right to left. Sweat dripped from the end of his nose, splashing on the ball below him. For a moment Will thought he was going to make his move, but then he passed to his teammate on his right, Brad's man.

Brad instantly moved in close, putting up his hand and playing tight. Will's man moved forward, bumping into him before posting up. He quickly got the ball back.

Will knew what was going on. The guard wanted to post him up to use his length and power and had just moved into a better position. Will's feet were just inside the key. He moved in close, putting his left hand on the player's shoulder, but didn't press too hard. He guessed the Knox guard wanted to make a move and drive to the basket more than he wanted to shoot.

Bouncing the ball twice, the guard backed into Will, trying to muscle him back. Will let him move forward, but made sure he didn't give too much space. Then he felt a hand go on his back just above his waist. He tried to shake it off, but it only dropped to his shorts, actually giving them a tug. Will had double-knotted the drawstring and thankfully his shorts stayed firm. Then all at once the hand shoved him hard in the backside, sending him stumbling forward. At the same time, the guard spun to his right. Will ended up crashing headfirst into Brad's chest. Brad had swooped around and was trying to go for the steal.

Brad yelled in frustration as Will bounced back, sprawling to the floor at his feet. The Knox guard easily scored on a layup as his teammate with the bowling ball body blocked out Nick from providing any help.

The Patriots crowd let out a collected groan as the Knox supporters screamed in delight.

"What are you doing, man?" Brad screamed down at Will. "Nice pick, you idiot! You took out your own team."

Will squeezed his eyes shut and opened him, shaking his head. "I was pushed," he mumbled.

Nick grabbed him from behind his shoulders and pulled him up. "You okay, man?"

Wincing, Will nodded. "My knees hurt the most," he said.

"What hurts the most is your sorry defense," Brad told him. He turned to Glen in disgust. "Toss in the ball, hurry!"

"Hold up!" the ref at midcourt yelled, blowing his whistle. "You all right, son?" he asked.

Mr. Moore stared out onto the court, but Will raised his thumb and nodded.

"Okay, let's play," called the ref.

Mr. Moore bit his lip, his face unreadable.

The clock ticked down and the Cannons now led by four. The game looked to be slipping away. Brad took the ball in and rushed up the court. He never slowed. Blowing by his man, he entered the paint and threw up a wild shot as two yellow jerseys shut off the lane.

"Foul, man!" he screamed as the ball bounced off the backboard, not getting close to the rim. The nearest ref just stared without blowing his whistle.

Big Mike saved the play, charging in from behind and grabbing the rebound. Making sure nobody was behind him for the block, he laid the ball up and in. The clock ticked below fifty-eight seconds in a two-point contest.

"Time out!" Mr. Moore cried, stopping the clock. He motioned for Jared from the bench. "Go in for Nick. We need your height for rebounding."

It was a short timeout, and after telling his players not to foul and keep the ball out of the paint, Mr. Moore drew up an offense play. "Once we get the ball, give it to Brad. Brad, you take it hard to the basket and go for a layup or draw a foul. But if you see no lane, kick it out to either Mike or Will. They'll be on either side of you. Jared, you and Glen just crash the rim and look for a rebound. Got it?"

Brad grunted and nodded. "Just as long as your son doesn't pick me," he muttered.

Ignoring him, Mr. Moore sent out his team.

Nick, drenched in sweat, slapped Jared's shoulder on his way to his seat. "Go get it, dude. Watch out for their small center guy. He's handful, man."

Jared nodded, rubbing his thigh. He knew bowling ball shorts all too well.

The Knox Cannons, clearly exhausted, did their best to run down the clock. There was a forty-second shot clock for middle school and they used every second they could before throwing up a three from the corner. Coming up short, it bounced high off the rim. Jared threw his body into bowling ball shorts and leapt for the rebound. The whistle shrieked and the ref on the baseline pointed right at Jared.

"Number 4!" he snapped. "Foul for pushing! That's the sixth team foul. One more and we shoot free throws."

"What!" Brad screamed. "Come on!"

Bowling ball shorts just grinned. There were now only seventeen seconds left on the clock and the Cannons had the ball under the rim.

"You have to foul now!" Mr. Moore cried. "As soon as the ball is in, foul and give them the free throws."

Will had other ideas. The Cannons opted for a long pass out to midcourt. Will patrolled that area and bowling ball shorts thought he could arc the ball over the shorter player. Will saw the ball coming and leapt as high as he could, deflecting the pass. The ball bounced free and Big Mike dove for it with two other Knox players. The big man in the black jersey managed to snare the ball and throw it back, right to Jared.

"Give it!" Brad yelled, rushing over. He snatched the ball from Jared's hands and rushed up the court.

The screaming reached a new level as the clock ticked down to less than ten seconds.

Jared quickly remembered Mr. Moore's plan and sprinted after the ball, heading to the basket. Brad dribbled down the middle, passing midcourt when three Knox defenders cut him off. Big Mike and Will were both open on the wings as Glen labored to catch up to the play with Jared.

Instead of passing, Brad juked right and then left, spinning away from the pressure and somehow managed to break through. He dropped his shoulder and made for the basket. Bowling ball shorts jumped to meet him and Brad hesitated, keeping his dribble. On the right side of the basket, Will cut in calling for the ball.

"Here!" he cried. "Pass!"

Instead Brad ducked under the Knox defender, moving right into Will's path. Will's eyes widened and he jumped out of the way. Brad barreled by, just missing running over his smaller teammate. Thrown off course, Brad ended up under the basket. Jared had charged the rim from the other direction, ending up right in front of Brad.

Jared opened his hands for a pass, but Brad instead jumped forward trying to throw up a reverse layup. Bowling ball shorts spun around and contested the shot. Flinching, Brad slammed his backside into Jared's chest, sending both boys tumbling to the ground. The ball bounced once on the rim and then fell off, just as the buzzer sounded.

Stomping his feet as he lay on his back, Brad covered his face with his arms. His chest heaved with exhaustion.

Next to him, Jared wondered if it was tears or sweat dripping down the eighth grader's face. He slowly sat up and hugged his knees to his chest. He looked up at where Will stood behind the basket with his hands on his hips looking lost. The ball lay at the shorter boy's feet.

All around them the Knox players jumped for joy as the crowd sat back in stunned silence. The game had ended.

"Come on, boys," Mr. Moore called, walking onto the court. "Put your heads up. That was a great game. We just came up short."

His team was slow to follow.

"Did we win?" John asked, clapping his hands. "We won, right?"

Nick sighed dejectedly beside him. "No, man. We didn't win. Let's go shake hands."

For a second John looked confused, but then he shrugged and grinned. He remained the only one smiling for the Patriots after shaking hands with the Knox players. He happily ran back to the bench to help Angie clean up.

The rest of the players stood around with bowed heads and troubled faces.

"We should've had that one," Glen muttered, summing up the general feeling. "They were good, but we should've won."

Brad grunted and glared balefully at where Will and Jared stood. "We would've had that one if certain players didn't try to help the other team!"

Mr. Moore frowned and started to say something when a loud angry voice interrupted.

"Look!" roared Brad's dad, running from the bleachers. "I don't know where they dug you up, *Coach*, but they'd better throw you back. You and your runt of a son cost us the game."

Mr. Moore narrowed his eyes. "Excuse me, but you're not allowed on the court."

"I'm a parent just the same as you!" Brad's dad had pale blue eyes and now they bugged out as they tried to stare down Mr. Moore. He stood a good two inches taller and had a wider girth.

Still, Will's dad just stared back and didn't back down. "I'm sorry you feel bad about the game, but I think you need to calm down and leave the court."

"Come on, Dad," Brad said, embarrassed, going to the balding man. "It's over. Let's just go home."

"No, I won't just go home. Not until I know this … this man won't be running this team anymore." He turned to Mr. Hackett. "Who put him in charge to begin with?"

Will licked his lips and nervously started for his dad. "Um, Dad …" he said.

Mr. Moore just held up his hand to his son. His ears burned red as he took breaths to control himself. "Don't worry, mister," he said tightly. "I was asked to help out for this game only, but I see it was a mistake. I don't repeat mistakes. I'm through here. Come on, son." Turning on his heel, Mr. Moore walked away. "I'll be in the car, Will. Grab your stuff and let's go."

All the players stood there stunned. Even Brad couldn't lift his head. Jared turned to Mr. Hackett who'd walked on the court when the yelling started.

The PE teacher ran a hand through his graying hair and tightened his lips. "Okay, everybody," he finally said. "Show's over. Coach Swopes should be back tomorrow. Let's get your gear and move out of here."

John laughed as one of the team balls escaped his hands and rolled onto the floor. Brad's dad narrowed his eyes when seeing him. "Retards and shrimps, what a team. Come on, Brad. You should've won that one."

Mr. Moore dropped Will off in the driveway and immediately backed out his car and drove off. The ride from the school had been one of silence. Sighing, Will hefted his sports bag and limped into his house. His bruised knees from his fall with Brad had finally started to hurt.

Chapter 38

Mr. Moore ended up at General's Pub, a local bar he passed on his way to and from the gym he worked at. Switching off the car engine after parking, he blew out his breath. He'd never stepped foot in this bar before, or in any bar for over twelve years. But after what he'd just been through, he needed a drink. Just one.

Stepping out, he breathed in the cold fresh air and stared up at the night sky above him. He'd almost lost it back in the gym. He'd almost lost it in front of his son and a whole team of kids. But he hadn't. Instead, he'd looked like a coward who walked away instead of standing up for himself and his son. In the army it'd been much simpler. In the army you knew who the enemy was and you knew who your friends were. And you could do something about it.

Inside the pub, he was met with loud music and the thick smell of smoke and beer. He passed by the tables and sat on a stool at the end of the bar.

"What'll it be?" a beefy man with more hair on his face than his head asked.

Mr. Moore swallowed and scratched his thigh. Then he took a deep breath. "I'll have a soda," he said tightly. "Just give me a Coke."

Frowning, the man nodded. "Nothing else?"

Mr. Moore's hands trembled, but he nodded. "Nothing else."

"Hey!" called a voice behind him. "Who's that I see? If it isn't the illustrious basketball coach from the middle school!"

Mr. Moore's shoulders stiffened. He slowly turned and saw three men at the table against the wall by the door.

The man sitting on the outside of the table grinned at him from underneath a mess of dark greasy curls and a Budweiser ball cap. "Me and my friends just got back from the game," he drawled. "I didn't think you'd be here. I figure you'd be hiding in a hole somewhere."

Mr. Moore nodded and then turned back to the bar. "Better make it to go," he muttered.

The bartender gave him a funny look. "We don't do that here, man," he said. He set a glass of Coke in front of Mr. Moore.

The guy with the ball cap had clearly been drinking. His buddies laughed as he got up and sauntered over to Mr. Moore at the bar. "How's your son taking it?" he asked, blowing hot breath smelling of beer in Mr. Moore's face. "He's crying, I bet."

Mr. Moore turned to the man and just smiled. "Do you have a son on the team?" he asked.

"Nope. And if I did, I would pull him right off." Then he blinked at Mr. Moore. "Come on, man. You're drinking soda? What, you can't handle a real drink?"

"Hey, Sam, lay off him!" said a deep voice from another table. "Stop trying to cause trouble."

Sam only grinned. "What, Mr. Coach? What are you going to do now? Let me buy you a beer."

Mr. Moore frowned and looked at his soda. Then he turned to Sam and smiled. "No. I'm going to buy you a Coke. Enjoy it." With that, he slammed down a five-dollar bill, got up, and walked out. It wasn't until he was outside that he realized his hands were shaking.

Instead of going to his car, he walked around to the rear of the pub, not really knowing what he was doing. At the dumpsters he saw a wooden crate leaning next to a broken mop handle.

All his pent-up anger came pouring out. "Okay, chumps," he muttered. "Let's see how you like it ..."

Without stopping to think, he gave in to his rage. Grabbing the mop handle he found himself pounding the crate. He hit it over and over, feeling the slats smash. Splinters exploded around him. Finally, the handle broke through the crate and struck the metal dumpster, shattering.

Mr. Moore felt his anger shatter with it. Panting, he dropped the broken stick and bent over, out of breath.

"Feel better?" asked an amused voice behind him.

Turning, he saw a brawny man with a thick mustache watching him, standing against the back entrance of the bar. "Remember me? I'm Coach Marsden from football."

Mr. Moore rose to his full height and nodded in recognition. He gestured at the destroyed crate. "Sorry about that," he muttered. "Kind of let my emotions run away for a second."

"Don't be sorry," Mr. Marsden told him. "I should be the one apologizing. I'm the one who told Swopes to call you if he ever needed help." The football coach sighed and ran a hand over his smooth, round head. "I was at the game tonight too. I saw everything."

Mr. Moore chuckled without humor. "No worries. I knew what I was getting myself into."

"Yeah, well ..." Mr. Marsden cleared his throat. "You might want to know this. A parent started talking before the game ... about how you're Will's father and that you were trying to take over the team to give him more playing time."

"Yeah, I know. I think I met him."

Mr. Marsden shook his head. "This guy wasn't Brad's dad. He's somebody I've never seen before, maybe not even a parent. He started riling up a bunch of parents and kind of set off everyone." Mr. Marsden scratched his bare head. "Now that I think about it, he was near Sam Pherrins at the time. That's the jerk at the bar back there."

Mr. Moore gave a start. But then he shrugged. "I guess there's more than one jerk in the world.

"You got that right," Mr. Marsden agreed. "The world is full of them." He grunted. "I just wish so many of them weren't parents."

A short time later, after thanking Mr. Marsden, Mr. Moore walked back to his Corolla. On his way he passed a faded Dodge pickup. He couldn't tell in the dark, but it looked red.

After showering and picking at his supper of leftover ravioli, Will lay on the couch in shorts and a T-shirt with icepacks over his knees. Angel had watched Jimmy during the game and was now putting him down to bed. Mrs. Moore had just returned home and heard about the game, blow by blow, from Will during supper.

Coming in from the kitchen, she crouched by Will's head, brushing hair from his forehead.

"It's okay, honey," she said. "I promise you your dad will be fine."

"Ha," Will muttered.

"Move over, Will. I had a long day too."

He lifted himself up on his elbows, allowing his mom to sit and slide her lap beneath his head.

"Mom, will Dad ever be okay? I mean, cured so he could get a real job?"

His mom stroked his hair and sighed. "He's trying, baby. He really is. We just have to be patient and always be there for him, just like he's always there for you in sports."

"Today didn't go so hot."

"Not everything goes our way, Will. But as the saying goes, where there's a will, there's a way."

"Ha, ha, Mom."

"I know." She sighed. "I'm afraid I get my sense of humor from your father. And about his job, Will, he is getting one. Do you know what he does during the day while you and Jimmy are at school?"

"Well, yesterday he short-sheeted my bed."

Mrs. Moore smiled. "Besides that." Her voice grew serious. "He writes. He sits in our room at his desk writing."

"Really?"

"It's like his therapy, I think."

Will lifted his eyes, looking back up at his mom. "What does he write about?"

"All sorts of things. He doesn't let me read everything, but he writes about his experiences in the war, his family … But lately I think he's been writing about you, Will. One day he'll be a published author. Just you wait."

"Yeah, well, I bet his first book is a joke book."

"Not funny, Will."

Mr. Moore made sure to stop by Will's room when he returned late that night.

"Hey, champ. It's me again. I just wanted to say … Well, I just wanted to say, I'm really the tooth fairy. Sorry, buddy, but I never told you before."

"Ha, ha," Will mumbled.

"Can I come in?"

"Sure, Dad." Will sat up as Mr. Moore stepped into his room, taking a seat on the edge of his bed. He kept the lights off, so the two sat in darkness.

"I'm really sorry about tonight, bud. I thought I was doing the right thing with the coaching thing, but I guess I was in a little over my head."

"Everything is over my head, Dad."

"Hmm. Sorry, champ, but that joke came up short."

"Ha."

The two sat in silence for a while. Then Mr. Moore cleared his throat. "I, uh, just want you to know. I went to the gym tonight … I did stop someplace first, but I decided to workout instead."

"You went to a bar?" Will asked.

"Yeah, maybe. Don't tell your sister. But I didn't drink anything. Not even the water. In any case, bud, I may not make the next few games of yours, if that's okay."

"Sure, Dad. I understand."

Mr. Moore sighed heavily. "I don't understand. I don't know why people act the way they do, or why I act the way I do sometimes. But I do know I love you. And I don't want you to see me lose control … I almost did back there. Thankfully, you kept your cool. That helped me. Well, in any case, I want you to know I'll always be there for you. Always. Okay, champ?"

"Yeah."

"Good. Now get some sleep. After that ugly loss you need some beauty sleep." Smacking Will's back, he stood up.

"Dad?"

"Yeah, bud?"

"I love you too. But you're still not funny."

As Jared walked into homeroom the next day, Gary greeted him with a wide smile. "Hey, beanpole. I heard you guys had a great finish yesterday. From what I understand you were one of the MVPs. For the other team."

Jared ignored him, going straight to his seat without making eye contact with anyone. He knew some of the kids had been there to the end.

"What happened?" Marshall asked loudly.

Gary chuckled. "Oh, you wouldn't want to know, Marsh. There was sweat and tears involved. Mostly tears for beanpole."

Giselle stood abruptly from her desk and glared at Gary. "Why don't you shut your hole, Gary?" she said. "You were a complete jerk last night! I wanted to stuff my pom-pom up your fat nose, and if you don't shut up right now I might do it with my fist." She then turned to look at Jared and stuck a hand on her narrow hip. "You guys did great, Jared. It wasn't your fault you lost. You'll get the next game."

Jared's mouth dropped open and he hastily closed it. "Uh, yeah," he said. "Thanks."

Marshall took off his glasses and cleaned them. "I think I need to be attending more basketball games," he said. "They sound interesting."

Gary just slouched in his seat, looking utterly chagrinned. He didn't say a thing when Big Mike walked in.

Jared had typing that day, so didn't get a chance to see any of his teammates that morning except for Ryan. Ryan just gave him a cold look and ignored him. Then at lunch Ben arrived alone at the table.

"Will and Nick said they had an English project to finish in the library," he explained apologetically as he took a seat.

Angie grimaced. "It's amazing what happens when jocks lose. All of a sudden they don't want to be seen anymore."

Jared glared at her. "That's not fair," he said.

The girl dropped her gaze guiltily. "I know, I'm sorry … I just can't believe what Brad's dad said last night."

"Yeah," agreed Ben. "And Mr. Hackett just stood there." He flicked a strand of hair from his face. "Sometimes I don't understand teachers."

Angie nodded. "I still think there's something funny going on around here." She exchanged glances with Jared.

Before Ben had arrived, Jared had caught her up on all the things that had happened, like the red pickup nearly running him and Will down, and overhearing Coach Swopes's odd conversation with Mr. Drydon after their first game.

Both wondered if that was why Coach Swopes had mysteriously fallen sick. Angie did confirm that the elderly gym teacher had shown up that day. She'd stopped by the gym that morning and said he looked perfectly fine. Jared never mentioned to her, nor did he tell Will, the strange message on his bag. He'd colored over it with sharpie but could still see the writing. *OOPS*. What did it mean?

Jared glanced at John, who happily sat between Angie and Ben eating his crust-free, white bread sandwich. He wished he felt as carefree and happy as John looked.

Chapter 39

The Patriots had little time to recover from the Knox Middle game. That Friday after school Coach Swopes had all the boys sit on the bleachers for a talk before practice. He'd heard all about what had happened at the game and promised changes. At the same time, he expected the boys to be teammates on and off the court.

"No more of this bickering," he said. "We're the boys' team trying to become like men."

Angie, listening, made a face. She sat in a chair to the left of the bleachers near where John sat between Jared and Will. "I've seen a lot of men bicker and fight," she muttered. "Where does he think boys learn it from?"

Jared just looked at her and then over at Will. He still hadn't gotten a chance to talk with him. He just wanted him to know he still had his back.

"In any case," Coach Swopes was now saying, "the Knox game is over and done with. A lot of mistakes were made, but we're moving on."

Jared understood where the coach was coming from. The next game was on Monday against their archrivals, the Hamilton Dragons. The Dragons, according to Nick, had won their first two games by a combined fifty-six points. There was no time to feel sorry for their loss.

"We haven't beaten Hamilton in any sport for three years," Coach Swopes said, continuing. "We need teamwork and better decision making if we're going to end that streak."

"Then why aren't we practicing?" Brad muttered from near the top of the bleachers. He'd mumbled an apology to the team before Coach Swopes's talk, but had pointedly avoided looking at Will.

It was a valid question many of the boys had and was never really answered. The practice session ended with the team running laps and doing a couple of shooting drills. That was it.

"I have some business to take care of tonight," Coach Swopes explained as he blew his whistle to end practice early. "Everyone have a good weekend and rest up for Monday. Remember. We haven't beaten Hamilton in any sport for three years. Let's end that streak!"

Being a Friday, nobody really complained. After a long week of school and the tough basketball loss, most were ready for the weekend.

Before leaving the gym, Jared wanted to ask Will about playing at the apartments the next day. He changed into his school clothes quickly and came out where some of the boys were still shooting baskets.

At the far end of the court he saw Will in deep conversation with Ryan. Nick and Ben were shooting behind them. It was just like old times. The four were friends leaving Jared on the outside. They hadn't invited or even told him about staying late to shoot. Abruptly Jared turned when Will laughed at something Ryan said. He went straight to the office to call his mom for a ride home, reaching her just in time. If he'd waited a few minutes later she'd have left with Kelly for dance rehearsal.

The only consolation Jared had that weekend was the fact that it poured on Saturday. He spent the weekend watching football alone.

The Washington Middle School basketball teams rolled into Hamilton just after four on Monday, December 15. It was a day and date Jared would not soon forget.

As the teams carried their bags off the buses and made their way to the gym, they were greeted by a large handmade sign hung over the school's gym entrance. With a picture of a purple dragon burping up a colonial tri-corner hat, it read in big block letters: *Dragons EAT Patriots for Snacks.*

"Cute," Giselle said, waving her pom-pom at the sign as she led the cheerleaders into the school.

"I hope we give dragons indigestion," Nick said, walking in the back with Will, Ryan, and Ben.

Ryan snorted. "Yo, man. I hear last year we almost had a riot with these jokers."

"Just focus on your game, boys," Coach Swopes said, shuffling after them, stooped over his clipboard. "We didn't come here for trouble. We came here to win."

"That might be trouble," Ben said, swallowing hard.

Jared came last. He hung back with Angie and John, to help them carry the bulky ball bag and basket of water bottles. He'd rather do that than walk in alone with his so-called team.

John had ridden with the boys and sported the team's black shorts with his matching jersey. Officially, in accordance to his dad's wishes, he was now a member of the team.

Angie hadn't been happy about it and had made Jared promise to sit with him. Now she gave Jared a tight smile. "I told him he didn't need to help anymore, but he insisted."

John smiled. "I'll get the water," he said. He happily ran toward the building with the water bottles.

"I don't blame him," Jared said, watching him go. Immediately he felt his face start to flush. "I mean, you need a lot of help."

Angie dropped the ball bag on the sidewalk and looked at him. She'd stopped painting her lips and nails black some weeks before, but still wore jeans with holes at the knees. Right now she had on a tight black hoodie over a blue T-shirt. Brushing back her hair, she frowned.

"Okay," she said. "But how come you aren't with your friends?"

"What?"

"Why aren't you with Will?"

Jared bit his bottom lip and shrugged. "I don't know," he finally said. "Sometimes I … Well, I can't tell who my friends are all the time," he finished lamely.

Angie gave him a look and then smiled. "Fine. If you want to help, grab this bag. It kills my shoulder."

From the boys' bus, Mr. Hackett sat in the driver's seat, watching. As Angie and Jared made their way to the school, he pulled out his cell phone and made a call.

The Patriots girls' team lost by forty points and had been held scoreless at halftime. As the boys took the floor, the gym was rocking. The gleaming white walls had a thick purple stripe that ran the length of each side twenty feet high. In the middle of the far wall facing the stands, just above the stripe, hung a line of championship banners. Three of the banners, including one from the year before, were for basketball.

Jared stared up at the banners and then at the stands, filled to capacity with kids and adults, nearly all decked out in purple and gold. A small, but boisterous gathering of Patriots fans sat in the far section at the other end of court. He didn't see Mr. Moore among them, but he did spot Brad's father. His arms crossed over his girth and his face pulled in a sour expression, he sat in the bottom row staring hard up at the banners.

"Come on, boys," Brad called loudly. "Let's get in lines for layups! It's game time, baby!"

"Yo, Brad!" called a voice from the opposing side. "Is that your hotshot guard over there? He looks like a tripping hazard."

A tall, well-built boy, with a faded buzz cut ambled to midcourt wearing his purple and gold jersey with obvious pride. Acne marked up his otherwise good-looking face, and he smirked at where Will knelt by the center circle tying his shoe.

Brad nodded at the Hamilton boy and went to meet him, leaving Glen in charge of the layup lines.

"Hey, Colton," he said. "Long time no see." He exchanged high fives and chest bumps. "You still playing travel?"

"Nah, man. I had it with my coach. He never played me right. Besides, why play travel when I can be a star right here at my home school?"

Brad chuckled, but didn't look too amused. "Yeah, dude, but good luck tonight. You're going down."

Colton laughed. "Yeah, right! All the talk about you guys is this hotshot guard the size of a pencil. I'm supposed to be guarding him all night."

Brad frowned and shook his head. "Whatever, dude," he said. Turning, he went back to the layups. He didn't look at Will as he passed him.

Will stood and stretched when Colton beckoned to him.

"Hey, runt!" he called. "You're done tonight!"

Will turned to him and raised his eyebrows. "Who are you?" he asked. "The manager?"

"Ha," Colton said. "I would kick your skinny backside here to kingdom come, but I don't think I could find it in that mess of shorts you're wearing. You'd better be careful out there. You might slip through a crack."

"My foot is going to slip through your crack if you don't back off," Nick said, coming to stand behind Will. He glared at Colton.

"Oooh," Colton said. "Nice. You have a bodyguard. You'll need one."

"And you need a facelift," Nick told him.

Will just stared and shook his head.

"Hey!" shouted the Dragons coach before Colton could reply. "Get away from there and start warming up! Come on!"

"See you on the court," Colton said. "Not you, little man. Just your fat friend. You, I might trip over." He winked as he turned back to his team.

"Hey, Nick and Will!" Brad shouted. "Stop gawking and lineup!"

Jared walked slowly to the layups line and went to stand across from Will. He'd seen the exchange with Colton. "If anything happens," he murmured, "I'll be ready."

"What's that?" Ben asked from in front of him.

"Uh, nothing," Jared said. He bit his bottom lip and waited for the game to begin.

Chapter 40

As the horn sounded, announcing the start of the game, Coach Swopes gathered the players together around him.

"Don't worry, boys. I'm all out of pep talks," he said. He glanced over his shoulder at the screaming crowd and nodded. "That's your pep talk right there. For the past five years their basketball team kicked us in every direction but up. Every one of those people came here to see you lose. Let's disappoint them tonight, okay? Same lineups for now, boys. Let's go!"

Will and Nick exchanged looks. It was an interesting opening speech at best. They took a seat on the end of the bench. Jared looked their way, but saw Ryan sit next to Nick and he went to the other side of the bench. He didn't understand Ryan at all. One moment he was distant and cold and the next he was trying to be Will's best friend. The only thing Jared could figure … Ryan treated Jared like he shouldn't exist.

As the whistle blew, he turned his focus to the game.

It started out well for the Patriots. After two slow starts in the previous games, Brad knew he had to do better, especially when everybody seemed to buzzing about Will. Big Mike won the opening tip to Glen and scored the first basket of the game from a nice lob from Brad. After a good defensive stop, Brad scored the next basket, beating his man off the dribble and hitting a runner in the lane when nobody picked him up. Three minutes later and the Patriots had a 10 to 4 lead.

Near the end of the quarter the Patriots started to tire and the Dragons started a comeback. Colton, the point guard for Hamilton, had scored on three straight possessions. When the buzzer sounded to end the first, the Patriots clung to a 16 to 14 lead.

"Okay, substitutes," Coach Swopes called, looking down on his clipboard. "I said there'd be changes and this is it. We're going with an eighth-grade team, plus Mike, and a seventh-grade team. Seventh graders, you guys are up. I want Will, Ryan, Kyle, Nick, and Jared. Ben, you and Tom stand by. If I see anybody on the floor not busting their tail, you'll go in for them."

Jared shot off the bench and wiped his hands on his shorts.

"You guys better keep us in the lead," Brad said loudly as he took a seat. "We worked hard for this. I'm not leaving this school without beating Hamilton."

Will scratched the front of his short hair causing it to spike up and looked ruefully at Nick. "No pressure on us, right?"

Nick burped in response.

When Colton saw the lineup coming from the Patriots' bench for the second, he laughed. Then, pounding the floor with both hands, grinned at Will. "Bring it, little man!"

Colton stopped laughing after Will brought it. After the Dragons missed a long three, Will leapt in front of Colton for the rebound and put the ball on the floor, scooting down the court and scoring a layup before anybody could catch him.

Glaring, Colton took the ball and tried going right at the smaller player, but Ryan pounced from the side, knocking the ball away. Will scooped it up and raced down for another layup.

After Will hit a three and made a pinpoint pass to a cutting Ryan for another layup, the lead had ballooned to eight. It was 23 to 15, with the Dragons' only point coming off a foul shot after Nick caught the arm of the Hamilton forward.

Jared had two rebounds, but had yet to touch the ball on offense. He didn't mind. Offense still proved to be his weakness, and besides, Will was humming. The team started feeding into his energy.

"We got this, guys!" Nick hollered as they set up on defense. "Let's hold them here!"

Kyle pounded the floor, mocking Colton.

Seeing this, the guard's face flushed red, his acne popping out like polka dots. Taking the ball, he tried to cross up Will and get by. The small guard stood his ground and Colton ended up running into him, knocking him to the floor.

Immediately the whistle blew. "Foul on offense, number 23, charging!" cried the ref, pointing the other way.

"What!" Colton shouted, slamming the ball down.

"Watch it, son," the ref told him. Both refs were tall with dark hair and brown skin. With hard faces, they didn't look ready to be intimidated by mere kids. "You want a tech, just keep it up."

Colton just snarled at Will and ran back.

"Nice!" Ryan said, pulling Will up. "That's the way to take it!"

Will rubbed his chest ruefully. "Fine, then you take it next time," he said ruefully. "That hurt."

Nick and Kyle came in to congratulate him, but Jared hung back. He couldn't help but feel as if part of the scenery. Then it happened.

On the next possession, Will threw the ball down to Jared, who'd established position on the right block, close to the stands. A huge, hefty boy with a mane of wild red hair pushed on him in the back. Colton immediately left Will to double him up. Jared didn't dare try to dribble as hands surrounded his face. He tried turning toward the basket, but had nowhere to go.

"Here!" Will called, shifting along the three-point line. "Pass it out, Jared!"

Jumping, Jared threw it out to him, feeling the big kid shove him in the small of the back. He flew off the court, sprawling onto the floor under the basket. Looking up, he saw everything happen as if in slow motion. Will caught the ball, lined up a shot, and fired it off, just as Colton charged at him.

Colton didn't even try for the ball. His eyes wild with fury, he extended both arms and shoved Will hard in the chest just as the boy reached his highest point. The ball arced high up before falling short. The boy flew backwards, smashing into the stands. He struck Brad's dad right in the stomach, bouncing off to the side before slamming into the wooden seat next to him. He'd managed to brace the fall with his hands, but his body striking sounded like a clap of thunder.

The entire gym gasped and shouted. The cheerleaders screamed in horror.

Whistles from both refs shrieked as Colton stood staring at Will's fallen body with a look of shock.

Then Jared smashed into the Dragon player. He didn't even remember getting up. All of a sudden he was screaming as he charged at Colton's back, striking his shoulder with his forearm.

Colton went down like a chopped tree. He banged to the floor and lay stunned, having just thrown up his hands to protect his face at the last moment.

More whistles screeched and parents jumped from the stands.

"Hold it! Hold it!" roared one of the refs. He ran over and grabbed Jared from behind, pulling him back. "Everyone hold it!"

Players from both benches started for the floor, but Coach Swopes, showing an amazing burst of agility and speed, hustled to midcourt and put up both hands.

"Stop right there and get back to your seats!" he shouted.

Big Mike stepped in front and stood next to the coach. "Listen to him," he barked. "Shut up and sit down. We ain't doing this!"

The Hamilton players also were hustled back to their seats.

It took over five minutes, but eventually things calmed. Jared stood with his chest heaving on the baseline as a lady trainer from Hamilton attended to Will. Colton had staggered to his feet and stood rubbing his shoulder, staring at Jared. He looked to be in a mixture of shock, fear, and anger.

Jared just felt numb. He'd never done anything physical or violent to another person before. Sure, he'd been in a few scraps with his brothers when little, but they had been mostly pushing and name-calling.

Nick came up to him and put an arm around his shoulder. "Hey, man. I don't think that was legal, but nice job. That jerk deserved it."

Jared just barely nodded.

Ryan stood by him awkwardly scratching his head. He looked as if he wanted to say something, but didn't know how. Finally, he sighed. "Yo, man. That was some hit."

The crowd still buzzed but gave a loud ovation as Will got up and painfully climbed from the stands. He had a cut on his lower lip and appeared shaken, but nothing appeared to be too serious. Holding a towel to his mouth, he ducked his head and limped to a table behind the scorer's table for more treatment.

The ref who'd grabbed Jared after the shove blew his whistle. "We got multiple fouls on both teams," he announced loudly. "We have a flagrant on 23 purple and a flagrant on number 4 black. Both players are disqualified."

"Sorry, man," Nick said, patting Jared's back.

Jared barely heard him. He felt as if someone had just punched him in the gut. He couldn't believe it. He'd been kicked out. For the first time in his life he was disqualified from sports for his behavior. Stumbling forward, he made his way to the bench, tears stinging his eyes.

As he arrived, Coach Swopes gave him a sharp slap on the backside. "Good job, Cook," he said. "But I never want to see you do such an idiotic thing like that again. Go take a seat."

He was surprised to see nearly all his teammates standing, waiting for him. Glen ran forward and smacked his shoulder. "Nice, man! That's what I'm talking about!"

"Beanpole has a spine after all!" Darius said. "I haven't seen you mad, like ever!"

Even Big Mike gave him a head nod.

It still didn't change the fact that he'd been ejected. He made his way to the last seat and fell into it. As he did, tears fell with him.

"You want some water, Jared?" Angie asked softly, coming up behind him.

Jared just shook his head.

"Here, then." She draped a towel on his head and left him alone.

Just before halftime, Jared heard somebody behind him. Turning, he saw Will limping with an icepack in his hand. A Band-Aid was stuck on his chin just below his lip. Wincing, he took the seat next to Jared and groaned.

"Sorry," Jared mumbled.

Will nodded. After a moment he nudged Jared's arm. "I missed what you did," he said. "I was too busy eating wood. But I did hear it."

Jared shook his head, reliving the image of seeing Colton spread across the floor. "Yeah ..."

Will nudged him again. "Hey, Jared. Really. I don't think Colton is going to mess with me again. Thanks, dude."

Feeling better, Jared relaxed and managed a grin. "Next time you want to sit in the bleachers, use the stairs."

Will winced. "Okay, man. You can't make me laugh. My Band-Aid's ripping."

As the game continued, the Patriots couldn't finish what they'd started. All their energy had been sucked out by the incident. After halftime, the Dragons started to dominate and eventually won 62 to 51.

Both Jared and Will remained at their seats as the teams went to shake hands. Coach Swopes didn't want to offer any of the Dragon players a chance to retaliate. He didn't have to worry. The Dragons were just happy to get off with the win. Colton left the line and came up to them, shuffling his feet. His eyes were red and face puffy.

"Sorry, man," he said to Will, sniffing. "I, um, sort of lost it out there."

"Me too," Jared said to him, getting to his feet. "I'm, uh, sorry for hitting you. I hope you're all right."

"Now I am," Colton told him. "After you knocked some sense into me." He squeezed his eyes shut. "Oh, man. My parents are going to kill me."

Will's dad picked him up straight from the game after getting a call from Coach Swopes. Before leaving, he made sure to shake Jared's hand and tell him not to worry about anything. "It's good to stand up to bullies," he told him. "I'm sorry you got in trouble yourself, but I'm sure your parents will understand. Thanks for watching out for Will."

Jared nodded and trudged towards his teammates.

At the bus, Mr. Hackett just stared at him and shook his head. "Cook, I heard what happened. I never knew a Cook to fly off the handle."

It was a quiet bus ride back.

Jared didn't have to worry about his parents. When he got home that night, courtesy of his tired mother with Kelly in the back, nobody even asked how he did. In the car his mom only asked if he'd won and then said too bad, maybe next time when he'd told her no. Kelly, exhausted from her schedule, had fallen asleep in the backseat.

Jared went straight to the shower and then to bed without speaking to his brothers.

Chapter 41

The school week dragged on after the infamous game with Hamilton. It was the final week before winter vacation and all the teachers and kids were anxiously waiting for Friday. It felt a lot like practice for waiting on Christmas Eve. At least for Jared, after Monday's game, Will, Nick, and Ben brought him back in the fold. Will arrived at school walking stiffly with bruised ribs and a sore knee. He limped through the halls with his scraped chin surrounded by well-wishers.

Both Jared and Will were minor celebrities, as news of the game spread through school. Kids that Jared had barely ever seen came up to congratulate him and slap his shoulder. He didn't understand it. None of these kids had been at the game and none had ever paid the slightest bit of attention to him before. Some of his classmates had not even known his name. Now everywhere he went teachers and students called him out, gave him smiles, and treated him as a hero. Gary and Chaz glared at him during English, but Giselle went out of her way to give him a smile, causing Jared to blush.

"Welcome to middle school fame," Angie told him at lunch when he expressed his feelings. "Don't worry, by January you'll be long-forgotten."

Jared frowned and watched John happily bite a teddy graham. "I certainly hope so," he said.

He looked across the cafeteria to where Will and Nick had been delayed. Giselle and Stephanie had pulled them to their table to fawn over Will's injuries. While Will looked embarrassed, Nick was doing his best to get Stephanie's attention, to no avail. John,

Jared realized, was the only kid he knew who treated everyone the same, no matter what.

One student still ignored him, treating him as if he didn't exit. Ryan had turned cold and distant again, avoiding not just Jared, but also Will, Nick, and Ben. Even at practice he stayed away from the group. Ben said he was just going through tough times and would snap out of it. Jared didn't think so.

"Hey, Jared," Angie said, bringing his attention back to the lunch table.

"Yeah?"

"One good thing about your fame … you're getting better."

Jared frowned. "Better at what?"

"You don't always say 'what' to every question now."

"What?"

Angie giggled and threw a pickle at him.

The Patriots had one final game on Thursday before the break, but it was against Newsome Middle, a small school from the upper end of the county. Their team came to Washington with more hope than talent. Half their roster was made up of kids around Will's height, but none had the athleticism. Jared was suspended a game for his actions against Hamilton and so had to sit on the bench. Will dressed for the game, but Coach Swopes also had him sit out, to rest his knee and ribs. They watched as the Patriots ran away with an easy 67 to 35 victory.

During the game, Jared had a lot of time to think. The crowd was sparse compared to their first home game and he'd easily spotted Marshall sitting by himself in the middle of the row behind the Patriots cheerleaders. Seeing Marshall, and thinking how he'd felt about wanting to make a friend before meeting Will, caused Jared to think about other kids. A lot of kids were alone, he realized. He remembered what Angie had said about Sarah.

After the game, he begged his mom to let him do some Christmas shopping. Exhausted, but pleased to have a thoughtful son, she complied. The Christmas spirit could be contagious.

The next morning, Jared roamed the halls carrying a wrapped package. He desperately wanted to find Sarah, but at the same time hoped she'd decided to skip the last day before break. He'd spent almost thirty minutes rehearsing what he would say if and when he found her. In his bathroom mirror it had come across smooth. Now his mouth and throat had become frozen like the North Pole.

Just as the first bell rang, announcing the start of homeroom, he spotted the shaved head walking beside a tall thin girl with dyed, shiny black hair. Buzzed to stubble on the sides and left long and flowing in the middle, her hair hung past her boney shoulders.

As he followed them, Jared couldn't help but think Sarah's companion's hair resembled a long, black tongue licking her back. He wrinkled his nose at the image. Both girls wore skinny black jeans and black leather jackets and their walk was slow and methodical.

Jared felt his will power drain with every step. All his lines from rehearsal turned to mush. "Christmas," he murmured to himself. Clearing his throat loudly, he lengthened his stride and pulled even with girls.

"Uh, er, hi, Sarah," he muttered. "I, er, remember you read … er, you might like this." He shoved the wrapped package at the surprised girl.

Her companion's eyes widened and she stared at Jared. "What about me?" she asked.

Jared faltered, but then he swallowed. "Yeah, I got something." He took his backpack off his shoulders and put it on the ground. Unzipping it, he pulled out *Once and Future King* by T.H. White, one of his favorite books. "If you like vampires, you should like this," he said, handing it to the girl.

"I-I was only joking," the girl stammered, taking the book, clearly pleased.

"Oh, it's okay," Jared said. "I read it four times already and I found this copy in the library for a dollar." His face reddened. "I, uh, meant to give it to somebody who might like it."

Sarah frowned. "So are these books also from the library?"

Jared quickly shook his head. "Uh, no, I picked those out especially for you. I, uh, remember how we used to pick books out together. I, er, gave you some of my favorites. I gotta go. Bye!" He grabbed his backpack and practically ran from the girls.

"Jared, wait!" Sarah called after him. Jared paused and turned. "Th-thanks," she said. "Thank you. I mean it."

The other girl nodded and hugged her book close.

Nodding, Jared gave them a wave.

"Merry Christmas!" called Sarah's companion.

Jared entered the winter break with a mixture of disappointment and the overwhelming excitement of Christmas. His disappointment came from missing basketball and not being able to see his friends. Coach Swopes had scheduled only a single volunteer practice during the break, for the twenty-ninth, four days after Christmas. The high schools were playing in tournaments and he encouraged the players to attend the games instead and practice on their own. All Jared had to practice on was his stupid tree branch and a soccer ball. Will and his family were going to visit his grandparents up in Maine. He said he should be back for the voluntary practice.

Jared sighed as he sat in his room on the first day of break. Usually, his mother would have Christmas music playing from Thanksgiving night to well past New Year's Day. She would spend the weekends baking pies and cookies, saving them all in the freezer for Christmas. This year, with Kelly's dance schedule increasing and Carey's increasing mobility, she'd only had time for baking a few pies when Jared and Kelly were at school, and no cookies.

On the first day of break, the Nutcracker less than a week away, Kelly's rehearsals only increased. She and her mother, with Carey, would be stuck in rehearsal all day and most of the night. His father went out shopping and Jack was out with Rick, both trying to pick up girls to take to the movies.

Lying on his bed, Jared had his radio playing a mixed CD of his favorite Christmas songs and had an open book of *A Christmas Carol* in front of him. He wished he had somebody around to enjoy the time with. Then his door opened and George walked in.

"What is that trash you're listening to?" he asked. "Put on some real music, man." Going over to the radio, he switched off the player and turned on the radio to a rock station.

Jared bit his lip and made sure to say nothing. Sometimes, it was bad to wish for things that might come true. Grabbing another Christmas CD, he quietly exited the room and went downstairs. He ended up curled under the tree with the music playing loud on his mom's stereo system. He fell asleep with a smile on his face just as the Ghost of Christmas Present showed up.

Winter arrived a few days later and the temperature hovered just above freezing. Jared spent his days reading, listening to

Christmas music, and playing outside. Basically, he spent it avoiding his brothers. Kelly's Nutcracker finally came and Jared sacrificed an evening with his parents, watching a nonsensical story with too much dancing and not enough sports. Still, he enjoyed the music and Kelly looked nice, he guessed. Afterwards, Kelly and their mother were so exhausted they pledged to sleep until New Year's.

Then, on the day before Christmas Eve, Kelly surprised everyone by staying up all night making Christmas cookies. She and Jared decorated them the next morning while their parents did last-minute shopping. George came by and swiped a few, but Jared didn't really care. They at least had cookies for Christmas. His greatest surprise came the next day.

Waking up on Christmas morning had to be the greatest feeling in the world. Jared always woke before dawn and spent an hour in bed listening to Christmas music on headphones. Then, just as the sky paled in the window, he crept down to the tree, turned on the lights, and admired the presents and the family manger scene.

His mom always set up the manger scene on a dresser by the tree, high enough to keep from Carey's prying fingers. It was in this moment that anything could happen. Any and every present he could imagine might be under the tree somewhere with his name on it. Of course, he usually never got what he really wanted, but that was okay. It was the hope and expectation that made it so exciting.

For this Christmas Jared was left even more disappointed than usual. He'd gotten boxes of school clothes, a few books, and a music CD. Then, after all the presents had been unwrapped, and his mother was in the kitchen making hot cocoa, Jared's father called him to the garage. Jared went with a huff, thinking he needed to take out the trash. Instead, his father showed him a large rectangular cardboard box nearly the size and width of a bookshelf lying down.

"This one didn't want to fit under the tree, Jared," his father said, his eyes twinkling. "I think your brothers are outside with a few other odds and ends to go with it."

"You got me a new bookcase?" Jared asked, frowning. Then his mouth dropped open. It wasn't a bookcase. It was a brand-new basketball hoop.

"We got it for the whole family," his father said, smiling. "But I'm willing to bet who's going to use it the most."

As Jared cried out and ran to the box, the garage door lifted open and Jack peered in, wearing a goofy grin.

"Merry Christmas, bro," he said. From behind his back, he produced a new basketball. "George has got a few bags of sand out here to put in the stand to keep the hoop up."

Jared was speechless. "I … I don't know what to say," he muttered. "I mean, thank you. Thanks a million. Thanks two million!"

George snorted, coming up behind his older brother. "Don't thank us," he said. "We were just sick of you embarrassing us by throwing a stupid soccer ball at a tree."

Jared just grinned.

Kelly helped him assemble the hoop that afternoon. By sunset, Jared had the hoop up and operational. His first shot hit nothing but net.

"Great!" Kelly said, clapping her hands. "Now you can invite Will over and I can finally meet him!"

"All right boys," Coach Swopes said, looking over the eight boys gathered on the morning of the twenty-eighth, "I'm glad to see some of you still like to play basketball." He sighed, looking a bit worn, "Why don't you all put any personal belongings in your lockers and come out ready for practice. Hurry up, now."

Most of the boys who did show up had arrived with fancy new phones and other gadgets. Brad showed off a new Apple phone and cordless headphones. It was ten in the morning and some of the kids looked as if they'd just woken up.

As Coach Swopes finished talking, Brad stood up, yawning loudly. "Come on, boys. Let's get this practice over with. I got things to do and people to call!" He led the way to the lockers, pumping his head to a loud beat. "I'm texting Colton right now, dudes," he said tapping on his phone. He looked back at Jared and grinned. "I'm asking how the floor tasted and telling him we'll see him again in the championship."

Jared ducked his head. Darius and Glen both smacked his back as they went by to put up their phones and jackets. The guys were never going to let him forget the Hamilton game. He drifted back to where Will and Nick remained on the bleachers. They both just wore long-sleeved shirts and shorts and hadn't brought any belongings with them. Will's legs were covered in black sleeves.

"How's your knee?" Jared asked Will.

Will grinned, slapped his legs and stood up. "They're good now," he said.

He pulled up his shorts to show off black matching leg sleeves with padded knees that went from his ankles to his mid-thigh.

"Man, put down your shorts," Nick told him, wincing. "Nobody wants to see that white. You're blinding me!"

Will let go of his shorts and stepped on his friend's foot. "Ha. Let's get a ball and start shooting. You already shoot like you're blind."

"Sure, man" Nick said, standing, "but I'm going to knock you down and test your pads." Then he looked at Jared. "Oh, uh, sorry man. I didn't mean to bring up, um, Hamilton."

Will slapped the back of Nick's shorts. "You and your two rear ends," he said. "You're always blowing out the wrong thing from the wrong end."

Jared just laughed and said he'll be there. First he had to drop of his new jacket in his locker. The mystery thief had yet to be found and nobody felt good about leaving anything valuable out. He was surprised to see Mr. Hackett in his office as he ran into the locker room.

"Cook," his PE teacher called, stopping him. "I hope you don't run anybody over today."

Jared's face burned. "Uh, no, sir."

"Good. Have a happy New Year."

Chapter 42

As Jared walked back out, he was surprised to see Angie and John sitting on the bleachers just outside the locker room. John had his eyes glued to the court where the boys were shooting around.

"Hey, Jared," Angie said, sighing. "John doesn't know what volunteer means. He just had to be here."

"Oh, hey. That's great," Jared said. "I mean, it's good to, uh, see you … and him. Uh, hi, John. I better get to practice."

Besides Brad, Darius, Will, Nick, and Jared, only Kyle, Teddy, and Tom showed up for the practice. After sprinting drills and having the boys jog three laps while dribbling a basketball, Coach Swopes had the teams divide up to scrimmage four on four.

"Full court?" Kyle asked.

"Of course full court!" Coach Swopes said. "What type of question is that?"

"I just ate a lot," Kyle said, holding his stomach. "I don't want to blow chunks, that's all."

Coach Swopes just shook his head. "If I don't see hustle out there, we'll do more running at the end of practice. Let's go!"

Jared teamed with Will, Nick, and Tom against Brad, Darius, Teddy, and Kyle. It started as an even game with both teams trading baskets, but then Jared got hot.

Knowing his offensive struggles, Teddy began the game playing off him, choosing to guard the basket. Will found Jared wide open on the baseline. Instead of passing back as usual, Jared went up for the shot and nailed it. On the next possession Will again found Jared alone on the baseline. Again Jared hit a jumper.

"Big man is on fire!" Nick called, slapping Jared's shoulder as he ran back to defense.

"Guard your man!" Brad yelled at Teddy. "Come on!"

Will started feeding Jared the ball every chance he got. Jared responded with three more made baskets in a row. He hit a jumper over Teddy, and then, posting up, threw up a hook shot that hit nothing but net. On this third basket, he pump faked, causing Teddy to jump, and then dribbled once to the basket before soaring for an easy layup.

"Somebody ate their Wheaties," Coach Swopes called. "Nice work, Jared!"

John started clapping and cheering, causing Brad to glare his way. "Maybe we should put John in for you, Teddy," he growled.

Teddy just wiped his face. "He's too tall and now knows how to shoot," he grumbled. "It isn't fair."

Jared's excitement carried over to defense. He blocked two shots, including a layup attempt by Brad, and controlled the middle, shutting down drives and snatching up any rebound in his area.

After an hour of hard playing, Coach Swopes blew his whistle to end practice.

"Okay, boys, good job. Grab your stuff and go have yourselves a happy New Year!"

Jared dragged himself off the court feeling elated. He'd never played that well before.

As he sat on the bleachers, Will and Nick came up to him, both grinning.

"What did you get for Christmas, man?" Nick asked. "Basketball skill?"

Will sat next to Jared and stretched. "It was just all those great passes he got," he said.

Nick snorted and reached down, slapping Will across his stomach. "Yeah, right, man."

Jared smiled. "Actually, I got a hoop for Christmas. I've been practicing."

Will paused in retaliating against Nick. "Really?"

Nick just stared at him. "Are you serious? You mean you didn't even have a basketball hoop before? Good grief!"

Jared shrugged. "I do now."

Just then they heard an angry yell from the locker room. It sounded as if someone was being murdered.

Jared felt his heart skip and Will gave a start.

"What the world, dude, is that?" Nick said.

Then the yell came again. This time they could hear Brad's voice. "Somebody stole my stuff! Which one of you"—Jared blinked as his next words came out in a string of curses—"took my stuff?"

Brad ran from the locker room, his sweaty hair a tangled mess and his face red with fury. His nose and eyes were scrunched in a snarl. "I'm serious! I'm going to kill whoever did this!"

"Watch it!" Angie snapped at him. She stood by John, who'd been gathering the balls and putting them on the rack. "You're scaring him!"

John now stood quivering, his hands pressed tightly to his side.

"I don't care!" Brad roared. "Get him out of here! Maybe the retard is the thief!"

"Don't you dare call him that! He wouldn't take your stupid stuff!"

"He was the last one in here!" Brad snarled back.

Jared's face burned. During the scrimmage, John had gone back in the locker room to fetch water bottles, but before that Jared had been the last player in the locker room, putting up his jacket.

Coach Swopes rushed out from his office, his face grim. "Everybody calm down! Right now!"

"I can't be calm!" Brad said, his chest heaving. "My locker was robbed!"

"What was taken?" asked Coach Swopes. "Are you sure you just didn't misplace it?"

"I didn't misplace anything! I put my phone and headphones in my locker and locked it tight. Now it's gone. Some—"

"Watch your language, Brad," Coach Swopes snapped as Angie covered John's ears. "We'll look around and see if we can find everything."

"We'd better!" Brad said. He suddenly squeezed his eyes shut and wiped his eyes. "I just got those for Christmas."

In the end, nothing was found. All the boys went to their lockers and did a thorough check. Only Brad had been robbed, but there was no sign of the culprit and no sign of Brad's phone or headphones.

Brad's dad arrived and demanded to have all the boys searched. Coach Swopes, looking gray and tired, only shook his head. "Nobody could stuff headphones in their shorts," he said.

Still, the boys, looking somber, lined up at midcourt and one by one showed Brad their belongings.

Jared stood with Will and Nick on the end, clutching his jacket. He felt sorry for Brad and wished it all had been some mistake. Why couldn't Brad just remember he'd dropped his stuff anywhere else? He couldn't believe one of his teammates to be a thief.

"Sorry, man," Kyle said as Brad went by him. He held up his own phone. "This is mine. No thief here."

"Shut up," Brad snarled at him. He glared at Will, but swept his eyes angrily past Nick and Jared. "One of you," he called loudly, "is a dirty thief!"

Standing behind him, his dad had both hands shoved deep in his jacket's pockets. He looked mad enough to spit fire. "What about him," he growled, jerking his head at where John and Angie stood. "That re—that kid over there. We didn't check him."

"Leave him alone," Angie said, moving to stand in front of John. "This is ridiculous!"

Coach Swopes sighed. "I keep telling them, don't bring valuables in here. Anything you bring with you is at your own risk."

Brad's dad looked ready to pop the basketball coach in the face.

"Okay, now," barked Mr. Hackett, coming from the locker room. "I just checked everyone's lockers. There's nothing to find. Whoever did it probably snuck in through the back way and is now long gone."

Brad left with his dad seething and threatening to sue. The remaining boys slowly trickled out to the parking lot, very subdued. Jared's great practice fizzled to a sour end.

"Hey, Jared, you want a ride?" Will asked him as they left the school. Nick had already said his goodbyes and left the back way, walking to his house.

"Uh, sure … that would be great. I told my mom I would call and sort of got distracted."

The two sat on the curb to wait for Will's dad. Will put his knees up and rested his chin on top. The cut on his chin had faded to a faint mark.

"Man, so what do you think about Brad?" he asked.

Stretching out his legs in front of him, Jared just shook his head. "I don't know," he said slowly. "I still can't believe somebody robbed the locker room during practice.

"You think it has anything to do with all the other stuff happening?"

Jared frowned. "Maybe. I still don't understand any of it."

"Me neither. Hey, what are you doing today? You want to go ice skating?"

Jared just blinked and looked at him. "What?"

"My sister is taking me this afternoon." He laid his chin on his knees looking at Jared. "You don't have to go."

Swallowing, Jared thought quickly. Kelly, now free of dance for a while, had wanted to hang out with him. They'd planned to shoot baskets and maybe go to the mall that night.

"Uh, I actually kind of promised to hang out with my sister. She's in sixth grade, and ..." His voice trailed off.

Will lifted his head and shrugged. "She can come too.

"I was afraid you'd say that," Jared said. He knew Kelly would be only too happy.

Washington County's one and only ice rink was housed in a huge rectangular building, located behind a busy shopping center about twenty minutes from Jared's house. His mom was happy to give Kelly and him a ride, especially when hearing Jared would be meeting a friend. She'd met Mr. Moore and Will when they'd dropped him off after basketball and quickly had agreed ice skating would be great.

"Now I know," Mrs. Cook said, glancing in the mirror back at Kelly and Jared. The two sat in the middle seat of their minivan with Carey between them in her car seat.

"Know what, Mom?" Jared asked.

"Now I know why Kelly wanted to meet this Will so badly. He seems like a really nice boy."

Jared groaned and rolled his eyes. "This," he said firmly, "is not happening."

Kelly only grinned and fluffed her curls. Her blue eyes danced with excitement. "This is *so* happening, Jared. Don't worry. I won't embarrass you. Too much."

Will and his sister Angel stood outside the rink waiting for them. They both wore jeans and hoodies. Will had a brand-new Golden State Warriors hoodie, bright yellow and blue. Two sizes too big for him, it made him appear even younger and smaller.

"You two have fun," Mrs. Cook called as Jared scrambled from the van.

"I will!" Kelly said. She smoothed down her black dance jacket and wiped her hands on her jeans before following her brother.

Jared rolled his eyes. "I probably won't. 'Bye, Mom. We'll call when we're ready."

Mr. Cook blew a kiss. "Take your time!"

"Hurry up!" Will called to them. "My sister needs to rent the skates and has to know your shoe sizes."

Jared dropped open his mouth. He'd forgotten all about bringing money.

Will grinned when seeing his reaction. "Don't worry, dude. My sister will pay for everything, right?" He looked up at his older sister.

Angel smiled. "Anything for my little bro," she said, mussing up Will's hair. "You must be Jared's sister," she said to Kelly.

"That's me!" Kelly said, grinning shyly. "I've been so busy with dance that I haven't been to any basketball games this year."

Will scratched his chin. "Yeah, well, it's a good thing you missed the last one. Come on, let's get the skates!"

Angel laughed. "Hold on, kid! We love skating," she said over her shoulder as she opened the door. "In Maine that's all we did over Christmas, but this is our first time here. Do you both skate much?"

Jared and Kelly looked at each other before shaking their heads. The only ice they'd ever stepped on was ice cubes during summer picnics. Occasionally puddles would freeze in the winter, but that was the extent of their skating experience.

"We go roller blading," Jared offered. "Does that count?"

"Close enough," Will said impatiently. "Come on!"

Inside was a warm room that reminded Jared of a locker room with a snack bar. Just inside the door was a counter to rent skates and beyond that there was a wide-open space with metal benches. In the right corner, a stand sold hot chocolate, coffee, burgers, fries, and an assortment of candies and chips.

Being the Christmas holidays, the room was swarming with kids and adults and littered with shoes. Swinging double doors led to the ice rink. Through a window behind a row of tables on the far wall, Jared could see the large sheet of ice filled with skaters.

Angel got everyone's shoe sizes and soon started passing out ice skates. "You kids go ahead on the ice," she told them. "I'll stand back and watch for a while."

Will looked at Jared and rolled his eyes. "She means she'll check out all the guys. When she sees one she likes she'll go out on the ice and fall in front of him."

Angel laughed and flicked him in the head. "Watch it, kid. Now I hope *you* fall."

"Ha," Will said. "Not a chance."

Kelly took her skates and held them up by their tangled laces. "Um, does anybody know how to put these on properly?"

Will looked at her, his mouth opened. "You've never laced skates before?"

Angel grinned and pushed him forward. "Go help her, little bro. Meet me back here at the first Zamboni break and I'll buy us all hot chocolate."

Shortly after, as Jared tentatively stepped out on the ice, finally figuring out how to get his laces properly done, Kelly and Will were already zooming way ahead. He shuffled forward and carefully pushed off, surprising himself how fast he moved. He had to windmill his arms to keep from falling.

"Great," he muttered. "I forgot ice is slippery."

"Jared?" called a familiar voice behind him.

Startled, he tried to turn and found both his feet slipping out from under him. He fell back on his backside with a painful thump, banging his elbow on the hard ice.

"Ohmygosh, are you okay, Jared?" Angie called, rushing to his side, skating easily across the ice. Jared stared at her in surprise.

"Jared's here!" cried John, skating from behind her. "Hi, Jared!"

Both wore the same clothes from basketball practice and had probably come straight from there. Angie had her usual dark jeans and black hoodie. John wore black athletic pants with a white stripe and matching jacket. A blue winter hat covered his golden hair, revealing his bright, nearly angelic, face.

Amazingly, John skated effortlessly, looking almost more comfortable on the ice than he did on regular ground.

"What are you two doing here?" Jared couldn't help asking, cradling his sore elbow as he tried to push himself up with his free hand.

"Careful, you're going to fall again," Angie said. She took his shoulders and helped pull him up. Jared slipped a little and nearly sent them both down.

"Sorry," he muttered. He wiped ice pieces from the back of his jeans.

"No worries," Angie laughing. "I can't believe you're here!"

Jared looked at her and quickly averted his eyes. "Yeah, I'm, uh, here with Will and my sister. They're right … There they are."

Will darted across the ice towards them with Kelly giving chase. Jared couldn't help but feel slightly jealous about how fast his sister seemed to be picking up ice skating. Her dance obviously helped her as she gracefully slid her feet over the ice, laughing as she tried to grab Will's hood.

Seeing Jared, Will slid to a sudden stop, throwing up pieces of snow.

Screaming, Kelly waved her hand and plowed right into his back. They both went down in a heap at Jared's and Angie's feet.

"Are you two okay?" Angie asked.

"Let me guess," Will said, his right cheek pressed to the ice with Kelly lying on top of him. "You don't know how to stop, right?"

Kelly laughed as she got up. "I do now. I just need to crash into somebody."

"Ha, ha," said Will. "Next time pick your brother."

"Sure," Kelly said, pushing herself up. She reached down and tapped Will's head as he got to his knees. "Oh, by the way. You're it." Laughing, she skated away.

Will got to his feet ruefully and looked at Jared. "Nice sister you got," he said with a grin. Then he noticed Angie and John. "Hey, it's a basketball reunion! Hi, John."

"Hi, Will," John said, grinning widely.

Angie smiled. "We come here a lot. John loves to skate."

Other skaters moved around the group, giving them dirty looks.

"Keep it moving," grumbled one of the adults. "Too many kids here."

"Merry Christmas to you, too," Angie said to his back. "Uh, we'd better keep moving."

The four started around the oval at a slow pace, much to the relief of Jared. John wanted to demonstrate his skating to Will and the two went ahead a few yards. Angie and Jared watched as John showed off crisscross skating and his ability to jump without falling.

"I'm impressed," Jared muttered. "I can't even stand without falling."

"You'll get used to it," Angie said. "When John first started he couldn't do anything."

"So you do come here a lot, huh?"

"Oh, yeah. Mr. Drydon has a pass that lets us skate any time the ice is open."

Jared bit his lower lip, frowning. "Speaking of Mr. Drydon, do you, uh, have you seen anything strange? I mean, after what happened with Brad, do you think that is related to everything?"

Angie's face clouded and she shook her head. "I don't think so. I feel bad for Brad, even if he is a jerk. But Mr. Drydon has been different. Of course, it could be the holidays, but he seems much happier these days. I mean, he's been busy and all, but it's like he finally found some peace." She gave him an embarrassed look. "I'm really starting to think I sort of imagined everything else."

Jared frowned. He hadn't imagined the writing on his back or the writing on his sports bag. Of course, that could have been some sort of prank, but then there were the mysterious locker room robberies, not including his missing twenty dollars.

"Yeah," he said doubtfully. "Maybe."

Just then Kelly came barreling by and caught his arm. They both ended up smacking into the glass wall.

"Sorry, Jared! But I really don't know how to stop!" She tossed back her hair. "But, ohmygosh, this is so much fun!"

Will turned from where he stood with John. "I can teach you," he offered.

Kelly's face lit up like a Christmas tree. "Really?"

Jared rolled his eyes.

"Sure," Will said. "Anything to keep you from running me over again. You want to come too, John?"

"Sure!" John said. "Let's go!"

Angie and Jared watched them glide away. Angie then turned to Jared and lifted an eyebrow. "Are we really letting them get away from us? Come on!"

She shot forward and, having no choice, Jared rushed to follow. After skating slow for a while he'd found his balance and quickly found ice skating to be very similar to roller blading. Throwing his knees forward, he swiftly caught up to Angie and the two flew up the ice. Jared could turn easily enough, but like his sister, he had no idea how to stop.

"Watch out!" he cried.

Ahead of him, Will turned and immediately pushed Kelly and John out of the way. Jared flew by and rattled the glass boards with a resounding thump. He fell back, landing with a thump back onto the seat of his pants.

"Taking a break already?" Angie teased, skating up to him, sliding to an easy stop.

Jared only groaned. "I think I'm going to take it slow for a while."

"Sure, here." Angie bent forward and offered him a hand.

As Jared took it, he couldn't help but feel heat rise to his face. It was the first time he'd ever held hands with a girl not related to him.

Angie perhaps read his mind and she ducked her head shyly.

Only Will clearing this throat spurred them to action. "You two okay?" he asked innocently.

"Oh, yeah," Jared stammered, instantly starting to pull himself up.

"No, Jared!" Angie screeched as his sudden jerking on her arm caused her skates to slip out from under her. With a yelp she fell across his lap.

Kelly plowed into them next. She'd moved in to help keep Angie from falling, but ended up lying over her back.

"Ooof," Jared groaned, bearing all the weight. "I'm, er, sorry."

Angie and Kelly only laughed.

"Dogpile!" Kelly said.

Will just shook his head. "Come on, John. Let's get out of here. They're hopeless."

Eventually, Kelly moved off to chase after Will and John, leaving Jared and Angie to skate slowly around the oval. Neither spoke for a while as they watched Kelly and Will dart through traffic ahead of them, followed by John.

"They look cute together," Angie finally said.

Jared coughed and nodded. "Yeah, I guess so." He found himself smiling. "Kelly has actually been waiting for this moment for a long time."

Angie chuckled. "Yeah, I bet ..." She then sighed. "I know how she feels."

"What?"

"Nothing. Let's just skate."

Chapter 43

The five kids left the ice together when staff members started clearing the way for the Zamboni to clean the ice. Angel stood waiting for them. At seeing Angie and John, she instantly invited them to join the group for hot chocolate.

"No worries," Angel said cheerfully when Angie tried to protest she had no money with her. "My dad gave me his credit card. This will be on him."

The group found a table and soon were laughing and joking over cups of hot cocoa. Kelly and Will had hit it off immediately. When the Zamboni finished, they immediately threw away their empty cups and headed back to the ice.

"We have to stay here," Angie said, sounding disappointed. "Mr. Drydon is coming to pick us up any minute."

John frowned at hearing the news. "Okay. Next time I'll skate longer, right, Angie?"

"Sure, John," Angie replied, "but it'll have to be next time."

"I'll stay with you," Jared blurted. "I mean, I could use a break from skating." He blushed.

Angel smoothly stood up, gathering her pocketbook. "In that case, I'd better head to the ice before my brother does something stupid. It was good meeting you, Angie. You too, John."

When she left, Angie and Jared stared awkwardly at the table with John between them. Somehow it felt much different than when they saw each other at school during lunch.

"So, uh," Jared said. "Are you enjoying being the manager yet?"

Angie brushed back her hair and smiled. "Yeah, well, the jocks can be a pain—"

"Angie, John!" snapped an angry voice. "It's time to go. Now!"

Shocked, Angie and Jared glanced up to see Mr. Drydon staring at them from in front of the skate rentals window. He did not look happy, especially at seeing Jared. His face turned to a severe frown and he glared.

"Uh, I'd better go," Angie said, quickly getting to her feet. "Come on, John. Your dad is here."

"Daddy!" John said, quickly running to Mr. Drydon.

The principal just took his son by the shoulder and pushed him toward the door. He waited for Angie to move in front of him and quickly herded her out as well. As he left, he threw one last look back at Jared. It did not look friendly.

Jared felt his blood run cold. If Drydon had been happy lately, it had all changed now. The look he'd given Jared could be described as murderous.

He shivered as he grabbed his cup of hot cocoa only to find it empty.

On the ride home, Kelly asked Jared what had happened.

"What?" Jared asked, shaking himself from a daze.

After Mr. Drydon had left, he'd returned to the ice in a distracted state at best. Kelly and Will whizzed around the ice playing tag with a group of other kids while Jared had just skated listlessly in ovals until the next Zamboni break when he'd called home to be picked up.

"Did you and, um, Angie have a fight?" Kelly asked.

Instantly Jared's face started to burn. "No!" he said. "Nothing like that at all! I'm just tired ..."

Kelly looked at him for a second and shrugged. "Okay, Jared," she said. "But thanks for inviting me. Will and I had a great time."

Jared just rolled his eyes.

Jared didn't see Will again until the Monday following New Year's when they returned to school. It would end up becoming one of the worst days of Jared's life.

"Jared Cook to the main office, please," blared the loudspeaker, interrupting Mrs. Donavon's New Year's announcements during homeroom. *"Jared Cook to the main office please."*

Jared frowned. He'd never been called to the office before and couldn't think of a good reason why that would change.

"Ooo, man!" Gary said. "Somebody's in trouble!"

"Gary, that's enough," Mrs. Donavon said. "Jared, go ahead, sweetie. I'm sure you just left something on the bus."

"'Bye, sweetie," Gary whispered to him as Jared went past.

Even if he knew Mrs. Donavon to be right, Jared couldn't help but feel his stomach clench. Something about being called to the office always made him expect the worst. But what could he have done wrong? "Is this about Hamilton and my suspension?" he wondered aloud as he walked through the empty halls.

Expecting the worst was not enough to prepare him for what he found.

Mr. Drydon stood in front of the office flanked by Mr. Hackett and Coach Swopes. None of them looked very happy. Mr. Drydon stared coldly at Jared while Mr. Hackett gave him a hard look. Coach Swopes just looked angry and confused. However, his anger wasn't directed at Jared.

"This is preposterous," he said as Jared approached them. "Jared is a good boy."

Hearing him say that only increased Jared's tension, and his eyes widened in fear and confusion.

"After what happened at Hamilton, I'm not so sure you can say that," Mr. Hackett said gravely.

Mr. Drydon just stared at Jared with his steel blue eyes. "Do you know why you're here, son?" the principal asked with a neutral voice.

Jared shook his head, not trusting himself to speak. It was the first time Mr. Drydon had ever spoken to him directly. He was surprised to find himself nearly the same height as the principal, but he definitely felt much smaller under the cold, unwavering gaze.

"Let's just get this over with," Coach Swopes said. "I'm telling you, this is crazy."

Mr. Hackett cleared his throat. "We need you to open your locker, Jared. There's been a, uh, tip that says you have something in there. Something that doesn't belong."

Jared froze. He'd just used his locker early that morning. The only thing inside were his books for class. He did have a copy of *The Power of One* by Bryce Courtney, but surely that couldn't be a problem. He'd read much worse in Mrs. Donavon's class.

"Is there anything you want to tell us?" Mr. Drydon asked him. "Now's your chance."

Jared just wrinkled his brow and shook his head. "I-I don't have anything."

"Just go to your locker and open it, Cook," Mr. Hackett said. "If this is a misunderstanding then you can go back to class."

It turned out to be a misunderstanding, all right.

Dazed, he walked back to the Pathfinder hall, feeling numb all over. He reached his locker just outside the door of Mrs. Donavon's room. He knew some of the kids had seen him go by with the principal. The three teachers stood just behind him, waiting impatiently.

"Hurry up and open it," Mr. Drydon commanded.

"Beanpole busted," he heard Gary's muffled voice say.

Sweat beaded on his forehead as he spun the lock, finding the combination. *What could possibly be in the locker? Maybe it was a cruel prank*, he thought.

The door popped and instantly Mr. Drydon yanked it open, nearly banging it in Jared's face. Mr. Hackett shoved Jared aside and reached in. He pulled out a sandwich-sized Ziploc bag. It was half full of crushed dried green leaves.

Coach Swopes groaned. "Oh, no," he whispered.

"Sorry, Cook," Mr. Hackett said, "but you are now busted. I never took you for a weed smoker, but middle school is when kids like to experiment."

Jared just stared in absolute shock. He'd never seen the bag before and certainly knew it wasn't his. He didn't even know what weed looked like … until now.

"My office, now," Mr. Drydon said, licking his mustache. "With the size of that bag, I think we need to call the police after your parents, son. Now let's go!"

Jared's mind raced and his heart started thumping wildly. He felt tears welling up in his eyes. His mother would be at home right now …

It was impossible, so how had the bag of weed appeared? Who would have put it in his locker?

Suddenly he felt as if somebody pulled a cork out of his throat and his breath returned, blowing out like an air pump. "Wait," he said. "This, this is just a mistake."

"There's no mistake, son," Mr. Drydon said. His mouth formed a tight smile. "You were hanging out with the wrong people and now have to pay the consequences."

"I'm sorry, son," Coach Swopes, sounding old and forlorn. "I never thought you were like this."

Jared shook his head. He'd been framed. He knew this. All he had was a prayer and a far-out hope. A few months before he would be a crying mess right now. His body would have shut down and he'd have rolled over. But now he knew he wasn't alone. He had friends behind him. He had a team behind him. Jared looked at Coach Swopes, pleading with his eyes.

"Coach," he said, "you know I'm not. That's not weed … it's just basil. Basil and some, uh, oregano mixed in." He remembered back on Halloween and the bag Ray had held out. He hadn't gotten a good look at it then, but it did look similar to the one in Mr. Hackett's hand now. He prayed he was right.

The three adults stopped in their tracks. Mr. Hackett and Mr. Drydon exchanged looks of surprise.

Coach Swopes just frowned. "Is that true?"

Jared certainly hoped so. "Uh, yeah … Check it."

Mr. Drydon bit the bottom of his mustache but nodded. He handed the bag to Mr. Hackett.

Frowning, Mr. Hackett opened the bag and sniffed. He used his finger to pick up one of the shredded leaves and gave it a lick. "It's basil all right." He stared hard at Jared. "How did you—what in the world are you doing with basil in school?"

Jared felt his life rush back through him and nearly collapsed with relief. He figured Gary and Chaz were the culprits. He knew it had been a wild shot about it being basil, but had hit nothing but net.

"Uh, uh, I, uh, like to use it at lunch," he babbled. "You know, uh, lots of times the food here is bland."

"Just go back to class," Mr. Drydon said, sounding disgusted and more than a little surprised. "I'll keep the bag for now. If you want it, come see me later."

Jared had no plans on seeing the principal later.

Gary looked surprised and disappointed when Jared returned to the classroom, but he lacked a guilty look.

"What happened, beanpole?" he asked him. "Last time Drydon and Hackett came at me like that I got three days suspension for bringing water balloons to school."

Jared bit his tongue and stared at him. Gary met his gaze and actually looked more curious than anything else. Shaking his head, he just returned to his seat.

After homeroom, Jared tracked down Chaz, pulling him into the boys' bathroom across from the gym.

"Chaz," he said bluntly, "I'm being completely serious. Did you or Gary have anything to do with putting something in my locker?"

Chaz gave him a look like he was crazy. "What are you talking about, man? You're tripping. Why would we go near your locker?"

Jared stared hard at Chaz, but Chaz only looked back, genuinely confused.

"Fine," he muttered. "Tell me the truth. Do you guys still sell fake weed to kids?"

"Man, get off of me," Chaz said, ducking his gaze. He made to pull away when Big Mike's frame blocked the entrance way.

"Shut up and answer the question, Chaz," Big Mike said coolly.

Sighing, Chaz broke down and his shoulders slumped. "Okay, uh, yeah. Sometimes."

He admitted to having bags of fake weed around, but knew nothing about Jared's locker or trying to frame him. He did, though, admit to having one of his bags disappear in gym during the week before winter break.

When Chaz had finished his confession, Big Mike had gone. Pulling away, Chaz quickly ran out leaving Jared utterly confused … and more than a little scared. Who'd had set him up and why?

Being the first day after a long break, the schedule reset made it an odd day. For Jared, it was indeed an odd day in more ways than one. As he headed to the locker room for PE, Angie ran to meet him at midcourt.

"Jared," she said, her voice low, "I, uh, want to apologize about the skating thing."

Jared tried to grin, but found it too hard. "It's okay, I—"

"Mr. Drydon is just worried about bad influences for John, and well … I don't think I can sit with you at lunch anymore. Sorry." She ducked her head, hiding her face behind falling hair. Without another word, she ran to the girls' locker room.

Jared felt like another sucker punch nailed him in the stomach. He barely knew what they did during PE class.

When lunch came, Jared didn't bother with the cafeteria. He'd had enough with all the sneaking around and the little games being played. Something was going on and it had to do with Mr. Drydon and the PE teachers. He meant to confront Coach Swopes and ask him directly.

Jared slipped into the empty gym and quietly walked across the court toward the teachers' offices. He'd seen Mr. Hackett head into the teacher's lounge by the office and hoped Coach Swopes would be alone.

Just as he reached the door, he heard voices and he instantly froze.

"I *need* to see Mr. Hackett. Now."

"Sorry, son," Coach Swopes said. "He's at lunch right now. He's probably in the lounge, and students aren't allowed there."

"It's an emergency."

"I can't help you, Ryan. Anything you want to tell me? I've noticed you haven't been yourself the last few weeks. Is something bothering you?"

"N-no, sir. Not yet. I'll, I'll just come back." For a brief moment Ryan sounded lost and scared.

Before Jared could react, he realized Ryan would be exiting the office and heading right for him. Caught in the open, he hastily backed a few steps and pretended to be just arriving when Ryan came bursting out of the locker room, his face tensed.

Seeing Jared, his eyes widened in surprise. Then he glared. "What are you doing here? Are you trying to spy on me?"

"Wh-what?"

"Yo, man. You heard me, man!" Ryan clenched his fists.

"I-I just got here," Jared stammered. "I just wanted to see Coach Swopes."

"He's not in there," Ryan said. "Go away, man."

Jared made to argue but then heard a door close in the locker room. The lock clicked.

"Yeah, okay," he muttered. Reversing his steps, he walked from the gym, forcing himself not to speed up or show his anger. He could feel Ryan's eyes burning into the back of his skull.

Exiting the gym with no appetite for food, he spent the rest of the lunch period in the library trying to read. All he saw were a jumble of words and he read the same page three times without making any sense of it.

Chapter 44

That afternoon, Jared's hot touch in practice abandoned him.

"What happened, man?" Nick asked him after Jared missed his fourth shot in a row during a warm-up drill. "Last week you were like Dirk Novinsky before he got old, and now you're shooting like his grandma."

Jared grimaced and shook out his hand. "Just not feeling right," he said.

He looked across the gym where Angie sat reading a book at the bleachers. John sat next to her watching the drills intently. Sighing, he ran a hand through his sweat-soaked curls.

Before practice he'd tried to catch Will and Nick at their lockers, but as he approached the back room, he'd heard Ryan's voice and had instantly turned around. He'd wanted to talk to them about Ryan and ask about him. Why did Ryan want to talk to Mr. Hackett? Coach Swopes was his PE teacher and coach. It made no sense. Something wasn't right … And it seemed to be getting worse in an awful hurry.

"Dude, where were you at lunch?" Will asked him. They were standing in front of the side basket just to the right of the entrance. The drill had each one taking turns shooting ten shots each. While one shot, the other two fought for any rebounds. So far Jared gave plenty of rebounds. "Nick and I had the table to ourselves."

"Yeah," Nick grunted as he tossed the ball to Jared. "It was awkward, man. Just the two of us. Now if it was Stephanie Baker and me …"

"She would've been bored out her mind," Will finished for him. "What?" he cried when Nick shoved him. "You never talk to her!"

"I'm just waiting for the right moment," Nick muttered embarrassedly. Then he grunted. "Sort of like I'm waiting for the moment Jared shoots again."

"Oh, uh, sorry," Jared said. He threw up another brick that clanked off the side of the rim. He was very aware of Ryan standing at the main basket behind him. He could feel his eyes, still burning into his skull.

Jared struggled for the rest of practice, dropping passes, missing defensive switches, and even airballing another free throw during a scrimmage. Finally, it ended and he started to rush to the locker room when Coach Swopes called him over.

Jared gritted his teeth. Ben and Ryan had amazingly left immediately for the parking lot without changing. Ben had a church meeting that night and was Ryan's ride. That meant Nick and Will would be alone for him to talk to, if he could just get there.

"Everything okay, Jared?" Coach Swopes asked.

Jared flicked his gaze where Nick and Will were just disappearing into the locker room.

"Uh, yeah," he muttered. "Just had a bad day."

"I know," his coach said. "I was there. I'm sorry about Mr. Drydon and the basil thing."

Jared blinked. He'd almost forgotten that had happened that very morning. "Oh, yeah," he managed to say. Behind him, he heard Angie and John gathering the balls.

"Look, Coach, I—"

"Jared, look at me. I'm getting too old for this. Not the coaching. I love the coaching. It's ... it's the other stuff."

Jared frowned, suddenly taking an interest. "What other stuff?"

"Oh, you know ... each administration wants things done certain ways." Coach Swopes rubbed his forehead as if it trying to put a hole in it. "I don't understand it myself ... But Jared, for some reason Mr. Drydon has it in for you." Jared felt an icy grip close around his heart. The old coach continued, looking and sounding his age, add a few years. "I ... Well, I know you tried to see me at lunch today. I'd just finished a long conversation with Drydon. He wanted to know about you, son. I ... Well, I'd be careful if I was you. Make sure you stay out of trouble."

Jared could only stare. "I, uh, okay ..." Then he blew out his breath. "I don't understand."

"Neither do I, son. You're a good boy, Jared. I think Mr. Drydon has a lot on his mind and is taking out his stress the wrong way." Coach Swopes nodded toward John. "He's worried about John, I think. Don't take it personal, but do keep your nose clean. Look, er, I got to go. I have a meeting with my financial advisor. See you tomorrow. Don't forget, we have Berkshire! Tomorrow, I have new shirts for you boys. Buses leave before the bell as it's going to be long drive. Get some sleep and get your touch back. We're going to need you."

Jared just stared as the old, stooped coach shuffled from the gym. "How can I focus better after that?" he mumbled.

Feeling utterly lost and confused, he went to the bleachers and collapsed in a seat. Angie and John left the gym without glancing in his direction. For a long while Jared just sat and watched as his teammates trickled from the locker room. He didn't see Will or Nick.

"You ready for Berkshire tomorrow?" Nick asked, putting on deodorant. "It's a long drive, man. Like two hours, so be prepared, dude."

"Maybe you can use the time to come up with something to say to Stephanie," Will told him, pulling on his long-sleeved shirt. The two were just finishing changing, but taking their time.

"Shut up, man. Hey, I hear you were hanging out with Jared's sister over the break. Some guys saw you ice skating together."

Will gave him a look and frowned. "Yeah. And we talked. You should try it with Stephanie." He stood and pulled up his Adidas pants.

"Ah, whatever." Tossing the deodorant into his locker, Nick grabbed his shirt and tugged it over his big frame. "Hey, speaking of Jared, what's up with him? Where is he?"

Shrugging, Will sat on the bench and started pulling off his sweaty socks. "I don't know, but I think that he and, um, Angie might've had a fight."

Nick lifted his eyebrows. "Jared and Angie?" Then suddenly he sniffed. "Hey, man. You smell that? That isn't your feet, is it?"

Will frowned and inhaled. "No way ... that's ..." His eyes widened. The funny smelling cologne started drifting into the room, growing stronger. "Nick, we gotta get out of here!"

Nick dropped his belt and staggered back. "Oh, man, this is bad ... This is what I smelled on Halloween ..." He tried to cover his nose, but still going backwards, tripped over the bench. Sitting down hard, he toppled backwards, landing on his side. After a soft moan, his body went still.

Will watched his friend go down and felt his own senses failing. Stumbling back, he ran into the row of lockers. His eyes started to droop and he felt his knees buckle. Then he felt himself falling. He never felt his body strike the floor ... and it never did.

As Will started to slide into unconsciousness, the hunter smoothly appeared in the doorway. He sprayed a misting bottle in front of him and wore a mask and gloves.

Quickly he moved forward and caught the sinking boy. He gently lowered him to lie over his knee. In the kneeling position, the hunter put down the bottle and supported the limp body.

It would be so easy to kill the boy now. But it wouldn't do. It didn't come to that. Yet.

"So we meet again," he said, sounding amused.

Carefully, he shifted and grabbed the boy by the armpits. He laid him onto the bench, stomach side down so his arms and legs dangled to the floor.

"Hopefully this will be the last time, buddy boy. For your sake." He reached into his back pocket to pull out a sharpie. His other hand pulled up Will's shirt, exposing his back. "How can I make this clear ..."

Before he could write, a sudden noise caused him to whirl around.

When not seeing his friends emerge for some time, Jared frowned and decided to find Will on the bus. He figured the two left through the rear entrance since Nick lived in that direction.

Inside the locker room was quiet and still, confirming his suspicions. He grimaced at the sharp sickening odor of old smelly clothes mixed with strong colognes. He'd missed his friends.

Sighing, he'd just popped his lock when his eyes started to water. He swung open the door, but paused as the smell only increased.

Wrinkling his nose, he suddenly gasped. He knew that smell and knew what it meant. He looked toward the back room and suddenly grew afraid. Not stopping to think, he grabbed his school shirt from his locker and held it over his nose. Then he raced for the back room.

He reached it just in time to see a large figure kneeling over Will's limp body laid across the bench. His shirt had been yanked up and the figure held a black sharpie. Nick lay in a heap on the floor beside the bench. The figure, who Jared saw to be a heavy man with blond hair, turned to stare at him, his eyes going wide over a white mask covering his face except for his eyes.

"Hey!" Jared shouted through his shirt.

Instantly the man threw the sharpie at Jared and grabbed a spray bottle by his feet. Then, after the briefest of hesitations, he snatched something from Will's open locker behind him.

Jared ducked from the sharpie and charged into the room, oblivious of the danger.

Squealing like a pig, the man squirted the bottle once and then dashed to the rear entrance on the right. He crashed into the door at full speed, swinging it open with his body. Without a look back, he disappeared into the darkness.

Jared ignored him. He could smell the fumes from the bottle and his eyes smarted. Fighting off any urge to sleep, he ran to Will's side and shook him by the shoulder.

"Will, wake up!" When the boy didn't stir, Jared took a breath into his shirt and held it. Then putting the shirt across his neck, he grabbed Will from under the shoulders and yanked him up and off the bench. Fighting hard not to breathe, he dragged the boy from the back room, thankful for Will's slight build.

Once he passed the bathroom, Jared lay the boy down and knelt low to the ground, drawing in deep breaths. The air proved fresher here, something he never thought he'd ever think in the boys' locker room. After four good breaths, he put the shirt back over his mouth and went for Nick.

Dragging Nick did not prove to be as easy as Will. The large boy lay in a heap on his side with his cheek pressed against the floor. Jared didn't even try to lift him. Kneeling at the large boy's side, he rolled him over to his back. Nick's mouth parted open and he breathed easily, but never stirred.

Wrapping his shirt around his nose and mouth, Jared took Nick by the ankles and started backing his way from the room.

He strained to move the large boy across the floor. Just as he made it into the small hall by the bathroom, Nick's eyes fluttered open. "Huh, what?" he said groggily. Then he saw Jared standing over him holding his ankles.

"Hey!" he roared, kicking wildly. "Get off! What are you doing?" Jared instantly let go, falling backwards, landing on the seat of his shorts.

"Are, are you okay?" Jared sputtered, shaken. He dropped the shirt from his nose and mouth. The harsh fumes had mostly dissolved, leaving behind the musky locker room smell.

"What the heck, man!" Nick cried, sitting up. He winced and held his head. "What happened? What did you do to me?"

Jared blinked. "Huh?"

Nick shook his head painfully and suddenly stared at Jared. "Hey, where's Will?"

"Right behind me. I got him out first. You, uh, I found you guys."

"Yeah, right you did." Nick pushed himself to his feet and rushed past Jared to where Will lay. His shirt had ridden up to his armpits, exposing his skinny ribs and flat stomach. Nick was relieved to see the stomach rise and fall.

"You okay, man?" he asked, crouching at his side.

Will's eyes started blinking and he groaned. "Where am I?" he asked. "What happened?"

"Back in the smelly locker room, man. I think we both passed out."

"Great," Will muttered. He shuddered as he rose to a sitting position. Looking around him, he ruefully pulled down his shirt. "How did we end up here?"

"That's what I want to know," Nick said, looking back to glare where Jared sat.

That was when Ryan barged around the corner of the lockers, looking furious.

"What's going on here?" he demanded. Then his eyes found Jared. "There he is. There's the stinking thief!"

Will looked up with his large brown eyes going from Jared to Ryan. He had confusion plainly written on his face. "Huh?"

Chapter 45

Jared had almost no chance to defend himself. He was so shocked to see Ryan and hear himself be called a thief that he couldn't speak for a second. It didn't help him that the noxious fumes still hung around him from the back room.

"I heard you guys back here and went to see what was up," Ryan said, glaring at Jared, "and what did I find? That tall dude had his locker wide open. With a whole bunch of stolen loot sitting right on top."

Jared coughed. "No way," he wheezed.

"See for yourself," Ryan said. "Yo, man. I told you this dude was bad news."

Jared got to his feet shakily. "I saw some guy back there," he said. "He was trying to write on Will. I stopped him."

Will and Nick exchanged glances and then looked up at him.

Ryan snorted scornfully. "Sure. What did he look like? Where did he go?"

Jared frowned. "I don't know … he had a mask on. I've never seen him before. But he ran out back. I was too busy grabbing Will and Nick to get a good look."

Ryan shook his head. "Yo, man. That's a bunch of bull. If that's true, how do you explain your locker?"

"I don't know what you're talking about," Jared said, his head clearing and anger growing. "Why are you here anyway? I thought you went with Ben."

"That's what you wanted to happen, huh? I decided to take the bus home," Ryan said mildly. "I had a feeling you were up to something. Guess I was right."

"Let's just check his locker," Nick said as he got to his feet. Reaching down, he helped Will up.

The smaller boy shook his head groggily, still dazed. They silently let Jared pass between them and then followed him and Ryan to Jared's locker.

Jared blinked in confusion. "I never put that stuff there."

Right on top of his folded pants was an assortment of watches, phones, and other items that he'd never seen before in his life.

"Right," Ryan said. "Let's see what we have. I see a new phone and pair of nice headphones. I wonder if Brad would recognize them. I heard he got robbed over the break. And what's this on top? Will, isn't this yours, man?" Ryan pulled out a small black wallet from Jared's locker.

Will's eyes widened. "Yeah, I think so. I got it for Christmas. It was in my locker …"

Ryan tossed the wallet to Will. "It was in Jared's locker, you mean. He was robbing you guys."

Jared just shook his head. He couldn't believe it. The second time that day he'd been framed … "I didn't do it."

"Then how did it end up in your locker, man?" Nick asked. He sounded mad. "Who else could have taken it? Besides, I remember you coming out last from the locker room when Brad's stuff went missing."

Jared just shook his head. "No—I …" Seeing the disbelief on his friends' faces, Jared's voice stopped working.

Will fingered the wallet, still slightly dazed. "How did he take all the stuff without getting caught before?"

"Easy," Ryan said. He flicked his gaze at the bin of old clothes. "He just hid everything in the old clothes bin until nobody was around. I bet he stuck around today to bring it all home. He heard you two clowns back there and saw some easy marks."

"Yeah, but how?" Nick said. "I mean, we both smelled it. Something made us pass out."

Ryan rolled his eyes. "Probably your own farts, man. Yo, I don't know how he did it, but the point is that he did do it."

"But why?" Will asked, still not believing it.

"Isn't it obvious?" Ryan said. He stared straight at Jared. "You're new to this school, Will. Before you came, this beanpole was a total loser with more snot than friends. I remember him picking his nose last year, talking to himself. He stole this stuff to feel cool. And then you came along and he tried to make you his friend. He did all he could to be friends with you, man. I saw him staring at you the first day of school. Sure enough, he tried to steal you away, too. But I've been watching him."

Will just stared at Ryan. "Huh?"

"Yo, don't you get it?" Ryan cried. "He steals anything he can't have. He took the phones, the headphones, and was trying to steal your friendship, too. Isn't that right, Jared?"

Jared just stared, his mouth refusing to work. Then all at once, he ran from the locker room. He couldn't take it.

"Wait! Jared!" Will called after him. "Come back!"

"Let the thief go, man," Ryan's voice said. "He's history."

Jared raced into gym, never slowing as he sprinted across the basketball court and into the hallway. He didn't know where he was going or what he was doing. He just knew he needed to escape. Through the main doors to the school he saw the activity bus parked out front and immediately took off down the hall to the left. Nobody was in sight and he kept running. Turning the corner, he ran past the computer lab and kept going until reaching the end of the hall where the doors to the dumpster were.

Slamming the doors open, he staggered out and collapsed against the side of the school, falling to the ground. Then the sobs came and he remained there for a long time. The cold and dark didn't bother him. They were his only friends.

Finally, his tears spent and his face encrusted with salt, he staggered to his feet and made his way to the front of the school. He still wore his practice shorts and a T-shirt and a cold wind bit into his skin. Jared didn't mind. He wore the misery like a heavy coat. Bowed down, he reached the main doors and knocked. The bus had long gone. Eventually Mr. Harold the janitor let him in and allowed him to call home for a ride.

Jack answered and said he would come. "Mom is taking a nap," he told Jared. "She's still recovering from Nutcracker rehearsals and the holidays."

Jack had gotten his driver's license over the summer, but still lacked a car. He welcomed any chance to drive, especially at night.

Jared bit his lip as he hung up the phone. He didn't even bother checking the gym for his backpack and other stuff. Tomorrow he would have to face that battle … if not sooner.

He wouldn't be surprised if Mr. Drydon had already called his parents to accuse Jared of being a thief. Just thinking about it brought a fresh batch of tears.

"I can't cry," he muttered. Wiping his eyes, he left the office and waited by the door.

Mr. Harold mopped the floor behind him, but said nothing. He'd seen his fair share of messes and knew which ones he could handle and which ones to leave alone.

Jack pulled up in the minivan. He barely gave Jared a look when he climbed in the back.

"Tough practice?" Jack asked.

Jared only grunted. Once he got home, he ran up to the shower. Right after, he went straight to bed without supper and without comfort. The next day would only be worse, he knew.

Will lay back on his pillow with both hands cradling his head, deep in thought. His clock read past midnight, but sleep eluded him.

He heard a faint knock on his door and it opened a crack. "You awake, champ?" his dad asked softly. "I couldn't sleep, so I decided to bother you."

Will gave a faint grin. He didn't know how, but his dad always knew when Will needed him.

"Ha," he said. Moving his hands, he pushed himself up and scooted over to let his dad sit next to him. "I was just thinking."

Mr. Moore coughed. "That's always a dangerous thing. What's eating you? You've been a zombie all night since basketball practice."

Will put his knees up and hugged them to his chest. "Dad, what do you do if you have two friends, but one is a liar and a cheat? And you don't know which one it is?"

"That's a tough question … I'm guessing you're having trouble at school?"

"Something like that."

Mr. Moore sighed and clapped a hand on Will's knee. "Son, I've learned people sometimes make it their mission in life to be hard to get along with. It's tough to know who your real friends are. But I've found if you're patient and you keep your eyes open the truth comes out. Life has a way of revealing people's true character. So my advice is, get some sleep and leave your worries out. Maybe they'll go away before morning."

"Not likely," Will muttered.

"Well, at least you won't be too tired to deal with them."

Jared at first refused to get out of bed. He decided to just lie there and tell his mother he felt too sick for school. As soon as he woke up, he remembered what had happened and felt a painful lurch in his stomach. There was no way he could face middle school again.

Then George stomped in the room. "What are you doing, you idiot!" he snarled. "Mom's been calling for ten minutes! I missed the bus and she's taking me, so you have to get ready yourself."

Jared tried to ignore him. Grunting, he rolled over to face the wall.

"Are you listening, idiot?" George stalked to his bed and in one quick move ripped the warm covers away.

Jared instantly curled into a ball. He'd been so upset he hadn't changed into pajamas and wore just his boxers.

"Get up," George demanded, "or I'll make your back so red you'll think you had a sunburn."

Defeated, Jared rolled to a sitting position, glaring balefully at his brother.

Seeing him, George laughed. "What's wrong, man? Don't you have a game today? Or did the coach finally cut your sorry behind. See you, loser." George stalked out, slamming the door. "Be down in two minutes, or I'll be back!" he hollered from the other side.

Jared staggered to his feet and found himself getting dressed. A short time later he stood at the end of the driveway with Kelly, waiting for the bus.

"Good grief, Jared," Kelly said, staring at him. "Where's your backpack? And don't you have a game today? Where's your uniform?"

Jared felt his face go red. He wore jeans and a heavy checkered sweater. His sports bag and backpack were still at his gym locker ... or more likely confiscated by Mr. Drydon. "I'm not playing today," he mumbled.

Kelly just lifted her eyebrows and fell silent. She bit her bottom lip as the bus appeared.

Jared went straight to homeroom and sat in his seat without retrieving his backpack. He figured that would come later. Big Mike walked in wearing a black T-shirt with red lettering over a gray hoodie. The T-shirt had WMS across the chest with the slogan, *We're WON Together* below it.

Mrs. Donavon frowned when seeing the shirt. "Really, proper English would be nice. I'll have to talk to your coach about that." Then she looked at Jared. "Jared, where's your shirt? Didn't you hear the announcement for all basketball players to stop at the gym?"

Jared shrugged. "I'll get it later," he mumbled.

Big Mike just gave him a look.

At the end of homeroom, Jared headed out to find his next class when he saw Marshall walking by with a huge smile plastered on his face. Seeing Jared, he held up his wrist, showing him a gleaming silver watch.

"I got it back!" he said. "I told you I wouldn't let them get me!"

Jared blinked. "Uh, how, where did you find it?"

Marshall pushed up his glasses. "Mr. Swopes found it in the locker room this morning, along with a lot of other stuff. He said it'd all been dumped on top of the bin with all the clothes." The tall boy twisted his lips in a grimace. "I know some jerk took it, but at least they turned it in." Then he glanced at his watch. "Oh, I have to run. I don't want to be late!"

Stunned, Jared found himself walking down the hall to the gym. He found himself engulfed with a bunch of sixth graders. As he entered, he spotted Kelly coming out of the girls' locker room. Seeing him, she smiled widely and ran over to him.

"Jared!" she called. "What are you doing here?"

"Uh, just going to get my backpack."

His sister smiled, a tad wickedly. "Hang around for a second and my friend Callie can meet you. She's been begging to get the chance."

Jared grimaced. "Maybe later. I got to go."

"Wait, Jared. I saw Will before school."

Jared stopped, his blood running cold. He turned to his sister. "And?" he said, his voice nearly choking.

Suddenly shy, Kelly balanced on her back leg and rotated her toe in front of her. Batting her lashes, she grinned. "If you change your mind and go to the game, tell him 'hi' for me."

"Right." Jared left his sister and waited for the sixth graders to clear the locker room.

Taking a deep breath, he forced himself to go see what remained of his own locker. He was surprised to find it locked and in good order. Quickly spinning the lock's combination, he snapped it open. His backpack, sports bag, and pants from yesterday were just where he'd left them. Even his school shirt that he'd used to cover his nose had been replaced.

Stunned, he stuffed his clothes in his sports bag, taking that with his backpack to his next class.

Jared didn't know what to think. It was as if yesterday with Ryan had never happened.

Chapter 46

It'd happened. All his fears came rushing back when during typing Ms. Jackson got a call from the office. Putting the phone down, she told Jared that the office wanted to see him.

Gary snorted, but said nothing. Ryan sat in the farthest seat possible from Jared. He stopped his typing and actually half stood when Jared stumbled to his feet. For a brief moment, the boys locked eyes. Ryan actually looked slightly scared. Then he abruptly sat back down behind his computer.

All of Jared's fears were for nothing. The office just wanted to give him his basketball uniform, freshly washed and pressed. His mother had dropped it off for him along with his basketball shoes.

Jared spent lunch in the library. He wanted nothing to do with basketball. But just before the final bell, when the announcement came for all basketball players and cheerleaders to head to the buses, he went out with team. He was going to Berkshire.

The journey to Berkshire was a long and quiet one … a painfully quiet one. Brad had stepped on the bus last and had yelled for quiet. He'd worn his new headphones, glaring at his teammates. "I know one of you is the thief," he'd said loudly. "Whoever it is had better quit the team before I find him." Then he'd swaggered to the back, sitting in a seat by himself.

Nobody had really talked since. Most played with their phones, listened to music, or stared out a window. Nick and Will sat together in the middle, while Ryan slouched near the back, right in front of Brad. Jared had chosen the first seat behind Coach Swopes.

With only sixteen boys, counting John, and a single coach, there were plenty of seats to choose from. Ben had been the only player not to make it. He stopped by, saying he didn't feel well and had to go home.

"Oh, here, Jared," Coach Swopes said, tossing back a black T-shirt. "I'm glad you made it."

The team had changed in the locker room before going to the buses and Jared grunted his thanks as he pulled the shirt on over his jersey. He felt the shirt should read *LOST together*.

As Mr. Hackett drove, he kept mopping his brow with the back of his hand. It was a cold day outside the bus, with temperatures in the lower 40s, but the heat blasted inside.

Glen, also overheated, tried to open a window but barely got it halfway down before it got stuck.

"Hey!" Mr. Hackett bellowed, almost sounding panicked. "Leave the windows alone! They don't work on this bus! All windows stay closed!"

Glen tried to put the window back up, but it wouldn't budge. "Cheap foreign junk," he muttered, settling back in his seat.

Jared stared out the window, wondering what to expect. He knew he'd been framed and the only way possible had to have been by Ryan.

He remembered the masked man grabbing something from Will's locker. He had to have snatched the wallet, run around the school, and then given it to Ryan to plant in Jared's locker. The only problem, who would believe such an unlikely story? And why hadn't Ryan ratted on him to Brad? Was he waiting for the game to start so he could tell Brad and embarrass Jared more?

He wished he could talk to Will and Nick, but didn't dare try now. They'd seen him get on, but hadn't made eye contact. He had no idea what to expect from them either. In the seat across the aisle, John happily stared out the window, trying to count all the cars. At least John had smiled at him. He seemed to be the only one happy on the bus.

It was nearly eighty miles to Berkshire and took a two-hour drive. First they took the highway north toward Richmond before getting off on a lonely road with a single lane going in either direction. The road cut through miles and miles of trees. Nearly an hour went by without Jared seeing a single gas station or restaurant.

Finally, they arrived at a small town and soon reached a sprawling brick school with a huge gym in the back.

"Okay, boys!" Mr. Swopes called as Mr. Hackett followed the girls' bus into the back parking lot by the gym. "I know Berkshire doesn't look like much, but this town lives and breathes basketball. Just about every kid plays the game as soon as they walk and they dream of wearing their school uniform. So far they're undefeated this year. Expect the whole town to show up for the game. There's not much else out here, so basketball is a big deal. Let's get ready."

The coach stood and faced the team, but got very little in response. Perhaps it stemmed from Brad's less than rousing pep talk before the journey, or maybe it was just from the long trip, but the Patriots did not come ready to play. After the Patriots girls got waxed by fifty points, losing 72 to 22, it was the boys' turn.

Coach Swopes had not been kidding about the whole town showing up. The entire bleachers were filled with bodies and the floor on either side had a crowd of mostly men in standing room only areas. The entire wall facing the teams' benches was packed with fans. Very few, if any, Patriots fans made the long journey. Brad said his dad was somewhere in the crowd, but if he was, he wisely kept quiet.

The Berkshire Flying Eagles ran out on the floor in sky blue uniforms with dark blue lettering. Their shorts featured a yellow streak of lightning on the sides. The crowd roared their appreciation.

"Look at them," Glen said, staring over his shoulder at the opposition from the layup line. "There're like twenty of them. And they're all taller than me."

"I think they put steroids in the water here," Kyle muttered.

"Just focus on our game," Coach Swopes said, clapping his hands, a little halfheartedly. Mr. Hackett had remained on the bus, leaving the stooped coach to deal with the bench. He looked even older and more worn.

Jared kept silent. He kept thinking that at any moment Ryan, or Nick, or even Will, would jump in his face, accusing him of being the thief. He flicked glances over at Ryan in the next line, but was pointedly ignored.

Ryan stood behind Tom with his arms crossed and his face a mask. He looked a million miles away. When it was his turn, he barely caught the ball and then missed the layup.

Will also ignored Jared. He grinned at something Nick said as he caught the ball and dribbled for the basket. Then he too missed a layup.

Brad slapped his hands together in frustration. From the stands they could hear fans laugh and jeer.

"They can't even hit layups in warm-ups! We're going to cream them!" a voice shouted.

"Good show, boys!" called another voice. "Don't worry, we'll show you how it's done!"

The Flying Eagles wasted no time showing the Patriots up. They took control right from the tip, quickly jumping to an 8 to 2 lead. It seemed like they were everywhere. Pressuring, boxing out, diving for loose balls, a Berkshire player rose to the task. The Patriots, on the other hand, fell apart. By halftime it was 27 to 12 in favor of the home team.

Brad stormed into the locker room, livid.

"They're killing us out there!" he cried, stamping to the center of the locker room. "We're not even trying!"

The visitors' locker room was a small, dank room in the back of the gym with dim lighting. Hard wooden benches bolted to the floor faced the center with rows of shelves behind them. Sitting on them, the team looked at Brad with gloomy faces.

Nobody but Big Mike had done anything to be proud about. The big forward had scored ten of the Patriots' points. At times he looked to be playing on a team by himself.

"What's wrong with you guys!" Brad yelled. He glared specifically at Will. "You're supposed to be the hotshot, you're playing like pot!"

Will had played only a few minutes. After committing three unforced turnovers, a foul, and missing all three of his shot attempts, he'd been sent to the bench. Pursing his lip, the smaller guard just stared at the floor.

Jared had done even worse. He didn't even get a single rebound in three minutes of playing time and actually had never even touched the ball. His man scored three easy baskets against him. He rubbed the side of his curls miserably, biting his bottom lip.

Coach Swopes just stood at the doorway watching. He decided his coaching wouldn't make a difference on a night like this and allowed the players to either pull together now, or fall completely apart.

"Look, guys," Brad said. "You seventh graders might not care, because you have another year. But this is it for us eighth graders. We're 2 and 2 now. If we keep losing, we have no chance for the playoffs."

Kyle shot to his feet angrily. "Then why don't you start leading us instead of yelling at us! I didn't see you do so great out there either!"

"I did better than you!" Brad shouted.

"Hold on, man!" Glen yelled over them. He stood and moved to the center of the room. "Look, man. Nobody is perfect. We all have bad nights." Then he looked a Brad. "But Kyle has a point."

"No, he don't," Darius muttered. "He has a goose egg. And so do you."

Glen ignored him. "Brad, man, you bellyached about your phone and headphones and that got us messed up. Let's just play basketball, man! Right now we're not even a team."

Brad glared at his friend. "Whatever, man. You're right, we're not a team. We have an old husk for a coach and a retard for a manager. What else should I expect?"

Thankfully Angie and John were out on the court getting things ready for the second half. But Jared suddenly found himself on his feet.

"Take it back," he said, his voice turning low.

"What's that?" Brad said, turning to him with a frown. "You, string bean, have no room to talk."

"Neither do you," Jared said. All his fear and stress suddenly dissipated. He'd been so focused on himself, so scared about his own fate, he'd forgotten all about John. Whatever was going on, he, the most innocent kid among them, seemed to be at the center.

Jared'd had enough of it. If John couldn't stand up for himself, then he would do it for him. All his anger and confusion boiled over and unleashed at Brad. "You've been calling him names and treating him like something you stepped in. John is not retarded. He's a person and he's a member of our team. You leave him alone."

Brad blinked and stared. Before he could say something in retaliation, Big Mike stood up, his bulk standing beside Jared.

"I agree," he rumbled. "Shut up and play ball."

The score ended at 76 to 42. Berkshire utterly destroyed the Patriots.

Utterly dejected, the team slumped back into the locker room with their heads hung low. Coach Swopes closed the door as the last player trailed in. He didn't want the boys to go to the bus just yet.

"Soak it in, boys," he rumbled. "This is what it feels like to fall to pieces. To be humiliated. When we aren't together, this is what happens." He then stood silently. Nobody spoke as they sat in misery.

Finally, after what seemed to be an eternity, Coach Swopes sighed. "Okay, then. Let's leave all the despair behind. Leave it in this room and keep it there. Get your stuff and get on the bus. We have a long ride ahead of us. I don't suspect we're going to do much talking."

Jared quickly got up and grabbed his bag. He just wanted to get out of Berkshire and get home. None of the players looked at him as he hurried out of the gym and headed to the parking lot.

He was surprised to find Will already standing there, still in his uniform with his sports bag slung over his shoulder. He still even wore his leg sleeves, and with his black team T-shirt over his jersey, he nearly blended in with the night. Only his pale skin kept him from being totally invisible as he stood dejectedly in the shadows where the streetlamps didn't reach.

"Hey," Will muttered, not looking at Jared.

Jared grunted. Thinking back, he hadn't seen Will enter the locker room after the game. He must have grabbed his stuff and slipped right out during the handshakes.

"Hey," he muttered back.

"Nice job standing up for John," Will said, kicking at the sidewalk. "I'm glad somebody said it."

Jared shifted his feet. He looked at where the buses were parked. The girls' bus was already loaded and had its engine running. Mr. Hackett sat idly behind the wheel of the boys' bus. Jared narrowed his eyes.

"Speaking of John, where is he? And where's Angie?"

"They were loading the bus," Will answered, staring out in the parking lot.

Berkshire's gym was a separate building from the school. Outside lights and streetlights from the parking lot bathed the area in harsh orange light. But behind the gym, by the main school building, they could see nothing but inky darkness.

From the darkness they heard a muffled scream.

"Angie!" Jared said tightly. Dropping his bag, he ran toward the noise. All despair from the game transformed into fury.

"Wait up!" Will called after him.

Angie and John had just finished loading the unwieldy ball bag in the bottom of the bus and were organizing the water bottles outside the bus door, making sure they were empty, except for a few for the ride. Coach Swopes never wanted full water bottles on long bus rides, fearing a water fight might break out.

"John, you go dump these over in the grass," Angie said, handing him two full bottles. "I'll get the rest."

"Okay, Angie," John said.

Angie watched him go, happily carrying the bottles to the grass across the parking lot. Then she got busy. She wanted the bus packed up and ready to roll as the boys came out. Spending an extra second in Berkshire was an extra second way too long, in her opinion.

"Hey, who are you?" she heard John's voice ask.

Looking up, her eyes grew wide. In the grassy area, in the dark shadows, John stared as if seeing something.

"What are you doing?" Angie asked sharply, getting to her feet. "Who's there?"

"There's one more water bottle, Angie," John said. "I'll get it."

All her warning systems started going off.

"Wait, John. Stay there." She ran across the parking lot. As she reached the shadows, she saw two ghostly figures loom forth.

"Hello, there," muttered a hoarse voice. "Great game tonight."

"You two should've played. Your team would have done no worse," a thin, whiny voice leered. They both sounded male and a few years older than Angie. In the shadows they appeared like wraiths, but she guessed them to be high schoolers.

Angie grabbed John's shoulder and pulled him back.

One of the figures lunged forward, throwing out his arms. "Boo!"

She screamed and kicked him in the shin.

"Bad mistake, girlie," panted the other figure as his friend swore, hopping back from Angie. "We were just messing around. Not anymore." The figure lurched forward. He smelled like cheap cologne and bubblegum.

John stood still and hugged himself, too scared to move.

Angie bit back her fear. "Don't lay a hand on us," she hissed.

Before the two figures could decide what to do, Jared charged from the parking lot. "Hey!" he called. "Hey!"

Swearing, the two figures immediately bolted, racing deeper into the shadows.

"Are you okay?" Jared demanded, pulling up at her side, breathless.

Will came up right behind him. "Who was it?"

Angie felt her hands shaking and her knees wouldn't stop trembling. "I-I think just some stupid teenagers. They, they wanted … I guess they were just messing around." She took a deep breath and pulled herself together. "Th-thanks, guys. I'm sure they're gone." She turned to John. "It's okay, John. They're gone. Everything is okay."

The trembling boy nodded, but never dropped his arms or looked up.

"Just in case," Jared said grimly. "Let's get back to the buses. Do you want John to ride with you?"

John immediately popped up his head and shook it vigorously. "I'm part of the team," he said. "I ride the team bus."

"Fine," Angie said in a grim voice. "Then I am too."

Chapter 47

When Mr. Hackett saw Angie boarding the bus with John, he just about had a conniption.

"What?" he cried, rising to his feet to block her way. "You can't ride this bus, Angie!" Jared had been climbing up behind her and saw the PE teacher's eyes bug out. He sounded more panicked than angry. "You're supposed to be with the girls!"

As the boys started trickling out, the bus with the girls had gone ahead, getting a head start.

"Sorry," Angie said, throwing back her hair and not backing down. "It's too late for that. Besides, John needs me."

"She can sit in the front with me," Jared said quickly.

After gaping with his mouth open, Mr. Hackett finally sat back down, looking slightly stunned. Swallowing, he composed himself, but his voice sounded a little shaky.

"Fine," he muttered. "Get on, but don't make trouble. Girls aren't allowed to ride a bus alone with boys. You can get me fired for this."

"I'll be good," Angie told him, not caring.

"We'll see," muttered the teacher.

Everyone took the same seat they'd had on the journey there, so Jared could only look at where Will and Nick sat in the middle. He still had no idea what had happened after Ryan had accused him of being the thief and he'd run out.

Sighing, he laid his head against the window and stared miserably out as the bus rumbled to life and pulled away from the gym.

Jared had just started to drift off when he felt the bus ease to the side and pull to a stop. Blinking, he looked around him and saw they were in the middle of nowhere. Outside the windows was nothing but pitch-black darkness. Not a single car appeared in front or behind them.

"What's this? What's going on?" Coach Swopes said, lifting his head, sounding as if he just woke up. "Where are we?"

"Sorry," Mr. Hackett called out. "But John needs a restroom break. Everyone sit tight. It'll only be a minute. Angie, you come too. I don't want John to panic out here."

Angie sat in the outside seat next to John and stared across the aisle at Jared in confusion. "He never asked for one," she hissed. She turned to John. "Do you need the bathroom, John?"

"Sure, okay," said the boy. "Let's go."

Angie stifled a groan. "Jared," she whispered. "Can you come too? I, I don't feel comfortable with Mr. Hackett out there." The only light came from the shine of the bus's headlights, but even in the dark Jared could tell Angie was scared.

Jared nodded and quickly stood. "I, uh, have to go too," he said.

Mr. Hackett stared at him and then seemed to deflate. "Okay, Cook," he said. "Let's make it snappy."

Angie grabbed Jared's arm and gave it a squeeze. She zipped up her jacket and made sure John did the same.

Jared felt warmth spread up his spine and to his face.

"I'll go too," Ryan said quickly from the back. Like Will and Jared, he still wore his uniform.

"Come on," Brad groaned. "Are you kidding me?"

The other boys were too tired or too dejected to care. They buried their heads in phones that no longer carried service.

"Just come along," Mr. Hackett called, swinging open the doors. "Stay close to me. We're in the middle of forests and if you get lost out there, you may never come back. Find a tree next to the road, boys, but move away from the bus. Oh. To keep your privacy ..." He switched off the motor and dimmed the lights, plunging the entire bus into darkness.

"Man, this is now officially creepy," Nick said, elbowing Will's ribs.

Other boys started to stir and muttered.

"Just calm down," Coach Swopes said loudly. "After how we played, it's good to reflect more in the dark. If you don't like it, close your eyes and get some sleep."

Jared stepped into the cold night and immediately hugged his arms around his chest. He still wore his uniform with his new shirt. Taken by surprise by Angie's request, he didn't think of putting anything else on. He noticed Ryan was similarly dressed.

John and Angie at least wore jackets and pants.

Thankfully, they had a mostly clear sky overhead. In the darkness, faint moonlight climbed through the trees and Jared saw they were pulled on the side of a narrow road with a shallow drainage ditch just beyond the pavement.

"Watch out for the ditch," Mr. Hackett warned. "Let's move in front of the bus. I don't want any accusations of people staring through the window. Angie, stay near John." The teacher spoke in a normal volume, but he sounded strained. "Hurry up! Move it."

Jared shrugged and walked forward.

"Yo, man," Ryan whispered at his back. "I got a bad feeling about this. Like, really bad."

Jared stopped and turned toward him. Ryan sounded scared, even more so than Mr. Hackett.

"What are you talking about?" Jared asked him, unable to keep the fury from his voice.

Then Ryan moaned. "Oh, no."

Mr. Hackett had parked the bus perpendicular to a side road, right at the intersection. Jared hadn't noticed it in the dark. He saw it now because a pair of lights rounded a bend and headed straight towards the bus. The lights never slowed down.

"What are you thinking about, man?" Nick asked Will. "You look like you're about to poop your pants. Jimmy would be proud."

The smaller boy shrugged as he peered out the window at the dark shadowy trees. "Ha, ha," he said, his face relaxing. "I just don't know about anything right now."

Nick grunted. "You mean Jared and Ryan, right?" He sighed. "You know Jared is the thief. He had your wallet. Besides, you heard what Ryan said. He just played us, man."

Will frowned as he blew warm breath on the window. "So he knocked us out too, right? Because you didn't smell that bad. And what about Angie and John? Are they thieves too?"

"They're part of it, I guess. Maybe she and Jared are partners, or something."

Will turned to him and lifted his eyebrows. "Really?"

"Well, sure, man. It would make sense ... I guess."

"Ha. Only if you watch too much TV."

"You still should've turned in Jared yesterday. Protecting him only made things worse. Look at how bad our team played today."

Nick's face suddenly lit up from headlights and he squinted.

"Speaking of looking, I wish that car would turn off its brights, man."

The lights only grew brighter as an approaching vehicle barreled towards them from the other side of the bus. Boys around them started to grumble. The lights poured through the windows, blinding anyone looking in that direction.

"Yo, man!" Glen cried. "What the heck!"

"Berkshire jerk!" Brad snarled, even though the bus had long since left the town.

Will flinched and turned his face from the light.

As the lights seemed to fill the bus, they could hear the rumble of a big engine behind them.

"Sounds like a big truck," Nick said, sitting up straight, alarmed. "And it's not slowing."

"Hey!" yelled Kyle. "That thing isn't stopping!"

"Look out!" yelled Glen. "Look—"

"What the—"

The lights lit up the inside of the bus for a brief second and then seemed to swallow it whole as a sudden darkness flashed. At the same instant, a loud crunching sound split the air and the bus bucked and shuddered.

Boys screamed. Many of them flew back at the impact. Nick turned to shield Will and felt his body blast forward. He slammed into Will's side, crushing the boy against the window. Will's head cracked against the glass.

"Will!" Nick yelled. He realized it wasn't his body doing all the moving. The entire bus slid sideways before suddenly dropping a foot. It then started tilting.

"Help—" screamed a voice, only to be cut off as bodies flew across the bus, all smashing on the side wall.

Then a tremendous boom shook the entire bus as it crashed on its side before going still. Only the screams remained.

Nick's eyes flashed open and saw he still lived. All around him he heard whimpering and crying. Boys were moaning in pain. One of them, sounding like Darius, screamed for help. Nick found himself lying on the floor on top of Will, only it wasn't the floor. It was the side of the bus. Up above him, in reality the opposite side of the bus, he could see faint light. He knew this had to be the headlights from the maniac truck that had hit them. The bus now lay on its side.

His right shoulder hurt like crazy and his head rang like a church bell, but otherwise he seemed okay. Gingerly, he moved his shoulder, instantly gasping in pain. Using his uninjured arm, he quickly pushed himself up.

"Oh, man. Will!"

The boy lay on his side, slumped against the window, his body curled in a fetal position. "You okay, man?"

Not breathing, Nick felt for a pulse and was relieved to feel a warm neck and steady throb.

"Yo!" Brad's voice called. "Everyone okay?"

He got mostly moans and cries of distress in response.

Glen cursed loudly.

"If you need help and can hear us, call out!" Brad said, climbing from behind a seat, he stood on the window near it and peered down the gloomy bus.

"Man, I think I broke my arm," Glen said, sounding sick. He cursed again.

"I'm okay," Kyle said. "I just feel as if somebody kicked me in the chest with steel boots."

"Who was that maniac?" Tom said. "He ran right into us!"

"Shut up!" Brad yelled. "If you're okay, check around. If somebody needs help, help them! Everyone who can, move out from the seats, but watch your step. Check for life, man."

Nick looked up and down the windows at his feet. Sports bags and bodies littered the space. Thankfully, most of the bodies were moving.

Darius's voice lowered to a whimper.

Nick patted Will's shoulder and got slowly to his feet. "I got Will down here. He's unconscious."

"Yo, I just woke up," Howard moaned. "My back is killing me."

Brad pulled out his cell phone and cursed loudly. "Great, guys. We have no service here." He turned on the light feature and started going down the end of the bus, checking out the damage. Other kids with phones also turned on their lights.

"Hey, I found Coach Swopes here!" Kyle's voice cried at the front, sounding panicked. "He's not moving and there's blood all over his face!"

Will remained unconscious as Nick moved to help Brad and Kyle lay their coach flat, pulling him gently from his seat.

"Should we really move him?" Kyle asked nervously. "I mean, what if his spine is injured?"

"I doubt having his head upside down was helping," Nick told him.

"He'll be fine," Brad said, his voice more pleading than confident. "It'll all be fine. Now go and help the others."

Nick carefully picked his way back to where Will lay and lowered himself to a sitting position. He couldn't believe what had just happened. "Oh, man …"

"N-Nick?" Will then said weakly, sounding confused. His eyes fluttered open.

Nick immediately knelt to his side, shining a cell phone light in his friend's face.

"Will, you okay, man?"

Will frowned but nodded. Besides a small cut above his right eyebrow, he suffered no worse than a headache and bruised ribs. Groaning, he stiffly sat up and blinked at the carnage around them.

"What happened?"

"We got wrecked," Nick told him. "And now we're stuck."

It took a while, but eventually things calmed down to a mild panic. Besides Coach Swopes, Howard, Darius, and Teddy appeared the most seriously injured. Teddy had been unconscious, but woke up screaming about his knee killing him. Howard couldn't bend his back, but assured everyone he could feel it. Darius had been sitting just near the impact and had slammed head first into the opposite wall when the bus fell. At first he hadn't been able to move his legs, but after some time he got back some feeling. Still, he wasn't about to get up anytime soon.

The rest of them suffered mostly bumps and bruises.

Brad stayed with their coach. After laying Coach Swopes on his side, he checked for injuries, desperately wishing an adult would get up and take charge. The coach suffered a deep gash just above his right temple and his breath sounded hoarse.

At first Brad looked about to lose it, but Big Mike appeared at his side.

"We need to stop the bleeding," the stocky boy said. "Grab the first aid kit."

Relieved to have some direction, Brad quickly did so, clawing his way to the front and yanking the box free from above the windshield by the stairwell. Looking out the front window, he started to shake in terror. The engine still growled from outside and he could see reflections from the headlights. Then all the light backed off and the rumble of an engine retreated. The maniac seemed to be leaving and the bus plunged into complete darkness except for the cell phones.

At first Brad felt relief, but then the truth crashed down. The stairwell lay on the ground, proving useless as an exit. And the windshield looked too thick to bust through.

"You good?" Big Mike snapped at him. "Hurry up!"

"Yeah, but we have a big problem. We're trapped in here." Brad turned and tossed Big Mike the first aid box. Then he raised his voice and called, "Hey, guys! Look for a way out of here!"

It was difficult to see or navigate because of all the seats being sideways. It was even more difficult finding a way out of the bus.

"The back door is stuck," Nick called. "Man, it's jammed tight."

"So is the emergency exit," Kyle announced in disgust. He pushed at the small hatch, originally positioned on the roof of the bus, but now on the side. "It won't give an inch."

It was final. They were trapped.

Minutes later, Brad, still acting as if in charge, stood in the middle of the bus with all those able to stand grouped around him.

Glen stood beside him cradling his right arm, his face tight with pain. "We can try the emergency window above us, but I doubt it'll work."

"How come?" Brad asked him.

Glen sighed. "Just a feeling. It feels like we're trapped on purpose. Remember all the windows being stuck? Now all the exits are jammed tight. I don't think this was an accident, man."

A gloomy silence descended as the boys processed Glen's words.

"So, how do we get out?" Kyle then asked, his voice trembling.

"What's even going on out there?" Bob wanted to know, scratching his curly head. "I mean, where're Mr. Hackett and the others?"

Nobody had an answer. The bright lights had not returned, cell phones still provided the only light. The front windshield faced only dark woods. They couldn't even see the road when looking out.

"Just keep calm," Brad said, breathing hard. It was not an easy thing to do.

Nobody felt brave enough to move any of the injured, so those who couldn't stand lay pretty much where they'd fallen. It felt as if they were all trapped in a large tomb.

"Hold on!" Nick suddenly said. "The window! We got one partially open, remember?" He pointed up at the half-open window near the back of the bus.

"Right," said Brad. "And who's going to fit through that crack?"

Everyone turned to where Will stood at Nick's shoulder. His large eyes blinked and then he grinned. "Sure, guys … but I'll need a boost."

Minutes later, Nick stood under the opened window while Will climbed up to his left shoulder with Big Mike lifting him up from the back. He used the sideways seats to lean on for support.

"Okay, man," Nick said. "Good thing you're light, but my shoulder is killing me, so you'd better get out quick." He wrapped his arms around the back of Will's legs.

At first Will slipped, but Nick managed to catch him. Gritting his teeth, he pushed Will up towards the window.

"No way can he fit through that," Kyle mumbled, watching next to Big Mike.

"Shut up," Big Mike grumbled. "He'll make it."

Will barely managed to fit his head through the slot and reached up his right arm, gaining a hold of the outside of the bus. Cold air bit into his face as he stared into the darkness around him.

"I don't see anything," he called down. He struggled to pull himself out, but after the game and crash, lacked the strength. "Um, I could use some help," he called down.

Nick gritted his teeth and pushed up his legs. "My shoulder is killing me!"

Will twisted his narrow hips and tried to wiggle through but couldn't make progress.

"Told you," Kyle muttered.

Big Mike shook his head. Stepping close to Nick, he reached up and slapped the back of Will's shorts. "Get up out of here, you pasty!" he snapped. Grabbing Will's shoes, he pushed up with all his might.

Crying out in pain, Will felt his stomach and sides scrape against the window edges but suddenly found himself lying on top of the bus, gasping for a breath.

Below him the boys cheered.

"Go find Mr. Hackett!" Brad told him. "Oh, and here! Somebody lift up my cell phone. Will, find service and call for help!"

Will turned to the opened window and reached down his arm to get the phone. Then he rolled to a sitting position on a window and stared around him. It felt as silent as a graveyard and twice as spooky.

"Not a nice view from down here, man!" Nick shouted up at him. "What do you see?"

"Nothing," Will said truthfully, shivering. "It's dead silent."

The bus had fallen off a shallow incline from the road. Whatever and whomever had crashed into them no longer remained. Under the faint moonlight he only saw the shadows of trees.

Then he frowned. "Wait, there's something up the road. I see some lights."

"Be careful," Nick warned from below. "Something's not right about this, man."

"I'll be careful," Will said, slowly getting up. The cold air caused his grogginess to fully fade. He gingerly walked down the side of the bus to the front. Reaching the end, he carefully climbed down to the side of the motor before jumping the last few feet.

Just as he landed, he felt strong arms grab him, yanking him into the shadows. He hadn't been careful enough.

"I've been waiting for you, buddy boy," whispered a hoarse voice. A hand cruelly clamped over his mouth holding a damp cloth. It pressed hard.

Will tried to scream, but found it impossible. His mouth and nose filled with vapors. Eyes wide with fear, he struggled, but quickly weakened. Familiar fumes overcame his senses and he felt his body start to wilt. Then he went completely limp.

The last thing he saw before surrendering to darkness was the crumpled body of Mr. Hackett sprawled in front of the overturned bus. The cell phone dropped from his useless hand.

Chapter 48

Jared and Ryan watched in horrified shock as an enormous pickup barreled down the road, blowing past a stop sign before slamming into the side of the bus.

Angie screamed in panic behind them.

"Stay back!" Mr. Hackett yelled. "Just stay back." He sounded terrified, but not totally surprised.

Neither Jared nor Ryan listened. Almost as if in slow-motion, the bus slid into the ditch and started to tilt. The pickup never stopped pushing. Its engine strained as it propelled the truck into the bus's side. Metal screeched and protested until all at once the bus fell over, slamming to its side with a terrible crunch. The truck jerked to a stop.

Jared could hear the screams of pain and terror from inside the bus. Both he and Ryan sprinted to the terrible scene.

Then the driver's door of the pickup opened up and a tall figure jumped out.

"What do we have here?" he said, almost pleasantly. "Boys, don't you know you're supposed to be inside the bus?"

Letting out a strangled yell, Ryan swerved toward him, but the man calmly lifted a hand and sprayed from a bottle he held. Mist blasted in the running boy's face.

Ryan reacted as if slapped by an invisible hand. He instantly staggered on his feet and veered sharply away from the figure. Then his legs buckled. With a moan, he crashed to the side of the road.

Calmly, the man squirted the fallen boy's face three times while covering his nose. Ryan kicked feebly and then went still. The man calmly walked away from the limp body, heading for Jared.

Jared had stumbled to a halt upon seeing the man step from the pickup. Now he nervously backed away.

"Y-you're the guy in the locker room," he said. His heart raced and his mind started to panic.

The man grinned. About an inch taller than Jared, he had thick, wavy hair brushed from a clean-shaven triangular face with cold, dark eyes. His muscular chest heaved as he sniffed the air. "And you're the boy who keeps getting in the way. Hold him, Hackett."

Jared stiffened, but reacted too slowly. The PE teacher had snuck up behind him and now grabbed his arms, locking them in a tight embrace.

"No!" Angie screamed. "You're supposed to be helping us!"

"Shut up!" Mr. Hackett yelled at her. "Just stay back! You shouldn't have come."

Jared tried to struggle free, but froze in fear.

"Listen to your teacher," the man said, grinning. He walked up to Jared and peered into his eyes. "Teacher always knows what's best. Remember that, boy."

"What are you going to do, Hunter?" Mr. Hackett asked, his voice full of fear.

The man's eyes widened and he raised the bottle, but he didn't spray it. Instead he brought it down hard, slamming it across Jared's face.

"Don't use my name, numbskull. Children are listening."

Jared tried to duck, but felt the blow knock him sideways. Tumbling from Mr. Hackett's arms, he crashed to the ground and saw stars. He tried to get up, but never saw the second blow fall behind his left ear. He fell into oblivion to the sound of Angie's screams.

Angie retreated as the man turned from Jared's fallen form to stare at her.

"And what are you doing here?" he asked her, sounding curious. "You weren't supposed to be part of this. The directions said to keep you out of it. Hackett, you sure know how to mess things up."

The PE teacher looked at the bus nervously. "I'm doing the best I can to keep this from getting out of control."

"Too late for that," the man said snidely. He looked back at Angie.

The girl started to scream, but it died in her throat. Caught in the bright headlights of the pickup, the man's face watched her with an amused interest. He didn't seem angry at all, but wore a strange look on his face, as if trying to solve an unexpected riddle.

Swallowing, she turned to run, but saw John. The boy lay on his side huddled in a ball in the grass. His mouth moved, but no words came out. She saw his eyes were wide open, but he didn't seem to be seeing anything. He had crawled into his hidey hole. She couldn't leave him.

"J-John," she moaned.

Just then lights from a car sped into view up the road. She felt a faint spark of hope and ran toward them.

"Help!" she cried. "Help!"

"Come back!" Mr. Hackett yelled at her. "Angie! Wait!"

"Let her go," the strange man said, grinning. "This game is getting more and more interesting. New rules are about to come into play."

Angie stumbled to a halt, surprise registering across her face as a familiar Honda Civic turned off the road, sliding to a sudden stop.

"M-Mr. Drydon?" her voice squeaked.

"What's going on here?" her principal demanded, climbing out of the car looking irritated.

Angie started to say something, but saw Mr. Drydon wasn't talking to her. He glared over her head at Mr. Hackett.

"This wasn't the plan!" he sounded angry, even furious.

Mr. Hackett crossed his arms and squeezed his lips tightly.

"Yeah, well, what was I supposed to do?" he complained. "She forced herself to ride with John and your maniac had his directions. He told me this would happen." He glanced back at the fallen bus, wincing as moans and screams were plainly heard. "I couldn't get a girl hurt." He stuck out his jaw. "I have my limits."

"And I have mine," the strange man grunted. He stepped behind Mr. Hackett and crushed the bottle against the back of his head, much harder than he'd hit Jared.

With a faint grunt, the PE teacher had no time to be surprised as he crumpled onto his face and lay still.

"Next time," the man said pleasantly, "do what you're paid to do. Nothing else. And don't call me by my name, or call me a maniac." He glanced up and grinned at Mr. Drydon. "Looks like we'll have at least one fatality for this 'accident,' Mr. Drydon. I'll drag the body to the bus and it'll look like he got hit by shrapnel in the crash. He'll be dead by morning."

Mr. Drydon wiped his mustache and closed his eyes. Opening them, he said, "Just do what you have to do. Angie, come with me. Now."

Angie just shook her head, her body in shock. She couldn't believe what she was witnessing.

"Come with me," Mr. Drydon repeated calmly, "or others will join Mr. Hackett's fate. Believe me. I'm trying to help you."

"Why are you doing this?" she asked, her voice quavering.

The principal ducked his gaze. "You wouldn't understand." He looked up at the man. "Hunter, hurry and move the truck. I want to be out of here as soon as possible."

"Sure," the man said. "But don't worry. Nobody drives this road this time of night." He grinned at Angie. "You probably didn't notice this, but Mr. Hackett took a different route from Berkshire. Right now, nobody on this earth knows where you are, except for us. Isn't that a comforting thought?" Whistling, he proceeded to take Mr. Hackett by the legs and drag him to the bus.

Angie just shook. Her entire body shuddered and she found it difficult to breathe. What had just happened? Why was Mr. Drydon doing this? It was all too much to take in and process.

Then Mr. Drydon was behind her, grabbing her arm. She tried to wrench free, but the larger man's grip tightened. "Think of John, Angie. Let's not hurt him anymore. Come to my car. We'll wait there."

"Wh-what about John?" Angie asked.

Mr. Drydon blinked and released her. "Oh. Yes. John. You won't leave without him."

Sighing, he reached in his pocket and pulled out a plastic bag with a cloth. Turning away, he pulled the cloth from the bag and went to his son. Without a word, he knelt down and pressed the cloth over John's face. The boy's tension ebbed away as his body slowly relaxed.

Angie watched in horror. At first she thought he'd meant to help his son, but now she knew better.

"You monster!" she yelled. "You monster!"

She rushed at him, swinging her fists, but he merely turned and gave her a sad smile.

"I didn't mean for this to happen, Angie. Believe me."

Angie's last view before darkness was the cloth coming at her.

She never felt Mr. Drydon dragging her to his car or heard the pickup roar to life and back from the wrecked bus.

Angie next became conscious of lying on wet grass next to the huge tires of the pickup. John lay beside her, but before she could think why this would be, darkness swallowed her up. After a while she became dimly aware of voices.

Her consciousness swam somewhere above her and it felt as if she was sinking in a deep, black pool. Her mind fought hard to kick to the surface and eventually the voices became clear.

"What a night," a man said, almost cheerfully. "When laying out Hackett back there, I found one loose kid at the bus, but put him down. And he's the one I wanted."

Immediately, Angie pictured the tall, evil man called Hunter. He'd hurt Jared … Jared, where was he?

Mr. Drydon said a curse word in reply. "This isn't how it's supposed to go," he muttered. "You weren't supposed to wreck the entire basketball team! You were supposed to just keep them trapped inside until John got lost! Everything is going wrong!"

"Sorry, but I made the call," the hunter said, his voice hardening. "It's my game. You want your boy to die of exposure, right? This was the best way to make it happen. Too many other kids got involved and had to be put out of the way. Even that didn't go right, thanks to your bumbling PE teacher."

"You told him you'd ram the bus, didn't you?"

"Maybe I hinted at it."

"But you didn't tell me."

"You didn't want to know the details, remember? We got your boy out in the cold, that's all you care about, right?"

Mr. Drydon let out another curse. "Don't call him my boy! I just wanted a simple accident! Now I have three other boys and Angie to deal with. And I'm their principal."

"Won't be a problem," the hunter told him. "I'll explain in a minute, but first let me go gather up your other boys. I'd hate for them to wake up alone in the dark."

The voices faded as Angie dozed off, yielding to darkness. She just wanted to sleep and wake up to find everything back to normal ...

Jared was on fire. Every shot he took, he nailed. Berkshire had no way to contain him. Taking the ball up the floor, he juked by a defender and went for a layup. Then all of a sudden George jumped from the ceiling and swatted the ball away. "You can't play basketball, loser!" he shouted. Jared waved his arms as he crashed toward the ground, going into the floor headfirst. As he hit, the floor turned into ice cubes. He opened his mouth to scream as he sank into the ice.

Suddenly, he woke up with a sharp pain pulsing inside his head. It felt as if somebody was slamming a basketball against his skull from the inside. And he was freezing. His lips chattered and for a minute he thought he really did lie in ice cubes, but opening his eyes he saw dark blades of grass in front of his face.

As the fuzziness of his dream faded, the reality of his horror returned. Lifting up his head, he saw the fallen bus. Instantly, he squeezed his eyes shut and grimaced. He woke from a bad dream only to enter a real nightmare.

"What happened?" he muttered. Then it all came back. Mr. Hackett pulling John off the bus for the bathroom, the pickup slamming into the bus, and then the crazy driver attacking him. The man from the locker room who'd attacked Will!

Wincing, he pushed himself up from where he'd fallen. Touching his head gingerly, he found a lump behind his ear and felt his bruised cheek on the left side of his nose. At least the cold kept the swelling down.

"Oh, great," he muttered. His feet felt like rubber.

Then he heard low whistling and mumbling. Blinking, he peered up and instantly drew in a sharp breath.

On the road, the figure of a man knelt over a limp body. He was pulling on the body's leg, yanking off something dark, and Jared could see pale skin reflect off the moonlight. A flashlight lay on the side of the road, aiming toward the trees.

Jared felt his blood surge and he forgot about his own injuries. He lurched to his feet.

Ryan lay on the grass where'd he been gassed and still appeared unconscious. Gritting his teeth, Jared started for the figure on the road. He knew who it had to be.

"You won't need these, buddy boy," murmured the figure. "Nothing to keep you warm, huh?" Then his back stiffened. "I know you're there," he said loudly. Reaching back, he snatched up the flashlight and shined it on the body.

Jared's worst fears were confirmed.

Will lay on his back, the legs of his shorts were bunched up around his thighs and his shoes had been pulled off. The figure had yanked off the leg sleeves.

Now holding them in one hand and the flashlight in the other, the figure turned to face Jared. "Keep coming at me and I'll ram these down your throat. But I won't kill you. Instead I'll choke the life out of your little friend here. If you want him to live, stand still and don't move. Got it, buddy boy?"

"You'd better listen to him, Jared," Ryan's voice croaked from near Jared's feet. "I-I know one thing about him. He's not lying."

The man grinned. "Yes. Listen to your friend, Jared. Friends don't lie."

"He's not my friend," Jared mumbled, his fists clenched and knees trembling.

The man barked out a laugh. "Yeah, I guess you could say that, all right. Still, he's telling the truth. Now, how 'bout you slowly walk over here. If you want this little kid to live past ten, pick him up nice and easy. You carry him. If you try anything funny, he'll die. And you'll watch it happen. You come too, smart boy who's not a friend. Both of you are coming with me." His voice grew hard. "Let's go!"

Jared had no choice. The man seemed crazy, like he wanted Jared to do something rash. Biting his lip and fighting back tears, he went to Will. His heart thundered against his chest and it seemed to climb toward his throat. He'd never felt fear like this. Only for Will's sake did he keep his body moving.

First, not daring to look at the man, he put Will's shoes back on, slipping them over the small socked feet. Then he carefully slid an arm under Will's back and lifted him up to a seated position.

"S-Sorry, Will," he mumbled.

The unconscious boy's head had lolled back, but he otherwise looked to be sleeping peacefully. Jared knew better. His skin felt like ice.

Jared never asked for help. He didn't want the filthy hands of the man or the traitorous hands of Ryan touching his friend. Taking a firm grip on Will's unresisting wrists, he crouched down and shifted his body around so Will faced his back. Then pulling Will's arms up around his shoulders while bending forward, he reached down and gathered up Will around his waist. As the unconscious boy leaned against his back, he shifted his hands under Will's thighs and, using all his remaining strength, hefted him up to carry him piggyback style. He ignored the strain on his knees. It was awkward, but Jared managed to stand and shift his friend to a better position.

So with Will draped over his back, Jared hunched forward and slowly turned to face the cause of all his pain. As a limp burden, Will proved heavier than he imagined, but Jared would not let his friend down. Not again.

"Nicely done," the man said, sounding disappointed. He turned to Ryan, who'd gotten stiffly to his feet. "Okay, you come on over. You two walk side by side on the road." He pointed up the road to the right of the overturned bus. "Head that way."

"Where're we going?" Ryan asked sullenly.

The man grunted. "You'll know it when you see it. But to answer your question, we're going to a very cold and a very dark place. You won't like it a bit."

He cackled wickedly and forced them to walk on. Rounding a bend in the road after about a quarter of a mile, the man tossed Will's leg sleeves into the darkness.

"Almost there, buddy boys," he said maliciously. "You two gonna make it?"

Jared, hunched forward, slowed to shift Will to a higher position, but made no comment. Ryan walked next to him like a lonely zombie. The man just snorted and cackled some more.

On the other side of the bend they reached a very surprising sight. Hidden behind a clump of trees, the oversized pickup was parked next to a small car Jared instantly recognized. Mr. Drydon leaned against the front door looking impatient and nervous. Seeing them, he knelt down over a dark shadow by his feet and shook it.

"Angie, wake up!"

Groaning, Angie opened an eye and stared up at her principal. Instantly, she started to scream, but Mr. Drydon clamped a hand over her mouth. "Stop screaming, or I'll knock you out again! Your friends are here." Letting go of her, he nodded toward the road.

Angie sat up and drew in a sharp breath when seeing Jared and Ryan. Then she saw Will slumped over Jared's back and moaned. "What's going on?" she wailed. "What's happening? Why?"

The man behind Jared and Ryan chuckled. "Those are some million-dollar questions, huh, Drydon?"

"We'll discuss details later," the principal snapped. He ran a hand through his mustache nervously. "So what's your great plan?"

"Right now? Right now it's to get these boys up in the pickup." He kicked the back of Ryan's shorts, knocking him forward. "Go pick up the retard," he commanded. "He's snoozing by the girl. Put him in the truck and you climb in after." He then turned to Jared. "You and your friend get in back too. Don't move fast enough and I'll have to help. And you wouldn't like that."

Ryan didn't look at Jared as he followed orders. Like a robot following a crude program, he gathered up John in his arms and hefted him up. Carrying his burden like he carried a giant baby, he walked stiffly to the pickup and gently lifted John up over the side. The boy tumbled in with a thump.

Turning, he then looked at Jared, his face lost in the darkness. His slumped shoulders said it all. Without a word, he went to help Jared, taking Will from his back.

"Sorry, man," he muttered softly as he lowered Will down. "My fault."

Jared made to resist, but at hearing the shame and regret in Ryan's voice, he let his friend slide free. They were all in this together.

"Shut it and hurry," the man snapped.

He and Drydon looked on without remorse.

Jared felt his whole body go numb as he climbed into the back of the truck without a word. Kneeling next to John's slumbering body, he leaned over to take Will from under his arms. He pulled the unresisting body up and over the side. Ryan stood looking at him for a moment and then swung himself up. Both knew trying to fight would be futile. Even if one of them made it into the woods, it would mean leaving Will, Angie, and John behind. Besides, where could they go? They were in the middle of nowhere, in the middle of a cold and terrible night.

Soon all four boys were either sitting or lying in the back. Ryan and Jared crouched miserably with the two unconscious bodies between them. Neither spoke.

"Good job, boys," the man told them. "That's how to follow directions. Your principal must be proud." He went to the truck and hopped on the back.

"Just tell me the plan," Mr. Drydon said irritably. "What are you doing with the kids?"

"Well, let's review," the man said, crouching to face Jared and Ryan. The boys stared back, trying to hide their fear. They didn't do a good job. "Mr. Hackett, the illustrious driver of a school bus, gets lost. He has a terrible bus accident. At the time of the accident, some kids were outside the bus trying to take a leak. One of them is a special needs kid and he goes off wandering in the woods. The other boys of course try to find him. What happens? They all get lost and end up … dead."

With that, he pulled another spray bottle from his belt and sent mist all over the back of the pickup. Ryan and Jared had no choice but to join Will and John in unconsciousness.

The man cackled harshly as the bodies slumped.

Chapter 49

Angie tried to scream, but Mr. Drydon grabbed her around the face and yanked her against him. "Stop it, or you'll join them!" he hissed. He looked up at the man. "What's the plan with the girl? What do you propose to do with her?"

The man hopped down from the pickup, covering his face with his shirt to escape the fumes.

"Girls are too smart to follow dumb boys out in the woods. I'm leaving her in your hands." He pulled his shirt down and grinned. Moonlight reflected off his teeth. "Principals know best. Just follow your heart, Drydon. You're part of this too, don't forget. I'm not doing all your dirty work. You'll have stain on your hands, just the same as me."

Mr. Drydon flinched, but made no comment.

Lifting a hand in a lazy wave, Hunter headed for the driver's door. "I'll be off now. Once I drop the boys off on their little excursion I'll head on home. You do what you have to do and call me tomorrow. But you'd better get out of here. The last thing we need is you at the scene of this very unfortunate accident."

"Great, just great," Mr. Drydon mumbled as the man slammed the door of the pickup. It sounded like a gunshot. He watched it rumble to life before turning onto the road. Instead of following it one way or the other, it cut across it, bumped over a small clearing before finding a narrow lane hidden among the trees.

Watching from where she stood in front of Mr. Drydon, Angie blinked back tears. She never would've known the road existed if she hadn't just seen it used. The boys were gone.

As the lights vanished into the darkness, Mr. Drydon yanked on her arm.

"Ow!" she cried, instantly snapping back to her own problems. "Why are you doing this? Why are you trying to kill everyone?"

"Shut up, Angie." He yanked open the driver's door and roughly threw her toward the front seat, not letting go of her arm.

"Stop it!" Angie shouted. "You're hurting me!"

"Just get in the car. Now!" He sounded nervous and suddenly dangerous. He stood blocking her escape, keeping her pinned against the car.

Jerking from his grip, Angie quickly climbed over to the passenger's seat and immediately tried to open the door on the other side, but it didn't budge.

"Sorry," grunted Mr. Drydon as he slid behind the wheel, slamming his door closed. "Because of John, I have child locks installed." He held up an electronic key. "You're not going anywhere."

Angie turned to him and couldn't keep the tears from falling. "Why?" she wailed. "Just tell me why you're doing this!"

Ignoring her, Mr. Drydon reached back and pulled out a large metal thermos from the backseat. He unscrewed the lid and took a sip. He immediately winced. "Ouch, that's hot."

Angie glared at him. She'd always loved the smell of coffee, but now it made her sick to her stomach. "I hope it burns your filthy tongue off!"

Mr. Drydon looked over at her and took a deep breath. His voice went calm, which made it sound even more dangerous. "You wouldn't understand, Angie. But the only person who was supposed to be harmed tonight was to be me. You and your friends messed it all up." His voice sounded almost sad.

Angie blinked and scrunched up her face. "Excuse me? You hired that whack job out there to hurt *you*?" She took several deep breaths. "I don't think so!"

"It's true. I ... I've had a hard life. Angie, if you could understand, it can still be okay."

"You're out of your mind."

"Perhaps." He sighed. "You don't know it, but those boys out there ... any one of them could've been my son ... one of them *should've* been my son. Then this never would've happened."

Angie looked at him incredulously. "You want to kill your son. That's it, isn't it? That's how you get hurt. What about *him*?"

"My son … that boy, that boy doesn't feel hurt. That boy doesn't feel anything."

"That's not true, and you know it!"

"No!" Mr. Drydon roared, his mustache quivering. "I don't know it!" He turned on a small light on the dashboard to see his coffee and Angie saw blood vessels pop from his forehead. "The only thing I know is that I once had a good life. I had a wife who loved me and a job with prestige and enough money to live a happy life. Then …" he closed his eyes as if in pain. "Then my wife got pregnant. It was supposed to be the proudest moment of my life! And we had John … and that, that *thing* ruined everything."

"He's your son!" Angie cried. "How can you say that?"

"He's nothing but a useless husk of a person!" Spittle flew from his mouth as he screamed. Taking a breath, his voice lowered, but the hot rage remained. "We should have gotten rid of him when we had the chance. He ruined my life! Do you know what it's like to live twenty-four hours a day, seven days a week, with a crying, whining child who has no more common sense than a vegetable? My wife ran out on me because she couldn't take it! I couldn't take my job anymore! Every time I thought I found hope and happiness, John's presence would rear its ugly head. I came to this place for a fresh start, but every day I came home to John! I lost everything because of him!"

Angie blinked back tears as she fought through her shock. "How, how could you say that? He loves you!"

"He doesn't know what love is! Love takes work and he does nothing. Judge me if you like, I don't care. In today's world there's no such thing as right and wrong, it's just about timing. If you do something at the wrong time you're a criminal. But the same thing at the right time, you're a saint. Think of slavery. Less than two hundred years ago we owned people like cattle." He blew out his breath. "And now we're allowed to kill unwanted kids every day, but only if done properly. If I had him destroyed before his birth, we would be in a better place and nobody would've batted an eye. We should've had an abortion. He never should've been born."

Angie just stared at him in revulsion. "H-How can you say that?"

Mr. Drydon stared out his window, avoiding her stare. "Grow a few more years and you'll understand. You have no idea what it's like working in a school and being a principal surrounded by normal kids … only to come home to John. To meet a woman, only to bring her home to that … that creature. John took my life and it's high time I get it back!"

"You're … you're worse than that man. You're a monster."

Mr. Drydon now looked over at her. "No, I'm like most people on this earth. You push us far enough and we'll do anything to make it better. Grow up. There's no right and wrong in this. If destroying unborn babies is perfectly okay, then what's wrong with waiting a few years?" He snorted. "John certainly won't know the difference."

He paused to take another sip of coffee. Angie could only stare at a man she'd thought she'd known. Then the principal continued, bitterness pouring out like a faucet left running.

"For years I was left alone with him. People called me a saint. Why? Because I didn't go crazy, I guess. But did they ever help me? Did they ever realize the pain I had to endure coming home to a broken child every day? Of course not!" His face twisted in self-righteous anger. More spit flew from his mouth, striking the mirror. "Tonight his long-awaited abortion finally happens, just twelve years too late."

Then taking a deep breath, he fought to regain control. After another sip of coffee, he looked over at Angie. "And now I'm left with you." His voice dripped with sarcasm. "The social outcast who tries to feel special by helping my special needs son. You're not special. You're just a fool. Do you know how hard I tried to keep you separated from other kids? I wanted this to happen the easy way. Nobody else hurt. In a way, tonight is your fault, Angie. Your fault. Everything was set for a quick and easy job, but you and your friends made that very difficult. I didn't want it to be like this."

"So you wreck a bus full of kids," Angie said bitterly. "You're a real hero."

Mr. Drydon just snorted and sipped more coffee. He stared out the front of the car and didn't look at her. "You're too young to understand," he muttered. "The only life that truly matters is the one you have. That's one lesson my life taught me very well."

Angie shook her head. "I do understand. Do you know why I liked being with John? Because he's everything good about people. Too bad his father is the opposite. You're foul, festering evil."

Mr. Drydon grimaced. "Maybe in your eyes I am. But do realize something, Angie. Those boys in that bus are probably all still alive, thanks to me. I had Mr. Hackett modify the bus so there's no way out, but that was to protect them." He smiled bitterly. "You know, these old buses are so unreliable. Tomorrow the police are going to think the windows and emergency doors malfunctioned and the bus should've failed inspection. But really, I had it done. I saved the boys, Angie." He breathed out fiercely and swallowed. "I didn't know the bus would be tipped, but I did know those boys needed protection. Sure, now they'll be stuck for a while, but eventually they'll be freed, not knowing a thing." His eyes narrowed. "Now, if they were ever to learn of what I just told you, then that would be very tragic indeed. I protected them the best I could, Angie. Unfortunately, I don't think I can do the same for you."

Angie cringed from him, but strangely felt more anger and disgust than shock and horror. Mr. Drydon, she saw, was more pathetic than scary. It was the other man called Hunter, who took the boys, that chilled her blood. Drydon was a coward at heart, a coward who wanted others to do his dirty work. Talking to her, she realized, was him trying to justify his actions to himself and work himself up to harming her. She couldn't believe she'd once looked up to him.

Glaring at him, she said, "You only think of yourself. Let me guess, you wanted John to go away and then you collect life insurance, or something."

Clearly irritated, Mr. Drydon wrinkled his nose. "Something like that, yes. I need a fresh start. Besides, that boy owes me for the twelve years of misery he brought me. I still have a woman waiting. So sit tight and let me make a phone call. Soon it'll be over …" Mr. Drydon went to take another sip from the thermos, but first paused to blow on the hot contents.

"The only misery is you, Mr. Drydon," Angie said bitterly. "You brought it on yourself with your selfishness and hate. You should've seen John for how he really is. A better person than you'll ever be."

Angie suddenly slammed her hand against the end of the thermos, jamming it into Mr. Drydon's face. Steaming coffee splattered his face and neck, running down his shirt.

Jerking with shock, Mr. Drydon's eyes bugged out and he lost hold of the thermos. It toppled right on his lap, spilling more scalding coffee.

Screams ripped out of his throat. Angie ignored these. Along with the thermos, he'd also lost grip of his key.

"My face!" he screeched, thrashing wildly.

Angie grabbed at the key, snatching it from the dashboard where it'd landed. Clicking off the child locks, she yanked on the handle next to her and threw open the door with her shoulder.

Scared out of her mind, she tumbled onto the cold grass below.

"No!" screamed Mr. Drydon behind her. "Come back!"

Rolling to her feet, she flung the key toward the woods across the road and sprinted for the bus.

Mr. Drydon's screams of pain and fury followed her.

"I'll get you for this! You'll pay for this!" he roared.

Angie did not look back.

Inside the bus, things were getting desperate. The air hung heavy with sweat, blood, and despair. Only the cracked window provided hope for fresh air, and it proved not enough.

"What happened to Will?" Nick kept asking. "I don't believe this ... Where could he have gone?"

Their real hope had disappeared with Will. The boy had climbed out several minutes before and had vanished. Just like Mr. Hackett and the others.

"Just shut up and help us find a way out of here!" Brad snarled. "Then we can find out for ourselves."

Big Mike and Kyle had already reached up and tested every available window, but had found them all stuck. So were the emergency exits.

Big Mike kicked the back door of the bus savagely. It didn't budge an inch.

"It's hopeless," Tom said. "We're all going to die!"

Darius moaned where he lay near the front of the bus with the other badly injured, Coach Swopes, Howard and Teddy. The coach remained unconscious.

"Shut up!" Big Mike roared. "If we can't open the door, we bust it down!"

Nick brightened. "Yeah, man! We can do that!"

"Right," Glen muttered painfully. He cuddled his injured arm close to his chest and his face glistened with sweat. "How?"

"This is how," Big Mike grunted.

He stepped back on the windows at his feet to face the now sideways emergency door. He had to stoop slightly to fit his broad shoulders between the row of sideways seats and the curved roof of the bus, now acting as the left wall.

Crouching into a football position, he snarled and threw himself at the door, slamming it with his shoulder.

"It won't budge, man," Brad said. "I tried it. It feels like something has bolted it from the outside."

"Then let's break the bolt!" Nick cried. "Come on, Mike! Let's do this!"

Both boys took turns throwing their shoulder into the door. They had to move out of each other's way to fit in the narrow space between the bus's "old" ceiling and backseats. The other boys, those who could stand, stood back to cheer them on. After several minutes of their banging, the door wilted and cracked open a few inches.

"It's working!" Kyle shouted excitedly. "I see a crack! Fresh air!"

"Not even Will could fit through that," Glen said scornfully.

"Quick!" Nick yelled. "Somebody bring me something to wedge in there."

Tom found a broom stick wedged against the "floor" and a seat. He quickly brought it to the back.

"Somebody jam it in the crack," Nick said. "Start to pry open the door, but don't pull too hard. Just give some tension while Mike and I pound away."

"What about your shoulder, man?" Brad asked. He took the broom and slid between the seats by the back, wedging the broom into the crack.

"What shoulder?" Nick said. "It feels great!"

Fifteen minutes later, Big Mike launched his shoulder into the door and there came a tremendous crack. The door buckled and then snapped open, swinging down on the ground with a thud.

Brad yelled in triumph, dropping the cracked broom.

"Freedom!" screamed Kyle, yanking back the broom as Brad let go. "We did it!"

Everyone not too injured cried out with glee. Hope had suddenly appeared.

Because of the angle of the bus and the sideways seats, they had to exit by crawling over and through the back door. Big Mike and Brad made it out first and then started helping the other boys, the ones who could move on their own.

Glen stayed in the bus to look after those too hurt to be moved. Coach Swopes had opened his eyes, but seemed too dazed to understand what had happened. He remained, along with Teddy, Howard, and Darius. The rest climbed out like they were resurrecting from a tomb.

"What now?" Kyle asked excitedly as he stretched out his bruised and battered arms. "I don't see anybody out here, man." Shivering, he put up his hood from his hoodie.

Before leaving the bus, Brad made sure all the boys had on their pants and hoodies over their uniforms, and jackets if they had them.

"Will!" Nick shouted. "Jared, Ryan! Where are you guys?"

He got no answer.

"This is spooky," Kyle said, his voice dropping to a whisper. "Where'd they all go?"

Brad grunted. "We need to find a signal for a phone," he said. "Will took mine, so somebody else has to use theirs. Move around!"

"We just need to find Will and the others!" Nick cried. He started calling loudly as he went the length of the bus. "Will! Where are you?!"

The others called, but Brad didn't let anyone stray too far.

"We need to stay close and keep warm until help arrives," he told the boys. "Everyone especially stay out of the woods. If you need to take a leak, use the side of the road. Nobody else is allowed to go missing."

"Hey!" Tom shouted. "I found something!" He crouched near where the front of the bus rested on its side. "Brad, I think it's your phone!"

"And I found Mr. Hackett!" Kyle cried. "He's not moving, man!"

Chapter 50

Angie peered around a tree, watching the fallen bus. She'd slipped into the edge of the woods when nearing the bus and hearing the boys break free. Remembering Mr. Drydon's words, she didn't want to bring doom to any of the boys. She knew the principal and that man were crazy. They were very capable of killing them all without a second thought.

"Will!" Nick cried out near her. "Where are you?!" He reached the back of the bus near the rear tires. Stopping, he stared out into the woods, just to the right of Angie's position. Even in the darkness she could make out his pain and frustration.

From the other side of the bus came an excited cry. "I got a signal! I got a signal!"

"Call 911, pronto!" Brad yelled.

Taking a deep breath, Angie stepped from behind the tree and hissed. "Nick, come here! Quietly! Don't let anybody hear you!"

Nick had turned toward the excited voices, but now paused. "Who's there? Is that you, Will? Jared?"

"It's me, Angie! If you want to find the boys, hurry up!"

Nick glanced around and hurried towards her. He crashed into the brush, nearly running her over.

"Angie, what happened? Where's everybody else? Where's Will?"

"Hush!" Angie cried. It was too late. Two more figures ran toward them.

"Who's there?" Brad demanded. "Nick, is that you?"

"Don't say anything," Angie pleaded. "If you want us to live, just keep your mouth shut."

Nick hesitated but then nodded. But his weight shifted and a branch snapped.

"We're coming in after you, whoever you are," Brad said. "Ready, Mike? Let's go!"

Angie groaned as the other two boys crashed their way into woods. She stepped out from behind Nick and waved them over.

"Angie!" Brad said in surprise. "What's going on?"

"She knows where the others are," Nick said, sounding worried.

Angie sighed. "I know where to find them, but you'll have to trust me. Nobody else can know and we have to stay dead silent. I mean it. Follow me and don't open your mouth until I say it's okay. I'll tell you everything once we're clear of the bus. If you don't want to trust me, then turn around now."

Brad just grunted. "I don't know what's going on, but if our teammates are in trouble, then we're coming for them."

Big Mike grunted in agreement.

"Are you sure?" Angie asked, sounding relieved to have the help.

"No doubt," Brad said.

"What about the others?" Nick asked, nodding toward the wrecked bus.

"The cops and ambulances are on the way," Brad said. "If we wait, we—"

Angie hissed, "No! Nobody else can know." She sounded frightened. "It's life or death!"

"Yo, Brad," Kyle called loudly from the other side of the bus. "Where are you?"

"You're crazy," Brad whispered as he crouched down. He brushed back his long hair and shook his head. "Fine. Okay, Angie. Lead on."

Nodding, Angie turned and headed into the thick woods. As she did, she heard a car's engine start in the distance. Her heart jumped. Mr. Drydon must've had a spare key and now seemed ready to make his presence known. She had to get away.

"Let's hurry," she said. As fast as she dared, she moved along the tree line parallel to the road.

The bright headlights of Mr. Drydon's car swung over and past them as they headed to the bus. As soon as Angie saw the lights, she ordered the boys down.

Amazingly, they followed her orders without protest. Then they were back up and rushing through the dark woods. It took longer than Angie thought possible, and at first she thought the mysterious road had vanished, but suddenly they plunged onto the narrow dirt lane, covered in tire ruts.

"They went down this," she said grimly. "Some crazy guy is trying to leave them in the woods to die. If anyone on the bus finds out about it they're going to die, too. That car that passed us is part of it." She'd tell them later about Mr. Drydon. She didn't want any of the boys to chase after him now. His time would come once Jared, John, Ryan, and Will were safe.

Big Mike smacked a fist in his palm. "What are we waiting for?" he demanded. "Let's find them!"

As they broke into a run, Angie had a disturbing thought. When trapped in the car, Mr. Drydon had wanted to make a phone call. She guessed it would've been to someone to deal with her— somebody to kill her for the cowardly principal. Since he wouldn't be calling Hunter, Angie had to wonder. Who else did Drydon know who would kill innocent kids?

The pickup jerked to a stop just above a steep gully. The lights went black and stillness settled.

Ryan opened his eyes and stared up at stars shining from on high over dark silent trees. Their long trunks looked like arms stretching up and their bare branches like terrible claws trying to tear down the stars. He shuddered, rolling to the side. He hated the outdoors.

He struck a still body and remembered where he was and what was to happen. The coldness sank into his bones, chilling him from head to toe. He shivered as the truck door creaked open.

"Oh, so you're awake," the man said as he stepped from the truck and looked in the back. "You know, Indians used to live in this area. I found a few arrowheads here."

Ryan sat up and stared at the man, too cold to be afraid. Even in the faint moonlight he could see the man smile, enjoying this.

"Eat my shorts," he muttered.

"No thanks."

The man walked around the truck and stopped at the tailgate, resting his arms on the back of it. Ryan shifted his body warily to face him.

"They're about the only protection you're going to have in this weather. You'll need them. You know, the Indians had a tradition. When a boy turned twelve, he was sent out in the wilderness to survive with nothing but a knife. No clothes and no food, nothing but his instincts to guide him. I read a story about it once when I was about your age."

"At least he had a knife," Ryan muttered.

"Yeah?" The man straightened and reached in his pocket to pull out a pocketknife that he snapped open. Holding it by the blade, he extended it toward Ryan. "If you want it, hop down. I'll give it to you."

Ryan stared at him and then slowly got up. Pins and needles seemed to stab him from head to toe and he took a moment to gather himself. Then he carefully climbed over the side, not knowing what the man intended, or what *he* would do if he really got the knife.

Just as his feet touched the ground, the man flipped the knife over and all at once stabbed out, slicing into Ryan's shoulder.

The boy jerked with surprise and then gasped in pain. Before he could react further, pain exploded in his middle.

The man had followed his stab with a knee right into Ryan's stomach.

Ryan started to cry out, but lost his breath as he fell in a heap, clutching his stomach with his left hand. His right arm dangled limply at his side. Fire seemed to rage between his elbow and shoulder.

"That's for betraying your friends," the man said pleasantly as he closed the knife and slipped it into his pocket. "Instead of a knife, you get knifed." He chuckled without humor. "If it makes you feel any better, you were going to die no matter what. You're a loose end that needs tying up. Now, buddy boy, enjoy the rest of your night. It'll probably be your last."

He grabbed the back of Ryan's shirt and half pulled, half dragged him to the edge of the gully. He paused for a moment and then flung the boy down.

Ryan cried out briefly and then went quiet as his body slammed into dark oblivion, rolling wildly over damp leaves, stabbing into fallen branches. He finally crashed into a tree near the bottom and went still. He couldn't even whimper.

Back on top, the man whistled as he returned to his truck and pulled down the tailgate. Reaching in, he grabbed Will and Jared, each by a shoe, and dragged them to the edge of the tailgate.

"The game is over for you two boys," he said pleasantly, as he got both boys lying on their backs. "Nice playing, but you lose."

Taking a handful of each shirt by their sides, he yanked them down off the truck, at the same time kneeling to let their unconscious bodies fall to his shoulders. Neither one stirred.

Humming, the man easily lifted them up and made his way to the gully's edge. There he dumped their bodies down, sending them tumbling after Ryan. Neither boy made a sound.

Good old John came last. When the man returned to the truck, the boy had his eyes open but lay rigid.

The man laughed. "You won't last five seconds out here, boy."

Grabbing him roughly by the legs, he manhandled the boy down. Pulling him up by the back of his pants and his collar, the man carried John to the edge of the drop. John squirmed at first, but then went rigid as a board when he saw the seemingly bottomless darkness before him.

"Goodbye, kid," the man said. He threw John down the gully and listened to the thumps and rattles of leaves. He knew the gully dropped at a steep angle for about twenty feet before leveling off in a thicket of trees. Some of the boys may never wake, and if they did, they'd have nowhere to go. John would only be a burden. They would all die.

For a moment he stared down into the blackness and frowned. The knife stunt was stupid. It left a mark on a body that had no natural explanation.

"Oh, well," he said with a sigh. "Guess that means I'll be out tomorrow to check on the bodies and hide some evidence."

For him, it just meant the game got to continue a little bit longer. That made him smile. He'd read another story long ago—a story about a man who hunted people for sport. It had ultimately changed his life.

Moments later, the truck roared to life and continued down the earthen road. The hunter couldn't wait to get home. His parents were making roast beef for dinner. Grabbing his phone from the seat next to him, he called his pa.

"Hey, Will. Wake up. Get up!"

Will opened his eyes to freezing cold and darkness. He felt a hand shake his shoulder.

"Come on, man," Ryan's voice said above him. "We can't sleep out here."

Will drew in a sharp breath and started coughing. "Okay," he said weakly. "I'm up … Wh-what just happened? Where are we?"

"Probably our grave," Ryan muttered. His voice sounded tight with pain and held only despair.

Will sat up and stared sleepily around him. "Is that why it's so cold?" he asked, shivering.

Bright spots of moonlight dotted the ground of an otherwise dark, shadowy forest. A cold wind blew through the trees above him, cutting into his bare arms. He found himself sitting in damp leaves at the base of a forested gulch. He only wore his basketball uniform and sneakers. Hugging his bare knees close to him, he tried to figure out how he had ended up here.

He remembered climbing out of the bus and trying to find help … then that smell … Will shivered.

Ryan knelt next to him, clutching his right arm, and shuddered violently. "Help me get Jared and John. We have to get moving."

"I'm awake," Jared muttered. "I'd rather not be, but I am." He sat up in a dark shadow on the other side of Ryan. "The last thing I remember is being in that pickup truck. I'm guessing this is the cold, dark place that guy talked about." His body shuddered. "I'm, I'm freezing."

Ryan staggered to his feet. "Yeah, this would be it." His voice sounded hoarse and weak with pain. "Oh, man … it hurts."

"What's wrong with you?" Will asked, looking up.

"Man, you mean besides the fact we're dumped in the middle of the woods, in the freezing cold, with nothing but basketball uniforms?" Ryan said. Then he groaned. "That punk cut me before he left. He got my arm."

Jared instantly got up. "What?"

"Who cut you?" Will asked, his entire body trembling. "Last thing I remember is getting out of the bus … Then I smelled that cologne stuff."

"We'll tell you later," Jared said, wincing as he stood. "Just know we're in big trouble. What happened to you, Ryan?"

Ryan told how the guy slashed his arm before tossing him down the hill. He left out the reason why the guy did it. "I think we need to get back up there and follow the road to find a way out of here. It has to lead somewhere."

"Sure, but which way do we go?" Will asked miserably. "Where are we?" He couldn't keep his body still.

"We came in a pickup," Jared explained to him. "We were all knocked out, so we could be miles away from civilization."

"Yo, man," Ryan groaned. "Not the time to think that way. Right now, man, it's we move or we die here. I'd rather move."

"First, let's check your arm," Jared told him.

Branches covered most of the moonlight, but they could barely make each other out.

Ryan dropped his hand from his right arm. The sleeve just above his elbow on the Patriots basketball shirt had a nasty rip about two inches in length and oozing dark blood.

"Great," Ryan moaned. "I'm either going to freeze to death or bleed to death."

"Or talk to death," Jared said grimly. He took a deep breath and yanked off the new T-shirt he wore over his uniform, instantly squeezing his arms to his sides, trying to fight off the cold. "I b-barely wore this sh-shirt," he said. "Oh, well."

"Man, I hope it's clean," Ryan muttered.

Jared tried to laugh, but sneezed instead. "I certainly didn't sweat in, in it t-tonight. I rode the b-bench."

Will fought to his feet and looked around. "Hey, did you say John was here too?"

"Yeah, I think so," Ryan said. "You were conked out and missed the crazy stuff, man. Apparently we're all part of some plan to get rid of John." He sighed. "I … I have a lot to, uh, apologize for."

"Later," Jared told him. "Right now … let's just … live." He found a stick and shoved it into his shirt, stabbing the cloth hard. Once he punctured the cloth, he put his fingers through the hole and ripped the shirt to make it one long cloth.

He was surprised to feel in control and not panicky. It was almost like it was a relief to finally figure out the mystery. Not everything was clear, but he at least knew the who and why.

Unfortunately, it came a bit late. But he wasn't about to give in to Drydon and his murderous friend, Hunter. He wrapped the ripped shirt around Ryan's arm, making sure to cover the wound before tying it tight.

"Let's get John and find someplace w-warm," he said.

A few feet up the side of the steep ravine, Will found John lying in a tight ball, not moving. He could see the whites of his eyes in the moonlight.

"Hey, John," he said gently, trying to keep his voice from trembling. "Are you okay?"

John made no response.

Will put a hand on his shoulder and rocked it, much like he did with Jimmy when his little brother was scared in the dark, after their parents fought. "Look, John, it's me, Will. I'm with Jared, and Ryan. We're here with you and, um, we need to get moving. We're going to, um, find Angie. Are you ready to go?"

John's eyes blinked once and he looked up at Will.

"I want to go home." he said.

"Yeah, good plan," Will said. He grabbed John's hand and helped the boy to his feet. "Let's start moving that way."

Soon the four boys staggered up the hill together. They pressed as close to each other as possible, with John and Will in the middle, trying to use each other's body heat to keep warm. It took several minutes of slipping and sliding, but they finally managed to reach the road.

"Which way?" Jared asked.

"Left," Ryan said. "I'm pretty sure that's the way the pickup went, so we know it has to lead somewhere."

As they walked huddled together, shivering in the cold, Ryan started talking.

"Yo, dudes," he said guiltily, "I keep waiting for one of you to ask me my part in all this, but you're both either too nice or too dumb to do it."

"Ha," Will said, his teeth chattering. "I-I'm j-just too c-cold."

Even John shivered, and he wore his jacket and long pants.

Jared grunted. "Just keep m-moving. Rub your arms and keep the blood g-going. Go ahead, Ryan. T-talk. It'll k-keep our minds off freezing."

"Okay, then … I'm sure you already know, Jared," Ryan said guiltily, "but I'm the thief. Well, mostly …" He explained how his mom had to raise him and his two brothers, but could never afford anything. "Ben's like family," he muttered. "He and his folks saved us. They helped my mom get a job as a receptionist and got us out of some filthy apartment. Yo, man, they gave us a lot when we needed it … So I owe them. I owe Ben a lot. So when I saw Ben …" Ryan took a deep breath. "You have to understand. Ben's parents are strict. They don't give him much. So, he, he sometimes wants things he can't have. One day after football practice I saw him go through a kid's locker. The kid had forgotten to lock it."

Jared gave a start and Will staggered at the news.

"Ben's the thief?" Jared asked aloud, in disbelief.

Ryan sounded deeply ashamed, but also relieved to finally confess.

"At first. It was crazy, man. Ben had his hand in this dude's locker taking some money when I heard Mr. Hackett coming in. I didn't think. I told Ben to hide in the toilets and tried to shut the locker, but I got busted, man. Mr. Hackett comes in and sees me. What does he do? He calls me straight to his office. Man, I know I'm busted. I'm busted like a broken TV. But I never let on about Ben. I tell you guys, I owe him too much. If his parents knew about him thieving, man, I don't know what would happen. It'd ruin him. Anyway, so I go in Hackett's office and you know what? That dude, he just looks me in the eye and asks how would I like to work for him … I nearly lost my mind, but I'm serious. He tells me either I work for him, or I was a goner. He'd pin every break-in on me and get the cops involved. So I told him, yeah, I'll do it. Man, I'm serious. I became his personal thief, man."

Ryan went on to explain how Mr. Hackett would point out which students to rob and what to take. He'd supply Ryan with the locker combination and give him time to sneak in the locker room alone.

Apparently, Mr. Hackett had a gambling addiction that he hid from his wife and needed cash on the side. If Ryan refused to help him, the teacher just threatened to turn him in, placing all the blame on his shoulders. He told Ryan over and over that nobody would believe a poor kid like him, emphasizing his brown skin, against the word of a respected teacher.

"Besides that, guys," he confessed, speaking softly. "He guaranteed me the starting QB position next year for football. And gave me a cut of all the money he got … I've been saving with Ben to get a laptop. He never knew where the money came from."

"H-how much money did you g-get from gym lockers?" Will asked.

"A lot," Ryan grimly answered. "I took cash, phones, shirts, gold chains, iPods, even a Kindle, man."

He swore he'd never spoken to Ben about the deal. He'd just told him that Mr. Drydon couldn't prove anything and had let him go. Since then, he'd carried the burden of protecting Ben while putting himself in danger by acting as Hackett's stooge.

Then everything changed when Mr. Drydon entered the picture. It happened a few days before Will went streaking for the towels and had lost his shorts.

"It was me, Jared," Ryan said apologetically, "who stole your money for your sports physical."

He told how Mr. Hackett had found some sort of knockout spray hidden in the supply room. The PE teacher thought it had been part of old medical supplies from years ago and wanted to test it out.

"He figured we could up the thieving to a new level," Ryan said miserably. He sighed. "Now I know, Will, how you and Nick got conked out on Halloween. But, I swear, man, I had no idea then. I think Hackett just wanted to see how the stuff worked." He grunted. "And I knew you had money for the physical, Jared. I was stupid, man. I didn't really think it would do anything … but, as I'm sure you all know now, it's pretty effective."

Jared bit his lip. He'd never forget the hurt and fear at waking up to find out he'd been robbed.

"And," Ryan continued, sounding amazed, "then you *still* showed up for tryouts, man. I resented you big time, Jared, after that. It got to be like poison, man. The closer you got to us, the more I had it out for you."

Ryan said he got real scared when hearing from Will how Mr. Drydon had brought a stranger to meet with Mr. Hackett. He knew it had to be about the spray theft and thought the stranger would be a cop.

"Yo, dudes, at first I thought I would be blamed for everything and arrested, but then I got scared for Will."

Apparently, Mr. Drydon had visited Mr. Hackett before and had hinted about knowing about the thefts, but seemed okay with it for some reason. Ryan figured something wasn't right about the principal, and sure enough, Mr. Drydon didn't get Mr. Hackett in trouble.

When Ryan went to return the towels to Mr. Hackett, he learned everything.

Mr. Drydon and the man, Hunter, used Mr. Hackett in much the same way Mr. Hackett used Ryan. Mr. Hackett and Ryan were forced to work with them, or be turned over for their crimes. The only difference, Mr. Drydon played for higher stakes. He went after people to hurt them. Mr. Hackett didn't like Drydon one bit, but was trapped, much like Ryan.

"Drydon was real mad at Hackett for stealing the knockout stuff, until he heard how it was used. Then he thought it was good to hurt you, Jared."

He took a deep breath and confessed to lying by telling Mr. Hackett it'd been Jared and not Will who'd snuck by their meeting to get towels.

"I told him the shorts were yours, Jared. He was too stupid to notice they were too small. Man, he took me straight to Drydon and I met that Hunter dude. They got really bent on getting you after that, man. Mr. Drydon didn't want any kids being friendly with John and knew John liked you." Ryan paused for a breath, obviously ashamed.

Jared kept silent, but felt his cheeks grow warm against the cold. He remembered John waving to him with Mr. Drydon watching back on Halloween. Beside him John didn't say a word, but had to be hearing everything.

Ryan then continued. "That's why you got set up on the second shower day … I helped spring the trap. I made you go for towels. Hunter was waiting and tried to scare you off."

Ryan did promise up and down that he had no idea of Mr. Drydon's ultimate plan. He just knew he got angry when people got close to John. He had thought Hunter would just scare Jared and get him to quit the team. Only it didn't happen. The animosity toward Jared only grew.

Mr. Hackett had promised Ryan once Jared was off the team he would be free to go—Drydon and Hackett believed Jared to be a threat for some reason.

"Which you were in the end," Ryan admitted.

Of course, everything backfired and then Ryan had started feeling really guilty. At first he thought Drydon just wanted his son left alone, but then he started thinking it had to be more. He remembered Halloween and figured Hunter had been inside the building then. It could not have been for good reasons for John. By then he was in way too deep to just back out.

He'd been the one to frame Jared as the thief. Mr. Drydon had also wanted to warn off Will, hoping to scare him away from John and Jared at the same time. Hunter had it all worked out—he would scare Will and cause him to go against Jared. Originally he planned to put a nasty warning on Will and then hide the stolen items in Jared's locker later that night—so the next day there could be a surprise locker inspection staged. Jared had ruined those plans, so it went to backup mode, which pretty much happened how Jared had guessed. Hunter had Ryan cover for him. After pretending to go with Ben, Ryan had snuck to the side of the school to watch the side entrance. When Hunter had raced out, Ryan had taken Will's wallet and sprinted back to the gym. He'd then planted the wallet and some of the stolen goods from Mr. Hackett's office in Jared's locker.

"Sorry, man." Ryan muttered. "You even left your locker wide open."

Only once Will and Nick had hesitated, not totally falling for it, Ryan knew it had to end. Hunter had been furious when the stolen goods were returned without pinning the thefts on Jared, but then acted as if it didn't matter.

That's when Ryan had gotten wind of some big plan happening at Berkshire, but again promised to know nothing of the specifics. He did get Ben to skip the trip. He was ashamed to have his friend find out about him being a real thief, and even more afraid that Ben would find out how it had all started to protect him. Ryan had wanted to admit everything to Coach Swopes, but knew he had very little leverage. All he had was his word against a principal and PE teacher. He needed proof, but had no idea how to get it.

Ryan blew out his breath. "I … I'm really sorry, man. I really am a … a real jerk. I didn't know what to do. I felt lost. But I finally came to my senses when I saw you, Jared, stand up for John. Man, back in the locker room, I really saw you, Jared. I confess, man. I pegged you as a nobody who would bend and break like a dried-up string bean. So did Mr. Drydon. When I saw you stand up to Brad, man, I knew I was the string bean. You got guts, man. That's when I told myself I'd do anything to make it right. I had to fix what I did … but I didn't act until too late." He sucked in his breath and let it out. "So there you guys have it. Man, I did some bad stuff. Real bad stuff."

It was a long, cruel story, at times nearly unbelievable, but having lived through it, Jared and Will never questioned it. At least it took their minds off their cold, miserable walk. For a time, they walked in silence.

Jared stared at the dark, leering branches sticking out on either side of them. It felt like walking between rows of sharp, crooked teeth. At any moment, the teeth would close in and smash them to pulp. He imagined Ryan must've felt trapped between Mr. Hackett and Mr. Drydon, two sharp-toothed monsters bent on prodding him on a similar miserable path leading to doom with no end in sight. He shivered.

"Gr-great st-story," Will finally muttered. "Wh-when I was five, I once st-stole a candy b-bar."

"What?" Ryan asked. Then he laughed hoarsely, before gasping in pain. "Man, but I bet you didn't get your friends in a pickle like this."

Jared coughed. "Let's w-worry about g-guilt after we're w-warm, okay?"

Just as he spoke, a cold wind struck from behind and the boys flinched. Even though still above freezing, the temperature was plunging. The branches waved and snapped, like the teeth clicking in anticipation.

"Keep moving," Ryan said, sounding weak. "Keep m-moving …"

Slowly, hunching low, they continued to trudge through the inky darkness. Guided only by choppy moonlight escaping through the maze of the toothy tree limbs, they followed deep tire ruts in the road. Pressed close, they used each other for support and warmth. They had no clue where they were going.

As they moved onward, Jared cleared his throat. Though he stooped low, trying to escape the cold, he still felt a flicker of warmth inside. He knew it took guts for Ryan to spill everything they way he had, even if it was too late. Wounded and scared, Ryan had done the right thing in the end.

"It's okay, Ryan," he said, breaking the silence. "You w-were just trying to h-help your friends." He felt his teeth start to chatter. Next to him, he felt John also shivering.

"Wish I could help them now," Ryan said softly, his voice faint. He tried shifting his shoulders, but instantly groaned.

Around them, the branches started to chatter louder as the wind grew bitterly cold and knifed through, hitting into their backs without mercy.

Will tripped and nearly fell, saved by Jared grabbing his arm. "I don't think we're g-going to m-make it much f-farther." He walked with his shoulders bent and hands wrapped inside the front of his jersey. His bare shoulders had no protection.

"We're s-so going to fr-freeeze," Ryan said through gritted teeth.

Jared suddenly stopped and stood up straight. "W-Wait. I got an idea," he said, "but it's going to take a whole lot of forgiveness and trust for it to work."

"I forgive," Will said quickly. "Do it."

"Me too," Ryan added. "I mean, I hope … you all forgive me."

"Done," Jared said.

John kept silent as he hunched his narrow shoulders forward and stared listlessly forward.

Jared still wondered how much of Ryan's story John heard or understood.

"Al right," he said, "I read this in a western, but they used cow guts instead."

In the faint moonlight slipping past the web of branches, Ryan and Will stared at him.

"Cow guts?" asked Ryan.

"J-just trust me," Jared said, growing more confident. "Everyone move off the road and l-lie down, uh, sort of close. Real close. Actually, get in a ditch. That m-might work best."

Too cold to argue, Ryan and Will led John to a ditch and helped him lie down between them. Jared then started piling leaves over them, finding only dry leaves on top of the surface. He packed them in as tight as possible. Then mumbling apologies, he climbed into the top, lying on top of his friends, wrapping his arms around them tight.

"Hug tight, guys. Hopefully our body heat gets trapped," he explained.

"Yo, man, I hope we survive the night," Ryan said crossly, "because if our bodies get found like this, it'll be an embarrassing death, man."

The boys never had to spend the entire night in the ditch. As they lay in the uncomfortable position, feeling some warmth seep into their worn-out bodies, lights appeared on the road, heading in their direction. They came from the opposite way they'd been traveling.

Jared sat up, instantly alert.

"Ouch!" hissed Will. "That's my leg your knee is on."

"Hold on, man," Ryan said, grabbing the back of Jared's shirt through the leaves. "What if it's Hunter coming back to check on us?"

"Then he could put us out of our misery," Will said, scooting out of the leaves and sitting up. "No offense, guys, but this is the worst sleep in my life." He brushed leaves from his face. "And we're still freezing."

The lights never reached them. They abruptly swung left and went up a hill before disappearing into the trees, only as they vanished, the engine cut off. The vehicle had parked.

"Hey, look!" Jared said excitedly. "I think I see a light up there! It might be somebody's house!"

"You think it's safe?" Ryan asked, doubtfully.

"H-Ha," Will said. "Is it s-safer out here?"

The boys quickly got to their feet, pulling a sleepy John up with them. John acted more and more distant and became almost like a frightened puppy, going whatever way Will went.

They cut across the road and up the hill through the trees. As they drew closer, they saw more lights and soon found themselves looking at the back of a small house built in a grassy clearing. An old red pickup had parked on the side where a long driveway started going toward the front before being lost in the trees.

"I don't see Hunter's pickup," Ryan said in relief. "I think we might be good!"

Jared hesitated but then the cold wind blew and his body shook. "Let's go find out," he said grimly.

Chapter 51

An older man with a head of thick gray hair and a wrinkled brow answered the door. He looked down through thick glasses perched on his clean-shaven face.

"What do we have here?" he asked, taking in the sight of four unkempt boys standing outside the door, three of them shivering in basketball uniforms. His eyes widened in surprise. "We never get visitors out here. Where'd y'all come from and what in the tarnation happened?" He stared at their bruised faces and Ryan's bleeding arm incredulously.

"We, we got lost," Ryan said. Wincing, he tugged at the bloody shirt wrapped around his arm.

"You got more than that, son," the man said. "Your arm is bleeding worse than a butchered deer."

"Who is it, Henry?" called a woman's voice from the back of the house.

"Some kids, Lisa," the man called back. "Y'all better come in," he said to the boys. "You're already half-frozen." He moved aside and motioned them inside. "I don't suppose you boys are from the bus accident back on Route 32, are you?" he asked. "We just got news of a basketball team in a bad accident just a little while ago. If so, you're a long way away." He had a deep jovial voice with a slight southern accent that instantly put Jared at ease. He sounded like somebody's grandpa.

The boys gratefully stepped into the warm home, entering a small hall with white walls and tan carpeting.

Jared sighed, feeling the blast of warmth enveloping his body. Pain shot into his fingers as they began to thaw and it numbed his thinking. It just felt good to have grown-ups take charge.

Ryan coughed. "Do you have a phone, uh, mister …"

"Oh, sorry, son. I'm Henry Lynch." The man wiped his hands on his jeans and offered it Ryan. Then he hastily put it back down. "Right. I forgot. You have a nasty wound."

From the room on the left, a woman with long, brown hair streaked with white entered, wearing tight jeans and a heavy wool sweater. Her face, etched in wrinkles, went wide with concern as she saw the boys.

"My goodness! You boys look like the earth swallowed you up and didn't like the taste! And you must be freezing."

"We, uh, just need a phone," Ryan said.

The woman held up her hand. "Not until you all have hot showers and warm food."

"Better listen to her, boys," Mr. Lynch said, giving a wink. "This is my better half, Mrs. Lynch. She done raised four boys and never gave in to none of them. Tell you what, while some of you boys shower, I'll patch up the arm and give a ring to the police. I'll let them know we found y'all and y'all made it."

"We have two showers," Mrs. Lynch said, wringing her hands. "Poor dears. One is upstairs and the other is down. You'll have to take turns, but while you shower, you toss out your clothes. They look and smell like they need a wash more than y'all do."

Will squirmed slightly, but felt his legs shiver. A hot shower sounded great.

Jared just looked at him and shrugged. He just wanted to surrender to warmth and safety.

"Uh," Ryan said, but then grimaced as his arm started to thaw. "I guess that's good. But what do we wear, uh, while waiting?"

The woman laughed. "Y'all can just put on some of Henry's shirts. Don't you worry, they're extra-large. They'll be nice and comfy while your clothes take a tumble."

"You come with me, son," Mr. Lynch said to Ryan. "I got some first aid in the kitchen."

"The rest of you follow me," said Mrs. Lynch. "I'll fetch some towels and Henry's shirts."

Jared and Will exchanged glances.

"What about John?" Jared whispered.

Will glanced at the boy looking forlorn beside him and shrugged. "I'll take him with me," he said with a sigh. "I've had some practice with Jimmy. If he doesn't know what to do, I'll get him started."

Thirty minutes later, the boys sat around a small round table with steaming bowls of creamy soup, smelling richly of potatoes, in front of them. Their hair damp, they each wore large, heavy shirts and were wrapped in blankets.

Ryan had his arm heavily wrapped in white bandages and held it stiffly to his side. Mr. Lynch had told him it would do for now, but he'd need some stitches.

"Eat up, boys!" Mrs. Lynch said. She brought out two glasses of white milk.

Mr. Lynch followed her with two more. "Make sure you boys drink this up, too," he said to them. "We made it with our special recipe. It's perfect after a long day like y'all had."

"Thanks," Will said, taking his glass.

"Yeah, thanks," Ryan echoed.

Jared took the milk and set it in front of the soup. As he stood under the hot shower he'd been thinking and started getting an uneasy feeling. Something was bothering him, but he couldn't think of what it could be. The blow to his head still gave him a headache and trying to process his thoughts proved painful.

On his right, John eagerly accepted his milk and started gulping it down immediately. He didn't touch the soup.

"How's the milk?" Mr. Lynch asked, leaning in.

"Oh, uh, good," Ryan said, swallowing hard after several gulps. "It, uh, has a little bit of an aftertaste."

Will frowned as he put his glass down. He'd quickly drunk half of it, but didn't look too eager for more. He wiped a milk mustache from his lip and eyed the soup with distaste.

"Well," Mrs. Lynch said brightly, "y'all eat your soup and then maybe take a nap. Y'all have to be tired." Humming, she vanished into the kitchen.

Ryan blinked and shook his head. "What about … what about the phone?" His words sounded slightly slurred.

"I'll take care of it," Mr. Lynch said. "Anybody want more milk, just ask."

Will slouched at the table and his head started drooping. He tried to lift a spoon, but it fell from his fingers.

John yawned widely and stared around, as if confused.

Biting his lip, Jared glanced at Mr. Lynch. The old man no longer appeared so jovial. He rubbed his jaw almost gleefully. Then his eyes settled on Jared. "You're not thirsty, are you, son? Want some water instead?"

"Uh, no thanks," Jared said quickly. "This is, uh, fine." He grabbed his milk and pretended to take a sip. When the man looked away satisfied, Jared poured a good portion of the milk in his soup.

"Ah, man," Ryan muttered tiredly. "I can't keep my eyes open."

"You boys should go lie down and maybe eat later," Mrs. Lynch said, returning with a beer in her hand. She put the bottle down and rubbed her hands together. "Come with me and I'll show you some beds."

"You all can eat more in the morning," Mr. Lynch said, grinning widely.

Jared felt his heart beating wildly. He had a bad feeling the special milk recipe contained a very strong sedative. Feigning wooziness, he got up after Ryan and Will. He had to help a wobbly John get to his feet.

The four boys staggered after the cheerful woman, barely clinging to their blankets. Mr. Lynch followed close behind, his hands flexing in anticipation.

Jared's suspicions were confirmed when Will, his body wilting, all at once collapsed on the stairs.

Mr. Lynch swiftly stepped in and gathered the boy up in his arms. Winking at Jared, he moved to the side to let him and John stagger by. Jared felt his heart skip but he did his best to appear too woozy to think. The old man cradled Will and followed.

"Too tired," Ryan muttered.

"Sleep is coming, dears!" Mrs. Lynch said with false cheer. "Almost there."

She led them up a narrow stairwell to a small hall where she opened the first door on the right. She showed the boys into a wide room, almost entirely empty except for a queen size bed and dresser. A musty rug lay on the floor in front of the bed, but the walls were bare and in need of a paint job.

"One bed fits all," Mrs. Lynch said cheerfully.

Ryan just groaned as he staggered in before collapsing on the bed. He just barely made it to the pillow, tugging his blanket over his shoulders before closing his eyes. In seconds he started to snore softly. John managed to crawl next to him and also went down. Mr. Lynch dumped Will on the other side and stared expectantly at Jared.

Jared blinked drowsily back before climbing onto the bed. He nudged Will as he crawled beside him, but the boy never stirred.

Pulling a blanket over himself and Will, Jared lay down and closed his eyes. His ears were wide open.

"Are they out?" Mr. Lynch said, his voice sounding much harsher.

The old woman cackled. "You betcha. Our recipe could put a rooster down at sunrise."

"Good," grunted the old man. "I already gave Sam and the boys a call. They'll be here in the morning."

"Where's Hunter?" Mrs. Lynch asked. "He didn't stay very long and never had any supper."

"You know our boy. He got mad 'cause I told him you made potato soup instead of roast beef. He grabbed some cold grub and headed out in the woods. He wanted to spend the night out there. You know him, he wants to spook a deer, I suspect." The old man chuckled. "Our boy is a strange man. He won't kill the animals, but he sure likes to eat them."

Mrs. Lynch sniffed. "Our boy only kills the prey. Little does he know, we got the prey right here awaiting him! Which one is it, do you think?" she asked, sounding suddenly excited. "Maybe we should take him now and get it ov—"

Jared snapped his eyes open and bolted up to a sitting position. "No!" he shouted. "Stay away from us!"

With Jared being tall, Mr. Lynch had given him a night shirt that went down to his calves. When crawling onto the bed and pulling up the blanket, he'd made sure to pull the bottom of the shirt over his knees so he could run and move easily if needed.

The old couple stared at Jared in shock, as if he'd just risen from the dead.

The old woman recovered first.

"You clever boy," Mrs. Lynch said, her beady blue eyes turning cold. "How did you know?" she asked.

Jared bit his bottom lip and took a deep breath. "I saw the pickup. It's a red Dodge. Did one of you try to run me over last month?"

"Don't know what you're talking about," Mrs. Lynch said with a frown.

"It could be any red pickup," added Mr. Lynch, sounding more curious than angry. "What tipped our hand? We were extra careful."

Jared glared at him. "Why would a guy trying to kill us drop us so close to a house? He'd only do it if he knew it wouldn't help us. Also, I didn't see any TV in here. How would you know about a bus accident with basketball players?"

"Clever," snorted Mrs. Lynch. Her eyes gleamed with cruelty. "We'll leave you alone for the night, but tomorrow, I'm afraid your cleverness won't help you. You'll notice, there're no windows. And if you did escape, we *are* the only house for miles. You won't get far dressed like *that*.

"Pleasant dreams," sneered Mr. Lynch.

They both moved to the door and Jared knew this was his only chance. He threw his exhausted, bruised body into action. Tumbling from the bed, he tried to race through the door, but felt a terrible fog descend on him.

The basketball game, followed by the knock to his head, and then the freezing walk had left his body ill-prepared for action. The hot shower only made his body crave rest.

Screeching, Mrs. Lynch shoved the old man in front of her as Jared stumbled sideways. Just as he righted himself, the door slammed hard.

Yelling, he charged it, but heard a lock click as he grabbed the doorknob. Groaning, he turned his back to the door and slid to the floor.

"Sleep tight, dear!" Mrs. Lynch called from the other side of the door. "You may never get another chance!"

Jared rested his aching head against the door as the cackling woman retreated. They were trapped.

He tried to stay awake and keep guard over his friends, but his eyelids started to drop. Feeling injured and with an empty belly, his body had no energy left. Jared felt himself slip away as he curled up in his oversized shirt.

The girls' bus arrived back at Washington Middle just after 10:00 p.m. It wasn't until 10:30 that parents started to get worried about the boys' bus. Shortly after, came the first call about a bus accident.

Mr. Moore raced into his house and shouted for Angel. He'd been waiting for Will in the school parking lot when he'd gotten a call from Glen, telling him about the accident and that Will had gone missing in the woods. The boy sounded hurt and scared. "Something bad is happening," he'd told Mr. Moore. "Something real bad."

"What?" shouted Angel, annoyed. "I'm studying for a test tomorrow!" She appeared at the top of the stairs and peered down, ready to argue. Seeing her dad's face, her face went ashen. "What is it?"

"Get in the car!" Mr. Moore said grimly. "Your brother is missing!"

Jack yanked George from the computer, telling him to get his rear in the minivan. "I got a call from somebody from Jared's school," he said, carrying two heavy jackets under his arm.

"What did Jared do now?" George grumbled, stumbling toward the stairs.

"That's what I want to know," Jack said with no trace of humor. "He's gone missing out in the woods somewhere."

George broke into a run.

Mr. Moore and Angel spent most of the drive in grim silence. Her mom stayed back with Jimmy, but not before making sure they'd promised not to return without Will.

Angel gasped as the Toyota Corolla zoomed onto the highway, but didn't protest.

She clenched her hands tightly in front of her when they pulled around a slower car, nearly clipping its bumper.

"You know how we go to church every Sunday?" her father suddenly asked, not taking his eyes off the road. "This is a good time to start using those prayers." His voice sounded hard, but strangely calm.

Angel nodded stiffly. Then she swallowed hard. "Dad," she asked, "you do think Will is okay, right?"

"That's why I want you to pray."

"Did you? Did you pray when you were in Iraq?"

Mr. Moore didn't answer for a moment. Then he nodded. "I prayed every day I spent over there. That's how I made it back home. Now we have to pray your brother makes it home."

Angel tightened her lips. It was the deepest conversation she'd ever had with her dad. If only it hadn't taken Will disappearing to make it happen.

Neither spoke a word for a long time after. Mr. Moore's foot barely left the gas pedal and they made the drive in less than an hour and a half.

When they neared the scene of the accident it was after midnight, but emergency lights lit up the sky like Christmas.

Angie winced for thinking of something so cheery on such a horrible occasion.

What seemed like hundreds of cars and pickups were parked along the road leading up to the scene. Before reaching them, Mr. Moore turned his car into the grass and hit the brakes. As it jerked to a stop, he shut off the motor.

"What are you doing, Dad?" Angel asked. They were about a half mile from the flashing lights. "Aren't we going over there?"

Mr. Moore took a deep breath. "Will's not over there, Angie. Remember what I always say when entering a new environment?"

Angel slowly nodded. "We're checking the perimeter."

Mr. Moore smiled without humor. "He's somewhere in the woods." He turned and looked at his daughter. "When Glen called he said this wasn't an accident. Somebody had locked all the bus doors and windows. We need to find some clue on what direction they took Will. I hope you said your prayers."

Angel covered her mouth and drew in a deep breath. Tears sprang from her eyes. "Oh, Will," she whispered. "He could be anywhere."

"He's in those woods," Mr. Moore said. "And I'm going to find him. And when I do, pray for whoever took him."

"I'm going too," Angel said quickly. "You're not leaving me here just to watch the car."

"I know. I need you to come." Mr. Moore looked at his daughter. "You've always been my rock. The light of reason. Angel, I need you with me to keep me from flying off the handle. If I find out who's responsible for this … I need you near me." He took a deep breath. "And I know Will needs you, too. I'm not always the best father, but I know my kids." He abruptly opened the driver's side door. "Now let's go. Do what I say and stay behind me. We're going hunting."

Mr. Drydon stood to the side of the fallen bus, staring into the dark, forbidding woods with no expression. He wore a jacket over his chest, now swathed in bandages and ointment from the spilled coffee. His chin and neck also glistened with ointment. The lower regions still burned. So did his anger.

It had all started as a foolish idea … a stupid dream. Somebody had asked him what his life would be like if he didn't have John to deal with. At the time, he'd brushed it off, but the idea had lingered. Deep in his mind, it had sat festering, slowly poisoning his soul. What would he do without John? How much better would his life be?

Later, when the same person asked him again, over drinks on a late Friday night, the idea took off. Mr. Drydon started to dream of ways to make John disappear. Soon he became obsessed with it—especially when that same somebody made it clear she'd love him without his son in the way.

That was what caused Wayne Drydon, principal of Washington Middle School, to be standing in the freezing cold, suffering from burns all over the front of his body. It was all out of love.

He blew out his breath and watched it puff in front of his face like a tiny cloud. Sure, storm clouds were gathering, but his plans still had a very good chance for success.

Mr. Hackett remained unconscious and was now on the way to a hospital, along with Coach Swopes and most of the boys. Almost all the injuries were superficial wounds and the hospital visit would be for checkups. Only three of the boys, along with Coach Swopes, suffered from serious injuries, but none were deemed life-threatening.

All because of Hunter Pherrins and his crazy game. Mr. Drydon leaned his head back and shut his eyes. He'd just wanted a simple accident. Something to take John out of his life without being traced back to him. That was it.

If he wanted John just dead, he could've handled it by himself. How many times at night did he stand over his son holding a pillow? Or thought of slipping too much "medicine" in his food so he'd never wake up? But he was no killer. Besides, he couldn't have any suspicions about his involvement.

He'd thought Hunter could do it with no problems. But it turned out Hunter was more than just a killer. He was a killer who enjoyed it. He had to set up a perfect scenario, had to play his game.

It could have been worse. And with Angie missing, it could still get much better. He knew Hackett wouldn't talk, if he ever recovered. He was up to his neck in it and would just get himself in prison, too. Besides, if it all worked out, Hackett would be getting fifty thousand bucks for his work—paid by Drydon himself. He just needed to take care of Angie.

He sighed heavily, watching more of his breath puff out. He never should've let her get away. She must've taken off with the other missing kids—three other boys had vanished from the bus. Hopefully they'd all end up lost and ultimately dead. As a principal, this was catastrophic, but if it went in his favor, he could come out a grieving beacon of light. Nobody would fault him for stepping down and moving quietly away.

He heard a commotion behind him where a search party was being organized.

"Where's my son?" demanded Brad's dad, Mr. Williamson. Clearly angry, the father pushed his way through the crowd of concerned parents, students, and citizens. "Where's Brad?"

He headed straight for the principal. With so many cars with their lights on, it proved impossible to hide.

Turning to face him, Mr. Drydon put on a mask of sympathy. As a principal for so many years he'd learned to show empathy to distraught parents. It was like a game to him. Parents come to him upset, he listens, coddles them, and then they go away.

"I'm sorry, Mr. Williamson," he said gravely. "It seems like both our sons are missing." Mr. Drydon fought hard to choke up and even managed a tear, mostly from the pain of talking. His chin, neck, chest, and lower regions screamed in agony. "I, I'm afraid John panicked during the crash … he was off the bus at the time and ran into the woods." He closed his eyes, using the burning pain to make him appear more sympathetic. "He got lost. Your son, Brad, and some of the other students went searching for him. I'm very thankful for that and I just hope and pray everyone is found safely."

Mr. Drydon swallowed bile. He hated this and knew he was talking too much. He just wanted the parent to go away. "I'm just about to join the search party myself. I think you should, too. I can understand how you feel in this difficult time … John. My John doesn't like the woods."

Mr. Williamson shook his head and then blinked. For a moment he looked ready to turn away, but then his head shot up and he glared at Mr. Drydon. "How come you were here so fast, Drydon?" he asked. "Glen said you came right after they broke out of the bus. How did you even know where to look for them? They're over a mile off their route. Only the phone's GPS found them."

Mr. Drydon sucked in his breath, wincing from pain as he ducked under the parent's glare. "It's been a trying time for us all, believe me. We have to be strong right now."

"Just tell me," Mr. Williamson said, sounding angry.

The principal snapped up his gaze. "I'm afraid I don't appreciate your tone, Mr. Williamson. This is a time for us to come together. But if you must know, I was following the bus after the game, but then it took a wrong turn and I lost it. When I finally found the turn, I came to …" Mr. Drydon paused to swallow hard, trying his best to produce tears. "I came to the scene. Seeing the bus flipped, I … I couldn't believe it. I panicked and even dumped hot coffee all over myself. As a father and as a principal, I'm doubly heartbroken over this tragedy."

Mr. Williamson ducked his head and wiped his nose. Then he looked up with a face of fury.

"Liar!" he yelled. "I was at the game, just like I go to every game! I've never seen you there! You never go to the games! You never cared for your son! You never cared!"

Mr. Drydon's eyes widened with surprise and he stood there stupidly as the enraged parent stepped forward and belted him in the nose.

Policemen ran up and pulled Mr. Williamson back. Mr. Drydon stared up at the stars and felt excruciating pain. His burns were on fire and he couldn't feel his nose. From somewhere a sob left his throat.

He hoped John's body would soon be found so he could go home, but knew this wasn't possible. The area the searchers assumed as John's last whereabouts had to be miles from where Hunter dumped the brats.

He just hoped Angie would never be found. She was the final threat to him. The girl had to be lost forever … or Mr. Williamson's punch would be the least of his worries.

Chapter 52

Mr. Moore skirted around the crowd, the flashing vehicles, and the parked cars. He walked with a purpose, but also with a sense of stealth. His body leaned forward and his eyes scanned the moonlit road beyond the crash scene.

Watching him, Angel was reminded of a cat, searching for prey. "What are you looking for, Dad?" she whispered.

"Anything that doesn't belong. Keep your eyes open. You take the right side and I'll look on the left." He pulled out a small flashlight and handed it to Angel. "I see better with my night eyes," he said, "but you might want this."

Silently, they worked through tall grass and cut through a small thicket of trees. Coming out, they arrived at a bend farther up the road from where the accident occurred. They could see the glowing lights from around the turn, about two hundred yards on their right. They were about to cross the road when Angel let out a squeak.

"Dad, look!"

Her light pointed to two dark shadows lying just off the pavement. In the dark they looked like nothing more than roadkill. Then Angel's light revealed them to be much more than that. Each was a black, padded cloth, about two feet long.

"Aren't those …"

"Will's leg sleeves," Mr. Moore confirmed flatly.

"Why would he take them off out here?" Angel wondered, knowing she wouldn't like the answer.

"He didn't. Somebody else did. Leave them there for the police to find. Maybe they'll come to the same conclusion. Now come on. We're getting close to something."

"Which way?" Angel asked. She'd never seen her dad like this. All sense of humor had been shut off. He moved and acted with a firm confidence that allowed nothing but respect. She didn't dare protest.

"Just follow me."

Moving away from the pulsing lights of the accident scene, Mr. Moore trekked along the road, sweeping the area for any other clues.

Angel flashed her light side to side in his wake, desperately hoping to find something, anything. After a few hundred yards more, they both discovered the fresh tire marks in a small clearing just off the road to their left.

"Could be from any car," Mr. Moore muttered. "But I doubt it. Looks like two sets of tracks and one came from a fairly good-sized truck."

His sharp eyes followed the deeper set straight to the road. "Come on. It went that way." He pointed across the road.

Swallowing hard, Angel rushed to keep up with her dad. Sure enough, they easily found a trail of flattened grass on the other side of the pavement. Something heavy had gone through and not too long ago. By morning the grass would likely be up tall again and hide the trail completely.

Angel's light found the hidden road at the edge of the trees shortly after. The tracks headed straight into it.

"Let's go," Mr. Moore said, his voice flat. "We got him."

Soon after, Angel's light discovered sets of footprints trailing the same tracks.

Angel had to rush to keep up with her dad.

A heavy pounding at the door startled Jared awake.

"Morning time, boys!" called Mrs. Lynch from behind the door. "I got your clothes ready. I suggest you make yourselves decent, 'cause here I come!"

Jared blinked stupidly as the door pressed into his back. Caught by surprise, he could only crawl out of the way as the door swung open. Mrs. Lynch walked in carrying a pile of neatly folded laundry.

Jared stumbled to his feet and quickly shook sleep from his eyes.

The woman chuckled at seeing him. "Tried to stay awake, did you? You should've gotten your rest like the others."

"What's your problem?" Jared asked her. "Why are you doing this?"

The woman blinked at him. Then her nose curled in a snarl. "You don't know what you're talking about, boy." She dumped the clothes on the floor. "I'm leaving the door open. Use the bathroom, get dressed, and get downstairs. If y'all ain't down in twenty, you miss breakfast." She smiled wickedly. "My boys should be here by then. So if you want to run, be my guest. They'll enjoy hunting you down."

When she'd left, Jared roused the others, breaking them from a deep, confusing sleep. When he gave the news they were really just prisoners, Will groaned and fell back in the bed.

"This nightmare will never end," he said.

Ryan just wiped his eyes with his good hand and shook his head.

"Sorry, guys," he mumbled. He went to the pile of clothes and started picking his stuff out. "I have a bad feeling it's only beginning."

From down below, they heard the slam of a door and rowdy voices. Mrs. Lynch's sons, it would seem, had arrived.

The boys quickly dressed and took turns in the bathroom. They had no other option. Soon Jared led the way down the stairs. Ryan, holding his aching arm, followed close behind. Will brought up the rear with John. They were back in their basketball uniforms, but remained in their nightmare. It was only going to get worse.

Mr. Lynch greeted them at the foot of the stairs. "Don't y'all look bright-eyed and bushytailed," he said. "Grab yourself some oatmeal, boys. Enjoy it."

He stood at the bottom of the stairs and grinned up with malice.

The boys ignored him as they passed by to the kitchen.

Three big men sat around the table. The closest one to them had a mess of blond, greasy curls hanging from a Budweiser cap. He turned to them with a wide grin.

"Hail the conquering heroes!" he said loudly. "It's the great basketball team! Heard you boys got wrecked last night."

A tall man with a grizzled chin of dark whiskers sat on his left and clapped his hands mockingly. His fleshy cheeks shook like jelly and his hatchet nose snorted like a pig. "Yeah, they did," he said.

The other man, to the right, just glared balefully. Short and squat, he had a sharp chin chiseled from stone with wide shoulders that looked more like football pads.

All three men had beer bottles in front of them. Empty bottles lay scattered on the floor at their feet.

Swallowing, Jared wondered what time it was. Through the window he saw pale sunlight and guessed it to be fairly early in the morning.

"Come join the table," the man in the hat said. "Any of you want a drink?"

The grizzled-chin man laughed. "Don't be like that, Sam. You might scare the poor things. Look at them." He cleared his throat. "Boys, I'm Corey. These are my brothers, Sam, and that mountain of muscle over there is A.J. We're your hosts today."

Ryan moved to stand beside Jared. "You dudes have serious problems," he murmured.

"No we don't," Sam said, lazily tipping back his bottle, taking a long drink. "You boys are the ones with the problem. Trust me on that, boy."

"You already met our fourth brother," Corey drawled. "Hunter's the one who led you boys to this place." He then nodded at Will. "You must be Will … You probably don't know this, but we're your neighbors, boy." He grinned wide, showing off yellow teeth. "We're the Pherrins. I nearly ran your sorry little hide over not too long ago. Remember that, boy?"

Will gave a start and Jared sucked in his breath.

Blinking, Will stood very still. He remembered what his dad had said about the Pherrins. They liked to hunt deer … with pickup trucks. He licked his lips and glanced nervously at John.

John had not smiled or spoken more than ten words since the bus incident. Now he stared blankly at the floor.

Suddenly he looked up, as if snapping out of a daze. "Is it breakfast time?" he asked. "I'm hungry."

The men roared with laughter.

"Hey, Ma!" Sam shouted. "The little boys want breakfast! Make it a good one, it might be their last!"

Corey snorted. "So now we know the retarded one. Too stupid to be scared."

"What should we do while we wait for Hunter?" Sam asked, sipping on a beer bottle.

A.J., the load of muscle, grunted and grinned. He spoke for the first time. "Ain't that obvious? Look at them. They want to play basketball, so that's what we'll do. We play ourselves a basketball game!"

Jared shivered as the men laughed again. He didn't like the sound of that.

"First they eat," Mrs. Lynch, who was really Mrs. Pherrins, said. "We want them to keep up their strength, right?"

"Sure, Ma," Sam said. "But not at our table. We don't want dead meat sitting with us."

The old lady cackled. "You heard my son. Get your bottoms on the floor and don't try nothing but my cooking!" She kicked the empty beer bottles, causing them to roll under the table. "Hurry up, now."

Shortly after, the boys were forced to sit on the floor and eat bowls of thick, gooey oatmeal, washed down with glasses of warm water.

Absolutely famished, the boys ate in silence and didn't worry about being drugged again. It would probably be better if they were. When they finished their last bites, they were told to leave their bowls and put on their sneakers. It was basketball time.

The boys had no choice as they were herded outside, back into the cold. Sam and Corey pushed and prodded them around to the back of the house.

A.J. stood waiting for them. Holding a basketball under his arm, he wore a nasty smile. "Hey, boys," barked his unfriendly voice. "You ready to play?" He stood in a dirt patch near the edge of the woods, just beneath an old rusted rim attached to an old, faded board nailed to a tree.

"It's us three against you kids," Sam said, grinning toothily. His teeth were a jagged, jumbled mess. "Call your own fouls. If you dare."

Ryan crowded next to Will and Jared. "We have to get out of here," he hissed. "They're going to kill us."

Will flicked his gaze at John. The boy stood hunched over, looking terribly confused. After eating he hadn't said a word, but clearly knew something bad was happening. Will feared he was lost in his hidey hole.

"We have to find a moment to run," he whispered back.

"Hey, no huddling!" Sam yelled. "That's a foul!" He came forward, shoving Will hard in the back, sending the boy flying forward, sprawling into leaves, landing heavily on his hands and knees.

"Watch it!" yelled Ryan, but Sam merely slapped Ryan's injured arm.

Gasping in pain, Ryan's knees buckled and he nearly went to his knees.

"Let's go, boys," A.J. called. "Ball in!" He threw the ball hard at Jared. Jared managed to catch it, but stumbled back.

A.J. leered at him. "If any of you boys try to run, that retard is mine!" He made a fist and punched it into a meaty hand.

Jared swallowed and took a deep breath. It would be a basketball game to the death.

The next several minutes were agony. John stood staring in confusion as Will, Jared, and Ryan went against the three men. The brothers positioned themselves in a triangle around the boys. Every time Jared or Will tried to dribble in, the nearest brother would set upon them like a wild beast, shoving them down, kicking out their legs, or yanking on their jerseys.

Ryan stood to the side, cradling his injured arm while looking on with fury. Next to him, John stood with his wide blue eyes watching it all soundlessly. Every time the ball rolled free, one of the men would chase it down and toss it back into the fray.

Finally, Sam tripped Will again, sending the boy flying back to the ground. "Not in my house, boy," he chuckled, stepping squarely on the back of Will's shorts. "We kick tails here."

The boy squirmed to shake it off.

Staggering back, clearly drunk, Sam laughed. He reached down and took up the ball, tossing it to Jared. "Your turn, tall boy."

Will had gotten up and brushed leaves from his stomach. His deep brown eyes flashed with anger. "Give me the ball," he told Jared.

"What are you going to do?" Jared asked miserably.

Will spoke low and hard, glaring at Sam. "Trips right, blue 42," he said. "We're running it up the middle."

Ryan's head snapped up. He recognized the play from football. It was a dive play where the lead blocker crashed through the right side, clearing a way for the back. He knew trips would mean Jared, John, and him. They were supposed to run while Will acted as lead blocker. He got it mostly right.

"On my signal," Will said, looking over at Jared.

Jared blinked in confusion, but saw Ryan nod toward the trees. Swallowing, he shuffled back to stand next to John.

"Follow me," he whispered. "Okay?"

The boy looked at him briefly but showed no comprehension. His bottom lip trembled. Then he gave the briefest of nods.

"Let's go boys!" Sam. shouted. "Let's see this fancy basketball play!"

Will dribbled once toward him. Sam stood right in front of the basket. His legs spread wide and his hands went up at his sides. He licked his lips in anticipation.

A.J. closed in from Will's left and Corey from the right. Will stared only at Sam. Suddenly, he picked up his dribble and held the ball like a baseball. Stepping forward, he flung it as hard as he could right at Sam, striking the man with a dull pop right between the legs.

The ball acted like the lead blocker.

Sam made no sound as his eyes popped out and he crumpled to his knees. Corey and A.J. blinked in momentary confusion.

"Now!" Ryan yelled. "Run!"

Jared pushed John forward. "Run!" he screamed "Into the woods! Follow Will!"

John stumbled once, but seeing Will race for the trees, his own legs started moving and soon his arms were pumping as he sprinted forward. Jared followed right behind him. From his right he saw Ryan leap over a bush, landing in the trees, clutching his arm where the bandage had a red stain.

"Get them!" hollered A.J., breaking from his stupor. "They're getting away!"

Sam only moaned and fell on his side.

Shouts and cries spurred Jared onward. He knew the men were now after them. He pushed himself to run faster and harder than ever before.

Amazingly, John not only kept pace, but pulled ahead. The boy ran wildly, but never seemed to tire. Hs jacket became a blur in front of Jared as he followed the best he could, ducking branches and weaving through trees.

He'd quickly lost sight of Will and Ryan. All he cared about now was getting away from the three brothers—getting as far away as possible.

Fear overrode any and all physical pain as Jared crashed through bushes, ignoring thorns tearing at his arms and legs. Twice he nearly tripped, but he would not stop. His chest felt as if on fire and his legs started protesting, but he only bit his lip and kept going.

Then, all at once, he burst into a small clearing just in time to see John trip over a hidden root. The boy crashed down hard. He immediately started screaming.

Will stumbled to a stop and leaned heavily against a tree, breathing in deeply. His chest burned and sweat dampened his hair. All of the running he'd done with his dad had finally paid off. He'd run as hard as he could for what seemed like hours, but in reality he knew to be only several minutes. Occasionally, he heard a distant cry of one of the brothers, but they were far off. Now he somehow had to find Jared, Ryan, and John.

Still resting against the tree, he bowed his head and took deep breaths as he grabbed his knees. Running had been a gut instinct. But now they were lost in miles of woods with murdering brothers hunting them.

He took a few more breaths to settle his heartbeat. Suddenly a high-pitched scream broke the silence, causing the hairs on the nape of his neck to stand on end.

Instantly, he straightened and pushed off the tree. But before he could take a step, a hand reached from behind him and grabbed the back of his waistband, tugging his shorts back.

"Going somewhere?" purred a nasty voice. Something wickedly sharp pricked the back of his neck.

Will froze and he didn't dare move a muscle.

"I see you ran from my brothers," the familiar voice whispered in his ear. "I sort of hoped that would happen. I've been waiting for this for a long time, boy."

The far off screaming continued nonstop.

The voice chuckled. "That sounds like the retard. That's too bad for you. That poor kid likes you. I planned to use you as bait to find him. Guess you're not needed anymore."

All at once the hand tightened on his waistband and yanked down, ripping his shorts down to his knees, exposing his boxers. Will felt a hard push from behind and he staggered forward, tripping over his shorts. Landing on his chest, his hands catching his fall, he instantly rolled to his back.

Terror gripped him as he saw a sharp knife poised in the hand of a mad man.

Holding the knife comfortably, a man with thick blond hair grinned wolfishly down. Will knew this had to be Hunter, the one who'd taken him from the bus.

"I just wanted you to see me," Hunter said conversationally. "This is the fourth time I got you, boy. But it's the last time, too."

The hunter's eyes widened with glee and his lips curled back in anticipation as he suddenly lunged forward, stabbing down with the knife.

Somewhere nearby he heard a scream.

Panicking, Will kicked up with his legs, raising them both to block the knife.

He heard a solid thunk, and for some reason the man tripped forward. The boy felt a burning sensation rip across his right thigh as the large man fell past him, landing just to his right.

"Leave him alone!" roared an angry voice.

Will sat up and blinked in surprise.

Big Mike stood before him, wielding a heavy branch like a sword.

Nick and Brad appeared behind a clump of trees with Angie between them.

Seeing Angie, Will hastily stood and pulled up his shorts to cover his boxers. His eyes were still wide in fear and amazement.

"Get behind me!" Big Mike yelled at him. He stared past Will at the fallen man. "Now!"

Will quickly complied with Nick running to meet him, pulling him in a half embrace.

"I got you, man," Nick told him. "I got you!"

Brad and Angie moved to stand with them. They all looked at where the man slowly rose to his feet, turning to face Big Mike.

"Where did you come from?" the man asked, frowning. He gingerly reached back and felt his head. It came back sticky with red.

"Shut up," Big Mike snarled. "Take a step closer and I'll smash your face in next."

The man blinked at him and shook his head. "I thought I had him," he muttered. He looked down at the knife and unexpectedly smirked. "Well, well. I think I got him after all." Raising his eyes, he held up the knife to display a dark red stain on the blade. "Didn't miss, after all. Did I?"

Angie gasped and Will felt his right leg start to tremble. He could feel warm liquid trickling down. At first he thought he'd wet himself, but looking down he saw it was red.

"You're bleeding, man," Nick said, sounding slightly shocked.

"What now?" mocked the man. "You going to come at me with that branch? Do it, tough guy. Let's add more blood." All at once, he tilted his head back and yelled. "I have some over here! Sam, Corey! One of you get your sorry hides over here, pronto! I got four of them!"

A call answered him, not too far away. "Where you at, Hunter? I'm coming!"

"Follow my voice!" Hunter yelled, grinning wickedly at Big Mike.

"Let's get out of here," Angie said worriedly.

"You're sick," Big Mike growled, still holding the branch in front of him.

Hunter started to grin wider when the large boy suddenly flung the stick at him, swinging it like a baseball bat, but letting go. Hunter tried to duck, but was caught by surprise.

The branch shattered across his face, dropping him like a tree freshly chopped.

Screaming, he dropped his knife and clawed at his face.

"I'm coming!" roared a voice in the woods, getting awfully close. "Hang on, Hunt!"

"Run!" Brad shouted. "Let's go!"

No encouragement was necessary. Big Mike turned and waved them ahead of him. The group took off into the trees without a glance back.

"I'll get you!" Hunter roared behind them. "You're all dead!"

"Where to?" Angie cried, voice catching with worry.

"Anywhere but here!" Brad roared back.

Will, already winded, started feeling a sharp pain with every step and the right leg of his shorts became plastered to his skin. Blood soaked his sock. He gasped for a breath.

"Oh, man, Will's bleeding bad!" Nick said, worriedly.

Will faltered and Big Mike swooped behind him. He barely slowed as he reached down and grabbed up Will, lifting him up before tossing him over his shoulder.

"Don't stop," Big Mike grunted. "We keep going."

A trail of blood dripped behind him.

Chapter 53

Jared ran to John's side and desperately tried to quiet him. All of John's pent-up frustration, confusion, and fear had been released and, rolling around, he just kept screaming.

"John!" Jared cried, kneeling by the boy. "You have to stop! They're going to hear us! The bad guys, John!"

"Yo, man!" Ryan cried, stumbling through a bush to them. "What's he doing? I thought he'd been caught!"

"I don't know," Jared said, his voice panicky. "He needs Angie, or something."

Just like that, John's crazed eyes blinked in confusion and he stared desperately up at Jared. "Angie?" he asked. "Angie is here?"

"Uh … I don't know," Jared stammered, but Ryan cut him off.

"Yes, she's here, but we have to find her," Ryan said. "Let's go."

John started gulping deep breaths, but his eyes remained on Jared.

Jared couldn't look away from the large blue eyes, suddenly full of trust.

"I don't know if she's really here," he said slowly. "But we have to go. Those are bad men trying to hurt you."

John nodded. "I know," he whispered. His bottom lip trembled and Ryan sighed with exasperation.

Then John took a deep breath and blinked away his tears. "I don't like being alone. I want Angie now."

"Let's find her," Jared said. "Okay?"

Remarkably, John let Jared pull him up. He wiped tears from his eyes and nodded. "Okay, Jared. I want to go home with Angie."

"Me too," Jared said. "But right now we need to be quiet. Let's keep away from the bad men."

Then they heard the loud voice call out from deep in the trees on their left.

"I have some over here! Sam, Corey! One of you, get your sorry hides over here, pronto!"

Jared and Ryan exchanged glances. They both thought of Will. Without hesitation, they started toward the voice, but kept their eyes and ears open. John walked between them, his hands gripping Jared's arm tightly.

"How bad is it?" Nick asked, too afraid to look.

"Bad," Angie admitted. She knelt in front of Will, wiping away a mass of congealing blood from his thigh.

Will squeezed his lips together as he held up the right leg of his shorts. "I'm right here, you know," he muttered.

Even in the cold, his hair was dark with sweat. More perspiration trickled down his cheek.

"Lucky you are," Angie told him. She had half of Brad's basketball shirt in her hand, cleaning the wound as best she could. "You could be dead."

"Where did you all come from?" Will asked, staring in fascination at the gore. "I mean, you guys just popped up from nowhere."

Big Mike sat against a tree staring out into the woods. He grunted.

Nick shook his head wearily from where he stood leaning against another tree opposite of Will. "Man, you don't want to know. After we broke out from the bus, Angie called to us and told us what happened. Man, we followed that dirt road all night! I've never been so tired before."

"We weren't going to give up," Angie said fiercely.

She put down the cloth soaked in blood and tried to keep the worry from her voice. "Okay, don't move. I'm going to tie this as tight as I can."

Taking up the other piece of Brad's shirt, she wrapped it around Will's thigh and pulled it tight, causing the boy to suck in his breath.

"The good news," she said, "I don't think any major artery got cut. Or you'd definitely be dead."

"That's great news," Will said faintly.

"Come on, guys," Brad said impatiently from where he stood guard watching the trees on the opposite side from Big Mike. "Let's find the others and get out of this place."

"Sure, man," Nick said. "Where do we look? I think we're lost, and I'm sure they're just as lost."

Angie finished her knot and tapped the back of Will's calf. "You'd better walk careful, Will. You don't want to lose any more blood."

Nodding, Will got stiffly to his feet. "How did you find this place in the first place?" he asked as he limped gingerly. "It's not near the road and not exactly well marked."

"We got lucky," Nick told him, yawning despite the circumstances. Dark bags clung beneath his bloodshot eyes. "After we fell asleep for a few hours or so, we woke early in the morning and heard a truck drive by from somewhere. That kept us going. Then we heard some voices."

"But that's when we saw that man." Angie shuddered. "We could've stepped on him. He was lying in the grass just staring at, like, nothing."

"Yeah," Brad added, "we were taking a bathroom break when Big Mike saw him from a hill. We hid behind some trees and just watched him."

Nick cleared his throat. "And I lay right behind the tree Mike used for his toilet, man. It felt like we stayed there for hours. Then we heard some yelling and the man got up like a jack-in-the-box, or something. We kept back so he wouldn't see us and followed him straight to you."

"Glad you did," Will said with feeling. He shivered and hugged his arms close around his chest. "You dudes saved my life."

"Ah, man, sorry," Nick said. "You got to be freezing." He went to pull off his hoodie and immediately gasped in pain. "Shoulder," he grunted. "Mike and I kind of ran into the bus door a few too many times." Gingerly, he removed his hoodie and tossed it to Will. He still wore his long-sleeved basketball shirt over his uniform. "Don't worry, man. My shoulder needs the cold. It's on fire."

"Thanks, man," Will said. He pulled on the hoodie, much too large for his small frame. Finished, he blinked embarrassedly at Nick. "I hate being small," he muttered.

"At least you're warmer," Nick told him, grinning.

Angie couldn't hold back a small laugh. "You look cute, Will."

The oversized hoodie went down to almost his knees and his hands disappeared in the sleeves. Will frowned and then wrinkled his nose. "Wait, Nick," he said. "You said you hid where Big Mike took a leak?"

"Yeah, man. Our man Mike baptized it, dude."

Big Mike just grunted. "You guys are idiots," he growled.

"Uh, guys!" Brad suddenly hissed. "I think I see something! We need to get out of here! Someone's coming."

Angie drew in a sharp brief. "We need to run," she whispered.

Big Mike shot to his feet and scooped up Will again, carrying him like he was a little kid. "Everyone shut up and let's go," he said.

Will's face wore a sheepish look as his head rested on the big youth's bouncing shoulder. He at least felt warm.

Jared never saw it coming until too late. One moment they were ducking under a low branch of a tall oak, heading toward a shallow incline, when all of a sudden A.J. Pherrins leapt out from behind the trunk, right into Jared. His elbow up, he caught the boy in the forehead, sending him flying backwards. The elbow landed squarely on the bruise he'd gotten the night before. Jared fell heavily into the layer of fallen leaves and briefly saw stars.

"Got you!" roared Sam, jumping from behind a neighboring pine, just to the right.

"Run, John!" Ryan screamed. He threw his body between John and the attacking bully.

John's eyes grew wide, but he turned and dashed into the trees.

"Your mistake," Sam grunted, wrapping Ryan up with his arms, squeezing tight. He all at once let go and Ryan fell to the leaves, gasping in pain. Sam then kicked him hard in the backside. "This is what you get for running! We never got to finish our game!"

Ryan clutched at the ground with his unwounded hand and tried to get up. Just as he got to knees, Sam kicked him viciously in the ribs and he collapsed back down.

"I … give …" he whispered hoarsely.

"No, boy," Sam said, grinning maliciously. "I give. You take."

Meanwhile, Jared tried to clear his head, but found himself being pulled up by his collar.

A.J., his face going red with effort, yanked him up off the ground and into the air. Jared could smell the rotten odor of old beer on the man's breath.

"You'd better call that retard back, boy," he hissed. Then he flung Jared back. Landing on the seat of his shorts, Jared rolled to his side, panting.

"Hey, retard!" Sam yelled. "We got your puny friends! Come back before we hurt them!" He reached in his back pocket and pulled out a small handheld walkie-talkie.

"Okay, Hunter. We got some boys, but we're missing the main ingredient. The retard's gone."

"*Let them live,*" crackled the radio in response. "*Corey got chicken and ran back to Ma and Pa, so it's just us. Keep them with you and be patient. The main ingredient won't go far. Use the kids as bait. Bring them with you and head my way. I have the other group tracked. You'll cut them off if I don't reach them first.*"

"You got it, brother," Sam said in the walkie-talkie. "The race is on!"

"*It's a game. Remember that. Let's end it.*"

"Two down," A.J. growled, glaring over at Jared. "Let's fetch the rest."

"We have to keep him awake," Angie said worriedly.

Several minutes had passed and they'd managed to find a narrow deer path they now followed, totally lost. Brad led the way, scouting ahead. Nick walked in the back and looked worriedly where Angie checked on Will's thigh. Blood leaked from the shirt and dripped down his leg. His sock and shoe were dyed a bright red. He now lay slumped over Big Mike's shoulders, his arms dangling.

"I'm awake," he muttered. "Kind of." His body resembled limp spaghetti.

"Hey!" Big Mike said. He boosted him up and slapped his backside hard. "Stay awake, Will. Come on now."

"Sure, man … We still on for basketball Saturday?" Will asked, his voice barely a whisper.

Big Mike grunted. "Soon as you can stand on your own feet," he said. "You need the practice, man. You dribble like my granny."

Will chuckled weakly. "Who's your granny? Steph Curry?"

Big Mike jostled him and gave him another smack.

They were just coming to a rise that loomed over their heads when they heard a loud cough. Instantly they froze.

"They have to be over here somewhere," a voice said from just over the rise. "Hunter said this is the spot to find them, and he ain't never wrong."

"Yeah, well, at least we got our boys," another voice said. "You boys sit real tight right here. Your friends will show up soon enough. Like A.J. said, our brother ain't never wrong."

"You guys are crazy," Ryan's voice said, heavy with pain. "You know you're going to pay for this."

"Sorry," snorted the first voice. "Nobody knows you boys are out here. And nobody will ever find out about it."

Brad dropped to the ground and motioned everyone to get low. It was unnecessary. Nick, Big Mike, and Angie had all crouched soon after hearing the voices.

"What now?" Nick whispered, his voice tight with fear.

"Get off the trail," Angie hissed. "Come on!"

The group scooted into the trees, not stopping until several yards away from the rise. Will, now fully awake, sat up in Big Mike's arms.

"You have to do something," he whispered urgently. "Those guys are crazy. They're playing some sick game where we all end up dead."

Brad wiped his lips and shuddered. "Like what do we do, man?" he hissed. "They have knives."

"They also have our friends," Nick said grimly.

Angie's face went white with fear. "Th-they have John and Jared too, I know it."

"How many are there?" Big Mike asked Will.

"Altogether, there're three brothers and that Hunter guy. There's an old man and woman, but they're probably at the house. All of them are mad crazy."

"So what do we do?" Brad asked again. "At least two of them definitely have Ryan."

"Get crazier," Big Mike said flatly. "Will, you're staying here. Angie, you too."

"What if that, that man comes back?" Angie hissed back. "Will won't be able to do anything."

"Hide in a tree," Brad said. "Get up high and he'll never spot you."

"It's winter, Brad," Angie whispered, exasperated. "All the leaves are gone. He'll spot us easy."

"Not all the leaves," Big Mike said. "My mom likes holly trees. They protect small birds from larger birds trying to catch them."

Nick raised his eyebrows. "Whoa, man, that's the most you said about—"

"Shut up," Big Mike snapped.

He carried Will to a young holly tree, ducking under the spikey leaves. The trunk was about six inches in diameter and it had several sturdy branches starting around six feet up.

"Reach up and grab a branch." He smacked the smaller boy's back. "Stay up there until we come back."

Waiting for Will to grab a branch, he pushed him up from his posterior, settling the boy on a well-hidden branch about eight feet from the ground. "Your turn, Angie. Watch out for Will. Make sure he don't do nothing stupid."

"Ha," Will mumbled.

"You all better be careful," Angie muttered. "If I have to come and rescue everybody, you'll all be in a lot of trouble."

Big Mike just grunted and squatted down and took her hand, allowing her to step on his massive thigh and pull herself up the branches.

"You kids be good," Brad said. "Just hang out until we get back."

"Hilarious," Will murmured. His head started drooping.

Angie, from a branch right above him nudged his shoulder with her sneaker. "Stay here, Will," she said.

"I'm in a tree, Angie. I'm not going anywhere."

Jared leaned back against the trunk of a broken oak tree. It had been struck by lightning years before and the fallen trunk left a jagged stump behind. The stump showed signs of new growth now dormant for the winter. Jared hoped he would live to see spring.

"From death to life," he muttered, feeling the solid stump behind him.

"That you, Jared?" Ryan asked. He lay on his side next to Jared, panting in pain. His right arm lay sunny side up. Blood leaked from the bandages put on by Mr. Lynch, who was actually Mr. Pherrins.

"Uh, yeah," Jared said. "Just talking to myself."

Ryan grunted. They were on a narrow deer path just next to a small rise. Neither boy wanted to move.

The two Pherrins brothers stood on top of the small rise about twenty yards from them. After searching the trees around them, they turned back and started their way again.

"Here they come," Ryan said. "I hope John somehow makes it out. Better to die free than by these freaks."

"We're not dead yet," Jared said. They also weren't tied up, or anything. The Pherrins brothers almost wanted them to run, just so they could hunt them down again.

Ryan, though, wasn't about to go anywhere. After a long painful walk, after being captured, they were told to sit where they were. Ryan had just about collapsed and since ceased to move. Every breath, he said, felt like somebody stabbing him in the chest.

"Yo, man. You should get up and run," Ryan said. "Go find John and try to make it out to a road somewhere."

Jared blew out his breath. "I won't leave you."

A.J. had already said if either of them tried to escape, the first one caught would die. They only needed one boy alive to lure John into the open.

Ryan grunted. "Yo, we cool then? I mean, are we friends?"

Jared blinked. "Uh, yeah … Of course."

"As a friend, I think you should leave."

"As a friend, I think you have poor judgement."

Ryan snorted and gasped in pain. "I … can't argue with that …"

The Pherrins brothers returned and stood in the middle of the trail, waiting impatiently.

"Where's that stupid boy," A.J. muttered. "If he don't come out quick, we're gonna hafta to dump these two and go hunting."

Sam chuckled. "You're probably right. That retard is so dumb he could just be about anywhere."

"Like right here?" said a voice behind him. Brad stepped out from behind a tree and flexed his arms.

Sam and A.J. stared at him in shock.

"Now, just who are you?" Sam demanded, scratching the side of his hat.

"John's friend, man. Don't you call him retard again or I'll cram my fist up your mouth and rip out your vocal cords."

Painfully, Ryan rolled to a sitting position and widened his eyes. "Brad, what are you doing here?"

"Something stupid," Brad told him. His eyes never left the brothers.

"That's what I was afraid of, man," Ryan said with a groan.

A.J. blinked and suddenly grinned. "Looks like we got an appetizer before the main course. And this one looks big enough to eat right now." He reached back and pulled out a knife from his pocket. "Come and get it, big man." Snapping the blade open, he approached Brad, his legs and hands spread wide.

Sam watched, grinning. "Get him, little brother. Let's water the ground with red."

Brad eyed the blade and nervously stepped back. "Uh, guys?"

Nick and Big Mike both sprang from behind trees on either side of Brad.

"Hey!" shouted Nick. "You want some of this? Come and get it!" He had a rock in his hand, which he lobbed at A.J.'s head.

The robust man watched the rock with disdain and went to catch it. That was when Big Mike stepped in with a thick branch and laid into his chest with a hard swing.

The branch smacking against flesh sounded like a gunshot.

Eyes bugging out, A.J. staggered back, just as the rock fell, bouncing against his left shoulder. His knife fell from his stunned hand.

Crying out in pain, he went to a knee. Instantly Big Mike was on him, swinging the branch again, this time at his head.

"No!" roared A.J. Throwing up a hand, he parried the blow, knocking it aside. Then he flung himself not on Big Mike, but on Nick, thinking him to be the easier target.

"Help!" Nick cried, going down underneath the bulky man's weight.

A.J. snarled like an animal as he punched and scratched.

Screaming, Brad charged him from the front and Big Mike attacked his side. Still, the big man fought on, using his elbows, hands, and head to keep the three boys at bay.

Sam snarled when seeing the two other boys appear, but had held back. He flicked out his tongue as if tasting the air. Then, smiling, he calmly pulled out a knife of his own. Slowly, he eased toward the fight, going for Brad's back.

Jared leapt to his feet. He and Ryan both cried out warnings, but the three fighting boys were too busy dealing with A.J. to listen.

Without thinking, Jared charged Sam's back. Just as the man look poised to strike, he leapt forward, sticking out his chest. Screaming, he slammed his bony chest into Sam's head. The man went down like a pile of bricks. Jared rolled free, his chest feeling as if on fire.

As he sat back up, he saw Sam blink stupidly and then stare at Jared. His eyes narrowed in hatred. "You'll pay for that, boy!"

Two feet away, A.J., his face red with fury, threw off Big Mike and punched Brad hard in the gut, sending him reeling back into a tree, where he bounced off before collapsing to the ground.

"Ah, no," Nick said. No!"

A.J., his chest heaving, giggled as he reached both hands toward Nick's neck.

Then all of a sudden a solid thump sounded and A.J. jerked his head up. A stone fell down his shirt and a red dot appeared just above his left eye. The dot started leaking blood.

"Leave those kids alone!" shouted a girl's voice.

A.J. put a hand to his head and saw the blood. Before he could react, Mr. Moore jumped through the brush, leaping on top of him and taking him to the ground.

Angel stepped from behind a tree and yelled. "Want Moore? You got him!"

A.J. snarled, but quickly found himself straddled by a smaller, but stronger, faster, and much madder man. Mr. Moore never hesitated. He threw down a punch on A.J.'s neck and went up to his knees, pressing them deep into his stomach.

A.J. choked and groaned at the same time. He tried to roll free and Mr. Moore chopped down hard against the side of his neck. The Pherrins brother stiffened and then relaxed, his body going still.

Sam stopped his attack on Jared at seeing the new arrival. Still holding his knife, he stood up slowly.

Mr. Moore rose from A.J. to face him.

"Remember me?" he asked. "I bought you a drink in a bar. You never did say thank you."

As Sam's eyes widened in recognition, they failed to recognize the fist coming straight for his face.

As Mr. Moore spoke, he'd also advanced, throwing a right hook as he did.

Sam went down, dropping the knife. His body bounced on the leaves and lay next to his brother's, also not moving.

"Where's Will?" Mr. Moore snapped.

Chapter 54

The hunter sniffed the air and frowned. He could smell the scent of blood and knew he had to be close. He'd been trailing the kids for the past thirty minutes and should've found them by now. Searching the ground, he saw crumpled leaves in front of him, as if they'd been kicked around by a group of kids, but where were they? He sniffed again.

Bending close to the ground, he started staring hard at the leaves, trying to determine a discernible path in the carnage. He walked under a holly tree. As he did, he felt a drop on the back of his neck. It was a chilly day, but far from cold. It was also cloudless and full of sunshine.

Frowning, he reached back and wiped the drop. Bringing his hand down, he saw a red smear across his fingers. A smile pulled on his lips. "Gotcha."

All at once, he stood and reached up with his hands.

Will and Angie both sat as still as statues. They'd seen the hunter emerge from the trees and start searching the area. Angie had her hand around Will's shoulder, trying to give comfort. And then all at once the boy vanished with a startled yell.

Will's yell went quickly silent. He'd been sitting with his back against the trunk and legs straddled over a branch. Strong hands grabbed his ankle, pulling sharply. Instant pain erupted between his legs and then he was falling off to the side. The ground rushed to meet his shoulder. Landing heavily, he lost his breath. His cut thigh shot stabbing pain up his spine.

Groaning, he went limp as hands slammed into his back and started pulling him up.

"No!" Angie shouted. "Leave him alone!" She dropped down a branch and jumped on the hunter's back, but he effortlessly bucked her off, sending her flying through the air before rolling in a heap of leaves.

"Nice of you to drop in," the hunter sneered. He had Will up on his feet and then up in his arms before twisting him and dumping him over his right shoulder.

The exhausted, injured boy had no fight left and succumbed to the capture. As his waist bent over the man's shoulder and his arms flopped down his back, Nick's oversized hoodie slipped down, bunching up around his head. He fought to keep his eyes open as warm liquid dripped down his leg.

The man turned to Angie and snarled. "You can come quietly, or not. I don't care. But if you want to see buddy boy here live, I suggest you do come." He savagely threw up his shoulder into Will's middle. The boy's body bounced and then hung limply, like a stuffed doll. Nick's hoodie tumbled to the ground as Will's consciousness followed. The boy blacked out.

The man chuckled harshly and patted the back of the unconscious boy's knees. "You'd better hurry before buddy boy here bleeds to death. I can feel his blood all over me." Then his face tightened and his nose wrinkled.

Angie heard a faint hissing sound. Not only did Will lose his senses, but he also lost control of his bladder. A dark stain formed just below Will's waist on the front of the hunter's shirt and it wasn't all blood.

Realizing Will had involuntarily relieved himself, Angie got to her feet unsteadily. Fear gripped her insides like a vice. She looked at the hunter, horrified.

He now resembled the beast he was. Big Mike's branch had opened up a wide gash just above the bridge of his nose. Both his eyes were turning a dark shade of black. Scratches lined his cheeks. Dried blood covered his forehead and lower parts of his face, giving him a crazed, maniac look. His wide smile, rimmed with red, only made it worse.

He carried Will like he carried a dead animal and seemed unbothered by the wetness staining his shirt.

"Buddy boy wet himself," he said, sounding almost cheerful. "That's what they do just before dying." His face suddenly twisted in a sneer as he bared his teeth at Angie. "You'll be next if you don't listen. I know our little lost friend is close by. If I had my guess, I would say you two are like his security blanket. Now get over here!"

Angie, trying hard not to whimper, could only comply.

The hunter forced her to walk in front of him as he carried Will's seemingly lifeless body over his shoulder.

He spat a gob of blood that had trickled to his mouth. "Call his name, girl," he told her. "Call it loud."

Angie bit back tears. She hoped the other boys were making out better. "J-John? I-if you're there. Run. Don't come here!"

The hunter laughed. "Boys like that can't think. They're too slow. He'll come. That's all he knows to do." He jostled Will's body with his shoulder. "Right, buddy boy?"

Will drifted in and out of consciousness, dimly aware of being manhandled by the murderous hunter. Dull pain throbbed from his thigh. He could hear Angie's voice but couldn't see her. The cold finally snapped him awake and total consciousness returned.

Blinking his eyes, he found himself hanging upside down over a man's shoulder. His basketball jersey had bunched around his chest, so his back lay exposed to the cold. He smelled the sour odor of urine and felt the dampness in his shorts. It helped focus his thoughts. Will gulped as his predicament became clear. He hung upside down over the shoulders of a murderer. His chin bounced against a scratchy blue sweater just above an ample backside covered in blue jeans.

Come on, boy, he heard his father's voice in his head. *Think! How do you get out of this one?*

Impossible, Will thought. *I'm too small, too cold, and too weak … I just want to sleep.*

His dad's voice wouldn't let him. *After all those workouts, that's all you got? Come on, Will! Where's there a Will, there's a way!*

Ha, ha … Will started to drift off when he felt the man's shoulder plunge up into his stomach.

"Call the boy," snarled the man, squeezing Will's legs tight. At first Will thought the man spoke to him, but then heard Angie sob.

"He won't come! He's too smart for you!"

"He's nothing but a retard, girl. He'll come. He just has to hear you scream. Keep walking or I'll make it happen."

Tilting his neck, Will's vision cleared. He ignored the pain. His dad wouldn't want him to give up. Not without a fight. His brown eyes widened as they spotted a chance.

The belt holding the blue jeans had a small walkie-talkie attached, right next to a sheathed knife. Will stared hard at the knife. He just might be able to reach it.

Licking his lips, he started to swing his dangling arms loosely, seeing if he could take hold of the hilt. His fingers brushed the walkie-talkie, but he came up short with the knife. If only he could grow another few inches!

Then his eyes blinked again. The knife lay on the man's left side, making it a long stretch. But if he reached straight down … he could make it to the man's waistline. His dad was right. Where there was a Will, there was a way.

Just then he heard Angie gasp. "John!" she cried.

"Where?" the hunter demanded, jerking to a stop. "Where is he?"

"Run!" Angie cried.

Will felt his body buck, bouncing on the man's shoulder. Angie cried out pain.

"Shut up!" the man snarled. "Or I'll kick you again. Get out here, boy!"

"No!" John's voice shouted. "Leave them alone!"

"Get out here," growled the man. "Then I'll leave your girlfriend alone."

John's voice wavered, but held firm, coming from in front of the man. "Stop it!" he said. "Stop hurting Angie! Put down Will!"

"Sorry," the hunter chuckled. "I can't hear you. Come over here and tell me."

"No, John!" Angie sobbed. "Go! Run! Run away!"

Will wasted no time. He wiggled his hips a little, trying to get up higher on the man's shoulder without alerting him to his intent. The grip on his back thighs tightened. Will only had one chance now. He grabbed the back of the sweater with one hand and pulled it up, exposing the man's fleshy back and top of his gray underpants. With no hesitation, his other hand grabbed the waistband of the briefs and yanked up as hard as possible. He gave the biggest wedgie of his life.

At first Hunter squirmed uncomfortably in confusion. Then as the waistband went way up, he threw back his head and screamed.

Will didn't let go as he pulled back with all his might, but then the man started clawing at Will's thigh, ripping at his injury.

Crying out, Will let go. He started wiggling and twisting his body, fighting to clamber down the man's back. He knew how to get out of holds because of his dad. It made it easier wearing his large basketball shorts.

As Will's momentum carried him down the man's back, his shorts, slick with blood and urine, went the opposite direction and he slid right out of them and straight out of the hunter's grip. Will crashed to the ground and rolled to his back, stunned for a moment.

Hunter stumbled forward, dropping the soiled shorts and cursing savagely. He turned to glare at Will with a murderous rage. One of his hands tried to pull at the backside of his jeans, but it only made him look ridiculous.

Angie sat on the ground with John standing next to her. Both looked shocked at what just happened. They were in a small clearing in the woods next to a dry spring, but neither ran to hide.

"Will," John finally said. "Your shorts came off. And you're bleeding."

Sitting with his wet boxers plastered to his skin, Will only slid away from the man. His whole body felt ready to quit and his thigh, streaming blood, seared with a raging pain. His eyes stared wildly at the man.

"You're dead, buddy boy," the man spat. Fresh blood flowed down his face as his contortions reopened the wound from Big Mike. Reaching to his belt, he drew out the knife. The blade gleamed wickedly.

"Angie," John asked fearfully. "What do we do?"

Angie got to her feet. "I, I don't know," she mumbled. Then she looked at John. "But stay out of your hidey hole, John. Now's not the time for that."

"I know," John said. "We have to help Will."

"If you harm us, you'll pay," Angie cried loudly, trying to keep the tremble from her voice. "You'll get caught!"

"Nobody knows you're out here," the man snarled, turning his glare on her. "You two are next." He winced and moved to spread his legs awkwardly. "Ah, that hurts! I'm so going to gut you for that!"

Faint voices called from the woods caused him to flinch. Once again, he was proven wrong.

"Will! Angie!" cried a girl's voice.

Then a man's voice boomed out. "Where are you, Will?"

Will's eyes went wide. "D-dad?" he asked, dazed. At first he thought it had come from his head, but then Angie shrieked.

"Over here!" she screamed. "Quickly! He has a knife!"

Hunter hesitated as he looked between Will and Angie. The knife started to shake in his hand.

Will crawled backwards, hope surging through his body.

"I'm coming!" his father's voice called. "Hold on!"

"Not possible," Hunter said hoarsely. He squeezed his eyes shut and opened them. The knife trembled as he unsuccessfully tried to fix his wedgie.

"Hurry!" yelled Angie. "Help!"

Jared appeared first. Hurtling bushes, he crashed through branches before bursting into the clearing with no thought of safety for himself.

Nick had led the way to the holly tree with Jared, Angel, and Big Mike close behind. Mr. Moore and Brad followed at a slower pace as they helped Ryan.

The injured boy had to walk slowly between them. They'd attempted to carry him, but that just made his ribs hurt more. The crude bloody bandages on his arm had been removed and replaced with Angel's sweater. The cut hadn't been too deep, but it'd been reopened multiple times and he'd lost a lot of blood.

When they'd found the holly tree empty of Will and Angie, Jared had felt a cold burn flow through his body. Fresh blood dotted the leaves below the tree, right next to where Nick's hoodie lay abandoned.

Mr. Moore had left Ryan when seeing the scene. It was he who'd found the blood spatter creating a trail heading east towards the climbing sun, now high overhead. He and Angel had called out for Will and Angie just as Jared took off, following the blood trail.

Jared had quickly left the others behind, even as they called for him to wait. He could not do that. Especially not after hearing Angie's cries. He'd run towards Angie's voice until seeing the man. Then he'd charged blindly.

Now, seeing Will sitting in a small grassy clearing with a crazed man standing over him with a knife, his mind went blank. He felt nothing. He just knew he had to get there in time.

Angie and John stood behind the man, but were kept at bay. Instead of attacking, the man swung his knife around him like an arrow, pointing it at John, then Angie, and finally at Will. He seemed to be in pain as he kept picking at his backside with his free hand. At seeing Jared, he turned to face him.

"What's this?" he growled. "That's not right!"

Jared ignored him as he charged into the clearing, throwing his body past the man and diving to a crashing halt at Will's side.

Will looked at him and gave a weak grin. "Hey, big guy," he said, his voice thick. "Glad you dropped in."

Jared whirled around and got up in a crouch. He put an arm on Will's shoulder and glared up at the man. "It's over," he said. "Your brothers are already captured."

The man just sneered. His face, a mask of blood, caused him to look more beast than human. "You lie. You're going to die with your friends, boy."

Mr. Moore's voice boomed out again, getting closer. Angel's voice also joined him.

"Will! Angie!"

"Where are you?"

"Here!" Angie yelled. "Hurry up!"

Instantly the hunter's face turned to stone. His swollen eyes narrowed. "Not possible," he muttered. "I had it all set up!" He glared balefully at Will and Jared. "It's all your fault," he hissed. "You ruined my game."

Jared tensed his muscles. The man looked poised to strike.

"Over here!" Angie yelled.

She went to sneak behind the man, but Jared shook his head at her. The man was like a wounded wild animal and would attack anything close. At the moment his focus lay on Will.

"Should've killed you when I had the chance," he wheezed, moving drunkenly forward. He breathed heavily as he waved his knife side to side. Fresh blood ran down his bruised, swollen face. Hunching his shoulders, he took another step towards the fallen boy. "You still lose. I'll kill you before they reach me. They'll only find your body, boy, buddy boy."

Will trembled, but could barely move to retreat. He eyed the knife. Angie screamed and covered her eyes.

"Leave us alone!" Jared yelled. Then he dove in front of the knife, his long frame missing the blade by inches. Landing at the man's feet, he threw himself at the man's ankles, grabbing the large right foot with his hands while slamming his shoulders against the man's shin.

Hunter grunted as he tripped on impact. Crying out, he fell over Jared and landed heavily just in front of Will. All at once, he sucked in a deep breath and made a choking sound. He did not try to get up.

Jared turned to his side and looked back. Will blinked owlishly, and then desperately scooted backwards. He had no real need.

The hunter's blade had finally found a mark. He rolled slowly to his back and raised his head. His knife had rammed into his gut, going several inches deep just below his ribcage on his right side.

"I … I stabbed myself," he said, sounding amazed. "I …" His voice ended in a whimper.

Jared got to his feet and walked to Will, taking a wide path around the man.

"You okay, Will?"

Will nodded briefly. "Better than him," he wheezed. "Y-You saved my life."

Mr. Moore crashed through the brush seconds later. Seeing the hunter as no longer being a threat, he rushed toward Will. Angel hurried right after him, followed closely by Nick. Big Mike and Brad had been left behind to help Ryan.

Mr. Moore went straight to his son. Ignoring the blood, he pulled Will up and wrapped him up in a tight hug, lifting him bodily off the ground. Then he gently placed him down, supporting the small of his back with both his arms.

"You, bud, have no shorts on," he said. "Why are you standing in the cold in your underwear?" He was kind enough not to mention the acrid smell of urine.

"Ha," Will responded, giving a slight grin. He leaned into his father and promptly fainted. His father held him tight in his arms.

"What do we do now?" Angie asked, slightly nervous. She had John tightly at her side with her arm locked around his shoulders.

Jared and Nick stood behind them. The four kids grimly watched the sad scene of the hunter, sitting in the grassy clearing, clutching the protruding knife handle. He looked nervous, confused, and scared all at once. His eyes darted wildly around and couldn't settle.

"Sh-should we help him?" she asked.

"Don't go near him," Mr. Moore commanded. He bent over Will and was busily working on his bloody thigh. He'd torn off his gray Army hoodie and now used it as a fresh bandage.

Angel sat, cradling her brother's head on her lap. He looked to be sleeping peacefully and had a slight smile on his lips. She looked worried, but watched her dad work silently. She'd never seen her dad in action before. Now that she had, she could only feel pride. With her father there, she knew Will would be okay.

His deft hands still working, Mr. Moore continued talking. "That man is an injured snake. He'll lash out at anything that moves too close, even if it's help." He grunted. "People like him are why I joined the army so long ago. The world should be free of their kind."

Angie shuddered and moved closer to Jared. No one spoke until Angel looked at her dad.

"How do you do it?" Angel asked.

Mr. Moore didn't look up. "Do what?"

"Stay so calm. I mean, I'm the one about to freak out."

"It's my job. I'm supposed to protect you and Will. Right now all you kids are my responsibility. I'm just thankful everybody is now safe."

Hearing him, the hunter glared up with pure hatred. His eyes were mostly swollen shut, but still managed to convey pure malice. His breathing sounded labored, but still came steady. "I'm not through, yet," he taunted. "I'll still come after you."

Mr. Moore finished tying the makeshift bandage and stood up slowly. He looked at where the hunter sat and shook his head.

"It's over," he said loudly. "You're not going to harm another soul on this planet except your own."

The hunter laughed and then started coughing painfully. "I had your boy's life in my hands four times … Four times I could have slit his throat."

Mr. Moore's eyes tightened. "If you try to hurt my son, or any other child again, I'll—"

Angel pulled Will up to a sitting position, sliding his still unconscious body on her lap. "Dad," she said. "We need to go. He needs a hospital, and so does Ryan."

Big Mike and Brad had Ryan between them as they slowly made their way to them. Ryan's injured arm rested tightly against his body and he could only move in a painful shuffle.

Mr. Moore slowly let out his breath and nodded. "All right, kids. Let's get everyone together and head out."

The hunter laughed harshly. "Good luck with that," he wheezed. "You'll never find your way out with those hurt kids. I'll still get your boy in the end. He's going to bleed out."

Angie shuddered, pulling John tight. "How do we get out of here?" she asked, looking around fearfully. "I don't know where we are, or even what time it is."

Nick groaned. "It'll be impossible, man. Just finding this place in the first place was hard enough."

Mr. Moore ignored the hunter. "Don't worry about that. We'll head out in style." He turned to the hunter and grinned. "Courtesy of our host here, we have a nice heavy-duty pickup truck waiting for us."

The hunter's eyes widened. "No," he gasped.

As a precaution, not wanting to leave a trail to his parents, he'd parked the truck a mile from his house the night before. He'd moved covertly through the woods for his supper and then spent the night sleeping in the woods. He'd thought he'd left the truck well hidden.

"That's how we found you all," Mr. Moore said, still looking at the hunter. "Angel and I followed the tracks pretty much all night until we found the truck hidden behind some trees. Funny, but it had a banged-up bumper with some yellow paint on the front."

"You won't find it again!" the hunter spat. Blood flecked on his lips, but he didn't seem to care. His eyes smoldered at Mr. Moore. "You may be a good tracker on a dirt road, but you've no idea where you are now!"

"Sorry, bud," Mr. Moore said, pulling out a compass from his pocket. "I learned how to navigate in places a whole lot tougher than your little backyard. And thanks for leaving the keys in the ignition, along with your wallet and driver's license, Mr. Hunter W. Pherrins. Funny, but I also found a strange spray bottle on the front seat with some sort of chemical. I'm sure the police will be very interested in it."

Hunter Pherrins wilted and his whole body seemed to sag.

Mr. Moore grinned without humor. "Don't worry, we'll send them back here as soon as we can, so sit tight. I'm sure they'll have a lot of questions for you. So whatever you do, don't pull the knife out. It's funny, but that's the only thing keeping you alive right now."

Hunter could only stare in undisguised loathing as Mr. Moore gathered up Will and led the group towards Big Mike and Brad, who supported Ryan between them.

"You'll have to forgive me," Mr. Moore mumbled to Angel as they walked. "I'm almost hoping he pulls out that knife."

Angel coughed and looked back. "I know, Dad. Me too … But you did the right thing. It's his choice now." She put a hand on his back. "I think I understand now, about how you worry about us so much. I … I just want to say, I love you, Dad."

Mr. Moore only hefted up Will to a better position and grunted. He always preferred speaking by his actions rather than words.

Their last view of the man Hunter Pherrins was of him reaching back and trying to pull out a terrible wedgie while not disturbing the knife stuck in his belly. Tears leaked from his eyes.

It took a slow and painful walk through the woods, especially for Ryan, but they eventually made it to the dirt road. Once there, Mr. Moore had Ryan sit with Angel while he carried Will and led the rest of the kids to the pickup.

John grinned widely when he heard they were going home.

Mr. Moore had Jared sit in front to support Will. The smaller boy looked pale, but breathed evenly as he lay against Jared's shoulder. The rest sat in the back.

"You're a good friend, Jared," Mr. Moore told him as he turned the key. "Will is lucky to have you."

Jared just pressed his lips tight and looked out the window. He felt like the lucky one.

Soon the pickup drew to a stop by Ryan and Angel. Then it was time to go home.

Jared remained squeezed in the front with Will leaning against his shoulder, breathing softly. Ryan sat on the other side of the smaller boy, clutching his injured ribs with his bandaged arm, taking slow careful breaths. He'd climbed in through the driver's side with Mr. Moore's help and had met Jared's eyes as he settled in his seat.

"Sorry again," he mumbled. "You still forgive me?"

Jared reached across Will and grabbed Ryan's uninjured hand. "We're shower brothers, remember? There's nothing to forgive. Especially since you saved my life."

Ryan grunted and nodded.

Before climbing in the back, Angel checked on Will and patted Jared's shoulder.

"My little bro is in good hands," she said. "Thanks, Jared. For everything"

Jared ducked his head. He still felt like the lucky one.

Mr. Moore started the engine and told the boys to hold on. "I'll go slow, but it's going to be a bumpy ride."

"That's okay," Ryan wheezed. "It sure beats walking." Then he moaned as the truck pulled out and hit a rut.

Jared reached over and tapped Ryan's elbow. "It'll be okay. You want me to tell your story?"

Ryan looked at him and nodded. "I would," he said, "but it hurts too much to talk … tell everything, man."

So as Mr. Moore drove in grim silence, Jared told everything. He started with Mr. Hackett forcing Ryan to rob for him and ended with Mr. Drydon's plot to kill his son.

Listening, Ryan closed his eyes and let tears run. They were tears of joy mixed with tears of pain. It felt good to let go of his burden of guilt.

Will slept blissfully on, using Jared's shoulder as a pillow.

Mr. Drydon carefully wiped his bloodshot eyes with the back of his hand as he paced along the road near the accident scene. He now had two black eyes and a swollen nose to go with his burned chin, neck, and lower torso. Every step sent bolts of pain shooting up and down his body. To make matters worse, his pants now chafed against his raw, burned skin.

He'd spent half the night with the stupid search party, stomping through empty woods yelling useless names. And through it all, he'd yet to receive a single text from Hunter Pherrins. He'd meant to call Hunter's brothers to take care of Angie, but now didn't dare. He didn't need those buffoons getting in the way. Hopefully Angie took care of herself.

The only good thing, his image as a concerned parent and devoted principal had grown. He'd just finished an interview with a local newspaper reporter who'd commended him for his tireless work in looking for the missing boys.

A newscaster had tried to do an interview, but Mr. Drydon had only allowed a brief question, letting it be known he needed to keep searching for his son.

"First to arrive on the scene, the principal of the middle school and father to one of the missing boys, Wayne Drydon went straight to work in searching for the lost children," the newscaster had said by way of introduction. "As you can see, he even suffered numerous injuries in his efforts. And still he has not left the scene. All thoughts and prayers are with him in this time of need …"

Mr. Drydon kicked at the grass. He had actually left the scene four times to find a signal for his cellphone. All he had were voice mails offering sympathy and support.

Where was the sympathy and support back when John was throwing himself on the floor and screaming all night? Where were they when his wife ran out on him with that sorry excuse of an art teacher? The art teacher had shown sympathy, all right. He'd started giving his wife afterschool lessons of therapeutic art to cope. Mr. Drydon's face burned at the memory.

He grew especially upset when not seeing any message from a certain assistant principal from his old school. She'd promised to be there for him, just as soon as he found a place for John. She wouldn't consent to a deep relationship until John had been taken care of, as in put out of the picture. Well, he had taken care of John. That at least brought satisfaction to Mr. Drydon's otherwise miserable day.

If only he could find out what happened to Angie. Kicking the ground in frustration, he resumed his pacing. Some stupid brothers of one of the missing boys had discovered the fire road with fresh tracks earlier that morning and that was the big discussion now. He didn't worry too much. Plenty of local hunters used the back roads and fresh tracks were no big surprise.

Still, he stayed around this road keeping his ear open for any talk of following it, or any word of kidnapping. So far it had been nothing but sympathetic small talk.

Everyone just came out to help to make themselves feel better, he thought. They'd help, no problem, just as long as the cameras and news people were there.

Then, from deep in the woods he heard the rumble of an engine. It steadily grew louder.

Licking the tip of his mustache, Mr. Drydon frowned and stared down the narrow dirt road. His eyes widened in fear when he saw the grill of a familiar truck turn a corner and head straight at him.

"Hunter?" he mumbled. "What are you doing?" Too surprised to move, he stared in fascination at the approaching truck.

The Pherrins' heavy-duty Ford pickup braked to a stop just in front of him. Glare from the sun prevented him from seeing inside the cab.

"What in the h—" he started to say when the driver's side window rolled down.

"Good afternoon, Mr. Drydon," a familiar man's voice said pleasantly. Not Hunter. Mr. Drydon, starved for sleep, couldn't place the face or think of a name, but knew he should know him. "I've got some good news and bad news, all in one. We found your son."

Mr. Drydon's eyebrows nearly shot to his forehead and he stepped back. It felt as if a sledgehammer had just knocked him between the eyes.

Then a very familiar figure hopped down from the back and he saw Angie standing in front of him. The girl stared up at him with no fear.

"You're wrong," she said. "There is good and bad in this world, Mr. Drydon. You just have to use your heart to figure out which is which. And you don't have a heart."

Mr. Drydon just stared speechlessly. Then he turned and started running. He pushed by two teen boys and ignored a voice calling for him to stop. As he reached the road, he saw a crowd of people coming his way. They'd seen the kids. They didn't care about him. If he could just get lost in the crowd …

A man stepped directly into his path and slammed into his chest. Mr. Drydon blinked rapidly to clear his vision and found himself staring into the fuming eyes of Mr. Williamson. The angry father brought up his knee, right into Drydon's belt area.

A moment later the principal knelt on the pavement holding a most painful area between his legs, trying hard not to cry. In less than an hour he'd be in a police car wearing handcuffs. The pain would only intensify.

Chapter 55

As Jared climbed out from the pickup, leaving Will to his dad, he felt the weight of the world come crashing down. He couldn't believe it, but it was only one day after the Berkshire game. A crowd started cheering and ran towards him. There had to be at least a hundred people. Jared bit his bottom lip and went to stand in the background. He doubted any were there for him. He wondered if his family even knew what'd happened—his brothers probably didn't notice anything missing. Just as he thought this, two familiar faces charged forward, heading straight for him.

"George?" he said dazedly. "Jack?"

Before he knew it, his brothers had him in a tight embrace. George, Jared noticed, had tears in his eyes.

With the sudden arrival of the missing children in a pickup with a damaged front, the questions started to abound. Quickly, police cars and ambulances filled the area and authorities had to hold back the crowd.

Statements were taken and arrests were made. Will and Ryan were both loaded on ambulances and whisked to a hospital. Mr. Moore had to stay to talk to police, but Angel rode with her brother, who'd awakened long enough to give her hand a squeeze.

Big Mike later went to the hospital to check out his shoulder. It turned out he'd carried Will and fought the Pherrins brothers with a cracked shoulder, courtesy of busting down the bus door.

Jared, Nick, Angie, John, and Brad were all checked out on the scene and treated for mild injuries. Mostly they suffered from dehydration, hunger, and shock. Nick's shoulder turned out to be only bruised, but he was too ashamed to even allow a sling after hearing about Big Mike. Big Mike had never complained once during the whole ordeal.

Poor John had no place to go. His mother lived in California and wanted nothing to do with him. She'd hung up when getting a call about his disappearance. Angie quickly stepped in and adamantly refused to let him go anywhere but her place. Her mom supported her, and after a lot of hemming and hawing from social workers, John was allowed to stay with Angie on a temporary basis, until a foster family could be found.

Angie's mom started applying to be a foster parent that very moment. John took it all very well. He wanted to see his daddy, but didn't mind being with Angie. He was just glad to be away from the bad men.

Hours passed before Jared finally got to climb in the minivan with his brothers. It was well after sundown and nearly all the crowd had left. Only a few police remained to secure the scene. He'd just eaten an entire large pizza from Domino's and felt exhausted. But he wasn't ready to go home.

"Uh, Jack?" he asked as his older brother got behind the wheel.

George climbed beside Jared, making sure he had his seat belt on and felt comfortable. Usually George would sit in the front and blast his rock music without noticing Jared's existence.

"Yeah, Jared?" his brother said.

"On the way home, can we stop at the hospital?"

Instantly his brothers were all over him.

"Oh, man," George cried. "Are you hurt?" He started feeling Jared's arms.

"What's wrong, Jared," Jack asked, nearly climbing over the front seat to him. "Where are you hurt?"

"Hey, stop!" Jared cried, pushing George away. "It's not that!"

Shaking his head, he sighed. His head no longer hurt, but most everywhere else still ached. Bruises and scratches covered most of his body and the doctors thought he had a slight concussion, but he was allowed to go home on the promise he would rest.

"Then what is it?" Jack asked.

"I just want to check on ... on some of my friends." Jared couldn't help cracking a smile. It felt nice saying that.

George sat back in relief. "That's it?"

Jared relaxed in his seat. "That's it."

The nurse at the reception desk took one look at Jared walking into the lobby with his brothers and instantly rose to her feet and smiled warmly. "You must be from the Washington Middle basketball team. I just want you to know, all your friends are going to be okay. Even your coach is awake and alert."

Jared let out a breath of relief. He wore an open jacket and his grimy basketball jersey underneath. A dark bruise covered his left cheek and he walked with a slight limp. Jack squeezed his shoulder behind him. Jared had been lucky.

They were at Lady of Mercy Hospital, a small Catholic hospital only twenty minutes out of Berkshire. It was the closest to the accident scene but far from the homes of the players.

"A lot of the boys have already been here and released to their parents," the nurse told Jared and his brothers, "and some have been transferred to Washington General Hospital, just to be closer to family, of course. Anybody in particular you're looking for?"

"Uh, are Will Moore or Ryan Mahome still here?" Jared asked her.

The nurse flicked a strand of blond hair from her forehead. She had a few lines around her eyes, but still looked relatively young.

"Yes, they just got here some hours ago. It's supposed to be just family allowed to visit, but ..." She gave Will a wink. "My son used to play at Berkshire Middle. He always considered his team family. Hold on and I'll get their room numbers."

They had put Ryan and Will in neighboring rooms on the third floor. Jared and his brothers rode the elevator in silence. Exiting, they navigated a mostly quiet hall, past a nurse's station, and found the rooms both with their doors wide open.

"At least drink your water, little bro," he heard Angel's voice say from the first room. "You need the fluid. Your skinny little body is like dried out paper."

"Ha, ha," Jared heard Will mumble. His voice sounded weak and sluggish. "You're my sister, not my mom."

Jared went to the doorway and tentatively knocked on the side.

"Will?" he said.

His friend lay in a bed wearing a hospital gown with a blanket covering his lap. He had a dark bruise just above his right eye, from knocking into the window on the bus crash, and an IV sticking in his right hand. His face was pale, but seeing Jared, his eyes lit up and he gave a tired smile.

"Hey, big guy," he said. "My sister is trying to make me eat puke. Tell her to stop."

"It's not puke, kid," Angel said, rising from a chair by Will's side. "It's spinach, and it smells ..." She wrinkled her nose after bending down and sniffing a tray of food on a stand by the bed. "It smells like puke. Still, drink the water."

Jack and George came up behind Jared and stood awkwardly at the door.

Seeing them, Angel smiled. "You two must be Jared's brothers." All at once, she bit her lip and swallowed. "Your brother ... Jared, he saved Will's life." Looking at Jared, her eyes started welling up. "I'll never forget what you did."

Jack and George stared at their younger brother, shocked. They had yet to hear what exactly happened.

"Uh, yeah," Jared mumbled embarrassed.

Angel quickly wiped her eyes. "If you want to see my little bro before he goes out, you'd better hurry. He lost a lot of blood and needs the rest, so the doctor gave him something."

"Yeah ... puke," Will mumbled.

"Okay, kid," she said. "You don't have to eat it." Getting up, she went over and gave Jared a big hug. "Thanks for taking care of my little bro." Looking up at Jack and George, she nodded to the hallway. "Come with me and I'll tell you about your awesome brother."

Jack swallowed and coughed. He couldn't take his eyes off of Angel. "Oh, er, you're Will's sister?"

Angel smiled at him. "I'm Angel."

Jack quickly ran a hand through his hair. "Oh, uh, yeah, I believe it. Er, I'm Jack."

Jared and Will looked at each other as the three left the room. They both cracked a smile.

"So, uh, you going to be okay?" Jared asked, going to Angel's chair.

Will's eyes were already drooping but he gave a brief nod. "Still there," he said, tapping his right leg. He briefly pulled up the blanket and bottom of his gown to show Will his heavily bandaged thigh. He'd been out while they'd stitched it up, but knew it had taken a lot.

"Sorry," Jared muttered as Will covered the injury back up. On the TV hanging across the room a basketball game played on mute. He knew Will wouldn't be playing for a while. He thought Will had drifted off to sleep when the boy's hand reached over and touched his arm.

"Jared?" Will whispered. "I'm afraid to sleep. Every time I close my eyes I see that guy and his knife."

Jared swallowed. "I'll be right here, Will. I won't leave until you're asleep." He grasped Will's hand and squeezed it.

"Thanks, Jared."

"Sure. That's what friends are for."

"Yeah ..." Will's eyes blinked opened and his voice grew faint. For a moment he sounded like a little boy. "Jared? You won't tell anybody I wet myself, right?"

Jared's eyes widened. After everything that happened and Will was worried about *that?* Then he gave a slight smile. "Honest, Will, I was so scared I thought that was me. I won't tell."

Will gave a small sigh and grinned as his eyes slid shut. "Thanks, big guy."

The two boys stayed together for the next several minutes, not talking. Jared watched as his friend slowly relaxed and started breathing evenly. His hand went limp and Jared gently placed it on Will's chest before standing up.

He couldn't help but feel a pang in his heart. Will looked so young and vulnerable in the bed, so void of energy and life.

On the TV, the players played on, always searching for their best shot, but Will wouldn't have a chance. Not for quite some time.

Jared met Angel in the hall. She leaned against the wall talking with Jack and George in low voices. Seeing him, Will's sister smiled and reached up to tousle his grimy hair. "He's asleep, huh?"

Jared nodded. "How, uh, long is he in here for?"

Angel frowned. "I'm not sure. My dad should be coming here soon and wants to bring him home tonight, but I don't know. The cold weather helped slow the blood flow, but still, it's bad. The doctors want to put more fluid into him and keep him for observation. Will really just needs a lot of rest and can do that better at home." She chuckled briefly. "Knowing my dad, I expect he'll be home sometime tomorrow. He hates hospitals and is good at getting his way."

"Could, could I stop by then? I mean, tomorrow, to, uh, check on him, to see how he is?" Jared asked.

Angel looked at him kindly. "I'm sure that'd be fine, Jared." She shook her head. "I still can't believe it … I see it in my head over and over. My dad and I, we saw it all from the trees. I actually froze, but my dad kept running." She paused to swallow. "When I saw you standing there, facing that beast as he came at you and Will with the knife …" She shuddered. "I thought he'd stabbed you when you fell like that. Then you got up and tackled him. What were you thinking?"

George and Jack stared at him in amazement. They hadn't heard this part.

Jared ducked his head, embarrassed. "You know, it's like basketball. When things get desperate, you just take your best shot."

"Well," smiled Angel, "I'm glad you did."

Before leaving, Jared stopped by Ryan's room, but found the boy in a deep sleep. He learned from Angel that Ryan suffered from three broken ribs and he had his arm wrapped tight in a sling. Angel comforted Jared by saying she would stay near Ryan until leaving with Will. Ben and his family were on the way, bringing Ryan's mother with them. Jared hoped everything would work out. In the end, Ryan nearly gave his life to make things right.

As the Cook minivan pulled away from the hospital, another ambulance arrived, followed by three police cars, all with flashing lights. Hunter Pherrins had been found huddled behind a tree clutching the knife's handle, crying. His brothers and parents had already been arrested at their home.

When Corey had found Hunter with a smashed face from Big Mike and had learned more kids were in the picture, he'd panicked and had retreated back to the house. He'd tried to convince his parents to flee with him. Mr. and Mrs. Pherrins had never listened. Hunter had never failed a hunt before, and they'd said everything would be fine. Then Sam and A.J. had staggered in, bruised and beaten. Collapsing at the table, they'd demanded beers. Corey had slumped down next to them. Not long after, the police had arrived and the brothers had given up without a fight. Their parents had hollered and cursed, but in the end had been dragged out in handcuffs. They had truly lost.

Jared and his brothers got home late that night, but found all the lights in their house blazing. His mother and father rushed from the house and practically tackled him as he climbed out of the van. Kelly, carrying Carey, joined the pile, and Jared could only return the hugs. George gave him slaps on the back and Jack just grinned. Jared finally felt as if he'd arrived home.

Washington Middle never closed, but on Wednesday, the day after the horrible accident where many students were injured and seven remained missing, including the principal's son, the entire school had gathered in the auditorium to support each other and have access to grief counselors.

On Thursday, the students again gathered in the auditorium to celebrate the recovery of the missing students and deal with the shock of their principal and one of their PE teachers being arrested for trying to murder their basketball team. Again, counselors were available.

Kelly went to endure the ordeal, saying she needed to update all her friends, but Jared stayed home. He slept until around noon and went down to find his mother making a stack of pancakes. There were two plates full of them, but she had more on the griddle.

"I kept making them while you slept, Jared," she told him, giving an embarrassed smile. "I wanted to make sure you got yours hot."

After his large breakfast, Jared asked his mother to give him a ride to Will's house, which she did without question.

As their minivan pulled up in front of Will's yard, Jared saw Jimmy standing in a pile of leaves, throwing them in the air. Jared didn't notice any missing cars so he knew Will would be home.

"I'll stay here, Jared," his mother said, glancing back to where Carey slept in her car seat. "You shouldn't stay too long if he's resting."

"Thanks, Mom," Jared told her. He leaned over in the passenger seat and gave her a kiss on the cheek. "Love you, Mom."

"I know. I love you too."

Seeing Jared, Jimmy dropped the leaves in his hand and raced to him, throwing open his arms. "Jared!" he cried. "What are you doing here?"

Jared had no choice but to catch the boy, nearly falling back in the process.

"I just came to see how Will is doing," he said.

Jimmy straddled Jared's sides and leaned back to look at him. "Will is still sleeping on the couch. He's been sleeping for like a million years!" Kicking his legs, he hopped down. "Do you want to see him?"

"Oh, uh, maybe not."

The little boy didn't wait for an answer. He raced to the door and waved for Jared to hurry.

Biting his lip, Jared followed but made sure to knock before entering.

Jimmy just rolled his eyes. "Come on, nobody cares."

Angel opened it and grinned at seeing Jared. "You look much better cleaned up," she said. "Come in, but keep it down. We got back around four in the morning and put Will on the couch. He hasn't moved since."

Jimmy proudly guided Jared into the TV room where Will lay on his side in a cocoon of blankets with his head propped on two pillows.

"I didn't go to school," Jimmy whispered. "I get to miss two whole days."

"I'm glad you can still count to two," Angel said dryly, reaching down and messing up his hair. "Come on. Let's go outside and let the kid sleep." She looked at Jared and pointed to the ceiling. "My dad is up there writing a storm, so we have to keep quiet for two reasons. I think writing helps him not worry so much. If you're hungry I have two batches of cookies in the kitchen." She grinned. "Baking is how I keep from worrying."

"My mom is the same," Jared said, grinning. Even after all the pancakes, he still felt hungry.

Shortly after, Jared sat on the front stoop with Angel, eating chocolate chip cookies and drinking milk. Jimmy had resumed playing in the leaves. As Jared finished his third cookie, a shiny blue pickup truck pulled in behind the minivan.

Jared felt his heart skip a beat. He hadn't had many good experiences with pickup trucks in recent days. He relaxed when he saw the passenger door open and Brad hop out. Glen followed him, arm in a sling. From the other side, Mr. Williamson stepped out, looking a little ashamed, but also resolute.

"Jared!" Brad cried seeing him. "Yo, man! What are you doing here?"

"Man, it's great to see you!" Glen said.

"You boys, uh, go ahead," Brad's dad said awkwardly. He waved at Jared and nodded at Angel. Jared noticed he had a bandage wrapped around his right hand. "I'll wait here … Call if you need me."

Jimmy stared at the boys and went to sit by his sister.

Angel stood and greeted Brad with a smile. "Hi, boys. I'm guessing you're not here for me. Will's not up, though."

Brad coughed and looked down at his feet. "Uh, actually we're not here for Will." He looked up at Angel. "Is your dad around?"

Angel just raised her eyebrows and nodded. "Jimmy, go tell dad he has some visitors. I'll go in and get some more cookies. Take a seat, guys. Sorry there aren't any chairs."

Immediately, Jimmy raced into the house, calling for his dad.

Rolling her eyes, Angel followed him in. "So much for peace and quiet," she said.

Chapter 56

Mr. Moore walked down the stairs slowly and thoughtfully. He held Jimmy in his arms. Before going out, they stopped and looked in on Will. They could hear Angel outside making small talk as she passed around cookies.

"Why is he sleeping so much?" Jimmy asked, leaning his head on his dad's shoulder.

"Well, buddy, you know how your brother is so short, right? Our bodies grow the most when we're asleep. And Will has a lot of growing to catch up on."

Jimmy frowned. "So baths are to water us, huh?"

"Exactly."

"Ha, ha," mumbled Will from the couch, not opening his eyes. "You're hilarious."

"I knew you were faking, champ," his dad said, sounding relieved. "I have three of your basketball buddies out there. Any guesses why?"

Will opened his eyes and sighed. "Our team is wrecked." He sounded more depressed than groggy.

Mr. Moore sighed. "Yeah, maybe. But I'm going to see what they have to say." He put Jimmy down and pushed him toward the couch. "Jimmy, you stay with Will and make sure he doesn't sprout roots."

"Daaadddy," Jimmy said. "Can I at least get a cookie?"

"Sorry, bud, but you've got enough chocolate on your face to tell me you've had more than enough."

"I only had four," complained the little boy.

Outside, Mr. Moore leaned back against his front door to face Brad and Glen. Jared stood on the porch off to the side, watching curiously. Brad had told him the reason for their visit and he waited to hear the answer.

"We, uh, were wondering if you would coach the team," Brad mumbled. "You know, Coach Swopes is going on leave and is retiring. He won't be coming back."

"I understand," Mr. Moore said. He flicked his gaze toward the pickup truck. "What about your dad, Brad? Is he happy with you being here?"

Brad's face reddened slightly. "My dad is the one who suggested this." He scuffed his shoe on the walkway. "He gets into it too much, but he's really sorry."

Mr. Moore sighed and pushed himself from the door. He crossed his arms over his chest. "I don't know, boys. I appreciate the fact you came to me to ask. I'll have to think about it. Right now I have a lot on my mind."

"Yes sir," Glen said. He gave a sad smile. "To tell you the truth, Mr. Moore, I doubt we have enough uninjured players left to even have a team."

Brad exhaled. "Yeah, who's even left?"

Glen started to run through the names. The seriously injured from the bus included Howard with a wrenched back, Teddy with a torn knee and broken leg, and Darius, who it turned out only sprained his neck, but still would be bedridden for several more days. Big Mike had a cracked shoulder and had left the hospital the night before in a sling. Glen's broken arm along with Ryan's and Will's injuries put the team down to only eight usable players left. Who knew how many still wanted to play, and if they did, most of them were bench players.

"We have Brad, Jared, Ben, Nick, Kyle, Tom, Scott, and Bob," Glen finished. "That's it."

Mr. Moore winced. "You'll need more players than that," he said.

The door cracked behind him and slowly swung open. Will blinked groggily in the sunlight as he stiffly limped out wearing gray sweatpants and a loose-fitting long-sleeved shirt.

It was a mild winter's day in the high 50s and Mr. Moore, Jared, Glen, and Brad all wore pants and hoodies.

Will flinched from the cool air, but yawned. "Hey, guys," he said, cracking a slight grin.

"Hay is for horses and you're not supposed to be walking yet," Mr. Moore admonished him. He instantly knelt. "Come sit and keep pressure off that leg. I don't want to bring you back for more stitches."

Looking sheepish, Will sat on his dad's knee and hunched his shoulders.

"Will, dude, it's awesome to see you!" Glen said, sounding genuinely pleased. "When you disappeared from the bus the other night we were freaking out."

Brad nodded. "I'm glad you made it back," he added.

"Me too," Will said, looking over at Jared. Then he wiped his nose. "You forgot one player."

"You've been listening," Mr. Moore accused, giving his left thigh a light slap.

"Who did we forget, man?" Brad asked.

"Isn't John part of the roster?" Will asked.

There was a moment of silence and then Jared coughed. Surprisingly himself, he said, "Yeah, isn't he?" he said. "He is down as a player."

Brad wrinkled his nose, but then relaxed. "You know? After all we've been through and all he had to go through, if he comes back and wants to be on the team, I think we should let him." He folded his arms in front of him. "I know I'm no saint, man, but I do know one thing. John is definitely a teammate from now on. I'm not calling him no names, not anymore."

Angel came out with more cookies and nearly dropped them when seeing Will. "Kid!" she shouted. "The doctor told you not to get up today!"

"So give me a cookie," Will mumbled defiantly. "I'm starving."

After Glen and Brad left with Mr. Moore still promising to think on it, Jared spent a few more minutes with Will until the smaller boy started to slouch and close his eyes.

"Back to rest, champ," Mr. Moore said, moving his arms around him to scoop him up from his knee. "Remember, tomorrow we have our three-mile run."

"Dad, really?" Will protested. "I'm not a baby. You don't have to carry me."

"It's not you, Will," his dad said as Angel opened the door for them. "It's your size. Sometimes I get confused on just how old you are."

"Ha, ha," mumbled Will. "See you later, Jared. Come back tomorrow and we can play Mario Kart again."

Before he left, Angel pushed a bag of cookies into Jared's arms and echoed Will's request. "You're always welcome, Jared."

Angel followed her dad into the house and stood to watch him settle Will back on the couch. He knelt and covered him with a blanket just as Will drifted back to dreamland.

"Dad," she said, hesitating. "I just wonder. You know your PTS thing? I think I understand a little better now. I just want to know how you deal with it. I mean, you must've seen horrible things in the army and had to face a lot of stress. Just that one night looking for Will has messed me up. I mean, when I thought we lost him, I nearly had a heart attack. I still wake up in the middle of the night thinking about it."

Mr. Moore rose and looked down at his sleeping son. "It's just one breath at a time, Angel," he said softly, his eyes sad. "One day at a time. You hold on to what you love and never let go. Then you've just got to have faith that things will get better. When you fall, you get back up again. You and your mom know that I haven't always done a good job, but I won't give up." He looked at his daughter. "Eventually it gets better, just as long as you don't give up."

He straightened and cleared his throat. "There. That's my preaching for the day. Now go rescue your cookies from Jimmy. And wash his face before your mom comes home. On the double!"

Angel grinned. "Yes, sir!"

Jared did make it to school on that Friday. Many of the players had yet to return and he became an instant celebrity. His homeroom, much to his chagrin, gave him a standing ovation. It was the first day of "normal" classes since Tuesday, the day of the accident, but nobody really focused on learning. Everyone talked about the basketball team and their twisted principal. During English, Gary and Chaz left him alone, but Giselle came back to see him. Big Mike had yet to return and she took his seat.

"I just want you to know, Jared," she said, "the cheerleaders took a vote and you're one of the top five cutest boys on the basketball team. If you ever want a date to the Winter Dance coming up, let me know." She winked at him. "I could hook you up."

Jared blushed and coughed. But then he looked at her and bit his bottom lip. "Actually," he said, "there is a huge favor you can do for me."

"Sure, Jared," Giselle said. "After what you did, I'll do anything for you."

"Anything?" Jared asked, lifting his eyebrows. He glanced to where Marshall sat hunched over in his seat, reading a book.

"Well, almost anything," Giselle amended quickly.

At lunch, Jared avoided his usual table, leaving it empty. Instead he walked up to Marshall and tapped his shoulder.

Behind Jared, Giselle gripped her bagged lunch tightly, holding it close to her stomach. She took a deep breath and looked a little sick. When Marshall looked up from his history textbook, she stepped forward and stared into his eyes.

"Marshall, you like me, right?" she asked.

Marshall sat up with a jerk. His book tumbled to the floor. He responded by pushing up his glasses and opening and closing his mouth without making a sound.

"Well, I can't date you," Giselle quickly continued, "but I can go to the dance with you. Is that okay?"

Marshal bobbed his head up and down and still struggled to find words.

"Great," Giselle said, sounding disappointed. She plopped her lunch bag next to Marshall and sat down.

Jared, grinning, took the seat next to her.

"Wh-what are you doing?" Marshall spluttered.

"Sitting here," Giselle replied. "Look, if I'm going to dance with you, I have to know you're not a creep. I'll eat lunch with you every day, and as long as you don't creep me out, I'll go to the winter dance with you. Agreed?"

"Uh, ah, sure," Marshall said.

"Great," Giselle said. "Now, let me talk to you about fashion …"

Jared sat back in his chair and looked over at the empty table where he'd always sat. It felt like a very long time ago when he felt lost and alone eating there. Now … Well, now he had plenty of friends. They were just all absent.

Ryan had left the hospital and was recuperating with Ben's family. Ben, according to Nick, wouldn't leave his side. Nick had shown up to school that morning, but had left early for a doctor's checkup. His shoulder had also suffered in breaking down the bus door, but he assured Jared it would be fine.

"I still can't believe Big Mike carried Will with a busted shoulder," he'd said in wonder before leaving. He'd met Jared in the hall on his way to the office. "But hey, I hear we might still have a basketball team, man. I'm definitely going to be ready for that."

Angie had yet to return to school. She'd called Jared the other night, surprising him, and said how John was having a rough time adjusting. He missed his dad and wanted his old room. Angie's mom and dad were still trying to become foster parents, but were having trouble with the system. Angie wasn't even sure if John would ever return to Washington Middle again.

"Tell him," Jared had said to her, "that if he does, the basketball team needs him. We're short on players."

"*What? Really?*" Angie had cried through the phone.

"Heard it straight out of Brad's mouth … I think he's changed. You won't be hearing the 'r' word from him anymore."

Angie had gone quiet for a while. "I think all of us have changed," she'd finally said.

They'd discussed a little bit about the basketball situation. With Coach Swopes gone and Mr. Hackett arrested, and definitely fired, Angie didn't see the point of even continuing the season. Still, she'd hung up promising Jared she'd tell John how the team missed him.

Jared's thoughts were rudely interrupted by Marshall's hand grabbing his arm and shaking it.

"Are you listening to me?" he asked.

"Marshall!" Giselle said. "Be more gentle! All I said was have you ever thought about wearing contact lenses! And a haircut and a new wardrobe."

Marshall stared at her, flustered, and then at Jared. "Are you hearing this, Jared? Girls are more trouble than I thought."

"That's a *huge* compliment, Marshall," Giselle said. "Just take everything you think about middle school and tell yourself you're wrong."

Jared just stared up at the ceiling. He couldn't wait for things to go back to normal.

"Hey, champ," whispered Mr. Moore. "Will. Will!"

His son groaned and moaned, twisting in his blankets. Suddenly his eyes shot open and he stared wildly around the room.

He lay on the couch, but gripping the cushions underneath tightly. His legs had been moving as if trying to run. The wound on his thigh throbbed with pain.

"It's okay, Will," Mr. Moore said gently above him. "You were dreaming. Just a dream …"

Will slowly exhaled and took deep breaths. He'd been dreaming of the Pherrins brothers chasing them through the woods with sharp knives and driving pickup trucks.

His parents had thought he'd been sleeping the night before and had talked in low tones.

Apparently, bodies had been discovered buried in the backyard of the Pherrins' home. Police had uncovered a grisly game where the Pherrins would kidnap hitchhikers and let them loose in the woods, only to be hunted down and killed …

Mr. Moore's friend in the police had provided him with details even the newspaper knew nothing about. When asked why he didn't just hunt animals, Hunter Pherrins had looked surprised.

"Why would I do that?" he'd said. "They're the only good thing left on this earth. It's the people who cause the problems."

It turned out he'd known Mr. Drydon from his school days. The two had met in their high school's outdoor club and became sort of friends. The friendship had soured when they'd been caught, along with Hunter's brothers, nabbing pets from families of kids who'd made fun of them. The pets were set free in the Pherrins' woods and Hunter would go to work hunting them down. Mr. Drydon's parents, from a well-to-do family in the community, had covered it up as a hunting accident and Mr. Drydon had quickly distanced himself from the Pherrins, but had never forgotten them. He'd kept in touch with Sam Pherrins over the years. When he decided to get rid of his son, Hunter was the first person he'd called.

Will had heard all of this and now couldn't stop thinking about it. Even under warm blankets, he shivered.

Mr. Moore crouched by his son and patted his arm. "Believe me, Will. I understand what you're going through. It won't be easy, but you'll get through this. Trust me."

"How?" Will asked. His breathing calmed but he kept a tight grip on the cushion. "I keep seeing him."

"Right now you need to take your mind off of him." He patted his shoulder. "Will, I decided to coach your team. Starting Monday, I have to start practices again. I'm going to need you with me."

"Ha," Will said, not sounding amused. "What could I do? I can't even walk without crutches." The doctor told him that to allow his thigh to heal he needed to keep all pressure off it for the next several days. His dad had brought the crutches home the previous day, but he'd not used them yet.

"I don't know, champ. You could watch your dad fall on his face."

"That might be worth it," Will said.

Chapter 57

Jared also suffered nightmares. In his latest, he saw Hunter Pherrins with his large, wicked knife going after Will. Jared tried to run and save his friend, but his legs wouldn't work. It felt as if he ran in thick mud. "No!" he screamed. The knife plunged down and he woke up sweating.

"Hey, idiot!" George called from the doorway. "You might be a hero, but now you're late for school!"

Jared groaned as his heartbeat slowly settled. He rolled over onto his back. It was Monday morning, time for another school week. The only thing different was a call from Mr. Moore. The night before he'd called asking Jared to bring his basketball clothes with him the next day. He needed him in the gym right after school.

"D-does this mean you're our new coach?" he'd asked.

Mr. Moore had sighed on the phone. "*It means you boys need a shot at healing. Playing ball right now is probably the best shot I can give you. So I hope you make it. Will should be there, too.*"

"You better come now!" George bellowed from the hall, snapping Jared back to the present. "I just missed my bus and Mom is trying to make you pancakes."

Jared breathed out. It was nice to have George back to normal. He'd been extra nice the last few days.

"I'm coming already," he said, rolling out of bed, falling to his knees. Then he grinned. "I have basketball today."

"Hey, Jared!" George yelled from the stairs. "Have a good day! I ... I'll see you later."

Jared frowned. "Great," he muttered. "George is not back to normal." He raised his voice. "Uh, yeah. I'll see you."

Ms. Jackson greeted the boys as they arrived for practice that afternoon. She'd stepped in to replace Coach Swopes officially, but confessed she knew nothing about basketball. She did, however, know about tutoring.

After having everyone sit on the bleachers, she walked to the midcourt in high heels, wearing a gray suit jacket and matching skirt. With her, she'd brought Mario and two other boys Jared recognized from playing basketball with Big Mike.

"These are your new teammates," she'd said by way of introduction. "They *will* maintain their grades and *will* join the team."

Mario started to grin, but Ms. Jackson's glare caused him to duck his head.

"Yes, ma'am," he said as the other boys nodded vigorously.

Ms. Jackson beamed. "Good. Now go do running stuff until your real coach comes."

Led by Brad, the boys who were able got in a line and sluggishly ran up and down the floor. Many still had bumps and bruises that needed to be loosened.

Mr. Moore showed up with Will five minutes later. The slight boy hopped in on crutches and watched with a sheepish grin as the whole team ran up to him, including Big Mike. After everyone exchanged high fives with him, he settled in the first row of the bleachers to watch. Big Mike sat next to him, but didn't glance his way.

Will had yet to thank the larger boy for saving his life—literally carrying him out of danger. He glanced at Big Mike's injured shoulder and sucked in his breath. Big Mike had literally sacrificed his life for not just him, but the entire team. Will knew what not playing basketball meant to Big Mike.

"Hey, Mike," he said. "I just want to say—"

Big Mike cut him off with a glare. "Shut up, Will," he snarled. "Just get your leg better and get your little heinie back on the court. If you don't, I'll kick it all the way back to Berkshire."

Will grinned faintly and nodded. "Okay, Big Mike."

Big Mike snorted. "The story got out, man." He ducked his head, embarrassed. "I got a call from the NBA. Some player got me a scholarship to his summer camp, okay? Don't tell nobody, or

I'll break your other leg." He abruptly got to his feet and stalked onto the court to join the team huddled around Mr. Moore.

Will raised his eyebrows and felt his mouth hanging open. "Sure, dude," he finally said to himself. He wondered which player did the kindness, but knew Big Mike would never tell. Crossing his arms over his stomach, he relaxed and let a smile cross his face. Big Mike deserved the break. His talent and modesty would carry him far.

On the court, Mr. Moore had the team introduce themselves to him and to each other, making sure the new players felt welcomed. Then he had everyone scoot in close.

"We're more than just a team, boys. We're a family now," he said gravely. "Don't forget that." He cleared his throat. "Now back to basketball. Our game from Thursday has been postponed to the end of the season." Mr. Moore stared at the boys facing him, making sure everyone listened to his words. "That means we're still at two wins and three losses with only four games left. If we want a chance at the playoffs, we need to play hard and fight for every game."

"Playoffs?" Kyle scoffed. "Shoot, man. Let's just talk about finishing a game."

"No, I'm talking about playoffs," Mr. Moore said coolly. "That was the goal coming into the season, and just because … well, we're not going to let anything throw us off that course."

"Like a murdering principal and his homicidal friends?" Nick asked.

"Especially not that. Look. You're kids, and deserve to live in a world free from that garbage. Unfortunately, that's not the reality. Evil is all around us, boys. People suffer from it every day. It doesn't matter your age, race, or gender. Now, we have a choice. We can accept this, or we can fight it. The only way to fight evil and win is by destroying it. The only way to do that is through love. It's something I learned the hard way in the army. Believe me, boys. What you all did on that night … what you boys did was to show your love for one another. You stood up for each other and ultimately crushed evil. I know some of you suffered and continue to suffer." Mr. Moore glanced around at the faces watching him.

Ryan, Darius, Teddy, and Howard were the only boys from the team still absent. Big Mike and Glen, both with arms in slings, stood in the back. The huddled team stared at their coach without blinking. Nobody had a phone out or a hint of a smirk. They were focused and attentive.

Taking a breath, Mr. Moore continued. "Now it's trying to worm itself back in our heads and our minds. It's been crushed but not destroyed. It's crawling around, lurking and waiting for us to doubt. So let's not do it. Let's not let it rise up again. Let's continue to show love for one another. The best way to do that right now is to play ball and play for each other. No more egos. Right now we're all Patriots, and one thing about Patriots, they never give up. So, I don't think we're giving up on the playoffs just yet."

Kyle nodded solemnly and coughed. "Uh, yes sir."

"Count me in," Brad said.

"Let's do it," Nick added.

Ms. Jackson clapped her hands from where she stood at the door. She'd nearly slipped in her heels and now stayed close to the hall where the floor wasn't so slick. "Listen to your coach, boys!"

"You heard the lady," Mr. Moore barked. "On the court and on the line. Let's put some fire in those legs, boys!"

There were two other absent key members of the team. Angie and John had yet to return.

Then, with a few minutes left of practice, Jared heard a shout from the door. Ms. Jackson jumped out of the way as a boy sprinted past her, wearing a Patriots basketball uniform.

"Wait, John!" Angie yelled from the hall. "You forgot to tie your shoes!"

Two weeks later the Patriots were riding a four-game winning streak and managed to sneak into the playoffs as the fourth seed. None of the wins were pretty, and each came down to the final minutes, but the Patriots had prevailed. For their reward, they would face Berkshire, the undefeated top seed, in the semifinal. The game would be away at Berkshire.

On the morning of the big game, Angel gently eased her brother's door open and crept in. "Will?" she asked. "You awake?"

"Really?" Will muttered. "Why do you always ask that after you wake me up?"

"Hey, kid," Angel said, crouching by his bed. "I'm just trying to be polite."

"Ha, ha. By waking me up at six in the morning?" Will flipped onto his stomach, his head tilted to face his sister.

"Watch it, little bro, I know your tickle points. I could always wake you up *that* way. Are you running with Dad today?"

Will groaned. "You mean running *from* Dad?"

Angel smacked his backside. "I told you to watch it, kid. You know he's just trying to get you ready."

Squirming, Will rolled to his side and nodded. "Yeah, I know …"

On his last checkup the doctor had removed the stitches and had said if all went well he could be cleared to play in time for the championship game … if they made it that far. Just in case, his dad had been getting him moving and stretching as much as possible. He'd bought Will a bike that past Saturday so Will could ride while he ran. Their morning workouts had resumed that Monday.

Then at every basketball practice, even when he still had the crutches, Will had to shoot baskets on one foot, over and over. John accompanied him and, while the rest of the team practiced, the two were at a side basket. John fetched all the rebounds until, finally, after the third day, Will started coaching him to also shoot. Now the two were firm shooting partners.

Will breathed out. "Angel, you know … I haven't had a bad dream all week."

"That's good, little bro."

"Yeah, but today, I don't know. We're going back there today."

"Don't worry, kid." Angel's voice grew serious. "You're *not* going past that road where the, uh, 'accident' happened. Besides, Mom, Jimmy, and I are driving there. You could always go with us."

Will shook his head. "I'll be okay. Maybe. Dad will be on the bus. He'll probably make me do jumping jacks in the back or something."

"Ha," Angel said, giving his head a rub. "Now who's trying to be funny?"

"That's the problem," Will grumbled. "I am being serious."

"Just another game, fellas!" Brad cried out when leading the team onto the bus later that afternoon.

Nick grunted from behind Will.

"Is he serious, man?" he asked. "It's just another game?"

"Hey, dude," Will said with a grimace. "At least you get to play in it. I have to sit and watch." He'd at least dressed out for the game. His old shorts were now police "evidence." Under his new shorts, still too big, a heavy bandage wrapped in red medical tape surrounded his wounded thigh. He'd tried jogging earlier, but knew sprinting was not an option.

"Don't worry," Kyle said, climbing in the bus in front of him. "We got you, Will." He'd become a starter in Will's absence and developed into a lethal midrange shooter and serviceable defender.

Jared stood silently behind Nick and slowly breathed in and out. He knew this game would be much bigger than just a semifinal basketball game. Going back to Berkshire meant going back to a whole bunch of painful memories and lingering nightmares. It meant remembering how close he came not just to dying, but also watching his friends suffer.

As if sensing his thoughts, Will slipped out of line and moved back to Jared's side.

"You ready, big guy?" he asked, nudging his side.

Jared gave a start. Then he grinned. "Not even close."

"Just think of Mario Kart," Will said. "Stay in your lane and don't mess up."

Jared grinned. He'd slept over at Will's house last Friday night with Nick, and the three, with Jimmy, spent the entire night playing video games. And Mr. Moore *still* got them up before six the next morning to exercise.

"Sure," he said. Then he lost his smile and bit his lip. "I just don't ... I don't think I want to make this trip. But I know I have to. I'm not even talking about basketball."

Will looked down at his sneakers and nodded. "I know what you mean." He looked up and slapped Jared on the shoulder. "Don't worry, dude. You were there for me. I'll be there for you."

"Yo, dudes," Ryan grumbled as he walked stiffly to the side of the bus with a basket of water bottles. "That sounds like a cheesy song, or something."

His ribs were still sore, but much better. However, after confessing his part in the crimes, he'd been suspended from the basketball team for the rest of the year. Now he accompanied the team as a student volunteer assistant manager, something Mr. Moore made up on the spot. Ben's confession of being the original thief had helped his cause. Ben had been benched for a single game for his part.

Will grinned slightly. "Ha."

"Okay, boys!" Mr. Moore yelled as he jogged from the parking lot. "Hurry up on the bus! We don't want to be late!"

"Maybe we do," Bob muttered as he climbed up the steps. "We lost by like thirty points last time we played. And then we *really* got wrecked."

"Yo, man, that's because I wasn't on the team then!" Mario said, grinning widely as he followed Bob. "You know the rule, when in doubt, give the rock to Super Mario."

Jared hefted up his sports bag and sighed. "Here we go," he said.

Will grinned and smacked the back of Jared's shorts as he climbed up. "If he's Super Mario, you can be Luigi."

"Hey, man, who would I be?" Nick wanted to know, stopping at the top of the stairs.

"The fat guy in the way," Will said. "Hurry up, man."

"Whatever, dude," Nick said. "You're that Daisy girl, then."

Will raised his eyebrows. "Speaking of 'that girl,' when are you asking Stephanie to the dance?"

Nick coughed and quickly headed inside the bus. "I'm just waiting for the right time, man," he called over his shoulder. "You know, after we win the championship."

Will rolled his eyes and carefully stepped up after Jared, mindful of his thigh. "It's Tuesday, dude," he told Nick. "Thursday is the championship game and the dance is Friday. Won't that be too late?"

Nick just sat in a huff.

"Guys!" Brad shouted. "Are we talking about the game, or a dance?"

"Dance!" Mario yelled. "We're going dance all over Berkshire tonight!"

"Shut up!" Big Mike snapped, getting on the bus behind Will. "Let's just get there first."

Jared smiled as he waited for Will to slide in one of the front seats by the window before taking a seat next to his friend.

Big Mike grabbed a seat behind them. He still had his shoulder in a sling, but acted as an assistant coach. With his guidance, Jared had turned into a formidable down low presence. With Nick and Mario at his sides, the Patriots ruled the inside of the court.

In the past four games they'd dominated the boards and shut down the lane when on defense. On offense, they worked together setting screens and picks and fighting for offensive rebounds. Mr. Moore directed his team to keep sending the ball down low. Then if there was no shot, kick the ball out to Brad and Kyle. The strategy wasn't perfect, but it worked.

Angie and John were the last to climb on board. They sat in the seat across from Jared and Will, John taking the window seat. Angie smiled over at Jared and let her hand hang down in the aisle, just a few inches from Jared's knee. For the past two weeks Angie did almost nothing but smile. Her parents had been approved to take John in and he was now officially her foster brother.

She'd confessed to Jared that John sometimes still missed his dad, but at the same time was much happier with her family. "My dad said they found a whole bunch of sleeping pills and bottles of chloroform solution in Mr. Drydon's house," she'd told Jared at lunch one day. "Poor John was put to sleep whenever he bothered Mr. Drydon."

Jared had asked how Mr. Drydon could've gotten all the drugs without causing suspicion. What he'd heard from Angie had nearly caused his blood to freeze.

Apparently, Mr. Drydon had gotten them on the sly from Mrs. Pherrins, set up by Sam, whom Mr. Drydon would meet at a bar. Mrs. Pherrins, it turned out, had once been a high school science teacher. She'd been fired years earlier for teaching her class about so-called government cover-ups, and after several accusations of using chemicals on students. This happened around the time Hunter had gotten in trouble for hunting pets with Mr. Drydon. Soon after, the Pherrins had yanked their kids out of school and disappeared into the woods. Before leaving, Mrs. Pherrins had managed to nab many chemicals from her school, taking them with her. The Pherrins had pretty much vanished until the boys, aside from Hunter, returned to town some ten years later.

Remembering nearly being run over by the pickup with Will, Jared knew exactly which neighborhood the brothers had moved into.

The brothers had kept close ties with their parents and their brother. Sam, managing to get a custodial job in a local doctor's office, had supplemented his mom's stash with stolen pharmaceuticals. Along with over-the-counter sleeping medicine, Mrs. Pherrins had been able to concoct all sorts of knockout drugs and chemicals. These she'd passed on to Hunter, as well as to black-market buyers such as Mr. Drydon.

When hearing it all, Jared had shaken his head in amazement. The whole family seemed to be wacko. He'd lost his appetite and had ended up tossing his lunch without a bite.

"Jared? Hello?"

Angie's voice snapped Jared back to the present. "Uh, yeah?"

"Did I hear something about a dance coming up?" she asked.

Jared quickly looked out the window past Will. "Uh, what?" he mumbled.

Angie just giggled. Her hand swung and knocked Jared's knee. "We can talk after the game."

Jared didn't dare look at her. Beside him, Will became very interested in running his finger across the window. He looked to be tracing a heart.

The Patriots girls hadn't won a single game, so a second bus wasn't needed. The cheerleaders were all carpooling and would meet them there. They'd offered Angie a ride, but since the last trip to Berkshire she'd become part of the team. No one questioned her presence. After Ms. Jackson and Mr. Moore climbed on, the driver shut the door and soon the bus pulled away from the curb. They were on their way.

Chapter 58

Once the bus hit the highway, the joking and fooling around fizzled and a somber quiet settled over the bus. When it pulled off the highway near Route 32 to cut through the heavy woods, Jared could feel the tension rise. Soon they would be near the wrong turn Mr. Hackett had taken.

The whole team had on their black uniforms and sported new long-sleeved T-shirts over their jerseys. This shirt featured a picture of a basketball printed on the front with WMS in red above it. Below it simply read, *'LOVING IT!'* They were designed by Mrs. Donavon, who'd tried to go out of the way to make sure it had no grammatical errors. Originally she wanted it to read *"WE ARE ALL LOVING BASKETBALL."*

"Now's the time, boys," Mr. Moore's voice spoke up. "If anybody has something on their mind, speak it now."

At first there was silence, but then Brad spoke up. "You know, that night … I thought I was going to die. Everything I thought was important … like my phone, I suddenly realized was kind of useless. Man, you guys … You guys are what's important to me."

"Amen, brother," Glen said.

The floodgates opened. Different members of the team took turns to speak, letting out their feelings and fears.

Jared and Will sat silently, listening. Neither one needed to speak. They both knew they had each other's backs and that was enough. When the bus reached Berkshire, the team was ready.

"We're no longer a team," Mr. Moore said as they pulled into the school. "Now we're a family. Let's play for each other and, win or lose, not forget that."

The Berkshire fans knew all too well what had happened on the last visit. When the Patriots bus pulled into the school, over a hundred fans waited for them. Many of them carried signs like *BERKSHIRE SUPPORTS THE PATRIOTS!* and *NEVER AGAIN!* They wanted the Patriots to know they were sorry about what had happened ... but they also wanted to win the game.

Nick stared out the window and shook his head in amazement.

"Man," he said, "I'm going to hate destroying all those people's hopes tonight."

Ryan snorted. "We'll see if they're still cheering when we leave."

As the team climbed down to head to the gym, they received a huge ovation. As team captain, Brad went first and he nodded his thanks as he led the team across the parking lot to the gym.

Jared followed with John and Big Mike close behind. Angie wanted John to reach the gym without incident, so had him get off right after Brad and had asked Jared to watch out for him. She remembered what had happened in the parking lot the last time they were at Berkshire. Big Mike would watch their backs.

Seeing the crowd of men, women, and children, all clapping, Jared doubted there would be any ugly incidents. He felt his face go warm. John grinned and waved back while Big Mike just glared with his head held high. He never acknowledged the crowd.

The rest of the team quickly exited after them.

Ryan slapped Will on the back when the smaller boy ducked his head in embarrassment.

"This is for you, little dude," he said.

Will stopped and pretended to ram an elbow in Ryan's ribs. "Ha. And this is for you."

"Just get to the gym, man," Nick said, pretending to wipe a tear from behind them. "I'm going to lose it." He shoved his sports bag at Ryan's back. "And you can carry this, dude. Since you're a manager now."

Turning, Ryan took Nick's bag and promptly dropped it. "I have to go and make sure there's a bench big enough to fit your big behind."

"Quit holding up the line," Mario complained. "All this cheering is going to my head."

Grunting, Nick took up his bag. He nodded to the crowd and followed Ryan. "Some great manager you are," he mumbled.

As the team made their way to the gym, Angie headed to the side of the bus to unload the equipment from the storage bins. Typical boys, she fumed. They had to soak up the cheers. Nobody stayed behind to help her. As she reached the storage bins, two teenagers slipped from the crowd and awkwardly approached her. Both had their hands stuffed in their heavy jackets and looked ashamed.

"Uh, hey," said one, a tall, pimply boy with tufts of straw blond hair sticking from his winter hat. "We, uh, wanted to apologize."

His companion, a shorter, rotund boy with a round face and broad forehead, nodded. He pulled a hand from his pocket and brushed back his dark spikey hair. "It was us who scared you last time you were here. You know, in the dark that night …"

Angie turned to them and put her hands on her hips. "If you're really sorry, you can help carry this bag and cooler to the gym. Then you'll promise never to do such an idiotic thing again!"

"Uh, yeah, sure," the taller boy said, bobbing his head. "Definitely."

As Jared went to the layup line, he stared in wonder as Angie marched into the gym, leading two gawky teens carrying all their supplies.

"Now that's a great manger," Nick said, beside him. "Man, she's something else." He smacked Jared's shoulder. "Don't forget the dance is Friday."

Will coughed from behind him. "I'm sure Stephanie won't forget."

Nick turned to give him a sour look. "Shut up, man. Go sit on the bench."

Will only grinned and cut in front of him, receiving the ball from Kyle. "The doctor said I can start jogging. So you better win tonight so I can play on Thursday!" Taking three dribbles, he neatly laid the ball up and in, but made sure to jump and land with his left foot, keeping his weight off his injured thigh.

Whatever the reason, guilt, nerves, or overconfidence, the Berkshire Flying Eagles came out flat and never found their rhythm. Early on, Mario, Nick, and Jared formed a brick wall down low and ate up every rebound close to them. The Flying Eagles started settling for long-range shots, and when they didn't drop, tried to force the ball to the rim.

By halftime Jared had two blocks and three steals. He also scored eight points, half on easy put-backs.

Will and John sat side-by-side watching, with Will explaining what was going on in the game and where John should be if he were playing. So far John had yet to appear as a Patriots player, but Will hadn't stopped hoping. His dad didn't want to embarrass John or cause him to be overwhelmed.

"I'll wait for a blowout," he kept telling Will. "Either we're up by a lot, or down by a lot, then I'll put him in." With the Patriots lacking a deep bench, a blowout seemed only possible if they lost. So far, they kept winning.

They ended up taking down Berkshire by a score of 51 to 46. The Flying Eagles had started hitting three-pointers late, but not enough. Brad sealed the game with free throws and the Washington Patriots had made the finals.

The next night Will had just put his head on his pillow when he heard a faint knocking at his door. He rolled on his back and blew out a deep breath. He wondered who his night visitor would be this time—Angel, or his dad.

He was surprised to hear his mom's voice.

"Honey," she said softly. "Can I come in?"

"Um, sure, Mom," he said, sitting up and scooting back to lean against his pillows. "Is everything okay?"

"Of course it is," Mrs. Moore said, coming into his room. She breathed in deeply and frowned. "Well, besides the sweaty boy smell in here, everything's okay."

"Ha, Mom," Will said, but he grinned.

His mom still worked hard and often still came home late. He knew it was part of her job and they needed the money, but he missed her. She hadn't been able to take very much time off when he'd been injured, and when she did he'd mostly been sleeping. It was nice having her visit now. It was like he had her all to himself.

"I'm serious, Will. This weekend, win or lose, I'm washing all your clothes. Twice." She sat on his mattress next to him and patted his shin. "How's your leg?"

"Great. I'm all set for tomorrow."

Mrs. Moore nodded. "I just hope you're not rushing back too soon."

"Trust me," Will said, slapping his bandaged thigh. "It's more than ready."

"I'm sure you are too, Will." She sighed heavily. "I know it's been tough for you. But when I heard the news of you being lost and then your dad calling and telling me you'd been stabbed ..." She all at once leaned over and hugged him tightly. "I nearly lost it, Will. I nearly lost you ... Your dad ... Your dad is the greatest person in the world. I just want you to know everything is getting better." She released him and patted his shoulder.

Will squirmed, but didn't complain. "He's doing real good as a basketball coach."

"So I hear. I think it's been good for him. His writing is getting along nicely too. That's why I came here, Will. Yesterday he told me he's nearly done with his first draft of a story. Do you know why I've been coming home late so many times?"

Will licked his lips. "Your work."

"Not just that. I've been meeting with some people in the publishing business. They're very interested in your father's writing. What I'm trying to say is, your father just might become a published author very soon."

"I just hope it's not a joke book, then."

"It'd better not be. It has a lot to do with you. Now, he doesn't have an ending yet, but tomorrow that just may change. No pressure, but go out there and win."

"Ha. Sure, Mom."

For the first time all year, Jared woke up before George. It was the morning of the championship game and pale light barely lit the windows. His head against his pillow, he lay still for a few minutes basking in the silence.

The day had come. Unbelievably, the Patriots, with Jared a key member of the team, were in the finals. Thinking about his life way back in September, seemingly a lifetime ago, he couldn't help but smile.

Basketball had changed his life. And then it had also almost ended it. For a moment, his smile wavered. The events after the first Berkshire game still haunted him. His external bruises had all but faded and now barely marked his face. The internal bruises still had a long way to go. Ironically, only basketball kept the bad dreams at bay.

And now he had one game left. After all he'd been through, after all the team had gone through, he hoped it ended in victory.

With a groan, he rolled out of bed and stood up to stretch.

"By tomorrow morning my season will be over," he said softly to himself.

A month ago those words would've struck like a punch to his belly. But now he smiled. He knew that, win or lose, he'd still have his friends.

Shrugging off his pajamas, he stood shivering in the cold air. It felt good. Good to be alive. After the Berkshire night, little things no longer bothered him. Then he shivered. Okay, so the cold still bothered him.

He quickly pulled on jeans and a T-shirt, all carefully laid out the night before. George slept on and would not ruin Jared's morning this time.

Over the T-shirt he pulled on his jersey and then tugged his new long-sleeved basketball shirt over that. Saving his socks for last, Jared headed for the bathroom feeling wide awake and ready to play.

Unfortunately, the game wouldn't start until seven that night, over twelve hours away. Jared still had to get through an entire school day.

As he left his room, Jared could smell pancakes cooking downstairs. He was not the first of the family to be up.

After finishing in the bathroom, he made his way down to find his mom standing watch over the kitchen counter where three golden brown pancakes steamed on the griddle. She looked tired, but perked up at seeing him.

"Jared," she said in surprise. "You're up early."

"Not as early as you, Mom." He sucked in his breath as he gave his mom a quick hug before going to grab a glass for water.

"I, um, I'm sorry for not helping out as much lately," he mumbled as he filled the glass at the sink.

"Nonsense, Jared! Your job is to live your life as a boy. I'm supposed to be doing the work." Her mouth curved into a smile. "Besides, George has been pitching in. Yesterday he even folded the clothes."

Jared nearly choked on his water. "George?" he coughed out. "Really?"

"I know it was him, because all the socks were mismatched. If you get your sister's shirts mixed in with yours, you'll know why."

Jared grunted. "I'll just give them to Jack. He'll wear them no problem."

"Oh, Jared. Go sit and let me bring you some pancakes. You have a big night ahead of you. Just remember, Jared. Your brothers love you very much."

Jared nodded as he sat. He still remembered how his brothers came to him that day after being lost in the woods. He would not forget again. Family was not always easy, but it was always there when needed.

Glancing at the clock on the microwave, he sighed. Still twelve hours and eight minutes before tipoff.

Thankfully for Jared, most of the students and teachers also had their minds on the game that day. School flew by with easy classes full of well wishes until it ended with an impromptu pep rally to see the team off. Even Gary and Chaz wished Jared luck. Then it was game time.

For the championship, the team had to travel to Hamilton Middle for a rematch against their rival. Hamilton had only one loss on the year and that was against Berkshire. Being a higher seed gave them home advantage, but as Jared jogged onto the court behind Nick and Will, it didn't feel like it.

The Patriots fans had turned out in droves and took over half the bleachers, filling the entire right side with red and black shirts and sweaters. Kids and adults alike were standing and yelling their support. Teddy, in a wheelchair with his broken leg in a plaster cast, sat just next to the bleachers, along with Darius and Howard, both in padded chairs. Darius no longer needed a neck brace, but still could hardly turn his head. It was the first game back for the injured players and they were given a rousing ovation.

Jared spotted Sarah Powers and her friend in the first row. Seeing him, they both waved. Marshall had also made it and sat facing the cheerleaders. Wearing a GAP hoodie and a ball cap, he was almost unrecognizable.

"Good grief, man," Nick said in wonder, "look at all these people." He tousled the front of Will's hair. "They're all here for you, man. No pressure. I mean, every eye will be on you when you step on the court. And it's only the championship game, man."

Will gave him a sick grin. "You've been hanging around my parents too much."

"Not at all," Nick told him. "I'm just suggesting if you ever get the ball in a big moment, just pass to me or Jared. The big men rule, man. Right, Jared?"

"The big men have big heads," Will told him, brushing down his hair. He'd just gotten a haircut the day before and it felt smooth and sharp.

Nick grunted and smacked the back of his shorts. "And little kids like you have no rear ends, so no more sitting on the bench. Today you're playing, man!"

"Cut out the chatter!" Brad yelled at them. "Get in line and do your layups!"

"Who made him boss, man," Nick muttered.

"We did," Jared said. "Remember we voted him team captain."

"Oh, yeah," Nick said. "What were we thinking?"

The three had wandered near center court and now headed sheepishly to the lines.

Ben turned to greet Nick and Will, brushing back his messy blond hair. He licked his lips nervously.

Jared stepped back, knowing the three boys had some catching up to do.

Ben hadn't hung around them since the first Berkshire night, mostly due to guilt for not being there and being the cause of Ryan's involvement. He'd started suspecting Ryan's strange behavior had something to do with his thieving. On the night of the Berkshire game he'd confessed everything to his parents and had gotten a long lecture on right and wrong, but also one of forgiveness.

He'd returned to school the Monday after Berkshire, relieved to have his guilt in the open, but had yet to fully incorporate himself back with his friends. He and Ryan remained tight, but he'd avoided Nick and Will, no longer sitting with them at lunch or during classes. Only Ryan convinced him to stay part of the basketball team. Ben couldn't quit when the team needed him most. Since Ryan couldn't play, he wanted Ben there for him. Since then Ben had stopped using his locker and always went straight to his parents after practice and games. Mr. Moore had suggested to Will to give Ben space and time.

Now Ben nodded awkwardly and looked a little sick. "I hope your dad doesn't put me in, Will," he muttered. "My stomach is in knots."

"Knot funny, man," Nick said.

Will gave a small smirk and elbowed Nick's side. "If only middle school had teams for comedians."

Ben stared at them with narrowed eyes. "So you guys aren't mad at me?" he asked.

"Nah, not yet," Nick told him. "Wait until you miss your first shot. Then you're in for it."

Will elbowed Nick again. "Ben, with guys like Nick around I need all the friends I can get."

Ben let out a deep breath like he'd been holding it for weeks and grinned. Just like that, the awkwardness lifted like yanking off an old Band-Aid. "I still hope I ride the bench," he said. "Look at all these people."

"No worries, man," Nick said, rubbing his side. "They're all just staring at you."

Ben grunted. "Yeah. Maybe John can play for me," he said ruefully. He nodded at where the golden-haired boy took the ball in the next line.

His emerald eyes gleaming with excitement, John dribbled awkwardly to the basket before tossing the ball hard against the backboard, missing the rim entirely. His face still lit up in pure joy as he skipped towards them.

"He certainly has the energy for it," Nick said.

Will just nodded and licked his lips. "Maybe."

Chapter 59

The Hamilton crowd applauded politely for the Patriots when the team was introduced, but more than one student from their crowd laughed and scoffed when seeing John run out with his hands flapping and face beaming.

"Awkward!" yelled a boy from the front row.

Big Mike stared in that direction and glared. Immediately the titters stopped. Even with one arm in a sling Big Mike managed to look intimidating.

The applause increased dramatically when the Hamilton Dragons trotted out onto the court in their purple and gold for their introductions. Colton led the way. Seeing Will, he gave a brief wave and then turned his back.

Being a championship game, the teams and crowd stood for the National Anthem and then the horn sounded for the game to begin.

"Let's go, gentlemen!" one of the refs called. An older man with iron gray hair and a matching mustache, he blew his whistle sharply, holding up the game ball.

"Okay, boys, this is it," Mr. Moore said. "Same starting lineups hit the floor. Brad, Kyle, Jared, Nick, and Mario, let's come out running!" He pulled Will aside and crouched in front of him, staring in his eyes. "Tell me, champ. How's the thigh?"

"Great, Dad," Will said. "I'm ready. Really." He patted his thigh and pulled up the shorts' leg to show the tape job over his bandage. He wore his leg sleeves and his pale skin around the tape gleamed in stark contrast to his black clothes.

Immediately Nick put up a hand to his eyes, acting as if blinded. "Hey, man!" he cried as he pretended to stumble past him to the court. "Pull that down! You trying to blind us?"

"Ha," Will said, smoothing down his shorts. "Remember how not funny that one was last time you said it?"

Mr. Moore put a hand on Will's back. "I'm still going to hold for the time being. I don't want to risk you getting new stitches unless I have to."

"What about John?" Will asked. "Is he going to play?"

"We'll see, champ." He patted his back. "Go take a seat with him and tell me how he's feeling."

Will smiled. "He feels like he always does. Happy to be here."

By the middle of the second quarter, nobody on the Patriots looked happy. Even John sensed impending disaster. The Dragons, led by Colton, took it to the Patriots right at tip off. Jared, being slightly taller than Mario, took the jump but had mistimed it. The Dragons' center tapped the ball out to Colton.

Colton had learned his lesson from the last time they'd played. His eyes were focused and face a mask of determination. He took the ball right at Brad, as if going for the rim. The Patriots guard backed down, giving space. Then, right behind the three-point line, Colton pulled up and drained a high-arcing shot.

On the Patriots' possession, Jared got the ball low and put up a quick shot that barely grazed rim. The Dragons took control and ran down the court, scoring on a layup. So it continued.

Soon it was a 13 to nothing game, with Hamilton in firm control. The Patriots couldn't hit a shot and had forgotten how to play defense.

Mr. Moore tried a timeout to steady their nerves and then tried substitutions. He looked at Will, but went with Bob and Scott.

Ben took a seat next to Ryan with an ashen face and looked ready to throw up.

Early in the second quarter Mario made a hook shot and Brad managed five quick points, but the Dragons still held a 21 to 9 lead.

"Okay, Will," Mr. Moore said, running a hand through his hair.

He glanced across the court to the bleachers where his family sat. Angel had Jimmy on her knees, watching the game intently. His wife, who'd taken off from work early, sat beside her, gripping her hand tight.

"I hope this is the right thing to do," he muttered.

"What? Are you putting in John?" Will asked him. He pulled up his front collar and nervously wiped his mouth

"No, champ. I want you in for Kyle," his dad said. "You and Brad have to work together to find lanes. Either go to the basket, or draw defenders and pass. Got it?"

Will nodded and pulled off his warm-up shirt. Handing it to his dad, he straightened his jersey and stretched out his right leg.

"Feel good, champ?" his dad asked. When Will nodded, he slapped the back of his son's shorts and sent him to the scorer's table.

Seeing him coming into the game, Colton dribbled the ball off his foot and out of bounds for the Dragons' first turnover.

As Will jogged on the court, he received a standing ovation from the Patriots fans.

Colton trotted over and nudged his shoulder. "Good luck, man," he said. "Don't run into any bleachers."

Will licked his lips, tucking in his jersey. "Ha. Sure, man. Just watch out for number 4."

Going to the sideline, he passed the ball in to Brad and it was game on.

Brad dribbled to the left side, crossing midcourt and then passed over to Will.

"Go ahead, man," he said. "Let's see what you got."

Will held the ball and looked for a pass down low.

Jared ran across the baseline to the corner near the bleachers, trying to open up the defense and give Will a lane to drive. But Will had his lips tight and large brown eyes open wide. He didn't bounce the ball as he pivoted his foot and passed the ball back to Brad.

"He's so small," Jared heard a woman say near him. "Look, he's just over the ref's belt line!"

"Why is he out there?" another woman said. "He could get hurt."

Brad dribbled forward and then sent it back to Will. "Take it, man!"

Colton set up in front of Will and shook his head. "Watch for the pass!" he called.

"Time's running down!" Mr. Moore shouted.

Will dribbled to his right, but still looked lost.

Jared, gritting his teeth, ran across the court to the opposite corner to be on the same side as Will.

"Remember!" he yelled. "Take your best shot!"

His mouth parted, Will looked at him and gave a slight nod. He all at once crossed to his left and then dove into the lane, slicing towards the basket.

Colton was caught off guard and recovered too late. His hand brushed the side of Will's jersey as it went by. Immediately two big men closed down on Will. Jared broke to the basket and Will sent a bounce pass between the big men, right into Jared's path. Grabbing the ball, Jared scored an easy layup.

"That's it!" Brad said. "Get back in the game, man!"

Colton took the ball and went right at Will. He knew Will hadn't played in weeks and was coming off a badly injured thigh.

Will kept his hands up and guided Colton into the center of the lane, where Jared waited.

Colton suddenly found himself in front of the basket with Jared in front and Will hounding him in back. Picking up his dribble, he struggled to find a pass, but could only twist in frustration as one of the refs blew his whistle for a three-second violation.

Will grinned and slapped Jared's shoulder. "Nice help, big guy."

"Anytime," Jared said. Then he looked down at his friend. "Remember you told me the rim is like a giant cookie jar?"

Will lifted his eyebrows. "Yeah?"

"It hasn't gotten any smaller since you've been away. You should reach in and try it."

"Yeah, but what happens when I miss?"

Jared grinned. "That's why I'm here. I got your back and your rebound."

Will rolled his eyes, but nodded. Taking the ball in, he dribbled up the court. He briefly hesitated and then charged into the lane. This time only one big man went to cut him off, but just inside the three-point line, Will tossed up a floater that found only net. Just like that, Will was on fire.

At halftime the Dragons had 27, but the Patriots had 24. Will accounted for ten of the Patriots' points on his own.

"You still feeling good?" Mr. Moore asked as the teams headed back on the floor from the locker rooms.

Will nodded. He rubbed his thigh. "So far."

"He's on fire!" Nick said, walking past and pretending to be burned when he smacked Will's shoulder.

Mr. Moore rubbed his jaw. "I'll put you back out there, but know they're going to guard you tight. Look for the pass first and shot second. But …" He mussed up the front of his hair. "Man, champ. Remind me to get you a haircut."

"Ha, ha, Dad. But what?"

"If you have a shot, take it."

At the start of the second half, Brad and Will took up top while Mario, Nick, and Jared resumed their down low work. Just as Mr. Moore predicted, the Dragons started in on Will. On the first possession of the half he got hacked hard by a stocky boy with thick dark hair. As Will dribbled by him, the kid karate chopped Will's right arm, missing the ball completely.

Will winced as he grabbed his wrist.

"More where that came from," the boy growled, trying to intimidate Will.

Jared straightaway came from the side and bumped the boy, knocking him a few steps.

"Watch it!" he cried. "More where this comes from, too!"

Both refs immediately blew their whistles and called for order. The ref with the iron gray mustache gave Jared a warning, but not a foul.

"I see what you're doing," he growled gruffly at Jared, "but keep it in the rules, son."

Jared nodded and glared at the stocky boy.

Colton chuckled. "I warned Coach to lay off you," he said to Will and then he looked over at Jared. "I promise, I'm laying off."

Jared just bit his bottom lip. He got the ball on the side from the ref and threw it in to Will at the whistle. The dark-haired boy immediately latched on to Will's hip, waving his hands and bouncing on his feet.

Will faced him down, dribbling from right hand to left hand.

"Watch it!" Mr. Moore called. "They're playing a box-and-one. Spread the floor and look for cuts!"

Nick set a screen for Jared, and Colton moved down to cut off passing lanes.

All at once, Will dribbled to the right and stopped. Taking the ball, he flung it hard across court to Brad, wide open behind the three-point line. The Dragons were caught watching the ball. All the purple clad players had followed Will with their eyes and had shifted their feet in his direction. Brad calmly took the three and rattled it in.

The next few minutes went back and forth with both teams scoring on put-backs. Then, with the scored tied at 36 apiece, Will took on his dark-haired defender, beating him clean. Driving down the lane, he searched for a pass or path to the basket. The defender rushed to catch up and jumped at Will, extending his arm. Jared stepped in front of the defending center, blocking him off and got a clear view.

Will tried to jump when the dark-haired boy crashed into his left side. Will landed with all his weight on his right leg and it instantly buckled. Crying out, he flung the ball at the basket and then slammed into the floor, the dark-haired boy on top.

A whistle shrieked and Jared found himself rushing in. He felt himself reaching for the dark-haired boy's hair when he caught himself. It could've been an accident, or it could've been on purpose. He didn't know, but he also didn't have to get ejected.

Taking a deep breath, he glared at the defender. "Get off of him and get to your bench before you get it."

"You heard him!" Nick growled, coming to stand by Will's shoulder.

"That goes for me too," the gray-haired ref said.

The dark-haired boy quickly got to his feet and retreated to his bench, looking scared.

The ref followed him and issued a warning to the Hamilton bench. "No more rough stuff," he said loudly. "Next one is a flagrant and ejection."

His partner, a tall man with nut-brown skin nodded. "That goes for both sides. Now let's play ball."

The Hamilton coach made a face, but made no argument.

Will remained on the floor for a few more seconds. He lay on his stomach taking deep breaths.

"You okay, man?" Nick asked.

"Yeah, just great," Will muttered. He looked up at Jared. "Help me up, but be careful."

Surprised, Jared reached down and grabbed Will's wrist. Will pushed himself up to a kneeling position and made sure to push off with his right leg, showing his dad it was okay. At the same time, he stared at Jared while offering resistance with his hand.

Jared bit his lip and yanked up his friend, using all the strength he had.

"It's open, isn't it?" he asked.

Will took deep breaths and gave a brief nod. "Maybe," he said tightly. "I felt something rip."

Jared shook his head. "You can't play," he whispered.

"Two shots, black," the gray-haired ref said. "Number 21."

Jared went to his spot for the free throws and bent over with his hands on his knees.

Will slowly walked to the line. Bouncing the ball, he looked once at Jared and then the rim. He swished the first shot and then the second before trotting down the floor for defense. As he turned to set up at the top of the key, a red drop splashed to the court under him.

"Time out!" Mr. Moore shouted. Not waiting for the whistle, he hustled on the court before the ref could stop him. He ran straight to Will. "Let's go, boy. To the locker room. Now."

"I'll go too," Jared said quickly. "Scott, check in for me!"

The refs now blew their whistles and waved their hands.

"You can't run on the court like that, Coach!" the tall one yelled. "Technical foul on the coach for the black team."

"Whatever," Mr. Moore said, kneeling down. He pulled up Will's right shorts' leg. A dark red stain marred the white tape around the boy's thigh. Beneath the tape, the top of his leg sleeve was soaked in blood.

Seeing the blood, the refs widened their eyes. After a brief conference they had the technical foul stand. Rules were rules and coaches weren't allowed to run on the court during play.

"Sorry, Coach," the gray-haired ref said gruffly. "Hope your boy is okay."

Nodding, Mr. Moore looked over where Ms. Jackson sat on the far end of the bench watching with interest. "It's all yours, Angela," he said.

The woman sat up as if her chair had just been charged with electricity.

"What?" she gasped. "What do I do?"

Mr. Moore pressed a hand over Will's shorts and squeezed hard. "Put Scott in for Jared and pray my son didn't do something really stupid."

Will sighed. "It's not that bad, Dad."

"We'll see," Mr. Moore said. "Put your hand here and hold tight." He then put Will's left arm over his shoulder and grabbed him around the waist. Standing, he hoisted up his son and carried him quickly to the locker room. Will looked embarrassed, but made no argument. As Jared followed, Colton made both free throws, tying the score again.

In the locker room, Mr. Moore put Will down and yanked down his shorts.

"Quiet!" he shouted when Will made to protest. "Let's see that cut. Jared, go grab a first aid kit. There's one just to the right of the door."

When Jared got back with the kit, Mr. Moore had the tape unwrapped to reveal the bloody bandage oozing red.

Will sucked in his breath and squeezed his eyes tight as Mr. Moore removed the bandaged and started cleaning it with alcohol pads Jared got from the kit.

"It's not too bad," he muttered. He gave his son a light spank. "Well, champ, you only got a partial tear. I'll bandage it up for now, but you're done for the game."

Will sucked in his breath and nodded glumly. "When you're done, Dad, I need to talk to Jared. It's for an end of the game play."

From the screaming and cheering out on the court, they knew the game remained tight.

"What's on your mind?" his dad asked. "I'm listening."

Will licked his lips. "You'll need Brad for this, too."

Chapter 60

Will limped out of the locker room with Jared and his dad right behind him. The scoreboard showed the Patriots down by four points with only fifty-two seconds left.

"Hurry up and get ready," Mr. Moore muttered, running a hand over his head. "If your play works, I'm shaving my head bald. I'll get all your haircuts at once."

"Ha," Will said. "That's a deal."

"First we need to score, and get the ball back," Jared said worriedly.

Mr. Moore grinned. "After all this team has gone through, that should be a piece of cake."

Sure enough, Brad threw the ball in to Nick, who drew a double team. Faking a shot, he instead jumped and passed the ball back out to Brad. Wide open, Brad swished a three.

The crowd roared and rose to their feet. There were forty-five seconds left and ticking away. The Dragons used every second they could of the forty-second shot clock and then Colton threw up a three that hit the front of the rim. Brad boxed out the shooter and grabbed the rebound.

"Time out!" Mr. Moore yelled just as he reached the bench. There were four seconds left on the clock.

Ms. Jackson put a hand to her heart and sighed with relief. "Thank goodness," she said. "You gave me some gray hairs today."

"I'm about to give myself some gray hairs," Mr. Moore muttered. He raised his voice. "Everyone, to me. I have a play that, er, Will and Jared drew up. I hope it works. And John, go to the scorer's table. You're in for Nick."

The crowd started muttering in shock when John raced to the scorer's table. Jumping up and down, he hopped onto the court.

"Number 1 is on the court, why?" demanded the Dragon coach.

Behind him, some of the Dragon fans started laughing.

"What is this, a charity game?" shouted a man.

"Our coach can't be serious," a Patriots father said loudly. "What are you doing?" he yelled.

Mr. Williamson, sitting in the front row, stood up and turned around. "That boy is part of the team and has every right to be on that court. If you don't like it, cry about it, but do it someplace else!"

"He's just trying to distract us," a Dragon mom yelled. "Letting a special kid play is nice and all, but it's not going to make us feel sorry for him. See? Look, he's just standing under the basket!"

"Ball in!" yelled a ref, blowing his whistle.

Jared took the ball. Brad, Kyle, and Mario were on the floor. They were the best shooters left on the Patriots. Brad particularly had been having a hot night. He'd hit four threes in the game.

"Watch number 23!" the Dragons' coach yelled, pointing at him. "Keep the ball away from him!"

Mario ran up and set a pick for Brad near midcourt while Kyle sprinted to the right corner, leaving the middle wide open except for John. Using the pick, Brad broke free and slashed to the middle, four feet beyond the three-point line. Jared threw him the ball and Brad immediately started dribbling to the right. After two dribbles, he leapt up and threw up the ball. All the defenders rushed him at once, their arms extended. Only, Brad never shot. Instead he'd passed it to a wide-open John.

John caught the ball and pivoted to the basket. Eyes wide, he jumped and put up the shot. It hit backboard and then swished into the net just as the buzzer sounded.

It had been a shot and a move he'd worked on with Will and Jared for over a week. At the end of every practice Jared had been joining the shooting session with Will and John. Will had had Jared pass the ball in to John before each shot. It had paid off.

The Dragon fans screamed in dismay and then unleashed a flurry of loud groans as the shot went in. Colton and the other players covered their faces in shock. Their coach fell to his knees and stared speechlessly onto the court. When his mouth finally worked, he said, "Cheater!" Nobody listened.

The Patriots fans, led by their cheerleaders, had erupted. The bench cleared as the players stormed the court to tackle John. Only the coach and his son remained.

Mr. Moore dropped his clipboard, his face etched in disbelief. He turned to where Will now knelt on all fours where he'd plunged from his seat as soon as John had caught the ball.

"I'm shaving my head bald," Mr. Moore said, still stunned. Then he went over to help his son up. "You know ... I've been writing a story ..."

Before he could finish, Will launched himself into his dad's arms. Mr. Moore caught him in surprise and held him tight.

Will threw his arms around his dad and hugged him even tighter.

"I know, Dad," he said. "Now you have an ending."

"Yeah," his dad said in a daze. "I guess I do." He shifted Will's body up to a more comfortable position. "I guess I do," he repeated, grinning.

Will loosened his grip and sat back in his father's arms. "Just one thing, Dad."

Mr. Moore looked at him and raised his eyebrows.

"Make sure you make me over five feet."

Mr. Moore bounced Will up and sucked in his breath. "Sorry, champ. But my story is too crazy to be fiction."

"Ha, ha, Dad. You can put me down now."

Leaving his dad shaking his head in wonder, Will limped over to where Jared still stood, rooted on the sideline where he'd thrown in the ball.

"I can't believe that worked," Jared said, still stunned.

Will smiled. "Hey, why not? It was our best shot, right?"

Angie nervously went to stand between them. "Should I go and try to rescue John?" she asked.

"Rescue him from what?" Will asked. "He's loving it!"

Brad had John on his shoulders and the entire team was jumping and screaming around them ... well, almost the entire team.

Will nudged Jared and pointed.

In the back of the celebration, Nick stood in front of Stephanie Baker. His eyes popped open at something she said.

Turning, he wildly searched the gym before making eye contact with Will. Then he threw up his hands in frustration.

"You already asked her for me?" he shouted, his voice nearly lost in the celebrations. Then Stephanie grabbed his arms and pulled them down. She said something to him and smiled.

Nick all at once jumped up and pumped his fist. "She said yes!" he cried. Then he promptly fell to the seat of his shorts.

Jared looked at Will. "What was that about?" he asked.

The smaller boy grinned. "I knew Nick would never get around to asking Stephanie to the dance, so I asked her for him." He turned to Jared and licked his lips. "Um, speaking of the dance … I was wondering … is your sister going?" Suddenly he sounded shy and he ducked his head. "I mean, is it okay if I ask her?"

Jared blinked. "You might make her head explode, but go ahead. She's somewhere in that crowd."

He then turned to where Angie had started drifting toward John. Now it was his turn.

"Angie!" he called. "Angie!"

Angie saw him and ran back and threw her arms around his neck. "Oh, Jared, thank you for everything! I never saw John so happy before!"

Jared gulped. "Does this mean it's okay to be a jock?" he asked.

Angie released him and stood on her tippy toes to deliver a kiss on his cheek.

"Does that answer your question?" she asked shyly.

Jared's eyes went wide and he nearly swooned.

"Uh, yeah … So, will you go to the dance with me tomorrow?" he blurted.

Angie responded by kissing his cheek again, just as Jared's parents and brothers emerged from the crowd, running to him.

"Jared!" Kelly screamed, scooting in front of her brothers. "OMG!"

Angie hastily backed away and gave a nervous smile.

Will's eyes widened and he patted Jared's shoulder before trying to slip away to meet his own family. Kelly quickly blocked his path, sprinting the final fifteen feet to stand in front of him.

"You were hurt, Will!" she said. "Are you going to be okay?"

Will grinned at her. "Don't worry. I can still make the dance … If you can make it."

Kelly shrieked and threw her arms around his shoulders, giving a big hug.

"Ooh, watch it," Will said, half choking. "My leg …"

Instantly Kelly let go and started walking him to where his family waited. Jimmy rode on Angel's shoulders next to their mother. Jimmy raised his arms in victory and nearly toppled backwards.

Meanwhile, George reached Jared and pounded him on the back. "Wow!" he cried. "I still can't believe it! You *do* play basketball!"

He sounded truly amazed and Jared had to keep from rolling his eyes.

"Great game, Jared," Jack said, slapping his shoulder. "Amazing."

His mother and father beamed as they stopped before him. Then his mom adjusted Carey in her arms and lifted her eyebrows. "And who's this lovely young lady behind you, Jared?" she asked innocently.

Angie had stepped back, ducking her head embarrassedly.

"Oh, uh, Mom," Jared said, blushing furiously, "this is Angie … She's my date for the dance tomorrow."

Angie lifted her chin and waved shyly. "Nice to meet you, Mr. and Mrs. Cook."

Mr. Cook grinned. "I'm sure it was nice meeting our son, too."

George's jaw dropped. "Wait. Y-you have a girlfriend, too?"

Later, as the team packed up their belongings and readied to head back to the bus, Mr. Moore had Will sit on the front row of the now empty bleachers. As soon as Mr. Moore finished his coaching duties, he would take Will to the hospital and have his leg re-stitched.

Jared emerged from the locker room first. Carrying out his bag, he dumped it on the floor before sitting next to his friend. He would be going home where his parents were throwing together a victory party.

The two boys didn't say anything as they basked under the gym lights where the scoreboard still read: Visitors 61, Home 60.

Nick found them there and collapsed to a seat on Will's other side. He was followed shortly after by Ben and Ryan. The five boys just sat in exhausted silence.

"Man, I'm so tired I could sleep through the weekend," Nick finally said with a groan.

"And miss the dance?" Will asked, not even lifting his head. "I guess Stephanie would be relieved."

Nick was about to give a retort when John and Angie walked hesitantly toward them. John carried a bulky paper bag in front of him and wore a stubborn look on his face.

"Um, okay, boys, John has a gift to give you all," Angie said, sounding slightly embarrassed. "I have no idea why, but he picked it out himself and is very insistent that you guys get it."

Smiling wide, John reached into the bag and pulled out an extra-large bottle of Herbal Essence Garden shampoo.

"I admit," Angie said apologetically, "sometimes I don't understand John … Uh, guys?"

The five boys could only stare in shock.

"Angie," Jared finally managed to say in a strangled voice. "Did John, um, sometimes shower at school?"

"Yeah, I think so. Mr. Drydon sometimes worked late. Why?"

The boys didn't say a word as they numbly watched John hold the shampoo out, grinning ear to ear. They'd finally discovered the true founder of the shower brothers.

Then Nick cleared his throat. "Welcome to the crew, man. I always knew you were one of us."

Angie just stood there watching with her eyebrows raised, arms crossed, and shaking her head. "It's now official," she said. "I'll never understand boys."

THE END

About the Author

Gregory Saur is the author of many novels for young readers, including *Diving Catch*, *Soccer Star,* and *Panterror! The Epic Babysitting Adventures of Rachel Pugsley*. His novel *The Pond Scum Gang* was shortlisted for the Gertrude Warner Book Award for Middle Grade Readers in 2017. Born and raised in Virginia, he spent some of his best years in middle school, partly because that was where he found his love of basketball. He's been known as the "bricklayer" when on the court.